CINEMA 7

a novel by Michael J Moore

A HellBound Books Publishing LLC Book
Austin TX

Michael J. Moore

**A HellBound Books LLC
Publication**
Copyright © 2021 by HellBound Books Publishing LLC
All Rights Reserved

Cover and art design
By Kevin Enhart for
HellBound Books Publishing LLC

www.hellboundbookspublishing.com

From Michael - thanks Cait

Acknowledgements

As always, I thank God for the breath I breathe and the ability to craft a story like *Cinema 7*.

I'd also like to thank Cait Moore, who was the first to proofread and critique *Cinema 7*, who has supported me more than anybody in my journey through the world of literature.

To my brother and sister, Adam and Alice Murphy, thank you for inspiring certain elements of this story.

Special thanks to Carly Rheilan, who selflessly gave *Cinema 7* a second proofread and helped Cait and I identify a couple of early inconsistencies.

My infinite gratitude to James Longmore and HellBound Books. James welcomed Cait and I into the HellBound family.

To Brooks Laughlin, with whom I consulted on police procedure, and Dr. Raj Patel, who helped me to make medical sense of the anomalies in this story, thank you both for your contributions. Any inaccuracies are my fault, not theirs.

To Connor J Jackson and Augustus Cooper who were among those to read this novel in its early drafts and my good friend P.S. Traum, an unofficial scholar in the horror genre.

Finally, I'd like to thank Schlock Webzine, University of Brighton's Dissections: The Journal of Contemporary Horror, and Soteira Press, who published excerpts of this book as a short story.

If I've left anyone out, email Cait and I and let us know we owe you a drink and an apology. We're good for both.

Michael J. Moore

CINEMA 7

Michael J. Moore

Prologue

The bed was shaking, and Kim was afraid because it was dark, and it was almost like the earthquake that had happened one night before Mom told her what an earthquake was. To make matters worse, raindrops were tapping on the roof of the trailer, and it sounded like giant spiders scurrying around up there.

Kim could have handled another earthquake. She was four, and earthquakes couldn't hurt you—not the little ones that happened in Washington, at least. But this was no earthquake because only the bed was shaking. The rest of the trailer was as still as the car the next-door-neighbors kept on blocks. She knew because it had happened last night, too, and that time she might have thought it was an earthquake, had the monster not been in her room.

The shadows had been there, though, like they were now. Lots of them. Thin, wavy ones, that looked like snakes crawling up every wall. So, she'd rolled off the mattress, but the floor hadn't moved. Neither had her dresser or toy box. Only the bed, which just kept shaking the way Mom's phone did whenever Daddy called from jail. It made the picture of Cinderella on her blanket almost seem like she were dancing.

The shadows had swayed like seaweed under water, and then Kim had glanced at the mirror above her dresser and seen the monster's eyes, glowing orange—the same color as her one-piece pajamas—staring right at her like she were a bowl of ice cream. She'd screamed so loud that her throat burned, and she'd run to Mom and learned her lesson because Gus was over.

Gus was here again tonight, so Kim didn't dare scream. The bed shook, and the shadows squirmed, letting her know the monster was back, but Kim wasn't going to look in the mirror again. She'd known he was coming anyway, because he'd been here every night for close to a week.

So, she hugged the stuffed dog she used to think would keep her safe, feeling her pajamas stick to her body from sweat. Her chest heaved up and down, up and down, and she wanted to cry, but didn't because that only helped if somebody cared that you were crying.

A gust of cold wind blew her red hair over her eyes.

"Stop!" she whispered, releasing her grip on Dog McGee, and brushing her bangs so fast she slapped herself in the face. "Please, just go away! Leave me alone!"

Then the monster laughed, and Kim couldn't hold the tears back any longer because he had never laughed before.

It had all started under the bed. The very first night, she'd just thought there was a mouse down there, running around and scratching at the carpet. It had scared the living daylights out of her anyway, so she'd gotten Mom, and they'd spent nearly half an hour searching for the pest.

That happened for a couple of times, then toys started moving and falling onto the floor, and Mom had taken a wooden spoon to Kim's bottom for not being in bed. When Kim swore it was a ghost playing with her toys, and not her, Mom had hit her again for lying. But when the shadows appeared, Kim knew it was a monster, and not a ghost. She didn't tell Mom until the next day after Gus left.

The monster's laugh wasn't like anything she'd heard before. It was almost a whisper, because it hissed and whistled like the wind. Kim cried and sniffed as he continued to laugh, and the bed continued to shake. She used to like the rain on account of it reminding her of running under the sprinkler in the summer. Now she hated it because if it wasn't so loud, Mom would have been able to hear the bedposts as they tapped the trailer's floor, then she'd believe her.

The monster whispered her name, and she covered her eyes with her hands, pressing so hard she saw red.

"Please just stop!"

"Hahahahahahaha! Are you afraid, Kim? Oh, baby, you don't have to be scared. I just wanna play with you."

Then she knew it didn't just sound like the wind. It *was* the wind. It was icy-cold, like she was lying next to a fan. It made her think of orange and green leaves, blowing along the sidewalk. It shouldn't have been able to form words, yet she could understand it perfectly. She felt her bottom lip curl into a frown. Every muscle in her face scrunched up without her consent.

"Oh Kim," the monster whispered. "Are you gonna cry, pretty girl? Are you gonna cry out to your mommy now? She doesn't care, baby. You know that. She's just gonna hit you with a spoon, or make you eat soap for telling lies. Don't cry to Mommy, Kim. Play with me instead."

That's when Kimberly Brenton lost control. It started deep in her stomach, and grew in volume faster than Mom's car could even pick up speed at a green light. She let out a long wail, crying like a newborn, and the bed stopped shaking but the shadows still danced on the wall, letting her know the monster hadn't left. So, Kim kept crying until heavy footsteps appeared in the hall. The door flew open, and the room filled with light, causing the shadows to finally vanish. Mom stood in the doorway looking like a tall, thin clone of Kim, her straight red hair flowing over a baby-blue robe.

"Kim? Baby, what is it?"

Kim stopped screaming, stared at her mom attempting to catch her breath. The music Mom liked to dance to while she cleaned, played lightly from somewhere outside the room. Kim was aware her face expressed nothing less than pure agony, but she was unable to do anything about it. She opened her mouth to tell Mom about the monster, thought about the spoon, hiccupped, and shut it again. She wiped away tears and snot with the back of her hand.

Mom didn't take another step into the room, just locked eyes with her daughter, and Kim knew what was coming next.

"No. No. No. Don't even think about it girly. You're not sleeping in my room. For fuck's sake, Kim. You're four years old."

"Mommy—"

"No Kim. This is BS. You know I don't wanna hear about any monsters tonight, don't you?"

Kim sniffed.

Mom raised her voice. "Don't you?"

"Yes Mommy. I just—"

"You just nothing! You always do this when Gus is over, don't you?

"No."

"Oh?" Mom let out a fake laugh. "But I think you do. I think someone's a little jellyfish. But listen up, 'cause Mom needs a life too. So, I don't wanna hear another peep come outta this room tonight. You hear me?"

Kim told her mom that she'd heard.

Mom said, "But do you understand?" then turned her head toward the hall. "What? Why? Dude, just smoke in the room. No. Just open the window. Yeah. I'll be right there."

Gus's hand appeared around Mom's waist. He smacked her bottom, then he was gone. When Mom looked back, she was smiling, but her expression quickly went flat.

"Do you, Kim?"

"Mom, I just—"

"Uh-uh. No more noise. You're going to sleep. Do you understand me?"

"Yes. I understand."

"Good." Mom smiled again. "Always nice to have an understanding. You know I love you, right?"

"Yes."

"Then what do you say?"

"I love you, too, Mommy."

"I know you do, baby. Now get some sleep."

With that, she killed the light, shut the door, and the monster laughed again, the cold breeze that accompanied his voice nipping at Kim's face.

"See, Kim? See? Didn't I tell you she wouldn't care?"

As Kim's eyes readjusted to the dark, she saw the shadows once again dancing on the walls.

"My Mom cares!" she hissed back, refusing to cry again. "She loves me."

"Hahahahaha! She does, does she? Then tell me, Kim. Why won't she believe you about me?"

"Because," Kim spoke through a frown. "You hide every time she comes in. You won't let her see you!"

Her hair tossed in an extra strong gust of wind as the monster said, "Because I shouldn't have to, should I? A mother who loves her daughter would believe her. I needed you to see that, baby. I need you to understand so we can play together." The snaky shadows grew thicker, and stretched across the walls, reaching for Kim like they wanted to tickle her. Every muscle in her body tensed, she trembled. Outside, the rain continued to tap the aluminum roof like a giant was pouring a bag of rice over the trailer. "Don't you wanna play with me, Kim? We'll have so much fun together. It's almost Halloween, and I wanna dress you up like a princess and take you trick-or-treating. It'll be so much fun you won't know why you were ever afraid."

Kim's voice came out in hiccups and yelps, but remained a whisper as she asked, "What are you gonna do to me?"

"What do you think, baby?"

"Please. Please don't kill me. I don't wanna die. I swear I'll be good."

"But you have to, pretty girl. You have to die first, then we can play. I just need you to remember one thing, okay?"

"Please," Kim sniffed.

"Don't yell, Kim. You don't want your mom to get the spoon, do you?" The shadows were so big now, that only small slivers of light existed in Kim's bedroom. Two bright orange eyes appeared just over her face, glaring down at her, and the freezing wind blew so hard that her hair went absolutely wild.

That was it. Kim could take the spoon. She could take the strap from Mom's suitcase. She could take whatever punishment awaited her. Sucking in a deep breath, she prepared to scream. But a thick shadow covered her face, as another wrapped around her wrist. Then the other wrist. Two more coiled on her ankles, and Kim's body was stretched across the twin-sized bed like the letter X. She couldn't move. She couldn't scream, because she couldn't even breathe.

The wind howled and whistled as the room grew so cold it was like being in a freezer. The monster said, "Remember, Kim, your mom let this happen because she doesn't love you. She's a liar. All she cares about is that guy in her bed. What's his name? Russ? Raul? Oh, yeah. Gus."

Kim tried to kick, to fight, to scream through her nose, but that was covered too. Her eyes averted to the right, where Dog McGee sat smiling, his cloth tongue sticking out of his mouth, his black plastic eyes staring into hers. She felt hot tears once again pouring down either side of her face and into her ears. Before she could stop herself, she wet her pajamas. Her body jerked, and after what seemed like forever, her ears began to ring. The room spun briefly, and Kim went to sleep, but the monster didn't let up.

The bed started vibrating again, but this time it was because Kimberly Brenton was going into convulsions. When her heart finally stopped beating, she soiled herself as the shadows uncoiled from her limbs. The one on her face slithered into her mouth, and once its tail disappeared, Kim's eyes popped open, but she still didn't breathe. Her heart still didn't beat. She sat upright, looked around, and climbed out of bed, walking barefoot to the door.

Twisting the knob, she opened it slowly and carefully, so it didn't squeak too loud. The entire house was dark, but Kim saw everything perfectly. Mom's door was shut, a few feet down the hall, on the left. Kim shut her own door, and tiptoed past it, hearing Mom's music inside, and her bed moving as she made the noises she always made at night when Gus was over. Kim had opened the door once and seen her sitting on his belly, bouncing up and down, up and down, then she'd crept back to her own room giggling before she earned a spanking for being out of bed.

Kim walked through the living room, where Grandpa's old cuckoo clock hung high up on the wall. Mom's gray cat, Silas, hissed at her from the couch, then darted across the room as she stepped into the kitchen. Sliding a chair quietly from the table to the counter, she climbed up on the seat and stood looking at everything she wasn't allowed to play with. Toaster. Blender. Mom's glass baking dish which needed washing. A black ashtray with cigarette butts sticking up like tree stumps.

A wooden block full of knives with smooth black handles.

Kim selected two of the smallest ones, the ones Mom used to cut her meat. Taking the ashtray as well, she hopped down as quietly as she could, and made her way once more through the living room. She stopped at the entrance to the hall—two knives in one hand, dirty ashtray in the other—and stared down at her closed bedroom door. Silas growled like a lawnmower from somewhere out of sight, but Kim paid him no mind. She could still hear all the noises coming from Mom's room; movement, moaning, music.

Kimberly watched, and waited for nearly seven minutes. Then, just before eleven, she cocked her arm back and sent the ashtray hurling toward her bedroom door. Grey ashes flew everywhere, and butts landed softly on the brown carpet just before it smashed into the thin wood.

The movement in Mom's room stopped abruptly, then the bed squeaked, her door flew open, and the dance music grew louder. Mom appeared, completely naked for a fraction of a second, before she pulled the robe over her pale body.

"I don't know. She's flirting with an ass-whooping, is what she's doing. What the—did you spill an ashtray?"

"No," Gus called from out of sight.

"Sure?" Mom treaded carefully through the butts, and headed toward Kim's room, reaching for the door. "Dude, there's a—"

THOOOONG! The clock wailed as its tiny doors swung open and the bird flew out, mounted to its perch. *COO-COO! COO-COO! COO-COO!*

Mom jumped startled, shook her head, then gripped the knob, as Kim took off at a full sprint down the hall, a steak knife in each hand. Mom didn't hear her approaching over the noise of the clock.

COO-COO! COO-COO! COO-COO!

Kim passed Mom's open door, catching sight of Gus in her peripheral. He lay nude on her bed, his legs open, his penis pointing to the ceiling.

COO-COO! COO-COO! COO-COO!

Mom still hadn't opened the door when Kim reached her.

COO-COO! COO-COO!

Reaching up, Kim thrust one of the serrated blades into her mother's lower back, just inches to the left of her spine, and pulled it back out watching dark blood expand on thin baby blue fabric. Mom gasped, pressed her palms and chest against the closed door. Kim stabbed her again, this time with the other knife, on her right side. The second it came out, Mom spun around and screamed, backing into the door, then sliding down and landing on her bottom. Two red lines trailed above her, and her robe opened, revealing her ta-tas as she grasped at the rug with both hands. Her eyes looked like they wanted to fly out of her head.

"KIM! WHAT THE—NO! AAAHHH!!!"

Kim thrust one knife after the other like a gorilla beating the dirt, stabbing her Mom in her face, in her neck, in her bare chest.

"Carrie?" Gus's voice rose over the music. "Babe, you good?"

But Mom couldn't answer because all she could do was scream and cry, and try to shove her daughter off her. A gargling noise came from her mouth, followed by hissing. She choked and fell limp, but Kim didn't stop stabbing her because the monster was right. She was having fun. Then she was grabbed by her hair and thrown down the hall, where she landed on her back and saw Gus's naked butt. He was standing over Mom.

"WHAT THE FUCK!" He leaned down and took her face in one hand, moved it around. His fingers left bloody streaks on her cheeks when he finally let go. Mom just stared at the corner where the wall met the ceiling, her mouth open like there was something she wanted to say, dark red liquid decorating her body and face in splotches. Gus stood up straight, turned and glared at Kim wide eyed. "What the fuck did you do?"

He was a pretty boy. Even at four, Kim knew this, had heard Mom's friends say it all the time. He had blond hair, which he shaved on the sides, and it looked like he combed it all day. Kim always laughed when he put his finger with the teardrop tattoo under his eye, so it looked like he was crying. His penis wasn't pointing to the ceiling anymore, but shriveled and attempting to hide inside his body like a turtle.

"Jesus, Kim. Holy shah—What the fuck did you—?" He took a step forward. "Kim, gimme those fucking knives!"

Kim jumped to her feet, bared her teeth and hissed like Silas had. Gus stumbled back, falling over and landing on top of Mom. He cried out and slid over, so he was sitting next to her, and her head toppled onto his shoulder. Kim smiled, turned around and walked off, leaving bloody footprints in the hall. Behind her, Gus seemed to be exhaling with the beat of the music in Mom's room.

Kimberly Brenton opened the front door, stepped out into the cold night, and made her way through the trailer park, a knife in each hand. Rain washed over her, leaving crimson puddles in her wake.

As she passed a home with a motion sensor out front, the porch light clicked on, casting her shadow on the wet gravel. It looked like tentacles—like the shadow of an exaggerated squid—or like snakes coming off the little girl's body, dancing and swaying in every direction.

Chapter One

Just before eight on Friday morning, Kyle McIntosh was making his way through the crowded gymnasium, and thinking about Claudia Rocha, when he walked right into the ass of a girl he had never before seen. She was taller than him—which wasn't saying much, as he was still waiting to hit the growth spurt adults kept promising would arrive someday—and wore jeans, a sweater, and a knapsack, rather than a backpack.

Almost involuntarily, he scanned her body, which appeared to have been sculpted to distract the eyes of sixteen-year-old boys. Then she whipped her head around so fast the tips of her black hair hit him in the left eye. Blinking in an attempt to keep it from watering, he began to apologize, but when the world came back into focus, she was gone, replaced by the angry face of a baldheaded Mexican kid he had seen around, but never met. He was accompanied by others, who all carried binders under their arms, as gangbangers at Mount Vernon High often did.

"You fuck my cousin," the kid spat over the noisy crowd, which was so thick Kyle was sure he was being mistaken for somebody else.

Rubbing his eye, he replied, "What?"

"Your name's Kyle, right? Kyle McDonalds?"

"McIntosh."

"Whatever, fool! You fuck my prima, Claudia, like a little bitch. You call her a fucking cunt, you puto."

And because the kid was so close Kyle could feel his breath on his face, and because Kyle had only been in a handful of fistfights (and rarely came out victorious), he explained that there had been a misunderstanding and Claudia had been his girlfriend only last week.

"The fuck?" the cholo retorted. "Your girlfriend? Think I don't know that? She ain't your girl no more, fool."

"I know."

"That's right you know."

"Yeah. That's what I said."

"I heard you."

This interaction went on for a while before the cholo, whose name turned out to be "Silencer," informed Kyle that if he ever spoke to his cousin again, he would get the bitch slapped right out of him.

"She got a new vato already, and he ain't no stupid white boy like you. She got a real man."

So Kyle said he understood, and then made his way to the far wall where he and his friends spent their mornings. He smelled flowery perfume before catching sight of Laura Cunningham's buttocks stretching a pair of black leggings to their elastic limit. She would've looked like she was standing alone against the wall had it not been for a set of pale, white hands clutching at the thin, blue tank-top around her lower back. Jesse Gerrard, who was short like Kyle, and much thinner than his curvy girlfriend, didn't peek around her to say 'hi,' or even acknowledge that Kyle had arrived, and though he and Laura never seemed to stop making out, Kyle doubted it had ever gone any further.

Painted on the wall directly behind them was an angry-looking bulldog in a spiked collar, baring its teeth and flexing its front legs over the letters, "MVHS." The artwork was done in a lime-green and white, which had invoked pride in generations of Mount Vernonites. Laura's positioning in regards to the image, and the movements of her head, gave the impression that the school mascot was getting more action than her boyfriend.

Next to her and Jesse, a chubby girl with strawberry-blond, curly hair waved to Kyle, and offered a strained smile.

"Hey Tara," Kyle said as a hand landed on his shoulder, causing him to glance up into the eyes of his best friend.

Dobey kept his jet-black hair just long enough that he could comb it backwards, and wore a trench coat that made him vulnerable to jokes of looking like an agent from The Matrix. This, Kyle knew, was resultant from poverty rather than a failed fashion sense, as the coat had been acquired at a secondhand store. But Dobey had great posture, and acted like he dressed intentionally, so girls didn't seem to mind.

He narrowed his eyes, and asked, "Did you get jumped by a bunch of Mexicans?"

"What?" Laura finally spun on her heels, revealing her boyfriend's messy brown hair and vacant smile.

Kyle told them what had actually happened, and then asked why the whole school was gathered in the gym. Stepping so close to him that her plump, blue jean-clad hip was pressed against his, Tara declared, "It's some kind of an emergency assembly over what happened last night."

Kyle tilted his head.

"Don't you watch the news?" Laura asked.

"Yeah. I mean—I don't know. Why?" What he didn't mention was that he had been too busy thinking about how much it hurt getting dumped to care about anything on his television screen.

Dobey said, "Haven't you heard what happened last night in the trailer-park?"

"The one by your house—or—your apartment?"

"No, fool. The one on Urban Ave. Behind Bargain Thrift."

"Wait—the one by *my* house?"

"Uh—yeah. Kind of."

"Yeah," Tara said. "The one with the restaurant out front."

"Where Claudia lives?"

A silence commenced, which wasn't long—no more than a fraction of a second—but so synchronized that Kyle wanted to stick his head into his backpack to hide his face because it hadn't been pretty enough to keep the girl he loved. Then a high-pitched squeal echoed off every surface in the gymnasium, causing most of its occupants to cringe and cover their ears. Principal Stack's voice appeared, robotic and thunderous, and the murmuring of the crowd dissipated until all that could be heard was static and Stack speaking between heavy breaths.

The bleachers were extracted on both sides of the gym at the same time, causing the crowd to gasp and constrict like a cold scrotum in the center of the court. It brought to mind a trip to Disneyland Kyle's family had taken just a few years ago. The walls in the waiting room of the famous Haunted Mansion had closed in, giving the impression its occupants would be crushed.

Fortunately, Kyle and his friends were positioned at the end of the bleachers, and avoided being caught in the overdramatic crowd. The entire student body was instructed to find a seat, which took close to a half hour, as people filed up the steps, then traded spots, climbing over each other to be by their friends.

The conversations were even louder than before, making it impossible to make out anything Stack was saying, so Kyle and his group just followed the kids who seemed to know what they were doing. They sat at the top of the bottom part of the bleachers, Kyle between Dobey and Tara. If she'd sat any closer, she would have been on his lap. Dobey made jokes, and Laura cuddled up to Jesse, but Kyle might as well have been watching it all through a thick fog. His mind was set on repeat, taunting him over and over again with Silencer's words.

She got a new vato already. And he ain't no stupid white boy like you. She got a real man.

And though there had been no evidence it was even true, he knew it was, knew she had moved on already after being broken up for less than a week. That she'd probably moved on before they had even parted. The worst part, though, was that now he knew why she had dumped him.

He wanted to confront her. To make her tell him the truth. That she'd left him for another guy. That she'd been seeing this guy while she was still with him, probably even sleeping with him. Hell, probably? Of course, she had. But for how long? And who the hell was this mystery person?

Looking across the gymnasium, at the bleachers opposite him, he scanned the mesh of various colored clothing, draped over mostly white and brown skin, as if he could somehow catch sight of her and who she was sitting with. Whom she was cuddled up to? Who this *new vato* was? But who said he even went to Mount Vernon High? What if he was older? Or from Burlington or Sedro Woolley?

Tara put her lips against Kyle's ear, said, "I don't think she's here," and Kyle's entire body was overtaken by a shiver that drew his shoulders to his jawline. She retracted, smiled bashfully. "Sorry. I don't think she's here."

"Who?"

"Claudia. That's who you're looking for, right?"

"What? No, I was just—"

"Looking for Claudia and whoever she might be sitting with. You wanna know who the new guy is, I'm sure. I don't blame you. That's messed up, dude. I don't think she's here today, though. I haven't seen her anywhere, and remember, that happened in her neighborhood. I saw on the news this morning; they had the whole street crime-scene taped. The bus probably didn't even run there. Did you really call her a cunt?"

"Yeah."

"And that's why you broke up?"

"No."

"Didn't think so."

Dobey said, "She is a cunt. She got a new boyfriend already? She was probably cheating on you the whole time. You can do way better anyway, bro."

Kyle supposed it was nice of his friend to lie to him. He asked, "What the hell happened in the trailer park, anyway?" Then he grew sick to his stomach, as another thought finally managed to overpower Silencer's words.

What if she was involved? What if something happened to her?

The crowd began to fall silent in a wave that seemed to start at the bottom of the bleachers, and move its way up. Kyle looked down and saw a six-foot gray bulldog in a white and green MVH T-shirt standing in the middle of the basketball court, somehow looking solemn in spite of the fact that it was limited to one facial expression. A whole crowd of adults, who he recognized as teachers and other staff was pouring in as well. Miss Rachel, who taught her health class that the secret to a long life was lots of sex and lots of vegetables, wiped tears from her face as she stopped next to the mascot.

Mr. Stack veered away from the rest of the faculty, a cordless mic in one hand. It squealed as he brought it to life. He slapped it with his palm a few times, causing hollow thuds to reverberate throughout the room. He wasn't a thin man, or a fat man. He wasn't muscular either, Kyle suspected, but it was difficult to tell because he always wore a gray or black business suit that concealed his physique. He was merely tall and stout, with a full head of salt-and-pepper hair. He scanned one side of the gym, then the other, raised the mic to his face.

"I suspect by now we all know why we're here."

Miss Rachel's body jerked. She hiccupped like a car with an empty gas tank attempting to start its engine.

Stack said, "My apologies for the mess that this morning's been, but as you can imagine, nobody could've seen this coming. Some of you, I'm sure have caught the news already. Others have heard it from your fellow students. And I'm sure the story's been spun a thousand ways already, so we're gonna go ahead and talk about it here. But first—as your faculty, we've had to make a few very difficult decisions today, one of which is whether or not to cancel school and send you all home in light of last night's tragic events."

Like every principal Kyle had ever known, Mr. Stack was a born performer. He paused, letting what he'd just said sink in, and a noticeable anticipation fell over the crowd, like a jolt of electricity. It was tension in which nobody seemed to breathe, lest they miss the news that something good had sprouted out of the ashes and they'd get a day off from school.

"And as your faculty," Stack raised his voice, "we've decided there's no way in hell we're not gonna be here for you today. We're bulldogs. Pack animals. And though what happened last night was an abomination, and we're all feeling the effects of it, bulldogs don't run and hide when times get tough. We stick together and work as a unit to get through it—whatever it may be."

The canine mascot raised both hands, pumping its fists, then dropped one and speed-bagged the air with the other. The crowd seemed to deflate like a bouncy castle without its plug. Kyle's eyes had taken on minds of their own, now searching the stands obsessively for his ex-girlfriend.

"So, I'm gonna encourage you—all of you—to take the same position. Be a bulldog. Step up to the plate today and support one another. Lives were lost last night, and some of those lives may have been dear to many of you. There aren't enough of us teachers to go around, but you know what? There *are* enough of *you*." He did a complete three-sixty, pointing at every segment of the gym. "There *are* enough of *you*."

The mascot pointed as well, nodding as it went around the room. Miss Rachel, it seemed had finally run dry of tears, she stood amongst the other teachers, yet appeared more alone than any of them. Kyle suspected somebody she knew had been involved.

Stack said, "I want everybody to look at the person on your right, and the person on your left. Are you feeling down? Talk to one of them! Tell him or her how you feel! And be that person for someone else as well. Maybe if whoever's responsible for last night's atrocities had had that someone, last night never would have happened."

Speaking out the side of his face, Dobey said, "Is it just me, or is something about this speech royally fucked up?"

Tara hushed him, but Kyle ignored them both, continuing to scan the crowd. Every word that spilled out of the principal hit harder than the last. People were *dead.* Maybe even Claudia. The fabric of his jacket rubbed together, zipping so loud that a pair of girls sitting in front of him glanced back as he reached into his pocket and fished out his iPhone.

"And if that's not enough," Stack went on. "We're bulldogs too. Us. Your faculty. If talking to one of your fellow students just isn't enough, come find a teacher. Find one of our wonderful counselors. Hell, come find me. I'll lend an ear."

Keeping the white phone in his lap, Kyle opened his text box, and found the last message he'd sent to Claudia—

—*ur a fucking cunt. u know that?* —

—to which, there'd been no response.

He typed, *r u ok?* and pressed send, watching a new dialogue box appear on the screen. In his peripheral, he caught Tara staring down at the iPhone, but paid her no mind.

"Now," Stack went on. "We don't know a whole lot yet about exactly what did happen last night, and you're bound to hear rumors. Unfortunately, that tends to be how people cope with this type of thing.

"Don't believe any rumors. Confirm everything you hear in passing. And just to keep the gossip to a minimum, we're gonna discuss the incident this morning. So, without further ado, I'll hand you over to Mr. Levendowski."

Stack turned toward his faculty, extending the microphone. The mascot began to raise both fuzzy hands repeatedly like a sorcerer over a cauldron, clapped, inviting applause from the crowd. And though a few random students joined in, most just stared unbelieving as Mr. Levendowski, the PE teacher, emerged from the faculty in a blue tracksuit, and accepted the mic. He raised it to his mouth, placing his hand on the dog's back.

"Why don't you go ahead and take a seat, Brent."

The mascot stopped what it was doing, looked at Mr. L, tilting its head.

"Go on, champ. I'll take it from here."

So, the dog disappeared and Mr L, stuck his chest out and said, "I'd like to be able to answer whatever questions you might have pertaining to the events of last night, but unfortunately that could take all day. So instead, I'll present the facts to you as I understand them."

Holding up six fingers, he said, "Last night, at least six people were killed in the trailer court on Urban Ave." Then four fingers, "Four young children are missing, and the police have—" one finger, "one man in custody this morning." Waving that finger like a wand to emphasize his points, he went on. "At this point, that's all that's known. That, and the fact that these were definitely murders. Anything beyond these facts is either speculation, rumors, or just plain lies.

"At this point, nobody's going home early, however, after school today, you can follow the story on the news. The police believe the missing children to be alive, and are actively searching for them. Four Amber Alerts have gone out, and they've asked that if any of you see any peculiar activity, you call them immediately. They've also requested that we ask you not to go out to Urban Avenue—"

Whatever else was said faded out as Kyle grew lightheaded, and found it difficult to breathe because the trailer park on Urban Ave wasn't very big and six dead people made it much too likely one of them was Claudia. Then, his phone vibrated in his lap, he glanced down at the screen, and he'd never been so grateful to see the words *fuck you. leave me alone* in a text message, because even though Claudia hated him and had a "new vato," at least she was alive.

***

Kim ran up the stairs because James was chasing her. It was pitch dark, but she could see just fine, as her eyes had lights in them. Orange ones. She and the other kids had discovered the power worked in certain parts of the building, but they didn't need it, and though there had never been a discussion about it, they'd been keeping it dark.

James was eleven, older than the rest of them. He was tall, and had red hair like Kim, only he had a face full of bright freckles to go with it. Mom always liked to make jokes about how she and Kim were the pretty type of gingers, not the creepy kind.

They had been playing tag for a while now, and James was "it." Kim suspected he liked being it, because he was taller and faster than the rest of them, yet he kept letting them catch him. She giggled and laughed as she ran, and her heart didn't speed up like it used to, because it didn't work anymore.

Kim knew she was dead. Her lungs worked, taking in air so she could form words. Her eyes and ears worked, and she could think and move her body—no problem—but she was dead all right.

She'd known she was going to die in her bed, because the monster told her. And she'd been so sad, and felt so let down because her mom didn't care. Because Mom let her die just so she could be alone with Gus. Then, when she'd woken back up, she hadn't put any thought into the matter of being dead or alive one way or the other. She'd just been angry. *Friggin pissed,* as Mom would have said. She'd been so angry that all she wanted to do was kill Mom. Not just wanted it. It was something she needed. Like a hunger. And not just her mom, but her dad, too, because her dad should have been there to protect her, but instead he was in jail.

So, she'd taken care of Mom, then left because she wasn't just Kim anymore, and her thoughts weren't all hers. The monster was living inside her now, and inside the other three kids who were running up the stairs, with her.

She hadn't known about the lights in her eyes until she saw the others. They weren't bright—not as bright as the monster's, at least—just dim, orange bulbs, and every time they shone on one of the kids, she saw his or her shadow, only it was the same shadow that had been on her walls whenever the monster was in her room. Like dancing snakes flowing out in every direction.

It hadn't occurred to her that she was still dead, either, until James pointed it out, showing them all that they no longer had a heartbeat. That if they didn't talk, they could hold their breath forever, and not get dizzy. That they could stick knives into their bellies and not feel a thing (Kim hadn't tried this last one, but Telma had, had even found it funny).

James was also the one who'd known the building the monster had led them all into was an abandoned movie theater. He said his dad used to point it out to him when they'd drive by, and tell him how he'd seen movies here when he was a kid. The Cinema 7.

Jose reached the top step first, and for a fraction of a second, pranced on all fours, before springing to his feet and sprinting around a corner. Then Telma and Kim emerged side-by-side at the same time, giggling with James behind them growling like a bear.

"Raaarrr! I'm gonna get'chu! I'm gonna get'chu! I'm gonna, gonna, gonna GET'CHU!" He caught Kim around the waist and hoisted her into the air, spinning her around, and around, and pretend gnawing at her belly. "I got'chu!"

She squealed with glee, kicked and waved her arms, because her happiest memories were of playing like this with Dad when he'd still loved and protected her from monsters.

All four of them were in their pajamas, except for James, who apparently slept in nothing but a pair of Superman undies. The front half was stained yellow. Kim knew why, because she had wet herself as well when the monster killed her. In fact, she had done more than just that, and her orange onesie was dirty on both sides and down the legs too.

"Ggggrrrr!" James nipped at her playfully. "Rarararararara! That's good stuff!"

All three of the others had lived on Kim's street, and she'd seen them, but never spoken. Now she wished she had because they were having so much fun together. Jose was younger than her. Telma, however, was four like Kim, and wore a long white T-shirt with pink undies underneath. None of them wore shoes, and even when Jose stepped on a nail, he'd only laughed and pulled it out.

Telma and Jose ran back, laughing and punching at James, so he set them down, got on his hands and knees, and let out the biggest, loudest growl yet. This set the younger children into an absolute frenzy. They cried out between giggles, and ran circles around him, taunting and tempting him to catch one of them.

They had been playing like this almost since arriving at the Cinema 7, and Kim couldn't remember a more blissful experience in her four years. It wasn't because of the games, though. She'd played games plenty while she was alive. Sure, Mom wasn't always in a great mood, and didn't let her play whenever she wanted, but that wasn't it either.

Everything was different now. Kim wasn't afraid. She wasn't sad. She wasn't lonely. She wasn't even bored. She was happy, and she was having a blast, and the monster had been right, because she didn't know why she'd ever been scared in the first place.

They laughed, and they played, and they teamed up on James, wrestling with him on the dirty carpet. Then, at one point, the wind started blowing inside the theater and every one of them stopped abruptly, stood up and silently made their way down the stairs, through the screening room where there had once been seats mounted to the cement floor, and out the door.

***

At lunchtime, Kyle and Dobey crept off-campus and stood between small, one-story houses in a gravel alley, passing Dobey's metal weed-pipe, which had a Batman symbol on its stem. It was turning out to be a particularly gray Autumn, and though it was only raining lightly, the wind made it difficult to keep a lighter aflame. When they'd finished, and were making their way out, Dobey lit a cigarette, and asked Kyle why he hadn't told him Silencer was Claudia's cousin.

"I didn't know," Kyle replied. "I mean, she never mentioned him to me."

"Whatever," Dobey blew out a long cloud of smoke. "He's a pussy anyway. His brother's in prison for shooting someone—in fact, remember Calvin?" He offered the cigarette to Kyle, and Kyle declined. "That's right. Always forget you don't smoke. Except ATF, that is." Droplets of water streamed down his black sunglasses, which he wore no-matter the weather.

"ATF?" Kyle asked.

"Alaskan Thunder Fuck. That's what kind of weed you just had. My uncle just got a couple pounds of it at the shop. I'm getting more later, so I'll kick you a bud or whatever. You remember Calvin though? He got killed behind Madison School last year. Silencer's brother's in prison for pulling the trigger, but who cares. Fuck Claudia and her whole family. You're the prettiest little blond kid she ever missed out on."

Faking a laugh, Kyle informed his friend that his hair was brown as they emerged from the alley, onto a residential street with no sidewalks, set on a steep hill. Across the road, a plastic skeleton hung from a noose, tied to a tree in somebody's front yard. It swayed ever-so-slightly, smiling like there was no place it would rather be. Both boys stared at it for a while, and though it was likely by design that the topic hadn't come up, Kyle found himself wondering if they were having the same thought.

Halloween's in a week, and somebody's out abducting children. How fucked up is that?

Then a bright purple Volkswagen Beetle pulled up so quietly it might as well not have had an engine. The passenger window slid down, and some pop song slowly died in volume until nothing could be heard accept a female voice, saying, "Excuse me? Pardon?" Only it came out, *Pah-don?*

Kyle was used to hearing accents. Mount Vernon's agricultural conditions encouraged the inflow of migrant workers, and the town was at least half Hispanic (the other half mostly white, of course). But this accent wasn't Hispanic, was unlike any he'd ever heard outside of television. He guessed it was one of two things, and just as he was having this thought, Dobey stepped up to the car, leaned down and said, "Yew sound like yah frum lown-dun!"

Giggling came from inside, then, "Very good! Well, close at least. Though I did just move here from London, I was born in Australia. But I imagine the two accents don't sound much different to a yank, now, do they?"

Smiling, Dobey said, "A yank? Short for Yankee? Ah, an American joke!"

There was clapping, then, "You are smarter than you look, sir! What about your friend though? I think we met briefly this morning. In fact, I may owe him an apology. Hello? Hey there."

Continuing to lean over, Dobey turned and gave Kyle a questioning look. Kyle stepped up and peered down into the car. A tall thin girl whose hair matched the black leather interior looked out through brown eyes, traced with dark liner. Without thinking, he said, "You whipped me in the eye with your hair."

She giggled again, and Kyle felt his face flush. "Did I? Well, I knew straightening my hair this morning wasn't such a brilliant idea. The ends are like a bullwhip, aren't they? And I was gonna apologize for the dirty look I gave you, but this just keeps getting worse, and worse, doesn't it? You're not gonna need an operation, are you?"

"Excuse me?"

"I mean, you're not gonna lose the eye, I hope."

"No. I mean—I—"

"I'm pulling your chain, mate. Honestly, I didn't mean to be a bitch this morning. I thought you were just being a boy, and walking into a cute girl's bum. By the time I'd realized otherwise, you'd already dashed off. Here," she reached into her center console, produced a blue can, "would you accept a Pepsi as a peace offering?"

Dobey sucked on his cigarette, causing the tip to light up and ash to fall onto the ground. He said, "If you don't want it, I'll take it. My mouth is as dry as Cleopatra's snatch."

"Because she's dead," the girl in the car said. "Lovely." Then, looking at Kyle. "So, what do you say, mate? Forgive me?"

So, Kyle said he forgave her, and Dobey could have the soda, which he slipped into one of the pockets on his jacket.

"I'm Marie, by the way. If you can't tell, this is my first day at your fine school. I was wondering if I might trouble you for some assistance."

Dobey grinned with one side of his face as he pushed his sunglasses up, so they rested on top of his head. "I guess that would depend on what type of assistance you're looking for." Sticking his hand into the Beetle, he said, "I'm Dobey."

Marie shook it. "Well, I've just learned that the legal age to purchase tobacco products here is eighteen. And as I'm only seventeen years of age, that's created a problem for me. Then, I saw you, with that Olympic torch in your mouth, and I can't imagine you're eighteen—so, I was wondering if you might be able to help me purchase a pack of Marlboros somewhere."

Dobey reached into his pocket, produced a pack. "You need a cigarette?"

"Oh, God no," she laughed. "I don't smoke those awful things. I'm buying them for someone else."

"Damn," Dobey put his pack away. "You make friends fast. Tell you what. My uncle owns a pot shop downtown. Gimme a ride, and I'll get him to sell you a pack of Marbs."

"Great! A marijuana store, I take it?" She looked again at Kyle, and her smile was the polar opposite of the expression she'd given him this morning. "Will you be joining us—I don't think I got your name?"

"Naw," Dobey reached in the window, unlocked the door. He tossed his cigarette onto the gravel before opening it and climbing into the passenger seat. "Kyle's gotta get back to class."

Marie looked disappointed. "Well, I hope we'll be back in time for class as well."

"We will." Dobey shut the door. Grinning at Kyle, he said, "Meet me later, I'll still shoot you a bud." Then the window rolled up, and a couple of seconds later, the car pulled onto the road and Kyle watched as red brake lights disappeared down the hill. Across the street, the skeleton continued to sway in the wind and smile like it found something that had just happened very funny.

***

The thing about pot, was that it helped Kyle forget about Claudia, about how much it hurt to get dumped, about how fucked he was without her. But it only helped when there was somebody around to laugh with. When there wasn't— after Dobey got into the car with the new girl and left—Kyle was alone with nothing but his own thoughts and a heightened sense of them at that.

So, he trudged to the top of the hill, sat on a block of concrete which was set in place to keep vehicles from driving into a certain alley, and looked out at the dirty street, which didn't even have lines to separate the two lanes. After a while, he brought out his phone. It was 12:44. Class didn't start again until one, so Kyle opened his text messages and read, *fuck you. leave me alone*, over and over again for a while, thinking of how scared he had been at the prospect Claudia might have been a murder victim.

But *fuck you. leave me alone* meant she was alive. She hated him, and she had a *new vato* even though they hadn't been broken up a week, but six people had been murdered in her neighborhood, and she hadn't been one of them. So, he guessed he should be content, because even if she didn't want him anymore, he had told her he would always love her—no matter what—and he had wanted her to be happy, and most of all safe. But he wasn't content, because no matter how much he'd meant the words when he had said them with shining, pathetic, puppy-dog-eyes, he could never be content without her.

He scrolled down, read a few "how's your day?" messages from just last week. He should have known. Should have seen it coming. In retrospect, it had been telegraphed even in his text records, which had become increasingly less personal in the days leading up to their split. In the fact that she had been less willing to spend time with him. But Claudia always had an excuse, didn't she?

I can't. My dad's making me go to Seattle with him today.

Sorry, not feeling too good. Gonna sleep a while.

Helping around the house. Talk later.

She always had a story, something to say rather than, *Sorry, Kyle. Can't talk now. Busy sucking off someone else. And by the way, he's a real man. Not some stupid white boy like you.*

He selected an image which she'd sent Saturday evening—less than 24 hours prior to the loathed breakup text, and watched as a tiny makeup clad Claudia in an even tinier bikini filled his screen. She stood in front of a full body mirror which was mounted to the door in her bathroom, holding a breast in one hand and her pink phone in the other, while flashing her patent duck face kiss.

He wanted to hate her. If for nothing else, he wanted to hate her for this picture. It wasn't the only one like it she'd ever sent, but it was the only one she'd ever sent the day before sticking a knife in his heart. All he could do, however, was hate himself for not knowing at the time that this one wasn't taken for him. It was taken for her *new vato* and sent to him merely because Claudia was a narcissist, and needed everybody to know how pretty she was with her clothes off. It didn't matter that Kyle already knew. She needed him to always remember what he'd once had.

He felt hot tears building up just below his eyes. They contrasted with the cold air around him, and almost felt good. Comforting. Still, he blinked a few times and held them in. He wasn't going to cry. But it quickly became clear that he might not have a choice in the matter, and his lips tightened, pressed together so hard a paperclip couldn't have slipped between them.

Then the phone vibrated in his hand, announcing an incoming text, and for reasons that only made him hate himself more, a tiny ray of hope sparked inside his chest, accelerating his heart rate as he scrolled up. But the message wasn't from her. Attached to a local number he didn't recognize, were the words, *where u at?*

He responded, *who's this?*

donkey fool.

donkey fool?

fuck autocorrect lol its dobey.

oh. lol.

using new girls phone on way back have bud for u where u at?

Kyle glanced around for a landmark, and saw a small group of children approaching from the direction of the high school. And because he was still feeling the full effects of the ATF, he thought nothing of it at first. Then it occurred to him that there was something off about the way they were dressed. In fact, one of them, a tall redheaded boy, wasn't even dressed at all. He wore a pair of stained tighty-whities with some design on the crotch. The others were much smaller, and all wearing some form of dirty pajamas.

Then Mr. Levendowski's voice played in his head, *The police believe the missing children to be alive, and are actively searching for them,* and Kyle flew to his feet, dropping the iPhone onto the wet pavement.

"Holy shit." He bent down, snatched it back up with trembling hands, then squinted for a better look at the approaching children. There were four of them. Two small Hispanics—a boy and a girl—and a slightly taller girl with fire-red hair flowing over orange one-piece pajamas. It only took a second for Kyle to realize he knew her.

"Kim!" He started walking toward the little girl who lived next door to Claudia. She was no more than twenty feet away now. "Kim. Jesus. Let's get you—"

But he stopped short and dropped the phone as instant sobriety fell over him like a bucket of ice had been poured on his head. His spine straightened like a popsicle stick, he felt his jaw hanging from his skull, and he knew he needed to run, but at the moment, his body was refusing to obey.

All four children were smiling like they were merely out on a field trip, and their parents hadn't been murdered last night, and Kyle understood why like he'd never understood anything in his life, because each one of them had bright orange lights in their heads where eyes should have been. And now, they were closer, maybe ten feet way, maybe less.

"NO!" Kyle yelled, took a step back, stumbled over, scrambled to his feet, scooped up his phone on the way. "NO! GET THE FUCK—"

Kim's mouth and terrible eyes opened wide. Her pajamas were stained in dark splotches which Kyle knew were bloodstains. All four of them were decorated in them. Kim sucked in a deep breath, then gasped, "Kyle!" her arms outstretched.

"FUCK NO!" Kyle turned, kicked up mud as he took off at a full sprint past the concrete block he'd been sitting on. He ran between a chain link fence, and the backs of old houses, then emerged onto a street with slightly nicer homes with thin trees in their front yards. He didn't stop, took a left and kept running downhill as fast as he could, his backpack bouncing off his buttocks.

This road had sidewalks, with cars parked against them, so that's where he ran. An old man stood in a doorway, staring at him as he passed, but he refused to stop, because he was still too close to the horrible children. Hanging a right into another alley, he saw a blue minivan in his peripheral, driving up the hill.

Kyle ran until he came to the back of a church he'd often passed, but never been inside. Then he stopped, leaning on the building, and trying to catch his breath. His lungs were on fire. His legs ached. He couldn't remember a time in his life when he'd been more afraid of something he'd seen.

Another text came in. *you want this shit or not? where are you dude?*

Kyle closed out his text box and dialed 911.

Chapter Two

Walla Walla was always either too hot, or too cold. It seemed moderate weather didn't exist in Eastern Washington, and Gabriel Brenton suspected that's exactly why they'd placed a prison here. Right smack dab in the middle of a burnt up, yellow field.

This morning, the field couldn't be seen through the fog. Gabe knew this without actually looking, because that's the standard the administration used to declare a fog line and deny prisoners access to the big yard. This could have been a good thing, had there not been a small yard attached to the side of Fox Unit.

The whites required mandatory workouts five days a week, and these mando sessions had to happen at the first available opportunity. That meant mornings, in whatever yard was opened. Today, it would be the small one, which wasn't actually a yard, but a fenced-in cement patch with a basketball hoop and pull-up bars.

It was the booth officer announcing fog line over the intercom that had initially awoken him in the small concrete cell. Then, the sound of his cellie, grunting beneath him on the bottom bunk. Even though the light was off and there was no sun beaming in the window by his bed, Gabe put his forearm over his head, as if shielding his eyes.

"Why can't it be a thunderstorm?" Zack moaned. "Lock us down, please!"

Gabe stretched, yawned.

Zack went on, only the frog in his throat seemed to have suddenly vanished, and his voice took on a playful note.

"What's the benefit of having the keys if you can't even cancel a workout for a day?"

"I can," Gabe finally said in a monotone that he knew was partially the reason he'd been put in charge of the whites in F-Unit. "Then tomorrow, when someone snitches to Brent that I didn't make you guys work out, I'll be gone and someone else'll have the keys and you can bet he won't cut you guys any slack."

"Dude, Brent's in G-Unit. No one's gonna snitch on you for doing 'em a favor."

"No?" Gabe half-grinned at the cream-colored ceiling, which was only a few feet away from his face. He threw the wool blanket off himself, and cold air nipped at his shirtless chest. Zack, though only a year younger than him, thought like a child. As did most of the men in Walla Walla. As had Gabe just two short years ago. He couldn't pinpoint the exact moment in which this had changed for him, and assumed it had been a gradual metamorphosis, but it seemed to have happened surprisingly faster than it did for others.

At twenty-four, being a shot-caller was practically unheard of. Some had done twenty years, putting in work through self-sabotage and acts of violence, all in anticipation of this esteemed title. But it hadn't worked that way for Gabe, because though experience and willingness to work were important for climbing the ranks in a prison car, they weren't everything. They weren't even the most qualifying characteristics.

There were guys in the unit who'd been around for longer, done more, and would still be here long after Gabriel Brenton was nothing but a distant memory to the Department of Corrections. They were all train wrecks though, and had any of them been allowed to drive, the whites would have been quickly headed for a car wreck.

Zack said, "Naw, dude. Why would they?"

Gabe sat up. He had to slouch to keep from hitting his head on the ceiling. He hung his legs over the edge of the top bunk, looking briefly out the small rectangular window on the cell's steel door. "Okay," he said. "Sure. Yeah, I'll go ahead and call off the workout today. Then if Brent *does* send someone after me, maybe *you'll* get the keys."

"What? Come on man. You know that's not what I—"

"That's what everyone wants," Gabe cut him off. "The whole unit. Every white guy at least. And why? So, they don't have to put in work? It's not like it's fun being in charge. It's actually a burden. You gotta be responsible for everyone else's actions, and everyone's trying to cross you out so they can have your position."

"Yeah," Zack said, "but that's not what I was trying to do, and you know it."

"Do I?"

"What the fuck, dude? Of course, you do."

Gabe hopped down in nothing but his white boxer shorts. His bare feet thumped on the cold cement floor, and a hollow thud resonated inside the cell. At six feet, the top bunk came up to the middle of his chest. Even in the dark, he could see the panic his cellie was attempting to conceal. He considered pushing it a bit further, then let him off the hook with a grin that suggested he'd just been poking fun. Zack smiled from ear to ear, broke out laughing. Gabe knew it was forced. Of course, it was because joke or no joke, what had been said was true.

Gabe went to the toilet and relieved himself. He wiped the metal seat, flushed, then washed his hands, and flipped the switch next to the shiny steel mirror, causing the room to illuminate. A folded photo of Kimberly on a hiking trail hung by the mirror. Had anybody pulled it from the brick, and unfolded it, he would have seen Carrie, who looked like a taller version of their redheaded daughter, and who Gabe had no interest in looking at or speaking to.

A black rosary made of thin string and plastic beads surrounded the picture, held in place by scotch tape, and positioned so it couldn't be seen from outside the cell looking in. A tiny black Jesus hung miserably from the cross.

Gabe washed his hands and took a seat on the metal stool at the desk next to his cellie's bed. He said, "You remember Skeeter?"

Zack's expression morphed so subtly the untrained eye may not have noticed. He was a smart kid, and he knew what came next. He wasn't yet disciplined enough to conceal it though, or the fact that he was already annoyed with what was going to be said. A few more months with Gabe, however, and he would be. "Of course, I remember Skeeter," he said.

"Then you remember what happened to him."

"A lot of things happened to that guy. You're gonna have to be more specific than that, dude."

"You know what I'm talking about," Gabe said.

"You sent someone after him."

"I had to take him off the line and you know that. But do you remember why?"

Zack took a deep breath, let it out slowly. He put his hands behind his head, causing the blanket to slide down, exposing a swastika, constructed of battle axes, which was tattooed on the left side of his chest.

"I'm not trying to make you feel stupid or talk down to you," Gabe said. "Just answer the question. You remember why I had to get rid of Skeeter, right?"

"Yeah."

"And?"

"'cause he wouldn't work out."

"Right!" Gabe smiled. "'Cause he wouldn't work out. Now personally, I couldn't give two shits whether or not any of you exercise. I don't think the bullshit cardio we're doing is actually making us any better in a fight. We should be trying to bulk up. Why you think the Samoans were able to smash out the Chicanos in the riot last year, even though they were outnumbered?

"But I don't make the rules. I just have to enforce them. You know why. And if Brent's making me send torpedoes after dudes for not working out, what do you think he'll do to me for not making you guys do it? Plus," he nodded toward his cellie's midsection. "You didn't have that six pack when you got here. Obviously, something's working."

"Whatever, dude," Zack ran both hands over his abs, pushing the blanket down as he did. "I had a pack before I came to prison."

"You had a dope-pack, you degenerate. Methamphetamine isn't a dietary supplement. You weren't fit, you were dying."

There was a knock on the door and both men looked to see a tall correctional officer with a beard, flashing a thumbs up. Gabe glanced down at the floor, decided it could wait another day to be swept, and waved a hand dismissively indicating he wouldn't be needing cleaning supplies today. The guard's face was indifferent as he disappeared.

"So," Zack said. "You're saying the workout ain't getting canceled."

"See? Those classes are paying off too. Maybe soon you'll actually get your GED." Zack gave him the finger. Cupping his mouth, Gabe yawned, then asked, "You ready, or what?"

"Yeah," Zack responded in the tone of a child who'd been told to do homework. "I guess." He sat up slightly, resting his weight on his elbows.

"Then grab it." Gabe said.

"Hold on, dude."

"We don't have all morning."

"I mean, we can always do it later. We got nothing but time."

"Yeah, or we could just do what we always do and get the day started on the right note. Come on little, bro, bring it out already while we still have some privacy."

"Fine." Zack reached up, lifted the corner of his mattress, and produced a thick book with a tattered blue cover. Written on the front were the words "Holy Bible." He handed it to Gabe and sat up.

"What's the date?" Gabe asked, glancing at the calendar taped above the small desk. "It's Friday? That makes it the—twenty-fifth. We're on Proverbs Twenty-

Five." He began flipping pages. "You wanna read today, or am I?"

"You go ahead," Zack replied.

"Cool. You pray us in then."

So, both men bowed their heads, and Zack began to pray.

***

Skagit County Jail would've seemed like a strange place to find God, had Gabe not come to believe it didn't work that way anyway. Since the day he'd slammed the phone into its metal cradle and stormed to his cell where he'd sat alone and cried into his palms because his wife of two years had told him about a man named Gus, he'd been convinced that *God* had actually found *him*. That he had wrapped massive, invisible arms around him and provided a supernatural comfort that had somehow carried him through a case in which he had faced a mandatory minimum sentence of ten years.

Seven months in jail, and Carrie didn't bring Kimberly to visit once. He'd wanted to blame himself. Everybody else seemed comfortable telling him he'd made his own bed when he committed first degree assault (Washington State's version of attempted murder), including his parents, who pushed this belief on him almost religiously.

And maybe believing he'd somehow sacrificed a relationship with his own daughter for the opportunity to cut some wino's head open with a switchblade would have brought him comfort. It would at the very least have shifted the blame, justified Carrie's indifference, and alleviated the ill feelings toward her which had wanted to settle inside him and rot for the past two years.

The problem was, no matter how hard he had tried, he couldn't blame himself. For the crime? Yeah. Of course. He'd done it. He'd plead. The charge had been dropped to second degree assault. And he'd taken a 48-month sentence on the chin without protest. But nobody told him he would have to lose his family over a bad decision made during a fight outside a bar. In fact, every time he thought back to his wedding day, all he could remember was being told the exact opposite.

For better or for worse. Through sickness and through health. Thick and thin. Over the mountains and through the woods. Blah, blah, fucking blah. It had all been lies, and when Gabriel Brenton had found himself at his lowest, Carrie, who he'd thought all through high school worshiped every footprint he'd ever left behind, had disappeared out of his life, along with his two-year-old daughter before he'd been incarcerated a whole month.

So, after that Dear John phone call, he'd locked himself in his cell, covering the window with a towel. Gabe had never been a religious man, hadn't even been a religious boy. Nobody ever taught him about things like church and prayer. But that day, without knowing why, and with tears pouring down his face, he'd cried out to God, begging Him to take away the pain, and that's how God found him.

Gabe took it easy on the whites. The workout was over in under a half-hour and nobody complained except Zack back in the cell. Lunch was a baked potato with some flavorless gravy containing a miniscule amount of meat poured over it. The food at Walla Walla may have contributed more than the workouts to its occupants' lean physiques.

Gabe and his cellie were both lying in their own bunks, waiting for shower time to be announced, watching reruns of an old sitcom on the small flat screen TV on the desk, when Gabe's name was called over the small speaker by the door.

"Yo," he responded.

"You dressed?" came the stoical voice.

"What do you mean?"

"CCO Conely wants you in his office."

Zack leaned out over the edge of the bunk and looked up curiously. Gabe just shrugged, hopped down, and changed into his prison issue Khakis, tucking his white T-shirt in, and telling the officer he was ready. A second later, the door slid open on its track and he stepped out into the big day room which was always segregated by race. He walked around the cluster of empty tables, the door by the control booth opened, and the CO with the beard and another stepped through.

The bearded officer said, "Brenton? We gotta go back there with you. I know you're cool and all, but it's just a precaution they make us take in these situations."

And Gabe felt the ground beneath his feet begin to sink, and he thought about his mother, his sister, Kim—everybody he cared about, because he'd seen *these situations* before, and every time it had meant a loved one had died. So, without a word, he darted past the two cops, toward his counselor's office.

***

The room was carpeted, and the walls were clean. There were no bars or metal doors, and Kyle wasn't handcuffed, but it was clearly an interrogation room. Not that he'd ever been in one before—in spite of the pot and occasional drinking, he'd never been in trouble with the law—but there was a mirror on one wall he could only assume was a two-way like the ones he'd seen on TV, and there were likely cops on the other side watching.

It was cold too. Even inside his jacket he found himself fighting the urge to shiver. He assumed they kept it this way, so criminals would be eager to confess to whatever they were being questioned about, and get the hell out of here. Other than that, and the mirror, however, it pretty much looked like an office without a desk or cabinets. A woman (wearing a flowery perfume that made him think of his Grandmother), who'd introduced herself as detective Bartlet, sat across the table and told Kyle that his mom had authorized her to look through his cellphone.

"Is that okay with you?" She had wavy brown hair, and wore black eyeliner that appeared to have dried and begun to crumble onto a layer of cover-up which barely concealed the crow's feet stretching from her eyes. Kyle knew plenty about makeup because Claudia wore it in what was probably excess.

"Are you *asking* me?" he responded.

"Well, yeah," Bartlet replied straight-faced.

"I thought you just said my mom authorized it already."

"She did."

"Then why are you asking me?"

Not missing a beat, she said, "Because, Kyle, I wanna make sure it's all right with you first. Respect is key here, right?"

"Sure. And if I say it's not okay—"

"Would you do that?" Bartlet squinted. She looked more like a lawyer than a cop—in a charcoal-colored pantsuit with three pens clipped inside her breast pocket—and her demeanor had been accusatory since they'd met.

"I don't know. I'm just asking."

"And so am I," she replied. "I don't see why a guy with nothing to hide would say I can't look in his phone. That doesn't make much sense, now does it?"

It didn't, he thought, *if, in fact, a guy had nothing to hide.* The last thing he needed, however, was this detective seeing the texts from Dobey about meeting up to give him weed. Especially if it led to the police tracing the number and calling the new girl. He didn't have to know her to be sure she'd snitch on Dobey's uncle for selling to a minor, and probably even get the shop closed down. Cannabis had only been legal a few years, and Kyle guessed the police still weren't pleased about it.

But that was a distant worry, which he only registered vaguely as he fought to keep his hands from shaking where they rested in his lap, because even now, close to an hour later, he still couldn't seem to shake the images of the impossible orange lights that had shone where eyes should have been in the heads of Kim and her friends. Not just in his memory, but they seemed to shine on the obnoxiously white walls like stars that faded briefly, then reappeared every time he blinked. Taking a deep breath, he said, "You know I called *you*, right?"

"Me?" She tilted her head.

"No. I mean, not *you*. I'm saying *I* called nine-one-one. So why am I being treated like a criminal here?"

"Do you *feel* like a criminal, Kyle?"

"What? Of course not. I said you're treating me—"

"Like a criminal." Bartlet's lips twitched like she might smile. She didn't. Instead, she said, "What would you say if I told you that I'd already looked in your phone?"

"I don't know. Big surprise?"

"There's no need for the attitude, dude." She tapped her fingernails, which were painted purple, on the table.

Kyle didn't respond, just dropped his gaze and watched as they danced on the stained wood.

"You know," Bartlet went on, "I know Mr. Collins. That's who was texting you, right? Just before we picked you up. Shawn Collins?" When Kyle didn't answer, she said, "There's no need to lie. I know his street-name is Dobey. Shawn's pretty popular around here, actually. He missed a court date a couple weeks ago, and we've been hoping to run into him at some point."

Kyle didn't look up, continued to stare at Bartlet's painted nails, noticing every blemish in the texture of the poorly applied polish. She'd stopped tapping, and though she had to have noticed him staring, she didn't react. Her hands were cloaked in skin that threatened to break into wrinkles at any second. He suspected she had been mildly attractive at some point in her life, and found himself tempted to ask her age (not because he cared, but because of some distant memory of learning early in life never to ask a woman her age).

He hadn't known Dobey had a warrant. His friend had been in juvie a few months ago, but he'd also been released, and Kyle just assumed the case was closed.

Bartlet sat back in her chair and said, "Okay, Kyle. You don't wanna snitch out your friend. I get that. Respectable. In a way that's gonna end you up on the same path as him eventually—and guess what. We'll be ready for you—but respectable, nonetheless. Tell me something though. Do you know the population of this town?"

It occurred to Kyle that he didn't, so he didn't answer.

"It's not a trick question. Do you know how many people live here in good ol' Mount Vernon, Washington?"

"No."

Finally, she smirked, and slapped the table lightly. "Lemme help. It's well under fifty thousand. And we have under fifty officers in our department. Of course, you still have the sheriffs and the Staties and whatnot, but that's beside the point. Think around one cop for every thousand people—and do you know how long the average knucklehead with a warrant manages to evade us?"

Kyle said he didn't.

"Under a month, Kyle. They never get far. You know why? Because they don't try. The criminals in this town never seem to think, 'Hey, I got a warrant, maybe I should get the hell outta town. Go somewhere bigger where I can just blend in.' So, to make a long story short, we'll catch your friend, oh, probably—" she puffed her lips out and rolled her eyes, "this week or next—and I don't care that you smoke a little weed, dude."

Kyle met her light brown eyes, opened his mouth to deny it, but before he had a word out, she cut him off.

"Save it, Kyle. Everybody smokes weed. That's not my department anyway. I solve the murders—and I'm good at it, too. I've been doing it a long time. You know I'm older than I look. So why don't we quit wasting time on some teenager with a shoplifting warrant, and talk about this bizarre statement you wrote."

Looking again at her hands, he said, "It's true."

"I know it is."

His eyes darted up and once again locked with hers.

She nodded. "That's right. At least some of it is. I also know some of it's bullshit. You seem like a smart guy, Kyle. I know you don't think I believe you left school by yourself just to get some peace and quiet. I can smell the marijuana on your clothes, and I called the number on your phone already. I know you were with Mr. Collins. And guess what? I know about the pot store his uncle owns downtown. So, let's nip all that in the backside right now, and get on the same page, because I also believe you saw those children. In fact, I know beyond a shadow of a doubt that you did. What I don't know is *where* you saw them."

"I told you—"

"I know what you said. And you wrote it in your statement too. Here's the problem, though, Kyle—and I don't expect you to know this—but statistically, every square inch within city-limits of any metropolis is monitored at any given time by no less than four cameras. Obviously, in a town like Mount Vernon that's reduced to two or three, but even so—worst case scenario—there should be footage from at least two cameras backing up any story. That is if the story's true. Can you guess how many are backing up yours?"

Her words fell over him like a bucket of cold water, yet her voice seemed to grow distant at the same time. It hadn't occurred to him that the police might not believe his story. Even though he hadn't thought to omit any of the details he, himself, was having trouble believing, like toddlers in bloody pajamas with orange glowing eyes. Why shouldn't they believe? It was all true.

He thought about the top of the hill where he'd seen the kids. Of course, there were no cameras. That's why students went there when they snuck off campus to smoke. He blinked a little too long, saw the orange lights on the backs of his eyelids, and quickly opened them again. Before he'd even thought about what to say, he heard himself telling her the neighborhood was residential, and that's why there were no cameras. That they needed to check all the ones nearby in the direction the children had come from.

Bartlet used the purple nail of her pinkie to scratch a spot under her eye, just missing the black liner. She yawned and said, "Well that's a good idea. Why didn't I think of that?"

Kyle pursed his lips, felt his body growing tenser by the second. He thought about movies he'd seen in which suspects told the cops they wouldn't answer any more questions without a lawyer, and it crossed his mind that

that was what he needed to be saying now. But why? Why should he need a lawyer, and why should he be a suspect? A suspect to what?

But something about her demeanor suggested she didn't suspect him of kidnapping those children. That maybe she knew already what he'd figured out the second Kimberly and her friends were close enough to see the blood on their clothes. That something had happened last night on Urban Ave that only happened in the part of the mind that entertains the impossible, and Bartlet was merely trying to ascertain how much Kyle had figured out already. That maybe this "interrogation" was nothing more than damage control.

But still feeling the need to assert his innocence, he told her again he hadn't done anything but call and report what he'd seen, and that now he knew never to do the right thing again. Bartlet just continued to grin like she thought the reaction she'd managed to pull out of him was cute. Then something occurred to Kyle, and he asked, "How do you know?"

"Excuse me?" She cocked her head curiously, but he suspected she knew exactly what he'd meant.

"You said you know beyond a shadow of a doubt I saw the kids. How do you know that?"

Folding one hand over the other, she said, "I'm not at liberty to disclose that information."

"Okay, then what is it you wanna know from me?"

Bartlet examined him a moment, then said, "Bring me the statement."

A couple seconds later, the door swung open and a tall, shiny-haired Hispanic-looking man in a white button-up shirt with a black gun resting under his shoulder stepped in and set a cream-colored folder on the table. He didn't speak, or address either of them, just left and shut the door behind him. Bartlet opened the folder and produced the single piece of paper inside—Kyle's statement—and for what may have been the next hour (there was no way of knowing as there was no clock in the room) they went over it together line-by-line.

She checked her phone from time to time, and asked questions like, "What do you mean, 'orange lights in their eyes?'" and "How do you know it was blood on their clothes?" But worst of all, were the ones like, "Don't you think it's a bit convenient these kids didn't use any streets with cameras nearby?"

When they were finished Kyle was sure she would make him write a new statement, specifying he had actually left school grounds to smoke pot with Dobey. But instead, she put the paper back inside the folder, stood up, and said, "Thanks Kyle. We'll get you out of here shortly," before turning to leave. When she made it to the doorway, he asked what time it was. She mumbled something he couldn't make out, and disappeared out of the room.

Kyle set his face down on his arms and shut his eyes, but his mind was worse than the interrogation room, because the first thing he saw was Kim and her own glowing eyes. He saw her mouth wide, her arms outstretched, and he still heard the air hissing through her throat as she sucked in a breath before saying his name.

And that voice. It was all wrong. It wasn't hers. It wasn't even human. But it wasn't *not* human either and that was the problem, wasn't it? It was choked and duck-like, as if she were speaking without a voice box. As if the air were merely being pumped by mechanical lungs out of a constricted trachea. Kyle didn't wonder why, because though he hated it, he already knew. It wasn't possible, and there was no way he would admit this bit to Bartlet, or to anybody, but he knew nonetheless.

She's dead. They're all dead. All four of them are dead, but they're alive at the same time and they killed their parents and if I would have let them, they would have killed me too.

Kimberly—what was her last name? He was sure he'd heard it once while hanging outside of Claudia's trailer, when the little girl used to run out of her front door squealing every time she saw him. When Claudia used to joke that Kim was trying to steal him away from her. When Kim's redheaded mother would sit on her porch smoking cigarettes and smiling at Kyle.

Carrie Brenton hung around her house in her blue scrubs because she worked at the nursing home on Division. And there it was. Her last name was Brenton. Kimberly Brenton. But she wasn't Kimberly Brenton anymore because Kimberly Brenton wasn't a walking corpse with orange eyes.

The more he thought about it, the more he became convinced. Not because of the voice, though, or the pale skin, or the swollen belly of the redheaded kid in the Superman underwear. No, those things had just confirmed what he would have suspected anyway because when he beheld those children, there was something missing.

Something he couldn't describe in his own mind, let alone words, because how do you describe nothing? It was a lack of something that he'd only seen one other time when his cousin had caught chickenpox at twenty-three, and his funeral had been an open casket and Kyle had sat in the pews feeling like his own soul had fled his body because he was the one who had given Curtis the pox, just two weeks prior.

It was that same nothing that he had experienced in his own body, and saw in his lifeless cousin's that those four children had harbored today, even though they were walking, moving, talking. And that had been more terrifying than any combination of glowing eyes and pale skin ever could be.

A few minutes later, the door opened and Bartlet appeared, holding his backpack. She told Kyle it was time to go, and didn't speak as she led him through a carpeted section with cubicle offices, then out into the big, open waiting area of the police station where a woman sat behind a service desk and his mother's wide hips filled a metal chair. Next to her, a set of tiny legs dangled from another as six-year-old Abel appeared hypnotized by an open magazine which sat on his lap.

Kyle's mother wasn't an angry woman (even when she was angry). She didn't have to straighten her blond hair, and her features were as pleasant as her personality. To top it off, she rarely handed out punishment, but the look on her face as she watched him approach informed Kyle that Bartlet had thrown him under the bus for skipping school to get high.

But then the detective told her that her son had done "the right thing," and been "very helpful," and she gave them both a business card with instructions to call if "anything new" came up. She reached into her pocket, handing Kyle his phone, and flashing an exaggerated wink. With that, she smiled at his mother and retreated back the way they'd come, her flat shoes slapping the tile floor and echoing until she was gone.

***

Skagit Valley College was small. Smaller than any college Marie had seen in London. Though it was quite confusing, because what was called a college back home was called a high school in the US. And Skagit Valley College would have been referred to as a community college had it been located in England.

Marie considered how strange it was to be not only sitting on the wrong side of the car, but driving on the wrong side of the road. Rain poured down all of the Beetle's windows, but she could still see the college's carpark—or what did Americans call it? A parking lot? — mostly empty. She'd passed it every day on her way to and from her home, but had no reason to stop other than there were likely cute guys hanging about. But even that wouldn't be necessary as Mount Vernon High School was co-ed, which had been the only positive aspect of moving, yet again.

Even in spite of leaving all of her girlfriends and Ian and knowing she wouldn't see any of them at least until she turned eighteen next year, the prospect of American public schooling had softened the blow. But that hadn't been the plan initially. In fact, her father had insisted fervently in the opposite, to the point they had almost wound up living an hour away from the apartment complexes he'd bought in Mount Vernon, in order to locate somewhere with an all-girls school nearby.

And based on what she knew of the public education system in the US, it was really the only move that would have made sense because Marie Franco had been top of just about every class at St. Paul's School for Girls back in London. She'd seen the evidence first-hand at Mount Vernon High today, when her class had learned math that she'd already aced at thirteen. And this was what Americans called senior year?

Across from the college, were the Sunset apartments. Behind the Sunset were the Silver Palms. Then the Woodlands. Her parents owned all three buildings, which sat amidst a cluster of others they planned to acquire eventually. And when Salvatore Franco wanted something, he got it because money was never an issue and Marie's father was a businessman who understood cut-throat tactics that would give Donald Trump a run for his money.

She'd been terrified to ask for public schooling. Not because he would say no, but because his fists were as rough as his business sense, and he seemed to enjoy using them just as much. Even in London where the lines defining child abuse tended to be thin, he hadn't hesitated to break her arm once after reading text messages between her and Ian. And though she'd wanted to believe her father had merely gone too far by mistake because Ian had been 19 and she only 15 at the time, she'd known better. The truth was, he was just a mean son-of-a-bitch, and unlike her sister, she was his intellectual equal—possibly even rival.

And her mother? Well, she didn't hit, nor would she dare utter a word of rebuke when her husband did. She was just there, and she enjoyed crocheting while she watched the news, and she looked enough like Marie that Marie hoped to God that she wasn't genetically predisposed to gain the weight that her mother carried at her age. Her sister was only twelve years younger than her, and had already begun to pack it on.

So, Marie hadn't asked. Instead, she had researched. She'd looked up everything she could find about the US. About Washington State. About the small town of Mount Vernon. But mostly about the local schools. Then she'd laid a blueprint that had started at Mount Vernon High, and ended at a medical school in New York. It was logical because she could breeze through the twelfth grade in the inferior public system where the work was much easier, and achieve her father's dream for her next year.

Skagit Valley College and the apartments appeared in her rear-view, and up ahead, old two-story houses sat in small yards. If she kept driving, which she had done once in the three weeks since arriving in Mount Vernon, the two-lane road would wind into the forest, which was actually quite aesthetic and unlike anything she'd seen in London. She hit her blinker and slowed down at an intersection where College Way met Waugh Road. Across the street, was a petrol station with a circular neon-green sign that read, "BP," suspended high up on a metal pole.

She'd prepared herself for a fight. Well, not a fight, but a beating. For her father to see through her plan and respond with the back of his meaty hand. It wasn't that he hated her, and wanted her to be unhappy. She'd always known this. He was just Italian and Catholic and sometimes girls needed to be reminded of their place in a family.

But she'd had to try, because though she had grown used to gowns and violins and teachers with perfect posture, she had craved a normal youth for longer than she could recall, and if she had to leave everything she knew behind, there needed to be a payoff. It wasn't even the idea of going to school with boys, really. Yeah, boys could be fun, and they made her laugh, but at the end of the day they were just boys. It was the prospect of normalcy that co-ed schools offered that had persuaded her to make the bold ask. Only it couldn't be a straightforward ask and she knew it, so she had used the one word that would give her a fighting chance.

A group of teenagers stood outside a small hatchback in the BP's carpark. Marie squinted to see if she recognized any of them from school, half expecting to spot Dobey, who she'd driven around for close to an hour today searching for his friend until well after lunch break was through. She didn't know if her resulting truancy had warranted a call to her parents, but suspected she might want to prepare herself for that as well.

The magic word had been *medical-school.*

And it had worked because the doors of opportunity had opened wide, but not Sal's eyes. No, her father had the coldest poker face there was, and would never reveal a feeling that didn't manifest in some form of anger. So, his approval that his oldest daughter had finally given in and decided to pursue the career which he'd been attempting to beat into her had only shown, when days later, he agreed to allow her to finish her year in a public school.

Mount Vernon wasn't as big as a suburb in London, but the kids at her new school cursed and fought and there was no mistaking that some of them were in gangs. She'd heard a story just today of a boy who was shot just up the street, and everybody seemed to do drugs and drink. All that was to be expected though, because she'd seen enough television to know what went on in the US.

Marie hadn't been to Australia since she was eight, and even though it had been nine years, she'd made a point in London to hold on to as much of her heritage as possible, which mostly just meant accent and lingo. It had made her exotic, different. Though she knew that she was easy on the eyes, being an Aussie in Europe had made her the center of attention in any given circle. Here, she was learning, nobody could distinguish between an Australian and an English accent anyway, though everybody seemed mesmerized every time she opened her mouth, and it was a curious thing.

But the most curious thing about her new home was that children were taken, and their parents killed last night, and there was no amount of American TV that could have prepared her for that.

She took the right onto Waugh and a hill appeared in front of her that was so steep it looked like the small Volkswagen shouldn't have been able to climb it. The neighborhood was wooded, but not heavily, and the houses got progressively nicer the higher she drove.

About halfway up, a horizontal, waist-high sign, which read, "Hilltop," sat on the right. From here, there were only mansions, and though Marie had yet to spot one as big and expensive looking as the one she and her parents had moved into three weeks ago, it was nothing compared to the one they'd left in England.

***

"Aw you gonna go to jay-oh?"

Kyle glanced in the rear-view mirror and saw Abel looking almost comical in the car seat he would soon outgrow. He was tall for a six-year-old, and had inherited a certain wideness from his mother. Though Tina McIntosh wasn't what most would consider obese, she was oddly egg-shaped, with hips that were so big they contrasted dramatically with her thin waist. Abel sat behind Kyle, who rode in the passenger seat of the Astro minivan.

Looking over her shoulder, his mom smiled and said, "What? Why would Kyle be going to jail, ya silly bird?"

"'Cause he got awested, didn't he?"

She returned her attention to the road and laughed. "Makes you wonder how he even knows what getting arrested is, doesn't it?" Her lips curved into a smile that may or may not have been forced. "Of course, Kyle didn't get arrested, brah. The police just needed his help with something. Can you say arrested?"

"Awested."

"Arrested."

Abel said, "Awested."

"Close. Ah."

"Ah."

"Reh."

"Weh."

"No, reh."

"Weh."

"Rrrreh."

"Rrrreh."

"Stud."

"Stud."

"Good," she said. "Arrested."

"Awested."

Some soft alternative song hummed quietly from the van's speakers. Kyle's mom said, "Okay. I guess that'll do pig," and Abel started making oinking sounds.

It was raining much harder than before, and the wipers squealed against the windshield while heavy drops drummed on the aluminum roof. The noises almost seemed in sync with each other like a percussion line. Kyle counted on his fingers—six days until Halloween— and made a mental note to look up the forecast later.

Bartlet hadn't snitched him out. And why would she? She was a homicide detective. Children were missing. Their parents were dead, and no matter how hard he tried, Kyle couldn't manage to convince himself the children he'd encountered hadn't been dead as well, and because of it he felt like something dead was in his stomach. Not rotting—it hadn't been there long enough for that—just lying where it didn't belong and causing a discontent.

He checked his phone, saw a few more texts from Dobey asking where he was. Some bordered on angry. He deleted them all, though it wouldn't make a world of difference if the police decided they did care about his extracurricular activities. They'd already seen the texts, plus they could probably just get them from the phone company anyway.

Abel laughed at his own piggy noises, then fell silent.

Tina McIntosh hadn't spoken more than a few words to her oldest son since picking him up from the police station. Now, without looking at him, she said, "Wanna talk about what happened?"

"What do you mean?" he asked.

"I don't know. Why don't you tell me?" She pulled up to an intersection where he could see Urban Fitness set in a huge parking lot just in front of Urban Ave. Normally, they would have taken that street home, and he would have glanced toward Claudia's trailer even on a rainy day like this, when it was unlikely she'd be outside. Today, however, he assumed Urban Avenue was closed, blocked off by police cars and crime-scene tape.

He said, "I'm not sure what you're asking."

"Okay—then let's start here: Are you alright?"

"Yeah."

Tucking a few strands of blond hair behind her ear, she examined him a moment, then said, "So you saw the missing kids from the news today?"

"I haven't watched the news today."

"But you know some kids are missing, right?"

"Yeah."

"And you saw them?"

"Yeah."

"And even though you haven't watched the news, you knew the kids you saw were the missing ones?"

"I mean, I guessed. I knew one from the trailer park."

She nodded, seemed to be considering this until finally, she asked where he saw them at.

"By the school."

"The high school?"

"Yeah."

"Really?"

"Why are you asking?"

"I'm just curious," she replied.

The light turned green, and she took the van through the intersection as the song ended and Kyle heard water splashing under the tires. Then a female DJ said something about a Halloween party in Seattle. His mom killed the stereo and asked where exactly the kids had been.

"By the school," he repeated.

"Yeah, I get that. But how close to the school?"

"I wanna go back to schoow!" Abel piped.

"Okay," Mom said, "Sounds great. You can go back on Monday."

"Okay!"

"I don't know," Kyle replied, knowing he was being backed into a corner, not sure he'd be able to avoid it. "They were like just up the street or something."

"Okay." She spoke slowly. "And you were like—?"

She knew something. Or maybe she didn't. Maybe she was just prying, which meant she at least suspected something. At this point it was either lie, and get in trouble if she knew the truth, or tell the truth and get in trouble if she hadn't known already. As he was having this thought, his mom went on.

"I'm not accusing you of anything. I just thought I should probably know what happened since I woke up today and I was still your mom and all. But be aware that trust is like a wee little ice-cube. If you break it, you can get it back, but it won't happen fast. You know I had to leave work early for this, right?"

Stalling for time, Kyle said, "Yeah, but can't Karen cover for you?"

"Of course, she can. And she is. But Fridays are particularly busy, and one receptionist isn't exactly ideal at a dental clinic. And if you can't tell, I had to pull Abel out of school early, too, because nobody would've been home when he got off the bus. He missed speech therapy, so I guess we're both pretty eager to hear the story straight from the horse's mouth. No offense, brah."

Abel said, "Yeah, brah!"

"None taken," Kyle replied.

"And—"

"And I was off school grounds, but it was lunchtime."

She hit the blinker, brought the van to a slow coast as they approached the railroad tracks just before Urban Ave. Kyle squinted out the windshield seeing that it wasn't blocked after all. Of course, it wasn't. How could it be? People lived there. His mom took the turn and drove slowly up the back road where there were four rows of gravel streets on the left, which were lined with old, beat up trailers on either side.

Abel cried, "Wook at the cop caws!"

But the only row with police vehicles was the first. The one with the tiny taco restaurant in front. The one Claudia lived on. Multiple trailers were surrounded by yellow tape, and a white van that said KOBO 4 sat in the restaurant's parking lot, but it was difficult to make out much besides that, two cop cars, and a couple officers in hoods, because the rain flowing down the Astrovan's windows obscured the view. Still, Kyle found himself scanning the area for Claudia. After they'd passed, his mom asked, "Is she okay?"

"Yeah."

"Well thank God for that at least."

"Yeah. Thank God."

"You know I've never been one to buy into conspiracy theories. I believe in the moon-landing and I don't think nine-eleven happened over oil. But I just keep thinking that whatever happened last night couldn't have been just some psychopath with a thing for kids." She sniffed and Kyle found himself staring at the side of her face, because he'd rarely seen his mom cry. She never did it for attention or sympathy. In fact, he suspected she would refuse a hug if it were offered. Then she blinked and there were no tears. She said, "It almost feels organized. Like whoever it was knew exactly which houses had exactly which children. Like it was tactical, I guess. Don't you think?"

And that's when Kyle McIntosh knew beyond a shadow of a doubt his mother didn't believe for a second that he'd seen the kids, because she thought they were either locked away somewhere, or dead.

At least she's right about one thing.

He wasn't going to try and convince her otherwise. His mother was an intelligent woman, and with that came a skepticism and need for validation which Kyle didn't have, couldn't produce if he wanted to. So, he told her he didn't know if it felt like that or not. He needed to see what they were saying on the news.

She turned onto a residential street where houses sat in yards with big trees in them which always gave the impression of driving through a dimly lit tunnel. "Are you allowed to be off campus during lunch?" she asked as if the previous moment hadn't even transpired.

"No," he said because he knew that if he was going to tell a lie he would need to be selective.

"So why were you—"

"I don't know. I mean, I do, I just—I wanted to be alone, I guess. I knew it was against the rules, I just didn't think it was that big of a deal. Like a small rule, you know?"

"Yeah. Sure. You know the guy you were named after? My brother?"

"Yeah."

"Well, he started out breaking small rules, then graduated to felonies. Now he's dead."

"Uncle Kyle died in a car accident."

"Drunk and high out of his mind, and on his way to pick up a bag of heroin. All of my siblings started breaking all the itty-bitty, little rules. Isn't that crazy?"

"Yeah. I guess."

"Seriously. Think about it. My mother had twelve kids, and how many of them are dead or in prison? That's why I tried to follow even the tiniest rules growing up. Because I saw what they were doing, and I wanted to be different. You know?"

Another drawback to having an intelligent mother, was that she always knew what to say so he couldn't argue. Not because she didn't allow it, or because she was even right, but because to her he was a book with large print and small words. Most of the time he didn't even know how she managed to manipulate him, so he'd learned just to go with it.

He told his mother she was right.

"I know I am."

"Mom's ah-ways wight!" Abel cheered.

"See? Even your brother knows."

"Yeah. He's smarter than me, I guess. Listen, I won't leave campus anymore during lunch. I promise."

"Pinky swear?" She exited the tree laden street, pulled onto Broad Road. In under a minute, they would enter the Stanford Development, which was the only upper-middle-class neighborhood in a two-mile radius, and which was also where they lived.

"Pinky swear," he replied.

"Good," his mom said. "And no more weed either, brah. It's not good for you."

***

Christina Bartlet, or Christy, as she preferred to be called, drove a silver Dodge Caliber because aside from the exempt license plates, it tended to be the most inconspicuous car on any given street, and a homicide detective had to be stealthy. Admittedly, even though Mount Vernon had an anomalous ratio of annual killings per capita, the vast majority were cut-and-dry gang-shootings. Last night's murders, however, weren't gang-related because even the gangbangers weren't this sick, and if they had been, they still weren't capable of causing the type of shit that was happening.

On a normal day, there might have been some country song or another coming from the Caliber's speakers. Today, however, wasn't a day for music and her wipers were as smooth as her car, so the only noises that could be heard were the sounds of raindrops tapping on the roof and her crackling handheld radio, which sat in the passenger seat next to a non-police-issue miniature laptop and the folder containing McIntosh's statement. Christy should have been in the passenger seat instead, enjoying the heated leather upholstery and napping while somebody else drove. Or just at home in bed. Or anywhere where she didn't have to be awake, which she'd been since around midnight. Illuminated blue digits on her dash said it was now 3:43 PM, and a charcoal colored sky suggested evening was quickly approaching.

The radio announced that somebody needed assistance with a traffic stop on 12th, in which the vehicle was registered to a violent felon. Yawning, she stopped at a red light on Riverside Drive and glanced in the rear-view mirror. Her eyes were bloodshot again, and had begun to droop.

"Go home," she told herself. "Get some rest, you crazy bitch."

But that was almost humorous, because both she and her reflection knew there was no way she would be able to sleep even if she *could* somehow convince herself to go home.

Kyle McIntosh had seen the missing children. There had been no doubt about it. Not just because he'd known information she had strategically withheld from the media—what each of them was wearing—but because he'd known about their eyes, and even the patrol units didn't know about them or the impossible squid-like shadows they'd cast under the streetlights on every bit of video they'd been caught on. And there wasn't much footage, either, because the little bastards had avoided surveillance so well there was little room to doubt it had been intentional.

She hadn't been entirely (or even slightly) honest with the McIntosh kid, though, because they had, in fact, been caught on camera after he spotted them. Not close to the location, but his statement had been enough to lodge a search of every possible route they could've taken to arrive there.

And quite an incompetent search it had been, because a squad of uniforms had been sent to conduct such search, while Christy and the small handful of informed plainclothes were at the station collaborating on the McIntosh interrogation.

She'd known from the jump that the kid's statement was true. Sure, she wouldn't have deserved her title or superior paycheck, had she not climbed through all the hoops associated with confirming what she knew, but the subtext of the meeting had been much simpler than that. Aside from details, which could have been acquired in a matter of minutes, she'd merely needed Kyle McIntosh to doubt his own story. And why shouldn't he? He was high out of his mind, and as far as Christy could see, not the sharpest knife in the drawer.

Still, it shouldn't have required four detectives, and had Christy slept last night, she probably would have sent at least one of them to head up the search for the children. But she hadn't slept, and they were dealing with something that policy and procedure didn't cover because whatever the hell it was, it was something inexplicable and utterly impossible. She hadn't slept, because from the time she had been called to the trailer park on Urban Avenue last night, she'd been heading up the case. She hadn't slept, and she'd made a bad call, and the bastards had gotten away.

The light turned green, and she took her foot off the brake, tapped the gas. A couple teenagers in hoodies jogged across the intersection, just missing the front end of the Caliber. She thought about Shawn Collins, whose picture had been pinned to the warrant board for a couple weeks, who she'd known nothing of before today, and who nobody at the station actually gave a damn about. She wondered briefly if he was under one of the hoods, then dismissed it because it was irrelevant.

Sending the uniforms alone to track the children had by far been the worst decision of her career. It wasn't because they were incompetent either. Far from it. But as soon as she'd taken a moment to reflect, it had occurred to her they were lacking the details they would need to look properly.

However, they did know certain things weren't yet being shared with the media. Like the fact that the missing children weren't kidnap victims, but rather parricidal maniacs. And their presence in the area suggested the redheaded boy's drug-dealing father, whom they'd been attempting to reach out to since the killings, had at last turned up at home. And though they knew the kids had thus far avoided surveilled areas, they didn't know about their glowing orange eyes or impossible squid-like shadows.

Christy wasn't a religious woman. She didn't read her horoscope in the morning paper. She didn't believe in the supernatural. She did, however, believe in evidence, had built a career on it, and the evidence all pointed to something not only paranormal, but pure evil—whatever that might mean. So had she, or somebody else who'd had the privilege of seeing the said evidence, been a part of the search, he or she would have checked the paths without cameras first. He or she would have followed the route that led to the one place no rational thinking person would expect four toddlers to cut through.

The cemetery by the high school.

When the uniforms showed up the children were already gone, and all that was found at the boy's father's home was a headless body in the living room, and tiny footprints in the bloody mess.

Hitting the blinker, Christy pulled into the turn-lane and prepared to take a left onto Fir Road, where an hour ago, just over the hill, her grandson Evan had been at Madison Elementary working his way through the second grade. A Dodge which was strikingly similar to hers pulled out of the parking lot of the Tesoro gas station on her right and drove off in the direction from which she'd come, kicking up water on its way. Her thoughts returned to the case.

The uniforms had managed to acquire footage from a security camera at the First Allegiance Apostolic Church, located on the opposite side of the cemetery before she'd finished the interrogation, and a short clip had caught the missing children skipping by. Only briefly (it added to an accumulated thirty-one seconds of footage of them which had been acquired since last night) and the officer who'd informed her over the phone had said, "Ya gotta pause it at juuuust the right time an' ya can see the redheaded boy holdin' his pop's head in a fuckin' shoppin' bag. Believe that shit?"

The light turned green, and Christy took the turn, not slowing down as she drove over the railroad tracks. On her left, she passed a cluster of old, abandoned warehouses with assorted colored windows that had mostly been broken out by kids with rocks. Then there was nothing but streets on either side of Fir with duplexes and apartment buildings, among three-and-four-bedroom middle-class homes.

In under a minute, the car climbed the hill and began to make its way back down the other side. Madison came into view on the left, the cemetery directly across the street. It had occurred to Christy, last year when Evan's teacher had taken her students on a field trip to see some of the hundred-year-old tombstones, that this had been a peculiar place to build an elementary school. And again, now as she considered that the only thing separating Madison from the high school was the historic graveyard.

It was surrounded by a chain link fence, which the kids had to have climbed on the high school side. Though Christy hadn't seen the footage or the decapitated body yet, she could picture eleven-year-old James Booth Jr. in his Superman underwear tossing a blood-logged shopping bag containing his father's head over the fence, and climbing like a little spider monkey to retrieve it.

She wanted it to make her sick to her stomach, knew it should have, but thirty years on the force had taught her that humanity was something that belonged at home, not work. And it was this ability to check her sentiment at the door (as well as other things) that secured her position as head of the homicide division still at fifty-two years of age.

Two dark-blue squad cars were parked just inside the cemetery's entrance, and a couple of uniforms in raincoats stood talking. She didn't slow down or acknowledge them, just hit her blinker and took the first left past Madison into the New Palace neighborhood where red and blue flashing lights lit up the heavily wooded street.

Most of the patrol vehicles littering the barely paved road said Mount Vernon Police on the sides, but a couple of Skagit County Sheriffs were here as well. Uniforms stood in groups watching canines sniff the pavement obsessively. House doors stood open as residents watched the scene unfold from inside. Christy guessed the news would be showing up any minute, as they were already in town anyway.

She pulled up behind a blue cruiser and killed the engine. Reaching into her glove compartment, she brought out a small bottle of Visine, turned on the dome light, and used the rear-view to apply the eye drops, careful not to smear her makeup. Then she killed the light and opened her door. Before she was even out of the Caliber, a tall dark-haired man in a MVPD uniform was approaching purposefully, slightly hunched over as if bad posture could somehow shield him from the rain. He stopped only feet from her as she shut the door and said, "Brian, please tell me I can finally go home and get some sleep."

"You can definitely go home and get some sleep." He squinted as he projected his voice over the downpour. "In fact, you probably should."

"Listen Brian, I'm sure you know this, but if you haven't located those children yet, every second counts. So, this isn't a time to be cute. Unless, of course you've found them. Have you found them?"

"Well, no."

"Then cut the crap and gimme an update."

"Listen, Mom—"

"Detective Bartlet."

"Right, uh—" he cleared his throat, "Detective Bartlet. You really should go home and—"

"Brian, I'm not gonna ask again. Are the dogs picking anything up yet or not?"

"Well, yeah. They did. There were traces of blood against the fence on the other end of the cemetery. Mostly washed away, but the dogs located enough to get a scent, so we started them there. They kept losing it, though, probably 'cause of the rain. But they were able to pick it back up and they led us that way." He pointed up the street, to where a dead-end lead into a patch of woods.

Christy glanced at the dogs, still sniffing the street and thought, *Then what the hell are they doing here instead of searching the woods?* Before she could ask though, her son went on.

"We got more dogs back there, but there's a creek."

"A creek?"

"You know, a stream."

"I know what a freaking creek is. Are you saying the kids crossed the water?"

"Well, yeah."

"And it threw the dogs off?"

"Ah, yeah. If the subjects cross a water source, the dogs can't—"

"Do you have units checking every route they could've taken on the other side of the creek?"

"Already on it," he said.

Another unmarked silver Dodge parked behind Christy's and Detective Rivas stepped out in a pair of slacks and a white button-up that instantly began to turn transparent as drops of rain soaked into the fabric. He wore his black Glock and extra magazines in his shoulder holster. His torso was long and toned, and he wasn't much older than her son. He stepped up next to her as she told

Brian to check every route without video surveillance first.

When Brian stood staring at her like she'd just told him his father had come back from the dead, she asked again if he'd already located the missing children, and without a word, he turned and jogged toward the other uniformed officers.

Rivas said, "You look like shit."

Almost involuntarily, she glanced down at his shirt, which was already pasted to his body, then back up at his face and tilted her head. "Aren't you just Prince Charming?"

"It's just your makeup," he said. "It's all smeared."

A uniformed cop instructed a woman holding hands with a young girl to please step back onto her lawn. Christy resisted the urge to look at her own reflection in the window of the nearest squad car and told Rivas everything she'd just learned.

When she was done, he said, "Listen, Christy, I'm not trying to overstep or anything here, but don't you think maybe you should call the feds in on this thing?"

"This isn't the fucking X-Files, Rivas. You think the FBI really has some secret department that specializes in tracking Chupacabra and the Boogeyman?"

"I don't know," he wiped his jet-black hair from his forehead. "I mean you see the documentaries—"

"To tell you the truth," she interrupted him. "I'm surprised the story's not out already from the employees we got the damn videos from. It'll go viral soon, though. Mark my words on that. And if there *is* some government agency that deals with paranormal shit, then you can expect Mulder and Scully to come knocking any time now to tell us they're taking over the case. If not, the news is just gonna have a fucking hay-day with whatever this is, and you can expect mass panic in this town. Either way, you might wanna keep your weapon handy."

Chapter Three

The forecast said it would rain on Halloween. Kyle had a tablet he often used when on social media, or websites that he felt compelled to delete from his browser history, but as he sat on his futon which was currently folded into a couch, listening to Post Malone sing about how his exes thought they were better now, he used his white iPhone to check the weather.

The blankets were put away neatly in the closet, and everything was tidy in a way that made his clean-freak mother joke that he was obsessive-compulsive. The only exceptions manifested in patches of short brown fur which stuck to the surface of the futon and carpet in random places. Their source: the tiny shivering bundle of a short-haired dear Chihuahua lying curled up next to him. He kept a lint roller handy, but it was just impractical to follow after Chewy all day and there was no way he was going to ban the dog from the only comfortable surface in the room, as he was currently in close competition with Dobey for best-friend status.

There were no trophies on shelves because Kyle had never played a sport. He might have, if he'd discovered at any point in life that he was coordinated, or good at one, but even a month of boxing lessons had served little more than to afford him the opportunity to learn that he didn't enjoy being punched in the face.

His walls were plain white, like everything else in the box-shaped two-story house. He didn't keep posters or pictures on them because everybody seemed to feel the need to stare directly into the camera and it always gave the impression the images were constantly watching. Once, when a cousin from out of state had visited, she had sat on Kyle's futon, her legs crossed, scanning his bedroom curiously before finally asking, "What are you into?"

He had stuttered trying to think of an answer, because the truth was, his leisure time tended to be spent at one of his friend's houses with Claudia by his side, surrounded by a cloud of marijuana smoke, and that was hardly a hobby.

It was supposed to rain all weekend, then Monday and Tuesday would clear up a bit. But Wednesday, the showers would return, and Thursday evening, Halloween night, would be an absolute downpour.

The song ended, so Kyle got into the music on his phone and selected to replay it. Chewy glanced up briefly as it came back on, then returned to his shivering nap.

Kyle thought about Claudia and wondered if she ever thought of him while she was with her *new vato*. He wondered if she would dress slutty on Thursday, then almost laughed because of course she would. She would probably go to some party in nothing but caution tape wrapped around her private parts, or a bikini with some form of animal ears, and she'd sit on her new boyfriend's lap while Kyle was out in the rain taking his little brother trick-or-treating like they'd agreed months ago they would do together.

Kyle's mom didn't talk much as she made herself busy around the house, responding to texts and preparing dinner from a recipe she seemed to be reading from her phone. Abel sat on the couch watching SpongeBob SquarePants and chanting "Ah-rrreh-stud" during the commercials until eventually he made his way downstairs to his bedroom.

Kyle spent most of the afternoon trying not to think about what he'd seen by the school, because, like his breakup with Claudia, thinking about it wouldn't make it any less real. The problem was, he could still see the lights from their eyes every time he blinked. It was as if he'd looked into the sun and burned his retinas, only worse because that would have gone away within minutes. Somehow, the tracers of the terrible eyes of the missing children had only managed to dim slightly.

Around six, he was downstairs watching a reality show that he guessed was scripted, but entertained him, nonetheless. Chewy's pointed ears had been flicking every few seconds as they always did at this time of night. Then, before Kyle even heard the car pull up, the dog flew to his feet like a jack-in-the-box and darted across the room barking maniacally and scratching at the bedroom door with his front paws.

"I don't know what your problem is," Kyle growled. "You know it's just Dad getting off work."

But he might as well have been a corpse, because Chewy didn't even acknowledge that he was speaking, just kept barking, which was more of a high-pitched chirp than anything.

"Okay, okay. Fine." Kyle made his way across the room to let him out, and before the door was even open the dog was trying to maneuver his pointed face into the crack. Squeezing his frail body through, he disappeared like a bullet out of the room, his claws scratching the carpet as he rounded the corner, and shot up the stairs.

After backtracking briefly to turn off the television, Kyle went to the door once again and gripped the knob. His mother had an almost eerie ability to get dinner exactly as his dad arrived home from work, which he guessed was meant to add to the simulation of a black-and-white sitcom home that she'd been engaged in his entire life. He also guessed that that, in itself, was no more than an attempt to forget what kind of home she'd grown up in.

He didn't mind the dinner conversations which always seemed reminiscent of an episode of Leave It to Beaver, but often wondered if they existed anywhere else in the universe besides his house and his TV set. Tonight, however, he wasn't looking forward to what would likely be the topic of discussion.

Opening his door the rest of the way, he instantly smelled sweet seasonings and chicken, which made him aware he was hungry. Then Abel's door—catty-corner to his—moved and his little brother appeared in a denim jacket with a red and yellow striped shirt underneath. A frizzy red wig sat crooked on his head. He raised a plastic serrated kitchen knife in one hand, and hopped out into the hall.

"Hi! I'm Chuuuucky! Wanna pwaaaay?"

Chewy continued to chirp, his barks mixing with Dad's voice and drifting down the steps. "Whoa! What's up, man? Well, hey there! Oh yeah? Oh yeah? Ah-buh-buh-buh-buh-buh-buh-buh!"

"What's up, Chucky?" Kyle raised his hand for a high five and his brother, who had worn his Halloween costume at least once a day since he'd gotten it last week slapped it. "Killer dolls eat dinner, right?"

Abel tilted his head, seeming to consider this, then gave a big, exaggerated nod.

"Then let's go get some food." Kyle stepped around the kid and made his way up the steps. Halfway between the first and second floors he saw his dog in front of the door dancing on his back two legs, barking and drumming at the air, staring up at the man who almost hadn't let Kyle bring him home from the rescue shelter two years ago.

"Hey," Kyle said as his dad reached down and scratched the dog behind the ears, then straightened back up.

"Okay," Dad squinted. "Chill out Chewbacca. Okay, buddy. Shut up already." Then to Kyle, "What's up, man? Heard you got yourself thrown into the slammer today. Whoa! Is that Chucky?"

Turning around, Kyle saw his brother slowly mummy-walking up the steps, toy-knife in one hand. "I'm gonna fuckin' kiiiiiw yeeeew!"

At first his dad just tilted his head, squinting, open-mouthed and speechless. Chewy, seeming to notice the change in mood, stopped barking and took off up the steps. Then their dad said, "What did you say?"

"Nuffing!"

"Well, it didn't sound like nothing. You know we don't use that type of language in this home, right?"

"Buuuuut I'm Chuuuuckyyyyy!"

"For fuck's sake." He shook his head. "Well listen, Chucky. Dinner smells really tasty, and my son Abel needs to eat so he can grow big and strong like his older brother. Think you could go find him for me please?"

"He's wight thew!" Abel pointed his knife at Kyle.

"Not Kyle. I mean can you go find Abel? Tell him to get changed for dinner and get upstairs quickly so we can all eat."

"Okay!" Abel turned and ran back the way he'd come.

Looking at Kyle, Dad said, "What the hell are you teaching your brother?"

"I didn't teach him that. You're the one who doesn't have parental controls on the TV."

Kyle's mom sometimes joked he was lucky hair recession skipped a generation. He'd been told it was passed down on your mother's side anyway. He often found himself hoping either theory was true, because Dan McIntosh's black hair grew around the sides of his pointy head like a cult-de-sac, and nowhere else. He kept it trimmed, but as far as Kyle knew, he had never shaved it to the skin to conceal the massive bald spot on top.

"So did they make you squat and cough?"

"What?" Kyle asked.

"You got arrested, right? Didn't they at least do a cavity search when they booked you in?"

"I wasn't arrested. I just had to go in and fill out a report."

Dan laughed and began to make his way up the stairs, using the wooden handrail to stabilize himself. It was a task which was never without considerable effort due to his left leg being made of fiberglass from just below the knee.

A few minutes later Abel was changed out of his costume, and the entire family sat around a wooden table under a chandelier. The small dining room was all that separated the living room from the kitchen. Tina made her husband pray before anybody touched their food.

Though his mother was the only person in the house who even remotely cared about religion, Kyle had rarely seen her utter a prayer out loud. She'd come home one Sunday during her church phase (which had lasted the whole of four months), and said she'd learned the husband is the spiritual head of every house, and therefore the designated prayer leader. In the three years since, not a dinner had passed in the McIntosh home, in which Dan hadn't pretended to speak to a God which Kyle speculated he didn't believe in – though speaking to a dubious God was a hell of a lot more tolerable than dealing with his wife's recent vegetarian phase.

If God responded tonight, Kyle didn't hear him, but the food was surprisingly good, so he said, "You found this recipe online?"

"Yup," his mom said. "Chicken ala—huh. Well, I'm gonna have to go read it again. It's chicken ala-something, though. It was on goodyfam.com. Isn't it amazing?"

Everyone else, including Abel, agreed that it was, in fact, amazing, so she said she'd remember the recipe. Then there was an awkward silence until Dan McIntosh seized the opportunity to regale them with one of his customary dinner tales of what had gone on at the hospital today, where he headed up one of the financial departments.

Kyle waited for the questions to begin about his own afternoon, but they never did, so halfway through the meal he relaxed and said, "So I checked the weather forecast for next week."

His mom didn't look at him, just twisted her fork into a tangled mess of angel-hair-pasta, and said, "Okay—?"

"Well, it's supposed to rain pretty hard on Halloween, and—"

"I saw that," his dad said through a mouthful of chicken.

"Dad!" Abel exclaimed. "Don't chew with your mouf open."

"I wasn't. I was talking with food in my mouth."

"What?" The boy's own mouth and eyes expanded in utter shock. "That's not good eithuw."

Dan laughed, and Tina said, "So you checked the weather, and—?"

"I mean, it's gonna rain most of the week anyway, but Thursday's supposed to be the worst. Like a downpour."

"Yeah. I saw that too. It's supposed to be like the wettest day of the year or something. That's a bummer, isn't it?"

"Yeah," Kyle said. "It's a bummer. I was just thinking, since I'm supposed to be taking Abel or whatever—"

"Actually," she interrupted. "I don't think that's such a good idea this year after all."

"What?" Abel shrieked. "But I wanna go twick-oh-tweeting."

"I know you do, brah. But this year's not exactly normal, ya dig?"

"Why's it not noh-mal?"

"It's not safe," his dad said, using his fork to tear flesh from a chicken bone.

"But I'm Chuuucky!"

"Well Chucky needs to be safe, too, doesn't he?"

"No!"

His mom said, "I know you're Chuuucky, brah. And we're still going trick-or-treating. I'm thinking I'll take you to the mall instead. They do trick-or-treating there every year. How's that sound for a compromise?"

"But I wanna go with Kyle!"

"Don't yell at the table. And Kyle can come with us, can't you Kyle?"

Kyle considered this, and felt something well up inside him that he didn't like. Not because he'd looked forward to taking Abel trick-or-treating. He had once upon a time, but that had all changed when Claudia left. It wasn't that he didn't value his baby brother's happiness either—far from it in fact. Abel was one of the best things that had ever happened to him. It might've been because his mom was right, it wasn't safe out there anymore, and he knew that better than anyone. But it was more likely because he knew that wasn't the real reason for her change of heart. The truth was, his mother no longer trusted him, and that was the price he'd paid for doing the right thing. Still, he said he'd go to the mall on Halloween.

Abel seemed to deflate. He said yeah, the mall sounded like a good compromise, but he was solemn after that, and Kyle couldn't help that it melted his heart a little.

***

Laura Cunningham posted a picture on Facebook at 9:33 PM, but it wasn't taken recently because the background showed a blinding sun, set against a light blue sky and she was wearing a pink bikini. The phone was held low and intentional so all that could be seen of her was the under curve of her ass, traces of her dark ponytail, and her forearm. She'd clearly taken it herself. Kyle clicked "Like" and in under a minute, she posted a smiley face in response. Then the music cut off briefly as his phone vibrated next to him indicating a text.

He was in his room and Post Malone was playing again on repeat, singing everything Kyle wanted to say to

Claudia. Chewy lay on his stomach on the futon, his head resting over his paws.

Tablet in his lap, Kyle picked up the phone, expecting the message to be from Laura, which would have been all right, though it would have been better if it was from Claudia. As it turned out, it was neither.

He examined the number. It was vaguely familiar, but he was unsure where from. The message didn't help to identify its source.

Hi.

His first thought was *Dobey,* who notoriously texted him from random phones because he didn't have his own. But "Hi," didn't sound anything like his best friend, and Dobey never would have capitalized a word, so he thought *Bartlet?*

But when he checked the number on the card she'd given him, it wasn't her either. His next thought was even more unsettling.

It's Kim. She's after me now that I've seen her and her evil eyes. She knows I know the truth and she's gonna kill me like she killed her mother.

That wasn't right either, though, because how could the child have known his phone number? Then again, how could anything he'd seen today have been real one way or the other? If toddlers could kill their parents and walk around dead with glowing eyes, surely, they could acquire a number which was available to the world on social media. He considered ignoring the text, but curiosity seemed to be knocking on the inside of his ribcage. Even Chewy raised his little head and stared at him expectantly. So, Kyle typed, *hey,* and pressed send.

The response was almost instant.

Where'd you run off to today?

The mattress seemed to sink beneath his body, threatening to pull him down and consume him like quicksand. His heart sped up, and his mouth was instantly dry because clearly it *was* Kim. It was her and her horrible, murderous friends. And if they could get his number, then why couldn't they figure out where he lived as well? He thought about every online account he had, and whether or not his address was posted. Of course, it wasn't, though, because nobody posted addresses on social media.

But what else is out there? Pictures of the house? Street signs? And what if she didn't use Facebook to get the number? What if she just knows because her eyes are orange and she's a fucking zombie, and not the four-year-old girl you used to wrestle with in Claudia's front yard?

Chewy tilted his head and blinked. Kyle typed, *what do you want?*

The phone buzzed.

Excuse me?

What do you want from me?

Well that's subjective, isn't it?

Subjective? What the hell was going on? The Chihuahua yawned, laid his head back on his paws as the song ended, then restarted. Kyle was losing it. There was no doubt about it, though the lights had finally disappeared from his vision. He didn't know when. At some point they were just gone. It hadn't made him feel any better, however, because now his own mind had been playing with the idea that maybe he hadn't seen what he'd thought he'd seen to begin with. And though that would mean there were no evil, murderous corpse-children wandering the streets, it would also mean he was out of his mind.

He typed, *Who is this?* and his thumb was just hovering over the send button when the phone vibrated again and a small image appeared. Without hesitation, he tapped it. The picture blew up, filled his screen, and he knew then why the number looked familiar.

The new girl lay back on a silk sheet, her hair flowing out in every direction like dark liquid spilling from her head, grinning up at the camera. She wore a gray sweater with a turtleneck, and Kyle found himself searching his memory for her name. Maria, was it? No, Marie.

The message was instantly followed by another.

Remember me yet?

As he read the words, he heard them in his head in her accent. *Remembah me yet?*

Kyle typed, *lol. yeah.*

Figured you thought I was someone else, which means you probably deleted all the messages your friend sent from my phone s'arvo. Thought a picture would help to remind you.

At first, he thought it must have been a typo, because this girl texted like she was writing an English paper for credit. Perfect grammar. Nothing misspelled. No fragmented sentences. He waited for her to send a correction, but nothing came in, so after a long pause, he typed, *s'arvo?* and pressed send.

Yes. S'arvo is how we say 'afternoon' in Australian.

oh. okay. I get it.

I want you to know, I'm very disappointed.

??

That you deleted my texts, she responded.

they were from you? I thought they were from Dobey.

Well they were. Obviously. But you still didn't save my number. I thought you forgave me.

for whipping me with your hair?

"Yes. Wasn't the Pepsi a sufficient peace offering?"

lol. yeuh. it was good.

Well, you wouldn't know that, now would you?

??

?? She mimicked his text and Kyle got the impression he was being mocked.

Feeling a sudden urge to prove he wasn't stupid, he typed, *what do you mean?*

You didn't drink it, did you? You gave it to your mate. So how would you know if it was good or not?

I've had Pepsis before.

Not that Pepsi.

Don't they all taste the same?

Negative, she texted. *In fact, that particular Pepsi was produced in a factory in London. They make them different because of laws regulating the sugar content of food in the UK. They taste very different from American Pepsis. Most people say they're much better, in fact. You see, when we moved to the US, customs allowed me to bring one case on the flight and that was my last can. I offered it to you as a gesture of good faith, because I felt bad for being such a b-word this morning. I really wanted you to enjoy it as a new experience.*

Kyle thought back to the blue can, tried to remember if there had been any indication it was anything but a normal American Pepsi. But the ATF had been using his perception as a chew-toy, and the can had been the same color as any other he'd seen. Not knowing what else to do, he typed, *really?*

Lol. No! I'm just having a go at you, mate! Why would a soda with less sugar taste better?

oh. lol. so they don't make it different in London?

A few seconds later the phone vibrated in his hand again, and the music cut off, but this time it didn't resume. The phone just kept buzzing, and the screen said he had an incoming call from Marie's number. Chewy looked up, stared at his owner wide-eyed. Kyle considered rejecting the call and bringing his music back to life, but then his dog glanced down at the iPhone and his face seemed to say, "What are you waiting for?" so he pressed accept and brought the device to his ear.

"Uh, hello?"

"Of course, they don't make it different in London, you silly goose. Why would they do that?"

"What? I mean, I don't know. You said—"

"It was a joke." She spoke in the singsongy tone of somebody who was smiling. "I was just busting your chops, mate. You really think they'd make Pepsi any different in the UK? The recipe's clearly what makes the product. Make it any other way and they might as well call it kangaroo piss, or algae water, or anything but Pepsi."

"Oh," Kyle replied. "Gotcha. Maybe you should invent those drinks. They might make you rich."

Laughing, the new girl said, "Yeah. Maybe. I'd have to call it something different though. If they knew it was kangaroo piss, they'd just go to Australia with a cup and get it the old-fashion way."

Chewy seemed to have once again lost interest at some point. He was coiled up like a short furry snake, heaving and breathing heavily. Both Kyle and Marie laughed, only Kyle's was half-forced. He said, "Yeah. Well, that's pretty gross. Do they do that in Australia?"

"Wouldn't surprise me, if I'm being honest. The men back home are exceedingly vulgar and obnoxious. It isn't uncommon to see someone running naked at a barbie with a piece of paper lit on fire between his ass-cheeks. But to tell you the truth, I haven't been there in years. We moved to London when I was twelve."

The phone buzzed again. Looking at the screen, Kyle saw another picture message from Marie's number. Only then did it occur to him she might be flirting. He considered how he felt about it, concluded that though she was very pretty and undoubtedly charming, there wasn't much room in his mind right now that wasn't occupied by either Claudia or the terrible children and their orange eyes. Still, his heart sped up as he selected to view the image, which would surely be whichever picture of the new girl had gotten the most likes on Facebook from various guys.

But instead, baby-blue water lining a light-brown beach filled his screen and Kyle found himself unexpectedly disappointed. It was an aerial view—like observing from a helicopter—and the beach was thin, and seemed to go on forever in both directions. People were everywhere, sunbathing and wading in the shallow water, but they were so tiny he couldn't make out any details of what any of them looked like.

Another text came through, which said, "That's Cairns."

"Hello?" Marie sang from his hand. "Are you still there?" Only it came out, *Ah you still theh?*

Putting it back to his ear, he said, "Uh, yeah. Yeah. I'm here. I just got your picture. So that's Cay—earns?"

"Oh! You got it. Figured as much. You know that thing the Pepsi was in today?"

"You mean a can?" He spoke slowly, and hoped a second too late she wouldn't take it wrong.

"Yep. Now say it plurally."

"Plurally?"

"Yeah. Like if you had more than one."

"Pepsis."

"No, not—"

"Oh, cans."

"There it is! That's how you pronounce Cairns. Anyway, that's where I grew up in Australia. Very working class, though the beaches are amazing."

A notification rang from the tablet. Looking down, he saw that Laura had posted a thumbs-up emoji next to the smiley face. He killed the screen, set the device down next to him on the futon's dark green mattress. "Yeah," he said. "That one's pretty nice. What do you mean by 'working class' though?"

"Hm. That's a good question, isn't it? Maybe I could answer it at some point tomorrow?"

"Tomorrow?" he asked, wondering if he'd crossed some line he wasn't aware of.

She said, "Well, I suppose it's good we got here. I probably shouldn't be on the phone all night anyway, but was thinking, since tomorrow we don't have school, and I don't know anybody in this town yet, maybe you could show me around a bit. I could meet you somewhere, or come by and pick you up in the morning. That is, if you don't have any prior engagements."

Before he even thought about whether or not he wanted to hang out with her, he responded almost involuntarily, "Uh, no. I mean, yeah. I don't have any plans. We could probably do something or whatever."

Somehow, he could hear her smile widen as she said, "Very good. I could pick you up in the morning, then? Make it an all-day thing?"

As it turned out, Marie was an early riser, even on the weekends. She offered to pick him up at seven, and Kyle said, "Jesus. On a Saturday?"

Giggling, she replied, "Is that not normal over here? Okay then. What time works for you? Eight?"

"Is ten cool?"

In the end, they settled on nine, and were just about to end the call when she asked again where he'd gotten off to "s'arvo."

"Oh. I just had to ah — well, I had to fill out a police statement."

She paused a moment, then said, "You mean about what happened today?"

"What. You mean last night?"

"No, today."

"You're talking about the kids that disappeared, right?"

"No, sweetheart. That was last night. I mean what happened s'arvo, right by where I picked up your mate. Have you not watched the news?"

He hadn't. Apparently, nobody in the McIntosh home had because he had no clue what the hell she was talking about. She told him everything they'd been going on about on the TV for hours, but even in light of what he had seen today, it was almost too farfetched to believe, so he politely ended the call, turned on his television, and began scanning channels for a news station that might be airing the story. It didn't take long to find one.

***

Abby Garner woke up in the dark to the taste of her own saliva, and wet fabric pressed against her lips. She'd been drooling into the red comforter, and the fuzzy material didn't soak up the moisture, just let it pool on the surface, then drip back into her mouth. Her first instinct was to resent Tim for making her buy a blanket from a stand on the side of the road just because it had an image of a pit-bull stitched into the fabric, then she registered what had woken her in the first place.

There was crying coming from the baby monitor.

Instinctively, she looked at the small plastic speaker which sat on the nightstand on Tim's side of the bed. Then she stretched her arms, groaned, and glanced at the digital clock next to it. Red lights announced, 12:22 AM. Tim lay motionless next to her. Even with his eyes shut, he managed to somehow brandish a vacant expression, but it was his light breathing that told her he was awake.

"Don't move or anything," she said. "I totally got it. Even though I have to be up in a few hours for work."

He didn't open his eyes as he said, "Thanks babe," rolled onto his back, and snored.

Abby kicked the comforter off, causing it to slide down his body as well, revealing a pale, hairless, chubby male figure in blue boxer shorts. She thought briefly of Jerome, because physically he was opposite to Tim in every way that a guy could be.

"Babe," he groaned. "What the fuck?"

Without responding, she rolled out of bed, felt the cold nip at her skin. Her pink underwear rode high on the right side, wedging between soft shaved skin. She pulled on the hems and they snapped quietly as they broke free. Then she attempted to tug her white tank top down over her exposed legs, only half awake and not yet registering that it was much too short.

Tim yanked the blanket back over his body and rolled into it like a chinchilla in a dust bath. Abby shivered, walking barefoot across the room. Then she cried out and almost fell over because a sharp pain bit at the bottom of her foot and shot up her ankle.

Tim's tired voice called from behind her, "Babe? You good?"

"No!" Abby pressed one hand against the wall to stabilize herself, raising her left foot and running her other hand over its sole. A small, pebble-shaped object dropped into her palm, and she knew instantly what it was.

"What happened?" Tim yawned.

In the other room, the baby continued to cry.

Abby said, "I stepped on a piece of your freaking bong and almost died!"

"You almost died?"

"You said you cleaned this up!"

"I did." He yawned.

"Then what's this?" Cocking her arm back, she launched the piece of broken glass toward the bed, knowing it would miss him and she'd likely just roll over on it in her sleep and get cut again. Just another reason to hate him.

"Babe, it was a three-foot-bong. We cleaned as much of the glass as we could find. I don't know—I thought we got it all."

"I don't care. I don't want that dumb-ass friend of yours over here anymore."

"But Joe's my nigger."

"Stop using that word!" She massaged her foot as she spoke. "You know I hate that word."

"What? That fool sells me ounces for fifty-a-piece. I'm telling you right now, that's my motha-fucking nigger."

Abby took a deep breath. Held it in. Let it out very slowly as she set her foot on the soft carpet and shifted back and forth to make sure she could handle her own weight. The pain was still present, but fleeting and bearable. She said, "You know what? You're twenty-one-years-old and you're not in high school anymore. Even when you *were* in high school, you weren't in high school. You're an idiot, and even our child knows it. That's why he's been throwing these fits every night."

Tim sat up on both elbows, yawned again. "Babe, it's like two in the morning. Can't we do a lecture tomorrow?"

"It's midnight, you moron. And no. You're gonna hear this now, because I'm getting tired of this. All you do is sit around all day, smoke weed, and play your stupid videogames, and it makes you stupid. Don't you get it? But I know that's not you. Know how I know? Because I knew you before you were such a loser, and you were smart. You were funny, and charming. That's why I was with you.

"But now, I don't know why I'm with you anymore, so here's what's gonna happen, Tim. Are you listening? You're gonna stop bringing that imbecile into my apartment, and you're gonna stop smoking weed."

Tim groaned. "What do you mean I don't do anything?' I take care of Malachi all day every day while you're at work."

"So, you're a freaking housewife?"

"What—?"

"Listen to me! Malachi is crawling now. What if he would've crawled over that piece of broken glass and cut himself? Or worse, what if he would've eaten it? And died!"

"What? Don't you think you're being a little overdramatic now?" He took a deep breath, looked up at the ceiling. "No offense."

"Fuck you. Get a job and stop being a loser."

"Babe, why don't you just come to bed? You gotta be at work early in the morning. We can talk about it tomorrow."

But there would be no talking tomorrow because Abby had been talking for the past seven months. She'd been talking since March eleventh, when she'd squeezed out this guy's spawn. And she had been tired of talking a few days later. Still, she'd done it anyway, because maybe she was wrong. Maybe he would listen and shape up. Be a man. She had kept talking because she hadn't been able to conjure up the backbone to stop, and just walk away.

Then Jerome was hired at the store, and he was tall, and he had a nice smile, and his hands weren't shy. So, Abby Garner had fucked him almost every day in her car for the past three weeks. He always called her a bitch just before he climaxed, and sometimes he spit on her back. She wasn't in love with him, and she knew she loved Tim, but the problem was that she hated Tim more than she loved him. They had been together since the eighth grade—seven years—and at some point, he had lost the ability to even breathe without wearing on the last nerves that she had left. But it didn't matter anymore. Not even the fact they had Malachi. None of it mattered. She had planned to end the talking soon anyway, so a broken bong in the bottom of her foot was as good of a catalyst as any, and midnight was as good of a time.

"I hate you, Tim. Don't you get it? You disgust me. Look at you. When did you stop caring about yourself? When did you stop showering every day? Listen to me. And pay close attention, because I'm done talking." She felt pride well up inside her at this last line, and let it propel what came next. "You're gonna stop smoking weed, and you're gonna stop bringing your goofy-ass-friends into my home. You're gonna get a job. Do you hear me? If you don't, I'm leaving you. But it won't be me who's leaving because I pay the bills. You'll be gone. Do you get it?"

"What the hell?" Finally, he sat all the way up, though it wasn't without effort because his flabby midsection attempted to push him back down. "Abby—"

"No. I mean it, Tim."

"Babe, please. Just come to bed."

"I'm not coming to bed! The baby's crying, you moron!" She flicked the switch next to the door and the room lit up, causing him to shield his eyes with his forearm.

"Uh! What the—the baby's not even crying anymore. He must've fallen back asleep."

"Yes he —" But before she could get another word out, she managed to stop herself, and glance at the monitor because he was right. There was no longer any noise coming from it.

"See?" he lay back down, but didn't move his arm away from his face. A patch of light-brown hair protruded from his pit, where Jerome had none, because either he shaved, or it just didn't grow in. "He's asleep. Come back to bed, please."

And because that seemed all he was capable of saying and she couldn't stand to hear it again, she said, "Fuck off," and turned, careful to watch where she stepped as she opened the door and exited the room. "Get that glass out of my bed!"

When she was in the hall, she paused a moment, listening for Malachi's cries, which she and Tim had joked when the child was born sounded like a pterodactyl's mating call. There was nothing, though. Not even the sound of Tim rolling out of bed to check the floor for additional glass.

And why should he? It was past midnight, and there was probably nothing there anyway. Maybe she was being too hard on him. But it didn't matter because they were spiraling now and there was no turning back.

Maybe he would take her seriously this time. Maybe he would do something with himself. Get a job. Clean a dish. At least take a freaking shower. Then again, maybe he wouldn't. And she wasn't backing down this time. This time she would throw him out. Not forever. They both knew it wouldn't be permanent, but while he was out crashing on couches and sending her text messages begging her to let him come home, her phone would be off because Jerome would be in his spot on their bed. Or maybe he would be on her side, calling her a bitch and spitting on her back, until she finally gave in and let her baby's father come home.

Abby's heart sped up and she felt a pleasant stirring beneath her stomach at the thought. Ignoring it, she tiptoed down the short hall, which was only vaguely lit from her bedroom. She reached Malachi's door in a couple steps, and slowly pulled the door open. Once inside, she shivered, feeling goose bumps stand up all over her bare legs because the baby's room was somehow colder than the hall. She glanced toward the window, where light from streetlamps outside seeped through small horizontal slits in the blinds, but couldn't tell if it was open. She walked over. Checked. It was shut.

"Jee-wiz," she whispered, looking down at her son who lay motionless on his back in the center of his crib. "We gotta get you outta here." He wore a baby-blue onesie and had kicked the thin, matching blanket off. It rested crumpled, down by his feet. "Come on," Abby reached in and scooped a hand under his mostly bald head. "You're gonna sleep with Mom and Dad tonight."

But she knew something wasn't right the second she touched him. It wasn't anything she could pinpoint because a sleeping child was just a sleeping child, but something was off. Missing. So, before she even felt her heart drop into her gut, she slipped her other hand under his back and lifted him more violently than she should have. But Malachi didn't move. His arms and legs hung at his sides like a ragdoll, and a trembling sigh escaped Abby's mouth as the floor began to move under her bare feet.

"Malachi? Malachi? Baby?" She shook him, lightly at first, then more vigorously but he was unresponsive. Before she knew she was doing it, she heard herself screaming. "TIM! TIM! OH SHIT! OH FUCK! PLEASE! MALACHI, WAKE UP BABY! TIM! GET IN HERE NOW!"

It ran in the family. Or did it? Was something like crib death hereditary? Or was it caused by something else? Something she'd done? Or hadn't done? She had heard the stories since she was young of how her father's baby brother had died in his sleep, and only now did she know she had failed her own child by not looking into the implications. She didn't check his heartbeat or breathing because it was obvious he was dead and she was holding him like a limp fucking cabbage-patch-doll and she knew she needed to set him down because she might pass out and she would drop him and then he wouldn't just be dead, but he'd be broken as well.

Thumping in the hall.

Tim appeared.

He touched the wall and the room lit up, revealing his flabby midsection and hairy thighs—but mostly his face, wide eyed and concerned. Abby didn't squint, but for a brief second, she hated herself, because she remembered why she loved her baby's father. He said, "Babe, what is it?"

"Take him," she groaned.

"What?"

"Take him. Take him now. Take him, Tim! Take the fucking baby from me, NOW!"

"Okay. Okay." He darted across the room and reached for his son. As soon as he touched him, the lights flickered, then died all at once and the room fell pitch-black aside from the minuscule light pressing against the outside of the blinds.

Abby gasped. She sniffed. Warm drops on her face made her cognizant that she was crying.

Tim said, "What the hell?" then brought some type of flashlight to life, and it crossed Abby's mind that she had fallen victim to one of his childish pranks.

But that wasn't right, because though Tim was childish, he didn't pull pranks. Not just that, but whatever he had was no flashlight. There were two bulbs, and they were both orange, and when they moved to shine on her, she backed up until her buttocks touched the cold wall next to the window, because they were set inside Malachi's eyes. They *were* his eyes.

They illuminated his face as he opened his mouth in a wide, toothless smile and reached for Abby.

"Mamamamamamama!" The voice was terrible. It wasn't her son's. It was forced and choked. High pitched.

Tim let out a shaky groan. "Oh, holy shit!"

"Mamamamamamama!"

Thin shadows danced on the walls like seaweed waving under water. Then the lights moved as he turned his head and gazed up at his father. Tim's eyes went wide, and he cursed, dropped the child who landed with a thump, then scrambled to his feet. Only he shouldn't have been standing because he hadn't learned yet. Malachi faced his mother and waved his arms like a bird right before he sprinted toward her.

"NOOOO!" Abby screamed, attempted to back up further into the wall.

"Mamamamamamama!"

"What the fuck is this?" Tim reached for the child, barely missing him.

Malachi made it to Abby, reached up, and drug his tiny fingers down her thighs, causing goose bumps to once again stand up all over her legs. Then he did it again. And again. It occurred to Abby he was attempting to scratch her, but his nails were too small and frail, and they were always trimmed.

"Mamamamamamama!"

"Tim! Do something, damn it!"

Tim flipped the light switch again, but nothing happened, so he dove at his son, scooped him up around the waste and hoisted him into the air just as something crashed in the living room. The sound of tiny feet tapping the floor filled the apartment, then more orange light appeared in the hall. Malachi laughed merrily, once again flapping his arms as so much of the light rushed into the room that there was no way not to see the crowd of children rush in accompanied by more shadows which gave the impression of hundreds of snakes crawling up the walls.

There were so many children—at least twenty—and they all had the same glowing eyes as Malachi. They were young. None of them could have been older than twelve, and some of them were carrying tools. A small, redheaded girl held two small steak knives. Another wielded a large axe he shouldn't have been able to even lift. A boy in a pair of underwear held an aluminum bat. Two of them had hammers. A tiny Hispanic girl even had a revolver. They were all laughing and squealing like they were in the playground, only their voices were sick and choked, just like Malachi's. Tim opened his mouth to scream, but the boy with the bat cocked it back and swung, barely missing Malachi, connecting with Tim's face, causing him to once again drop the child and stumble back into the wall. Then he was hit again.

Abby cried out as red-hot pain exploded where Malachi had been scratching her. Looking down, she saw the redheaded girl pull one of the knives out of her thigh, then thrust the other in, only higher. Abby leaned down and covered her leg, and a knife went through her hand and back out. Then one tore through her panties and punctured her vagina. She screamed, fell to the floor, curled into a ball, saw Tim's face contorted in agony as an axe removed his hand from his wrist. The blood that sprayed out of the stump appeared orange under the light from the children's eyes. Abby found herself wondering if Jerome would have worn the same ugly expression.

Then something collided with the side of her head, and there was a hollowness in her chest as the orange morphed briefly into a flash of bright red and the pain in her body began to fade. She blinked and looked up to see a boy raise a hammer with a fiberglass handle, preparing to hit her again. And he did, but this time on her lips.

The pain no longer registered, but she knew somewhere in her increasingly fogging mind that she needed to protect herself. To cover up. But she couldn't, because she was on her back now, and her arms were spread, pinned to the floor like a crucifixion victim. The larger children were sitting on them and smiling. The hammer crashed into her mouth again and she felt her teeth in her throat. Then again. The boy was focused. Precise. He was taking them out intentionally.

When he was done, Abby coughed as blood and teeth poured into her windpipe. She writhed weakly, but there was no strength to fight. Malachi appeared over her, his eyes bright and orange, the happiest smile she'd ever seen pasted to his face. He laughed as he stuffed his little hand in her mouth and shoved until everything below his elbow was buried inside her.

"Mamamamamama"

Abby kicked and choked. She gagged, feeling burning stomach fluid travel up her chest. She wanted to cough, but she couldn't even breathe.

"Mamamamamamama!"

Malachi blew a raspberry, then stuck his tongue out. Abby Garner thought about how much she loved her baby. How he had given her a sense of importance, and taught her to love in a way she hadn't known existed seven months ago. She stared up into his eyes and choked and kicked until finally the lights in his head disappeared because the whole world had gone black.

***

There was nothing but darkness. Kyle was so tired and so much that should have been impossible had transpired in such a short period of time that he thought he might never sleep again. But sometime after ten he turned off the news and killed the light in his room. He didn't even fetch his blankets and pillow, or pull his futon out into a bed. Just curled up in his jeans and T-shirt and closed his eyes and then there was nothing.

Until he opened them again and felt around for his phone. Bringing the screen to life, he squinted to see what time it was.

1:39 AM.

Then he realized what had kidnapped him from his slumber.

Abel was crying in the next room.

But before he could put any more thought into it, the darkness returned as Kyle fell once again into a deep, dreamless sleep.

Chapter Four

Kimberly was in the cemetery, and she was crying because it was dark, and she was afraid. Gabe knew it was his job to protect her, and he hated himself because he didn't know what to do. It was a foggy night. The kind of night you could tell was cold just by looking. He couldn't feel the cold, though, because it was just a dream and though he knew that, it was still too real to not scare the hell out of him. Crickets chirped in the distance, and the moon was distorted and fuzzy behind a thick layer of clouds.

The tombstones were moving and that was a problem because tombstones were made of stone and weren't supposed to dance, even in dreams. These ones, however, didn't seem to care what they were or weren't supposed to do. They swayed side to side like grass, tossing in the wind. Except for the one behind Kimberly. No, that one was alive. It was a concrete angel, with the face and body of a baby, and it was crying.

So was Kim. She was only a few feet away and her face was scrunched up in agony, soaked in tears, staring into his because he should have been there the night her mother was murdered and she was abducted, and now she was probably dead as well.

Probably? Who was he fooling? Of course, she was. Why else would she be visiting him in a dream?

She wore a white dress. A very pretty one that flared out at the hem. It was the same one they had picked up for her at the second-hand store on Riverside Drive for his sister's wedding. Only she shouldn't have been wearing it because she'd outgrown the thing already. The dress, however, seemed to have stretched in order to fit her again. She had been an infant the last time she wore it. Here in the cemetery, however, she was two—the same age she'd been the last time he'd seen her.

Her bottom lip was curled into a frown, and she just continued to stare into her father's eyes and weep. But there were no sounds, only this terrible scene which played as if on mute. Gabe tried to break the silence, to utter his daughter's name, but no words would form.

The stone angel flapped its wings, opened its mouth wide. It stopped crying and its expression slowly morphed into one of murderous anger. It pointed a finger at Gabe and so did Kimberly. Neither had to speak, because their faces said what they thought louder than any words ever could.

This is your fault. You failed as a father and as a man and now your wife and child are dead. Soon, you will be too.

A fear unlike any he'd ever known overtook Gabriel Brenton and finally he shouted so loud he woke up panting and covered in sweat. It was dark in the cell and the fact that he didn't hear heavy breathing told him he had woken Zack up as well.

"Sorry," he said.

"No problem, man." His cellie's voice was tired below him. "It's almost time to get up anyway."

"Is it?"

"Yeah. It's five-twenty."

"Oh."

"You good?"

"Yeah," Gabe lied, because he wasn't good. Though he hadn't yet been able to shed a tear over the situation, he was far from good because he'd learned today that his wife was dead, and her lover was in jail and his daughter was missing along with three other children. He wasn't okay, because more than twelve hours after Kim and the others had gone missing, somebody had shown up at the home of one of their fathers and cut his head off. He wasn't okay because whatever the hell was going on, his daughter was likely dead, or would soon be dead and he was in prison on the other side of the fucking state and unable to do anything about it.

Zack said, "All right, dude. Sure?"

"Yeah. I'm sure."

"Cool. Back to sleep then." Zack yawned, and a few seconds later he snored once and didn't speak again. Gabe knew he wouldn't be back to sleep though. It had taken him hours to drift off in the first place, and even if he could, it wouldn't be worth it because apparently his dreams were worse than his waking thoughts. So, he just lay on his back, staring up at the stained white ceiling until the alarm went off at six. Then he climbed out of bed, cleaned the cell, and pretended it was any other day.

***

There was no big-yard this morning, so he exercised with the whites along the fence in Fox-Unit's small yard, and that's when he learned eighteen more children had come up missing last night, and their parents were all dead. After the workout, he called his mother, who cried and said how horrific and bizarre the whole thing was, and then informed him there would be a funeral held for Carrie on Tuesday, and that his counselor had told her that he would likely be transported by DOC, and allowed to attend, provided he was shackled and cuffed throughout the service.

But did he really want to attend? At the end of the day, he was still a Christian. And though Carrie had turned her back on him when he needed her the most, and though she had been with another man, and though she had withheld a relationship with his child from him, she was still his wife, and like Hosea, he was commanded to forgive. He didn't have to forget, and unlike Hosea, he hadn't been ordered to re-embrace her as wife. Adultery was clearly grounds for divorce, but not cold-hearted indifference.

So sometime before lunch, as Fox News was airing a speech which the president was giving about the tragedy in his hometown, he took down the picture of Kim and the plastic rosary that had hung around it for the past year. Zack watched the TV from where he sat on his bunk as Gabe set the folded picture on the desk, then took a seat on the stool, the rosary hanging from his hand.

"I need to talk to you about something."

Averting his attention from the television, Zack said, "You see this shit?"

"Yeah. Yeah, I do. Listen man—"

"Bro, I'm sorry."

Gabe reached for the small flat screen, which sat on the desk. His finger hovered over the power button, as he said, "Mind if I turn this off? They'll be replaying it all day anyway, and I think I'm leaving."

"What?" Zack tilted his head. "Leaving where?"

"Listen," he pressed the button, and the screen faded to black, "I might go to the hole today."

"What?" Zack straightened up, examining his cellmate's face as if to determine if he was being pranked. "Come on, man. Don't do anything—"

"I'm not gonna do anything. Look, I talked to my mom this morning, and she told me when Carrie's funeral is."

"Gabe—"

"Just listen, man. Remember I told you they wanted to take me to the hole yesterday? When they told me what happened?"

Zack frowned. "You signed their contract, though, right?"

"That was just saying I was all right mentally. They do it with everyone who gets shitty news. It's not really for us though. They're just afraid we might freak out and do something crazy, then they'll have to deal with the backlash. Anyway, they told my mom they were gonna let me go to the funeral. They weren't supposed to tell her that. I had a cellie once before you, and when his mom died, they transported him to the service, but he didn't know he was going until the last minute. They do that so you can't call someone to come help you escape or drop off contraband."

Zack said it made sense.

Gabe said, "When they figure out they screwed up, they're probably gonna come get me and take me to the hole without access to a phone. Before they do—I mean *if* they do—I need to tell you the story of how I got this rosary." He raised the strand of black beads, letting Zack examine it. "There was a guy here before you showed up whose name was Jack."

"Isn't that the guy who shoved a chopstick in his dick and died?"

"It wasn't a chopstick," Gabe corrected. "It was a pencil. But yeah. He was out of his mind on meth. He told the doctors he had an itch inside his urethra, and he was trying to scratch it with a golf pencil. It worked its way inside, though, and lodged itself in his bladder."

"Jesus."

"Don't use the Lord's name like that. Anyway, Jack went into septic shock and died. It was sad because he wasn't always a mess. In fact, he was supposed to get the keys instead of me. I guess he did have a strange thing for sticking foreign objects into his pecker, though, because that's exactly where this rosary was supposed to go."

Zack squinted, his eyes still transfixed on the rosary, until finally he smiled. "Shut the—"

"I'm serious. I mean not the whole rosary. Come on, man. Just the beads. Well, some of the beads. A lot of the fellas do it. I don't think they usually use rosaries, but Jack thought it would be funny. Like blasphemous or something." Finally, he lowered the relic, setting his hand on his lap. "You know these guys think doing anything that could be seen as tempting God is just hilarious, right?"

Zack said, "Whatever, dude. You're telling me this guy was gonna shove beads up his pee-hole?"

"No. Not his peehole. They use a pen to poke a hole in the skin on their—well, you know—and then they put beads in it and let it heal."

"Dude!" Zack grabbed at his crotch, scrunched his face up.

"I'm serious. People get it done outside too. Only they do it at tattoo shops and get stainless steel ball bearings inserted. It's supposed to rub on a girl's g-spot during sex.

"So, Jack got this rosary from one of the Chicanos in the yard, but he found out someone was talking shit about him like ten minutes later."

"Who?" Zack asked.

"Nobody. Just some lame."

"Well, what was he saying?"

"It's irrelevant. Just listen, man. The point is, he reached over, put the rosary on me like a necklace, and said, 'Here. Hold this.' Then he went and beat the brakes off this guy. When he got out of the hole, they put him in G-Unit and I was next in line to be put in charge."

Zack's eyes moved to the door and Gabe glanced back to see a tall, bearded guard staring in the small widow. After a second, he moved on and Zack said, "So you're saying you think God gave you the keys to the white car?"

Gabe nodded.

"And you think this because of that rosary?"

"More or less."

"Don't you think that's just a little farfetched? I mean you've told me you don't even believe in Catholic relics, and the rosary was just decoration or whatever."

"I believe in signs. And I lied. You know since I've been in charge, I've done my best to run things in a way I thought was righteous, and I've done it all because of what I believe. I've reduced the violence here, and made all your lives easier. When I meet up with Brent in the library every week, I tell him everything's good in the unit, even if someone's fucking up because I don't want to have to have somebody taken out.

"And I've done it all on the down-low because the guys benefiting from it don't approve of my God. The same God who's appointed me to do them this freaking favor. I'm pretty sure I'm leaving, Zack, and I don't know why, but I think I was supposed to tell you all this. And to do this."

Gabe lifted the rosary in both hands and slipped it over Zack's head. Zack didn't object, just stared down at the floor for a long moment before asking, "How are you so calm, man? I mean after everything that happened with your wife and kid." He nodded toward the folded picture on the desk. "I'd be freaking the fuck out if I were you."

"I'm not calm," Gabe replied. "I am freaking out. I just don't—"

A knock on the door cut him off and somehow, he knew what he would see before he even looked back. The bearded guard had returned with two others and was once again staring in, all business. As the door's rectangular pass-through popped open, a metallic clicking echoed out in the day-room.

"Brenton? Come on over here and cuff up, bud. Gotta take ya to the hole."

***

Just past eight Kyle woke to Chewy scratching the door to be let out. He'd slept so hard it felt like he had just shut his eyes, though he recalled waking up briefly to the sound of his brother crying next door. Or had that been a dream? He checked his phone, saw no texts or missed calls, then let the dog out and sauntered into the bathroom where he relieved himself before peeling off yesterday's clothes and climbing into the shower.

It was Saturday, which meant his mom would be home, though it was unpredictable whether or not she would be out of bed yet. Abel might be. If so, he would likely be upstairs watching early morning cartoons.

Marie would be outside at nine to pick him up. He'd instructed her to call, rather than knock or honk her horn, just in case. Kyle wasn't sure what he was supposed to think of the day-date. Especially since receiving the text from her had been so freakishly random. And the picture of her lying on a bed? Mind you, it was nothing compared to the kinds of pictures Claudia had often sent him (and who knew who else?).

But Claudia was the epitome of narcissists. She looked good, and she knew it, yet for some reason she needed it reaffirmed constantly by other people. Marie looked good, too. There was no denying that. She wasn't like Claudia, though. That much was obvious. She hadn't been dressed overly provocatively. She hadn't worn a pound of makeup. It had been clear she was smart from the second she opened her mouth. In fact, she was probably the exact opposite of Claudia in just about every way.

As he rinsed shampoo from his head, letting it flow down his body like a foamy mudslide, he decided there was probably nothing more to the hangout than what she'd said on the phone. Why would there be? She *was* new in town. She *did* need someone to show her around. She probably would have texted Dobey instead, had Dobey had a phone.

Images of what he'd seen on the news last night flooded his mind, playing one after another in clips that were already fading into little more than foggy snippets. Images of a house, which he'd seen often because it was located less than a block from the alley where he and his friends smoked when they snuck off campus. From where he had been sitting at the top of the hill when he spotted Kimberly Brenton and her orange-eyed friends.

Images of yellow tape and police surrounding the house. Of paramedics standing by, waiting to haul out the headless body of the father of one of those horrible children. The man who they'd killed just after he saw them. Or had they done it before?

After. You know they did it after, because the blood on their clothes was old and dry when you saw them.

There hadn't been much information divulged on the news. Just that James Booth Sr. had been found decapitated in his home. That it was likely unrelated to the disappearance of his son because Booth was a known drug-dealer, who had been working for the Mount Vernon Police as an informant for years.

But that was bullshit because Kyle had been there. And what the news was failing to mention, was that the kids had been spotted in the area. By Kyle. That they were walking corpses who were possessed by something evil, and that they were killing their own fucking parents. He took a deep breath, held it in for a long moment, then let it out slowly and finally took the time to process what he hadn't had the energy for last night.

The new girl. Marie. Whatever this was, it had started when she showed up in town. Then it was her he had seen just before Kim and her friends arrived. And then she had texted him out of the blue, wanting to hang out, and Kyle knew he was nothing special and definitely hadn't made a point to make her want to be his friend—or otherwise—so what the hell was going on, how did it involve her, and why did it have to involve him?

He let the water wash over his head, down his back, onto the grime-stained plastic floor. What the hell was he even entertaining right now? That this new girl was some kind of a witch? The problem was, no matter how hard he tried, he couldn't reconcile anything that had happened without a scenario that was equally outlandish. Kyle didn't know what to think anymore because either the world had gone crazy, or he had. And why not? Maybe he was losing it because of Claudia. Maybe she had actually broken him.

He killed the water, then stood for a long moment staring at the wall in front of him. Claudia *had* broken him. That was a fact. Even if no children had turned up missing, and nobody in her trailer park had been found dead. Even if he hadn't seen what he had yesterday, and Marie wasn't new in town. Kyle McIntosh was still broken because Claudia fucking Rocha had a *new vato* who wasn't a stupid white boy like him.

Stop, he told himself. *Stop feeling sorry for yourself. People are dead. Children are dead, and all you can do is twist this in a way to make yourself a victim.*

But it wasn't that simple, and Kyle knew it, because no matter who was dead and who was or wasn't a victim, broken was still broken, and somehow, he seemed to be waking up each morning more so than the last. For this reason, he considered canceling on Marie. How could he possibly be good company in this state? Moreover, how could he not have thought of this last night? She had been charming though. Persuasive. And he suspected she hadn't even meant to be.

Cold air nipped at his skin, contrasting with the fleeting sensation left by warm water and kidnapping him from his self-torture. He brushed the curtain aside and stepped out of the shower, making up his mind as he pulled a white towel from its rack and began to dry off. He would go with Marie today, and he wouldn't talk about Claudia. He would make a point not to even think about her. He wouldn't entertain any ridiculous notions that the new girl might be somehow connected to recent bizarre events, and he would put forth a genuine effort to make a new friend of her.

Kyle stepped into a pair of boxer-shorts, and cracked the door. He used his towel to wipe steam from the mirror, then applied gel which gave his dishwater hair a darker appearance. Once he was fully clothed, he checked his phone. Still nothing. It was 8:46.

Slipping the iPhone into his pocket, he made his way upstairs and heard the electronic hum of a window-fan coming from his mom's room, which meant she was still asleep. So was Abel, apparently, as the rest of the house was silent.

Chewy met him halfway to the kitchen, his head down, his tail between his legs. Kyle knew as soon as he saw the dog that he'd messed up. Chewy moped over and pressed his tiny body against Kyle's shins, causing him to almost trip.

"Okay. Okay. Move. I already know what you did."

But the dog didn't leave his side as he stepped into the kitchen where a small puddle of urine pooled in front of the sliding glass door leading to the balcony that overlooked the backyard. For having a brain the size of a walnut, Chewy was a smart dog, and Kyle knew he had stood at the door until he could wait no longer. He must not have been done, either, because when Kyle slid it open, he darted out and down into the grass, his nails scratching the wooden steps on his way.

Marie arrived as he was soaking up the mess with a dirty towel. He knew before the phone vibrated against his leg, because Chewy went crazy outside. If Kyle didn't shut him up, his mom would wake and he might be stalled, so he flew out into the light rain, taking the steps two at a time, emerging into the backyard, and almost slipping on the wet grass. Running around the house, he saw his dog clawing the fence as if he could dig a hole in the wood and get at the intruder.

He scooped Chewy up, and held him to his face. The dog stopped yapping and gazed curiously through perfectly round black eyes into Kyle's, his little body trembling. The phone continued to buzz in his pocket, so he peered over the fence at the purple Volkswagen Beetle parked in front of his house. The passenger window slid down, and though she was too far away to make out her expression, she was staring at him with her own phone to her head.

Tucking the dog under one arm like a football, he fished his out and took the call.

"What in God's name is that?" Marie's voice sang into his ear.

"Uh—what?"

"Is that a rat?"

"Huh? No. It's a—dog."

"Well, that's not like any dog I've ever seen. That thing looks more like a shaved weasel. Or a hotdog with legs."

"He's not a Wiener-dog," Kyle replied. "He's a Chihuahua."

"You don't say?"

"What?"

Chewy kicked a few times, then resigned to just shivering at Kyle's side.

Marie said, "I'm wondering if something's getting lost in translation here. Maybe it's just a cultural gap, but you really don't seem to register humor, do you man? Of course, I know that thing is a Chihuahua! It was a joke! Are you gonna stand out in the rain all day, or come get in the car?"

"Right," Kyle replied. "I'll be right there."

"Brilliant! Just you though. No dogs allowed I'm afraid."

Ending the call, he ran back around the corner and galloped up the stairs and into the house. He set his dog down, threw his jacket on, and exited through the front door.

When he made it to the Beetle, the wipers were dancing across the windshield, and the passenger window was once again sealed. It was tinted so dark he could only vaguely see inside. When he pulled the handle, he heard R&B music, accompanied by the *ding-ding-ding* which indicated an open door.

Marie wore a pair of dark blue jeans and the same gray turtleneck from the picture in his phone. Her hair was straightened so flat it looked like a black waterfall pouring down her head. She was fiddling with her phone, and didn't glance up at first. Then she did and he saw she was wearing more makeup than the last time they'd met.

The sound of a gas powered propeller caught his attention overhead, and he gazed up in time to see a helicopter pass by so low he could read, "SIRIUS 7" painted on the side. He wondered briefly how long it would take for the story to slowly fade from the headlines, then returned his attention to Marie.

She smiled, and her dark brown eyes seemed to shine behind the black lines traced around them. "Is this like a vampire thing, or what?"

"What do you mean?" Kyle asked.

"Well do I have to extend an invitation for you to be able to get in?"

So, Kyle stepped out of the rain and into the Beetle, which smelled of new car and some sweet perfume that made him want to close his eyes and drift into a deep, relaxing sleep. He shut the door and the *ding-ding-dinging* curtailed as Marie put the car in drive and pulled onto East Stanford. The houses were all single and double story, lightly colored and placed mere feet from one another. Kyle's dad often reminded him this was the type of neighborhood in which it's mandatory for residents to keep their lawns neat and aesthetic. The street ran in a big circle, and she was headed the long way, so Kyle asked if she had been here before.

"Why is that?" she inquired.

"Well, you're going the wrong way."

"Actually, this road is circular. You can get out this way as well. Plus, there's an exit near the back, which will deposit you onto Urban Avenue."

"I know," he said. "I mean, how do you know that though? Unless you've been here before."

"Oh." She laughed. "Of course. Yes, I've been stalking you actually."

The song ended, and a DJ announced that Vice 93 was Seattle's home for hip-hop.

Kyle said, "Really?"

Giggling, Marie replied, "Yep. Sure have. You know you really should pull the blinds if you're gonna be wanking at night. The whole neighborhood could have seen that. Nice package though." She glanced at him, winked, then returned her gaze to the road.

Kyle felt his ears heat up as he faked a laugh. "Wanking, huh? I'm guessing that means masturbation?"

"And you're guessing correctly! Actually, I showed up a bit early and drove around the block, since you were so adamant about not leaving your house a second before nine. Plus, I do have access to Google Maps and GPS."

"Oh. Gotcha."

Then Post Malone began to play over the DJ's voice, and it was the same song Kyle had been listening to on repeat since Claudia left. But today was committed to not dwelling on Claudia, so he considered reaching out and killing it. Then he considered kicking her stereo as hard as he could, or ripping his own ears off.

Marie flashed him an inquisitive look, then asked if he was okay.

"Yeah," he said. "I'm good. I just—"

"Don't like this song?"

"What?"

"It's written all over your face sweetheart. Here." She silenced the music, then her eyes widened with realization. "That's right. You just had a nasty breakup, didn't you?" Kyle's own eyes narrowed, and his lips parted slightly. His first inclination was to lie, but he was saved the trouble when she said, "Sorry, mate. I know it's none of my business. Your friend was really worried when we couldn't find you yesterday. He thought you might've gone off the deep-end and done something silly. We drove around for quite some time searching for you, but honestly, I'd completely forgotten until now. I just assumed you looked solemn because of what happened last night."

Kyle shook his head because though Dobey was a loyal friend when it counted the most, his big mouth never failed to let him down.

"He was very concerned," Marie said as they reached the far end of the neighborhood. She hit the blinker, preparing to make the turn which would take them through a relatively new elderly community, and deposit the Beetle onto Urban Ave.

As she brought it to a full stop, however, her words replayed in Kyle's head, and he forgot momentarily about Dobey's loose lips. He asked what she meant by "what happened last night," but his body felt so light that had the panoramic roof been open in her car he might float away because he was pretty sure he already knew what he was about to hear.

***

Downtown Mount Vernon wasn't what one would normally picture when associating images with the word "downtown." It was the oldest, most rural part of the city, and it looked its age, with businesses set inside small historic buildings, reminiscent of movies depicting the old west. Most of them were currently strewn with costume spider web, and had skeleton mannequins and Styrofoam tombstones out front.

Marie asked why they called it downtown, and Kyle said, "I don't really know. I always just assumed it's what passed as a downtown a hundred years ago."

Nodding, she said that made enough sense.

They were in the Courthouse Café, a diner named after the Victorian building which sat directly across the two-lane street. Kyle wasn't sure how he felt about letting a girl pay for his food, but he was hungry, and she had insisted breakfast was on her. Moreover, he didn't have any money. So, they sat on opposite ends of a stained wood table, which had a jack-o-lantern constructed with papier-mache taped to its napkin dispenser, and he used a butter knife to cut into a piece of French toast. Next to them, a window offered a view of the small courthouse.

The restaurant was something straight from a movie, with a long counter in which customers could socialize with waitresses, view the chefs while indulging in whatever soup or pie was currently serving as the "daily special," and glance up periodically at a big suspended flat screen TV.

Urban Ave had cleared out for the most part, but the rest of town was swarming with news vans and police cars. Not just Mount Vernon PD, either. There were white State Trooper vehicles, brown Sheriff cruisers, SUVs— even something that resembled a tank on tractor wheels parked by the road on Riverside Drive.

There were more helicopters as well. Not just local news stations, either, but ones he had never seen on his TV. Marie said more children had disappeared. More parents were murdered. She'd promised to tell him the rest over breakfast. He could have just googled it. He had his phone in his pocket, and whatever had happened was clearly all over the news already. But instead, he had taken in the chaos that was unfolding in his town and tried to convince himself that it was all just some media prank, or even a fucked up dream.

But now they were here, and they were eating, and the diner was full of people who were talking about twenty-two missing children and close to forty dead bodies. So, as Marie stabbed at a cherry crepe with her fork, Kyle took a deep breath and said, "How are you not more—what's the word? Distressed?"

Staring into his eyes, she shoved a bit of the blood-red pastry into her mouth, chewed, swallowed, and tilted her head. "About the children?"

"About all of this." He motioned to the window.

She glanced out, then back at him. "I am. I mean it's terrible what happened. Don't get me wrong. I don't feel nearly as chipper as I probably look. I just—I don't know. I've learned to remain collected and level-headed in most situations. Plus, I may have heard about it sooner than most, as it happened in my father's buildings. So, I've had more time to process it all, I guess."

Outside, a car horn went off. Kyle peeked out the window and beheld a gray SUV, stopped in the road as a group of young Hispanics ran in front of it. They made it to the sidewalk and the SUV resumed motion, kicking up water as it passed the courthouse.

Kyle asked, "What do you mean 'one of your father's buildings'?"

Stuffing another bite into her mouth, Marie glanced down at Kyle's plate and said, "Don't you like your meal?"

"What?"

She swallowed, then observed, "You're not eating."

"No. I mean—yeah." He cut another piece of the toast. "It's good. I'm just trying to—"

"No, no, no. I get it. Honestly, you're totally right. Whatever's happening is just so bizarre that I really don't know how I'm supposed to react. It's terrible. I mean you read about other countries, and you read about America and the crime over here, but nobody hears about things like this happening." For the first time since picking him up, her upbeat expression wavered, and her shoulders slumped slightly. She didn't break eye-contact though, but seemed to be feeling him out, waiting to see how he responded.

So, he told her, "That's because things like this don't happen. This is the weirdest shit I've ever seen, and I've lived here my whole life."

"Really?"

"Yeah. Really."

"Well, that's a relief, I guess."

"Yeah. I guess."

"I haven't even told you what happened yet."

"No." He sipped coffee from a white mug which sat next to his plate, burning his tongue, but trying not to let it show. "You haven't answered my question yet either."

She squinted. "Pertaining to?"

"You said it happened in your dad's buildings. What does that mean?"

"Oh. Right. Well, we own some apartments in town. I mean my parents do. That's why we moved over here at least. Late last night, or early this morning really—around three—my father received a call from the police that his presence was needed at the buildings. So, he left, and he's kept my mother informed via phone ever since."

"Jesus," Kyle said. "You own apartments?"

"Yes. My parents do. They own real estate around the world, so we're always moving on account of their various business ventures. Though we did make it nine years in London. So, would you still like to hear what happened last night?"

Two overweight men in professional attire sat at the counter, their backs to Kyle and Marie. One of them glanced over his shoulder briefly, examining them, then returned to his own meal.

Kyle said, "I think I already heard it all just listening to people's conversations. Twenty-two more kids disappeared. Forty more parents died. Well, close to forty."

"You gathered that just from eavesdropping?"

"Well, I mean—"

"No, I'm not chastising you, mate. I'm impressed. It's eighteen children though, and close to thirty dead."

But he hadn't just heard one person spout off twenty-two and forty. It had been said in the diner more times than he could even remember. Moreover, he told her the numbers had been scrolled across the TV behind the bar since they'd entered the café. She glanced over at the screen, which displayed "Breaking News," across the bottom and said, "Oh. Very good. Impressive. It's still eighteen though. Eighteen and just under thirty."

"Are you sure?"

"Of course, I'm sure. I wouldn't say it if I wasn't, now, would I?"

"I don't—I mean—"

"It's twenty-two altogether. Four kids went missing Thursday night, and eighteen more last night. Make sense?"

Kyle nodded as she went on.

"Similar circumstances, though, only it wasn't just the parents who were murdered. It was the entire households. Siblings, aunts—everyone living in the houses. Well, the apartments in this case. The news stations all seem unclear as to the death toll, but it's thirty-seven, counting both nights. I know—well, obviously I know from my dad."

Collected and level-headed, Kyle thought. It was surprisingly easy to remain so, as somehow, hearing that the numbers were lower than he'd thought seemed to soften the blow. He nodded. Took another bite of his food. Considered trying the scalding coffee again. Decided against it.

"You probably know a lot, the news isn't saying, huh?"

The subtlest hint of a grin appeared in the corner of her mouth as she said, "Probably."

Kyle considered this. He wanted to know what she knew. Not just wanted, he *needed* it. Partially because allotting his mental energy to trying to piece this all together was serving to take his mind off Claudia, but more so because he couldn't seem to shake the sense that she was somehow involved.

But just coming out and asking would be the wrong approach, and he knew it. It would put her on the defensive and if she was hiding anything, it would kill any chance he had of getting information out of her. He needed to be sneaky—what was the word? Shrewd? The problem was, Kyle had never been a very sneaky guy. That had been clear from the time he had handed his mother's day gift to his dear mom at eight-years-old, wrapped and bowed, and declared, "It's not a necklace!"

As if she could read his mind, the new girl said, "What would you like to know, Kyle?"

"Huh?"

"Come on, mate. No offense, but you're an open book. If you wanna know something, just ask."

"I don't—I mean—"

Her grin morphed into a full-blown smile, and he noticed for the first time she had what may have been the straightest, whitest teeth he had ever seen. "Why don't we start with what you *do* know," she offered. "Then fill in the blanks."

Kyle McIntosh had no delusions of being particularly smart or strategic, but it didn't take a genius to recognize the power play. Marie knew that he knew something as well—probably based on nothing more than the fact that he'd told her he had spoken to the police last night—and she wanted to barter for knowledge. Or possibly just glean his.

And he wasn't opposed to sharing, so long as she didn't think he was a lunatic for what he saw, and her intentions were pure. But how did one predetermine either of those things?

A young, blond waitress appeared by the table with a glass coffeepot which was half-empty. She asked if either of them needed a refill, which they both declined. Before leaving, she flashed Kyle a smile that made him drop his gaze. Once she was out of earshot, Marie lowered her voice. "She looked at you like you were a sushi-wrap, didn't she?"

Kyle flushed. "I uh—"

"Oh, now don't play coy. We both saw it. Maybe you should try and get her number. I don't imagine she's much older than you. How old *are* you, anyway?" She finished off her crepe.

"Sixteen," he responded.

"Really? I assumed you were my age."

Kyle tilted his head. "How old are *you*?"

"How old do you think I am?" She set her fork down, carefully wiped her mouth with a napkin.

Examining her, Kyle pursed his lips. "I don't know. Let's see—so you already said you're not my age. And you thought I was about the same age as that girl—and as you—so you must be older than me. But you're still in high school—"

"For God's sake, man! I'm seventeen."

For the first time in days, Kyle let out a genuine laugh. He didn't feel it coming, either, or he might have tried to halt it. But before he knew what was happening, he was chuckling through his nose. Marie joined in and it only propelled his own laughter. Then it occurred to him that he had no clue what the hell was even funny, so they laughed together some more.

When they had both run their courses, Marie brushed a strand of black hair behind her ear and said, "Or I could tell you what I know first. I have a feeling we're both holding pieces of a puzzle that might make more sense if we put them together, though, don't you think?"

At first Kyle didn't answer, just felt the muscles in his face contract as his smile deflated. He examined her for any trace of dishonesty, then concluded it really didn't matter. Maybe she *was* being evasive and interrogatory. Maybe she *was* using her charm to her advantage. Maybe she was even somehow involved in what was happening to the children in Mount Vernon.

That last thought sparked a chill that started in his asshole and scurried up his spine as fast as a bolt of lightning, because for the first time, he became cognizant that something hadn't merely *happened.* It was *happening.*

Present tense.

Ongoing.

Yet still, it didn't matter because he was here, and he was convinced now he hadn't imagined the sound of his brother crying last night. Something was *happening,* and if he didn't begin to try and understand what the hell it was, Abel might go missing, and Kyle and his parents might wind up dead.

So, he made up his mind and told the new girl, "Yeah. You're probably right." Then he went first.

***

"If all—the raindrops were lemon-drops and gumdrops—oh what a rain that would be!" Kim sang, her arms out to her sides, as she spun around and around like a helicopter. There were so many kids now that the room was completely illuminated by the orange lights coming from their faces and every surface was covered in waving shadows. They were in the part of the theater that had once had a giant TV and chairs, and they were all dancing and singing the song Michael had taught them. More huffing and heaving could be heard than anything as most of them took in struggled breaths and sang through their swollen throats. A few of them still had normal voices. Even they had to suck giant gusts of air, however, and their bellies expanded like beach balls when they did. It made Kim laugh.

"I'd stand outside with my mouth open wide!" She looked at the ceiling. It was so far away that if she could fall up, all her bones would shatter like toothpicks when she crashed into it. Sticking out her tongue, she caught the pretend raindrops in her mouth, which was growing dryer and dryer. "Ah! Ah! Ah—ah! Ah! Ah-ah! Ah! Ah-ah! If all—the raindrops were lemon-drops and gumdrops—oh what a rain that would be!"

Michael liked songs. He liked to dance. He liked to throw James's daddy's head like a basketball. They had had it since yesterday, when there were still only four of them, but they hadn't thought to play catch with it until Michael showed up.

Last night had been the best night Kimberly Brenton had ever experienced. Even better than when she killed her mother. They had gone to the apartments where Mom's friend Gage lived, and then they had gone door-to-door getting the new kids and helping the ones who needed help finishing their families.

They knew where each new kid lived and which ones needed help, because the monster knew. The monster didn't need to tell them, though, because they knew what it wanted them to know, and that's just how it worked.

Kim couldn't be the one to kill last night, and neither could James, Telma, or Jose. Each child had to handle his or her own family. That's what the monster wanted. The others could only help, and oh how fun it was to help. Kimberly still had her knives, and she loved them very much. More than she had ever loved any of her toys at home (including Dog McGee).

She had loved sticking them into Malachi's mommy's legs, and using them to take out the eyes of Justin's dad. She had even considered using them on her boyfriend.

Kim wasn't sure what a boyfriend was, but Mom used to joke that that's what Kyle was when he would wrestle her in front of the trailer. And she liked him a lot, so she had wanted to wrestle him again yesterday with her steak knives. Kim had squealed with glee when James removed his father's head with the axe from his own shed. Yes. There was no doubt this was how a princess was meant to live.

Something collided with her foot, and she glanced down to see the severed head staring up at her, mouth open wide to catch all the pretend rain.

"Kim!" A duck-like voice croaked. She looked back up at Michael, who was older, like James. He wore a pair of green sweats, and a long white T-shirt with splotches of blood everywhere, and he was smiling from ear to ear. "Kick it back!"

The other children continued to sing, "I'd stand outside with my mouth open wide! Ah! Ah! Ah—ah! Ah! Ah-ah! Ah! Ah-ah!"

Kim kicked the head as hard as she could, launching it into the air. Blood splattered out in every direction in tiny droplets as it flew toward Michael. He caught it like a football and took off running through the crowd of dancing children. A second later, another boy's eyes went wide, and he chased after him.

"If all—the raindrops were lemon-drops and gumdrops—oh what a rain that would be!"

***

Kyle told Marie just about everything he knew, only omitting that he'd heard his brother crying last night. She sat across from him, straight-faced, listening and nodding from time to time. It was just past ten, and the Courthouse Café had begun to clear out. Only a few costumers remained, mostly sitting alone sipping coffee, and fiddling with cell phones. One man sat at the counter with a white mug, watching the TV, which still displayed images of Mount Vernon Police cars. If Marie thought Kyle was crazy, she gave no indication, and when he was finished, neither spoke at first.

Then, she said, "And what do you think it is?"

"What do you mean?" he asked.

"I mean what do you think happened to those children and their parents?"

"I don't know. I mean—I ah—I really don't know."

"I had a feeling you'd seen them."

"The kids?"

"No. I mean, yes. But their eyes."

"Wait, you saw them too?"

"No," she said. "Not me. My father. The police were being very secretive. They demanded the video surveillance, and didn't want to let him view it with them. But it doesn't work that way. I mean this isn't some nineteen eighties movie, in which you just hand over a VHS tape and go about your day. He needed to access and navigate the security system in order to allow them to review the footage on his computer."

Kyle said, "The footage of what?"

"The halls and the lobby and whatnot. There are cameras everywhere, you know. And my father is a very stubborn, and a very persuasive man, so I'm guessing he played the 'I don't speak English' card. He's uber Italian, and can get away with it, you see.

"So, he pulled up the videos in front of the police and saw them briefly before they rushed him out of the room."

"The kids?"

"The kids. Yes. The footage is all black and white in our buildings, but I heard him over the phone, and I can't say as I've ever known my father to be as worked up as he was over what he saw. He said it was like they had flashlights for eyes. He couldn't see that the light was orange, but you've clearly seen them, too, and you're saying it was. Did they have weapons?"

"What do you mean?" he asked.

"My father said they all had weapons. Like garden tools and knives and whatnot. One even had a gun."

"Jesus."

"Yes. So, you saw them yesterday, when there were only four. Were they carrying tools of any kind?"

Kyle thought back, picturing the terrible children and their orange eyes. The memory was becoming more of a blur as time passed, but it was still clear enough, and he hadn't seen any types of weapons, so he told her he hadn't.

She nodded, asked again, "So what do you think it is?"

"They're dead," he replied without hesitation.

"Pardon?"

"I don't know. I can't really explain it, but those weren't kids. They were walking corpses. I know it sounds ridiculous—"

"No more ridiculous than anything else that's happening," she interrupted.

Kyle nodded, then went on. "One of them was in nothing but a pair of underwear and he had a swollen stomach. They were all turning pale, and you could see veins, or blood-vessels or whatever. And I don't think they were breathing. It was weird. I mean, Kim said my name, but she had to suck in air first, and it came out choked and raspy. Fucking freaky, you know?"

"Can you show me?" Marie asked.

"What?"

"How she talked. I mean can you show me how her voice sounded?"

"I don't—I mean, yeah. I guess I could try. Why?"

Marie paused, apparently attempting to conjure up a sufficient answer. Then she said, "My father wants me to go into medicine, and I've had to read up on the topic quite extensively. I mean, I'm no doctor, but I may have some insight into your zombie-toddler theory."

"Zombie-toddler?"

Ignoring the question, she asked, "Did it sound like her throat was swollen?"

"Yeah, actually. It was like she was choking as she talked."

"Spoke," Marie said.

"What?"

"As she spoke."

"Oh. Yeah. As she spoke or whatever."

"Show me."

Taking a deep breath, Kyle closed his throat and groaned like something from an old George Romero film. "It was kinda like this."

The man at the counter turned and scowled at him, along with a couple others, including the waitress. Kyle supposed they thought he was making a joke out of what was being talked about on TV, and it caused his ears to heat up.

Returning to a normal voice, he continued, "Well, not quite like that, but you get the point."

"Right." Marie glanced around at the sour faces, which were slowly returning to their plates, then back at Kyle. "I wouldn't request a refill on the coffee, mate. I imagine we might get a double shot of saliva at this point. So, it sounded like her throat was constricted?"

"Yeah. Pretty much."

"And one had a swollen belly, and they were pale?"

"Pale-ish."

"Pale-ish." Her eyes glazed over, and for a moment she seemed to be in deep thought. Then, "Not sure why their throats would be swollen. But without taking anything off the table, let's assume they *are* dead. It could be pulmonary edema, which could indicate death by strangulation. Or perhaps anaphylactic shock. That's usually a reaction to a food allergy, in which the lips, or feet, or throat swells and the patient dies. Let me ask you a question. Did she appear to be choking, while trying to breathe before she spoke?"

"No. That's what I'm trying to tell you. I don't think she was breathing at all. I think she just sucked in a breath to push the word out. But yeah, it was like a choked breath, I guess."

Marie shook her head, examined Kyle the way Detective Bartlet had.

He said, "You don't believe me."

"Actually," she replied. "I think I do, and that's the problem."

Her words caused every hair on Kyle's body to stand up like a crowd doing the wave at a baseball game. For what felt like the longest moment that had ever transpired, a silence hung between them in which they just watched each other's pupils expand because they were likely having the most fucked up conversation of both of their lives now. Then Marie licked her lips and Kyle's parted because somebody needed to say something.

But before he could form a word, his phone vibrated in his pocket. Bringing it out, he glanced down and saw a text from his mom announced on the screen. He selected to view it, then felt his heart drop out of his rectum and roll down his pant-leg.

"Are you okay?" Marie's voice sounded miles away.

Kyle's body grew light. He took a deep breath, then peered up at the television, only now looking closely at where the news crews and police cars where all parked. His voice shook as he asked Marie which apartments her parents owned.

"Uh, the Sunset, the Silver Palms, and the Woodlands. Why?"

"On College Way?"

"Yes."

"Jesus."

"What is it?" She tilted her head.

"We need to go. Can you drive us there?"

"To my father's buildings?"

But Kyle was already on his feet. He dropped the phone back into his pocket, but the screen still read,

Where are you? Are you all right? Call me. Something happened in Dobey's building last night.

***

Kyle was almost to the door when Marie hollered, "Hold on. Of course, I'll drive you. Let me pay the bill first."

So, he stood at the counter and stared at the old brown building on the television as she paid with a credit card. He searched for any indication that his friend had been involved, but it was impossible to tell one way or the other.

Marie told the waitress "Okay then. Ta," as she slipped her card into her wallet, then dropped the wallet in her purse. She took Kyle's hand and began pulling him toward the door. At first, he didn't even notice, because he had always held hands with Claudia in public. Then he *did* notice, and wondered if this was how girls interacted with their male friends where she was from.

She pushed the door open and led him out into the rain, which had picked up significantly while they were in the restaurant. They both ducked, as if that would keep them dry, and Marie let go of his hand, putting her arm around his waist.

"Come on! Come on! Come on! Come on! Get to the car! Quick!" She picked up her pace, tugging him along, and without putting too much thought into it, Kyle threw his arm around her shoulder and jogged beside her. Then a voice appeared behind them, which only took him a second to recognize.

"Eh! What's up, fool?"

Stopping in his tracks, Kyle turned and saw the Mexican boys who had run in front of the SUV (how long ago? It must have been a half hour. What were they still doing out here? In the rain no less). And one of them was Silencer.

He wore a black jacket with the hood up, and walked a few feet ahead of the small pack, his head up, his chest out. He looked like he smelled something foul.

"What's up, fool? Remember me?"

"Hold on." Kyle let go of Marie. She kept her arm firmly around his waist though, like he might float away if she let go. "Come on, man. I don't want—"

"I don't give a fuck, homie." Now he was in front of Kyle. He pressed both fists into his chest, shoving him back a couple of feet and breaking Marie's embrace. "I told you to leave my prima alone, didn't I?"

His three friends were next to him. One of them, who wore a blue sweater with a huge logo that Kyle didn't recognize stitched across the front, spit on the sidewalk and cracked his knuckles simultaneously.

"What is this?" Marie frowned.

Silencer said, "You gonna let a hayna fight your battles for you, dawg? That's how you get down?"

"Excuse me?" Marie asked. "A what?"

Silencer glared at her, half-grinning, then back at Kyle. "Why don't you shut your bitch up, homie. Tell her men are talking."

"Listen," Kyle said. "I'm just trying to get to—"

"I beg your pardon?" Marie stepped up next to Kyle. "Who exactly are you calling a bitch?"

The other three cholos cupped their hands around their mouths and cooed. One said, "Ooooh. What's up, fool? This hayna gots an attitude on 'er!"

But Silencer didn't care. He shoved Kyle again. "Answer me, puto! Didn't I tell you to leave my prima alone?"

Kyle wanted to be mad. For the briefest of seconds, he imagined cocking back and throwing a wild punch that would knock this kid out, and watching his friends all run away like scared little animals. But that thought passed like a speeding car on the freeway, because Kyle had never knocked anybody out in his life, and even if he *could* (he couldn't), these were gangbangers, not chipmunks. They wouldn't run. They would fight, and they wouldn't lose, because they would do whatever it took to make sure of it. And, they probably had weapons.

Just as he was having this thought—as if in confirmation—Silencer slid a hand into his jacket pocket, and for reasons that Kyle didn't understand, he became aware of the cold. Of the heavy drops of rain streaming out of his hair and down his face. His gaze dropped and he felt his heart thump against the inside of his ribcage. In his peripheral, he saw Marie's eyes expand like wet sponges and they both took a step back.

Kyle thought, *gun,* and when the hand re-emerged for a second, he was sure he was right because it clutched shiny chrome. But then his fingers each slipped into small holes and Kyle recognized the object as a set of thick brass knuckles.

And because that wasn't a vast improvement from a gun, he said, "Come on, man. I left her alone. I haven't even seen her."

"You left her alone, 'what,' fool?"

"What?"

"Say my motha-fuckin' name, Kyle. Say, 'I left her alone, Silencer.' You know what time it is."

Two of the cholos did a sort of dance, cupping their mouths again and turning away momentarily to laugh out of sight. Then they turned back and one of them said, "Come on, Silencer. Fuck this vato up already."

But Silencer didn't look, or even acknowledge they were there, and Kyle flashed back to yesterday, in the gym. It had been apparent the young Latino had wanted a fight no more than Kyle himself. He'd merely been pumped up by his friends to initiate the confrontation. And again, he was clearly hesitating, either attempting to talk himself into committing violence, or out of it.

But today he had a weapon. They weren't on school grounds where there would be unavoidable consequences to a physical confrontation. Surely, he had vowed to do something the next time he saw Kyle, and if he didn't keep to that vow, he would lose face in front of his gang.

Silencer scowled. "So, you gonna just lie to me? That's what you gonna do? Think I don't know you texted her yesterday?"

Before Kyle could respond, Marie said, "Have you considered that perhaps you're the one who's a bitch?"

All three backup cholos laughed and cackled, flailing their arms over-exaggeratedly.

Baring his teeth, Silencer raised his metal clad hand and advanced on her. "The fuck you say to me, bitch?"

Without thinking, Kyle stepped in between them, pressed both hands into the kid's chest and shoved him as hard as he could. Silencer swung wild and stumbled back simultaneously. Everything started to move in slow motion, and Kyle was sure he would miss. Then he was sure he *had* missed because though his ears were ringing, he didn't feel a thing until Silencer recovered and all four cholos charged at the same time, like sharks closing in on their prey.

For a split second, he finally registered a sharp pain where the brass knuckles had collided with the left side of his head before the onslaught of punches began, landing one after another like machine-gun-fire to his face, his head, his body. He doubled over, bringing his arms up and hugging his face so he was in a sort of a standing fetal position.

Somewhere amidst the sound of ruffling polyester and shoes splashing in wet pavement, he heard Marie yell, "Oh come on, man! That's just unnecessary!"

Then he was on the ground, still curled into a ball, his eyes shut so tight that an electron couldn't have slipped in. A foot smashed into his lips, and he tasted blood as somebody landed on top of him. He smelled Marie's sweet perfume and felt her wet hair on his face. She wrapped her arms around him, covering as much of his body with hers as she could, then grunted, apparently hit by a fist or a shoe.

A car horn went off, Then another. Then somebody yelled, "HEY! WHAT THE HELL DO YOU THINK YOU'RE DOING? COME ON! COME ON! COME ON! GET THE FUCK OUTTA HERE! NOW!"

The blows stopped, and rubber slapped pavement as the cholos fled. Kyle opened his eyes, saw nothing but darkness at first because Marie's black hair still hung over them. He shook it out of his face and attempted to sit up, but she had him pinned down like a professional wrestler. Her stomach heaved against his side and her face was burrowed deep in his neck. Her black purse lay next to them in the rain, and only now did he notice the gold-colored emblem, which read, "COACH." It must have been very expensive, but she didn't seem to care if it got ruined. She had no intention of getting up or even dismounting from him.

"Are you okay, man?" the voice of their rescuer called from above. Glancing up, Kyle caught sight of a fat dark-skinned man with a ponytail and an X-shaped tire iron. His hair was messy, and he wore glasses that were too big for his face and a shirt that was too small for his body. A red SUV sat against the curb with smoke coming from its tailpipe, and the driver's side door wide open, blocking traffic. With considerable effort, he reached into his pocket, brought out a cell phone. "Those dudes're outta line, bro. Don't even trip. I'm calling the cops."

Ignoring him, Kyle said, "Marie?"

But she didn't respond, didn't even twitch. Just hung on him like a wet towel.

"Marie, come on. We gotta get up."

Finally, she moved, sitting up slowly as if she was just getting out of bed, and scanned the area. Kyle sat up as well and started to stand, but she threw her arms around him and sobbed into his ear, causing something to stir in his stomach that sent a chill over his scalp. He returned her embrace, hugging around her waist until she finally let go, grabbed her purse, climbed to her feet, and offered her hand. Kyle accepted it, but stood without her assistance.

Then something caught his eye, and he leaned over and scooped up Silencer's brass knuckles from the sidewalk. They were heavier than he would have expected, and he guessed it made throwing punches with them quite a task. Marie watched as he let them drop into his pocket.

The fat guy now held the phone to his ear, watching the two teens wide-eyed. "Nobody's picking up, bro. It's just ringing and ringing. It's all good though. I ain't in no hurry."

"They're busy," Kyle replied, touching the side of his head and wincing. He examined his hand and saw blood on his fingertips, but the rain quickly washed most of it away. As an afterthought, he told the guy, "Thanks."

"No problem, man. Those guys're fucked up. My nephew got jumped the other week, too, and he's only still in middle-school. Listen, lemme park my rig somewhere and I'll chill with you till the cops show up. In fact, why don't you hop in an' get outta the rain."

Kyle didn't think about it, just said, "We can't. We have to get somewhere. Listen, man, thanks again." He took Marie's hand and pulled her toward the alley that would take them to where her car was parked. She didn't hesitate when the guy tried to call them back, and within seconds they were jogging side-by-side.

Chapter Five

They ran through the alley and emerged behind a restaurant that smelled of some type of ethnic food Kyle had never tasted. The backdoor was open and a guy in an apron stood under a thin covering smoking a cigarette. He glanced in their direction, then disregarded them, tossing his butt into a coffee can, and disappearing inside.

The boardwalk was just across a three-lane street, which they traversed without hesitation, and that's where the Beetle was parked against the wooden rail where Kyle often stood with Claudia to watch the passing river. Now he could hear the rain as it splattered against its surface, but he didn't look. He had been under the boardwalk once with Dobey and some other friends to smoke, and knew a whole community of homeless people slept and spent their time just below his feet.

When they reached the car, Kyle was out of breath, but Marie appeared fine. She used the electronic clicker on her keychain to unlock the doors and hopped into the driver's seat without hesitation. Kyle opened the passenger door and peered in, but didn't move so she leaned over, gazed up at him expectantly, and he noticed that her eye makeup was smeared on one side of her face.

"Thought you were in a hurry?" she said.

"I am," he puffed. "But my clothes are wet."

"And?"

"Well, your car's really nice. I don't wanna mess up your seat."

"Then take them off."

"What?"

"Your clothes."

"No—I mean I know what you meant. I was just—"

"I'm kidding." She smiled. "Mine are soaking wet as well. What can you do? Just hop in and we'll sort it out later."

So, Kyle slowly lowered himself into the car and took a seat, hearing his pants squishing around beneath his bottom and finally taking the time to shiver. He wiped at his swollen lower lip with the back of his hand. It stung and left a thin layer of light-red blood on his pale skin. Marie pressed the ignition and brought the car to life, turning the heater up as high as it would go, and for a long moment, neither of them spoke, just stared out the windshield.

Then Kyle looked over at the side of her head, noticing that her hair, which had been straightened so nicely only moments ago, was tangled and messy like her makeup. He said, "You had my back."

She smirked. Returned his gaze. Nodded. "Yes. I suppose I did. Were those gang members?"

"Uh, yeah. I think so. Don't you have gang members in Australia?"

"Sure we do. I've been living in England for the past nine years though. Mind you, we have them there too. Quite different types of fellas than your friends back there. Who in the hell was that guy, anyway?"

"My ex's cousin."

"Are you sure?"

"Uh—yeah. I mean—why?"

"Well, you two hardly even know each other."

"How do you know that?"

"Well," she spoke slowly, "when he first approached you, he asked if you remembered him. That must mean you've only met briefly. How long were you with this girl?"

Kyle considered attempting to change the subject, or lie because it was headed somewhere, he wasn't comfortable going there with her. But then he thought *what the hell?* and said, "Seven months."

"And you just met this guy?"

"Yesterday morning."

Marie shook her head. "Oh sweetie. Don't be silly. If that were her cousin back there, you would've known him a long time ago. You must know he's full of shit."

"What are you getting at?" Kyle asked, even though he already knew.

"I'm saying that that guy is her new lover. Did you see how enraged he was that you'd even texted her?"

"Yeah. Well, there's a reason for that—"

"Do you know what my last name is?"

"What?" He thought back to whether or not he'd gotten her full name yesterday. Couldn't recall.

"It's not a trick question, mate. My last name. Do you know it?" She put the car in reverse and glanced into the rear-view mirror. "Oh dear. Why didn't you tell me I look like a zombie?" But she didn't stop to fix her makeup, just backed out and started to drive them across the mostly empty parking lot.

"Never mind," she continued. "Anyway, my last name is Franco. Marie Franco. That's as Italian as it gets. Believe me, I know Latin people are very protective of their female family members, because we're the same way. My cousin back home once beat a boy half to death for flipping my dress up on the playground. But what happened back there—in front of that restaurant—that wasn't a cousinly protectiveness. Not even brotherly. That boy was green as a string bean with jealousy."

Kyle considered this, as she pulled up to the lot's exit and hit her blinker. But before he put too much thought into the matter, Marie reached up, rubbed the back of her head, and winced.

"Did you get hit?" he asked.

"I'll be fine." She set her hand back on the wheel.

"Let me—" Reaching over, he touched the place her hand had been and felt his jaw clench almost involuntarily as red-hot anger stirred in his chest because there was a lump the size of a golf-ball back there. She winced again and leaned away from him. Kyle retreated and examined his hand, but saw no blood. "He hit you with the brass-knuckles."

"Well, I jumped in front of them, didn't I?" She stepped on the gas, ushered them out onto the street.

"It's still fucked up. You're a girl."

"Sweety, don't worry about me. I'm tough. Plus, I put myself in that situation, so I have only myself to blame."

Kyle shook his head. "You shouldn't have done that."

"A simple thank you would suffice."

"No. I mean, thank you. For sure. But I just—"

"—are too proud to let a girl get your back? That's a bit silly, don't you think? Would you have done the same for me?"

"Yeah."

"Then what's the problem? If we're gonna be friends, you're gonna have to learn to be a team player."

Kyle opened his mouth to respond but there was really no sufficient refutation to her logic, so he just nodded instead.

Marie asked, "Why do we need to go to my father's apartments so badly?"

He told her that Dobey lived in one of the buildings, then said, "You never took your turn."

"My turn for what?"

"To tell me what you know. I mean you said your dad saw them on video and their eyes were glowing, but that's it."

She pulled up to an intersection and replied, "My father only saw a few seconds of footage, and all he said was that they had glowing eyes and the devil's shadow."

Kyle examined her. "Devil's shadow?"

"Honestly, mate, I don't know what the hell that means. He's very Catholic. He said they had the shadows of snakes. Did you see anything like that?"

"No," Kyle responded without hesitation. "I don't think so."

"You still haven't answered my question either," she said as the light turned green.

"Which one."

Marie hit the gas. "What do you think is happening?"

Kyle took a deep breath, let it out slowly. "I think it's pretty obvious. The kids are killing their parents."

Nodding, she replied, "Unfortunately, I think you're right. Does Dobey have any siblings?"

***

The roads were relatively clear downtown, but traffic increased the closer they drew to the scene. Kyle told Marie that Dobey had an adopted sister, who was a year older than him, and a ten-year-old brother named Josh. When this bit of info came out, she drove faster.

College Way was absolutely packed, and police were directing traffic. Though the speed limit was normally thirty-five-miles-per-hour, it was impossible to go above ten for at least a one-mile-stretch. When they finally reached the cluster of apartments, Kyle rolled down his window for a better view. The entrance was blocked off, so they parked across the street at the college. The parking lot, which was normally empty on Saturdays, was packed with news-vans and the vehicles of people who had gathered along the sidewalk to stare across the street and snap videos and photos of the crime-scene.

Marie asked which building Dobey lived in.

Kyle thought a second, then said, "The brown one."

"You mean the Woodlands?"

"What? I don't know. The cheaper ones."

"Right. The older building."

"Yeah."

"That's the Woodlands. What do we do now? I don't suppose they'll let us onto the grounds."

"What about your dad?"

Marie shook her head. "No way, man. He'll be about as helpful as a tick on a koala's ass. Even if he did want to help out, do you really think the police would let him dictate who was allowed on the grounds?"

"No," Kyle deflated. "You're probably right."

"Do you have his number?"

"He doesn't have a phone. His parents do, but I've never saved their numbers because they don't like people to call him on them. He usually calls from somebody else's phone, or—hold on." Kyle lifted his bottom and dug his iPhone out of his pocket, seeing three more texts from his mom.

Hello?

Are you OK?

Call me now!

He'd set it to silent at the restaurant, but now he increased the ringer back to vibrate, where he normally kept it.

Marie fished in her purse, bringing out her own black phone. She examined the screen, typed something, and traded it for a circular compact mirror, which she used to assess the damage to her makeup job. Then she peered at him and asked, "Or what?"

Kyle connected to the internet. "Facebook." He opened Messenger and saw nothing from his best friend. There was, however, one message from Laura Cunningham.

wuts up kyle? wanna come over to my house?

It was sent at 9:32, about an hour ago and Kyle felt his body relax because though they ran in the same circle, Kyle and Laura had never hung out alone, nor would she have any reason to extend such an invitation. It must have been Dobey texting from her account, which meant he was at her house.

After what happened last night, the police would surely want to speak with everybody who lived in the building, and Dobey had a warrant. He had to be hiding, which was all right, because that meant he was at least alive. It would make sense for him to be contacting him from her account, in case the police were somehow monitoring his. Or Kyle's.

As he was having this thought, Marie said, "Would you be a dear and get me the wet-wipes from the glove compartment?"

"Sure." Kyle opened the glovebox, found them, and handed them over.

But what if it *was* Laura messaging him? Sure, they had never been the closest of the group, but every so often he swore he caught her giving him looks that suggested had they both been single, they might amount to more than just friends. And Kyle *was* single now. Laura wasn't, but he was.

And something was killing children. Possessing their bodies. Steering them like remote controlled fucking cars to kill their families. And that something had apparently swept through Dobey's building. And Dobey had a little brother. So Dobey was probably dead.

"Did he message you?" Marie asked as she cleaned makeup from her face.

"I don't know," he responded.

"You don't know?"

No, he thought. *I don't know. I don't know anything anymore. I don't know if my best friend is dead or alive, or how to even find out, or whether my own brother is going to wake up tonight and cut my head off in my sleep.*

But that's not what came out of his mouth. Instead, he said, "I mean, I'm not sure. He might have from somebody else's account."

"Well," she spoke slowly. "Can't you just ask if it's him?"

"No."

She paused, seemed to consider this. "Okay then. Well, is there another way to find out?"

"Yeah. Maybe. Would you be all right with taking me somewhere else?" He closed out Messenger and killed the screen.

She froze momentarily, then, holding the mirror and the wipe inches from her face like it had its own gravitational pull, she glanced at him and said, "Are you ditching me?"

"What?"

"Well, I thought we were spending the day together."

"We are—I mean, so did I."

"Well, you're not asking me to just drop you off somewhere, are you?"

"No."

"Then of course I don't mind driving you. We're kind of in this together at this point, aren't we?" She resumed wiping.

"Yeah." Kyle nodded. "Kinda."

He expected her to take at least ten more minutes to reapply her makeup, but instead, once the previous layer was removed, she put the kit away, dropped the used wipes into her purse, and set the rest on Kyle's lap. "Would you mind putting those away?" She combed the knots out of her hair with her fingers. "Where are we headed, now?"

At first, he didn't answer because it was the first time, he'd seen her bare face. Then her eyes narrowed, and the hint of a smile teased her lips. Kyle recovered, replaced the wipes in the glovebox and said, "Back down—"

Tap. Tap. Tap.

Marie's eyes moved first, pointed past Kyle, out the passenger window. They remained calm, however. *Collected and level-headed.* Then Kyle glanced over and saw Detective Bartlet looming over him in the same outfit as yesterday, pens protruding from her breast pocket and a chrome badge hanging from a chain around her neck. Her hair was drenched and there was no longer coverup concealing the circles under her eyes. She appeared to have aged ten years. A few feet behind her, the tall

Hispanic Detective stood in a black raincoat with the hood pulled over his head and his hands in the jacket's pockets.

Kyle's first thought was, *Marie. She was texting when we pulled up. Bartlet said she called her phone yesterday. This was all just a set up.*

But to what end? Even if Marie *was* texting her, and she *did* tell her he was here, he hadn't done anything wrong.

Before he could put any more thought into it, she rapped the knuckle of her index finger against the glass again. "Kyle. Why don't you go ahead and step outta the car?"

Kyle turned back toward Marie. Their eyes met and she shrugged.

Tap. Tap.

"Kyle. Get outta the car."

"Who is that?" Marie asked.

Ignoring her, Kyle opened the door, causing Bartlet to take a step back. He climbed out into the rain and dropped the phone in his right pocket, remembering the brass knuckles in his left along with something he'd heard before about them being illegal to possess.

As he shut the door, Bartlet and the other advanced on him at the same time, causing him to flinch involuntarily. She stopped and examined him a moment, then shook off whatever she was thinking and said, "I'll give you one guess as to what I'm about to ask, Kyle."

The male cop shifted once, then was as still as a statue, staring down at Kyle like he was something a waiter had set in front of him that he didn't want to eat. Bartlet brushed wet hair from her face and put a hand on her hip. Behind Kyle, Marie's door opened, but he didn't look back. Bartlet glanced at her partner and finally he spoke.

"Hey! Miss! Stay in your vehicle please!"

"Excuse me? Who exactly are you?"

The detective marched purposefully around the car, throwing his hood back and unzipping his jacket to reveal a badge identical to Bartlet's, along with his gun which rested in its shoulder-holster at his side. "We're the police. So, unless you wanna take a ride downtown in my car, step back in yours right now."

The door slammed shut, and the cop returned to Bartlet's side as Kyle said, "Am I in some kind of trouble?"

"That depends," Bartlet responded.

"On what?"

"I don't know Kyle. I'd say it depends on how long you decide to stand there with that smug look on your face and dick me around."

The rain had subsided slightly at some point, but it was still coming down in a light mist.

"I'm not trying to do that. I don't even know—"

"Let's cut the crap, dude. Where the hell is he?"

"Who?"

"You know who. Where's Shawn?"

"I don't know. I've been downtown at the Courthouse Café all morning. I just found out what happened over here." It wasn't a lie. Yeah, maybe it *had* been Dobey messaging him from Laura's Facebook, but he didn't know yet one way or the other.

"The Courthouse Café?" the male cop asked.

"Yeah."

"So, if I call my niece who works there right now, she'll tell me she saw you and," he pointed into the car, "her?"

"Yeah," Kyle stuttered, "I mean we—I don't see why she wouldn't. We were just there—hold on." He reached into his pocket and both officers noticeably tensed. What the hell was he doing? This was ridiculous. He hadn't even been watching the clock and had no clue what time they'd left the restaurant. But he was nervous as hell, and his body was on autopilot, so he brought out his cell phone and pressed a button on the side that brought the screen to life.

It was 10:46.

He said, "Like a half hour ago. We left at like nine—" he did the math as quickly as he could in his head (it took way too long), "—fifteen. Nine-fifteen."

Bartlet was incredulous. "Gimme the phone, Kyle."

"Why?"

"You really wanna go down that road?"

"I didn't do anything wrong."

"Do you pay your cell phone bill?"

"No."

"Didn't think so. Your mom does, and she gave me permission to look through it, remember?"

Kyle took a deep breath. His hand shook as he handed over the phone. She was a detective, and one didn't become a detective for being inept, or ignorant to details. She would check his Messenger, and with a clearer perspective than his, deduce that the text was likely from Dobey. Then, after following up on the lead, she'd arrest Kyle for lying. What was the term he'd seen on every cop show on television? Obstruction?

So, he stood trying not to appear too defeated as she snooped though his phone, the other officer peering over her shoulder like a raven on a roof. But he knew he looked as awkward and anxious as he felt. After the longest minute that had ever transpired, she handed the phone back with the text-message box still open.

"Kyle, I know you're hiding something from me. I don't know what it is, but I'll figure it out. I've been doing my job twice as long as you've been alive, and I'm particularly good at it. And when I do, I'm going to arrest you for getting in the way of a mass murder investigation. I'd do it now, and sort out the details later, but I'm terribly busy. So, count your blessings.

"In the meantime, I want you to pass a message to Mr. Collins when you see him. Tell him I already know he wasn't home when it happened. Tell him not to do anything stupid." Reaching into her breast pocket, she produced a soggy business card, offered it to Kyle. "Tell him to call me and we'll figure out his warrant. I'm not gonna haul him into juvie unless he makes me come looking for him."

Kyle accepted the wet card, tucked it into his pocket, asked, "What exactly *did* happen?"

She tilted her head, studied his face for a long moment. "If you don't know, Kyle, it's probably none of your business. Now get outta here," she turned and walked away, the other cop following at her side, "and call your freaking Mom, dude. What's wrong with you?"

***

The dog was onto something.

Noel Rowland had pulled into the old building which used to house the Cinema 7 on nothing more than a whim, but even barely into his late twenties, he'd learned during his six years on the force to trust whims. In fact, he'd learned it very early on during a traffic stop.

The car had been something straight out of a movie depicting Southern California in the nineteen-nineties. A blue Cadillac lowered on shiny chrome rims and every seat occupied by gangbangers. But you couldn't just notice a thing like that, because though anybody with half a brain could recognize a gang member in Mount Vernon, the physical characteristics (brown skin, shaved head) turned any cop who noticed into a racial profiling lawsuit magnet.

But 16th Street was a high crime neighborhood, known for drive-by-shootings and other types of violence, and the vehicle had been driving by suspiciously slow, and even more suspiciously past midnight. Rowland had been parked on a cross-street, watching for just such activity and the occupants apparently hadn't spotted his car.

But that's not when he'd had his whim. It was, however, when he'd waited for the Cadillac to pass, and pulled up behind it. And it was also when the car had sped up. Not to the point of speeding, but to the residential street's ten-miles-per-hour limit. So, Rowland had hit his lights and called in the plates and his location as he counted more than ten seconds before the car pulled up to the sidewalk.

He hadn't gotten a decent view of the occupants yet, but it wasn't difficult to deduce what types of people he would find inside. It was just a matter of how many there would be. He'd considered waiting for his backup before approaching, but that would just have allotted passengers time to swallow drugs, stuff guns under seats—even talk the driver into fleeing.

So, Noel Rowland had stepped out into the cold night, all five-foot-seven of him, and he'd made it halfway to the vehicle, before he finally *did* see the bald heads poking above backrests, and that's when he'd had his whim.

It was almost a premonition. They had guns. Not just a couple, either. No, they *had guns,* and they were prepared to use them. On him. So, he had drawn his own weapon and pointed it at the back windshield, skipping in reverse to his car in order to get behind the driver's door and direct them out and onto their faces.

There had been enough light from the looming street lamps for him and the driver to lock eyes in the rear-view mirror, though, just as the backseat passengers had turned and pointed weapons and bullets had flown through the window for the next eight seconds. Rowland knew because during the ensuing investigation, footage from his dash-cam had been thoroughly examined by internal investigations (Mount Vernon PD, hadn't yet adopted bodycams).

He hadn't fired back. Just hit the pavement facedown and prayed for his life, until the shots ceased and all that could be heard was the sound of squealing tires as the low-rider sped away. Ironically enough, he hadn't touched one bullet, and he legitimately believed God had answered that prayer, yet he'd lied his ass off about seeing the gangbangers' guns in their laps before he pulled his own. But he knew his co-workers talked shit behind his back. And they knew he hadn't seen guns, but how could he tell them that he'd just known?

As it turned out, the cholos had been about to do a drive-by just two blocks from where they shot at him. They were all rounded up within days and sentenced to marinate in prison cells until they were old and pruned— no longer a threat to the taxpayers of Skagit County.

Now, Rowland had had another one of his whims, only today he had a canine that lived to follow up on them, so the police issued SUV was parked behind the old cinema, next to an overgrown light-green field. The lot was big enough for teens to skateboard in if it hadn't been strewn with pebbles, but too small for drunk college kids to do donuts. Not that they would if it were bigger, seeing as the police station sat just across a two-lane street from the front of the building.

The dog had his entire head in an opening where an aluminum backdoor was bent outward in the bottom left hand corner.

The cinema was located on a back road, and the door had been broken for years. In fact, there had been one year, in particular, in which the place had been popular amongst local squatters. Noel and his colleagues had busted runaways and other trespassers inside nearly every week, until they finally figured out that breaking into a place across from the cop-shop wasn't a wise endeavor.

Rowland had been on his way into the station for lunch when the whim had overtaken him, and he had turned into the lot. He hadn't called it in. Not yet at least, because not only was it just a whim, but it was *his* whim and he'd be damned if he was going to be ordered to just wait around for somebody else to come and validate it. But now the dog was going absolutely crazy, and had half of his body inside, which meant he had either heard movement in there, or finally picked up a scent. Rowland suspected it was the latter. The rain had thus far not obstructed the canine's nose, which was by far the strongest sniffer in the department.

Gripping the lead with both hands, Rowland said, "Rocket! Rocket! Come on! Get back here!" Had anybody been listening, he would have given the command in German, but Rocket understood English just fine. They made a show of using the commands they had both been trained with in public, but in private the two had an understanding because in spite of how cliché it might seem, he took the canine home every night and they were best friends.

"Rocket! You stupid fuck! Hold on a second. We'll go in together."

But the German Shepherd wasn't having it. The lower portion of his body wedged itself through the opening, then, for a brief second, all that could be seen was his tail until that disappeared as well. The black lead started to slip in Rowland's palm, so he gripped it with both hands, but it was too late. It hit the pavement, then retracted into the door like a spaghetti noodle being sucked up.

"Shit!" In a desperate attempt, he stomped his heavy steel-toed-boot, barely catching the loop on the end, holding his breath, and praying it would be enough to halt the dog. He clenched his jaw so tight that he thought he would chip a tooth, then felt the tug under his foot and heard Rocket let out a yelp that echoed around inside the cinema.

Wrapping the lead around his wrist, he grabbed the door and wrenched as hard as he could, bending the flimsy metal until he thought he could fit through the hole. Then Rocket barked. Just once at first, followed by a momentary pause before exploding into absolute maniacal thunder that was distorted by its own echo. The dog pulled on the lead so hard that Rowland thought for a second his wrist would dislocate. Then he thought, *Somebody's in there.*

And if somebody, then why not the twenty-two missing children—well, twenty-two they knew about so far. After all, the little bastards had been exceedingly evasive. And though Bartlet and her small crew of plainclothes thought they were concealing something from the rest of the department, Fowler had been at the First Allegiance Apostolic Church just yesterday and seen the footage of the kid carrying his fathers severed head in a shopping bag.

It was no secret that those kids weren't abducted by some pedophile and buried out in the woods somewhere. They were killing their own folks. God only knew why, or what type of plague had fallen over them, but everybody on the force knew at this point and it was only a matter of time before it was leaked to the media.

Rocket continued to bark and pull as Rowland lowered himself onto all fours getting his knees wet and sticking his head in the door. "Rocket! Pst. Shut the fuck up, dude!"

But the dog paid him no mind, just barked and tugged, so Rowland lowered himself further and poked his head inside, anticipating the scent of the cinema, which always conjured up warm feelings associated with memories of his youth. It was some cross between the smell of a new-car and a warehouse, and somehow, even with all the seats and equipment cleared out, the place had maintained the aroma. On some level, he had been disappointed when the squatters had abandoned the building and there was no longer any reason to enter.

But that's not the smell he was hit with this time. In fact, there was nothing pleasant or surreal about what seemed to force itself into his nostrils like an electric current.

Noel Rowland had never had to deal with a dead body while on the force, but he knew the smell of rotting meat. The gap in the door allowed a decent view of the inside, but he jerked his head back out so fast it scraped the metal, sending a sharp pain down his spine that caused him to curse and his eyes to water.

He released the lead, and watched it disappear into the building as he clutched at the back of his head from where he now knelt upright on the wet pavement. The dog's barks grew louder at first, then distant. Then there was an unmistakable yelp that caused Rowland's stomach to flip inside him, and Rocket fell silent.

So, Rowland fell still.

The pain beneath his head vanished in an instant and his heart seemed to expand inside its cage. He lowered his head again, but didn't peer inside. Just placed his hands onto the wet pavement and his ear next to the opening. "Rocket?" He whistled. "Come on, boy. Come on outta there."

But Rocket didn't come. Didn't bark. Didn't even sniff. Not a sound could be heard inside, and Rowland knew it was time to use his radio, so he straightened back up and reached for the receiver, which was clipped to his shoulder, then paused. If the missing children *were* inside, and if they *had* done something to his dog (God forbid), then this would be big news. The biggest news.

It would be investigated deeper than any shooting involving gang members ever had, and likely by outside entities. Feds. He needed to be thorough at this point, and everything needed to be documented. Noel needed to activate his bodycam. So, he went for that instead, but before he touched it, a metallic scraping appeared above him, and he glanced up just as the door swung open to reveal a skinny redheaded boy in nothing but a pair of piss-and-blood-stained underwear with a Superman symbol over the crotch.

In one hand, he clutched a machete with a chrome blade that was streaked with blood, and blue veins could be seen beneath his pale, freckled skin like lightning bolts traveling up and down his limbs. They were most prominent over his belly, which was swollen like a beach ball, giving him the appearance of a pregnant woman.

Rowland knew instantly that his dog was dead, and that this was no child. It was a monster from a bad movie. But the skin, the smell, the distended gut—none of it was as horrible as the thing's eyes. They were a bright orange that brought to mind thoughts of Halloween decorations with electronic bulbs. They shone like flashlights, so bright that Rowland might as well have been staring straight into the sun.

Only this was worse, because the sun didn't have an agenda and these eyes did. They were predatory in a way that made him think of his father who loved to hunt, not for the meat, but for the thrill that he experienced from killing.

And the little fucker was smiling just the same as his father. Smiling and staring down at him like he was something caught in a trap. Something he intended to skin and pin to his wall like a trophy.

But that wasn't what he intended to do at all, and Rowland knew it, because he knew exactly who this kid had once been. James Booth Jr. had been among the first to vanish on Thursday night, and just yesterday, he had hacked off his father's head, not hung him on a wall.

And he still had a machete.

Like waking up from a dream, Rowland became cognizant of his hand, still hovering over his bodycam, and made a split-second judgement call that he didn't give a rat's ass whether he was investigated, fired, or even jailed for not following protocol, as long as his head remained attached to his body. He went for his gun instead.

Then more orange light appeared behind the kid and a deafening explosion erupted. Rowland grunted and the wind was knocked out of him as he fell over backward, clutching at his chest and feeling a hot indentation in his vest. He'd never been shot before, but it didn't take more than a second to figure out that that's what had happened. And even with the vest on, it hurt like hell.

Rolling into a ball, he went for the radio again, but then James Booth Jr. was standing over him, bringing the machete down on his wrist and though the pain didn't register at first, he felt the bone snap like a piece of kindling and screamed so loud his throat burned. Then there was pain and he looked to see his hand attached to his forearm by nothing more than a flap of skin and what was probably a tendon, blood spouting from the wound in repetitious bursts in sync with his accelerated heartbeat.

Soon, he was surrounded by pale children with glowing eyes, who reeked of putrid, rotten flesh, and shadows appeared which had to have been his panicking imagination, because they looked like the shadows of snakes rather than toddlers. The children laughed with terrible choked voices and grabbed a hold of his clothes. Some held weapons or garden tools, a couple even had guns. But others clutched brown, spotted, fur-covered limbs like they were toys or baby rattles. Rowland recognized Rocket's severed legs the instant he saw them.

Kimberly Brenton, who had also been among the first to disappear, thrust a steak-knife into Rowland's crotch and her mouth opened so wide and she laughed so happily it might as well have been Christmas morning.

Rowland screamed again, attempted to clutch at the point of impact with his missing hand. He had no children. No wife. He thought about his brother, Bill, as the kids began to drag him into the building. Bill worked for FedEx, and he made decent money. Though their mother had died of breast cancer, Dad was still alive, and he still loved to hunt, and he was very proud of Bill.

An infant who shouldn't have been walking, but was, wore Rocket's head like a hat, the dog's neck oozing blood down the baby's head and face, his mouth wide open, tongue flopping around the way it did when he hung out the window of Rowlands truck on the highway.

A boy with messy blond hair removed Rowland's gun, while Rowland kicked and yelled. He cried for help. For mercy. But he didn't dare reach for his radio because James Booth Jr. still had a fucking machete. Then one of the kids started singing a song from Rowland's childhood, "John— Jacob— Jinglehymer Smith! That's— My name too!" as he was dragged through the door, into the building that would have been dark had it not been for the impossible glowing eyes.

The rest of the children joined in. "Whenever I go out— The people always shout— There goes John Jacob Jinglehymer Smith! Na-na-na-na-na-na-na!" Their voices were all terrible. Choked and raspy.

Once they were inside the Cinema 7, one of them pulled the door shut and they all scrambled over one another to lay into Noel Rowland with their various weapons, laughing and singing like they were having nothing more than a day at the park.

***

It was warm inside the Caliber, and Christy Bartlet might have been tempted to fall asleep had her hair and clothes not been soaking-wet.

The McIntosh kid knew something. Bartlet hadn't become the department's lead homicide detective by not being able to recognize when somebody was full of shit. Especially a snot-nosed sixteen-year-old. He knew where Collins was, and he wasn't talking out of some misplaced sense of loyalty, but the problem with that was that he was going to get his friend killed.

Christy wasn't a monster, and she would take no joy in locking Collins up after his entire family had just been murdered. But it had to happen. Yesterday had proven that. The Booth boy had come for his father as soon as he was back in town. Not just him, either. The little bastards were killing as a pack, and that pack had significantly grown last night.

Now John Collins had joined, and he had murdered his mother, his father, and his foster-sister. Bartlet was sure that the only reason Shawn was still alive was because he hadn't been home when whatever evil was taking over these children had possessed his younger brother. But he would go after Shawn just the same, and the others would be with him. Christy could only hope they hadn't found him already, and she would before they did, because juvie was the safest place for him now.

The facts of the case were impossible, but they were still the facts, so they were all she had to go on in making educated decisions. And even those facts were slim pickings. Kids were killing their families. They had orange eyes and cast shadows depicting tentacles which didn't exist. Whatever anomaly was causing it all had struck like outbreaks, two nights in a row, and in two separate neighborhoods, yet they were coordinated, as the children from night one had shown up at the scene on night two as well.

If it was a disease, it wasn't medical. No matter how much Christy wanted to resist a belief in the supernatural, at this point that would only be a disservice to her intelligence and training in deduction. Not only were they projecting traits that could only be paranormal, but they knew things they shouldn't have. Like the second James Booth Sr. had pulled back into town, and when and where the second outbreak would strike.

That being established, they either weren't leaving Mount Vernon, or this knowledge didn't extend out of town. Otherwise, they wouldn't have waited to do Booth Sr. They would have just gone and found him in Everett, where he had spent Thursday night with his meth supplier.

Christy had almost slept. Almost. But it hadn't helped that she still couldn't shake the image of Booth sitting upright on his living room floor without a head. At first, she had assumed the children had left him that way. Then one of the medics on the scene had uttered two words with which she was familiar, but never thought she would acquire an image to associate with.

Lazarus Effect.

The way the body was positioned, there was no way it could have remained, had it been set manually. It was perfectly upright, like a big headless toddler, sitting on his ass to play with a LEGO set, spine sticking straight out of his neck.

The image itself hadn't been the kicker, but rather the thought of the body rising on its own, likely after the children had already left with its head.

The medic had explained nonchalantly, "It happens within minutes of death. No exceptions really. Body just sits up like the crypt-keeper and scares the hell out of anyone in the room. What makes this one unique is that they usually go back down. I suppose that's not the case one hundred percent of the time, but I've never heard of this. All as well, though, right? I always wanted to see it."

But Christy hadn't. She had never entertained any such desire, and had spent the hours between the experience and now trying to think about anything but the fouled-up memory which would likely haunt her the rest of her life, because forgetting something like that wasn't likely in the cards. So, when she'd agreed to go home for a couple hours and get some sleep, even she had known it wasn't actually going to happen.

Now she was following the purple Volkswagen because Kyle McIntosh knew where the Collins kid was, and if he was still in town, she needed to get his butt in a juvie cell before it ended up in a coffin. She tailed the car at what she believed to be a safe distance, but after two nights of sleep deprivation, her depth perception was so obstructed she might not have been very far back at all. And the roads were clearing out toward downtown where the teens appeared to be headed.

***

Marie started talking as soon as Kyle climbed back into the car, but he didn't because he still wasn't convinced, she hadn't set him up. It wasn't until they were almost downtown that she asked what was wrong.

"Nothing," he responded.

"Nothing?"

"Yeah. Nothing."

"Then why have you all of a sudden gone quiet, and what did those police officers back there want?"

Kyle snickered, shook his head. He was aware he was being transparent, possibly even exaggeratedly so, and that if he wanted to ascertain whether or not he could trust her, he should probably conceal his feelings. But it was too late for that anyway, as she had already sensed his change of tone.

He wasn't going to take her to Laura's house, though, that was for sure. He couldn't. The problem was, he had already told her Dobey may have messaged him from somebody else's account, and that that person lived downtown. If Marie was double-crossing him, she would text this bit of information to Bartlet, as soon as she figured out he was holding back. Bartlet would check his messenger. He needed to delete the text, and stall for time by taking Marie somewhere else downtown.

But where? That was the burning question, wasn't it, because there *was* nowhere else to take her. Even if he *did* know somebody downtown, the two of them would show up and she would figure out what was happening as soon as Kyle didn't mention Dobey or the message.

His other option, of course, was to just ditch her. To tell her he had changed his mind and he needed to be dropped off somewhere. Then he could delete the message and walk to Laura's house alone. But what if she *hadn't* set him up? What if he was just being a paranoid bag of dicks? Did she really deserve that?

Before he could put any more thought into it, she pulled to the side of the road, just short of an intersection that would take them over the viaduct, and into downtown. She killed the engine, causing the heater to go quiet as the wipers froze mid-stroke. Rain covered the windshield, obstructing Kyle's view just after a black two-seat-pickup passed, followed by a silver Dodge.

She said, "Well, speak on it, why don't you?"

"What?" he asked, even though he knew what she was playing at.

"What's on your mind, Kyle?"

"Nothing. Why?"

"Are you sure?"

"Uh, yeah. Of course."

"Look," she went on, "maybe I should just drop you off somewhere. Or take you home. When I invited you out, I really thought we would have a nice time. Then, last night happened, and we spoke about it, and I was under the impression we were trying to figure it out together. But now you're either hiding something, or you've decided you don't trust me. Or both."

"What?" Kyle tried his best to play it cool, but knew he was failing miserably. "Why do you think—"

"Hold on. Let me finish please. When those boys were attacking you back there, I dove right in the middle, and my head hurts something fierce right now. If you still can't trust me after I—I just don't think I've done anything to deserve the way you're treating me. I understand everybody has secrets, and I'm not the thought police, but people are dying, Kyle. A lot of them, and though we didn't come out and say it, I guess I just kind of assumed we were in this together."

That had, in fact, been the implication. Kyle knew it, but that was the issue, wasn't it? People were dying. He was no longer entertaining any ridiculous notion that she might be involved merely because it had begun around the time she moved to Mount Vernon. But it was too coincidental when Bartlet had shown up back at the college, he wasn't about to risk his best friend's freedom. So, what did you do when people were dying, and you didn't know if you could trust somebody who you were "in this together" with?

As if she could read his mind, Marie said, "Just ask, Kyle. When you want to know something, that's how you get answers. By asking the right questions."

And because there seemed to be no way of concealing his intentions from this girl, or arguing with her logic he nodded and said, "Okay. Did you tell the cops where we were?"

Seemingly appalled, she half-gasped, "Back there?"

"Yeah."

"You mean at the college?"

"Yeah."

"How in the world would I have done that? You were with me the whole time. You've been with me every second since we decided to go there."

"I know. I know. It's just—I saw you sending a text, and—"

"You thought I was texting the police? To what end? And how in God's name would I have gotten a number to send it to?"

"That detective—well she went through my phone yesterday. I mean when I was being questioned. She saw the messages from Dobey, and she said she called you."

"On my mobile?"

"Yeah."

"Well, did she mention me by name?"

Kyle thought a second before responding, "No."

For a brief second, Marie's eyes became slits. She shook her head before saying, "Listen sweetie. I'm gonna explain something to you. The police—no matter what country, I would imagine—lie. They tell lies and mislead in order to acquire information from people—especially when the stakes are high, and I'm guessing they've never been higher than they are now. I don't know what she wanted from you yesterday, but I can assure you that no police officer called my phone. If you'd like," she reached into her purse, "you can look and see for yourself."

Immediately Kyle told her no. He didn't want to snoop through her phone.

"No," she responded coldly. "I insist. Clearly, I could have deleted any calls from yesterday, but I want you to take a good look at the text I sent back at the college." She brought out the black phone and offered it to him, allowing a view of the back of her hand, which he just now saw had been scraped up during the altercation. He felt his body deflate and started to apologize, but she stopped him, growling, "Just look, for Christ's sake."

So, Kyle accepted the phone and brought the screen to life, seeing several missed calls and new text messages announced from a contact labeled "Ian." Marie leaned over, touched the screen and the notifications disappeared, replaced by a picture of an old looking bridge with two matching towers on it, which served as her background. She selected the text-box and Kyle saw a string of messages from "Ian," seeing that his contact had an international number attached to it.

They had been coming in, nonstop for the past half-hour, and said things like:

Hello?

Are you kidding me?

If you don't call me, consider us through.

Call me.

Pick up the damn phone.

And a response from her, sent around 10:30, which was when they were parked at the college.

I'm busy right now, Ian. Talk later.

Kyle handed the phone back to Marie. "Is Ian your boyfriend?"

"Something like that." She accepted it, dropped it back into her purse.

"Why are you ignoring him?"

"Because I'm spending the day with you, Kyle." She lowered her head. "I assume I still am, at least."

Kyle nodded. "Yeah. Look, sorry I was being a dick. The cops must've just seen me in your car when we drove by. I did have the window down." He paused for a long moment, considering whether or not to share the next bit of information, then concluded that she was right. At this point they were in this together. At least they were for now, because his family and his best friend very likely might be in danger, and she was willing to help. And if that wasn't enough, she had backed him up outside the cafe, and even gotten hit on the back of her head with brass-knuckles. So, he said, "Dobey has a warrant out for his arrest."

"Really?"

"Yeah. He missed a court date for a shoplifting charge. But I think his family was involved in what happened last night. In fact, I'm pretty sure they're— well—I don't think he should be in juvie right now. He needs to be with friends."

Marie nodded. "Didn't that lady say she wouldn't arrest him if he turned himself in?"

So, she had been listening.

Just then, Kyle's phone vibrated in his pocket. He brought it out and read another text from his mom.

Kyle McIntosh. Call me right now if you're okay, or I am calling the police.

Marie's lips curved upward so subtly he almost didn't see it. He knew she was going to say something like, *Maybe you're the one texting with the police,* so he spoke before she could.

"You said yourself, the police lie, right?"

"Yes. I suppose you're right. So, what's our next move then? Are we going to this person's house? The one who's account he messaged you from?"

"Yeah," Kyle responded. "I mean if you still want to."

Marie pressed the ignition button and the heater and wipers both came back to life. She hit the blinker, stared into the rear-view mirror as a gray minivan passed, then pulled back onto the road. "Just lead the way, mate. I'll take you wherever you want to go. You know, if I had been working for the police and trying to somehow use you to locate your friend, you really could have handled the situation better."

"Yeah?"

"Yes sir."

"How so?"

"Well, you revealed too much. I mean, really. That's a scenario which requires a poker-face. Learn to hide your hand. Think about it. I already knew you received a message from your mate on Facebook. I knew it was from somebody else's account—somebody who lives downtown, no less. The police would have everything they need right there, I'm sure." She chuckled as they pulled up to a red light at the entrance to the viaduct. To the right, was a neighborhood with beat up houses set next to the freeway. Across the freeway, was the river and an old smoke-tower painted to look like a giant red tulip with the words, "City of Mount Vernon" scrolled across it in thick, black lettering. She explained, "You would have been better off acting like you didn't suspect a thing, and attempting to mislead me. Now if I were setting you up, would I tell you that?"

Kyle supposed she wouldn't, and he really did feel like a Grade-A-Prick for the way he'd treated her. But there was still something that wouldn't stop bouncing around inside his head like a cockroach on a Pogo stick. He considered taking her advice and "acting" like it wasn't bothering him. The problem was, he wouldn't be able to fully trust her until he cleared it up, and moreover, he had no ambitions of ever being a poker player. So instead, he just asked.

"How long did you live in London?"

Marie hesitated just long enough for him to notice, then the light turned green, and she stepped on the gas, ushering them onto the bridge. She spoke slowly, cautiously, as she said, "Five years. Why?"

"Since you were twelve?"

"Yes." Her face gave no indication she appreciated the questions. "I believe I told you that last night in a text message."

"You did," he said, surprised that she remembered. "But earlier today, you said you've lived in England for nine years."

"Yes? And, your point?"

"You're seventeen, right?"

"Kyle," her voice took on a stern tone, reminiscent of a mother scolding a young child, "I've lived in England since I was eight. I told you my parents move around because they're into real estate. We lived in a different part of England before we moved to London. Now are you going to spend the rest of the day interrogating me? Because if you are, I have better things I could be doing with my time."

Kyle thought about it, and told her again he was sorry.

"Don't be." She shook her head. "Just cut it out and let's get on with what we're doing. Now I think it's only fair I get to ask *you* a question after all the bullshit you just threw at me."

Chuckling, he said, "Sure. Okay. Shoot."

She grinned, narrowed her eyes, focusing on the road ahead as they drove down the steep hill that would dump them off the viaduct. "Don't you feel a bit stupid right now?"

Kyle couldn't help but laugh as he told her he did.

***

Christy waited at the bottom of the hill, in the parking lot of the Skagit Steak House. She was sure the teenagers had noticed her tailing them, and that's why they had stopped. She had half a mind to take them in and threaten them with something preposterous, like prison time. It would be a bluff, but it might just work. And if it did, it might just save a life.

But instead, she waited, because she was tired as hell, and maybe they hadn't spotted her. Maybe they had stopped for some other reason, and they would pass, and she would pull up behind the Beetle again and be on with it. And as she was having this thought, that's exactly what happened, so she yawned as she put the silver Dodge in reverse and pulled out of the parking space.

***

Kyle called his mom. She was pissed. He was embarrassed because Marie listened to her chew him out for not telling anybody he was leaving the house. He had never had to announce his coming and goings before, though. He was terrified that she would order him home, but she didn't, just said to pick up the damn phone when she called.

They turned off Sixth Street, and down Nadler Lane, a residential road with old houses ranging in size. Laura's was a smaller one surrounded by a chain-link-fence, with an apple-tree in the yard. It was located next to the train tracks. There was a small apartment on the property, painted light blue to match the house. It probably would have been rented out, had Laura not lived in it.

Marie parked by the curb and she and Kyle stepped out of the car. It had stopped raining at some point, but Kyle could see his breath form clouds of fog in front of his face as he opened the gate and made his way up the gravel walkway leading to Laura Cunningham's apartment.

The sliding-glass-door was covered by a dark-blue curtain, which moved aside when they were still a few feet away, to reveal Dobey in nothing but a pair of black jeans with a cigarette between his lips. His abdomen was thin and defined, and a thin strip of dark hair led from his navel, down into his pants. His jet-black hair wasn't slicked back as it usually was, but parted in the middle and hanging down over his ears and one of his eyes. The visible one scanned Marie, and Kyle saw her tense in his peripheral. Then Dobey met his eyes and shook his head.

He opened the door, brushed his bangs from his face and said, "What the hell are you doing, dude?"

"You texted me," Kyle responded, not knowing what else to say.

"Why the hell would you bring her?" He pointed the cigarette at Marie.

"I don't—I mean she was with me when—"

"Come on fool." He moved aside, revealing Laura, who wore a red T-shirt, and was just pulling a pair of black leggings up over her wide hips. When she saw Kyle and Marie, she opened her mouth as if to speak, paused, then closed it again and turned away.

Kyle entered first and the smell of tobacco and cannabis filled his lungs. Then Marie, who he could tell was trying not to frown. The apartment was big, but Laura only had one room with a queen-sized bed against the far wall and a small TV set on a black crate. The screen displayed a male SERIUS 7 reporter standing outside Dobey's building with a crowd of police behind him, but the volume was all the way down.

There was an old scratched up nightstand by the bed with a few lighters, an ashtray, Dobey's Batman pipe, a digital clock which read, 11:02, and some other small objects scattered over its surface. Clothes littered the floor and there was an iPad sitting on one of the bed's white pillows.

A door on one wall led into the rest of the apartment. But in the years that Laura had lived here, that portion seemed to be under a renovation which had begun, but never completed. The floor back there was uncarpeted, and the walls stripped, displaying insulation that resembled pink cotton-candy. The only thing that was functional beyond that door was the plumbing in the bathroom, though there was no electricity, which meant Laura and whatever house guests she had over were forced to handle their business in the dark.

Dobey shut the door and the curtain as Laura recovered from her embarrassment and threw her arms around Kyle. At first, he didn't know what to do, then he returned her embrace. She clung so close that every inch of their bodies, it seemed, touched and she breathed deeply into his neck until Kyle felt his ears begin to heat up.

When she finally pulled her face away, her body remained close to his. She gazed into his eyes, and he saw that hers were red and saturated with tears. "Did you hear what happened already?" She sniffed.

"Uh—yeah. Maybe. Not all the details though."

She dislodged from him and extended her hand to Marie. "Hi. I'm Laura."

Accepting it, Marie offered a weak smile. "Marie."

"Let me ah—" she trudged over to a wall where a few metal folding-chairs leaned, and grabbed two. Unfolding them and setting them next to each other, she invited Kyle and Marie to have a seat, so they both did.

Dobey paced between the bed and the TV, sucking on his cigarette and dropping ash onto the floor, but he didn't speak so Kyle asked if it was okay.

Finally, he forced a high pitched laugh and ran a hand through his hair. But he didn't look at Kyle, just continued to pace as he said, "Yeah. Yeah, my whole fucking family's dead, but I'm okay. I'm just hunky-fucking-dorey, Kyle. It's all rainbows and unicorns for me. What do you think, dude?"

Laura stepped in front of him and put both hands on his chest, peering up into his eyes. "Hey." She spoke softly. "Relax, okay?"

"No!" He pulled away so swiftly that it was almost aggressive.

Laura flinched and threw her hands up. "Okay. Okay. Fine." She walked away and plopped down on her bed.

Finally, Dobey stopped pacing and looked down at Kyle. "Have you been by my place today?"

"Yeah," Kyle replied.

"And?"

"It's blocked off by cops and ambulances. News everywhere. A lot of people—well, I mean—"

"They died! A lot of people died! Including my parents! My brother! My sister!"

Marie shifted next to Kyle, and he knew she was thinking the same thing as him.

He still doesn't know that the children are doing the killing.

Dobey stomped over to the nightstand, snubbed his cigarette out in the ashtray, and picked up his weed-pipe and a lighter. He took a long pull, dropping the whole setup in Kyle's lap when he was finished. Without thinking about it, Kyle hit it while the cherry was still lit, then coughed as the smoke stabbed at his lungs. When he could finally breathe again, he offered it to Marie, who scrunched up her face and shook her head. Laura leaned over and accepted it instead, telling him "thank you," and taking a giant toke.

Marie coughed and fanned her face with one hand. Her expression gave Kyle the impression she was judging him, and for reasons he didn't quite understand, when the apparatus made its way back to him, he declined. Not that it made a whole world of difference, as he was already feeling the effects of the drug, but he swore he saw her in his peripheral, nodding approval. Or maybe he was just high as hell and imagining things.

Dobey plopped back on the bed, his arms splayed out at his side like a crucifixion victim and stared up at the dirty ceiling. "This is so fucked, man. I mean, I don't know what I'm supposed to do. I have a fucking warrant. They're gonna arrest me if I go home." Then he let out a yelping laugh that made Kyle sick to his stomach. "That's funny, right? Home? I don't even have a home to go to, do I? I can't go to juvie, dude. Not right now. I'll go fucking crazy in there."

Kyle said, "I know," because he didn't know what else to say.

Dobey sat up like a skeleton rising from an open coffin and examined his friend for a long moment. Kyle couldn't read his expression, but there was something about it that he didn't like. "Come talk to me, fool. Just you though." Looking at Marie, he held up a hand and said, "No offense."

She puffed her lips, shook her head. "None taken, mate."

So, they went into the other part of Laura's apartment where it smelled like plywood and dust and Dobey shut the door. They were in a dark hall, but enough light came in from a window in the living room—about fifteen feet away—that he could see his friend's solemn expression with clarity. In fact, the shadows cast over his face in the relative dark accentuated it in a way that was almost cartoonish.

Dobey lowered his voice to a quiet growl just above a whisper. "Dude, why the hell would you bring her here?"

"I don't know," Kyle replied. "I mean, she texted me last night and—"

Dobey set a hand on top of his head. "I left your number in her phone, didn't I?"

"Yeah, but—"

"My bad, man. I wasn't thinking."

"It's okay. She wanted to hang out since she doesn't know anyone in town, so I met up with her this morning and that's when I found out what happened."

"You didn't know yet?"

"No."

"Didn't you see the news? Or social media? Or anything?"

"No. I mean, I guess not."

"I don't know what to do, Kyle. I mean, I'm still trying to wrap my head around it all, you know? I just ah—I mean—I don't think I believe it's real yet. I keep thinking it'll turn out to be some twisted joke and they're all actually still alive. You think that could happen?"

Kyle proceeded to tell his friend everything that transpired since they last saw each other, only omitting the bits about being jumped outside of the Courthouse Cafe, and what he and Marie had speculated together about recent events. When he was finished, Dobey seemed to be considering how believable his account was. Finally, he asked, "And you're sure the kids you saw where the missing ones?"

"Yeah. I'm sure."

Thrusting his hands into his pockets, Dobey stared down at the floor for a long moment. He was too calm. Much too *level-headed and collected* for a sixteen-year-old whose entire family had been murdered last night. Though Kyle figured he had just now deducted that they weren't all in the funeral home. That his ten-year-old brother had, in fact, slain his parents and foster sister, and that he was now hiding somewhere with the rest of the homicidal children.

Still Kyle found himself wondering if he'd wept yet, and how he, himself, would react if the roles were switched. Then the memory of his own brother's wails last night flooded his thoughts.

"What about the new girl?" Dobey asked.

"I don't know, man. What about her?"

"Is she cool?"

"We'll, yeah. I mean, I think she—"

"I mean do you trust her?"

Kyle paused, even though he knew the answer already, had been pondering it all morning. He did it, he guessed, more for dramatic effect than anything, and he hated himself momentarily for it. "Yeah," he responded. "I wouldn't have brought her here if I didn't."

"Sure?"

"Yeah. Pretty sure."

"Okay. Then so do I. You think she'll give me a ride outta town?"

Another pause. Then Kyle said, "I don't know man. Where would you go anyway?"

"There's a cabin. I mean just up in Lake McMurray. It's on the water by Tara's house. It must be somebody's vacation spot or something because it's always empty. We party out there sometimes, you know. I mean there's no power or running water. I couldn't stay forever, but just for now while I figure shit out."

Kyle considered this, then asked, "Who?"

"What?" Dobey's brow furrowed.

"Who parties out there sometimes?

"*We* do. I've been out there with Tara and some friends before. I don't know, man. Jesus Christ. I'll make sure you get an invite next time. Are we really gonna do this right now?"

"That's not what I was—" Kyle shook his head. "Never mind. So, you were here last night when—well, when it happened?"

Dobey hesitated, then said he had been.

"You and Laura were—"

"Yeah."

"Is she still—"

"With Jesse? Yeah."

Kyle nodded, decided it was none of his business, said, "Okay, man, Let's get you the hell outta town." He turned toward the door, but before he could take a step, Dobey threw his arms around him and pulled him back, thumping his back with one fist.

"Thanks for coming, dude."

"Yeah." Kyle hugged him back then went for the door. "No problem. Come on. I think we need to hurry. I can tell you the rest of what I know in the car."

But he never got the chance, because as soon as he emerged back into Laura's room there was a familiar *Tap. Tap. Tap.* and Kyle's heart almost leapt out of his mouth because he immediately recognized the sound of Bartlet's knuckle rapping against the outside of the sliding-glass-door.

***

Multiple things seemed to happen all at once. Kyle glanced toward the chair, found it empty aside from Marie's gray sweater draped over the backrest. Then the bed, where she sat next to Laura, in a white tank-top that allowed him a view of her black G-string protruding from the back of her pants. He noticed for the first time that she was curvy like Laura. In fact, from the neck down, the only way to distinguish the two apart, was the way they were dressed.

Dobey said, "Who the fuck is that."

Marie was reapplying her makeup. Her face was now covered in foundation and one eye was lined in black.

Tap. Tap. Tap.

"Kyle!" Bartlet's voice was distorted through the glass. "Open the door, now!"

Turning toward his friend, Kyle growled, "Get the hell outta here! Use the back door!"

But Dobey was already in motion, sprinting into the living room. The sound of the door cracking, then of weather and traffic appeared, and Dobey cried out in pain. Kyle ran down the hall, and outside to see him squirming face down in the wet grass, mud covering half of his face.

Two uniformed officers were on top of him wrenching his arms behind his back.

One, who had a knee in the middle of Dobey's back, spoke into the radio clipped to his shoulder. "We got 'em. Suspect detained in the back of the residence."

Bartlet jogged around the side of the house, a walkie-talkie in one hand. She glanced down at Dobey who stopped fighting now that he was handcuffed, then up at Kyle. "You lied to me, didn't you?"

Marie and Laura emerged through the door and stepped up next to Kyle. Bartlet raised a painted purple fingernail and pointed it at Marie's chest.

"And you. Think I don't know who you are? I ran your plates, little girl. What would your daddy say if he knew the type of friends you were making around here?"

The two cops hoisted Dobey to his feet and he glared at Kyle as they led him around the house toward the front yard. Marie didn't answer.

Kyle said, "You followed me."

"I sure as hell did. Now you listen to me. Both of you." Looking at Laura, she hissed, "And you too. You're lucky I have more pressing business, or I'd haul every one of you in and lock you up for harboring a fugitive. I don't want to see any of you again unless I call your asses down to the station, do you understand me? Don't let me catch you around any crime-scenes any time soon. None of this concerns you. If I see you again, I'm taking you all to juvie." She glared directly into Marie's eyes. "And you can bet that pretty little car your daddy bought you on that, girl."

With that, she turned and began to follow the other cops, until her radio crackled, and a sound resonated from her side that caused every hair on Kyle's body to erect in unison like tiny little meerkats onto a predator.

"If all—the raindrops were lemon-drops and gumdrops—oh what a rain that would be!"

He knew the voice because he had heard it yesterday when Kimberly Brenton had opened her arms to him and wailed his name.

Kyle!

It was her. Choked and duck like. Dead. Only it wasn't *just* her. There were more—some with terrible voices like hers, others who still sounded like children. And they were all singing the same children's song. Into a police radio.

Bartlet raised her walkie-talkie and examined it as if it was an alien artefact as the children continued to sing.

"I'd stand outside with my mouth open wide! Ah! Ah! Ah-ah! Ah! Ah-ah! Ah! Ah-ah!"

One of the uniformed cops returned, his jaw hanging, his eyes wide with confusion. He looked at Bartlet, but she didn't return his gaze. Just continued to stare at her radio. Marie edged close to Kyle, so their hips were touching. Then Bartlet glared up at them and bared her teeth. She shook her head, and for a fraction of a second, Kyle thought she was going to try and somehow pin this on them. Then, she and the other cop took off jogging around the house as their radios continued to broadcast the horrible song.

"If all—the raindrops were lemon-drops and gumdrops—oh what a rain that would be!"

Chapter Six

The monster spoke.

It was getting harder and harder to move. Kim wasn't worried because worry didn't exist anymore. Only fun did. But when she walked, her legs didn't work the way they were supposed to. The way they always had. Her knees didn't bend properly anymore. Neither did her arms, really, but that wasn't presenting much of a problem because she didn't use *them* to walk.

It had been fun cutting up the doggy. And stabbing the policeman in his penis. She had laughed and danced as all the children sang songs and played with them both. Now Malachi was chewing on one of the cop's fingers. Michael was wearing his face.

Telma lay in her nighty on the cement floor of the old theater, curled up like a dead spider. Kim had watched as her movements grew short and jerky, the way hers now had. Then, Telma had bent over like Kim used to when Mom gave her a spanking and walked around like that for most of the day.

The lights in her eyes had faded too. And the shadows coming off her body had shrunk and shrunk, until they almost weren't even there. But Telma had laughed and played, and done what she could to help while they cut the police officer's clothes off him, then took out his eyes and his guts as he screamed and kicked and begged them to stop. She could barely move, but she made the best of it until finally she curled up and her lights disappeared along with her shadows, and she didn't move again.

Now the cop was everywhere. Bradley had a big sledgehammer, which he had used to break his head open after Michael used one of Kim's knives to cut off his face. His brains were all over the floor, and pieces of his skin stuck to the walls, and Kimberly Brenton couldn't move too good.

But nobody was moving anyway, because the wind was blowing inside the building, as the monster spoke. Kim hadn't heard its whistling, howling voice since it had killed her in her bed. There had been no reason for it to talk, because all the children knew its thoughts already.

And there was still no purpose, Kim knew. But it had started speaking anyway—for no other reason except that it wanted to—as soon as they had finished singing into the policeman's walkie-talkie.

"Look at you. Every one of you pretty babies. I'm so proud of you all. I hope you know that."

Every face in the theater lit up with glee just to know that they had made the monster proud. Malachi pulled the finger from his mouth and squealed, flapping his arms like a bird. Another little boy did a funny happy dance.

The voice made Kim want to dance as well. More so than when she had killed her mommy. More than when she thought of doing it to her dad. It was the sound of the wind, blowing yellow and orange leaves around on Halloween, and she wanted it to wrap itself around her and never let go.

"You're all princes and princesses. Every single one of you, and I'm so happy that you're mine. It's almost

Halloween, my wonderful children, and I can't take you trick-or-treating without costumes, so I need you all to start thinking about what you'd like to be this year. Figure it out before the good ones are taken."

As the monster spoke, every child's hair tossed so vigorously that it looked like they were floating under water. Then, Kim glanced up and saw its eyes. The same ones she had first seen in her bedroom the night before it had killed her. Huge and orange, just like hers. They hovered above the rest of them, and cast thick tentacle-shadows out in every direction like a silly octopus.

She knew the monster lived inside her and all the others, but she hadn't seen it like this since she was still alive. And though it had scared the living daylights out of her then, now it brought her a sense of peace and calm that she hadn't even known existed before. She knew that every child felt it, too, but nobody spoke. They all just hung on every word the monster uttered.

"I like it here. I like it very much. In fact, this is my favorite place in the whole-wide-world, and it makes me so happy to have all my favorite boys and girls here with me. But it's time to leave now. If we don't, Halloween could be ruined. So, I'm going to take you to another of my favorite places, and we're going to have fun on our way there, what do you say?"

Only then did the kids finally shout, "Yay!" in unison.

The monster asked, "Would you like that?"

"Yeah!"

"I can't hear you!"

"Yeah!"

"Are we ready to go then?"

"Yeah! Yeah! Yeah!"

"One more time! Say it like you mean it!"

"YEAH!"

"Okay! Good! Then let's get out of here! Everybody at once, before the mean, mean police show up to ruin everything!"

Kim wasn't sure who moved first. Somebody scooped up Malachi, and somebody else carried another baby, a little bigger than him. Then, the monster disappeared, the door flew open and like a stampede, they all ran out into the parking lot where they had first found the policeman.

They ran past his truck and into the field of tall, wet grass. Kim couldn't go as fast as the rest, though, and they kept passing her by. They were all bloody from head to toe, and a black girl who wore a T-shirt and stained white underwear still held one of the doggy's legs. She looked back at Kim briefly, then kept going.

Kim walked stiff legged and slow, and it made her think of something she had seen on TV. What was it called? A zahm-key? Soon everybody else was in front of her. Then they all disappeared into the grass, she was left alone in the parking lot, and for the first time since dying Kimberly Brenton began to worry, because she didn't want to be left behind.

She reached for an old trick that worked better when Dad was still home, but still worked a little after that, depending on what kind of a mood Mommy was in, or who she had over to visit. She scrunched up her face, and reached for the good old cry. But the cry didn't come because that part of her body didn't work anymore and there wasn't much water in there anyway. All she could manage, was a raspy, choking wail as she picked up her bowlegged pace, reaching for the field with a knife in each hand.

Then the grass split, and James's face appeared, streaked with blood that looked like fingers and was only a shade darker than his hair. He tilted his head and smiled before skipping out and scooping her into his arms the way Dad used to. He kissed her cheek, and she raised her shoulders bashfully. Then he ran back into the grass, Kimberly bouncing up and down in his arms.

***

Laura cried, but first her mom came outside in a pair of bright-green sweatpants and a stained white T-shirt that was so baggy it could have served as a sundress. She was overweight and her dark hair was tangled and wavy, contrasting with her daughter's perpetually damp ponytail. She watched three police cars—including one unmarked Dodge Caliber—speed away, then frowned and told Laura, "Get those kids the hell off of my property."

So, Kyle and Marie waited in the Beetle as Laura went inside momentarily, then emerged in a black North Face jacket, carrying Marie's purse and sweater. She climbed into the backseat, and that's when she started sobbing.

Her mother stood on the front porch, smoking a cigarette and glaring at the vehicle, so Marie examined herself in the rear-view mirror, shaking her head at the sight of only one eye traced with liner. Then she pressed the ignition button and pulled onto the road.

"He shouldn't be alone," Laura sniffed. "Not right now. It's just not right."

Neither Kyle, nor Marie responded as they went over the bumpy railroad tracks.

"He's not doing good," she went on. "He was trying to hide it when you showed up, but he really shouldn't be alone right now."

The houses grew smaller and dirtier the further they went back, and the trees in yards grew taller and thicker, causing it to seem darker. Leaning down, Marie squinted out the windshield and looked around, brushing a strand of hair from her face. "Where are we going?" she asked.

"I don't know," Kyle responded.

"I know what you're thinking," Laura said. "I know what it looked like when you showed up, but it's not like that. I mean I love Jesse, Kyle. You know that."

"I know," Kyle didn't look back.

"Don't say it like that, bro. You don't have to—"

"I wasn't. It's none of my business anyway."

"Yes, it is. Of course, it's your business. Dobey's your best friend. And I'm your friend, too. And so is Jesse. It's just that—I don't know, dude." She hiccupped a couple times, then cried some more.

Kyle had never been crazy about the sound of a girl weeping, but he was too preoccupied with his own thoughts to even consider comforting her right now. Bartlet had followed him. And why hadn't he expected her to? Both times he had encountered her, she had been set on using him to track down his friend.

Marie said, "I don't suppose we could go to your house for a bit?"

"No." Kyle shook his head. "Probably not a good idea."

"Right. Your mum may not be thrilled about you leaving again, would she?"

"Doubt it."

"Then I imagine our best option is to find somewhere to park until we figure out our next move."

"Yeah. Probably."

With a trembling voice, Laura asked, "What next move? What's she talking about?"

Marie glanced in the rear-view. "Well, we've gone a bit Hardy Boy's on this whole thing, I guess you could say."

"What?"

"Hardy Boy's. It's an old series about—"

"I know what Hardy Boy's is." Laura seemed to regain control. "Are you guys really trying to solve what's been going on? Like who's been taking the kids or whatever?"

Not who, Kyle thought, *What?*

"Essentially," Marie replied, "yes. Do either of you know of a carpark nearby that's inconspicuous?"

"A what?" Kyle asked.

"Oh, sorry. I keep forgetting, you call it a—"

"She means a parking lot," Laura sniffed, wiped her face with her sleeve. Then, when the water repellent material proved insufficient, she used the back of her hand. "Don't you watch Harry Potter, Kyle? There's the Green Apple. You'll have to turn around though."

Marie hit the blinker. "Is that the grocery store off the main road? I saw it on the way here."

So, they parked in the Green Apple's lot and at first nobody spoke. Then Marie asked, "Is anybody hungry?"

"No," Kyle said. "I'm still good from breakfast."

Laura stated that she was fine as well.

"Well, I'm famished." Marie opened her door and a helicopter somewhere overhead could be heard. "I'm just going to run in and see what they have to eat."

Once she was gone, Laura said, "You think I'm a slut, don't you?"

Kyle shook his head.

"I'm not. Just so you know. I mean, I know it looks bad, but I've never even slept with Jesse." She sat as still as an ice-sculpture as she spoke.

"Yeah," Kyle nodded. "I know."

"He told you?"

"No."

"Dobey did." It wasn't a question.

"No."

"Then how—never mind. Did you know about me and him? I mean, Dobey?"

"No."

"Kyle, I really do love Jesse."

"I know you do, Laura."

Finally, he heard the ruffling of windbreaker fabric, indicating she had shifted in her seat as she said, "Okay, I guess."

"I'm not gonna tell anyone."

"I know you're not, Kyle. You're a good friend."

"Thanks."

"Kyle, please don't be like that. I swear I'm not trying to hurt Jesse. I don't wanna hurt anyone. I just—"

"I don't care about Jesse," he cut her off. "And your business is your business. I'm not judging you."

"Then what's wrong? You can talk to me, you know."

And he supposed he should, if she was going to be along for the ride. So, he turned in his seat, saw her sitting back, her legs open the way a guy might sit, and filled her in on everything he'd told Dobey back at her house.

Just as he got to the part where he'd met up with Marie this morning, Laura glanced up and Kyle followed her gaze, seeing a feminine torso outside the driver's window and only now noticing that Marie wore a black bra under her white tank-top. The door cracked and she stepped in with a yellow grocery bag. Both eyes were now traced, and her hair was tied back into a loose ponytail like she had simply combed it with her fingers. She must have used the store's bathroom mirror. Kyle continued, and both girls listened, Marie nodding in agreement at times. He once again omitted the piece about his little brother.

When he was finished, Laura said, "You know it's not your fault he got arrested, right?"

"Actually, I think it kind of is," Kyle responded.

"Because you didn't expect the cop to follow you?"

"Yeah. Pretty much."

"Kyle, how the hell were you supposed to know?"

"Actually," Marie cut in, "she's right. There was no way to know we were being followed."

"No," Laura agreed. "But you guys should cut it out. Whatever you're doing, you gotta stop, or she's gonna lock you up too. You know that right?"

It sounded good. To just stop worrying about what was happening and be sixteen and carefree. The problem was, if he did, he would just start thinking about Claudia again, and then, tonight or tomorrow, or God only knew when, his six-year-old brother might just turn into a walking corpse with orange eyes and the devil's shadow, bent on slaughtering him and his parents.

And why not just say that? Why was he making such a point to conceal it? It had started with Marie, he supposed, when he hadn't been sure he could trust her. But any bit of outstanding doubt had fled when Bartlet arrested Dobey. Though Bartlet's threats to the new girl could have easily been manufactured to invoke trust from Kyle, Dobey was gone now. There would no longer have been a reason.

What purpose did it serve to hold back the information now? The answer was: none. So, he decided to divulge everything to both girls, but before he had a chance, Laura said, "They're not fucking around, Kyle. And you're not the Hardy Boys. Somebody out there's taking kids and killing their parents. That's serious shit, and if you keep snooping around either you're gonna get in the way, or they're gonna think you're involved somehow."

He stopped, bit his tongue, because she hadn't believed a word he had said about the kids doing the killing, or even that he had seen four of them yesterday.

She would eventually, he was sure of it. Everybody would. They would have to, because the facts that he knew couldn't be hidden forever. But for now, only Marie believed him, and probably merely because of what her father had seen.

Marie reached into her shopping bag. Produced a plastic bottle of Dr. Pepper. Offered it to Laura. Laura accepted it and thanked her.

Kyle considered how to convince her that he wasn't insane. That he had, in fact, seen children with glowing eyes, and that Marie wasn't lying about what her father had seen on the surveillance footage. Then Marie offered him a Pepsi, and their eyes met and hers were somehow prettier than usual, but there was also something there that hadn't been before. She was trying to tell him something. And because he wasn't sure what, he considered everything that it could possibly have been.

She thinks you're crazy.
She doesn't believe you.
Don't trust her.
Conceal your hand.

And every option, it seemed, required the same outcome. He needed to shut up. To change the subject. So, he told Laura that she was right, and he would stop snooping around, and she leaned forward and hugged him around the neck, brushing his cheek lightly with her lips, before sitting back and asking, "So what do we do now? We could roll out to Tara's in Lake McMurray. Her mom works Saturdays and guess what I still have." Reaching in her pocket, she produced a sandwich bag with bright green plant matter inside. She opened it, put it against her face and took a giant whiff. Even from where he sat a couple feet away, the aroma of skunk filled Kyle's nostrils. Laura said, "Snickerdoodles," which she often used to refer to weed.

"Actually," Marie piped. "I need to be getting home." Reaching into her purse, she brought out her phone and examined the screen thoughtfully. "My father needs me for something. Can I drop you off?"

"Oh." Laura sounded disappointed, "Uh—sure. I guess that'd be cool. I could just get out here, I guess. I don't feel like dealing with my mom's shit right now. Hey Kyle?"

"Yeah?"

"Wanna hang out? I really don't wanna be alone today. We could like, go somewhere and just kick it. Together, or whatever."

Kyle considered this, and he almost accepted the invitation too. But then, in his peripheral—there it was again. Marie was giving him that same look. So, he told Laura that he needed to get home as well, and he felt like a whole box of assholes, and he hoped like hell he was reading the new girl correctly.

Laura hesitated, then sulked. "Yeah. Okay. Well, I guess I'll see you then. Oh yeah! Here," she picked a small bud from the sandwich bag, offered it to Kyle. "Dobey said he was gonna give you—well that's for you."

Kyle knew Marie was waiting to see if he accepted it or not, and wondered briefly if marijuana was still illegal in London, because maybe that's why she seemed to be using her body language to pass judgement. But it didn't matter because, though, it was still illegal at sixteen, there were pot-shops all over Washington, and it wasn't considered a drug anymore. He accepted it and thanked Laura.

"No prob," she replied. "Thanks for the pop."

"You're welcome," Marie beamed.

Once she was out of the vehicle, Kyle asked Marie if she really needed to go home.

She half-shrieked, "What kind of a question is that?"

"I don't know," he choked because he had clearly misinterpreted the entire exchange. Glancing out the window, he saw Laura's legging-clad hips swaying like a piece of paper gliding to the floor as she made her way across the parking lot with her hands in the pockets of her jacket. He reconsidered going with her on account of it would be better than being at home and stressing over Claudia. "I just thought—"

"Of course, I have to go home, silly," Marie interrupted him with a devious grin. "But not until tonight. As of now, I believe you and I still have business to attend to, so point the way, navigator-boy. Maybe hide your drugs first though, seeing as how cops seem to be following us today."

***

The monster wasn't talking anymore, but the children knew what it wanted because they wanted it too. They wanted it so so bad. So very, very much. More so than they had ever wanted anything before, and that went for each and every one of them.

So, they ran through the field, and some of them got cut. But it was okay because no matter how deep the blades sliced into their skin, they didn't feel a thing. They were all so pretty and small. They were all so innocent, even with blood on their hands.

Then there were thorns that dug in their cheeks, and ripped at their flesh. But the monster's children just laughed, and the big ones carried the babies. Others had limbs from the dog, or tools, and James still had his daddy's head in a bag. They waved them around like toys from home and Malachi still wore the doggy's skull as a hat. Everything was good, because the monster was proud of them all.

Somewhere up front, Michael sang about apples and bananas. The kids who already knew the words joined in. Then the rest learned them too, just from listening. Soon there was a fence, which they climbed with ease. Then there were a road and some houses. Big ones and little ones. Dirty ones and clean ones. Some with cars out front, but the yards were mostly empty.

Except for one, where an old man was walking toward a little gray truck, with an umbrella in one of his hands. He saw the monster's babies and froze. Then he took a step back. And another. But it was already too late because they were too, too close, and they were having too—much—fun!

So, every one of them sang together as Carlos swung a long sword from his big brother's room that connected with the old man's knee. He cried for a second and fell to the ground, and then Brandon opened his head with a hammer and a smile.

The children didn't stop because they knew they needed to move. They knew because the monster knew. They ran through a yard and hopped over another fence. The bigger ones tossed the babies and fetched them on the other side. Kimberly hung on James's back like a little spider-monkey.

They ran through a backyard, but didn't stop to play on the jungle-gym. Hopping another tall fence, they sprinted some more in another backyard where a man stuck his head out of a door. A girl in pink pajamas shot him with a revolver and he fell so he was halfway out of the house.

The babies trampled him as they ran inside, emerging in a very clean kitchen where a woman stood over a stove. They all laid into her before she could even scream, and she was dead in seconds.

Next, they piled out the front where a minivan stopped in the road at the sight of them. There was a family of four inside and the children slayed them all and moved on, killing everyone in every vehicle who spotted them—seventeen people and one Chihuahua, which a girl named Livia brought with her because it reminded her of Grandma's doggy. They made their way across Winslow Street and under the railroad bridge that crossed the Skagit River.

Then, one after another, they waded in because it was one of the monster's other favorite places in the whole-wide-world. Soon they all disappeared beneath the surface of the green, murky water.

***

Kyle wasn't sure what the police did, or didn't know, or what they had managed to figure out based on what they had discovered thus far. Last night it might have been plausible that he was closer to the truth than they were, because he had actually seen four of the children. For all they knew, on the other hand, his story could have been no more than a potato sack full of bullshit.

But now they had also seen them on surveillance footage from Dobey's building. If they hadn't believed his statement yesterday, they did now because they knew everything he and Marie knew—probably more.

That didn't stop Kyle and Marie from searching for clues though. Kyle's reasons were simple. It took his mind off his breakup, and his family might be in danger. Marie's were still unclear, aside from the fact that it presented the opportunity to make friends in a new country.

What did ultimately end up stopping them from searching was that there was nowhere else to look that wouldn't get them arrested. So as the day grew progressively greyer, they spent it driving around and engaging in conversation about London and Australia, and she told him that he had held a much better poker-face with Laura. And that they had had to get rid of her because she clearly thought they were either crazy or liars and she would have only gotten in the way.

They had a late lunch at an El Piraton, a Mexican restaurant on Riverside Drive, where a mariachi band went table to table with acoustic guitars and a mandolin playing and singing for couples as they ate. Outside, it was pouring harder than before, and traffic had begun to pick up. Kyle and Marie sat across from one another in a booth set by a window sharing a huge plate of nachos. It was there that he learned that she wanted to be a lawyer.

"I thought you said you wanted to be a doctor," he replied.

"No," she separated a yellow corn-chip from a strand of melted cheese and dipped it in guacamole, "I said my father wants me to go into medicine."

"And you don't want to?"

Stuffing the chip into her mouth, she shook her head and crunched.

"Because you'd rather be a lawyer."

"You're quick, aren't you?" She swallowed.

Kyle's gaze dropped.

"Oh, don't be a big baby." Wiping her lips with a paper towel, she reached over and gave his hand a squeeze. "I was just having a go at you."

"It's okay," Kyle chuckled. "I know I'm no Einstein. I mean, people are always telling me I'm smart or whatever, but I think it's just one of those things where a Mom tells a little girl she's pretty, or she tells her son he's gonna grow up to be a doctor or a lawyer. Not that that's the case with you or anything. That's not what I—"

She interrupted, "Is it your mom telling you you're smart?"

"Well, no. I mean, yeah. She's said it before, but that doesn't really count, you know?"

Marie smiled. "Then why'd you use it as an example?"

"I don't know," Kyle stuttered. "I was just trying to make a point I guess."

"But the point's kind of moot if you're not talking about your mom saying it, because you said—"

"I know what I said."

Marie frowned. "Well, you don't have to be nasty about it, do you?"

"Sorry. You're right. I guess what I mean is I know I'm not really that smart. It's like people try and tell me I am, and it just makes me feel stupider. Like they're just saying it to encourage me or something. Does that make sense?"

Ignoring the question, Marie sipped brown soda from a straw sticking out of a glass without picking it up off the table. She asked, "Has it worked?"

Kyle grinned, shook his head. Then they both giggled, and it occurred to him that it wasn't going to take much effort to be friends with this girl.

She took another sip, continuing to smile around her straw, and Kyle chuckled some more.

"I'm just playing, mate. Listen, I went to a very prestigious private school back in London, called St Paul's. Basically, I was provided with one of the best educations there is, and my classmates were all either spoiled rich kids, or genius prodigies, and I can tell you this: You would have fitted in just fine."

"Right," Kyle snickered, wondering silently if he was being patronized.

"I'm not lying. I know you think I am, but smarts—real smarts, I mean—are summed up in potential to learn, rather than what you've learned thus far. Does *that* make sense?"

He considered this, then said it did.

Marie used one chip to scrape the cheese off another, then scooped the bare one in chunky red salsa, examining a giant piece of avocado, which she'd caught. "Trust me. I've known some stupid people. I mean, no offense, but you haven't met my sister."

"Does she go to our school?"

Chomping off the half of the chip with salsa on it, she said, "No. She's older than me. She stayed back in London, and I'm telling you right now, if she hadn't married a millionaire before she got fat, my parents would have been taking care of her the rest of her life. She's about as sharp as a tuning fork. You, though? You're not stupid. When I look across this table, all I see is brown hair, green speckled hazel eyes, and untapped potential. Are you any good at Math?"

Selecting a chip with a healthy amount of meat on it, he popped the whole thing in his mouth and shook his head.

"Didn't think so. I suspect your intelligence lies on the other side of your brain. Do you play music?"

"Nope."

"Draw?"

"Uh—" Kyle thought of praises he had received for rudimentary sketches he had done for book reports in elementary school. "Yeah. A little, I guess."

"No," she went on. "That's definitely a no. Do you write?"

"For school?"

"Sure. Why not?"

"Yeah. When I have to."

"And have your teachers often had to correct your—"

Before she could finish, the band appeared by their table, playing their instruments and singing something in Spanish that Kyle suspected was romantic. They were all male, dressed in flamboyantly bright shirts which were tucked into black slacks. The singer was overweight and had a moustache, but the other two didn't look out of their twenties. Everybody in the vicinity, it seemed, turned from their own conversations and meals to watch, and Kyle flushed because they must have assumed that he and Marie were a couple.

Marie said something to the band that he couldn't make out over the music. The singer smiled and nodded, as Kyle focused on the food until they moved along halfway through their song.

Then, because he wasn't eager to return to their previous conversation, he asked Marie who makes more money, doctors, or lawyers.

"It's all subjective," she said. "Depends on who you work for. Really, that's not why I want to go into law. It's just something I think I'd enjoy. I've been a good litigator since I was knee-high to a kangaroo, and I've always been good with deduction if you know what I mean."

The truth was, he had no clue what she meant but he nodded anyway and told her she was really smart.

"Thanks," she replied with a bashfulness that may have been manufactured. "Some girls are good at being pretty, and others, I suppose are good at being smart."

But Marie was both, and he found it difficult to believe she didn't know that. He suspected she was fishing for compliments; the way Claudia often did with every male she encountered. It was the only common denominator he'd discovered between the two so far, only Marie hadn't done it once until now. He considered telling her she was pretty as well, then hesitated.

Then he considered it again, but before he could, she asked, "What is it you want to say?"

"What?" his heart sped up.

"Back in the carpark. At the Green Apple. I sensed you were going to say something right before your friend basically called your story rubbish. What was it?"

Recovering, he thought back, and considered whether or not he still wanted to reveal the situation concerning Abel. But why not? At this point there was nothing to lose, so he lifted his own glass, took a drink, and crunched on a small ice-cube before telling her about the cries he'd heard coming from his brother's room last night.

When he was done, she seemed to go into deep thought for a long moment and he looked out the window at passing cars kicking up water on one of Mount Vernon's rare four-lane roads. It was turning out to be the earliest winter he could remember ever experiencing and it was so gloomy out there that they all drove with their headlights on in spite of the fact that it wasn't even three in the afternoon. Much too gloomy, Kyle thought, for October. Especially so close to Halloween. Not that it mattered, since at the rate things were unfolding in town there would either be a ban on trick-or-treating this year, or no children left to take part in the tradition.

Finally, Marie asked, "Did you go in the room and check on him?"

"No," Kyle responded, feeling a sense of shame that hadn't been there before. "I thought I was just dreaming."

"Well do you still think you might have been?"

"Maybe. But the more I think about it, the more I think it was real. I was just so exhausted, or I would have—I don't know. Anyway, when we were talking this morning and I told you about the kids' voices, you mentioned reasons their throats might be swollen?"

"Yes."

"What were they again?"

"Well keep in mind that I'm no doctor. I've only studied a bit at my father's insistence. But the two reasons I could think of offhand, were anaphylactic shock, or pulmonary edema."

"And what does that mean?" Kyle asked.

"Well, as I said before, anaphylactic shock usually happens as a result of an allergy. A patient will come into contact with an allergen and experience swelling, usually in the lips, feet, or throat."

"Like when someone's allergic to nuts," Kyle offered.

"Correct. And it can be fatal, which is why people with severe allergies will carry around an epinephrine pen in case of a reaction. Now assuming these children really are dead, as you say—" she held a hand up in a calming gesture, "—and I'm not doubting you, just thinking outside the box—then that could very well be the cause of death. To be perfectly honest, I'd be prone to lean more toward that theory than the alternative, because it might explain this anomaly in a way that almost isn't completely mad. It could be nothing more than a bizarre disease that somehow affects children under a certain age, causes a deadly reaction consisting of tracheal edema—that's swelling of the throat—and reanimates their bodies in a murderous rage."

"Yeah," Kyle snickered. "That's not crazy at all."

"Well, it's a whole lot more plausible—and agreeable, I might add—than the alternative."

"Which is?"

"Well, could you see any swelling?"

"You mean in their necks?"

"Yes," she didn't break eye contact, watched him thoughtfully as they spoke.

"No," he replied. "They looked fine—except for, well you know—"

"I figured as much. So, ruling out strangulation as C.O.D., for now at least."

"Cause of death?" he tilted his head.

"Yes. So, this is likely not the only alternative. And again, I'm no doctor, these are just my crude diagnoses. But it could be pulmonary edema."

"Oh—kay—" Kyle stretched the word out.

"So pulmonary basically means, to do with the lungs. And edema means—"

"Swelling, right?"

With a hint of a smile, she nodded. "Very good. It could be caused by any number of factors, including, but not limited to, suffocation. Either way, we would have dead toddlers on our hands. However, the latter option, in my opinion, pretty much takes any medical explanation off the table and you're left with something very paranormal, probably suffocating children in their sleep and possessing their cadavers in order to build an evil, murderous army of zombies—ridiculous as it sounds."

Kyle felt something dark and dirty fall over him, like a game his cousin had once played in which she'd cracked an imaginary egg on top of his head. He felt Marie's words pouring down him from every angle because even though everything they had talked about today had been pointing in the same direction, hearing it put so bluntly, transported it from the realm of theory, or even imagination, right into reality. And with that came real life danger.

He thought, *You always hear about bad shit happening, but it never happens so close to home. And if it does, it never happens to you, or to anybody you know. Sure, people get sick, and they grow old, and sometimes they even die. But nothing this big or this fucked up ever happens outside of TV. School shooters don't strike at your school, and people don't fly planes into buildings anywhere except on the news. Children don't die and come back to life to kill their families. Especially not in your home. Especially not Abel.*

"Kyle?" Marie reached over and once again placed her hand over his. Only this time she didn't retreat, but held onto him and titled her head, gazing into his eyes. "Are you okay, sweetie?"

Breathing heavily, he nodded and said he was cool. Then he asked if she really believed him.

"I'm still here, aren't I?" she responded.

"Yeah. But you said, 'assuming the kids really are dead,' like you're not convinced they actually are."

"I don't think you're even convinced they are," she replied. "We don't know enough to be sure, do we? It's just a theory at this point, but maybe it's the best we have. Who knows? I can tell you I'm not convinced they're *not* dead, if that's any consolation."

He nodded because he supposed it was better than he would have gotten from anybody else, and at the end of the day, she *was* still here. And now that he thought about it, she was still holding onto his hand like an anchor, keeping him from floating away.

"So, you think this means your brother's been targeted?" she interrupted his thoughts.

"No, I mean I don't know. His room's always been next to mine, and he's never woke up crying before. It's probably nothing, but I haven't been able to shake this feeling all day. I'm just worried."

"Then maybe we should go to the police. Well, maybe *you* should. I imagine they'd just tell me to piss off because I'm not family. But if they know everything we know—and I'm sure they do—then they'll have to listen to you and take some kind of precautionary measures, right?"

"Yeah. Or arrest me."

Marie sighed. "And do nothing." When Kyle didn't respond, she said, "I suppose that's the more likely scenario seeing as there's not enough evidence there to make a solid case. I mean a little boy cried. It really could be nothing, right?"

"And it probably is," he agreed.

"But on the other hand, it could be something. And if it is, and we just assume the former and disregard it—"

"Then Abel might be the next lucky boy to get his glowing eyes and the devil's shadow. And a garden tool, right?"

Without hesitation, Marie said, "Well I suppose we need to do something, don't we?"

Kyle took a deep breath, let it out slowly, swallowed a lump in his throat before stating, "I've been thinking about it all day, and I can't come up with anything except just going to my parents or the cops. I guess I could try to convince my parents to go to the cops, but I'm not really sure they would listen to me. They already think I'm just a stoner and a loser and my mom isn't likely to believe a word I say lately."

Marie offered an almost sympathetic look and squeezed his hand. "Well, we'd better put together a game plan then, haven't we?" She released him and reached into her purse. Bringing out her phone, she opened an app. "Let's take a look online for starters. There might be something helpful."

Kyle wasn't sure what could possibly be helpful online, but he was learning to trust this girl, who spoke and thought like an adult, and was clearly his intellectual superior. So, he didn't object as she began searching the internet for clues as to how to battle whatever evil was ravaging his hometown. Then they stumbled upon the news of what had transpired a few hours ago in a residential neighborhood off Winslow Street.

***

Noel Rowland's body cam had been useless. The Mount Vernon Police Department contracted with Axion, and unless manually activated, their products only recorded on a thirty-second loop without audio. It was almost like a sick prank that the thing had been the only piece of equipment that hadn't been either destroyed, or taken, seeing as checking it for potential footage had only served to waste precious time.

The Cinema 7 had been like a slaughter house, that hadn't been cleaned in weeks. The scent of putrid, rotting flesh was sickening and there were pieces of Noel Rowland's insides and outsides, along with crushed and splintered bone and his shredded uniform, strewn about the large viewing room in puddles of blood which had begun to dry. His handcuffs, his taser, his gun—they were gone, and his radio was smashed to bits. And the canine? Rocket had been mutilated worse than his owner, and only traces remained.

Bartlet hadn't been the first on the scene. The station had tracked the SUV and sent every unit nearby to the building, which was located right across the street. When she arrived, spotlights were being set up, and those inside already wore hazard-masks. She'd nearly vomited at the smell. Then she saw the child.

She knew instantly who it was, as four-year-old Telma Salazar had been among the first group to disappear. Now she lay in her oversized T-shirt on the cold cement floor, curled up and motionless. Her neck was twisted unnaturally so her head rested on her shoulder, and her arms were scrunched up like a T-rex. Her eyes were huge, almost to the point of bulging, as if in shock—or fear—and her jaw thrust to the side. There was nothing peaceful about how she lay.

Christy had turned and stormed out, taking in a gust of cold, humid air, then bending over and dry heaving. Now there was a chalk outline in the cinema, and Bartlet was in the hospital, where the little girl lay on a gurney, a gray-haired man in glasses and a white coat standing over her.

The room currently smelled of floor cleaner and rotting toddler. Bartlet had been here more times than she could count, but never with this medical examiner, and never on such a solemn note. Skagit Valley Hospital's morgue wasn't a dimly lit dorm, like what would have been depicted on television, but more what one might imagine would be used for surgery. Except that it was bigger, and the gurney clearly wasn't designed for comfort. Why would it be?

Rivas stood so close to Bartlet that their arms touched, but neither of them moved, or even seemed to be breathing. All three wore tortes-shaped masks over their faces, and cream-colored rubber-gloves.

The medical examiner poked at the body, running his hands over the surface of Telma's skin, the way a man might touch his lover. He gripped her little forearm and attempted to move it like she was nothing more than a cabbage patch doll, then glanced up at the two detectives and said, "Rigor mortis."

"Clearly," Bartlet replied.

He stared at her a moment, then proceeded. "It can clue us in early on as to how long a cadaver's been deceased, since it happens as a result of C-two-plus depletion."

Bartlet rolled her eye. "Meaning?"

"Well, we know about how long it generally takes—"

"What's C-two-plus?"

"Oh. Right. Sorry. It's just another way of saying calcium, which is what muscles use to unflex, or relax. When somebody dies, the calcium levels begin to slowly deplete until the muscles just go stiff, or in some cases," he pointed down at the body with his eyes, "contract. The process usually takes around forty-eight hours from the time of death.

"Usually?" Rivas asked. The mask, covering the bottom half of his face, accentuated his almond-shaped eyes, and somehow made him appear even more intelligent. Not that he wasn't a sharp detective to begin with, but Bartlet could imagine him as a doctor, himself.

"Well," the examiner went on, "it's not an exact determinate. Obviously, there are plenty of factors that could cause the time to fluctuate. Size of the cadaver, diet or health factors, and so on and so on. But forty-eight hours post mortem — give or take a few — is when we generally expect to see rigor mortis occurring. Mind you, I'll be able to give you a much more definitive estimate after I run all the usual tests." He glanced back and forth between the two detectives. "Will you be sticking around for that portion?"

Before Rivas could respond, Bartlet said, "No." Reaching into her pocket, she produced a small, flimsy rectangular mesh of paper. She peeled off a soggy business card and offered it to him. When he accepted and examined it like it might be covered in anthrax, she said, "If you would call me on my cell the second you know something, that would be great."

She didn't ask how long it would take because she had been through the process, and knew to expect that call within hours. Instead, she turned and walked out, hearing Rivas handling the niceties behind her.

The lobby to the ER wasn't any more packed than usually, everything considered, because everybody affected by whatever the fuck was happening, was dead. Apparently, even the people doing the killing were dead.

A set of automated doors slid open in both directions, and she stepped outside where it was only sprinkling now, but evening was beginning to set. Soon it would be dark out, then night would fall, and there was no doubt in her mind that the children would strike again. They would choose another neighborhood where more of them would turn, and they would kill, and they would ravage.

And there would be more this time. Thursday night there had only been four. Then, last night, eighteen. It was growing and tonight God only knew how many of them would turn, or die, or whatever the hell was happening to them.

As she made her way through the parking-lot, Rivas jogged and caught up to her. "What now?" he asked.

"What do you mean?"

"I mean what's our next move?"

Making it to her car, she dug in her pocket for her keys. When she found them, she brought them out, hit a button and heard the familiar "click" as every door unlocked simultaneously. "There is no 'what now'. We keep doing what we've been doing. Only we need to spread out more. Do it separately. We'll be able to cover more ground and follow up on more leads that way. You can take the incident on Winslow Street if you want. I'm onto something else." Only it was a lie, because she wasn't onto anything except a deep dread of having to face more reporters.

Or Feds.

She'd eaten her words when they'd shown up, only not all of her words because like she had said, it hadn't unfolded anything like in the movies. Nobody had flashed a laminated card and said, "I'm taking over this investigation," and it sure as shit hadn't been Mulder and

Scully, or any other top-secret unit delegated to the strange and unusual.

Just federal agents that were virtually indistinguishable from Bartlet and the other plainclothes, sent from an office in Seattle to offer support wherever it was welcome. And yet, she still had no interest in mingling with them. Christina Bartlet was a veteran homicide detective and she worked on the intuition which she'd developed as such.

Rivas hesitated like he wanted to object, but he didn't, and she didn't care. She didn't even tell him goodbye, just opened the car-door, stepped inside, and shut it again. As he strolled off, she started the engine and squeezed the wheel so tight her knuckles turned white because the facts were crystal-clear now, yet somehow even more impossible than before.

Her first instinct was to recommend a citywide evacuation of all children, pre-teen and under. But she knew that would never be declared, as the powers that be would sooner quarantine the town out of fear that whatever this was would spread. And maybe they were right, but maybe they weren't. That was the problem, wasn't it? There was no way to know how to combat an evil that you knew so little about. That, and the fact that her seven-year-old grandson, Evan, lived here in town.

***

Dark red blood rose to the top of the dirty water and floated away with the current. Nobody saw, though, because it was dark outside. The monster's babies didn't have to see to know it was happening, because they knew what it knew. Well, not quite everything, but they knew what they needed to know. They had to keep their eyes closed because if they didn't, passing cars might spot the orange light.

They had swum near the bottom of the river like little fishies, until they had reached the bridge by Broad Street. Now they were holding onto beams to keep from floating up to the top, Malachi's blood was floating, though, because a boy named Tyson had cut his hands off for him with a hacksaw, and now he was sharpening his wrist-bones on a big rock.

***

Kyle and Marie had a plan. They'd spent the latter half of the day coming up with it. It wasn't perfect, but there wasn't enough evidence to prove, or even really believe, that Kyle's brother had been targeted by whatever was changing Mount Vernon's children, so the plan was to continue to investigate, and they developed a sound enough method for doing this.

It was close to seven, and dark outside when the Beetle finally pulled up in front of the McIntosh house. Streetlights shone overhead through a layer of fog which was growing progressively thicker, but it wasn't raining anymore. Marie kept the motor running because she clearly had no intention of getting out, and at first, Kyle didn't move either, so she turned to face him, using her door as a backrest, but didn't speak. He couldn't quite read her expression through the dark, though it seemed to anticipate something.

She wants you to kiss her.

He shook the thought off before it finished playing out in his head, because it was clearly misguided as today had been no date. If the look on her face was urging him to do anything, it was to get out of her car so she could go home. But instead of moving to do so, he asked, "How far away do you live?"

"You know Waugh Road?"

"Uh, yeah. Off of College Way? That's where you live?"

"I suppose that's one way to enter. Yes."

Waugh was a long road that went almost all the way across town, and it looked very different depending on where you were. But it was known mostly for the small segment which contained cul-de-sacs on either side of a steep hill consisting of the only mansions in Mount Vernon. It made sense, he supposed, as her father owned apartment buildings. Not just that, but she'd said he owned real estate all over the world. They must be loaded.

Still, he asked, "On Hilltop?"

She nodded.

"Oh."

For a while neither of them spoke, then Marie brushed something he couldn't see, but guessed was a loose strand of hair, behind her ear. "So, tonight you'll do what we spoke about?"

"Yeah."

"And you'll call me if you discover anything new?"

"Yup."

"Then we'll meet back up tomorrow?"

"Yeah. I mean if you still want to."

She smirked. "Of course, I still want to, silly. 9am again?"

Kyle thought a second, then said, "How about earlier?"

"What? Earlier than nine?" Leaning in so they were no more than a couple feet apart, she laid a wrist over his forehead. "Are you feeling okay?"

They both laughed, and she set her hand in her lap, but stayed close, rather than returning to her post. Kyle's heart sped up because, again, he found himself wondering if he was supposed to kiss her, and it invoked a stirring in his lower region which caused his member to swell and press against the inside of his pants. He hoped she didn't notice, as he told her he just thought they should get an early start tomorrow, all things considered.

"Yeah, you're probably right." She seemed to deflate as she finally sat back against the door.

She did want it, you moron. She still does, and so do you. Quit being such a pussy, and just go for it. What's the worst that could happen?

But the answer was simple because maybe he was wrong. And if he was, she would reject him like Claudia had, and then it would be awkward, and he might not see her again tomorrow. Or ever aside from in passing at school.

He wasn't sure when it had started, but he liked her. It was probably when she had dived in the middle of the fight this morning. Then, while the day progressed, what he was feeling had become abundantly clear as he got to know her. What he wasn't sure of, however, was whether or not she liked him back. He suspected she hadn't had many male friends who didn't develop crushes on her, and her bubbly personality probably contributed to that as much as her looks.

As he was having this thought, along with a silence that probably lasted long enough to have become awkward, Marie peered over his shoulder and asked, "Is that your mum?"

Glancing back, he caught sight of his mother in a pair of jeans and a T-shirt, standing in the open doorway hugging her arms and staring at the car, light from inside radiating behind her.

"Yeah. I ah—I guess I should go. What time you wanna meet tomorrow?"

"Your call, captain."

"Seven?"

"Seven works for me."

"Okay then. I'll ah—I'll see you then."

With that, he climbed out of the Volkswagen and made his way across the damp grass feeling like the world's biggest sack of dicks.

***

Marie took the long way home, because otherwise she would have had to drive past the scene on College Way. She wasn't sure if it would be as chaotic as earlier, seeing as the police and media would likely be split between that and the new scene on Winslow Street, but either way she avoided both, by entering Waugh on the other end of town.

On either side of the Beetle, small houses sat in barely maintained yards so close that some of them almost touched. Very working-class. *Very pretty,* she thought.

Her head still hurt. The Hispanic kid had hit her rather hard, and though she hadn't touched it in hours, she suspected it was still swollen. She had never seen anything like what those boys were doing to Kyle, though, and she had just reacted without thinking.

It had been out of character for Marie Franco, because thinking was what she did best. It was what she was known for. She supposed what she'd said to Kyle was true, because some girls *were* known for being pretty, and others *were* known for being smart.

He was easy to read, and she knew he had almost corrected her, told her she was pretty. It's not what she had been after, though, and she'd felt stupid for even saying it the second it had come out of her mouth because she knew how he would take it.

And she *was* pretty. She had no self-image issues. But she had also been on his Facebook page and seen his ex, whom he'd gone on and on about, and that girl clearly wasn't known for her brains.

It hadn't mattered at the time, because though Kyle McIntosh was cute, she hadn't entertained any ideas involving him, other than exploring a potential friendship, or possibly meeting people through him. She still had Ian back home, and though going to school with boys was new and exhilarating, she had no intentions of stepping out on him with one. Not until she'd begun to get to know Kyle McIntosh at least.

She brought out her phone, selected his contact, and pressed "send" connecting to the car's speakers as it rang. A few seconds later, his groggy voice appeared.

"Ugh."

"Hello? Ian?"

"Christ, Marie. Do you know what time it is?"

Now that she thought about it, it was three in the morning in London. "Oh, jeez. I'm sorry. You're right, aren't you? Why don't I call you back later? In the morning? My morning."

There was silence on the other end, then Ian said, "Marie?"

"Yes?"

"Why don't you not."

She paused briefly, then nodded, even though nobody saw because she'd known it was coming. She hadn't known when, or who would say it first, but now that it was out in the open it hurt so much less than she would have expected. In fact, if she were being perfectly honest, she felt nothing. No joy. No sorrow. Only the indifference that accompanies the observance of events unfolding in their natural order.

Still, more out of a sense that the proper motions needed to be observed than anything else, she asked, as the houses on Waugh Road grew increasingly larger and more expensive, if he still loved her.

"When have we ever said we loved each other, Marie?"

"I don't know," she responded. "I guess I always just sort of assumed it was implied."

"So did I. But do either of us really think this is going to work? You and me? Long distance like this?"

And she didn't. She knew neither of them had actually planned for it to carry on once she'd moved out of the country, so she told him that, and they said they would always be friends even though they both knew that that was rubbish as well. And when she ended the call, she was just pulling up behind her father's pearl-white Escalade.

She paused and reflected inwardly for a moment just to make sure she wasn't subconsciously suppressing something that needed to be dealt with. She waited for tears, or even a hint of disappointment, and when neither came, she dropped her phone into her purse, climbed out of the car, locked it with a grin and approached the mountain of a house with an unexpected sense of relief.

The day had taken a curious turn, because though she couldn't pinpoint when she had begun to perceive Kyle as potentially more than just a friend, by the end of the evening she had unequivocally found herself hoping he would kiss her, or even say something indicating that he felt it too.

But that was the problem with nice boys, wasn't it? They tended to come with a shyness that made it nearly impossible to gauge their intentions. She sensed that there had been a mutual spark, and she had put out all the proper signals but received nothing definitive to go on in return.

The front door was made of thick oak, but would have been useless to stop an intruder because it was surrounded by stained glass on either side and above. Granted, the glass was thick as well, but it was still glass and could be broken with a large enough rock—or a garden tool.

She put her key into the lock. Gave it a turn. Felt the tumblers give. Pulled it back out. But before she could turn the knob, the door swung open revealing her father— tall, round and scowling—in a black T-shirt and a pair of slacks. At first, Marie froze because she knew this look all too well, and it manifested when the right combination of alcohol and rage had been introduced.

His eyes were bloodshot, and his posture slouched. His distended gut protruded more when he drank, because he made no effort to stand up straight or suck it in. Baring his teeth, he reached out and gripped her ponytail, which she'd tied only in an attempt to look cute for Kyle. Stinging pain shot from the lump on the back of her head, all the way down her spine, as she was heaved inside and thrown to the tile floor only feet from the landing of the staircase. Her keys landed next to her purse. Around the stairs was the entrance to the kitchen and living room, but here there was only Marie and her drunk father.

Salvatore Franco slammed the door, turned on her, and bared his fists.

Marie curled into the fetal position, but didn't dare speak as he leaned down and wedged one meaty fist between her bicep and forearm, pressing it against the side of her head and growling, "Where are you been? Huh? You answer me!" His knuckles dug into her temple with every word.

"I'm sorry!" was all she could manage, so he cocked his hand back and she clenched her jaw, her whole body tensing in anticipation of the blow. When it didn't come, it was almost worse than if it had.

"I don't ask if you sorry! Where are you been today! Do you know what is happen in this place? Huh? You answer me now!"

"Dad, I was out! I was out driving around, that's all. I know. I saw the news and the police, but I was just exploring and seeing the town. I'm sorry."

Then it *did* happen. It wasn't too bad, though, and probably wouldn't leave much of a bruise. Still, she cried because, though it wouldn't guarantee that he stopped, if she didn't it would guarantee that he *wouldn't* stop. She cried and she told him that she hadn't meant to upset him, and she didn't know he was worried about her. What she didn't say was that he hadn't even called or texted to tell her.

He didn't hit her again, but jerked her up by her arm and spit in her face. "You're done! Do you hear me? You're done with that school! You never go back! I see you today! I see you driving the car I buy you with the boy inside! You think I don't know what you do? YOU THINK I DON'T KNOW?"

He took a step closer so she could smell scotch and some type of meat on his breath, and her hands came up instinctively to block her face. This caused him to raise both hands like an untrained boxer.

She wanted to tell him that she hadn't done anything wrong. That nothing inappropriate had happened. But she knew her father. If she so much as opened her mouth at this point, he would shove his fist in it. So, she bit her tongue and blinked back tears as he went on.

"My daughter is prostitute! I give you everything! I do everything to give you future and this what you do?

You throw it away for nothing? You done! You hear me? Done!"

"Okay, Daddy."

Her mother appeared in her peripheral, a ball of yarn in one hand, knitting needles in the other. She watched the exchange absently, silently.

His jaw shook, and his chest heaved. Marie had made a mistake in thinking she had somehow been clever enough to get her way. In believing that she had actually persuaded the old man and it wouldn't all just play out to be no more than a short-lived fantasy. She had made a mistake because her father didn't even understand the root of his contempt toward his youngest daughter, let alone harbor any desire to combat it.

She knew though. She had always known. She knew every time he tried to beat his plans for her future into her, and when he had broken her arm only two short years ago. She knew that Salvatore Franco had to be the master of his universe and Marie had inherited enough of his alpha tendencies, to make her the only person in his home—and in his life—who was capable of threatening his kingship.

He didn't recognize it, but his subconscious did. Somewhere in the back of his alcohol-addled brain, was a big, fat baby, kicking and screaming and resorting to violence to avoid being out-smarted.

He didn't hit her again, and her mother didn't greet her after he stomped away. She just examined Marie for a long moment like something that could only be removed by an exterminator. Then she turned and followed her husband into the kitchen.

Marie tiptoed upstairs. She considered taking a shower, but thought it better to make herself scarce the rest of the night.

Chapter Seven

Tina McIntosh didn't greet her son with a smile, or even a nod as he made his way up the porch-steps, but it didn't matter because Kyle had known she was pissed before he'd even stepped out of Marie's car. It wasn't any one thing he could pinpoint in her body-language; he just knew his mother.

Or maybe his unconscious mind had already worked it out before he'd seen her. Not that he'd done anything wrong since the last time they spoke, but they hadn't exactly hung up on a positive note. The Beetle didn't turn around, but once again, drove straight and took the long way out of the Stanford Development, likely using the back exit.

Mom asked if he'd had a good time before he was halfway up the steps, and it occurred to him that Bartlet might have contacted her. Then, a few minutes later, when Abel was sent to his bedroom and Chewy put outside, and Kyle sat in the silent living room with both parents, where he was instructed to empty his pockets, he knew that he was fucked.

He could still smell the remnants of a tuna casserole while Dan McIntosh informed him that he was lucky he didn't call the police, then walked the marble-sized hunk of marijuana into the bathroom. The toilet flushed and he reappeared as Kyle's mother slipped her fingers into the holes in Silencer's brass knuckles and shook her head. She calmly told Kyle how disappointed she was, then confirmed his suspicion. Bartlet had called.

So, they took his cellphone and told him he was grounded until further notice. Not for the weed. Not for the illegal weapon. But for lying to a police officer and trying to hide a fugitive while children were being abducted and their families slaughtered in their sleep.

He considered telling his parents that that wasn't what was happening at all, but concluded that it would only be a waste of breath. He could tell them what he knew until his tongue had road-rash and they would just assume that he was out of his mind on drugs.

As he made his way downstairs, he prayed silently that he would be able to find Marie's profile online. It was unlikely she had friended anybody locally, yet, and it may still be linked to London, but he had her name, and he still had an iPad.

What he didn't have, he learned as soon as he was in the hall, was a bedroom door. It had been removed so all that remained were the hinges, like tiny severed limbs, sticking out at the top, middle, and bottom of his door-jam to taunt him. He examined the scene, shook his head, and stepped inside just as his father appeared and requested the iPad as well. Handing it over, Kyle sighed, plopped down on his futon. He watched as Dan McIntosh knocked lightly on Abel's secured door.

"Hello? Can I come in?"

There was movement beyond the thin wood, then it opened, and Abel's voice appeared cheery as ever. "Dad! You don't have to knock. It's yew house!"

"I know it's my house, buddy. But the polite thing to do is always knock, right?"

"Uh—wight!"

"Why are you wearing your Halloween costume again, turkey? You're gonna wear it out before it's even time for trick-or-treating."

"Because," Abel lowered his voice, "I'm fuuuckin' Chuuuuuucky!"

After a long pause, Dad sighed, shook his head, and said, "Why don't you go ahead and take it off and we'll have some ice cream. How's that sound?"

"Okay! "Abel squealed.

"See ya upstairs." He didn't glance in Kyle's room as he turned and made his way through the hall with his head down.

Kyle listened to his footsteps as they climbed the stairs. Then, once they disappeared, he stood on a chair, digging under the blankets folded and stacked on the overhead shelf in his closet. Bringing out an old, gray laptop computer, he tossed it onto the futon. Then he dug out the charger, plugged it into an outlet and concealed the entire setup behind his bed, just as Abel ran out into the hall, his tiny bare feet slapping the linoleum in rapid succession.

"Hey Abe!"

The footsteps petered out, before coming to a halt, but the child didn't speak. Kyle stuck his head through the doorway and saw him standing in a pair of bright green sweats and a black T-shirt with a Nike symbol over a breast pocket. His hands were at his waist, and he harbored an indecisive expression.

"Come here a second, man. Can I ask you a question?"

"Why did Dad take yew dow?" he finally asked.

"I don't know. I got in trouble. Come here, man. Lemme ask you something."

"I wanna go upstaiws and have ice-cweem, Kyle."

"I know you do. This won't take long. I just miss my brother. I haven't seen you all day. It'll be quick, I promise."

So hesitantly, Abel stepped into his big-brother's room, and Kyle asked him why he was crying last night. At first, Abel denied it. But Kyle said he knew he was crying, and he promised not to tell anybody if he admitted it. So, Abel stood rigid for a long moment in which Kyle could hear his own heart trying to pound its way out his chest, then the child's lips curled and his face scrunched up like he might cry.

Kyle pulled him close and wrapped him in a big-brother-bear-hug. "Ssshhh." He lowered his voice to a whisper, "It's okay, turkey. Tell me what it is. What did you see last night?"

Abel sniffed and he jerked against his brother's body, then finally he cried and said there had been a monster in his room and Kyle felt an electric chill surge through his body that caused goosebumps to rise from beneath his skin and his eyes to dampen because this was what he had feared, yet he had known somewhere in the darkest corner of his subconscious that it was true.

But he wouldn't succumb to full-blown tears, no way. Rather, he scooped his brother up and took the steps two at a time, the child sniffing and weeping like an infant in his arms. When he reached the top, Chewy ran in front of his feet and almost tripped him.

"Damn it!" He stepped over the dog, through the living room, and into the small kitchen where his dad stood over a huge bucket of chocolate ice cream with a scooper and two bowls. His mother was at his side, and they both turned to address their children with looks that suggested a serious conversation had been interrupted.

"What's this?" Tina's eyes expanded as she rushed over and took her youngest son from Kyle. "What's wrong, brah? Hey. Hey now. Come on." She bounced him. "Ssshhh."

Abel clung to her like Velcro as his dad placed a hand on his back. "What happened, buddy?"

But Abel didn't answer, just wept, so they both glanced at Kyle almost simultaneously.

Kyle said, "You need to listen to him."

"What?" His mom squinted. "What are you talking about?"

But Kyle couldn't say it because he had promised his brother that he wouldn't. So instead, he touched the six-year-old's shoulder, causing him to jerk as if startled. His mother turned away, shielding Abel's body with her own.

"What the hell did you do to your brother?"

"Nothing!" Kyle exclaimed. "I didn't do—just listen to him. There's something he needs to tell you."

"Well, what is it? You can see he's crying! Just say it for him, for the love of God!"

"I can't."

"Well, why the hell not?"

"Because I told him I wouldn't!"

"Jesus Christ!" Dan took Abel by the waist, peeled him off his mom and set him on the counter. Abel sniffed, frowned down at the bucket of ice cream, and stopped crying. Dad made bunny-ears with one hand and pointed at his eyes. "Right here, buddy. You want ice cream?

We'll have some after you tell me what's going on. How does that sound?"

Abel's chest heaved as he returned his father's gaze, his bottom lip curled again, and he shook his head.

"No?" Dad asked. "You don't wanna talk about it?"

Another shake, more exaggerated than the first and accompanied by a sniffle and a backhanded wipe of the nose.

"Oh—kah—did you do something you shouldn't have, and you think you're gonna be in trouble?"

"No!"

"Then what could possibly be so bad?"

But Abel didn't speak again.

"All right," Dad took a deep breath, "how about this,can Kyle tell me? Would that be okay with you?"

The little boy's face darted in Kyle's direction and his eyes expanded like balloons connected to an air compressor. He didn't shake his head or make a peep, but Kyle knew he was silently pleading for him not to tell.

But how could he not at this point? He had been sure Abel would, and he wouldn't have to. Now, however, *it was break his promise* — along with his baby-brother's heart—or lie. Make something up. But, though, Abel wasn't about to tell his parents what he had told Kyle about the monster in his room, he still might refute Kyle if he lied.

And if he didn't tell? Would Abel be changed? Killed in his sleep and resurrected, bent on murdering everybody in the McIntosh household? The first part of his plan with Marie had been to hear what Abel had to say, and if there was something there, get Abel himself to relay it to his parents.

But it was looking like he would have to improvise, so he told them himself. Not about what he and Marie had concluded. That would just cause them to dismiss whatever he had to say. He simply told them that Abel had informed him there was a monster in his room. As he spoke, Tina and Dan McIntosh stared down at him impatiently, but not Abel. The little boy's frown was no longer one of sorrow or fear, but rather contempt for his big brother who had betrayed his trust.

And did Kyle feel like a crate of donkey shit, sent oversees for no reason other than to stink up the ship? Of course, he did. It came as no surprise when Abel vehemently denied his claim. Or when their parents told Kyle to go ahead and call it an early night while they spoke in private with Abel over a bowl of ice cream.

Fuck it. That only meant that it was time to execute the second part of the plan. Before Abel or anybody else made it downstairs, Kyle rushed into his room and checked the charge on the laptop. It was at 33 percent, but it would have to suffice. He had wanted to find Marie on social media before he did what needed to be done next, but now there wouldn't be time. Unplugging the device, he crept into Abel's bedroom with it.

The second he stepped through the door, he was overcome by a cold chill. Not because there was any change in the environment—not that he could sense, at least—but because his brother's words were still playing in his head.

Thew was a mostew in my woom wast night.

He took a deep breath. Glanced around. Not for any monsters, but for a hiding place. A dark-blue blanket with pictures of computer animated cars with faces on them stretched across his twin-sized bed, and an old chest that almost matched the bed set, sat in the bottom of his open closet, serving as a toy box.

The closet was the most concealed place in the bedroom, and the door remained perpetually open, so Kyle activated the video camera application on the laptop and set it to record. Then he stepped up on the ledge of the toy box, nearly causing it to tip over. The toys clunked around loudly, and the bottom of the chest slammed back down onto the floor.

Shit. Shit, shit, shit.

He tiptoed out of the room and into his own as fast as a cockroach scurrying into the dark because he was sure he'd been heard. He tried not to breathe as he listened for footsteps coming down the stairs. But when there were none, he hurried back into Abel's room. Standing on the edges of the box in a more supported fashion, he set the laptop on the overhead shelf and leaned the screen in such a way that the camera was pointed at the bed.

Then he carefully climbed down and took a look, seeing that it was much too conspicuous. Conspicuous? Who was he kidding? It was obvious. Climbing back onto the toy box, he felt around on the surface of the dusty wooden shelf until his hand touched what felt like a notebook. He brought it down and examined it.

An old photo album. The kind which his grandma had in her house, and surely contained weathered pictures from some time before cellphones when cameras abounded. Out of the same curiosity that was said to have killed many-a-cat, he cracked it open and beheld a photograph the size of an iPad, which displayed a much younger Kyle, sitting on a red velvet platform, his hair combed to the side and his newborn brother in his arms.

It was the type of picture that was taken in a crude studio at the mall, by somebody who fancied themselves a photographer, and though he didn't remember the particular shoot, he had been through plenty of others.

Moreover, he'd seen this picture just about every day of his life, as it had hung in a chrome frame in the upstairs hallway for as long as he could remember. For reasons that he didn't understand, seeing it now invoked something inside of him that he knew needed to be suppressed, if only for the moment. He didn't flip to see what other memories the album held, but snapped it shut and set it lightly over the laptop's keyboard.

Then he reached up again, finding Abel's baby-book (and Kyle's for that matter), and some other random treasures that were stored where it was assumed nobody would tamper with them. He arranged them in such a way that they concealed as much of the computer as possible, while still allowing the camera to surveil.

If any fucking monster decided to show its face tonight, there would be proof.

***

Jose didn't curl up the way that Telma had. He was holding onto a wooden beam under the water where another bridge must have been before, and his body was stiff when it froze and didn't move again.

He dislodged from the beam and his eyes and mouth popped open, but there was no light in them as he began to float toward the surface of the river diagonally because he was being carried along by the current.

And though all of the monster's babies still had their eyes closed, they knew what was happening because the monster saw it all. One of them opened his. He was a tall boy whose black hair was as long as a girl's and swaying in every direction like their shadows always did. He was the only one who opened them because he was the closest to Jose, and if the others did it as well, there would be too much light and the people in the cars above would see.

He reached out and caught Jose by his pajamas, pulling him close and holding on tight. Then he shut his eyes again and waited like the rest.

***

Usually nobody had to tuck Abel in at night. He wasn't that type of child. He was very independent. But just after 9:30, while Kyle was watching the news with Chewy on his lap, and learning about a dead police officer found in an abandoned cinema across from the police station, his mother came downstairs with her youngest child and spent a few minutes in his bedroom with the door shut. Chewy, who had been shivering and staring at a spot on the wall, glanced up briefly as she passed, then set his little head back down.

This was probably the worst-case-scenario at this point, as his mother's fastidious attention to detail almost assured that she would spot the computer. But any attempt to lure her out would only set her on alert and increase the chances of being found out.

They were now talking on TV about the children. It had finally been leaked that they were responsible for the killings, and it was by far the biggest story in the nation—maybe the world. CNN and FOX seemed to be discussing it more than the local stations, however, and reporters were predicting a citywide quarantine.

Kyle snickered because he knew something that they didn't. It wasn't a virus. What good would a quarantine do against something that a six-year-old described as a monster?

Then it occurred to him *why* a quarantine was so likely. Virus or not, it wasn't striking sporadically. It had shown up in one neighborhood one night, and another the next. It did, in fact, seem to be contained to wherever it attacked, and both sights thus far had been in town. He couldn't help but think this bit of information would have significantly affected his and Marie's plan, had they worked it out today.

As he was having this thought, Chewy's ears twitched, Abel's door creaked, and his mom appeared in the hall. Dim light shone from Abel's bedroom as she and the dog briefly locked eyes, then she quietly shut the door and turned her attention on Kyle, staring for a moment before stepping through the doorless jam. Black yoga pants stretched over her wide hips, and a light-gray tank top revealed a thin layer of age-revealing fat under her arms. Blowing a strand of blond hair from in front of her eye, she said, "Got a minute to chat?"

But before Kyle could answer, she reached over, killed the power on his television-set and took a seat on the futon. Kyle scooted over, bringing Chewy with him, but the dog quickly hopped down, glared up at him irritably. He used his back leg to tackle an itch behind one of his pointed ears, then strutted out of the room as Kyle waited for his mother to speak. At first, she didn't.

Then she said, "I have to admit, it catches me a little off guard when someone can manage to confuse me. I don't always deal with it in the best of ways, I'll confess." She studied Kyle's face, waiting for him to respond. When he didn't, she went on. "I mean really? Weed?"

"I don't know." Kyle wondered if he had a reason to be ashamed, and promised himself he would put more thought into when it made sense to do so. "I was just—"

"Smoking weed, right? Why don't you go ahead and table the defense for now, brah. I was your age once, too, remember? Truthfully, it's not the weed—or the weapon—I'm upset about. And I don't think I'm upset, really. I mean I am—don't get me wrong—but I think that's the fruit of my disappointment, not the root. Does that make sense?"

Kyle told his mom that it did, then wondered why she thought he would lie about what Abel had said. What his motivation could possibly have been. Did she really think he wouldn't have come up with something more plausible if he were just trying to take the heat off himself? But of course, she didn't, because everybody knew Kyle McIntosh was no Einstein, including his mother. Not just that, but to believe him would be to call her other son a liar, and in light of recent events, Abel's word surely held more credibility than Kyle's.

Now his was no good to his little brother either. But why had Abel lied? Why had he been so terrified to tell her what he'd told Kyle? Unless it was Kyle that he had been lying to and there was no monster. And again, which option was most plausible?

"Don't you wanna know?" His mom interrupted his thoughts, furrowing her brow and forcing a smirk.

"Know what?" He scratched an itch on his face.

"The root. Don't you wanna know what the root of my disappointment is? I know if I were sitting in a room with no door, no phone, and no iPad, I sure as hell would wanna know why."

Kyle wanted to care, wanted to be upset that his parents had taken his belongings, his door, and with it, his dignity. He wanted to pout and maybe even cuss them out a bit. But at this point all that mattered was keeping them, his little brother, and himself alive. So, he heeded Marie's advice, and he concealed his hand, nodding like a bobblehead set on a dash and telling his mother that he wanted to know what the root of her disappointment was.

She took a deep breath and said, "Sometimes I think about my brother. The one you were named after. Have I ever told you how he used to protect me from our other brothers and sisters whenever they would mess with me? You know Uncle Jimmy, right?"

Kyle nodded.

"Of course, you do." His mom's eyes took on the far-off look that accompanied deep reminiscing. "He used to have this BB-gun. Jimmy did. It was a pistol that had this pump on the bottom of the barrel, and he'd make me flap my arms like this," putting her hands in her pits, she made wings out of her elbows, "and he'd say, 'quack like a duck!' and he'd shoot me with it if I didn't do it.

"But sometimes he'd shoot me even if I did. Isn't that crazy? Those BBs would make me bleed and leave welts in my skin for days. Tsh, sometimes even weeks.

"Anyway, one time Jimmy was picking on me, making me quack and shooting me, and I was crying, and Kyle just happened to walk outside and see it and he beat him up so bad that Jimmy didn't leave the house for two weeks." She chuckled "But he never shot me with that thing again.

"I really loved your Uncle, and I mean that. I know people always say this when someone dies, but with us it was true. There were twelve of us, and I've never been as close to any of them as I was with Kyle.

"When he started using that stuff, I knew it was the end of his life. I know this sounds crazy. I mean I was just a teenager and all of them were into something, but Kyle was always different. He could've done anything if he'd only had a fair start in life, but he couldn't do anything moderately, you know? I knew from the start that heroin would kill him someday, I just didn't know when."

She paused and Kyle wondered, *Is she trying to say I'm like Uncle Kyle? That I'm headed down that road and I'll end up dead? Or is she comparing me to Jimmy? Does she really think I would take advantage of my little brother to get myself out of trouble?*

All of a sudden, Kyle was overcome with the sense that maybe he *did* need to care what his mother thought. Not because it would make him feel any better about the current state of their relationship, but because maybe if he could somehow fix their dynamic, she would listen to him. Maybe she would understand that she had raised him differently and he was nothing like her siblings. She would remember that he had never been into trouble before, and that would at least earn him some credibility.

But the second he opened his mouth, she held a hand out and said, "Just listen, brah. Don't tell me it's just pot, and not heroin, because I'm not stupid. I already know that. And I don't think you're gonna end up strung out behind Shelly's Pizza or anything. I already told you, it's not the dope.

"I've always tried to make sure you had a better shot at life than I did, Kyle. I think you know that. And somewhere deep down in the bottom of my little heart, I like to make myself believe you appreciate it. What happened to you, anyway?"

Kyle tilted his head.

"You have a fat lip. Do I even wanna know? You know what, never mind. What I was saying was—" She paused, looked up to the right, then said, "You know he did it in front of me once. Your uncle. I was the only one at the house, which never happened, and he came home and neither of us were even out of high school yet, and he stuck that needle in his arm while I sat and watched. I was just like, 'jeez,' and I thought I would die right there. Can you imagine if I sat here and shot up heroin right in front of you? Wouldn't that just traumatize you for life?

"I don't know. Anyway, Kyle, I don't know what the hell is happening in this town, or why I keep getting calls from the police about you," she held a hand up again, "or who that girl is, but people are dead. A lot of freaking people are dead. This isn't a game."

Kyle McIntosh felt his soul deflate inside him, and he almost sank right through the bottom of his futon. In an instant, he came face-to-face with a sorrow that he never even imagined existed. He felt as if his heart was rotting in his chest because now he knew for certain she wasn't comparing him to her dead brother, whom she had loved dearly, but rather letting him know that she thought he was involved in the killings.

Poker face, he told himself. *Level-headed and collected. Don't show your hand. Don't you dare show your fucking hand. Don't cry or object, or even blink because if you do, you're all going to die. You, your mother and father who think you're capable of murder, and your brother—and haven't you betrayed him enough for one night?*

So, he sat as still as a statue and silently prayed that she would be done soon and go away.

She said, "So I guess the root of my disappointment is that you have all the opportunities that I never had, and I've worked my tired butt off to make sure of it. It just really hurts to see you blowing it, you know?" He nodded, and after a long pause, his mom stood up. "Anyway, get some rest and leave your brother alone tonight, 'kay?"

"Yeah. Sure."

"…and in the morning. He's had a rough night, so don't harass him." She began to walk off, but paused at the door, glancing back. "And just hang tight tomorrow. We'll talk more later, but don't leave the house. Got it?"

"Yeah," he replied. "Got it."

"Cool. Night, brah." With that she disappeared into the hall and up the stairs.

Kyle sat for a long moment willing himself not to feel anything because it didn't matter what she did or didn't think he had done. And the truth was, she probably didn't know what she thought anyway. All she knew was whatever Bartlet had filled her head with. But in all fairness, her lack of trust wasn't completely unwarranted, because tonight he planned to kidnap her youngest son and get him the hell out of Mount Vernon, Washington.

***

Chewy didn't come back downstairs, and Kyle hoped to all things sacred that the dog hadn't decided to sleep in his parents' bed, because it would guarantee his plan was thwarted. He waited until there was no more movement upstairs, then brought two blankets and a pillow down from his closet and arranged them on the floor at the entrance of his bedroom.

Abel's room was only feet away, and he would be able to hear any commotion inside. Dim light escaped through the crack between the bottom of the door and the straight edge, where cream-colored carpet gave way to the hallway's white linoleum, but it was thus far silent beyond the thin wood.

It was far from silent in Kyle's head, however, because though he tried to remain neutral and calm, he couldn't get his mother's words to stop playing on repeat. He tried to tell himself that he was just shaken up because he wasn't used to punishment of any sort—not from her, at least—but that wasn't the root of *his* unsettledness, and he knew it.

She had been so cold. So calculated with her words. They had been intended to strike a blow, yet there had been no affection in them. Kyle had become a threat to her world, and she wanted him to know that if provoked, she would easily choose to stop loving him.

And after tonight, that's exactly what would happen, because he was taking his brother out of this house. She might break down, and she might even cry, but she wouldn't accept a hug from her husband. No way. She would never let a man wrap her in his arms and comfort her because she was a strong woman.

It wouldn't last long enough anyway. It would be just enough time for a tear or two to push their way out of her and roll down her face. Then she would sit up straight and stop loving Kyle because he was a selfish little son-of-a-bitch who had kidnapped his baby-brother, and who was capable of mass murder.

But at least she would be alive.

So would his father and Abel, and Kyle might be wrong and maybe they would have been just fine if he didn't take his brother and leave town, but there was no way of knowing right now, so it had to be done. When this whole fiasco was over and children were no longer being possessed and compelled to kill, he would make sure Abel returned home. Kyle would be a fugitive, and eventually he would be caught and locked up, but it would be worth it as long as his family still had air in their lungs.

Then he found himself reflecting on how Kim had sucked in air in order to growl his name through a swollen trachea—if, in fact, Marie was right and that's why her voice had sounded the way it did (and he was sure she was). What did that mean, though? That they were strangled? *Suffocated,* she had said, right? Because there were no physical signs of strangulation on their necks?

But there was a fundamental flaw in the path they were taking to figure this whole thing out, and Kyle wasn't too dumb to recognize it. The flaw lay in the fact that they didn't actually *know* if these kids were dead. Sure, *he* knew. It wasn't just that they were pale and veiny, either, but that they were empty. Void.

How many times, though, had he been sure of something in the past and ended up being wrong? He knew he needed to open up to the idea that he might have made an inaccurate assumption early on and ran with it, and that such a fallacy could have easily set them on the wrong path to solving this thing. Or maybe he just didn't want to think about his brother being strangled or suffocated in his bed.

Either way, sometime between when he was having this thought and when he was trying to determine whether or not he would be able to follow through with what he intended to do tonight, he drifted off to sleep and dreamt that he was in Marie's car again. Not in the passenger seat, but in the back, lying with her on the black leather interior.

He was on top of her. Between her long legs. Kissing her, but they were both dressed. It was nice in a way he had thought only this morning nothing would ever be nice again and it stirred something in his chest that bubbled up and threatened to overflow out of his eyes.

He pulled away and gazed down into hers for a period of time that may have been a fraction of a second, or maybe much longer. It was impossible to tell, because it was one of those dreams in which time tended to be obscured. But he knew he was dreaming, and he knew what he wanted, so he kissed her again, letting his hand explore her waist, her ribcage, her breast.

Her own hand wrapped around the back of his head as her tongue slipped into his mouth and the car started to rock. It moved slowly at first, like a boat swayed by a gust of wind, then picked up momentum until it was shaking back and forth, back and forth, and Kyle once again pulled away from her because it wasn't them that were causing the commotion.

And even though it was a dream, he almost jumped out of his skin as blinding orange light filled his vision, because outside, more children than he could count stood all around the vehicle with their terrible hands and faces pressed against the windows, staring in. They pushed from every direction, causing the Beetle to shake and rock, but none of them spoke or made an effort to get in.

Marie didn't shriek. She didn't move, or even react in the slightest. Just lay on her back smiling up at Kyle. The child closest to him slapped a tiny palm against the glass and a hollow thud resonated inside the car that brought to mind thoughts of somebody beating on the outside of a coffin. Kyle glanced up and met the eyes of John Collins—Dobey's ten-year-old brother. His long black hair hung partially over an innocent, pale, blood-streaked face.

The car continued to shake until it was practically vibrating, and Kyle yelled so loud that he woke himself up and gasped because his heart was trying to beat its way out of his body. *No more sleep tonight,* he told himself. The dream had been so real he could still hear the shaking car. *What time is it?*

His eyes adjusted to the dark and he gazed up at the ceiling. There was no alarm clock in his room on account of he always used his phone or his tablet. Though it felt like he had barely dozed off, he suspected he had been asleep for a while.

The shaking continued, and he recognized the metallic squeal of Abel's bedsprings on which he had once made love to Claudia when nobody was home. Kyle grew instantly nauseous. He considered pinching himself to see if he was still dreaming, then flew to his feet faster than a piece of bread in a toaster and dove for his brother's bedroom. He wasn't even in the hall yet when he wrenched open the door, which sat kitty-corner to where his own should have been.

Two steps later, he was inside, where a small nightlight shone from an outlet low on the wall and it was almost cold enough to see his breath, but there was no longer any shaking. No rocking. Nothing but the sound of his baby-brother sobbing where he lay curled up on his bed, his decorative blue blanket at his feet.

Abel didn't cry out loud, just sniffed and whined as if trying to suppress his tears. His hands were over his eyes, refusing to look up as Kyle hurried over to him and touched his back. Abel jerked. Something brushed Kyle's ankle. He shuddered and jumped, realizing too late that it was only Chewy, here to see what the ruckus was. Abel started to shiver, but didn't remove his hands from his face.

"Hey," Kyle whispered. "Hey, turkey. It's okay. It's okay now. I'm here. It's just me, Kyle. Talk to me, buddy."

But Abel didn't talk. He shook his head vigorously back and forth and shivered and sobbed and Kyle wondered why the hell it was so cold in his room. His first instinct was to glance toward the window, but that was shut, as always.

His next thought was simply, *move,* because though he didn't know much about what he was up against, he *did* know that if he didn't do what he planned to do, now, he might never get the chance.

Leaning down, he scooped up the bony Chihuahua and set him on the bed next to Abel. Then he covered them both with the blanket and exited the room, securing the door behind him so the dog wouldn't leave the child alone.

He didn't turn on any lights as he tiptoed up the stairs. When he reached the top, he heard the window-fan coming from behind his parents' door on his left. Their bedroom sat at the end of the hallway, catty-corner to a bathroom, with two doors. One led into the hall, the other into their room.

Kyle stepped into the dark bathroom, his bare feet sticking to the linoleum. He put his ear against the thin wood and listened for any movement inside, but all he heard was the loud double-rotor fan, so he slowly inched the door open and made a point not to think about what might happen if he was caught. Tina McIntosh couldn't sleep without her fan, but the room wasn't nearly as cold as Abel's had been.

Kyle's father lay on his back snoring like a satisfied pig. His mother was on the other side of the king-sized bed, facing away from him, her entire body covered by the comforter.

He crept around the bed, taking both of their phones from where they sat on separate nightstands charging, only pausing briefly on his mother's side because next to hers sat the brass knuckles and what he thought at first was a cigarette butt.

But that wasn't right, because his mother didn't smoke. He picked it up, examining it closely, smelling burnt marijuana when it was halfway to his face, and thinking *What world is this?* because his mother didn't smoke weed either. But it *was* legal now, and he supposed that made it akin to having a drink at the bar. But had his father indulged as well? Of course, he had. He was the one who had pretended to flush it down the toilet when they took it from Kyle, which meant it had been his idea.

Shaking his head, Kyle scooped up the brass knuckles and his own phone, which sat next to his mother's. Once he was back in the bathroom with the door shut, the sound of his father's snoring disappeared into the electronic hum of the window fan. Kyle stuffed the roach, along with the weapon and all three phones into his pockets.

He was tempted to feel bad for stealing their phones, but it had to happen on account of he couldn't have them waking up and calling the police before he could get his brother out of town.

He took the stairs two at a time, pausing outside Abel's door briefly to listen for any commotion. When he heard nothing, he stepped over his two blankets and into his own room without turning on the lights. He dug his phone out, only now looking at the time.

11:43 PM.

Pulling up his text messages, he selected the most recent one from Marie and typed, *can u talk?*

When she didn't respond right away, he paced a few times, then called her. She picked up on the second ring.

"Hello." Her voice was soft, with the hint of a smile in it. "I was just responding to your message."

"Marie," he whispered. "Can you get over here?"

There was a long pause in which Kyle could hear his heart beating inside his ears. Then she said, "Kyle, I—"

"Marie please."

"What's happened? Did you get the video already?"

"I—I don't have time to explain. Please just come and pick me up. Like right now. If you don't, I don't think my family will make it through the night."

"Kyle, I can't. My father—just tell me what's happened. Maybe we can—"

"Marie," his voice shook, "do you trust me?"

"Well, yes. Why wouldn't I—"

"You said today that we're in this together, right? Did you mean it?"

"What? Of course, I meant it."

"Then come and get me, Marie. Please. Even if you have to sneak out. If you get in trouble, I'll make it up to you somehow. I promise."

Another pause, followed by movement on the other end of the line.

When Kyle could take it no longer, he asked, "Are you coming?"

"What do you think?" she whispered so quietly he almost couldn't make out her words.

"Thank you. Jesus, thank you so much."

"Ten minutes," she said.

"You can be here that fast?" He felt his body grow light because this was the craziest thing he had ever done, and it was really happening. "Okay. Pull up out front and turn your lights off. I'll be watching for your car. Listen, Marie, I mean it. I promise I'll make this up to you, okay?"

But Marie had already hung up.

***

Kyle stood in the middle of the room staring down at his screen, which displayed one of the factory wallpaper settings that came standard with the phone. It was nothing that he would ever recall if he never saw it again, just red, blue, and green lights which appeared to be moving across a black background and crossing over one another, creating diversely shaded squares and rectangles.

His breath was shaky. He could feel the cold from Abel's room as if he was still there. He considered going in and bringing his little brother into his own bedroom, but decided against it. Abel couldn't know they were leaving yet. Kyle was sure the boy would fight him tooth and nail on the matter.

Not merely arguing either. He would throw a fit, and scream, and Kyle would be lucky if his parents weren't woken. This would have to quite literally be a kidnapping, and it would have to come as a surprise. He might, he thought with absolute dread, have to subdue the child somehow. But how? By knocking him out? *Choking* him out?

Shaking off the thought, Kyle dropped the cellphone back into his pocket where it clinked against the heavy brass-knuckles.

Light, he thought, moving for the switch next to the door, but stopping inches from it. What if Abel was still awake? He would see the light seeping in from under the door, and it would put him on alert.

So, Kyle fished the phone once again from his pocket and activated the screen, shining it into his closet, and snatching up a pair of shoes and his black backpack. He emptied the contents and stuffed the two blankets from the floor into it, then slipped into the shoes and his jacket. He would wait until Marie was outside to wake Abel. Tossing the pack onto the futon, he paced again, checking the time every couple of minutes. After what felt like forever, he stopped, glanced toward his brother's door.

Fuck this.

He needed to check on him. Even if it did manage to upset the child. He needed to make sure he was all right. *Make sure he was still alive.*

Clenching his jaw, he made his way out into the hall and slowly and quietly opened the bedroom door. When he stepped inside, the first thing he noticed was that the temperature had begun to return to normal.

That's a good sign. It has to be a good sign. It means the monster's moved on.

But to where? If this thing was poised to strike in his home, then based on its patterns, that meant it would strike in his neighborhood. Any minute now, to be sure.

He needed to call the police. He needed to warn them, and maybe, just maybe, they would show up and do something to stop it. Even if Abel's monster had moved on to the next house, Kyle still needed to get the kid out of the Stanford Development right now.

His brother didn't stir as he approached the bed, just lay motionless, and for a second Kyle was tempted to entertain what would have been the worst thought that had ever passed through his mind.

Instead, he gripped the blue comforter over the face of an orange tow-truck, and decided he needed to wait to call 911 until he and Abel were safely inside Marie's car and headed out of the neighborhood. He tugged lightly on the blanket until a blue pillow appeared which matched the rest of the bed-set.

What the hell?

At first, he didn't believe his eyes, so he lowered it some more, and saw Chewy lying next to the pillow in a shallow pool of his own blood, tubular intestines protruding from his torso like a snake crawling out of his gut.

"Oh, holy shit!" Kyle backed up until he hit the entertainment center which sat against the wall, because the Chihuahua was practically inside-out, and his brother was nowhere to be found. A trembling "No" spilled out of him like warm water, and his stomach turned around and around, and the room started to spin, and Kyle was dizzy, and he was sick, and he needed to sit down, but he also needed to throw up.

Then the nightlight flickered. A subtle electronic buzz resonated from somewhere in the walls and the light dimmed almost in slow motion before it was swallowed up by the darkness and the entire room became one giant shadow.

The Devil's shadow.

Only it wasn't the Devil's shadow because it was nothing like what Marie had described. This was simply darkness. Before he even reached for the light-switch next to the door, he knew he would find it useless. The power was out. Had been cut.

Energized by a chill in his spine, he set his feet, prepared to run. To fly up the stairs and wake his parents. But he stopped short and ground his teeth because it occurred to him that they still wouldn't believe him. He could show them all the dead dogs in the world, and they would just assume that he had killed them. He needed proof, and if even a small portion of his and Marie's plan had succeeded, that would be on the laptop. So, he climbed onto Abel's toy-box, and tried his best not to think about his dog who had been so well behaved-that Kyle used to sneak him onto buses in his backpack. When the chest threatened to tip over and spill him and its contents onto the floor, he just stepped inside, crunching plastic toys underfoot. Bringing the computer down, he folded it shut, climbed out of the chest, and paused, only now thinking, *Oh shit. Abel.*

Before another thought could find its way into his head, he was in motion, flying around the corner and taking the stairs two at a time because it didn't matter what his parents did or didn't believe. They may have been dead already. When he was halfway up the steps, and in front of the front door, the distinctive sound of shattering glass appeared behind him, causing him to freeze in place for a moment, listening to an ensuing series of noises. Scraping. More shattering. Thumping. More scraping. Banging. Short footsteps. Coming his way.

"Kyle!"

At first Abel's voice caused so much relief to fall over him that it was like it had been dumped from a cloud, because it wasn't choked like Kim's had been and he didn't immediately register the orange light. Then he turned and saw the child standing at the top of the stairway in blue coveralls and a striped shirt, his red wig atop his head and bright illuminated eyes. He held a black-handled kitchen knife which was so humongous that under different circumstances it would have looked comical in his six-year-old hand. Only it wasn't the plastic one that came with his Halloween costume.

This one, Kyle recognized from the knifeboard which sat by the kitchen sink, and even under the blinding lights in his brother's head, he could see that it was dripping blood. But his shadow was the worst part because it wasn't just one shadow. There were dozens, coming off the boy in every direction, dancing and swaying on the walls and the banister like seaweed in a storm.

For a second, all the sounds coming from downstairs seemed to stop and all that Kyle could hear was the window fan in his mother's room. But it was louder than it should have been, which meant that the door was open.

Then Abel smiled from ear to ear and squealed, "Wook at me, Kyle! I'm fuckin' Chuuuuuuucky!" and the ruckus reappeared all at once, only closer now. Abel raised his knife overhead in both hands and scurried down the steps, his little feet slapping in rapid succession.

Kyle yelled, turned and gripped the doorknob. It was locked. The downstairs commotion crescendoed until it was right behind him, and orange light filled his peripheral, but he didn't dare look back. The shadows grew on the door like magic bean-stalks as he flipped the switch on the knob. Then the deadbolt. Then he twisted and wrenched the door open and saw his lawn filled with children.

They all had lights in their faces which overpowered the streetlamp that sat at the edge of the yard, and cut through a thick layer of fog hovering over the grass. Their shadows were the same as Abel's only there were so many of them that they looked like a mesh of black wire attempting to untangle itself.

Some of the kids were pale with blue veins showing beneath their skin. Others were soaking wet, their hair matted to their faces. Some wore pajamas, some underwear. Others, still, were completely nude, with swollen bellies and splotches of blood all over their bodies. Each one held some kind of weapon and the bigger ones were hoisting the smaller ones into Kyle's broken bedroom window which sat a mere couple of feet down and to the right of the elevated front door.

Kyle paused for a fraction of a second, as the children stampeded up the stairs. It was a fraction of a second too long because the light from their eyes was like standing next to the sun. Though he didn't glance back, he knew that Abel was at his heels now as well.

Without thinking, he kicked like a donkey, his sole connecting with his little brother and sending the child flying backward. But not before a sharp pain stung Kyle's calf.

He cried out, but didn't look at the wound, just stumbled through the door, pulling it shut behind him. Only then did he notice the odor. It was the scent of old food, decomposing in the bottom of a dumpster, and it was by far the most sickening air that he had ever breathed. But there was no time to think about it because the children in the yard were now turning their attention on him.

The door swung open and a boy with a samurai sword rushed out. He wore a two-piece plaid pajama set, which clung to his body because it was soaking wet, and water cascaded out of his mouth like from a faucet as he rushed outside.

The ones who had been climbing through the window ran around to the landing of the porch-steps and began to make their way up toward the house. Toward Kyle. So, he placed one hand on the wooden railing and hoisted himself up, doing his best to protect the computer. He stepped on the rail and leapt over the side where his mother's gray Subaru was parked in the driveway.

The ground was an entire story down, but Kyle landed on the roof of the car, feeling it indent under his feet, slipping on its moist surface, and landing hard on his back. The wind was knocked out of him but all he could think was, *The computer. Please don't be broken.*

The sky was black, covered by a thick layer of cloud which threatened to give way to rain.

"Kyle! You hewt me! Why'd you kick me, you jewk?"

Kyle's shoes slid as he scrambled to his feet and saw his brother descending the porch stairs with his knife hanging at his side and his head tipped back like the hood of a sweater, so he was staring up at the clouds. It bobbed and dangled as he walked, and the wig had fallen off, but he was smiling and speaking as if he didn't have a broken neck. Others were with him, pouring out of the house and running down the steps with shovels, knives, hammers—a black kid even clutched a hunting rifle with a wooden stock.

HONK! HONK! HONK-HONK-HONK-HONK!

Glancing toward the noise, Kyle saw the purple Beetle pulling up just behind his mother's car. The headlights were off, and he could see inside just enough to know that Marie's eyes were as wide as quarters. He didn't think, just ran and leapt off the back of the Subaru, barely landing on his feet as a deafening thunder cracked and echoed off the sky.

Then there was metallic scraping, and he knew without looking that another round was being chambered into the rifle. The Beetle's passenger door popped open and Kyle dove behind the seat as another shot rang out. He dropped the laptop onto the floorboard and landed on a pair of soft legs feeling the elastic fabric stretch and move over them as glass from the car door shattered and landed all over his back.

A feminine shriek wailed above, and the car jerked. Kyle pulled his feet inside and sat up. He saw Laura

Cunningham next to him, gripping her door handle, terror all over her face.

"What are you doing here?" Kyle choked.

In front of her, Marie turned the wheel, barely avoiding running over a baby in nothing but a bright white diaper. "We'll explain later!" she cried. "Shut the bloody door!"

Kyle reached for the door as another shot was fired. A slug crashed into the metal next to him, causing sparks to fly in his face. He retracted, then reached again, gripping the ledge where the window should have been, and pulling as hard as he could. It slammed shut and Laura screamed as Dobey's little brother, John, ran up and tossed an infant in a soaking wet blue onesie through the window.

Orange light filled the inside of the Beetle. The baby landed on its face, then hopped to its feet like a break-dancer and scanned the car wide-eyed. It was so pale that it looked like a porcelain doll, and it smelled as horrible as the entire crowd of them had. It had no hands, only pointed bone protruding from torn flesh on its tiny wrists.

Laura screamed again, took Kyle by the shoulders, and attempted to wedge him between herself and the child. But it paid her no mind, turning its attention to Marie in the front seat.

It knows she's driving. It wants to stop the car.

Then the infant made its move, crouching down, hopping higher than should have been possible, and landing in the center console next to Marie. In his peripheral, Kyle saw two children, who often rode their bikes in circles around the neighborhood, run out of a one-story house with what looked like hot pokers from a fireplace. He shook Laura off, hitting her a little too hard with the back of his elbow and grabbing the baby's onesie. It opened its mouth and water shot out like the nozzle of a hose, soaking the dash and causing Marie to shriek as Kyle pulled the kid into the backseat again.

It let out a shriek like a pterodactyl, landing on the seat and then running up onto Kyle's lap. Cold water soaked into his pants and splashed his face. It got in his mouth and he almost vomited.

"GET THAT THING OUT OF THE CAR!" Marie screamed.

"I'm trying!" Kyle shoved it off his lap. He needed to fling the damn thing out the window. He knew he did. The problem was, he couldn't. The thought of picking it up caused an anxiety which he'd only experienced when a kid in the fourth grade had brought a tarantula to show and tell and tried to pressure him into letting it crawl on his hand. The baby landed on its back, and he snatched it once again by the wet fabric. But it jabbed at his hand with one bony stump, and he let go just in time to avoid being punctured.

Kyle pivoted so his back was facing forward and saw the herd of toddlers a distance away, chasing after the Beetle which must have been going 40 miles-per-hour now, taking the long way around the neighborhood. The baby climbed back to its feet and gazed directly at Laura, who fell silent aside from her rapid breathing. Then it moved so fast that Kyle had no time to react, sprinting across the backseat, up her lap, and shoving its weaponized bone right into the clavicular portion of her neck.

"Oh, holy shit!" Kyle moaned as Laura choked and gargled, grabbing the baby around the waist with both hands and dislodging it from her throat, but before she had it out of her, it thrust the other wrist in right next to the wound.

"What is it?" Marie glanced back.

"JUST DRIVE!"

Dark blood pooled from the initial puncture, bubbling in thick bursts. Laura's eyes bulged like they wanted to fly out of her face. She clutched at her throat as the infant pulled its arm out and prepared to stab her again.

"NOOOOOO!" Kyle snatched it once more by its clothes, feeling them rip as he threw it onto the floorboard and struggled to get a shaking hand into his pocket.

Laura continued to choke and gasp. She slid down the seat, onto her back, both hands over her neck, blood oozing between her fingers and down into her jacket. She stared up at the ceiling and kicked Marie's backrest.

Then the baby crawled back onto the seat and shrieked, "Mamamamamamama!"

Kyle brought the brass knuckles out and fumbled to get his fingers into the holes. The baby went for Laura again, and he cocked back and brought them down on its tiny head as hard as he could, feeling it crack under the weight of the blow.

The infant collapsed facedown like a splattered insect, but continued to kick and flail with all four limbs, so Kyle hit it again. And again. He hit it in the head and the body, over and over again, feeling its frail bones snap and crunch with every blow. He didn't stop until it lay broken and motionless, spewing water from its face and a hole in its back where a rib protruded.

Then, and only then, did he pick the thing up. It hung limp in his hands like a marionette as he deposited it out the broken window. The other children were so far back they had disappeared. Kyle turned his attention to Laura, who was now squirming in the seat, writhing back and forth and struggling for breath. Her back arched and Kyle heard air hissing from at least one of the holes in her neck.

"Laura!" He leaned down, wedged his arms under her and scooped her up, pulling her close to his body. "Laura, it's gonna be okay!" Her warm blood oozed out in rhythmic bursts to the beat of her heart and soaked his shirt.

"What is it?" Marie's voice shook. "What's happening back there?"

"Hospital!" Kyle's voice cracked. He didn't care. "Get us to a fucking hospital!"

"Okay. Okay." The tires squealed as Marie sped around the corner in the back of the Stanford Development that led to the exit which would deposit them onto Urban Avenue. "I think I remember the way. Tell me if I take a wrong turn, please."

But then Laura's eyelids raised so high that they disappeared for a moment before dropping again as she stared off into nowhere. Her blood stopped spurting and began to just stream out of her like a waterfall as her heart stopped and she let go of her life in the backseat of a Volkswagen Beetle.

Chapter Eight

Kyle shook Laura Cunningham. He slapped her face. He thought of how people always gave CPR in the movies. Then he thought about how often he had imagined his lips against Laura's and it made him want to rip them off his own face, so instead of doing that, he slapped her again. He didn't know CPR, anyway, and even if he did, how would CPR unpuncture a throat?

It wouldn't. That's how. She was dead. She was dead because she had been in the car and the car had been in the midst of the attack because Kyle had called it there. He had been selfish, thinking only of himself and his family, and he had invited Marie to her own death. But Laura had caught it instead, and now she would never stand against a wall in the gymnasium making out with Jesse Gerrard, or spend another night with Dobey. Her lips would never again brush Kyle's ear when they hugged. However, knowing this didn't stop him from trying to talk her out of being dead.

"Laura." His voice was barely more than a whisper. "Laura, come on. Please. Don't do this." Then it grew louder as he began to lose control of himself like somebody had stuck a gas pedal inside him to the floor with a K-bar knife. "Don't fucking do this. DON'T FUCKING DO THIS RIGHT NOW! I CAN'T HANDLE IT! I REALLY CAN'T FUCKING HANDLE THIS RIGHT NOW! DO YOU HEAR ME? WAKE UP, DAMN IT!"

"What?" Marie's voice echoed inside his head as if from a distance. He glanced in the rearview mirror, met her eyes as the Beetle flew past the nursing-home, almost colliding with a parked truck and only slowing down when it reached Urban Ave. She didn't bring it to a full stop, but looked both ways, and took a left onto the empty street. "I'm going to get us to the hospital. Just be calm. I take a right at the light, correct?"

"Just forget about it," Kyle said between the deepest breaths he had ever taken. He knew if he kept hyperventilating, he might pass out, but he couldn't stop. And if he did pass out, so what? He would welcome the break from reality, because in reality all of his worst fears had just materialized in a matter of minutes.

Not just because Laura was dead, but his entire family as well. His mom. His dad. Abel. Even Chewy. He closed his eyes because tears were coming now. He shut them tighter than he had ever shut them before. So tight that the muscles in his face ached. Then it occurred to him that he was still clutching his deceased friend like an infant at his chest. He let go, felt her drop next to him, and scooted all the way over so he wasn't touching the body.

Marie asked. "What? What do you mean?"

But Kyle didn't respond because on the backs of his eyelids all he could see were orange lights and images of his baby brother with a broken neck, his head dangling about his upper back, smiling with a giant knife in his hand.

"Kyle. Hello? Kyle, I'm pulling over."

"No!" Finally, his eyes snapped open and were attacked by the freezing air hissing in through the open window. He stared straight ahead, refusing to look at Laura. "Don't stop. Please." He could hear the sobbing in his own voice, and he hated himself for it but didn't have the strength to fight it. Then he was sniffing, and he could feel warm tears streaming down either side of his nose, contrasting with the cold as he said, "Just—just get to the freeway. Get us out of this town."

Marie's voice grew meek. "But what about Laura?" she trembled.

When Kyle didn't answer, she slowed down to what he assumed was the speed limit, sniffed and wiped her face with the sleeve of her jacket. The Beetle pulled up to a red light where Urban Ave crossed with College Way and her shoulders raised, and dropped as she took deep breaths and let them back out, but she didn't move to turn and look in her backseat.

Sniffing again, she said, "Kyle, where are we going?"

"Just—ah—freeway. Just get to the freeway and go south."

"Why, Kyle? Why are we fleeing town? We've done nothing wrong, have we?"

"What? What do you mean?"

She took another breath, holding it in for an exaggeratedly long time before letting it out very slowly. Then her voice grew rigid and cold—almost stern—like she was talking to a rambunctious child. "Why are we fleeing, Kyle?"

But her tone only served to make him angry. On any normal night, it might not have. He might have even felt compelled to appease her, or somehow atone for whatever he had done to invoke the reaction.

Not tonight though. Not after what he had just witnessed. What he had just *experienced.* Not after he had broken his six-year-old brother's neck, then smashed every bone in some baby's body with brass knuckles. Not after his parents had been murdered and Laura Fucking Cunningham had died in his arms. Tonight, he cared about as much as he cared who won the local box-car derby this year.

So instead of acknowledging her attitude, he simply growled, "Why?"

"Excuse me?" Marie hit her blinker, prepared to take a right. "Why what?"

"Why was she here?"

"Don't."

"Don't what?"

"Don't do that right now."

"Do what? What the hell are you talking about?"

Finally, Marie lost it. She yelled, "Don't say *was,* okay? Don't say why *was* she here, like she's dead back there, because frankly, Kyle, I'm not prepared to deal with that scenario yet, if you can't tell! Maybe you should learn a thing or two about communication! How about that?" She slammed her palm against the steering wheel so hard that Kyle thought it might break. "So, can you do me a favor, and not speak about the girl in my backseat in the fucking past tense? And I will explain to you later why she is there. Would that be okay with you?"

He had finally stopped hyperventilating, but now it was his turn to take a deep breath. The light turned green, and Marie hit the gas. She took the turn onto College Way. He let it back out, and said that would be all right, but still refused to look down at the body lying next to him.

Orange lights filled his vision every time he blinked. It was just like yesterday, only worse because there were so many more of them now. It was like he had gotten way too close to the sun and burned his retinas. And the smell of the decomposing children didn't seem to be dissipating either.

"Can we roll down a window," he asked, in what was meant to be a monotone, but came out choked and whiny.

"It does smell something horrid in here," she responded. A second later all three windows which hadn't been broken slid down simultaneously, accompanied by the electronic hum of their motors. The freeway entrance was about a mile away, at the end of the street. Marie asked again why they were leaving town.

"Because," he replied. "I can't go to jail. Not right now. Not after—"

"Did you do something wrong?"

On either side of the Beetle, supermarkets, auto-part stores, and other businesses were mostly closed for the night in the part of Mount Vernon that probably should have been dubbed 'downtown'. College Way had four lanes in this area, and it was always lit up at night by streetlamps in big open parking-lots. It was mostly deserted now, aside from the Beetle and a silver SUV, which passed going the opposite direction, but the occupants paid no mind to the purple car with a dead teenager in the backseat.

"Of course not!" Kyle snapped. "Why would I—that was my family! You think I would—"

"Kyle, please calm down. I'm trying my best right now not to react, and I know you are as well. I know it's not ideal to be asked these questions right now, but you have to just relax. Take a deep breath. You say you didn't do anything wrong? Okay. I believe you. Why would you go to jail then?"

"Because, they won't care that my entire family—" he choked, took another breath. "You saw what they did to Dobey. They arrested him anyway. I can't let that happen to me. I'm not going to jail. I'll freaking lose it in there. I need to be out right now. Look, if you don't wanna help, I get it. I just—I don't know what else to do, or who else to ask."

"Did I say I don't want to help you, Kyle?" Marie pulled up to an intersection where College Way met Riverside Drive. "I snuck off and came to your rescue, if you haven't noticed. But if we really are in this together, I think it's only appropriate we have an equal say in decision making. All I'm trying to ascertain is why exactly we need to be outside of Mount Vernon to keep you from getting arrested. Don't you think that if they want you, they'll pick you up anywhere they find you, and send you back?"

"Of course, I know that. I just—there's a cabin a couple towns away. Dobey told me about it today. He was gonna ask you to take him there so he could hide, and I don't really know anywhere else. So—"

"Where's it located?" she interrupted.

"Lake McMurray."

"And how long will it take to get there?"

"To Lake McMurray?"

"To the cabin."

"I don't—I mean I've never actually been there. It's by Tara's house I guess, and she knows—"

"Who is Tara?" The light turned green, and she hit the gas.

"She's a friend from school."

"And she lives in Lake McMurray? Don't they have a high school there?"

Kyle found himself growing annoyed by the onslaught of questions. He asked if it really mattered whether or not Lake McMurray had a high school.

"I don't think anything is irrelevant at this point," Marie responded. "Two heads are always better than one and I'm merely trying to glean what's in yours in order to brainstorm and strategize together. How much do you trust this Tara?"

Kyle considered this, then said, "A lot. I mean, I don't think she would screw me over or anything."

"Unless of course she reacted emotionally, and therefore, irrationally. Correct?"

"I don't know," Kyle said. "What do you mean?"

"Well, is she friends with Laura?"

You mean was she? Kyle thought but didn't dare say out loud. Instead, he said, "Yeah. They're were—or they're like best friends or whatever."

Marie nodded. "Okay," she spoke slowly. "Best friends. Then is it possible that she might not be overly eager to help you hide from the police if you show up with her best friend in tow?"

"Jesus," Kyle said.

"Bear with me, Kyle, because if we're going to get through this, we'll need to avoid wasted movements."

Finally, Kyle glanced almost involuntarily down at Laura. Her eyes and mouth were wide, and her knees were still bent awkwardly, pressed against the back of Marie's seat. He quickly averted his gaze, focusing once more on the road ahead. "I thought you didn't want to acknowledge that she's—"

"I think we're bloody well past that, now, Kyle."

"Okay. Then what are you saying? We don't go to Tara's?"

"Do you think you can find this cabin without her?" Marie asked.

"No."

"And you know of no other places to go?"

"No. Nowhere."

"Then apparently we need her. But we can't very well show up with her best friend dead in the backseat, can we?"

"So what?" Kyle asked. "We dump her in the street somewhere?"

"Absolutely not." Marie drove toward another intersection just before the College Way freeway entrance, but she didn't move to take them into the turn lane which would deposit them onto Interstate Five.

Kyle said, "This is it."

"I know that's the freeway," Marie responded, "but we can't board yet."

She stopped at the light, and a red sedan pulled up next to them, poised to deposit onto the freeway. Kyle didn't glance over, just prayed silently that whoever was inside didn't look into the Beetle. But even if somebody did look, Laura was so low that all he or she would glimpse were her legs. There would be no indication that she was dead, aside from her blood all over Kyle's shirt and neck. Maybe even his face.

"Here's the problem," Marie continued. "If your friend Dobey was murdered, and this Tara's face was all over the news as a suspect and she showed up asking you to hide her, would you do it?"

"Of course not," Kyle responded.

"Right. And the police saw you with Laura s'arvo. They saw me, too, for that matter. As soon as her body's found, I can almost guarantee they'll be looking for us as persons of interest. And if Tara and Laura are—if they were best friends, you can bet that they'll question her almost immediately. No offense, mate, but I don't care how much you trust her. She'll roll over on you if they can convince her you killed her friend. If you want this cabin to be a safe haven for now, I don't think anybody can know that Laura's dead."

"Okay." Kyle swallowed a lump in his throat. "But why can't we get on the freeway?"

"Because," Marie hit the gas, passing the other vehicle and taking them straight through the intersection. "I know a place where we can hide the body."

***

Abel had stuck his knife into his own belly only a few minutes ago because one of the other kids had dared him too. It hadn't hurt a bit, and it had made a girl with piggy-tails laugh, so he had done it again. And again. And one more time just for fun. Blood and food, and something orange had oozed from one of the wounds, but most of it stayed under his Chucky costume.

Abel McIntosh's head bounced around, hanging off his neck bone. It rolled over his chest and hung like a necklace, and though he couldn't see with his eyes, he could with his mind. He could see because the other kids and the monster could see, and he was having the best time he had ever had. It made him wonder why he had been so afraid when the monster had first shown up under his bed. He had cried and cried every time it was there, and he had even begged it not to kill him.

But now he was in Gloria and Vanessa Fowler's house and the kids had their mom naked on the living room floor, with her arms wide like she wanted a big "I love you" hug. The fat kids sat on her arms and others sat on her legs. Gloria and Vanessa jumped up and down on her like a trampoline, laughing and wailing with glee as she screamed and cried, trying but unable to form words.

The girls were both older than Abel, but younger than Kyle, and Abel had only talked to them a handful of times while waiting for the bus to school. Now, he knew, they would be very close. They would be family because they all belonged to the monster.

Their dad was naked, too, but he hadn't been so easy to pin. So, a dark-skinned girl in pink undies had hit him in the head with a big sledgehammer and he had gone to sleep. Abel hadn't been in the house yet when it happened, but he knew. Then, when two boys had nailed his wrists to the floor, he had woken back up and tried to fight, but he hadn't had the energy to even yell. Now it was the mommy's turn to be nailed down.

Abel grew overly excited as one boy put the nail to her wrist and the other swung the hammer. As soon as it punctured her skin, though, she screamed louder than ever and arched her back, causing the girls to fall over and one of them to land on top of Abel. His throat broke in half and the skin of his neck stretched so far that his head was in his armpit. Somehow, he knew that it couldn't stretch any more. That if it came off, that would be it and the fun would be over.

Frowning, he raised his knife and prepared to bring it down on the screaming woman's belly, but a redheaded boy in Superman undies caught his wrist, looked into his orange eyes, and shook his head. It had to be Gloria or Vanessa. He had understood that since he had slashed his own parents' throats in their bed and wanted to kill Kyle next.

Finally, the woman was able to make words. "NOOOOOO! PLEASE DON'T DO THIS, GIRLS! DON'T HURT YOUR MOMMY ANYMORE! I LOVE YOU. GOD, I LOVE YOU BOTH! DON'T HURT ME AGAIN! PLEASE! PLEASE! PLEASE! PLEASE!"

But Abel knew the truth. The girls' mom didn't love them. When they told her about the monster in their rooms, she had sent them to bed without dessert. Then, the next night when they said it again, their daddy had spanked them both with the strap from a suitcase. Then, on night three, she had let them die.

The nail was hammered until the circular back almost disappeared into her skin, but she managed to get her other hand out from under the kids on that side and reach for her punctured wrist, screaming even louder.

"OH, FUCK ME! HOLY SHIT! PLEEEEEAAAASSSEEE NO MOOOOOORE! DON'T DO THIS TO ME!"

However, the bigger kids got a hold of her arm, wrenched it back, and it was nailed to the floor with the other. Then a baby dragged a metal gas can from the backyard across the carpet. It was funny because the can was bigger than her whole body. Vanessa covered her mommy and her daddy in gasoline and used a lighter from the fireplace to set them on fire. Then all the kids ran outside laughing and having a blast.

Even when the baby who had had the gas can stepped out last, covered in bright orange flames like the girls' parents. Only the baby wasn't yelling or fighting or showing any indication that it didn't like the fire. She was just as happy as the rest of them.

The monster had told Abel that he'd better not tell his parents about it because they wouldn't believe him and even if they did, they wouldn't care anyway. And even though the monster hadn't said so, Abel had assumed that if he listened, it would go away and leave him alone. Now that he thought about it, it made him laugh that he had ever been so silly.

The children were done with the Stanford Development because all the babies whose parents hated them had been gathered. And there were so many of them now, but it still wasn't enough.

They ran around the neighborhood, and the boy in the Superman undies gave a redheaded girl named Kim a piggy-back-ride. When they had made it to the back, where the old people all lived in a big hospital, the baby dropped in the middle of the road twitching and burning, but they didn't stop because they all knew it was over for her.

Abel couldn't talk anymore. Not with his throat broken in half. With one hand, he held his head up so the skin didn't stretch too far and break. He didn't want it to be over for him. It wasn't that he was afraid of it being over, he was just having too much fun.

They ran out onto the street where Kyle's girlfriend, Claudia lived and Abel considered going to her trailer and playing with her boobies. He liked when Claudia came over because she would let him sit on her lap and do that, as long as he pretended that he didn't know it was wrong.

The monster had already been in that neighborhood, though. That's where Kim and James came from, and other than Claudia's boobies, there was no reason to be there again. Plus, if they didn't hurry the mean-ol-cops would show up and ruin everything.

So instead, they went to the thrift store that was right next to the trailers and they smashed the windows out with their tools and went right to the aisle where the Halloween costumes were. Abel didn't need one because he was already fuuuuuucking Chuuuuuucky! But he grabbed as much of the stuff as he could carry anyway. They all did, and when the aisle was cleared out, they took it all with them into the field behind the store.

***

Kyle dialed 911 and reported the attack on his neighborhood. The dispatcher instructed him to stay on the line, but he instructed her to go to hell and hung up.

"Turn it off now," Marie said from behind the wheel. They were headed over a bridge that crossed the river into Westside Mount Vernon, which consisted of mostly forest and farmland.

"What?" Kyle asked.

"They can trace your signal. Turn the phone all the way off."

Without hesitation, Kyle obliged, and just before it shut down a call from an unknown number started to come in, which meant they must have been calling back. Reaching into his pocket, he brought out his parents' phones and considered tossing them out the window into the river. Then he shut them down as well. "Where are we going?"

"Just across this bridge," she said. "I was out here the other day and I think if we drop her off in these woods, she'll go unnoticed for a while."

"You mean at Riverview Park?"

"I don't know. Is that what this is?" They made it over the bridge and Marie hit the blinker, slowing down and preparing to make a left turn.

"Yeah." He heard the snappiness in his own voice and attempted to check it as he said, "People come here every day. There's no way they won't find her."

"Honestly, sweetheart, I doubt people will be out and about with their children anytime soon. Plus, it's been raining cats and dogs lately. Not exactly ideal weather for play-days at the park. We can't just leave her out in the open anyway. We need to take her out in the woods and hide her."

"What? You mean like in some bushes or something?"

"Unfortunately, that's exactly what I mean. Look mate, I'm not stoked about doing it, myself, but unless you want to end up in that jail cell you said you're trying to avoid, I think we both know it has to happen."

She brought the Beetle to a full stop, then killed her headlights and turned down the long gravel driveway leading into the park. As they approached the forest, it grew darker and somehow colder inside the car. They drove past the jungle-gym, and Marie parked as far out of sight as possible, though if somebody were really looking, they would still be able to see the bright purple vehicle from the street. They needed to hurry.

The car lit up when they opened their doors and only then did Kyle take the time to notice that Marie had her hair down and it was slightly tangled. She had washed off all of her makeup, and she wore a pink hooded sweater and blue jeans. She met his eyes briefly, then reached up quickly and killed the dome-light.

He took Laura's top-half, scooping her under her arms, and Marie held her legs. Together they hauled the body down a hiking trail until she grew so heavy Kyle needed a break. It was pitch black in the woods, and the river could be heard in the distance, accompanied by a symphony of chirping crickets.

"I can still see their eyes," Marie said as Kyle caught his breath. "It's like the lights are burned into my vision."

"Yeah," Kyle responded. "They do that."

"Will it go away?"

"It did yesterday. It took hours though."

"Oh dear."

"Come on." Kyle scooped up his dead friend, grateful that he could hardly see her face, but unsettled by the feel of her slippery blood.

After a few more minutes, they diverted from the trail, into thick sticker-bushes which scratched at his skin and pulled on his clothes and jacket. There was no way of knowing if the spot they chose would conceal the body in the daylight, but it would have to do, so they left her there and even though it was dark and difficult to see, Kyle made a point not to look back because maybe he would catch a glimpse, and he didn't want to remember her like this. As they made their way to Marie's car, neither spoke, but she walked so close that they touched from time to time.

Something scurried out from under the Beetle, startling them both and darting into the woods right before they climbed back inside. This time Kyle sat up front with her, and when they made it to the freeway, she failed to take the turn again, so he told her she had missed it.

"I know," she said. "I need to stop at an ATM machine. It has to be before we leave town, and it can't be one by the freeway, either, or they know which way we went. I have a feeling my card will be canceled within hours, and even if it isn't, I won't be able to use it without leaving a trail."

Kyle didn't object, just sat rigid, hoping she would be able to do what she intended before being pulled over—or worse. But exactly twelve minutes later, at nearly half past midnight, they were on the freeway headed toward Lake McMurray. The smell was, for the most part, gone, so Marie rolled up the windows, but it was still loud as hell and cold with one of them busted out. As she drove, she brought her phone from the center console and handed it to Kyle.

"Will you kill that please?"

"What?"

"Turn it off for me."

"Oh. Yeah." He hit the button on the side and the screen came to life, displaying the bridge he had seen earlier. It disappeared as he shut the device down, set it next to him on his seat and only now took the time to say, "Thanks."

"For?"

"You know—for coming to pick me up and all. I mean, you didn't have to do it."

The interstate was more active than the streets of Mount Vernon had been, and though there still weren't many vehicles, Kyle guessed it was better than being the only one on the road.

"Sure, I did." Marie didn't look at him, just stared ahead at the windshield. "Whatever the hell is happening back there is spreading, is it not?"

"Yeah," he nodded. "I guess it is."

"Don't guess. I assure you it is. Which begs the question, how far will it expand? I think at this point it's the responsibility of anybody and everybody who wants humanity to carry on becoming involved. Though you can bet that's not what's going to happen. Even if they wanted to, it appears that the police will put a halt to their attempts."

Kyle considered this and concluded that she was at least right about the police. That had been apparent just today, when Bartlet had threatened to have them both locked up if they lifted a finger to help. And under normal circumstances that would have made sense, but if Marie was right, and this was some twisted version of a zombie outbreak, then it did, in fact, beg many questions—one of which was how far it would go.

But she was wrong, and he knew it because there was something that he hadn't yet shared with her. So, he told her it wasn't a disease.

"Pardon?"

"Yeah," he said. "You're right. It's spreading, but it's not a disease or anything like that."

"I get what you're saying," she responded. "And I agree we can safely say that it's supernatural. I saw a boy with his head hanging off his spine, walking upright like it was nothing more than a day at the park."

Kyle felt his jaw tighten as he shooed away images of his baby-brother with a broken neck, or more accurately, a neck which he had broken.

Marie said, "However, the supernatural is merely science that we don't yet understand, right? I mean if you rode a time-machine back a few hundred years and lit a match in front of the wrong people, they would burn you at the stake for witchcraft, simply because they hadn't yet advanced enough in their knowledge of the world to know better.

"Therefore, even if this thing is paranormal—and it clearly is—that doesn't make it *not* a disease. Follow?"

"Yeah, but it's not."

"Oh-kay?" She invited him to elaborate.

He said, "That boy with the broken neck—he was my brother—"

"I'm sorry, Kyle."

"Just listen. It was my brother, and before all that shit happened, I mean earlier tonight, he told me there was a monster in his room."

Marie hit the blinker, changed lanes. "So, you're saying that it's an entity, rather than a virus."

"Yeah. I guess."

She nodded. "I saw that you brought the computer. Did you get it on video?"

"I don't know. I haven't had a chance to look yet. I had it recording when it happened though."

"Okay. Well, that's a start, isn't it? We'll be able to ascertain more once we can watch that video. Until then, it's probably pointless to speculate any further, as it will only lead us to conclusions that may be refuted by what we see."

Kyle agreed and then they were quiet until the Beetle reached the exit that would take them into Lake McMurray. He directed her down a heavily wooded street and instructed her to pull up next to a mailbox at the end of a long driveway and kill the headlights.

"What now?" Marie whispered.

"I don't know, but I don't think we have to whisper."

"Oh. Right." She elevated to a normal volume, and it caused Kyle to jump, because for some reason it sounded obnoxiously loud in his ears. "You know we can't call her, right? Our phones can't, under any circumstances, come back on."

"Yeah. I get that. She doesn't have a phone anyway."

"Oh. Well, do you think we could just drive around looking for this cabin?"

"No way," he said. "We'd never find it. There's too many of them out here. I'm gonna have to sneak around and knock on her bedroom window."

"Do you know which window it is?"

But before she finished, he was already opening the door. He stepped out into the cold, where he once again heard crickets, and saw his breath turn to fog in front of his face. Leaning down, he stuck his head inside and said, "I'll be right back."

Marie nodded, shivered. Kyle shut the door as gently as he could manage, but cringed because it was still too loud. Then he tiptoed around the mailbox and down the gravel driveway toward Tara's brown house which looked like it had been assembled a hundred years ago. It was made from old, dirty wood and gave the impression that it would fall apart in a storm. There was a big window next to the front door with a white curtain hanging over it, and as far as he could tell, it was dark inside.

Tara's room was all the way around the back, next to the one which her two younger brothers shared, but the last time he had been over—only months ago—her bed had been by the window.

He crept up next to her mother's silver station wagon and there was a "click," as the porch light came on illuminating the ground all around him. At first, he thought he was caught, so he ducked behind the car. Then, realizing that he had merely gotten too close and activated the motion sensor, he shook his head and hurried around the side of the house.

Taking a deep breath, he held it in and listened for the front door. When it didn't open after what must have been a whole minute, he exhaled and tiptoed the rest of the way to Tara's window, which was low enough for him to look inside and see her sleeping on her stomach in a dark blue T-shirt with only a sheet covering her bottom half. The shirt rode high on her midsection, exposing a chubby waist that hung off to one side.

It took a few rounds of tapping on the glass, and when she finally sat up and glanced out, her eyes almost came out of their sockets. She looked like she was going to scream, and he thought that she would, but then she slid the window up and asked in a hushed tone what the hell he was doing here and why he was covered in blood.

Only then did it occur to Kyle McIntosh that he looked like he had just murdered somebody. Why hadn't he thought of that before? But what if he had? What could he have done about it—stop at a Laundromat? He didn't want to tell her that his family had been attacked the same way Dobey's had, because he'd thus far been making a point not to address it. He knew he would have to eventually but wasn't ready yet.

He needed to get to the cabin, though, so he sucked it up and told her everything except how he had just hidden her best friend's body in the woods, and he did it in as few words as possible, rejecting any and every tear that threatened to push its way out of him. Three minutes later Tara pulled on a pair of jeans and a black hoodie, and squeezed her plump body though her bedroom window.

***

Kyle let Tara sit up front so he wouldn't have to explain the blood all over the backseat, and Marie was quiet when she got into the car. The more time Kyle spent with her, the more he was becoming convinced that she was the smartest, most calculated person he had ever met, and he suspected she was merely feeling Tara out.

Tara was full of questions at first—

"Is it really the kids doing the killing?"

"Were there a lot of them?"

"What do you think's causing it?"

"How did you manage to get away?"

—and Kyle answered cautiously, making a point not to lie, nor to offer up any information that would be too much for her to believe. It was clear in her tone that she knew he was being evasive, but eventually she let up.

The cabin was only a few minutes away. It sat on a big piece of property, surrounded by trees, with no neighbors to be found. There was no electricity, no furniture, no carpet. It consisted of two stories, but sat on the side of a hill so they were able to access the upper half from a ground-level door which was unlocked. Kyle could see his breath even inside.

Tara shut the door and threw her arms around him, pulling him close the way that Laura had earlier. "I'm so sorry, Kyle."

"It's okay," he lied.

"No, it's not. I don't even know how you're coping right now. I'd be freaking the fuck out, dude. I just want you to know I'm here for you. Whatever you need. I promise."

You wouldn't be if you knew what I just did to Laura, he thought.

She pulled away and even in the dark he could see that some of Laura's blood had gotten on her sweater. Marie stood off to the side holding the laptop and watching, but she still didn't speak.

Finally, Tara turned and offered her hand. "Hi. I'm Tara."

"Marie." She accepted it.

"Thanks for giving him a ride."

"You're welcome," Marie maintained a neutral expression.

"This guy means a lot to me. To all of us, really. I ah—I don't think our circle would be the same without him."

"Yes," Marie nodded, "he's quite popular, I've gathered."

"I like your accent. You're the girl from England, right?"

"Oh. Ah, yes. Have we met?"

"No." She chuckled nervously. "No, sorry. Dobey said he was hanging out with a girl from England yesterday, or the other day, or whatever. Then when I heard you talk, I figured it must've been you."

"Right." Marie smiled, nodded. "I don't imagine there's a plethora of English girls pouring into that school."

"No," Tara agreed.

"Well, I reckon our next move ought to be to look in this thing here." She held the laptop up, and Tara examined it, tilting her head.

As Kyle explained that he had recorded what happened at his house, he made sure to omit everything about monsters and zombie-toddlers. If there was evidence on the video, it would speak for itself. If not, she would just think they were insane—or lying.

There were empty liquor bottles and beer cans scattered about, and Kyle wondered why Dobey and the rest of them wouldn't clean up after their parties to avoid being caught when the owners finally showed up. He guessed it was somebody's vacation home, which his friends had only discovered this year.

They chose a spot on the hardwood floor where Kyle and Tara sat Indian-style and Tara lit one of many small candles that were lying around. Then she used it to light a cigarette. Marie knelt on the other side of her, setting the laptop on the floor, and Tara scooted close to Kyle, leaning into him so he could smell remnants of her fruity shampoo mixed with tobacco smoke. He had never seen her without her strawberry blond hair saturated with product until now. It was frizzy and tangled.

Marie leaned forward, placing one hand on the floor and fidgeting with the laptop and even in spite of everything he had been through tonight, Kyle found himself memorizing the shape of her body almost as an involuntary reaction. Tara sucked on her cigarette, causing the end to light up and illuminate her face, then she let out a long stream of smoke.

When Marie returned to an upright position, she fanned her own face and coughed. "Is there a trick to turning this thing on?"

"Lemme see." Kyle reached over and pressed the power button, holding it down and waiting. Nothing happened. "You know what?" he said. "It was at thirty-three percent when I set it up. I'll bet the battery's dead."

"And there's no power here," Marie stated.

"I didn't bring the charger anyway."

"Oh dear. Well, that figures, doesn't it?"

"I mean I almost wasn't even able to bring the computer. I thought I was gonna die."

"Oh my God, Kyle," Tara piped. "I'm so sorry. I'm just really glad you're okay."

Marie said, "No, no, no. I'm not faulting you, mate. I didn't mean it like that. I was simply saying it's Murphy's Law."

"What's that?"

"Anything that can go wrong, will."

"Oh."

"I mean what are we gonna find on this thing?" Tara asked. "Just video of the kids attacking you? They know it's the kids doing the killings already. They've been talking about it on the news all day. They're saying it has to be some kind of a virus that you can only catch if you're under a certain age."

In his periphery, Kyle caught Marie giving one of her signals. It was something in her body language, and it was so subtle that it was impossible to pinpoint exactly what she was doing, but he caught it nonetheless and understood perfectly what she was trying to say.

Poker-face, mate. Conceal your hand.

There was no need, however, because he still had no intention of talking about Abel's monster. The problem was, he didn't know what else to say. So, he paused just long enough that hopefully she would get the hint and think of something.

"They arrested Dobey today," she said, and Kyle thought, *She's a mind reader or we're just really in sync. Either way, it's almost freaky.*

"Yeah," Tara took a long pull from her cigarette and flicked ashes onto the floor behind her. "I know. Everyone knows what happened. It's fucked up."

"Right." Marie coughed again. "Well, they didn't even care that his entire bloodline had just been eradicated, did they?"

Kyle tensed. A chill fell over him like tiny spiders crawling on every inch of his body. Then his heart sped up as anger boiled inside his chest.

Tara said, "Dude! That's a fucked-up way to put it."

"Well excuse me for being so forward, but it's a fucked-up thing that's happened, and this police lady who took your friend today—excuse me, yesterday—she didn't seem to care that he was suffering. I'm merely saying, they'll take Kyle in a heartbeat and not lose a moment's sleep over it."

Tara took a deep breath, flicked her cigarette again. "You were there?"

"Pardon?"

"When they took Dobey. You were at Laura's house? You saw?"

"Yes," Marie nodded toward Kyle. "We both were."

"Oh. Well, didn't Dobey have a warrant?"

Looking at Kyle, Marie said, "I believe so. Did he, Kyle?"

"Yeah," Kyle said.

"Either way," Marie pushed. "She also told Kyle that if he showed up at another crime-scene, she would have him locked up, and frankly, I believe her. That's why we need to see what's on this computer, because if Kyle's managed to catch the right video, it could vindicate him and secure his freedom."

And just like that, she had overcame any objection that Tara could possibly raise, using cold hearted indifference followed by a statement meant to invoke sympathy for Kyle. He realized it had all been by design, intended to invoke a protectiveness for him, and it had worked because Tara was now nodding with every word like a bobblehead.

The anger which he had been feeling only moments ago drained out of him as if a plug had been pulled, giving way to yet another level of admiration for this girl who was so smart that it was nearly a superpower. He guessed that even that was orchestrated by her, and at first, he wasn't sure how he should feel about it. Then he concluded that he should probably be grateful that the burden of thinking hadn't fallen on him, because after all, Kyle McIntosh was no Einstein.

"Okay. Lemme see." Tara popped the cigarette into her mouth, letting it hang there and lifting the laptop to her face. She inhaled, activating the cherry and allowing a better view of the device. "I have a charger that should fit this at home." Her words were obscured with her lips wrapped around the butt, so she set the computer down and plucked it back out. "If you drop me off on your way out, I'll hook it up and bring it back in the morning. I'd stay with you, Kyle, but my mom'll freak out if I'm not home when she gets up."

Kyle almost told her that he'd be okay. It's not like he was going to be alone. Then Marie did it again, and he bit his tongue. Tara hugged him for longer than he would have liked before leaving, and Marie hung back just long enough to whisper, "Wait here. I'll be right back."

***

The bigger babies were good at climbing, so up the trees they went. That's where they stashed the Halloween costumes. All but Abel and the others who had brought theirs from home when the monster took their breath. They kept theirs on, then the bigger kids came down and together they made their way through the forest and out of Mount Vernon.

***

Marie made sure the dome light was deactivated before she let Tara back into her car. She couldn't allow her to see the mess in the backseat. If she did, however, Marie would think of something. She was already planning for worst-case-scenario, but it seemed best to avoid it if possible.

Tara was quiet during the ride. So was Marie, but when they were once again parked next to the mailbox at the end of her driveway, Marie asked if Tara had an extra blanket. "For Kyle," she said. "He'll freeze tonight without one."

"Oh," Tara hesitated. "Are you, ah—are you going back out there?"

"Oh no. I mean, I'm not staying. I have to be getting home as well, or my parents will freak. But I'd drop him off a blanket if you had one."

So, Tara disappeared for close to four minutes, returning with an old quilted comforter, that might have been some shade of gray, but it was difficult to tell in the dark. It smelled of cigarette smoke and dust, but it was thick and likely warm.

She pushed it through the window, setting it on the passenger seat, then lingered long enough for the air to grow awkward. She was looking to be comforted, Marie knew. To be assured that this new English girl wouldn't be spending the night in the cabin with Kyle. She even slouched when she finally did leave, and it was impossible to tell whether or not it was for show, or she had tried to conceal her feelings

Marie didn't care one way or the other. She wasn't a nasty person, and under different circumstances she might have felt something for the chubby girl who liked a boy who didn't reciprocate the sentiment. But it seemed rather insignificant in light of everything else that had taken place tonight.

Plus, it was hard to conjure up sympathy when one was sure that her father was going to nearly kill her for running away. Not just running away, but taking off in a car which was in his name, and would probably be reported stolen in the morning. Marie wouldn't merely be doomed to Salvatore's wrath, which would surely be worse than it had ever been in the past, but she would be a felon as well.

Moreover, she couldn't bring herself to sympathize with Tara because the more she got to know Kyle, the more she became convinced that he was worth her trouble, and all was fair in love and war.

When she made it back to the cabin, she brought the blanket inside, noticing that it seemed to have grown colder in the short time that she was gone. At first, she didn't see Kyle. The candle was no longer lit, and the big open floor appeared desolate aside from loose trash, scattered at random. Shutting the door, she called, "Hello? Are you still here?"

"I'm here." His voice was low and monotone—almost a growl—echoing from the far end of the room. Marie glanced toward it, and still saw nothing.

"Are you alright?"

"Yeah."

As she approached, her foot connected with an aluminum can, and it caused her to jump. She didn't see him until she was halfway across the room and her eyes finally began to adjust. He was sitting in a corner, his knees propped up, his head down. Without a word, she set the blanket on the floor and sat next to him, so close that they were touching.

"I'm good," he said without looking up.

"Okay. I got us a blanket. Tara let us borrow it. Well, she let *you* borrow it."

"Why didn't you want her to know you were staying?"

"It wasn't that."

"No?"

"No."

Finally, he glanced up, and even in the dark there was nothing short of pure agony scrolled across his face.

Marie said, "She wouldn't have cared that I was staying here. But it was clear that she didn't want me staying with *you*. I know you might not have seen it, but believe me. I know girls. She has it bad for you, and there's no way she's going to help you to shack up with someone else. Not that that's what's happening or anything, but for all she knows it is.

"I know you trust her, and I don't doubt she's a good person, but jealousy is a green monster, and it can make good people justify, in their own minds, doing very bad things. I just thought it best we keep things on an even keel. I'm glad you picked up on it actually."

Kyle nodded, looked down again. "She'll be by in the morning. Are you gonna hide or something?"

"Don't be silly," Marie chuckled. "We'll just have to tell her I showed up right before she did to help the two of you out. Unless you and I are on the news tonight, in which case we'll have to play it by ear, I suppose. You wanna talk about it?"

"About what?"

"Well, if we're still in this together, and I'm not just along for the ride, I imagine we'll have to eventually discuss whatever happened before I arrived at your house, but that can wait for now. Would you like to discuss what's on your mind?"

"No. Not really."

"Fair enough. You think you'll be able to sleep?"

"I don't really know, to be honest."

She nodded. "Well, would you lie with me so we can at least keep warm while I sleep? I would have asked for two blankets, but it would have aroused suspicion. This one's big enough that it should fit both of us though."

At first, Kyle didn't answer, and Marie's heart beat like a drumroll because she was sure he either never would, or he was thinking of an excuse to reject her. Then he said, "I killed the candle."

"Yes." Marie had always prided herself on her ability to remain neutral in just about any situation. An ability which she credited her father for, as it had arisen as a survival mechanism in response to his cruelty. Now, however, she was aware that her voice shook, and she couldn't help but hate herself a bit for it. "I saw that."

Kyle said, "I—ah, I've never been here, you know. I mean I didn't see any houses nearby, but maybe someone can see from across the lake or something. Or maybe people drive up to check on the place for the owners. I didn't want anybody to know I was here."

"Makes sense," Marie took a deep breath, recovered and listened because it was the right thing to do.

"Then I got kinda freaked out. I mean, I've never been afraid of the dark or anything, but I, ah—I mean I don't know."

"I think I get it," she said.

"Maybe. Or maybe you don't. I don't think I would've got it a few hours ago, to tell you the truth. I wasn't freaked out because it was dark though. I mean it wasn't because I killed the candle. It just happened to kick in around that time. It was this crazy feeling—and trust me, I know it's crazy—but this feeling like those kids were right outside. So, I opened the door and stepped like halfway out, and all I could hear was the crickets and the wind blowing through the woods and obviously there was no one there, but it still *felt* like there was." He glanced at her once again. "Does that make sense?"

Marie nodded, and Kyle averted his gaze as he went on.

"So, then it was like they were in the woods. But I know that's not true either. I mean even if they were coming this way—and I'm sure they're not—there's no way they could be here now. It's too far. I mean it would take all night on foot. But like I said, I know they're not coming here. It was just a feeling.

"So, then I realized why I was having it. And it was—ah, well I guess it was just because I was alone. I don't think I wanna be alone right now. So, what I'm trying to say is thank you for being here with me. We can talk. I promise I'll tell you whatever you wanna know about what happened tonight, but maybe later? Would that be cool?"

Marie wanted to give him a hug. To put her arm around him and hold him tight and tell him that he wouldn't have to be alone ever because she would always be here with him. It didn't even have to be true, as long it was true for now. She wanted to make him feel better. But she didn't dare touch him because he hadn't gone for a kiss yesterday, and he hadn't said he would lay with her, even just to keep warm. So instead, she said, "Yes. That would be cool. Maybe we could speak about it tomorrow."

After that there was a long silence, in which she was sure that she could hear the same crickets that he had just spoken of. Then he said, "I wish there was a broom in here. The floor's probably covered in about an inch of dust—or dirt." He climbed slowly to his feet and offered her his hand. Accepting it, she allowed him to help her up, then she watched as he grabbed the comforter and examined it.

He swept his feet across the floor, clearing all the rubbish by the wall away, and laying the blanket down. Then he kicked off his shoes and an irrational sense of relief fell over Marie.

"Your clothes are bloody," she told him. "I mean, so are mine after we—well so are mine. But yours are really bad. I was actually bewildered when Tara didn't ask about them."

Kyle laughed, and even though she could tell it was forced, it made what she meant to say next a bit easier.

"We should probably take them off anyway, as it will allow us to share body-heat. It's nothing sexual, but it well and truly is going to get cold tonight. It already is if I'm being perfectly honest, but it will only get worse, I can assure you of that."

She grew tense as she spoke, but before she had even finished, Kyle was slipping out of his jacket. He dropped it onto the floor, and Marie's OCD flared. She found herself resisting the urge to pick it up, fold it, and set it neatly somewhere. Then he took the hem of his shirt in both hands and brought it up over his head, and while his eyes were covered, hers scanned his slim body.

She averted her gaze quickly, however, then kicked off her shoes and began to slip her pants down, wiggling her hips and making sure not to look to see if he was watching her. The cold nipped at her skin like mosquitoes all over her legs, but she ignored it.

Bending down, she picked up the sweats and folded them so nicely that if somebody didn't know that her parents were billionaires, he or she would have assumed that she worked in retail. Then she set them down and pulled off her shirt, willing herself not to give in to embarrassment at the fact that she was now standing on the cold wooden floor of a dirty cabin in which she had broken into, in nothing but her socks, a black thong and an unmatching white bra.

Only then did she finally glance over at him, and as if she were standing in front of a mirror, he looked at the exact same time. He had been shivering, his hands up near his waist, but stopped, dropped them, and played it cool as their eyes met. Then both sets began to explore each other's bodies. It was brief—just a quick scan—but she knew that it didn't go unnoticed on either end.

Kyle wore blue boxer-shorts that were too baggy for his small frame, but he either didn't know this, or he was unapologetic, and therefore unscathed. He sat down and pulled off his socks as she folded her own shirt and set it on top of her pants. Then, he shivered again and lay back on the blanket, so she hurriedly slipped out of her own socks and plopped down on her side next to him.

Kyle was the first to break the silence. "Here. Lemme—ah—" He reached over her body, spread the blanket on top of them, and tucked it under his back.

"Thanks." Marie laid her head on his arm and her hand on his chest. His fumbled, seeming not to know where it belonged, so she caught it and set it on her waist. Then she reached out of the blanket and brushed hair from her face before returning to her previous position.

"No problem," he said.

That's when she felt him begin to grow beneath the surface of his boxers. It pressed against her, but he didn't pull back, or even flinch, and she found, to her surprise, that she didn't want him to.

Marie had only ever been with Ian. And even then, she had made him wait more than a year. That was what her father hadn't seemed to understand when he had broken her arm for being a harlot, in spite of the fact that she had still been a virgin at the time. She wasn't the type of girl to sleep around, or to give into a boy whom she had just met.

But somehow this was different. There weren't words for how—none that she could conjure at least—it just was. And it didn't even cross her mind to resist because what his body wanted—well she wanted it as well. So, she looked up and she pressed her face into his and instantly recognized the sensation of warm tears.

They fell out of him and onto her, soaking her lips. So instead of kissing him, she wrapped her hand around the back of his head and pulled him close as his body began to jerk against hers. He sniffed and he sobbed, and his tears wet her hair, and neither spoke for what had to have been the next hour. Then Kyle fell into a deep sleep, but not Marie. She lay awake most of the night with restless legs, contemplating what the next move needed to be.

Chapter Nine

Guards banged on Gabriel Brenton's door with a thick metal key, and woke him out of a dead sleep. It was only his second night in the Intensive Management Unit, and had it not been for the intimacy that he shared with his Creator, he knew it would have been torture. Not because the hole was so bad, but because being alone right now would have given him nothing to do but fixate on what had happened to Carrie and Kim.

But that's not what he had done. He had spent the hours between slumber and reading a Bible which had been left by whomever had occupied the cell before him, on his knees in communion with God.

He hadn't prayed for Kimberly to be okay, because he wasn't stupid and he already knew that she wasn't okay. She was dead somewhere, along with the others who had been taken. Instead, he had prayed that the Lord would receive her soul, and Carrie's as well. He had prayed for a heart to forgive his wife, who hadn't cheated on him, but rather turned her back on him at his lowest. He had prayed for peace and serenity for himself and their families. But most of all, he had prayed for a deeper walk with Christ.

As a result, his stay had been surprisingly peaceful, even in spite of all the banging and yelling under metal doors, which perpetually echoed within the unit, and sometimes induced insanity in those doing long stints. Then, when it had finally quietened down on Saturday night (or maybe it was Sunday morning), guards woke him up and informed him that it was time to go. It wasn't until he was cuffed, shackled, and inside the cage in the back of a white DOC van that he learned that Carrie's funeral had been moved from Tuesday to Sunday.

Even in late October, the fields in Eastern Washington were burnt yellow and brown, but Gabe didn't see them because it was still dark when they left the State Penitentiary in Walla Walla. The sun didn't attempt to shine through the clouds and the fog until just before the desert disappeared and all at once the landscape turned green.

And though tree-ridden Western Washington was his home, had been for most of his life, something about the change in setting made him uneasy. He figured that somewhere in the part of his mind that chose to entertain bleak possibilities, he had resigned to the idea that he might never see home again. That he might never leave Walla Walla.

It wasn't, after all, too farfetched of a possibility, as Walla Walla was the end of the line as far as Washington State correctional facilities were concerned. It housed the worst, most hardened criminals in the system, most of whom were serving life sentences.

Gabe had gone to a few of the church services advertised in the day room, and been mildly flabbergasted to see meek preachers, who volunteered weekly to step into the notorious penitentiary and attempt to deliver the Word in rooms which were packed with disinterested gang members having private meetings of their own. Once, even when he sat up front, the conversations had been so loud that he couldn't hear a word the preacher had said.

And it wasn't just a Nietzschean indifference toward good and evil which abounded there, but rather a cold-hearted affinity for the evil. Brutality was praised and mercy not merely frowned upon, but loathed, along with anybody who displayed or promoted it. Gabe realized early on that Walla Walla was the devil's playpen.

He had only wound up there by default due to his age and the violent nature of his crime. But once there, he had been forced to embrace—at least outwardly—the mentality and resultant lifestyle. If the whites found out about his faith, and what he did for them to keep the peace, it could mean his life. And if he had to take a life to protect his own or somebody else's, it would mean a life sentence.

So, when the bare landscape vanished, and the van was surrounded by trees, rather than giving into a sense of nostalgia, he shook off all notions that he was home because that wasn't true yet. Nothing was guaranteed until the day he stepped out of prison without metal around his wrists and ankles. This was merely a vacation, and one which he would have preferred not to be taking.

Not just that, but the forest brought to mind thoughts that he had thus far been able to reject. Thoughts of his daughter in a shallow grave somewhere amongst so many others that the ground was hollow.

Two correctional officers sat up front—one driving, the other, a chubby guy with a beard, who was there for nothing more, it seemed than to talk the driver's ear off—

but they hadn't acknowledged Gabe much during the ride until now, as the passenger turned in his seat and asked, "You hungry, man?"

Gabe had picked at a DOC issued sack lunch, consisting of a pint of milk, an apple, and two peanut butter and jelly sandwiches, but none of it had sat well with the motion-sickness he was feeling after not being on the road in such a long time.

When he didn't answer, the C.O. said, "'Cause if you can keep yer mouth shut about it, we was thinkin' we could get some burgers or somethin'."

Gabe had heard tales of prisoners in transport being given fast food by the guards, but just assumed that they were nothing more than bullshit fantasies, and with him they accomplished little more than to drive home how dehumanized he had become.

Prison food was so tasteless that somehow ramen noodles and other instant meals which could be prepared simply by adding water were practically delicacies to his tastebuds. If somebody tossed a rib on the day-room floor, he imagined men would swoop in and fight for it like dogs. A cheeseburger, even from the dollar menu at the drive-thru, seemed in Gabe's mind like some mythical treasure that didn't even exist anymore.

And now that he thought about it, the stories probably *were* bullshit, not meant to invoke jealousy in other prisoners, but to suggest that even the guards respected whoever was telling them. Gabe, however, always got the impression that they did respect him. They searched his cell. They saw the hidden Bibles. They knew he was in charge, and they saw the reduction in violence.

The thought of fast food brought the hint of a smile to his face, but he concealed it and told the guard that he could eat. What he didn't do was get his hopes up or even say a silent prayer about it, because though his prayer life had increased a thousand percent in the past two days, that's not what prayer was for.

Still, a half hour later, the van pulled to the side of the road, and the fat guard exited, sliding the door open, and tossing a children's meal next to him on the hard plastic seat. And though he wasn't given the beverage to go with it, it was still the best meal he had ever eaten.

***

Kyle woke up in the morning shivering because it was cold as hell. The blanket had come untucked from under his back and the humid air was pressed against his bare skin. Marie was asleep, breathing heavily on his chest. At some point in the night, he seemed to have wrapped his arms around her and not let go. Raindrops drummed on the roof so hard it sounded like there was a waterfall outside. It reminded him like a slap to the face that he had cried himself to sleep in *her* arms.

He had been so sure that he wouldn't be able to rest, and he had promised himself that he wouldn't succumb to tears again—not until this thing was over at least. But then she had laid with him and set her head on his shoulder, and something had happened inside his chest that hadn't happened since the day he had been sure he loved Claudia. He and Marie had both been practically naked, though, and Kyle had been feeling so many things all at once that he didn't know what was what anymore.

He had been sure they were going to hook up, and even after the night he had had, he was prepared to do it because maybe—just maybe—it would have made him feel better. Then, before he even knew they were coming, the tears had forced their way out of him, and Marie hadn't given any indication that she was judging him for being weak.

Still, he'd blinked and blinked, and he'd tried to order them back to where they came from because crying wouldn't undo anything that had happened, or solve anything for that matter. And to make it worse, every time he had closed his eyes, he saw the horrible fucking orange lights from the faces of the murderous children. But then Marie had touched him in a way that nobody ever had before. A way that said she cared that he was hurting. So, he had lost control and given into her.

Now he was awake, and the lights were gone, and Kyle was shivering, but he was fully erect under the blanket and pressed against her and it felt good, so he found himself wondering if it would be all right to give her a kiss.

It wasn't dark anymore, but it wasn't bright either. Glancing toward one of several windows, he attempted to gauge the time, and saw nothing but light grey clouds, blurred by thick rain. Maybe early-to-mid morning. Maybe later. It was impossible to tell in this weather.

A layer of dust coated the floor beneath scattered party paraphernalia behind Marie's head, and a few feet away, her clothes sat folded like they belonged on a shelf in a department store. Ironically, Kyle's clothes normally would have been folded with the same meticulousness. Last night, however, he hadn't had the energy to do much more than cry.

The place was a mess, and probably ridden with rodents and spiders, but it had kept them out of the rain. He glanced down at Marie again and thought, *You could probably do it. She might not wake up, and even if she did, she might not mind.*

Then he thought about his dog, lying dead amidst his own organs like an exploded hot pocket.

Stop it. Not today. You did that last night, and you even cried, and you got it all out. So don't do it again today. Don't think about any of them and don't you dare cry again. You already know this isn't gonna end well, and when it does, then you can think and cry all you want if you're still alive. But not today.

So, he shut his eyes and thought about the fight he'd had with Silencer yesterday. He thought about the brass-knuckles that he now owned, and whether or not the cholo would want to fight him again to get them back. He thought about the marijuana roach in his pocket. Kyle McIntosh thought about everything except his dead family and the body that he'd left in the woods last night at Riverview Park.

Then he thought once more about kissing Marie, and before he could put any more thought into it, he leaned down and placed his mouth right above her eyebrow, feeling his bottom lip, still slightly swollen. When he pulled away, he stared down at her for a long moment, until her mouth curved up into a smile, but her eyes remained closed.

"Good morning." Her voice was soft.

"Hey."

Finally, she opened them, gazing into his and yawning. "Goodness. What time is it?"

"I don't know. The phones are off."

"Right." She shifted against him, and he wondered if she felt what was happening beneath his boxers. Of course, she did. How could she not? She gave no indication though, and to his surprise, he wasn't embarrassed in the slightest.

"It must still be early," he said.

"Because your friend hasn't shown up yet?"

"Yeah."

She touched his chest, rubbed it lightly. "Are you cold?"

"Why?"

"You're shivering. Here—" Sliding her hand over the surface of his arm, she reached around him, her chest pressing against his, along with their lower bodies. It caused a wave of electric pleasure to sail over the surface of his skin, expanding out in all directions. He felt her warm breath on his neck as she tucked the blanket once again under him, then rubbed his back as if to heat it with friction. "Is that better?"

Kyle didn't answer. He felt his own breath growing shallow and his body tense. It wasn't because he was nervous. He wasn't. He had only been naked with Claudia and one other girl in the eighth grade, and with both of them he had been nervous as hell the first time.

But with Marie there was no anxiety. Not last night, and not now. He wasn't sure if she was exceedingly disarming, or they had crazy chemistry, but being here with her—like this—felt not only natural, but right. Even though being here with her, at its root, meant that something terrible had transpired. Somehow everything was exactly as it should be.

No, he wasn't nervous, but something was happening inside him. Stirring and stirring and brewing and bubbling and it had been triggered not by the kiss, but by her reaction to it.

She smiled. She was awake, or maybe it woke her up, but she smiled before she even opened her eyes.

And what was boiling inside Kyle was nothing short of red-hot desire for this girl. Maybe even love. And it was taking control of his most basic functions, and he had already kissed her, and they had slept naked together, and he had cried in her arms like a damn infant, so why not just give into it?

Before he even knew what he was doing, his eyes were closed, and her face was in his hand. His lips pressed against hers, and he reflected briefly on the fact that it was morning, and he hadn't brushed his teeth. Then her nails dug into his back, lightly at first, and her lower half nudged against his so hard that he felt his abdomen tighten and all thoughts of dental hygiene vanished like a ghost in the light.

He pushed back and her leg moved slowly up and over his body, brushing his skin on its way. She wrapped it around him and pulled him closer, her tongue slipping into his mouth. Soon they were rocking against one another, and his hand was exploring parts of her body that hadn't been affected by the cold.

He threw the blanket off them and climbed between her legs, kissing her neck, then working his way down to her breasts. Her fingertips combed the hair on the back of his head, and he opened his eyes as he took her black panties by the lace, slipping them down and wondering if she would stop him.

She didn't. Instead, she lifted her hips, then her legs, allowing him to easily slide them over her feet. Sitting up, he examined the thong for a moment, glanced toward her neatly stacked clothes, and began to fold it for her.

But Marie sat up and took it from him, tossing it to the side and reaching back with both hands to unclasp her bra. It fell loose and she tossed it with the panties as Kyle stood up and removed his boxers.

Then Marie was on her knees, and she took him in both hands and opened her mouth, but he pushed her back down and made love to her on top of the comforter even though it was cold as hell and there were still traces of Laura Cunningham's blood on his hands.

***

They lay together for a while after, and though Kyle could have laid there forever, they both knew they needed to be up and dressed before Tara arrived. Along with no electricity, there was no plumbing in the cabin, so Kyle went outside shirtless to relieve himself under a covered area by the door.

It was an absolute downpour, and it was freezing; he noticed the dried blood on his hands and forearms while he was holding his member. So, once he was done, he stepped out into the rain and began to scrub it off. When it didn't work, he used dew from nearby bushes, then went back inside, finding Marie fully clothed with her pink hood over her head. She slipped out the door without a word, bumping into him on the way.

She's leaving, he thought, picking his T-shirt up off the floor. *She's gonna get into her car and ditch you now.*

And as he was having this thought, her car-door opened and closed again, and he knew that he was right.

It was the sex. It wasn't good enough. And you know what? That's probably the same reason Claudia left. Even if it wasn't that, something about you will never be good enough to keep a girl around, and the sooner you accept that, the better it'll be for you.

He didn't move for the door, didn't even flinch. If she wanted to go, he wasn't going to beg her not to, or even raise an objection. He would sit alone in this cabin with nothing to do but think about all the things he had committed not to think about, along with the fact that he had been once again, abandoned. He would probably pace, and he might cry again, and maybe he would even break one of the many glass bottles on the floor and slice a couple of his veins open before Tara showed up.

Then the car-door opened and shut again, and Marie returned with her black purse hanging at her side. She strolled over and planted a kiss on his lips as he was examining his shirt, which was stiff and crusted with a thick layer of dried blood. She took it from him, then leaned down and picked up his jacket.

"Just put this on for now. We'll get you something else to wear later." Folding the shirt, she set it, along with her purse, in the corner. "Are you hungry?"

Kyle slipped into the jacket and zipped it all the way up. It had blood on it as well, but not nearly as much, and the polyester material would be easy to clean. He said, "Not really. Thirsty, though."

"You should eat anyway. You're probably hungry and you just don't know it because of your nerves. I was wondering if there's somewhere nearby where we could get food without being seen by too many people."

Kyle thought about it. There was a gas station by the freeway, with a small diner inside, but if the police were looking for them, and they had any suspicion that they were in town, that would be the most obvious place for an ambush. Lake McMurray didn't have much to it as a town, which was evident by the fact that it didn't even have a high school.

This begged the point that if they *did* suspect that Kyle was in town, it was only because they knew that he had a friend here, and they would be watching Tara's house. He had texted Marie, and called her right before the attack, so they would know that they were together as well and be looking for her car.

He told Marie this, and she went into deep thought for a moment, then said, "You may be right."

"I mean I'm not saying that's the case," he replied.

"I know. I know. But we do need to consider worst case scenario, don't we?" He didn't answer because it wasn't really a question. She seemed to be looking through, rather than at him as she spoke. "In fact, as much as I hate to say it, seeing as how we went through so much trouble to get here, I don't know if it's a good idea for us to stay. Especially with Tara planning to come back this morning.”

“Why not?” Kyle scanned the room, searching for a chair or even a bucket to sit on, and finding nothing.

As if on the same thought-wave, Marie took a seat on the blanket and said, “Because, if they’re watching her house in order to find us—or even just you—they’ll follow her here.”

“Shit.”

“Shit is right.”

“Then should we—”

“Probably, but not without a plan. We need that computer, and I need to know if there are any alternative routes out of this town which don’t involve passing Tara’s house or using that freeway ramp. First, however, I want to talk about something else. Would you like to sit down?”

Kyle hesitated, thinking, *Here it comes. She’s gonna tell you how you’re a really nice guy and she’s glad she met you, but she needs to drop you off somewhere and get home.*

She smoothed out the blanket next to her and gazed up at him expectantly, half-smiling, urging him with her eyes. So, he plopped down a few inches away, and she scooted so close they were touching.

“You asked me a question last night, and I wanted the opportunity to answer, and to hopefully hear what happened before I picked you up. Would that be okay?”

And though talking about what had happened wouldn’t be okay, or anything that even resembled okay (In fact, he might have preferred that she *did* ditch him, over having to relive last night), he knew that it had to happen. He’d known since the talk in her car, so he lied and said it would be okay, asking what question she was referring to that he had asked.

"Why Laura was with me," she responded. "You asked and I think that you deserve an answer." She took his hand, squeezed it tightly, setting it in her lap and not letting go. "I still think it's important we put everything we both know out on the table in order to move forward intelligently, don't you?"

Kyle took a deep breath, nodded.

"Good," she said. "Would you like for me to go first?"

"I don't know. I mean, I don't care."

"It's nothing major, I'm afraid. I mean, it might be, depending on how you view things. But I felt bad for the way we brushed her off yesterday, so when I got home, I contacted her via social media to apologize. Or at least to be nice and clear the air.

"She asked for my phone number, so I sent it and she called me from some boy's phone."

"Jesse's?" Kyle asked.

"I don't know. Does he live near Waugh Road?"

"Uh, no. Not really. He doesn't have a phone either."

"Then no. I imagine it wasn't Jesse's. I heard the guy in the background, and he sounded much older. She was at his house drinking or something, and as it turned out, he lived close to me.

"Laura was still very distraught. I didn't tell her anything that we had concluded together, but tried to comfort her. Then you called, and I told her to wait while I accepted it. When I switched back over and told her I was going to get you, she insisted I pick her up on the way. Well, she practically begged me.

"I suspected it was something to do with the guy, because he was in the background objecting and telling her to stay. But there was an urgency in her voice, and as a girl, I felt compelled to help. Plus, she said she could meet me outside, and it wouldn't even be out of the way. So, I picked her up and rushed to you, and I suppose the rest is history."

Kyle thought about whose house Laura might have been at. There was nobody in their social circle who matched the description though. He asked, "Why would that be something major?"

"Pardon?" He felt her hand tense.

"You said, 'depending on—' What was it you said?"

"Oh. Right." She released her grip, leaving his hand resting by itself on her leg, then brushed her hair behind her ear. "Depending on how you view things. Well, I suppose there's really not much of a reason to disclose this, but as long as we're operating with complete transparency—it's the way that I located Laura's profile."

Kyle's hand began to feel naked and awkward where it sat, so he took it back and attempted to rub a knot out of the back of his neck. "I don't get it."

"No. No, you wouldn't, I suppose. So, I may have cyber-stalked you a bit before I texted the other night."

"Cyber-stalked?"

"Not *really* stalked. I was being hyperbolic."

"What does that even mean?"

"I don't know actually. I mean, I know what it means," she giggled nervously, "but it may not actually be a word. What I meant to say, is: I was using hyperbole. It was an exaggeration. When your mate put your number in my phone, I used it to find your online profiles before I actually contacted you."

"Oh." Kyle considered this. "Why?"

"I don't know." She shrugged. "It's a new school in a new town. I didn't know anybody yet. You were a cute boy. Anyway, obviously I found Laura on your friends list."

He heard everything she said, but all that registered was "cute boy." He found himself wishing that she had shown up in Mount Vernon before all of this craziness had begun to unfold. But what if she had? Kyle would have still been with Claudia. Would their paths have even crossed, and if they had, would he have given her the time of day?

He supposed Marie had come into his life at just the right time for things between them to have unfolded the way that they did. But it was a time in which it seemed their story would have to end as a tragedy, rather than a romance, because it was looking like they would either end up dead, or in prison.

He told her everything relevant which had transpired from the time she dropped him off, until when she picked him up, and was relieved, but a bit perplexed as well that it invoked no emotion this time around.

When he was done, Marie said, "That's very peculiar."

"Yeah?" he snickered. "Which part?"

"I just wonder why they would be spewing water?"

"The river," he said matter-of-factly.

She tilted her head, inviting him with her eyes to elaborate.

"The river's just across the main road from my neighborhood. That must be where they were hiding."

"Really?"

"It makes sense, right? I mean if they're dead—which now I'm sure they are. Did you smell them?"

Frowning, Marie nodded.

"Then they could just hang out under water for as long as they have to, right?"

"I suppose." But her tone was skeptical.

"And it's not like they'd be holding their breath or anything. So, their lungs and their stomachs would fill up."

"Okay," Marie looked like she might vomit, "I get it. Enough please."

It's not like you had to see it up close, he thought, but didn't say. Instead, he said, "I hadn't thought about it when I called nine-one-one last night, or I would have told them to look in the river."

"You think they went back in there?"

"I don't know, but there's always the possibility, right? We should probably figure out a way to get that information to the police as soon as possible."

Marie said, "Slow down, sweetheart. Don't go getting ahead of yourself. Remember that all it takes is one wrong move and we're caught. For instance, even if we can make it out of this area, and we drive into the next town to make the call, they'll know we're moving south, won't they?"

"Well, yeah, but we can't just *not* tell them. People are dying."

"Of course. I understand that. I'm merely saying we need to be smart about how we do it. I don't see any point in making multiple calls, so we should probably find out what's on that laptop first. That way we can deliver all the information at once, don't you think?"

Kyle thought about it, then asked how they were supposed to get the computer if they couldn't wait for Tara to show up or even go near her house.

"Well obviously we'll have to go near her house," Marie answered. "It's just going to be a matter of how we get there, isn't it?"

***

They left the car where it was parked in front of the cabin and walked along the thin, wooded street toward Tara's house, keeping a close eye on the path ahead. The first sign of a police car—or any vehicle for that matter—

parked outside, and they would turn around and head back the way they had come. But the road was deserted. Nobody drove by, and even birds couldn't be heard singing over the rain as it poured through trees and bushes.

Marie ducked down and stayed close to Kyle, as if he could somehow protect her from the rain and he suspected that Ian was taller than her. And that if Ian were here, Kyle would be dead this morning because Marie wouldn't have shown up to rescue him last night. And that Ian had never cried himself to sleep in her arms, and he wondered for the first time why Marie had let him inside her because Ian was her boyfriend, wasn't he?

At one point, he glanced down a long driveway, and saw the front door of a two-story house slightly open, which meant that it must have been late enough in the morning for people to be up and about. So why hadn't Tara shown up yet? He thought about it, remembering that her mom took Sundays off. She was probably having trouble getting out of the house.

They didn't speak much until they were close enough to see Tara's old beat-up mailbox. Then they stopped altogether, and Kyle wiped rain from his face and squinted for a better view.

The plan was simple, because it was the only plan that made any sense. They would sneak around the house and hope that Tara was in her bedroom. It was unlikely that her mother or either of her siblings would be outside in the rain anyway.

As it turned out, it was clear. If the house was being watched, it was happening from somewhere in the forest, and even though Kyle was no Einstein, he knew the likelihood of that was slim to none.

But when they made it to the driveway, they found it bare. Tara's mom's car was gone. So, they peeked in every window, found the place empty, and broke in through one that was unlocked.

Kyle's computer was under Tara's bed, fully charged. But when he opened it and started to watch the video, Marie took him by the wrist and pulled him toward the door.

"Not here," she whispered. "We need to leave before somebody comes home."

He considered telling her that there was no need to whisper, then just followed instead.

***

Kyle grew sick to his stomach near the end of the video. There was close to three hours of footage, and the monster didn't show up until the end. After Tina McIntosh had tucked Abel in, the child had cried in his bed, silently with his pillow over his face for close to ten minutes. Then he had fallen asleep and there had been no activity for what seemed like forever.

Kyle and Marie sat on the blanket in the cabin, skipping over most of this portion. The bottom right-hand corner of the screen told them that it was close to ten in the morning. They had to stop and go back when they saw orange light hovering over Abel.

Marie gasped, covered her mouth.

They watched as it appeared, and it only took a second to register that there were two of them, like hovering bulbs, which shone as if they should have been accompanied by a smile. The wind was blowing, somehow whistling inside the boy's room, and Abel was laying on his side, sniffing into his pillow.

The shadows were everywhere. Every-fucking-where, but they were coming off the hovering eyes, like Medusa's reptilian hair, dancing and squirming on Abel's walls. The wind blew the child's hair, but it wasn't really the wind because it was forming words which made Kyle's bones want to crumble inside his skin.

"Why are you so scared, Abel? Why don't you like me? I'm not gonna do anything to you that you won't thank me for later. I just wanna take you trick-or-treating. You wanna go trick-or-treating, don't you?"

Abel whined something so quietly that Kyle couldn't make out what was said.

"You don't wanna go with your stupid brother. You know you don't, and so do I. He lied to you, didn't he? He said he wouldn't tell anyone about me if you told him, and it was a lie. A big, fat, stupid lie. And do you wanna know something else, Abel? I know you do, and I wanna tell you.

"He thinks you're stupid. He talks about you to that girl—what's her name? Claudia? The one with the boobies. He tells her you're retarded because you talk funny, and they laugh when you're not around. I'll bet you didn't know that, did you?"

Kyle's chest heaved and any fear that he had previously felt of whatever this thing was, began to dissipate, replaced by a rage that made him want to pick up the computer and smash it against a wall. He had never once in his life, not even before he was old enough to know better, made fun of his brother for his disabilities.

The monster went on, "Everybody thinks it, Abel. They all think you're a fucking dummy, don't they? Not me though. I know better. I know just how special you are, and that's why I'm here. It's why I chose you to come with me and all my other pretty children. I needed you to know, though. I needed you to understand how they all feel about you. You do understand, don't you, Abel?"

Abel let out another sequence of words, the only one of which Kyle could make out was, "Please."

Then the monster laughed, and the bed began to shake. Kyle's fear returned because even on video, the whistling laughter was the most skin-crawling sound that had ever tickled his ears. The bed shook like a gigantic phone set to vibrate, and the springs squealed the way they had when Kyle and Claudia had made love on top of it. The monster laughed and it laughed, and it grew in volume until the wind blew so hard that Abel's bedspread rippled, and his hair was tossed about.

The child squinted and opened his mouth. His expression hardened just before he pulled the covers over his face and curled into a ball underneath.

The monster said, "You know I don't need your permission, right? I don't need you to tell me I can do it, because I do whatever I want, whenever I want. I take what I want, and I want you, Abel. But you're gonna love being with me, I can promise you that."

Then the blanket flew off the bed like a tablecloth pulled by a waiter and Abel seemed to look directly into the camera. His eyes appeared as if they would fly right out of his skull as every shadow on every wall advanced on him like cobras. Some wrapped around his wrists, others around his ankles and he was stretched out toward the four corners of his bed. He opened his mouth again and Kyle tensed, bracing himself to hear his brother scream.

But before a sound could escape the six-year-old, another shadow fell over his face, covering his mouth as he writhed and attempted to kick and fight. The bed continued to shake and Abel's back arched, then the video ended because the battery had died.

Kyle sat wide-eyed, his jaw hanging, his heart thumping against his chest. He wasn't sure what he was feeling, aside from the fact that the floor seemed to be sinking beneath his bottom. Whatever had come over him, however, Marie must have recognized, because she straightened up and threw her arms around him, pulling his face into her chest.

His first reaction was to jerk away. But he wasn't sure he had the energy right now, so he didn't even try. Instead, he kept his hands in his lap, feeling his entire body stiffen as he stared into the pink fabric of her hoody.

At first, he thought he might cry again, and he didn't care that he didn't have the strength to fight that either, because he had just watched his baby-brother be smothered to death in his bed by a fucking spirit that claimed it wanted to take him trick-or-treating.

But no tears surfaced, or even threatened to try and find their way out of him. It may have been because he was dehydrated, but he suspected it was because the anger he was feeling overshadowed his sorrow, his fear—everything else that had ever existed inside him.

***

Kyle stood up. He paced. Marie sniffed, and he glanced down briefly and saw her wiping tears from her face. Then his foot collided with an empty cigarette pack and he focused on the dirty floor in front of him.

"He was dead. When I saw him lying in the bed, he was dead already. It was all just an act, so why didn't he kill me then and there?" But he wasn't actually asking anybody. Just thinking out loud.

"I think we need to move," Marie said.

Finally, Kyle stopped, glance down at her again, but didn't speak. Her face was flushed, but there were no more tears as she went on.

"Obviously they're not watching Tara's house, or we wouldn't be here. We would've been arrested already. But that doesn't mean they won't show up later. Maybe they're questioning her right now."

Kyle took a deep breath. "You think that's where she is?"

"I don't really know, honey. It makes sense that if they called her in, her mother would drive her, though, doesn't it?"

"Why do you keep doing that?"

"Pardon?"

"You keep calling me things like sweetheart and honey."

Marie's eyes narrowed. "Does it bother you?"

"I don't—I mean, no. But don't you have a boyfriend?"

"Excuse me?"

"Ian, right? Don't you have a boyfriend back in England?"

"Are you kidding me right now?" she raised her voice. "Do you think that I would have—Gee, thanks Kyle. Thanks for thinking so highly of me."

"What? I'm just going off what you said yesterday."

"Whatever." Marie crossed her arms. "I won't call you anything besides 'Kyle' from now on."

"I didn't mean—"

"I don't care, Kyle. It's unimportant at this point. We need to figure out what our next move is, don't we?"

But for some reason, it was important to him. Even in light of what he had just witnessed on his computer. He told her, "Look, I'm sorry. I didn't mean to be a dick. I ah—I'm really upset right now and I'm not handling it too good if you can't tell."

Marie paused, examining his face as if for any trace of insincerity. Then she smiled warmly and said, "'Too well', not 'too good'. And that's all you have to say. You didn't have to take it out on me."

"I know. Trust me, I'm really grateful that you're here, and that you showed up last night. I just—"

"Ian and I broke up."

"Oh. Sorry."

"Don't be. It's not your fault. It wasn't going to work, long distance anyway. Listen, I'm very sorry about what you just had to watch. You have every right to be upset right now. Trust me, I get it. But doing so won't accomplish anything positive or productive, will it? I'm here with you, and I'm here for you. At this point, I if I wanted to turn back, I couldn't anyway. My father is already going to kill me when this is over, and I have half a mind to think that my car is probably reported stolen by now, so that's one more thing we need to be thinking about."

She was right. Kyle knew she was right. Getting worked up would accomplish exactly nothing. The problem was, he wasn't sure anymore what it was he was supposed to be accomplishing. Was he merely hiding from the prospect of incarceration, or were they still trying to solve this thing? Either way, he supposed he would do well to remain level-headed and collected.

So, he took a seat next to her and cupped her face in his hand. At first, she turned away, as if to resist, then she closed her eyes and let him kiss her. Her lips weren't as soft as before, though, and she didn't push back with the same enthusiasm. He guessed he had managed to fuck up pretty good with his words and his overall attitude, but like she said, being upset about it right now wouldn't accomplish anything. So instead, he shook it off, folded the computer screen down, and they discussed what their next move would be.

***

In the end there was no choice but to return to the cabin. Not because it was safe, but because it was safer than anywhere else. Even if one of them had been old enough to rent a room, they could be traced that way. Marie had money. Not much, because the ATM had only allowed her to take out 300 dollars last night, but it was enough to get a T-shirt for Kyle, some basic hygiene supplies, and keep food in their stomachs for a while.

They used back roads which were surrounded by trees and fields on either side to drive a couple towns south, where Kyle called Detective Bartlet and told her everything they knew and where the laptop would be stashed. Then, when she tried to convince him to stay on the line, he hung up and destroyed his phone. Marie tried another ATM, but her card was canceled, which meant that the car would be reported stolen as well. So, they hopped into it and hurried back to the cabin.

***

The McIntosh kid was alive, and even in spite of all the children who weren't, this was a relief to Christy Bartlet. She hadn't found a body at the scene (not his at least), but God only knew what that meant. No teenagers had been possessed yet, but did that guarantee that it wouldn't happen?

And here she was, thinking words like "possessed," and considering exactly where it was that she would wind up if there was a such thing as an afterlife. The kids were dead though. They were up and walking, and killing and they were dead.

The call from the medical examiner had come in shortly after she left the hospital, and it had confirmed that the little girl had been deceased for days. Likely since the night she disappeared. That she had been since before she was caught on multiple cameras around the city walking and smiling, carrying a fucking ball-pin-hammer.

Kyle's call had come in just past 11, and coincidentally, Bartlet had been at the McIntosh residence at the time, standing next to a baby apple-tree in the front yard. She'd already seen his mother and father lying on the floor on either side of their bed with their throats cut, and even though it was likely that Kyle knew, that he had been home when it happened and somehow managed to escape, she made a point not to mention it.

The sight of his number on her vibrating phone had caused her to sigh and think two words that she rarely threw together.

Thank God.

But the children would find him. There was no doubt in her mind that they would hunt him down the way that they had James Booth Sr., and they would lop off his head, or cut his throat, or nail him to a floor and set him on fire. They would find him because they weren't children anymore.

Whatever had once lived in those tiny bodies was gone, replaced by pure evil, and that evil was bent on destroying whoever the child had loved in life. *Or whatever.* Abel McIntosh had even mutilated his dog— and with his bare hands, it appeared.

But not all the houses in the Stanford Development with young children had been hit, and though Bartlet knew in her heart that this was good news, it was fucking with her mind because it provided yet another mystery. Why had last night been different? Why not all of them like the other two neighborhoods that had been completely ravaged?

But that was a question that needed to be pondered on, as she remained productive throughout the day. For now, Christy needed to get Kyle McIntosh safe behind steel, brick, and bulletproof glass, the way that she had Shawn Collins. Only with Collins it had been as simple as serving an arrest warrant. McIntosh had never even been suspended from school, let alone acquired a court-date to miss.

But he was with the Franco girl. Of that, Christy was sure. And the Franco girl was driving around in a car, which her asshole whop father had reported stolen. So Bartlet made a call and requested that two arrest warrants be issued: One for Kyle, and one for Marie.

Then she hopped into her car and headed South on Interstate-5 toward Stanwood to recover a hypothetical laptop computer which Kyle claimed held evidence, crucial to her case. It may have been a setup. An excuse to lure her somewhere, and watch from a distance to see if she was alone.

And she *would* be alone, because if McIntosh and his little friend decided to approach thinking that it was safe to speak with her—well Christy carried a service pistol and two sets of cuffs.

Plus, the funeral of one of the children's mothers was being held in Stanwood today, and it might not hurt to be in the area, anyway, as the kid's father would be in attendance, and maybe—just maybe—the evil little sons-of-bitches would make an appearance for that reason.

***

Just before one, the funeral was about to start. Carly Brown and her husband were there, sitting near the middle of the small crowd, on the right-hand side. Neither of them cried, or spoke, or even looked back at Gabriel, who sat between the two armed guards, shackled and handcuffed to the chain around his waist. There was a fragrance in the air like that of a new car, and he found himself wondering if it was the insides of coffins that he was smelling.

His in-laws had never liked him much, but being sent to prison had absolutely assured that he remain forever ostracized from the Brown tribe. And had anybody asked Gabe how much he cared, he would have readily held up a hand, using his thumb and index finger to indicate less than an inch and said, "About this much." Who were they that they needed to be impressed anyway? The Browns lived around the same distance from the poverty line as his own family (which was pretty damn close), so becoming a Brenton hadn't been much of a leap for Carrie.

It didn't bother him that they hadn't, in any way, acknowledged him since he arrived at Clinton Funeral Home. What had, however, picked at him and even managed to dig its way under his skin, was the fact that his own mother was in attendance, and when she'd attempted to hug him, both guards had not only stopped her, but put their hands on her in the process.

Gabe had since been fighting the urge to entertain a plan to use his status back at the prison to order something not-so-pleasant against each of them. It didn't matter that they had given him food that could have cost them both their jobs, because Mom was Mom, and Gabriel Brenton had never let a man put his hands on his mother and get away with it.

And now that he thought about it, the fast food had been more of a slap to the face than a kind gesture anyway. He had been given a children's meal. Something that should have excited a dog, not a twenty-four-year-old man. And had he considered it at the time, he might have told them to take it home and feed it to their ugly wives, because it was nothing more than a statement that they believed him to be something less than human, to which they had mercifully decided to show an inkling of kindness.

But that aside, there was a cherry-red coffin sitting on a table in front of this murmuring crowd, with white flowers all around it and his dead wife inside, and these fat mother-fuckers had placed their greasy fucking hands on his mother.

It would be so easy to put a sharp piece of metal in some kid's hand and point one of them out. Then, once the facility came off lockdown, it would be just as easy to do it again. It would be an abuse of his power, and it would eventually lead to retribution against him by his own people, but first the jobs would get done.

There was music playing somewhere in the room. Piano. Slow. What you would expect to hear at a funeral, and for that reason, it was pissing him off. That, and the fact that he couldn't figure out where it was coming from. He didn't see a piano anywhere.

Then he saw two speakers, propped high on black poles on either side of the crowd. It must have been coming from them. Somebody must have had their iPhone plugged into a PA system somewhere, and his or her Pandora app set to the classical station.

The turnout wasn't what he would have expected had he actually taken the time to consider how many people might show up. Most of the seats were occupied, but then again there weren't many seats in this room. He wondered if every venue at Clinton Funeral Home was the same size, and what they would do if somebody more popular died in this town.

His mother kept glancing past the guards at him, and making comments in a whisper that anybody in a ten foot radius could hear. He didn't return her looks, though, or offer any response beyond a polite nod here and there because even though he was thinking terrible things about the apes who had had the audacity to touch her, she was beginning to wear on his nerves. He knew he was wrong for it, and that his expression probably didn't serve to hide what he was feeling, but he was finding himself powerless to gain control over the situation.

He only recognized some of the people in attendance, and only one of Carrie's two brothers was here. It was sickening. He knew that he should probably say a prayer for Doug, who was likely in some crack-house pulling a hypodermic needle out of his vein at this moment, but it was easier, instead, to burn with hatred for the junkie.

And just as he was having this thought, Gus Jenkins walked in with the sides of his head freshly shaved and his bleach-blond hair combed perfectly to the left. He wore some button up designer shirt, which reflected the dim lights hanging overhead, and matched his black slacks, making Gabe painfully aware at he was the only person in the room wearing an obnoxiously bright, white T-shirt and ugly tan jeans.

Gus glanced down at him briefly, then flashed a smile to the Browns, extending his hand to Carly. She accepted it and he wrapped the other around hers as they shook. Then her husband stood, and the two men embraced and Gabe was sure for a second that he would be able to break right through the chains that bound him and rip both of their fucking heads off.

The last he had heard, Gus was in jail, under investigation for Carrie's murder. But of course, he would be released after the other families were attacked the next night. And of course, Gabe wouldn't know, because he hadn't been able to call his mother from the hole. And of course, he would find it nearly impossible to have a Christian love for the man who was drilling his wife the night she was killed, and his daughter was abducted.

The music kept playing, and the murmur of voices belonging to people who had never done a thing for Carrie or her child continued, and Gabe found himself hoping that the pastor would begin the service soon, and that he would say something that triggered a spark of conviction inside him, because right now no matter how hard he tried, he couldn't bring himself to be the Godly man that he had been called to be, or even positive about anything.

It wasn't until a few minutes later that one of the guards said, "Damn, that's the preacher?" and the other smirked, and Gabe glanced over to see a thin woman in a black skirt that exposed defined, milky white legs from just above the knees making her way up the aisle. The conversations slowly died down until all that could be heard was the soft hum of the melancholy piano tune and her clacking high heels. Stepping up to the elevated pulpit, she looked down at what must have been a page full of notes for a long moment. Then the music died, and she addressed the crowd with what may have been the most piercing blue eyes Gabriel Brenton had ever beheld.

Before she even spoke, he heard his mother sobbing beyond the fat guard on his right, and he felt his jaw clench. Then the preacher took a deep breath and said, "We're gathered here today to remember a person who—"

—and before she uttered another word, multiple things happened, seemingly all at once. Gabe felt his lips curl almost involuntarily, and purse like a duck's bill. Something burned in his chest. As fast as a bolt of lightning, it shot up his neck tickling his face and he knew he would finally shed a tear. An orange glow permeated in his peripheral vision and a gunshot echoed inside the small parlor, so loudly that his ears rang instantly. The life fled from the preacher's eyes, leaving behind a vacant expression as she crumbled to the floor behind the pulpit.

Then more shots exploded, and the place erupted into absolute madness. The guard seated between Gabe and his mother fell forward, banging his head on the backrest of the pew in front of them, and landing awkwardly and motionless.

The people up front flew to their feet first, and a young girl wearing a pink jacket over her black dress—Carrie's cousin Emily—burst into tears. There were so many shots fired that nothing else could be heard, and bodies fell like air was being deflated from them. The guard on Gabe's right reached for the handgun on his belt, and glared down at him as if whatever was happening had something to do with him. Then his head dropped, landing on his massive chest and rested there as if it was where it belonged. Gabe looked back to see a little black girl in her underwear holding a sledgehammer and smiling, and though this was horrifying in its own right, what made it worse was that where her eyes should have been, were two bright orange lights, shining directly into his face.

"Oh, holy shit!" He flew to his feet and almost tripped on his shackles.

More glowing-eyed children poured in like water, each carrying a weapon of some sort, mostly household tools but some had knives and guns—one even had a samurai sword. Then there were flies buzzing about and a smell like the dump at the end of the week was in the air, and the girl with the hammer moved on as the kids spread out and went to work on the crowd as if it were merely a garden in somebody's backyard.

One child, a tall Hispanic boy in red pajama bottoms and no shirt, thrust a shovel into a woman's neck, stepped on it, and took her head off. Another put a pickaxe in Carrie's grandfather's spine. A tiny arm flew through the air and landed in front of Gabe, and he grew sick to his stomach when he saw remnants of Emily's pink jacket.

The children were mostly pale. Blue veins showed beneath their skin, and some of them had been mutilated in ways that they shouldn't have been able to survive. Others had swollen bellies, and a small boy in blue coveralls held his head on his shoulder with one arm. It appeared to be attached by nothing more than stretched skin. The lights in their eyes overpowered the ones on the ceiling, shining on black fabric and creating what could have passed for Halloween decorations had they not been accompanied by real life carnage.

And there were shadows. Horrible, impossible, snakelike shadows, which stretched over the entire scene. They squirmed and danced over quickly accumulating piles of bodies and up the walls like snakes, or seaweed swaying underwater in a windstorm.

Gabe gasped. He looked over and saw his mother lying on top of one of the guards. Her mouth and eyes were open. So was her throat, and blood was spilling out of it like a water-hose. Her body twitched and one leg kicked at the floor.

He thought, *Oh God no,* as people dived for the back of the room, and were shot by a line of toddlers blocking the door and clutching various types of guns. Some of them, to Gabe's horror, even stopped to reload. Then everybody ran for the front and the first to make it dived behind the coffin, tipping it over and spilling Carrie's body onto the floor.

Gus turned and locked eyes with Gabe, and Gabe saw that the Browns were both dead next to him. Then there was a blast that resonated above the others, accompanied by the cracking of wood and ricocheting metal. Even though the two men were at least ten feet from each other, warm blood managed to mist Gabe's face as half of Gus's head disappeared before he even hit the ground, revealing a thin boy with long, dark hair, holding a shotgun with a wooden stock. He grinned and pointed the weapon at Gabe.

Gabe froze because he was handcuffed and shackled, and it was all that he could do. But even if he could have dived for cover or lunged at the kid, he knew it would be useless. There were too many of them. Not just that, but they were strong. Fast. Much more so than they should have been, and they had already slaughtered just about everybody in the room.

So instead, he swallowed a lump in his throat, sat back down, closed his eyes, and said, "God please forgive me."

Screaming. Choking. Gargling. More gunshots. And then there was a throaty growling that belonged in a George Romero film. It was their voices. They were speaking, and though there were so many of them, and they were accompanied by so many other sounds that it was impossible to make out anything aside from a few random words like, "lemon-drops" and "smile big," hearing them form them made the whole thing somehow more terrible.

Gabe braced himself for death, because death wasn't really the end anyway. He waited for pellets to tear through his skull and the moment seemed to last forever. Then the screams died down and there was only one. A woman, crying, "Please! Please! Please! Please!" Then a crash and silence, aside from movement, the buzzing of flies, and the scraping of metal on metal.

Until they started singing, "The itsy-bitsy spider— went up the waterspout! Down came the rain and— washed the spider out!" Some had choked, growling voices, but others still sounded like children, and it was the worst thing that Gabe had ever heard. Worse than the screaming and begging of all the people who he knew that he would see dead all around him if he opened his eyes.

For the briefest of seconds, he thought, *I'm dead too and this is hell. I went to hell for the thoughts I had about Gus and about the guards and for my shitty fucking attitude right before I died. But most of all, I went to hell for not forgiving my fucking whore of a wife.*

"Daaaaaaaaaad." The voice brought him out of his thoughts and caused his eyes to pop open almost as an involuntary reaction.

"Out came the sun and—dried up all the rain!"

Like he knew there would be, there were bodies everywhere. They were piled on top of one another, and ripped open, and people's insides were out and strewn about. Everybody was dead, except for the children, but Gabe knew that that wasn't true because they were dead as well. They were circled around him in what must have been a twenty foot radius with only two in the center with him.

The boy with the gun, which was still aimed at his face, and Kim.

She was bigger than he remembered her, and she wore an orange one-piece pajama set, which matched her eyes and looked like it had been dragged through a septic tank and hung out to dry before she put it back on. Her skin hung from her face like she was ninety years-old, and she spoke in that fucked up voice. The lights in her head were dim compared to the others and her voice was strangled, along with her movements as she attempted to crawl over a pew while clutching two serrated steak-knives.

"Daaaaaaaad." She sucked in a shrieking breath and jerked her head to one side.

"And the itsy-bitsy spider—went up the spout again!"

Kimberly's arms were curled up like a praying mantis's, and she didn't seem able to unbend them. Her back was arched as well, she appeared to be having trouble with the slightest movements. So, a fat boy with a hacksaw, who was completely nude, stepped into the circle and hoisted her up and over as the rest continued to sing.

"The itsy-bitsy spider—went up the waterspout!"

The kid set her down, and then she was on all fours, crawling up the next pew, heaving and choking and staring into her father's eyes. "Da—daaaaad. Dad. Daaaaaaad!" She shrieked and inhaled between each word.

"Down came the rain and—washed the spider out!"

That's when Gabriel Brenton realized why he wasn't dead yet. They were saving him for Kim. And they had only come here for this very reason. Kimberly had killed her mother, and now she would finish the job with Gabe. They had all slaughtered their parents. The news stations either didn't know, or weren't reporting on it, but these children were dead, walking corpses, possessed by something murderous and *parricidal.*

He tried to remember if he had read anything in the Bible about this. In Revelation? Any of the Old Testament Prophets?

"Out came the sun and—dried up all the rain!"

The fat kid hoisted his daughter over another pew and set her on top of a dead prison guard—right next to Gabe—while the one with the long hair kept his shotgun leveled at Gabe's face.

Gabe returned his daughter's gaze and said, "The Lord is my Shepherd. I shall not want. He makes me to lie down in green pastures."

"And the itsy-bitsy spider—went up the spout again!"

"He leads me beside the still waters."

Kimberly struggled to twist her little body so she rested partially in Gabe's lap, and Gabe backed up so far that he thought he would push right through the pew. But he didn't move to get up because even if one of them didn't have a gun aimed at his head, and there weren't so many of them that escape would have been impossible, he was still handcuffed and shackled.

"The itsy-bitsy spider—"

"He restores my soul." Gabe's voice became rushed and desperate. "He leads me in paths of righteousness for His name's sake."

"—went up the waterspout!"

Kim raised one of her knives and pressed the tip against his lower abdomen, just above his pelvis. Her arm remained bent and awkward, but he had no doubt that she would have the strength to push it inside him. He shut his eyes as tightly as he could and sucked in his gut like that would do him any good.

"Kim! Kim! Kim! Yea though I walk through the valley of the shadow of death I will fear no evil! Kim, baby, I will fear no evil for God is with me!"

"Down came the rain and—washed the spider out!"

"Da—da—daaah—"

"HIS ROD AND STAFF THEY COMFORT ME!"

The singing stopped—

"HE PREPARES FOR ME A TABLE IN THE PRESENCE OF MY ENEMIES! KIM DON'T DO THIS! PLEASE DON'T DO IT!"

—and there was scraping. Buzzing. Movement. But not from Kim. She lay motionless. He could still feel the tip of her knife nudged against his belly, but there was no longer any indication that it would go any further, and the orange light pressed against the outside of his eyelids was beginning to dim, so he opened them and saw the children pouring into the aisle and walking purposefully out the back door in two single-file lines.

Kim lay stiff on his lap, a knife in each hand, her eyes wide open. Only there was no longer any light in them, just vacancy. The children picked up their pace, and soon they were running, a stampede of death, taking with them their shadows and their lights and their flies. But they didn't take Kimberly Brenton, so once they were gone, Gabe stood up and watched his little girl roll off his lap, and onto the floor.

He glanced at the closest prison guard, who lay face down between the pews. Then he squatted and found the handcuff keys. Removing his cuffs and his shackles, he pulled the pistol from his belt, finding it surprisingly light. He tucked it into his waistband, climbed over dead bodies, ran outside, to see a yellow school bus pulling out of the cemetery.

***

Marie's overall attitude had gone back to normal at some point, but Kyle couldn't shake the feeling that she was still upset with him, so once they were safely back at the cabin, and examining a peddle-boat which rested upside down on the raggedy old dock at the bottom of the hill, he told her again he was sorry for what he had said about her having a boyfriend in England.

"It's all right," she responded. "I understand. I must confess I can be a bit irrational when I'm feeling defensive. It's not your fault, I've just gotten so used to having to be on guard and combat accusations from my father, that I have a habit of taking it out on other people at times. I probably should have been more sympathetic toward what you were going through when you said it."

The rain had substantially subsided, and it was barely sprinkling, but a layer of thick grey clouds that hung low suggested that it would pick back up soon. In the daylight, it was even more apparent that the cabin was a perfect safehouse, provided the owners (or anybody who knew them) didn't show up. Even on the dock, or at the grassy water's edge, all that could be seen across the lake and in every direction were trees and bushes. The place was completely concealed, and the closest neighbors were blocks away.

Marie had bought Kyle a new black T-shirt and a pair of jeans, since the old ones had a slash in the back of one leg. She cleaned and wrapped his wound, though, as it turned out, he hadn't been cut deep enough to even need stitches. They now had food, water and a few other supplies in the car as well. Kyle had wondered if she would buy another blanket, so they didn't have to sleep together again. And though two blankets would be warmer than one even if they *did* sleep together, he hadn't floated the idea, or even glanced toward the bedding section of the store.

He asked if they were cool, and she smiled warmly and said they were. Then she dropped the question which he had known would come out eventually.

"Why do you use marijuana, anyway?"

"I don't know," he responded

She seemed to try and decipher encrypted writing on his face for a long moment, then said, "Well that's not an answer, is it?"

"What? I mean, I guess I just don't know why I smoke."

"Does it make you feel good?"

"Ah—not really. I mean it can."

"So, it does sometimes, but not always?"

"Why are you asking?"

"I'm not judging. I'm merely trying to understand what leads a person down that path."

"What? What do you mean 'that path?' It's not heroin."

Marie grinned, threw her hands up in surrender. "Okay. I'm simply curious is all. I was actually wondering if maybe there was something you might want to replace it with someday, that could make you happier than the pot does." She walked over and ran a hand over his head. "I like your hair without product. It makes you look a bit more rugged."

Kyle smiled, dug in his pocket, bringing out the brass knuckles first, then the marijuana roach. "See this?"

She nodded.

He tossed it into the murky water. "I don't really like it that much to be honest. I guess I just do it because my friends all do. It's like a social thing."

"Well, that's a bit silly," she planted a kiss on his lips, "don't you think?" When he didn't answer, she took the brass knuckles from him and slipped her fingers into the holes. "This is quite a clever weapon, actually. Hurt like hell, didn't it?"

Kyle felt anger flare up inside him at the thought of Silencer hitting her with them.

She said, "Have you ever thought about writing?"

"What?"

"Writing."

"I know. I mean, I get that. But writing what?"

"Well, I was going to suggest it yesterday at the restaurant, but we got interrupted by that band. I don't know why, but I have a feeling you're the creative type. We just need to figure out the best way to channel your creativity. Once we do, you may find a pleasure in art that greatly surpasses that of cannabis."

Kyle snickered. "I just said I don't even like weed that much."

"Okay. If you say so." She slipped the brass knuckles into the front pocket of her hoody. "Listen, I came across some research last night which may be helpful in understanding what's happening to those children."

He flashed her a questioning look as she went on.

"You see, I was thinking, and I couldn't quite grasp the concept of intelligent, strategic, walking corpses. Can you guess why?"

Squinting, he said, "I guess, ah—because if they're dead, then so are their brains?"

Marie smiled, and for the first time since he had made the comment this morning about Ian, her expression and body language seemed to genuinely soften. "Correct. So, I was wracking my own brain trying to think of how it could be possible, and I remembered something I had learned somewhere about a theory which states that consciousness can go on postmortem. So, I went online and searched for any research available that might back it up, and what I found was actually quite interesting.

"Now I had originally thought that they were claiming that consciousness went on for a short period of time after death—like a few minutes, you follow?"

Kyle nodded.

She said, "But Vanderbilt University has published research in which biopsies were done of human brains—taken from cadavers, of course—and the neurons were transplanted surgically into the brains of live rats. Now we know that certain parts of the brain are responsible for specific responses, so using something called a PET scan, they observed that the transplanted braincells responded to stimuli in much the same way that they would have in a human. Do you know what that means?"

"I ah—" Kyle paused and considered what he was hearing. "I think. You're saying that they put a dead person's consciousness in a rat?"

Her smile widened. "Essentially. Well, a small fragment of it, at least. Basically, it suggests that consciousness may go on long after death. Likely until the neurons—those are braincells—become broken down by decay. Mind you, the research is far from definitive at this point. But it could explain conscious corpses. It seems it's either that, that we're up against, or possession."

"Abel knew me," Kyle said. "He was dead. I mean his fucking head was hanging off his neck bone, but he said my name. He recognized me."

"Okay," Marie concurred. "Not possession then?"

Shaking his head, Kyle said, "No. That's not what I'm saying. He wasn't himself either. I mean, he was him, but he wasn't *him*, if that makes any sense. Like he had his mind, but he was also possessed by something. By that—thing on the video, or whatever."

Marie was silent for a moment, seeming to consider this. Finally, she asked, "So both?"

"Yeah. I think. How do you know so much about everything? I mean, are you sure you're only seventeen?"

For the first time since he knew her, she flushed, glanced down at her feet. "It's just a matter of applying oneself, really."

"Well maybe you should be a doctor after all. I know you want to be a lawyer and all, but you seem really good at this medical stuff."

Looking back up and meeting his eyes, she said, "Oh sweetie, that's just because you haven't seen me litigate yet. I'm beginning to wonder if your friend is coming back after all, aren't you?"

Just then, thunder erupted somewhere in the distance and within seconds it was pouring again. Heavy raindrops crashed against the surface of the green water, causing ripples to spiral out like soundwaves that covered every inch of the lake. The two teens stared into each other's eyes for a long moment, as if waiting for the other to make the first move, then, Kyle took Marie's hand and pulled her up the hill toward the cabin.

***

Tara never showed up, and Kyle couldn't help that he hoped she wouldn't. He and Marie's clothes were already soaked by the time they were inside, so they peeled them off and made love on top of the blanket again. When they were done, they cuddled for what may have been hours until Marie walked out to her car in nothing but her shoes, returning a couple minutes later with water glistening on her naked body, and plastic grocery bag in hand. It contained a pad of paper and some pens.

At first Kyle didn't know what to write. It had never crossed his mind to even try. But then, as he sat against the wall in his boxers and jacket, with the tablet resting on his knees, an idea came to him. Once he put the pen to paper, he found it nearly impossible to stop, so he just kept writing. Marie lay quietly, still completely nude and wrapped in the blanket next to him. She faced away from Kyle, but he suspected she was smiling. He wrote until it grew too dark to see what he was doing, then he peeled all his clothes back off and climbed in next to her.

Chapter Ten

Tara hadn't been pissed when she noticed that the laptop wasn't where she'd left it under her bed. Or when she figured out that Kyle had broken into her house to get it. Though she hadn't yet watched the video, she understood the importance of what might be on the thing.

She had connected it to the charger last night, and planned to look this morning before she took it back to the cabin. Then, her mother had declared that the entire family (which meant Mom, Tara, and the twins) would be going to Conway to see Tara's grandfather today, and she had almost smacked herself on the forehead when she remembered it was Grandpa's birthday.

She wouldn't be able to get out of the trip, and she knew it. Not even if she attempted to play sick. So, she'd spent the morning trying to come up with any excuse to get to the cabin and back before they left, but her mother seeming to suspect something, had watched her with the attentiveness of a hawk.

It wasn't until mid-afternoon, when they finally made it back home, and Tara had found the computer missing. At first, it had actually made her smile to think that Kyle McIntosh had crept into her bedroom. Something about it had been right, because of how wrong it was. It had been—risqué. Then her heart had fluttered at the thought that she may have left something embarrassing laying around. She had even checked her underwear drawer wondering if there might have been a rummaging intruder.

She'd told her mother that she was going for a jog, and Mom had said, "Great! Why don't you take Todd and Tyler?"

Tara had laughed and said, "I don't know if that's a good idea. I think I'm gonna go at a pretty fast pace."

"Oh, come on," her mother had snorted. "You know those boys can keep up."

And though the twins were only eight, she was right because they had always been exceptionally athletic. So, she'd waited another fifteen minutes while they got ready, changing into sweats and locating raincoats, and by the time they finally left, it was nearing two-thirty.

When they were halfway to the cabin, Tara was so out of breath that she'd thought she might die. Then it had begun to pour, and the boys had wanted to go home, but she'd refused.

She'd made them wait at the end of the driveway, which twisted on its way down to the cabin, and felt her ears heat up when she saw the British bitch's purple car parked outside. But only when she'd peeked in the window and saw them together, fucking on top of the blanket she had loaned to Kyle, had she finally grown pissed.

That night Tara lay in her bed and considered calling the police and reporting them both—and had she owned her own cellphone, she probably would have done it. She probably would have used her mother's cell to do it first thing in the morning, had Todd and Tyler not dragged them both outside that night with glowing orange eyes, and buried them alive in the yard next to their house.

***

Marie's voice was sleepy as she asked Kyle what he'd written. They had been lying together silently for hours, her nude backside pressed against his front, her head resting on his arm. Kyle was hugging her so close they might as well have been welded together. He had known she was awake, but suspected that, like him, she had been trying to get to sleep. It was cold and pitch-dark inside the cabin.

"I don't know," he responded, finding his voice groggy, clearing his throat. "It's not done, but I guess it's like an essay or something."

She wiggled her hips, scooted somehow closer to him and he felt her buttocks squish against his manhood. "An essay *or something?*"

"I mean, yeah. I guess."

"Well, does it follow the essay format?"

"Probably not. Does that make it not an essay?"

"Not necessarily. I think most reputable essays tend to deviate from formula. What's it about?"

"I just—ah, I guess I wanted to write about my brother."

Marie paused for a moment. Then she took his hand, interlacing her fingers with his and kissing his knuckles. She held it tightly and pressed it against her heart. When

Kyle didn't speak, she said, "Would you like to talk about it?"

"About my essay?"

"Or your brother."

"I don't ah—"

"Only if you want to, baby."

Something about hearing her call him "baby" rang different than "honey" or "sweetie." Maybe it was because in spite of what he had said earlier, those words didn't necessarily mean anything. Kyle had heard girls call their little brothers those names. But baby? There was really only one way to interpret that. And it was a way in which he was growing surer by the minute that he was very comfortable with.

"No, it's not that. I planned on letting you read what I wrote anyway."

"Oh. Then I suppose we can just wait."

"No. I think I do wanna talk." He took a deep breath. "Abel was—he was special, you know?"

She nodded, but didn't speak.

"I mean, he talked funny. He had like a speech thing."

"A speech impediment?" she offered. "That's not too uncommon. You said he was six, right?"

"Yeah, but it wasn't just that. He went to speech therapy and all, but they thought he might have this mild form of autism."

"Asperger's?"

"Yeah! You know about it?"

"It's quite common, honey. A lot of people have it. I'm not sure they can diagnose it at your brother's age though."

"I don't think they can. But a couple of different doctors told my parents he was showing some early signs. Anyway, sometimes he seemed like super slow. Like, if you didn't know any better, you might think he was retarded or something."

"Developmentally disabled," Marie corrected.

"What?"

"Retarded isn't a nice word."

"Yeah. I didn't mean it like—"

"I know you didn't. I don't take offense to it, personally, but some people might. Anyway, carry on."

"Right. Well, what was I saying? Oh yeah. So, he seemed like he was—*developmentally disabled*, but everything I read online about Asperger's said that it makes people socially awkward, but they're usually really smart. So, I always just assumed that if somebody his age had it, it would be easy to mistake their awkwardness for stupidity, you know?"

"Yes." She yawned, "I suppose that makes sense. So, you're writing a scholarly piece about early indicators of Asperger's Syndrome?"

"No. Nothing like that. I wouldn't know what to write anyway. I mean I'm not a psychologist. It's just an essay about my brother."

"All right. Well, it sounds amazing. I can't wait to read it."

"It's probably not," he said. "I mean, I've never really written before. Except for like school."

"You were writing for quite a while, today, though. Did it make you feel any better?"

"Was I? Yeah, I guess I was. I ah—yeah. It did feel nice."

"I think it's going to be great, Kyle. I have a feeling, and my feelings tend to be correct. Do you know what you're going to call it?"

"I have an idea. I'm not sure if I'm gonna use it for sure though."

"It's a working title."

"Yeah."

"Well?" She nudged him with her backside again, and gave his hand a squeeze as if she could pump the words out of him. "What is it?"

Kyle paused a moment, then said, "Abel's Monster."

***

He wasn't sure when he finally dozed off, but he woke up to Marie's elbow jabbing into his ribs.

"Kyle!" Her voice was a whisper, but it was urgent. It only took a couple of seconds to understand why, and when he did, he flew to his feet, nearly tripping on the blanket on his way up.

There was a growling engine, just outside. Not just any engine, either, but one belonging to a massive vehicle. A dump-truck, or an RV. Or a bus.

"Shit!" He bent down and felt around for his clothes as Marie scrambled onto all fours. "Get dressed! Quick!"

"What is it?" she hissed.

"I don't know." His hand touched soft fabric, and he scooped up her sweater, tossing it onto the floor in front of her.

She ignored it, scurried off the comforter, onto the dirty wooden floor. Then she was on her feet, shoving a pair of jeans into Kyle's abdomen. He quickly stepped into them without his boxers as she bent down and came up with what he assumed was her own pants, and began to dress.

The rumbling faded out and died, and both of them froze for a fraction of a second before Kyle sprinted, barefoot and shirtless toward the door.

"Baby no!" Marie cried, but he didn't stop or even slow down.

When he made it there, he put his ear against the cold wood and at first all he heard was his own heartbeat, pounding as if inside his skull. Then his stomach dropped into his rectum at the sound of gravel crunching under feet that couldn't have belonged to the police because the footsteps were too light. And it couldn't have been the cabin's owners, either, unless the cabin was owned by dwarfs—or fucking children.

And as he was having this thought and trying not to have a panic attack, something touched his shoulder and he jumped.

"Baby-baby-baby," Marie whispered. "It's me, okay? Relax. Is it them? Is it the children outside?"

A repetitious hollow thumping stirred up an unsettling sense of nostalgia inside him, making him sure beyond a shadow of a doubt that what was parked outside was a school-bus, and what he was hearing were tiny footsteps as they hurried barefoot down the aisle and out the door. Then metal scraped rocks. A shovel being dragged across gravel.

"Yes," Kyle trembled. "I ah—it's them. It's ah—"

She took his face in both hands and shoved hers into it. Kissing his lips she whispered, "Kyle, are we going to die?"

Their foreheads pressed together, and he could feel her breath on his mouth. He closed his eyes and put his arms around her waist. She was in her jeans and hoody now, but he could tell by the way the sweater slid across her skin that she had nothing on underneath. Pulling her close, he savored the feel of her body against his, etched the taste of her lips into his memory.

Then something metal clinked against metal, and he said, "Go get my shoes."

"What?"

"My shoes, Marie. They're on the other end of the room. Go get them for me, please. Hurry."

Without hesitation, she let go of his face and sprinted across the room.

He didn't wait for her to reach the far wall. Opening the door, he ran out and shut it behind him praying silently that she would be smart enough not to follow. It made no sense for both of them to die if there was a chance one could survive. He knew that the children had guns, and that they were fast, but maybe he could get a head start on the little bastards and lure them far enough away for her to at least get in her car and escape.

But as soon as he stepped out into the cold, and his feet pressed into the piercing gravel, he froze because the long yellow bus was parked diagonally, barricading the driveway. It had sounded so much closer from inside, and even if he could have run around the front or back end and squeezed his way between the vehicle and the bushes, the children were blocking his path.

It was raining, but an overhead cover rested above the cabin's door. He instantly saw his breath leaving him in thick clouds, and felt the humidity in the air pressed against his bare chest.

There were so many more children than there had been outside his house last night. There had to be at least a hundred now, forming a crowd which was no more than fifty feet away, making its way toward the cabin. Toward him.

Their eyes were bright and cut through the fog, casting their horrible shadows which stretched so far that they almost reached Kyle. The light obscured his view slightly, but not so much that he couldn't see their weapons and their smiles. Then a set of identical twins, who he recognized as Todd and Tyler, Tara's brothers. They both held old dirty shovels, but he refused to stop and dwell on what their presence meant. Kyle knew that he needed to move, and that he needed to do it now if he was going to save Marie.

Down the hill, he thought. *It's the only way now. If you lead them into the water, she won't be able to drive out, but she can run around the bus, or even into the woods.*

So, he set his feet and prepared to run, but then the children halted and so did he because what if he ran down to the water and they ignored him and went in the house to do to Marie what they had all done to their parents and siblings? The crowd parted on the left-hand side and Abel stepped out, his arm raised and clutching his head to keep it resting on his shoulder, lights glowing from his face.

The two boys locked eyes and Abel smiled but didn't talk. Kyle knew why.

He can't. His windpipe is broken in half like a fucking banana.

Abel wore every piece of his Chucky costume, except the wig. He raised the huge knife that belonged in the McIntosh kitchen and waved to his big brother with it. Then, all at once like their feet were spring loaded, the children burst forth, sprinting directly at Kyle, kicking up rocks and mud. Before he even understood what was happening, Kyle's legs were in motion, propelling him down the hill and toward the water.

He didn't look back, nor did he notice the sharp rocks under his feet. Then he was in the grass, and he must have tripped on something because the ground came at him, collided with his hands, and he rolled like a truck tire for a while before he was up and running again.

They have guns, he reminded himself. *You're not gonna get far because they're gonna shoot you and then you'll roll down the hill some more, only you'll be limp and dead before you reach the bottom.*

And as he was having this thought, the water appeared right in front of him before he had expected to see it. He tried to stop, but it was too late. Then he was falling. Splashing. Fully submerged, and it was so cold that he almost gasped, but stopped himself short of inhaling water. He needed to swim. To kick and paddle as fast as he could. To get far from the cabin. And they might follow because they weren't afraid of the water, but they would be away from Marie.

He planted his feet, feeling mud between his toes and stood upright. His body emerged from the chest up and he took a breath as children dived in all around him, plunking and kicking up water. One, a dark-haired girl in a nightie that clung to her tiny body, popped to the surface right in front of him, bobbing and smiling.

At first, Kyle thought she was clutching a doll close to her chest, but it only took a second to see that it was an actual baby. Not just any baby, either, but the one which he had destroyed in the back of Marie's car. She had lights in her head, but the infant didn't. Its skull was crushed and distorted, and it hung loosely in her arm like it was full of sand.

Something wrapped around Kyle's ankles, and his legs were pulled out from under him. His face collided with the girl's as he fell forward into the water before he could even suck in a breath. Tiny hands clutched at just about every inch of his body, pulling him down to the bottom. And though it was shallow, it was dark and thick with dirt and who knew what else. Still, he could see foggy images of their faces because of the light that their eyes provided.

Some people claimed that they weren't afraid to die. In fact, most of Kyle's friends did, likely in an attempt to appear tough. Not him. Now that he thought about it, he was sure that he had never made such an assertion, but now that it was happening it occurred to him that he should have been much more terrified than he was.

However, now that he knew there would be no fighting or getting away, there was only anger. The same rage he had felt when he watched the video of the monster lying to his baby brother before it smothered him to death, and Kyle thought, *I would embrace death if I could take you with me, you mother fucker.*

Still, he kicked and writhed and fought to get away. But there were just too many of them. They held him under, smiling while their hair and pajamas flowed like rapidly blossoming flowers. His back touched ground and one of them landed on his stomach. It was Abel, straddling him the way he used to when he was a baby and they would play together on the rug, only now his head floated and swayed in the water like a balloon in the wind. The skin of his neck was stretched so far that it was a miracle it hadn't broken.

For just a second, Kyle was ten again, talking into the video camera on his mother's cellphone with his newborn brother in his lap. He remembered everything, from the dim lighting in the living room, to the way Mom's air-fresheners—plugged into outlets—had smelled. His mother asked from behind the phone how he felt about his new brother and Kyle beamed with pride.

"I love him a lot, and I'm gonna play with him all the time and protect him from anyone who tries to hurt him!"

Then Kyle understood it wasn't really the monster that he was angry at, because the monster had only done what monsters do. He was pissed at himself because he had failed, and now Abel was dead and currently looked like a bobblehead.

Breathe. Kyle McIntosh needed to take a breath.

The orange lights hovered all around, with the children's hair swaying out in every direction like dancing snakes. Like the shadows which they shouldn't have been able to cast, but did. Abel was the only child not watching Kyle die because he had no control over where his head went.

Don't breathe. he corrected himself. *If you breathe, you die because there's no air down here for your lungs.*

Then there was the song which had resonated from Bartlet's radio outside Laura's house. It played in his head, and though he had never heard it before yesterday, and their voices had been sick and inhuman, he remembered every word and every note.

If all—the raindrops, were lemon-drops and gumdrops—oh what a rain that would be!

He considered Marie and what might have been between the two of them if they had only had more time together. Was it love? Maybe. Nothing like what he had had with Claudia, though, because with Claudia it had never just been straightforward. Their love had always been accompanied by discomfort and insecurity, and Kyle had always known that they had nothing in common aside from sex and the convenience of being together.

With Marie, there was more. And though, physically, she was every bit as attractive as Claudia, Kyle had hardly noticed until they had sat down and had a real conversation. And now, she had managed to become the only person he wished that he could say goodbye to, and this was how their story would end. But before he could put any more thought into it, his lungs reached the end of their capacity, and he knew he needed to take a breath, or pass out.

He arched his back and Abel looked like a tiny bull-rider, holding onto Kyle with only his legs. Kyle fought and twisted. He gyrated, until one wrist broke free, slipping out of the grasp of countless tiny fingers. He didn't think about what he did next, just reached up, took his brother by the hair and ripped his head clean off, feeling the skin snap like a rubber-band and watching blood float up from his neck like a volcano ejaculating lava into the sky.

Then the lights in Abel's eyes died, and all at once, every child released his or her grip from Kyle's body and his view became obscured as the water stirred and the orange bulbs floated toward the surface. He knew he had no choice but to follow because he needed air and it was a miracle that he was even still conscious.

Releasing the head, he sat up and watched his decapitated brother float away, as he planted his feet on the ground and prepared to propel himself up like a jack-in-the-box. But before he could push, the monster appeared in front of him, fiery orange eyes burning into his, and Kyle was overtaken by fear which started in his chest and expanded until even underwater he was covered in goosebumps. But it didn't last because as soon as it arrived, it morphed into a sadness deeper than any he ever imagined existed and he froze just long enough to suck in a lungful of dirty lake water.

***

Then Kyle McIntosh isn't Kyle anymore. He's the monster, only he doesn't know it because the monster hasn't become the monster yet. He's a she, and her name is Bridget, and she's only eight-years-old. Too many to count on one hand.

Bridget sits on her bedroom floor pulling a pink dress onto one of her baby-dolls, whose name is Betty. Betty always wears pink because it matches her rosy cheeks and her yellow hair. All the babies have their own colors, and they never share.

Bridget likes yellow hair, because it's what Mom has, but hers is dark brown, like Dad's. That's okay, though, because she likes Dad's hair too. It feels good to be Bridget. Better than hiding from Abel, and his army of homicidal kids, and definitely better than drowning in a lake. Though Kyle still knows everything about being Kyle, he knows everything about being Bridget, now, too.

There's a shelf that Dad built on the wall for all of Bridget's babies. It's made of brown wood, kinda long, and just low enough so Bridget can bring them down whenever she wants to play with one. Diapers, bottles, and other supplies sit on the shelf as well, because her babies need to be taken care of, but there are currently two babies missing, even though she's only playing with one. Bridget isn't stupid, even though Juanito said she was last week during recess. She knows that the babies aren't real, but she's very protective over them, and she loves them just like if they were. She can't wait to be old enough to be a mommy someday, so she can have lots of real ones to play with.

Tomorrow's Sunday, and the day after that she'll have to go back to school, which wouldn't be so bad if everybody hadn't laughed at her yesterday when they found out that she had kissed Derrin Terly.

She had been so stupid to do it front of Jessica, because Jessica always tells everyone everything. And why does she do it? Well, it's obviously just so people will like her. Bridget doesn't have too many friends, either. There's Jessica, and sometimes Jerrod Conrad plays tag with them, and that's pretty much it. Still, she doesn't feel the need to run around talking about everybody else all the time. But that's just Jessica, she guesses.

Bridget has a toy-box, and Kyle can't help but notice that it's a lot like Abel's. Another chest, only less beat up, and hers is pink, instead of blue. There's stuff in it too.

There's barbies, and there's LEGO, and some other toys that she's had since she was a baby, but she doesn't play with them very much because her babies take up a lot of her time. The carpet's tan, and Mom's vacuum is screaming just outside the closed door. Bridget zips up the back of Betty's pink dress.

***

Then Kyle was in the lake again and the monster was still there. Only it wasn't a monster at all. It was eight-year-old Bridget, in a baby-blue dress that was a little too big for her body, with her dark hair flowing out and dancing in the water like snakes. And though her eyes were still orange, they seemed to be pleading with him now to see what she wanted him to see. So, he returned to her memory.

***

Only it's changed now because though he's Bridget again, he's no longer in her bedroom. He's at the dinner-table, and Bridget knows it's made of marble. Mom, Dad, and her older sister Noel, who Kyle recognizes from school are all present. He's never spoken to Noel, but sees her around often. She used to have a nose ring, until Mom and Dad made her take it out.

The dining room is nice, and it's crazy, Kyle thinks, because it's all so real. He can smell the food and he can feel the warm air from the home's heater. But most of all, he can feel the lightness of Bridget's body, which is his body now, seated in the hardwood chair. He can feel a misgiving inside her tummy because one of her babies is missing.

Bridget doesn't know that the home is decorated like a rich person's house, because she's lived here her whole life. Kyle knows because it's hugely different from the one in his home. Dinner, however, is macaroni and cheese, and a chicken patty that Dad buys in big bags from Costco, and Kyle knows that that's not what rich people eat, because even in his middle-class home they ate better than this.

The house isn't big, either. Just nicely decorated. It's one story, with three bedrooms and a hot tub just outside the sliding-glassdoor, leading into the backyard. The blinds are shut, but Kyle knows it's dark and foggy out there because Bridget knows. There's a garage out back that Dad built, and it's bigger than the house is.

Mom and Dad are talking about a guy Dad works with named "Bud."

"So, he's watching this girl jog by," Dad says between bites, "and not paying attention to what he's doing, and he swings the hammer and doesn't even touch the damn nail. Completely flattens the tip of his finger."

Mom scratched her plate with her fork, gasps. "Cheese-whiz! Is he okay?"

Chuckling, Dad winks at Bridget and says, "Well, I don't expect to see him back on the site anytime soon."

Bridget fakes a laugh, even though she's not sure she gets the joke. She's been to Dad's work site plenty of times. It's changed throughout her life, but his crew is currently building apartments in Burlington. Dad is one of the bosses at his construction job, though, and he spends most of his time in the small, portable building that's used as an office.

He says, "Fortunately for the company, I just happened to be around when it happened. God knows the other yahoos out there would have lied so he could make a claim."

Mom clears her throat.

Dad smirks, says, "Right. Anyway, I wrote it how I saw it, and I don't expect anyone'll contradict me on the matter. He was being reckless, plain and simple. And I imagine that's what's meant when we're commanded not to chase after the lusts of the eyes."

The chicken patties are okay. Not as good as pizza, but better than lake water. Bridget's not hungry, but she picks at her food anyway. A chandelier hangs above the table in the small dining room. It looks like it's made of lots of pieces of glass, but Bridget knows they're really plastic, because Mom brings it down to clean it sometimes.

Noel doesn't look happy. She usually doesn't, especially not lately. She's skinny and has dark hair like Dad and Bridget, which she keeps tied into a tight ponytail. Though she's pretty, Kyle has never taken the time to notice because they've had no reason to ever have spoken.

Mom taps her fork against her patty, frowns at Noel.

Noel pretends not to notice, picks at her food.

Bridget's been itching to ask a very important question, and figures now is as good of a time as any. Looking at Dad, she says, "Has anyone seen Molly?"

Noel rolls her eyes. Dad wipes his mouth with a napkin. "Good Golly, Miss Molly?"

"No, Molly!" she snaps, not meaning to. She's so angry because Molly is her second favorite baby and she just knows somebody has stolen her.

"Whoa!" Dad throws a hand up in surrender. "Okay. Just Molly then." He smiles.

Mom says, "Molly's one of Bridget's dolls. You know that, Dad. The purple one."

"She's not purple," Bridget corrects. "She just wears purple because somebody has to."

"So, there's this thing on Wednesday," Noel says.

"Oh yeah?" Dad grins. "Wednesday night, I'm guessing?"

"It's not a party or anything."

"I'm sure it's not."

"Seriously."

"I wanna say we've already had this discussion," Mom pipes. Bridget deflates because clearly nobody cares that Molly is missing.

Noel's eyes widen as she says, "I know, but it's not what you think. It's not like that."

Dad shoves a bite of macaroni into his mouth and says, "Nobody in this house is doing Halloween this year. It's not open for discussion."

"It's not—that's not what I'm asking."

"Then what are you asking?" Mom's eyes are slits, but her lips threaten to curve into a smile if her daughter says anything too stupid.

Noel takes a deep breath, let's it back out. "So, you know Claudia, right?"

"Claudia Rocha?"

"Yeah."

"Oh," Mom snickers. "This ought to be real good. Let's hear it."

Bridget knows what's happening. Everybody at the table knows. The only one who doesn't seem to realize what everybody knows, is Noel. Kyle's heart leaps at the mention of Claudia, not because he still loves her (that's a matter he would need to evaluate further before making a ruling one way or the other), but because it adds an element of familiarity, and he's never known her to be friends with Noel.

Noel is lying, and it's obvious. Ever since Mom and Dad started going to church there have been no holidays: No Easter. No birthdays. Bridget was painfully aware that there would be no Christmas this year. And for the first time in her life there had been no pumpkin carving or shopping for Halloween costumes.

And though Bridget hates lies, she can't help but hope that Noel can make some headway here, because she hates not having Christmas even more. So, she bites her tongue and doesn't mention Molly again. But she doesn't forget either.

Noel says, "Well, Claudia's cousin is having a thing at her house. Like an alternative to Halloween, because her church doesn't celebrate it either."

"I'm not sure what you're getting at," Mom says.

"That's because I'm not there yet."

"We don't attend a church," Dad adds. "It's called a Kingdom Hall. And an 'alternative to Halloween' just sounds like an excuse to celebrate Halloween to me. Jehovah isn't fooled by semantics, even if fifteen-year-olds are."

"It's not that at all. I'm just saying—"

"I'm just saying 'no'. Nobody in this house is doing anything on October thirty-first. And you can hate me for it if you want, because I care much more about your spiritual wellbeing than I do whether or not you like my mode of parenting. We'll stay in as a family, and we might even pray together."

"Whatever." Noel shakes her head.

"What was that?"

"Nothing."

"That's what I thought."

Bridget tries not to show her disappointment, but she can feel her shoulders slump. She's never cared much about Halloween, but no Halloween means there will still be no Christmas, and it was bad enough in June when nobody told her "happy birthday," and there was no cake or presents.

So, she asks again about Molly, but nobody hears this time because now Noel is saying that it's unfair that she doesn't get to do anything because her parents decided to join a cult, and Mom is gripping her fork like she wants to stab her oldest daughter with it. Dad is getting angrier than Bridget has ever seen him, and then they're yelling and fighting until Mom slaps Noel across the face. But nobody seems to care that Bridget's second favorite baby is missing. So later that night, she starts thinking about all the places she remembers playing with her, and she finds herself outside in the dark with only Dante (who happens to be her fourth favorite baby), searching the front yard.

***

Dante is in a baby-blue jacket (even though it doesn't match his brown hair too well), and nobody knows that Bridget is outside. That's because nobody was in the living room when she crept out the front door. Noel was in her bedroom, listening to music so loud that Bridget could hear it from her own room, and Mom and Dad were out back in the garage where they have their serious talks.

It's cold tonight and she can see fog hovering over the lawn like a giant ghost under the porch-light. Bridget isn't wearing a coat, so she starts shivering as soon as she is out the door. Without thinking, she steps on the soggy wet grass in her favorite pink and red socks. They are instantly soaked, and she knows she'll need to take them off before she walks through the house, or Mom will see her wet footprints on the carpet and know that she snuck out.

Bridget doubts that Molly is out here. But she has to look because she's searched everywhere else she can think of, and she did bring the baby out today when she checked the mail for Mom.

The neighbors' yards are all empty, and Kyle can't help but notice that the houses are slightly older than the ones in the Stanford Development, and that this road-- wherever it is--has no streetlights. Though Bridget doesn't look, Kyle can see in her periphery that the house across the street is two-stories-high, and has a big window in front, which is covered by white blinds with light from inside pressed against them.

There's a cemetery in the yard. The tombstones are fake—made of plastic, or styrofoam—and they say RIP on them. There's an apple-tree in the yard which is covered by a giant spiderweb. They even have a skeleton, standing in the grass with his hand up like he's waving. Last year, Bridget's house had Halloween decorations, too, but Dad doesn't like them anymore, and Bridget still does, so she just looks at the Williamsons' now. On Wednesday night, there will be lights and music in the yard as well.

Bridget is beginning to feel like Juanito is right. She is stupid, because why would Molly be in the front yard anyway? Noel's window is right behind her, but Noel keeps the blinds shut too, ever since Bridget went outside once, caught her smoking there, and got her in trouble.

Bridget's feet are squishy and gross, and Kyle is beginning to experience unease because if she doesn't hurry up and get inside, she might get caught and Mom will take her babies for a week. And now that Kyle thinks about it, just losing the one is almost too much to handle. It causes Bridget to hug Dante close to her body, and Kyle thinks he might cry, but he knows it's not really him who's feeling this. It's her.

Still, he's freaking out, slipping into what he assumes is an anxiety attack because he feels her tiny heart beating against the inside of her chest like a snare-drum, and it's growing difficult to breathe. So, Bridget turns and glances back at the house, but it's so far away now, like she's in the water, and the house is the shore and she's floating, floating, floating away from safety.

***

Then Kyle was once again back in the lake for just a fraction of a second and he was choking and gagging, and the water was in his throat. In his chest. In his stomach. And he was vomiting. Watching a cloud appear in front of him. But Bridget was still there and even through the orange beams in her head he could see that she was crying.

***

A car is coming from up the street, and Bridget squints into the headlights. She can see the fog sparkling in their beams like diamonds just before they go out. Kyle is afraid because he's on full display under the porch light and as the vehicle gets close, it begins to veer toward the sidewalk in front of her house, slowing down, until it's parked only feet from him. But the house is so far away because Bridget and Dante are floating, floating, floating.

Only they're not floating. She's standing in the wet grass staring at the black car and so is Kyle because he is Bridget the Monster. He's standing, standing, standing, and he wishes that he was running because nobody has to tell him what comes next.

Exhaust smokes from the car's tailpipe as the driver's door opens, and out steps a man in shiny dress-shoes and slacks that match the night. His winter jacket, however, is grey and red. His dark hair is thin, styled with gel above his puffy cheeks.

"Par-done," he says in an accent that Bridget has never heard before, and which Kyle can't place. "Are you mommy and pappy home?"

He takes a step toward her, and she steps back. Her shoulders float up as if to shield her face and her hands grip the blue fabric over Dante's body. She nods but doesn't speak. The man is tall, and she feels teeny-tiny in his presence.

He doesn't seem to notice her discomfort. As she stares up at him, he doesn't even look at her because he's focused on the house, squinting as he reads the numbers nailed to the wall by the door. "Because I am looking for the house three one two five. This is it, yes?"

Recognizing her own address, Bridget feels a spark of excitement and comfort, because this man must know her parents. Maybe he works with Dad. But then she begins to panic again, because if he goes inside, he'll tell everybody that she was out in the yard by herself at night. So, without putting any more thought into it, she shakes her head.

The man cups a hand over his brow. "You sure?"
Bridget nods.
"Oh. Okay. Well, I am to deliver the candy to this house. For the Halloween? Are you knowing where I can find this house? Three one two five?"

Bridget feels tiny geese fluttering all over the surface of her skin, and her hair begins to stand straight up because now she knows that he's lying. Kyle has never been so afraid in his life. Not even when he first came eye to eye with the monster in the lake where he knows he's still drowning at this very second. Not even when he saw his brother descending the steps of their front porch with a kitchen-knife and a broken neck.

He needs to run. Bridget needs to run. She needs to turn and sprint as fast as she can inside the house. But the house is still so far away and this man who is lying, lying, lying is so close.

But then, before she even knows she's doing it, she spins and slips on the grass. She runs as fast as she can, feeling one wet sock slide down her foot, the tip flapping with every step. She doesn't stop. Just keeps running until something wraps around her waist like a giant snake, hoisting her into the air.

Dante falls from her hands. Bridget screams so loud that her throat burns, reaching for Noel's window even though Noel is inside listening to her music and there's no way she can hear. Then she's spun around so she's facing the car and a hand is placed over her mouth and her nose. She kicks and she kicks, and she feels her sock slip off her foot. She punches the man's arm, claws at his jacket which is made of scratchy material. He's too strong, though, and she can feel his plump belly pressed against her back.

"Sh-sh-sh-shhhhh," the man breathes into her ear. "No more. No more. You don't do this, okay? You be good girl."

Bridget can't breathe, just like Kyle under the water—just like Abel and all the monster's other babies in their beds. Kyle is crying, but not with his own eyes. He can feel hot tears streaming down Bridget's face. They contrast with the cold of the night and roll sideways when they reach the man's hand.

Bridget bites. She opens her mouth and closes it, chomping at the terrible hand, but it's just beyond her teeth's ability to reach, so she sticks out her tongue and tastes rough, salty skin.

He releases her face and wipes his palm on his coat, before opening the back door of his car. Bridget sucks in the deepest breath that she's ever taken and screams again as she's thrown into the backseat. Her face hits the seatbelt buckle. The door slams behind her and her ears ring so loud that she can hardly hear her own voice. She becomes aware that at some point she has lost the other sock, and her feet are dirty and bare.

It's warm inside the vehicle. It's warm and Bridget is afraid, so she scrambles onto all fours as the driver's door opens and the man takes a seat before closing it again. He adjusts the stick on the side of the steering wheel.

"You stop! You stop now! Do you hear me? You be good girl, and everything be okay!"

"NOOOOOOOOO!" Bridget screams. She finds the door handle and pulls. Kyle knows before she does that it won't work.

Then the car is in motion and Bridget is pulling on the handle again and again. She presses her palms against the warm glass and slaps as hard as she can. She scans the yard for Dante, but doesn't see him anywhere. Then the porch light turns off and for just a second, she grows hopeful, because it means that somebody is right on the other side of the door. Probably Dad. He's the one who always turns it off because keeping lights on runs up the power bill.

But the door doesn't open because Dad doesn't know that Bridget is outside. And the car is floating, floating, floating away, until the house disappears and finally, she remembers where she left Molly.

***

Marie saw Kyle's body floating face down and limp in the lake.

***

The laundry room. Just this morning, Bridget changed Chastity's diaper there, on top of a pile of clothes in a hamper. But she had Molly with her, too. She set Molly on top of the dryer, making sure that she was asleep, and somehow she forgot to pick her up on the way out.

So, Bridget might be a bad mommy.

"Why you do this?" the man asks as she crawls across the seat and tries the other door, finding it child-locked as well. "Why you no be good girl? You stop, please."

"No!" Bridget yells. "Let me out! Let me out now!"

"NO!" The car screeches around a corner, coming to an abrupt stop that causes her to crash into the backrest of the passenger seat. He turns and glares at her, baring his teeth. "YOU LISTEN! I say be good girl, you be good!"

Bridges sniffs. She can feel her face all scrunched up and she can taste her own tears. "Please," is all she can manage to say.

"What is you name?"

"Please."

"I ask you a question! What is you name?"

"Bridget." She moans.

"Okay. Why you do this, Bridget? Why you make a fight? I'm bad? I'm bad guy? I only want to take you for the trick-or-treat. You don't like this? You don't like candy?"

Wiping her nose with the back of her hand, Bridget shakes her head.

"This is bullshit! Everybody like the candy. So, you listen to me. You be good girl, I take you trick-or-treat, then I take you home. You keep making a fight, there will be trouble. Do you want trouble with me, Bridget?"

Bridget thinks about diving between the seats, escaping through the passenger door. But she knows it won't work because this man is too big. Too strong. He'll catch her, then there will be trouble. She shakes her head.

"Good," he says. "Then you sit."

Light fills the inside of the car, and the man glances up to see a truck approaching from the direction they had just come. For just a second, Kyle is filled with hope, even though it's unwarranted because it's become crystal clear at this point how Bridget's story will end. Bridget, however, doesn't know this yet, and she's the source of the ambition. The light fades as the truck passes without so much as slowing down.

Then Bridget cries. Not like before. Not loud. Now she cries like a baby because she knows that there's nothing she can do to change her situation, and she's sad, and she's afraid. She cries and she stares into the man's eyes, pleading with hers and hoping that he'll care that she's sad and show her mercy. Take her home. Let her go.

"You sit," he repeats. "I tell you this, you don't listen. Is it trouble you want?"

It's becoming hard to breathe between sobs, so she sniffs, and she sniffs, trying to make herself stop crying but it's just so hard. She shakes her head.

"Then listen to me. Sit and put your seatbelt, and there will be no trouble. We go do trick-or-treat, and I take you home. Come on." He looks around, then nudges her lightly into the middle seat. "Fast."

So, Bridget buckles up, but she still can't stop crying because it's only Saturday, and Halloween isn't until Wednesday.

***

They stop at a hotel, and Kyle reads the neon sign out front.

Sherman Inn.

They're still in Mount Vernon. He knows this place. He's never been inside, but he's passed it countless times throughout his life. The man drives around the back where it's dark and doors line the outside wall. He climbs out, opens Bridget's door and tells her again that if she doesn't be a good girl, there will be trouble. Then he takes her by the hand and leads her into a room marked "117."

The walls are dirty, and it smells like cigarettes inside. Like Noel sometimes smells. There's a bed, a table, and a small dresser that's rectangular and no taller than Bridget. It has a TV on it. The man tells her to sit on the bed and please be quiet. She does as she's told the best that she can, but it's so hard not to cry when she's scared.

There are pumpkins in the corner of the room, sitting on the floor between the dresser and the wall. They have faces carved into them, which seem to be laughing at Bridget. It only takes her a second to realize that they aren't real. They're made of some kind of plastic, and they're both the same size—a little bigger than basketballs.

On the far wall is a counter with a big mirror over it. Next to the counter is a door, which Bridget guesses leads into a bathroom. When the man walks toward it, she grows hopeful that he'll go inside, because if he does, she plans to run out of the room as fast as she can. But he doesn't go inside. Instead, he stops and picks something up off the counter, pausing for a moment before turning with a smile to show her what he has.

"You see? Very nice, yes?"

A dress. Baby-blue. There's a piece of cardboard clipped to the top, and a plastic bag with yellow hair in it.

A wig, Kyle thinks. Like Abel's Chucky wig, only blond.

The cardboard has a picture of a girl wearing the dress. She's older than Bridget. It says "Cinderella," and Bridget knows it's a Halloween costume.

"The princess," he beams. "Very pretty, yes?"

Bridget feels her heart racing again. Though she can't quite pinpoint how or why, she's aware that something has just gone from bad to worse. She thinks of Dante, who doesn't have blond hair, but always wears baby blue. Has anybody found him in the yard yet, where she dropped him? Do they even know that Bridget is missing?

"Bridget? Bridget, you answer me. You like the princess?"

Bridget starts to shake her head, then stops because it's a lie, and what if he knows? Will there be trouble?

"Bridget?"

"Yes," she pouts.

"Yes?"

Bridget nods.

The man smiles from ear to ear. His eyelids droop, and his face flushes a little. "Very good. Very good for the trick-or-treat. You put it on, but not here, okay? Somewhere else."

***

The pumpkins have lights inside them. They're battery operated, and their mouths and eyes glow bright orange. Kyle knows these lights because they now rest in the eyes of Abel and all of his companions.

Bridget is in an old, abandoned movie theater. The Cinema 7. The man brought the dress, the pumpkins, a bag of colorful hard candies, and a blanket from the hotel room. He parked around back and opened the door with a key before putting a hand on Bridget's neck and nudging her in.

Now they're upstairs in what Kyle guesses was once the projector room. It resembles a long hallway, with square holes in the walls on either side that likely overlook the screening area. The floor is carpeted, and the blanket is laid out with the synthetic jack-o-lanterns lit on either side.

The man slips out of his jacket, sets it next to one of the pumpkins. It's difficult to see anything outside the illuminated blanket, but she can vaguely see his beer belly beneath a black shirt which matches his slacks. Bridget's jaw quivers as she stands off to the side watching him scatter the candies over the surface of the blanket.

"You must forgive," he smirks. "I am not yet ready for you tonight."

Mother fucker, Kyle thinks. You were planning this for Halloween. You were gonna snatch a kid off the street, but then you saw her, and you made your move early.

With considerable effort, the man bends down and picks up the costume. He instructs Bridget to change into it and she's so terrified that she doesn't dare object, but her hands are shaking to the point that she can't even get the package open to bring out the wig. The man takes it from her, then ushers her onto the blanket, where candies in plastic wrappers stick to the bottoms of her feet.

She's told to take off her clothes as he opens the costume. Trembling, she obeys, but she doesn't cry again until she's standing in her undies, and he scans her body, then says, "Everything."

Kyle is crying too. Bridget is afraid. The man's eyes are like lasers, burning into her skin as she obliges, then pulls the Cinderella dress on as quickly as she can. It's a little too big, but it's okay because she's never been so relieved to be covered. She's told to choose her favorite candy.

"Eat," the man says. "You don't like the candy?"

"Yes," she sniffs. "I do."

"Then eat."

"I—I'm not hungry right now."

"Okay," he kicks off his shoes and steps onto the blanket with her. The orange light reflects off his, like that's where it's coming from. He places the wig on her head and brushes blond hair from in front of her eyes. "It's okay. This is all for you. You can eat now, or you can do it later."

Bridget's gaze drops, and she stares at his black socks. She's never been so conscious of how teeny-tiny she is. He touches her chin and she cringes, hiccups, scrunching her face and forcing back her tears. He raises her head so she's looking up into his eyes, and tells her that because he's been so nice to her, she must be nice in return.

***

The pumpkins watch everything. They watch with their bright orange eyes and their terrible smiles, and they seem to be enjoying themselves. But Bridget isn't, so she cries and at some point, she even tries to fight, but the man is just too strong. Too much bigger than her.

He's naked, and his round stomach has dark hair on it, but he never removes Bridget's dress. When the wig falls off, however, he doesn't put it back on her either. What he's doing hurts so bad that she screams, and she can hear her voice echo inside the theater, like another Bridget, screaming back at her, but she knows that nobody else hears.

He flips her over and bends her this way and that, and his breath smells like onions, and Bridget is trying not to throw up. She doesn't know how long it lasts. It might be a minute, or maybe an hour, but when he's done, he rolls over and pants. He tells her she wasn't a good girl like he said. He tells her that she's bad, bad, bad, and very dirty now.

Still, there doesn't have to be trouble. He will take her somewhere to wash off, and then he'll take her home. But only if she stops making a fight.

Bridget has never wanted to be home so bad in her life. She wants Dad. She wants Mom. She even wants Noel. So, she promises to be good, and asks if she can put her own clothes back on.

"What is the problem?" the man scowls, stepping into his pants. "I give you pretty dress, and you don't like?"

"I'm sorry," she says.

"What?" He pulls his shirt on, then his shoes and jacket.

"I like the dress. I'll keep it on."

"Come on." He takes her hand. "Leave candy. We pick it back up later. First, you wash off."

***

The orange lights from the pumpkins won't go away. It's dark in the man's car, and Bridget is once again in the backseat, but every time she blinks, she sees them. It's like she looked right at the sun in the summertime.

The man doesn't speak much as he drives, but every now and then, he'll ask a question like, "How old are you, Bridget?" or "What is you favorite candy?" and she doesn't dare ignore him or lie.

Kyle is less afraid now, because so is Bridget. The worst has already happened, and there's little left to fear. At least that's what she thinks until the man takes a left turn into Riverview Park, where it's darker than the rest of the world because there are woods here. Then, she once again begins to panic, and so does Kyle. Not because this is where he left Laura Cunningham's body, but because Bridget is afraid.

The man parks as far back as the car will go, then orders her out. When Bridget refuses, he takes her by the hair and forces her.

"I don't have shoes," she whines.

"It's okay. I carry you."

"Please, sir." She doesn't know why she says it. She's never called anybody "sir" before. She guesses she must have seen it on a movie or something.

But the man picks her up, the same way he did in front of her house. She kicks and screams just the same as well. Only this time he doesn't cover her mouth. Instead, he throws her at the ground so hard that she doesn't have time to break her fall with her hands. The sides of her body and head collide with hardened mud, and before she knows it, she's crying from the pain.

Taking her hair again, he presses his fist into her head and growls, "YOU STOP THIS! DO YOU HEAR ME? YOU MAKE A FIGHT ONE MORE TIME AND I GIVE YOU REAL TROUBLE!"

So, she stops fighting, but she still cries as he carries her along one of the park's many trails leading to the river. Soon the sound of flowing water appears, then they're on the beach, where he finally sets her down. She can feel sand between her toes as he begins to undress.

"You get in the water," he barks. "You get clean and I take you home."

But Kyle knows that this is bullshit, and by this time so does Bridget. She shakes her head, and one of them thinks, run.

The man is naked now. He bares his teeth and takes a step toward the little girl, who spins and sprints toward the woods. Then her foot collides with something—maybe a rock, she doesn't know—and she falls face first just before he scoops her up and walks naked into the river.

"I tell you! Do I not say it? I say be good girl and I take you home! Now stop this! Stop this fight and you clean you-self!"

He dunks her into the water until she's fully submerged, and it sounds like there's a swimming-pool inside her head. It only comes up to his knees, but he's bent over, holding Bridget by her hips and pressing her against the bottom. Water gets into her nose, and without thinking, she gasps. Then it's in her mouth and her throat. She's coughing, kicking and scratching, trying to get away. Trying to breathe. It's so dark down here that she can't see anything except the orange lights which are still watching everything—still laughing at her—and her hair as it floats around her face like dancing snakes.

And all of a sudden Kyle understands the lights in the children's heads and the horrible shadows they cast. He understands why the monster collects children like they're fucking dolls. And then Bridget stops fighting and begins floating, floating, floating away from the man. She glances back and sees her blue dress floating as well. It's attached to her body, which lay motionless in the river.

The man is scooping up his clothes and running away, disappearing into the woods while Bridget floats because she is not attached to her body. Her eyes are glowing, and her hair is still flowing, but her body is left behind.

***

Kyle was heavier than Marie had expected. Still, fueled by adrenaline and what may have been love, she managed to drag his limp body out of the water and onto the lake's grassy edge. Her shoes and clothes were soaked, and she was freezing, but she was sure that Kyle was still alive.

She didn't even check for a pulse or to see if he was breathing because if he *was* alive, and she didn't hurry, he wouldn't be for long. Rolling him onto his side, she began to pound on his back, feeling the hollow thud of his ribcage and hearing raindrops tap on the surface of the lake.

Up above, the bus's engine came to life as the children boarded. At first, Marie had assumed that the fact that they were leaving meant that Kyle was dead, and she had been tempted to weep as if that would do any good. Then, her brain had processed what her eyes were seeing. Kyle was still moving when they began to retreat. He was kicking and splashing like a fish on a hook, and he wasn't anything close to dead.

She hadn't even waited for them to pass before she sprinted down the steep hill, toward him, and their smell had assaulted her senses and made her want to vomit. They were disgusting and horrifying to behold. They held every variation of weapon, from swords, to carpentry tools, to hunting rifles. They were pale, with swollen bellies and there were so many of them that they made up a bloody militia.

They had been close enough that she had had to squint against the light from their eyes. So close that, had they wanted, they could have reached their short arms out and grabbed her. But they hadn't even paid her a second glance as they made their way up the hill toward their vehicle, and when she made it to the bottom, Kyle had been floating face down.

As she beat her palm against his back, she bared her teeth and thought of how he had deceived her, told her to get his shoes, then ran to his death like he thought he was some kind of a superhero.

"Stupid!" she shouted. "Stupid! Stupid! Stupid! Don't you even fucking think about dying on me!"

He coughed, and water shot from his mouth and his nostrils. Marie thumped his back some more until he vomited.

The bus beeped as it backed up, then moved forward. It drove back and forth, maneuvering itself until finally it pulled out of the driveway and disappeared leaving behind the smell of exhaust.

Only now, did Marie cry. She cried and she slapped Kyle again as he stopped vomiting and his coughing fit commenced. She cried because it felt like the weight of the world had been lifted from her. And now that he was breathing again, so could she. It occurred to her, almost painfully, that she had, in fact, fallen in love with this guy.

When Kyle finished coughing, he curled into a ball, and at first Marie didn't register the sounds of his agonizing moans over her own. Then they grew in volume and intensity and for reasons that she didn't understand, she became overwhelmingly aware of how cold she was. Kyle hiccupped and he groaned like an animal who had been pierced by a hunter's arrow, and it sent goosebumps fluttering over every inch of her skin because it may have been the most horrible noise she had ever heard.

She placed a hand on his bare shoulder, and he jerked so hard that she flinched, thinking he would fly to his feet and hit her. But he didn't. Instead, he just kept crying.

"Oh God! Oh God! It was so bad. It hurt so much. She was so—she was scared. She was fucking scared, Marie."

"What?" Marie didn't dare touch him again. "Baby, who? What are you—"

"She was just a baby. She was just a little—oh God, Marie. It was so—I can't even—" Then he cried some more, and though it seemed he was attempting to form words, what reached her ears was an intangible moan.

Fuck it.

She threw herself on top of him and he jerked again, but she pinned him to the grass and the mud, wrapping her arms around him and holding him tighter than she had ever held Ian, or anybody for that matter.

"Ssshhh. Sssshhhh," she whispered into his ear. "I know it was. I know, baby."

But his body grew so stiff that she knew he wanted to tell her that she didn't know anything. Still, she held him until his tears ran dry. Then, when he didn't move to get up, she held him some more. She held him because his entire family was dead, and he needed to be held and because she had never been so grateful than she was just because he was alive.

***

Kyle had never known true sorrow before tonight. Though he had thought that losing Claudia had invoked a pain incomparable to anything he would ever experience, he had been wrong. There was nothing like the pain, and the fear he had experienced when he came face-to-face with Abel's monster, and he could die happy if he never felt it again.

He and Marie rushed into the cabin, and he changed out of his new jeans and into the old dry ones. Marie slipped out of her sweater, and into her T-shirt, but she was stuck with the wet pants, so he gave her his jacket to wear. He placed his writing tablet back into the shopping bag, then tossed it into the backseat.

"I'm so cold," she shivered. "Will you drive for me?"

Kyle stood just outside the passenger door and told her he didn't know how.

"Really?"

"Yeah."

"Aren't you sixteen?"

"Yeah, but I don't have a car, so I haven't taken driver's ed yet."

"And you've never been behind the wheel?"

"No."

"That's so odd, don't you think? None of your friends have vehicles either."

"They're poor," Kyle climbed in and shut the door.

"Oh." Marie took a seat, started the engine, and in under a minute they were on the road.

He knew before he looked down the passing driveways that there would be evidence of entire families having been murdered because the monster had struck in Lake McMurray tonight. He made a point not to glance toward Tara's house as they passed, instead, bringing out his mother's cellphone and hitting the power button.

When it came to life, 7 missed calls and a few text messages were announced. Ignoring them, he checked the clock, seeing that it was 10:42 PM, then pulled up the calendar app.

Marie glanced over, asked what he was doing.

"I need to see something."

There was a tension in the air which suggested she wanted to ask him to elaborate, but she refrained.

He scrolled back an entire year, then said, "Halloween was on Wednesday last year."

"Okay baby," Marie focused on the road.

"I'm sorry. I just, I'll explain in a minute. I promise. I need to call Bartlet first."

"That policewoman?"

"Yeah."

"Are you sure that's a good idea?" She spoke slowly

"I don't know. We don't have a choice though."

"And why is that?"

"Because I think the monster's taking those kids trick-or-treating tonight."

***

The monster's babies parked their bus behind some trees, then they all piled out and made their way into the woods where they had left their Halloween costumes.

Chapter Eleven

There was no reception where Kyle and Marie were, so he checked his mother's text messages and saw something that may have made him sick to his stomach, had he not just been through an experience which would likely callous him for life.

A black man named Carl, had sent a photo of himself from the neck down, chiseled and completely nude, captioned: *Lunch tomorrow?*

But what was worse, was when Kyle scrolled down and saw that she had been leaving work to meet him regularly. He didn't read any further.

Once they were on the freeway, bars appeared in the upper corner of the screen, so he made the call. Bartlet was wide awake, and answered as if she'd already known that he had his mother's phone, and had been expecting his call.

"Hello Kyle."

He told her they needed to meet up, but had trouble hearing over the wind rushing in the broken window. The interstate was relatively empty, and Marie stuck to the speed limit.

"About time you figured that out," the detective replied.

"No. That's not what I mean. Listen to me, you have to promise you're not going to arrest me."

"Kyle—"

"No! There's something you need to know, and I think you're gonna need my help. Do you have kids?"

"I beg your pardon?"

"Do. You. Have. Kids?"

"I don't see how that—fine. Yes, Kyle, I have a son. He's all grown up now, and works at the department with me."

"Swear on your son's life that you're not gonna arrest me—or Marie—if I agree to meet you."

Bartlet paused, then said, "Okay, Kyle. I swear on my son's life that I won't arrest you."

"Or Marie."

"Or Marie. Cross my heart, hope to die. Do you feel better now?"

"No," Kyle responded. "Not really. Where are you?"

"Why don't you just tell me where you wanna meet, and we'll take it from there?"

"Not a chance. Tell me where you are."

"I'm downtown. At King's Port Pub. Know where that is?"

"Yeah. You're at a bar?"

"You wanna meet or not, Kyle?"

"Be at the boardwalk in five minutes."

He hung up and tossed the phone out the window.

***

There were some houses in the woods, so once they were dressed, that's where the children stopped first. There weren't a lot of homes, so they didn't have to spread out too far yet. They only split into three groups for the first round of trick-or-treating.

John Collins got to be Ironman. There was a boy named Daryl in his group, which was funny because Daryl was so small, but it sounded like an old person's name. Daryl was dressed as a bowling-pin with arms and legs. The first house they found had a barn next to it. It was tall and old with a picture of a jack-o-lantern hanging on the front door, which was the only Halloween decoration that there was, and John guessed that that was because they didn't usually get trick-or-treaters out here. It must have been three stories high, and it looked like it would blow over in a windstorm.

They crowded in the yard, as a dark-haired girl in a bumblebee costume tapped on the door with a hammer. Her name was Tiffany. John had his shotgun, but knew not to use it, or somebody might hear and call the police to come and ruin Halloween.

All the lights were off inside, and nobody answered, so Tiffany knocked again, only louder and harder. Then the wind blew, and the monster said, "Just go inside," so Tiffany reached up and twisted the knob, finding it unlocked.

She stepped in first, and the rest followed in a single-file line—the way that they used to at lunch, or at school on their way to the library. John was one of the first in the door, and though it was dark, the lights in his eyes allowed him to see everything.

It looked old and dusty on the inside as well. There was a flimsy wooden table by the door and a flight of stairs with a skinny, shirtless, white-haired man standing at the top holding a gun just like John's. He yelled, "Sweet Jesus! What in the name of—"

But the children cut him off, every one of them wailing, "Trick-or-treat!" in unison.

The old man's eyes were so wide that it almost made John laugh. Tiffany ran up the steps first, her hammer raised high over her head. When she was halfway up, the man lowered his shotgun, pointing it at her and pulling the trigger.

BOOM!

She flew back a few steps, then tumbled down the rest, but the lights in her eyes still shone as she giggled and climbed to her feet.

"What in the world is—" An old fat woman in a long, white T-shirt appeared next to the man and screamed, backing up into the wall and sitting down against it as the children all rushed up the stairs laughing and having a blast.

***

Kyle told Marie everything about Bridget and the man as fast as he could, and before he was done there were tears rolling down the sides of her nose. They were almost to the exit, which would deposit them into downtown Mount Vernon, so she began to veer right.

Sniffing, she said, "Are you sure it was real?"

"What do you mean?"

"I mean, maybe it was just a dream. You know testimonies from those who have near-death-experiences have reported, very bizarre—"

"Marie. It was real. It was—I mean, I wanted to think the same thing at first. In the vision, Halloween was gonna be on Wednesday, and this year it's on Thursday. So, I was like, 'It's not real,' or whatever. Then I scrolled back on the calendar to last year, and—"

"It was on Wednesday." Her tone was defeated.

"Yeah. The vision wasn't from this year. It happened a year ago, and I think she's been waiting to take revenge this Halloween."

"On Thursday?"

"No. I mean, not actually Halloween. On the night that the guy killed her. It was Saturday, but he called what he did to her trick-or-treating. It was Halloween for her."

"Goodness."

"Yeah."

Marie slowed the car down, pulled onto the offramp. "Kyle, how can we trust this woman not to ambush us right now?"

"We can't."

"Then why are we doing this? I mean, why couldn't you just have told her on the phone, what you've just told me?" The Beetle came to a stop at an intersection, and the sound of wind hissing into the car disappeared. Outside, the rain was now nothing more than a light sprinkle.

"Because," Kyle responded, "she's not gonna do what needs to be done to stop Bridget. We need to be there for it to happen."

"Then why do we need her at all?"

"Because we need to track down the guy who did this to her."

Marie paused, seeming to consider what she was hearing. He knew she understood what was being implied. Still, as the light turned green, she tapped the gas pedal and asked, "And then what, baby? What can we do that the police couldn't do without us?"

Kyle didn't look at her as he said, "We're gonna feed the mother-fucker to the monster he created."

*****

There were four vehicles parked along the boardwalk. Kyle recognized the silver Dodge easily as an unmarked police car. He was aware that the others could be cleverly disguised ones as well, and that even if they weren't, there could be cops hidden nearby.

It may have made him nervous before, but not tonight. He instructed Marie to pull up next to the Dodge. She didn't object, but her demeanor was rigid and hesitant. Once they were next to it, and the river was in front of them, she put the Beetle in reverse and kept the motor running.

Glancing over, Kyle saw the Hispanic cop who always seemed to be with Bartlet in the passenger seat. Bartlet sat behind the wheel. She said something that Kyle couldn't hear, then both doors opened, and the two officers exited the car.

"Baby, I don't like this," Marie's voice shook.

"It has to happen," Kyle said. Without another word, he stepped out into the cold, watching his breath turn to fog, and walking around the front of the Beetle. The detectives met him there, both shielding their eyes until Marie killed the headlights.

"I know what it looks like," Bartlet said, "but I gave you my word. This is just my partner. He was with me when your call came in."

"Detective Rivas." He extended his hand.

Kyle didn't accept it. He said, "We've met," and after a while, Rivas took it back.

Bartlet said, "Kyle, I'm having a lot of trouble with this. You know we could both lose our jobs if we let you and Miss Franco just walk away. I'm a woman of my word, though, but you gotta give me something to work with here for this to make sense."

"I'm not stupid," Kyle ran his hand through his hair.

"Nobody said you're stupid—"

"Just listen please. I'm not stupid enough to meet up with you if it wasn't important."

"Yeah," she nodded. "I gathered as much. Which is the only reason I'm taking this approach. Tell your friend to turn off her engine and come join us. If you were gonna get arrested, it would've happened already. Plus, it's not like she'd be able to evade one of our teams anyway."

So, Kyle turned toward Marie, but before he had said a word, or moved for her door, the engine died, and she stepped out.

Eying her up and down, Bartlet said, "You're soaking wet."

"It's been a rough night," Marie responded.

Bartlet shook it off, turning once again to Kyle. "Listen Kyle, I know you didn't have anything to do with what happened to your folks. That being said, I'm sorry."

For just a second, Kyle tensed, thinking, *She's about to arrest me after all. This was a trap, and I didn't just walk into it, I set it for myself.*

Then she went on, "So why don't we put all our cards out on the table. Yes, when we spoke yesterday, I was trying to lure you out so I could put you in juvie. There are things that I've learned about the nature of what's fallen on our community that have led me to believe you'd be safer there. In fact, had your friend Shawn Collins not been where he is, he would be dead right now, I can assure you of that. I still think you'd be safer behind bars, but I made you a promise and I intend to keep it.

"What I can't, in good conscience do, is allow you to drive away in that stolen car. I'm gonna insist that you two come with us. Marie, we're gonna take you home. Kyle, you'll be sticking with us until we figure out somewhere safe, and far away from this town for you."

That was it. Kyle had heard enough, and he wasn't about to waste another second. Fueled by adrenaline and anger, he snapped, "Would you shut the fuck up?"

"I beg your pardon, young man?"

"Do you not know the definition of 'important', or do you just not wanna hear what I came here to tell you? You think you know the nature of what you're up against? You don't know shit. So shut up and listen—at least for a second—then you can tell me how you intend to use fucking semantics to break your promises."

In his periphery, he saw Marie resisting a smile, and it caused him to do the same.

Conceal your hand, her voice resonated in his head. *Remain level-headed and collected.*

But Bartlet was anything but level-headed. She was pissed and she made no effort to hide it. Still, with no shortage of attitude, she invited him to go on.

So, he told her everything that he'd just told Marie, and by the time he was finished, both detectives' demeanors had softened slightly. Rivas said, "Jesus. He's talking about the Newport kid."

Bartlet glared skeptically at Kyle. "She has an older sister—what's her name?"

"Noel," Kyle replied.

"That's it, isn't it? She should be about your age. You go to school with her?"

"With Noel?"

She nodded.

"Yeah," Kyle answered. "But I've never talked to her. Why?"

"You would know what happened to her sister last year, wouldn't you?"

So, it was true. It was all true, and though having it confirmed validated that he wasn't crazy, it also made it so much worse because he had not only witnessed what had happened, but he had *experienced* it. As Bridget.

"I didn't know until tonight," he held his ground, tried not to sound like he was pleading with her to believe him.

"So lemme get this straight," Rivas spoke up. "You broke into a cabin in Lake McMurray, and that's where you've been hiding?"

"Is that all you heard?" Marie gasped. "Out of everything that he's just told you, all you took away was—"

"Why Kyle?" Bartlet cut her off. "If what you're saying is true, and everything that's happening is the work of Bridget Newport's vengeful spirit, then why in the world would she choose to reveal her secret to you and nobody else?"

Kyle took a deep breath. "I don't know. I mean, I think it's because I was drowning—you know, like how she died. It was like she related to me at the time. Or maybe she sympathized with me or something."

Rivas was checked out. Seeming not to have heard anything that was being discussed, he stated, "They're moving back north, then."

"What?" Marie tilted her head.

"They were in Stanwood this afternoon. You encountered them in Lake McMurray. That means they're coming back this way. Jesus, we better hope they didn't attack there."

"They did," Kyle said, wondering what the children had been doing in Stanwood.

Every head snapped in his direction.

"In McMurray?" Bartlet asked.

"Yeah."

"They picked up more children?"

"Yeah."

"For fuck's sake, Kyle. Don't you think you could've led with that?"

Stepping away, Rivas pulled a small handheld radio from his pocket and spoke into it in codes that Kyle didn't understand.

Bartlet ignored him, glared incredulously at Kyle. "It's still not adding up, dude. I'm calling bullshit on your story." When he started to object, she held up a hand, silencing him, and went on. "I'm not saying you're lying, because I don't know that yet. Maybe you heard about Bridget Newport and just forgot. People's subconscious minds retain facts all the time that they don't even remember learning, and it's highly possible you think you're telling the truth.

"And believe you me, I'm not being skeptical, either. At this point, I'm prepared to believe anything that speaks to the facts—ghosts or no ghosts. But there's a giant hole in your story that your subconscious either doesn't know, or seems to be forgetting."

"Yeah?" Kyle asked as Rivas stepped back into the circle, his walkie-talkie in hand. "What's that?"

"Well, you're spot on that Bridget Newport was raped and drowned a few days before Halloween last year. But there's no way you saw her spirit tonight, because she's not dead."

Marie opened her mouth, but no words came out. Kyle felt a chill run up the back of his neck as Bartlet continued.

"A couple people saw what happened from across the river and called nine-one-one. When the perp realized they were there, he ran away. Bridget Newport lives with her Mom and sister over on twenty-first street."

***

Loretta was dressed like a mermaid. And not just any mermaid. She was dressed like The Little Mermaid, which happened to be her favorite. She had a bright-green fin that hung off her butt like a tail, only it had two holes for her legs because she wasn't really a fish, and she had to walk.

She also had a nail-gun from Daddy's tool shed. It used to be heavy, but now it was easy to carry—even with one hand. It was the same one she had used to shoot nails into Daddy's head. Then into Mommy's eyes and tummy. Loretta liked trick-or-treating, had since she was just a little girl. She was five now, though, and everybody knew that five-year-olds were big girls.

They had been in a large group when they stopped at the houses in the woods, walking from home to home through sticker bushes and dirt, rather than using the roads.

Then, the trees had thinned out and light had appeared.

That's when the wind had whistled as the monster cried, "Don't forget to say 'Trick-or-treat!'"

So, they'd stepped happily out of the forest and into a two-lane road set on a hill. There were no businesses, but just across the street was a big fenced neighborhood with streetlights and houses as far as the eye could see. When a white car had come down the hill and stopped to let them cross, a group of kids had surrounded it, breaking the windows with their tools and pulling two women out into the street, where they cut them to pieces.

The kids had helped each other over the fence and when it was Loretta's turn, she had seen that the houses were covered in spiderwebs and other Halloween decorations. It had made her so excited that she had squealed with joy. Then they had spread out like confetti in water as every boy and every girl had gone his or her own way and begun knocking on doors.

Now Loretta was standing under the porchlight of a two-story house with her nail-gun, and there was a plastic skeleton in a rocking chair that made her think of Grandma. It occurred to her that she should pay Grandma a visit before the night was over. Then she knocked on the door.

In the distance, a woman screamed. Then choked. Then fell silent.

Loretta knocked again.

Somebody fired a gun. Then another. More screaming. More shots.

Loretta raised her fist once more, but before she could knock, the door swung open and a tall man in green sweatpants appeared, glancing around confused, then down at her. His eyes expanded like jellyfish as she raised her tool and ejected a nail into the bump between his legs.

"Trick-or-treat!"

***

They all piled into Bartlet's Dodge, and once inside, Kyle could smell alcohol from the detectives' breaths. They drove to King's Port Pub, where Bartlet dropped Rivas off outside a car which was almost identical to hers. The plan, which they hadn't hesitated to discuss in front of Kyle and Marie, was for Rivas to find out who was registered in room 117 at the Sherman Inn this time last year, while Bartlet and the "kids" went to the Newport home.

Kyle and Marie sat together in the backseat, her hand resting in his, and Marie shivered.

"Can we get the heater on?" Kyle asked. "She's soaking wet back here."

Bartlet reached forward and turned a knob, bringing the heater noisily to life. "Why are your clothes wet anyway? Wasn't Kyle the one who was attacked."

"I had a dry pair of jeans," he answered for her. "She didn't."

"I'm asking: If you were attacked, what the hell was she doing in the lake?"

"She saved my life," he gave her hand a squeeze because he hadn't yet taken the time to thank her. "Again."

She smiled and set her head on his shoulder, her wet hair touching his face.

The digital clock on the dash announced that it was just past eleven.

Bartlet said, "Kyle, I need to ask you a couple of questions."

Of course, she did. It would just be a matter of whether or not her questions were aimed with the right intent because they had thus far been nothing more than accusatory arrows, fired at him. She had seemed not nearly inquisitive enough for a detective who genuinely wanted to solve this thing and prevent any further killing. Kyle didn't have to invite her to go on.

"When you left your house last night, how were you able to lure the children out of your neighborhood without being killed?"

"What do you mean?" He kissed the top of Marie's head.

"It's not a trick question. How'd you get them away from your neighborhood?"

"I didn't."

"You were in Miss Franco's car, right?"

"Yeah."

"Well, did they follow you out of the Stanford Development?"

"No. I mean, they would've, but we were driving too fast. We went around the back entrance where the senior housing place is, but we ditched them before we were even close." He made a point to omit the bit about destroying the infant with Silencer's brass-knuckles. "Why?"

"It's just interesting, is all."

"What is?"

Bartlet hesitated, then said, "In all the other attacks, every kid on the street under the age of eleven was taken. But not in your neighborhood."

"Really?" Marie spoke up.

"Really."

Kyle opened his mouth, but she squeezed his hand and tensed on his shoulder, so he shut it again.

She asked, "Do you have any idea why it might be?"

As the Dodge pulled up to a stop-sign, Bartlet said, "I have a couple. And nice try, but I plan to spill the beans anyway because I'm gonna need straight answers from your boyfriend back there, and in order to get them, he needs to know exactly what I'm asking."

Stepping on the gas, she said, "So one, is that you *did* lure them out before they'd finished their business, and you just don't know you did. Maybe they were chasing you even when you were so far away there wasn't a chance of catching up. Maybe they left looking for you. But I'm not so sure that's the strongest of my two theories. See, there seems to be a common link between the homes that weren't attacked. I didn't get it, though, until I watched the video on that computer today."

"So, you found it." Kyle stated matter-of-factly.

"Of course. Don't you think if I hadn't found it, I would've brought it up by now?"

"Do you still have it?" Marie asked.

"I gave it to the feds, and believe me, it's kept them busy and out of the way since. But we can talk about the video later. The kids that weren't taken, were all either sleeping in their parents' beds, or had been comforted in some way or another when they told their families what was happening at night. In one case, a mother had even called to report that her daughter claimed somebody was sneaking into her room. Did your brother make any such claims, Kyle?"

Kyle took a deep breath and told her how Abel had confessed to him that there was a monster in his bedroom, but vehemently denied it to his parents. Bartlet nodded, seemed to be processing his account as she turned onto a lightly wooded residential street marked, "21st."

Without hesitation, Kyle said, "I think you're right."

"About what?" she asked. "I haven't even told you my theory yet."

"You're thinking she takes the kids whose parents and siblings don't believe them, right? Then she brings them back and all they want to do is kill their families for letting them die."

"Stop saying 'her'," Bartlet growled. "I already told you that what was on that video was not the ghost of Bridget Newport. In a minute you're gonna see with your own eyes, and I don't want you saying anything to upset the family when we're inside. And yes. That's what I'm thinking. I'd be suspended, pending a psych-eval, if I put it in a report, but at this point—all evidence considered—it's what I have to work with." She took a left into a parking lot and gravel crunched under the tires as the Dodge came to a stop next to a baby-blue, four-door, eighties model Honda which was parked in front of a small, two-story apartment building that sat between old houses with chipped and peeling paint.

Marie sat up, lessening her grip on Kyle's hand.

Kyle said, "This isn't it."

Bartlet killed the engine, along with the heater's electric howl. Turning in her seat, she narrowed her eyes. "What's the matter, dude? Don't know the place from your own vision?"

"Of course, I do!" He released Marie's hand. "This isn't it. She lived in a house, not an apartment."

Bartlet seemed to be analyzing some sort of evidence which was stuck to his face. Finally, she said, "Come on," and climbed out of the car. But when Kyle attempted to follow, the handle stuck, and for a fraction of a second, he was Bridget again, in the back of the man's car with child-locked doors. Then Bartlet opened Marie's from the outside and they both climbed out into the cold.

"They moved here a few months ago," Bartlet stated. "The husband lost his job and left the state, and Margaret Newport couldn't make the mortgage because she doesn't bring home enough, serving as her daughter's caretaker." She shoved a finger in his face, and he saw that only traces remained of her purple nail-polish. The rest seemed to have been scratched off. Or chewed. "You don't mention the old house, or anything you've told me tonight, do you hear me?"

"Yeah." Kyle swallowed.

"Why are we here anyway?" Marie asked. "If Bridget's alive and you don't believe his story, isn't this just a waste of time?"

"It's called detective work, little girl. We follow up on every lead and leave no stone unturned. If you didn't notice, I sent my partner to find out who was in that hotel room last year as well. And if you can think of a better use of my time, I'm all ears."

Marie brushed matted hair from her face, and looked away. Kyle stood speechless for a long moment, thinking about what he'd just heard, until finally he asked, "Why would Bridget need a caretaker?"

***

The Newports lived on the second floor, behind a door marked, "B-22." It was located up a set of stairs that was covered, but not inside the building, and there was another door directly across from it with a plastic glow-in-the-dark skeleton hanging below the numbers. A television could be heard in the apartment, accompanied by feminine voices. Kyle stood close to Marie as Bartlet knocked. Then there were footsteps, the door swung open, and the TV grew loud enough for him to identify the playful sound of cartoon voices and goofy sound effects. Noel appeared in black sweats that hugged her thin hips and a matching sweater, which was only half-zipped over a cleavage-revealing tank top.

It was dark inside aside from colorful flashing light coming from the television, which was placed somewhere that couldn't be seen from the porch. Still, Kyle could see that Noel's hair was different than it had been in his vision. It was short now, and tied back into a ponytail, with bangs hanging in thick strands on either side. She had a stud in her nose which may have been a diamond, or a cubic zirconia. She locked eyes with Bartlet, then Kyle, and it occurred to him that he hadn't even noticed before how different she looked in his vision, from the way he had been seeing her at school this year. He remembered Bridget reflecting on how her parents had made her take the nose ring out for religious purposes.

So, they've lost their faith, he thought.

But before Kyle could follow the notion any further, Bartlet said, "Hey Noel. Your mom up, by chance?"

Noel glanced back indifferently, then moved out of the way as Bridget's mother stepped barefoot into the doorway in sweats that were strikingly similar to her daughter's, and a baggy white T-shirt. She held a clear dinner-glass in one hand which contained a dark soda that Kyle guessed by her droopy eyelids was mixed with liquor of some sort.

She didn't smile when she saw Bartlet. Then her eyes landed on Kyle and Marie, and she shook her head. "No. No-no-no." She waved her index finger like a windshield wiper. "I don't know what you think this is Christina, but it ain't no scared-straight program."

"That's not why I'm here," Bartlet said.

"My daughter's not a museum exhibit. You take that shit somewhere else, you hear me?"

"Margaret, when have I ever treated Bridget like an exhibit?"

"Do you know what time it is?"

"Of course, I do, and I'm sorry to show up like this, but new information has surfaced pertaining to Bridget's case, and I'm afraid it can't wait. We need to see her."

Margaret washed down what remained of her drink, then glared at Bartlet. "It's been a year. A whole fucking year. You took DNA samples from my little girl, and you made her look at pictures after picture—ha! Like that would do any good! Your department's been so fucking incompetent that you haven't had a single lead that was worth a damn, and now, on tonight of all nights, you think you're gonna show up here and I'm gonna let you torment my baby some more?" Glancing at Kyle and Marie, she said, "And you have the nerve to bring these strangers with you?"

Kyle couldn't help but feel what Bridget felt when she had wished that someone—anyone—would care that her second favorite baby was missing. As he stood on this woman's porch and stared into her eyes, he was utterly let down by her. She had failed him, and because of it, he had been abducted by a stranger and had terrible things done to him.

And though not even an hour ago, he had been sure that nothing would be able to penetrate his emotional core again, he found himself crying like an eight-year-old girl. He hadn't known it was going to happen until there were tears streaming down his face, and all he wanted was for Bridget's mom to hold him and tell him that she would never let something like that happen to him again. That she was sorry, and that she would protect him next time.

But nobody put their arms around him, instead they all just stared unbelievingly, and somewhere in the midst of his sobs, he heard Bartlet telling Margaret that he and Marie were potential witnesses who may have seen Bridget with a man that night, and if they could confirm that it was her, they might be able to identify him as well.

By the time Kyle had gotten himself under control, Margaret was just caving, and though she didn't seem pleased about doing so, she moved aside and told them to make it fast.

As soon as Kyle stepped inside, the television came into view. It was a big flat-screen, mounted to the wall across from one couch which sat in the living-room. It was playing cartoons which shouldn't have been aired this late at night, and Kyle guessed it was connected to a DVD or a blue-ray player. Then Margaret turned on the light and all thoughts of what was on TV scurried away like cockroaches.

Bridget was there. She sat on the floor in front of the couch in what looked like a baby's car-seat, only much bigger, wearing a two-piece blue pajama set. Straps, which were identical to seatbelts, crossed over her shoulders and ribcage, creating the letter "x," and latching in the middle of her chest. Her arms curled like a praying mantis, and her face was distorted, her bottom lip hanging as she drooled over it. She turned her attention from the TV just long enough to lock eyes with Kyle and stick her tongue out.

"Aaaaaaargugubuh!"

Marie gasped and stepped so close to him that they were touching. Kyle almost moved away, but stopped himself, instead, staring down at Bridget like he was the child, and she was a cartoon. Only she wasn't a cartoon. She wasn't the monster, either. She couldn't seem to control her own body, and her arms and legs flailed about, but she was a little girl who had been ruined by the real monster, and as he gazed down at what she had become, he wanted nothing more than to find the son-of-a-bitch, and avenge her in the worst ways imaginable.

Then he saw the doll in her lap. A blond-haired baby in a purple dress. It lay awkward and motionless, as she turned her head and focused once again on the TV, and before Kyle knew what was happening, he uttered, "Molly."

***

The monster's work wasn't done. There were still babies to be had, so it moved as fast as it could from one home to another, hitting more houses and more neighborhoods than on any other night. Soon the streets were crawling with new babies, trick-or-treating in the Halloween costumes that their mommies and daddies had bought them.

***

Bartlet stepped up next to Kyle, gave him an evil eye. The door shut behind him and there was a hollow "thunk," which Kyle knew without looking was Margaret Newport's glass landing on the carpet.

Then Noel was in his face. "What did you just say?"

"I ah—" Kyle stuttered. "I—"

Bartlet asked, "Is this the girl you saw, Kyle?"

"No!" Noel spat. "What you said a second ago—say it again!"

Kyle didn't meet her eyes, just stared at Bridget, who jerked her head a few times and watched her cartoons with a vacant, yet, wide-eyed expression.

"I know about the dolls," his voice was weak. "I know she was looking for that one the night she was taken. Her name's Molly, and she always wears purple. Not because it's such a great look for her, but because somebody has to wear it."

"Kyle," Bartlet growled. "What the hell are you—"

"She was in the laundry room. On top of the dryer. I remem—Bridget remembered when she was in his car." Kyle felt the tears coming again. He pursed his lips and willed them back.

Margaret stepped up next to her daughter and bared her teeth, shoving her face so close to Kyle's he could smell her liquor-ridden breath. "How the hell do you know that?"

"Because I was there."

He realized a second too late that he had said the wrong thing. But before he could backtrack, Noel put her hands on his chest and propelled herself forward, shoving him with all of her weight. "YOU FUCKING SON-OF-A-BITCH! I KNOW YOU! I KNOW WHO THE FUCK YOU ARE! WHAT DID YOU DO TO MY SISTER?"

Kyle doubled over as he collided with the television set, causing it to come off whatever it was hooked to and crash noisily onto the floor. The screen went black as his eyes instinctively landed again on Bridget, who jumped startled, but stared at the commotion mostly expressionless. Then Margaret was on him as well, and both she and her daughter were hitting him in the head and the body.

"WHAT THE FUCK DID YOU DO TO MY LITTLE GIRL? ANSWER ME! WHAT DID YOU DO, YOU LITTLE SHIT?"

"Nothing! Nothing! Jesus, I would never— That's not what I meant! Please just hear me out."

The blows persisted, however, and though they didn't actually hurt—were akin to being hit with wet towels— the intent behind them was excruciating. The sting of the pain which was driving them. Still, he didn't straighten up until he heard Marie's grunts and glanced to see her behind Noel, her arms around the teenager, holding her in a bear-hug as she writhed and attempted to get away.

"Stop!" Bartlet exclaimed. "Stop it right now!" Then she was in the confrontation, wedging herself in the middle of it all and thrusting her arms out like a crucifixion victim. "Kyle! You just couldn't listen, could you? You couldn't keep your mouth shut!"

Margaret took a step back and panted, staring at Kyle like he was something that a neighbor's dog had left in her yard. But her oldest daughter continued to struggle against Marie's embrace.

"Get the fuck off me! Get your skanky hands off me, you bitch!"

"Just relax," Marie huffed. "Please. Just listen to what he has to say."

"No!" Bartlet barked. "Kyle, you're gonna shut your mouth here and now! Not another word from either of you! We're leaving. Margaret, I'm sorry. This was a bad idea, and I'll make it up to you."

All along, all Kyle could think was, *How? She's still alive. How in the hell can she be Abel's Monster if she's still alive?*

And, *they didn't care. They didn't care that Molly was lost. She tried to tell them, and they wouldn't listen because they were too busy arguing about Halloween and church and nose rings and everything except her second favorite baby. They made Bridget look for her all alone and then the man got her. He got her and he hurt her, and he put her in the water and look at her now.*

Kyle shook off the thoughts, which he didn't seem to have control over. He felt his lips curl back, and cold air nip at his gums as he bared his teeth. What he needed was what Rivas was after. The name of the rapist. And once he had it, he still needed Bartlet to track him down. Then he needed to ditch her somehow, because there was no way in hell she would allow him to do what needed to be done next.

As he was having this thought, Margaret frowned at him and spat, "No."

Noel writhed a couple more times, then stopped fighting. "What?"

"I said 'no'. You're not taking him anywhere until he says what he has to say, Christina."

Dropping her arms and letting her hands slap her hips, Bartlet growled, "Not gonna happen Margaret."

"Don't tell me what is and isn't gonna happen in my own home, Christina! You and your people? You're useless! You dropped the ball on my family and my little girl! I want answers, do you hear me? A whole year, and you still haven't told me shit! You say this kid's a witness? That you're onto something? Fine. I'll bite. But I'm gonna hear what he has to say too! Do you understand me? That's MY baby! MINE!"

Bridget's arms flailed more wildly than before, crossing over one another as she tried to rock against the straps. She let out another "Aaaaaaaaaaaaarg," that made Kyle's stomach roll over like a distressed old corpse in a coffin. Then she started kicking violently at the air with both shoeless feet until Molly rolled off her lap and onto the floor. "Aaaaaaargubuh!" Aaaaaaaguuuuuh! Guh! Guh!"

"Margaret!" Bartlet lost her cool. "Stop it! You're drunk and you're scaring your daughter!"

"Scaring her? I'm scaring her? Look at her! She's a goddamn vegetable! She's nine-years-old in diapers! She doesn't know her foot from a block of cheese. She eats baby-food, Christina! All she knows is that her cartoon's turned off!" Addressing Marie, she said, "Young lady, if you don't get your hands off my daughter, I'm going to break them."

So slowly and reluctantly, Marie released her hold on Noel, who turned and stared fiery darts at her.

"Noel!" Margaret snapped. "Cool your jets. Sit down. Everybody, sit the hell down!"

Bartlet held the demeanor and expression of a woman who wanted nothing more than to stand her ground, but just didn't have the energy. She stood rigid, yet somehow defeated for a long moment. Then, finally, she glared at Kyle and spat, "You heard the woman. Take a seat and tell her your story."

***

"If all—the raindrops, were lemon-drops and gumdrops—oh what a rain that would be!" Michael sang as he skipped up the street, machete in one hand, revolver in the other. There were lots of guns in the houses and the kids were collecting them all. They weren't knocking on the doors anymore, because the people were no longer answering. Now they just broke a window or a lock and went in and killed everyone.

But they never forgot to say "trick-or-treat" first, because it wasn't right to not say it when you were trick-or-treating.

There were bodies strewn out on lawns, hanging from trees—even nailed to the sides of houses. Some of the homes were on fire, even though it was raining, and Michael had never known fun like he was having now. A lot of the kids had climbed up on roofs and begun to shoot people in cars who were attempting to get out of the neighborhood.

Michael was wearing a white dress because even though it wasn't really Halloween yet, tonight was the night that the monster had chosen to celebrate it, and he had always wondered what it would be like to be a girl. As he stepped onto a nicely mowed lawn, he peered up at the cloudy sky and chirped, "I'd stand outside with my mouth open wide! Ah! Ah! Ah-ah! Ah! Ah-ah! Ah! Ah-ah!" and it was funny because even though he couldn't feel them, he knew that itty-bitty rain drops really were falling into his mouth.

A black car came screeching around a corner and gunshots erupted, one after another. The windows sang as they broke, then the car veered into the yard that Michael was in, missing him by just inches, and slamming into the side of the house. The horn went off, then didn't stop. Looking, Michael saw that the man who had been driving was lying face down on the steering wheel.

Then one of the back doors opened and a teenage girl and a golden dog both jumped out. The dog darted through the yard, and it may have gotten away, but Michael raised his gun and shot it right in the butt. It cried out and rolled onto its back like a bug, waving its legs at the sky as he walked over and chopped its head off with his machete.

The girl screamed, "No! No! No-no-no-no-no! Please don't—" But whatever else she meant to say was cut off as a group of children in assorted colored costumes closed in on her.

"Trick-or-treat!"

Her body was penetrated from every direction by various sharp steel objects before she even hit the grass. Then, one boy began to remove her leg with a hacksaw, starting just below the knee.

Michael opened his mouth to the sky and caught more raindrops, then broke out the nearest window, climbing into a house and emptying his revolver on the people inside. One man made it out the back door, but there were children out there waiting for him. Michael found a rifle, with six extra magazines, so he took them all up to the roof and that's where he waited and watched as over a hundred children continued to trick-or-treat.

***

Kyle had been sure he would cry again, but he must have finally run dry of tears, because by the time he was finished telling his story for the third time tonight, the only people in the room shedding them were Bridget's mother and sister.

They had sat on either side of him on the couch, leaning forward and hanging on every word. Noel had initially tried to pace, but her mother had demanded that she sit down. Kyle could smell a perfume coming off her which was reminiscent of one that Claudia sometimes wore.

Bartlet and Marie sat in wooden kitchen chairs that Margaret had dragged into the living-room. Bridget had calmed down at some point. She now stared up at a spot where the ceiling met the wall, and seemed to be trying to chew the inside of her face.

He was naming her dolls when Noel had jerked so subtly that he almost didn't catch it. Then she'd tried to blink back her tears, but eventually she'd just given into them. It wasn't until he talked about the blanket and the jack-o-lanterns in the Cinema 7, however, that Margaret burst into full-blown, audible sobs. When he described what happened at the river, Noel flew to her feet and dashed down the hall, into what he assumed was a bathroom.

He knew that the visuals provided by his own memory were so much worse than anything that their imaginations could use to attempt to fill in the gaps, but he still couldn't help but sympathize with them.

And though he didn't want to dig up any more turmoil than necessary, he had to ask, "How long?"

Sniffing and wiping her nose with the back of her hand, Margaret said, "'How long' what?" in the most deflated tone he had ever heard.

"How long was she—"

"Thirteen minutes. From the time that the couple across the river called it in, to when the medics arrived and managed to bring her back, she was dead for thirteen whole minutes."

"Jesus."

"Yeah. That's what I thought too."

"No," Kyle shook his head. "That's not what I—"

"Lemme make sure I'm hearing you correctly." Margaret still had tears in her eyes, but she seemed to have gained some semblance of control over them. "You live in one of the neighborhoods that was hit by the kids from the news, and your whole family was killed. Then you ran—" she squinted at Bartlet, "—because Christina wanted to arrest you?"

"For his safety," Bartlet's voice was flat.

Margaret held up a hand, returned her attention to Kyle. Nodding, she said, "Okay. I get that part now. So, you were hiding in Lake McMurray and the kids found you somehow—that I don't quite get—and they had my daughter's spirit with them? It sounds to me like you're trying to say that Bridget is causing all this shit. Is that what you're saying?"

"No," Kyle replied as Noel returned and took a seat closer to him than she had been before. "I thought so at first, but that's because the vision ended before she was revived, and I thought she was dead. Now, I ah—I think her spirit is causing it, but not her."

Every eye in the room seemed to zone in on him, as if he had just said that the world was flat.

Noel trembled, "Are you trying to say that her spirit left her and never came back? That my sister doesn't have a soul?"

"I didn't say that either."

"Then what?" she sniffed.

"I don't know. I mean I'm not saying that. I'm just telling you what I saw. Well, what I experienced. I didn't do this to her though. I swear I would never—"

"We know you didn't," Margaret said coldly.

"You do?"

She nodded. Took a deep breath. Let it out. "We've had a description of the person who did it for a year now. It wasn't the best, but you don't look like a middle-aged, overweight man to me. Unless you were there up until the point that he was spotted with her at the river, but frankly, I find it very unlikely that my little girl would be telling you about her dolls as she was being kidnapped and—" Another deep breath. Her eyes had dark circles under them that they hadn't had in his vision, and he suspected it wasn't because she was intoxicated. "You knew this one."

Leaning down, she scooped up the doll on the floor. "You didn't ask or second-guess yourself. You knew it was Molly the second you laid eyes on it. I knew this thing was the reason she went out that night. As soon as we figured out that she'd been taken, I knew I should have just helped her look for the fucking thing." Her grip tightened around the doll like it was a stress-ball, and Kyle was sure she would break into loud sobs again. But she didn't. Instead, her tears stopped altogether. Though her expression grew cold, there was a desperation in her eyes that seemed like it was only meant for Kyle to see as she gazed into his. "So, what now?"

"What do you mean?" he responded, even though he already knew what was being asked.

"We know the hotel. We know the room number and what night he was there, right?"

Kyle nodded.

"He used a key?" she went on, looking over at Bridget, who was still transfixed on the ceiling.

Kyle tilted his head, then a chill came over him because he understood what she was thinking, and why in the hell hadn't he, or anybody else caught it yet? "Yeah!" he exclaimed. "He had a key to the theater! He must own the place. Or maybe he knows the owner. Either way—"

But before he could finish, Bartlet's phone vibrated noisily in her pocket and she popped up like a piece of bread in a toaster, turning her back to them as she took the call.

"Talk to me, Rivas. Yeah. Not much better on this end. What'd you get?"

There was a long pause in which nobody seemed to even breathe. Kyle met Marie's eyes, and she offered the hint of a smile, which was meant to be supportive, and he appreciated her more than ever for it.

Then, Bartlet said, "Jesus. Yeah. I know who he is. Good. Go. I'll be in touch." She hung up, slipped the phone back into her pocket, and turned, addressing Marie. Moving her jacket to reveal her holstered black gun, she reached behind her and produced a pair of handcuffs. "Marie, stand up for me and place your hands behind your back. Keep in mind, I'll only ask nicely once."

***

Red and blue lights reflected off the cloudy sky and sirens screamed as police cars poured into the neighborhood like water. Then gunshots exploded from the roofs. Windows shattered and tires popped, causing sparks to fly from the pavement as the vehicles drove on their rims.

Some of them slammed into telephone poles or each other, but others kept driving as children swarmed them, tossing babies with weaponized forearms inside. Officers scrambled out into the rain, drawing handguns and firing on kids who didn't go down, but rather advanced on them with sharp objects and smiles.

Soon blue-uniformed corpses lined the street, the trunks of squad-cars lay open, and the monster's babies marched out of the neighborhood with police issued pistols and assault rifles to continue trick-or-treating somewhere else.

***

Kyle flew to his feet first, and Bartlet had her pistol out before he even found his balance. She held it with both hands, cuffs dangling from one as well, and leveled it at his chest.

"Sit the fuck down, Kyle! You're a half a step away from being in the same boat, and I have two sets of cuffs!"

"Whoa!" He threw his hands up. "What the hell? You promised! You swore on your son's life!"

"Shut up, and sit down!" Nodding to Marie, she said. "Up! Now!"

"Aaaaaaarrrrrrg," Bridget rocked in her chair, glanced down from the ceiling at the flat-screen on the floor. "Aaaaguh! Guh! Guuuuuuuuuuuuuuuuuh!"

Margaret and Noel watched silently from behind Kyle on the couch.

Finally, Marie said, "I don't understand."

Taking two steps back, Bartlet growled, "All you need to understand right now, is that I'm a police officer, I have a gun, and I'm giving you both a fucking directive. Kyle, you sit down. Miss Franco? Stand up and place your hands behind your back."

No way, Kyle thought. *No fucking way. She'll have to shoot me.*

And by her demeanor, he was sure she would. Still, Marie had saved his life twice. She had dived on top of him and shielded him with her own body when he was being jumped. She had left home to hide from the police and a militia of evil murderous children with him, though she didn't have to. He had no intention of putting his tail between his legs when she needed him.

But then she stood and placed a hand on his chest, gazing into his eyes and once again, a message was conveyed without words.

We don't have a choice.

She shoved him lightly, and he glided back down onto the couch. Then, she turned, said, "Okay," and placed her hands behind her back.

Holstering her pistol, Bartlet advanced on her and had her cuffed in a matter of seconds. Then she began to pat her down. Finally, Margaret spoke up.

"What the hell's going on, Christina?"

Pulling the brass-knuckles from Marie's pocket, Bartlet examined them, then set them on her chair. "My partner just got the name of the man who was checked into the Sherman Inn, room one-one-seven, at this time last year. That's what."

"So? If it was a man, why in the world are you arresting this girl?"

"Because," she checked Marie's socks, then straightened up, "it was her asshole father."

***

Most of the monster's babies stuck together until they went into the neighborhoods. Then they spread out, trick-or-treated in just about every house, and moving on to the next street as a group again. But the ones who had only been changed tonight, traveled in smaller groups on the other side of town. Some of them were even alone, with weapons that they found at home and used to kill their mommies and daddies. The majority of the Mount Vernon Police Force was dead, including those from the local Sheriff's Department, and the agents from out of town. Helicopters were buzzing overhead, shining lights and recording the commotion. The monster was having so much fun with its babies, but it still had another surprise in store.

***

Kyle felt as if he was sinking into the couch. His breathing grew rapid and he saw Bridget's mother and sister's chests heaving to the same rhythm. He heard the man's accent in his head, *You want the trouble with me?* and remembered Marie telling him that she was Italian.

Marie shrieked, "What?"

"Quiet." Bartlet brought out a small bundle of cash and set it next to the knuckles.

Kyle said, "Marie? Was your dad in the U.S. last year at this time?"

Marie's eyes expanded, and her jaw dropped. She hesitated for a long moment, then nodded. "Yes. I mean, yes. He ah—he was inspecting the buildings. Figuring out if—"

"Shut up!" Bartlet snapped. "Are you deaf, or just stupid?"

Ignoring her, Kyle asked, "Does he have an accent? I mean not just British, or Australian, or whatever. Does he have an Italian accent?"

Marie frowned. For the first time since he had met her, she appeared genuinely confused. "Of course, he does. But that doesn't mean—"

"Jesus."

Bridget attempted to stuff her hand into her mouth, missing by inches and pressing it into her cheek. Bartlet took Marie's arm and pulled her toward the door. "Come on, Kyle. You're coming with. And keep in mind that if you try anything funny, you'll end up in cuffs too."

Margaret hopped to her feet. "Christina?"

"No Margaret! My partner's on his way to her house right now to detain her father. He'll request a DNA sample, but if he refuses to give it, we'll have to let them both go until we can acquire a warrant. Do you think that some teenager's story about how he had a vision is enough to get that?"

"Then help me understand," Margaret spoke calmly. "How does arresting his daughter get you a warrant any faster?"

"Maybe it doesn't, but I think she knows something that she's not telling me. And she's not arrested. She's just detained for now."

It was a lie. Kyle knew there was no way Bartlet believed that Marie's father would tell her if he *had* done such a horrible thing. Who would ever tell his family something like that? She merely thought that if she showed up at the Franco residence with the man's daughter in handcuffs, he would agree to take a DNA test, maybe even confess.

And what if he did? What if he allowed himself to be tested? How long would it be before the results came back, and how many people would still die? Kyle suspected that even arresting him wouldn't make a difference, as he would be safe behind bars, where the children couldn't touch him.

"Then you believe him," Margaret pushed. "You obviously believe Kyle's story, or it wouldn't matter who was in that room that night, would it?"

Reaching up, Noel touched her mother's arm. "Mom—"

"No!" Margaret snapped. "None of this is adding up! You can't come to my home in the middle of the night and feed me a line of bullshit, when the mother fucker who did this to my daughter," she pointed to Bridget, "might be living a mile away!"

"It doesn't make sense," Marie murmured, though her expression was far off. She stared down at her feet on the verge of tears. "It can't be correct. There's no way it was my—"

Bartlet exclaimed, "I'm sorry, Margaret, but unfortunately for you, this is how it's gonna happen! And

I don't know what I believe! Kyle knows something. His story *is* adding up. Does that mean that every bit of it's true? Not necessarily. Kyle? Up! I left my radio in the car, or we would have known that all hell is breaking loose out there right now. My partner says it's a fucking madhouse on the streets. So, I highly recommend you don't make me ask again."

Marie stopped mumbling, took a deep breath. Kyle stared into the side of her face harder than he had ever stared at anybody before, begging her with his eyes to look at him. He knew she saw him in her periphery, but she refused to acknowledge it. Finally, he stood up and glanced at Margaret, then Noel. Then Bridget. He reluctantly made his way across the room as Margaret said, "I wanna come with."

Bartlet maintained her grip on Marie's arm, turned and swept Margaret's liquor glass out of the way with her foot as she reached for the knob. "Forgive me if I don't give a shit what you—"

But before she could get another word out, Kyle picked the brass-knuckles up off the chair, slipped his fingers into them and punched her as hard as he could in the back of the head. Margaret gasped as Noel flew to her feet. There was an audible "thud," and Bartlet crumbled to the floor, landing on her side with her arms splayed out like she wanted a hug. Her eyes were closed, and she didn't move, but to Kyle's relief, he could see her chest heaving.

"Holy shit!" Noel cried.

"Baby!" Finally, Marie met his eyes.

Ignoring her, he dropped to one knee and rummaged through Bartlet's pockets until he found a thin piece of metal which had to be the handcuff key. It only took him a second to get them off her and once he did, she threw her arms around him and pressed her lips into his so hard it almost hurt.

Pulling away just far enough that he could still feel her breath on his mouth, she said, "What are you thinking? Oh, baby, you're gonna go to jail. Why would you—"

He kissed her again for a long moment and savored her touch, her taste, her body against his. When he finally pulled away, he said, "We're in this together, right?"

Marie inhaled, cupped the back of his head. "Right. Yes. Check her, Kyle. Make sure she's okay please."

Kyle stepped back and glanced down at Bartlet, but he froze because Margaret was just coming back up with the detective's police-issued handgun. Noel stepped next to her mother and Bridget groaned as Margaret pointed the weapon at Kyle's face.

He slowly raised his hands, the knuckles still draped over one of them. "Listen—"

"Stop." Pointing the gun at Marie, she said, "Was it your dad? Did your father do this to my baby girl?"

Marie opened her mouth, and at first, she didn't speak. Then, in a weak voice, she said, "I don't know."

"You know! Of course, you know! He's your father for Christ's sake. There's no point in lying to me, or to yourself for that matter, girl. So, dig deep, and tell me right now, is your father capable of this?"

Finally, a tear streamed down the side of Marie's nose. She blinked twice, however, and there were no more. Then she nodded.

"Oh my God," Noel edged closer to her mother.

Margaret's features hardened, and for a second, Kyle was sure she was going to pull the trigger. He started to object, to beg her not to hurt the girl whom he loved. Then she lowered the gun and something that resembled sympathy appeared on her face. "I'm sorry."

Marie sniffed. Nodded again.

"Will you take me to him?"

"Yes," Marie's voice was weak. "Of course, I will. And I think we should bring Bridget as well."

Margaret's lips twitched, threatening to curve into a frown, as she said, "You bet your ass she's coming with."

Chapter Twelve

It was dark out and it was raining, and Gabriel Brenton was lost when the lights appeared behind him. Not physically, (he knew Stanwood well enough to know that he was walking along Columbus Street, toward Downtown), and not spiritually either. But emotionally and mentally he was a fucking wreck. As soon as he'd left Clinton Funeral Home with the guard's gun in hand, he knew that he'd screwed up. He would be charged with escape and given more time.

But wasn't that the destiny that he'd resigned to anyway? That one event after another would keep him perpetually in prison? And did it even matter anymore? The worst part was knowing, yet not stopping. Not turning back, or finding a cop somewhere and giving himself up. Surely there were cameras in the venue which would demonstrate his innocence.

But innocence was a subjective term, because if Gabe were really innocent, then why had God allowed his little girl to be possessed? And that's exactly what it had been, hadn't it? She had been dead as a doornail, and her body possessed by the devil himself.

Gabe wasn't a sensationalist, and he wasn't going to speculate on what it implied. He doubted it was the end of the world. But he was a Bible-Believing-Christian, and if possession happened in the Bible, then why not in real life? He had never considered that it could happen to a corpse, but he was aware that there were a hundred-and-one ways to interpret every word of every verse, and a hundred of them had to be wrong.

He was also aware that the husband is the spiritual head of every household, and though any family is susceptible to fall under attack, his had been defeated because he had failed as such.

He had known what he was doing when he ran. He hadn't been on autopilot like he had the night that he earned his sentence outside of that bar. He just hadn't cared at the time what the consequences would be. So, he'd hopped a few fences, and hidden in a toolshed in somebody's backyard, listening to sirens as they rushed to the scene, and silently praying for hours before he finally crept out.

Columbus was a residential street. The houses were mostly two and three stories high, and only a few years old. He guessed that it was past midnight, as there had been exactly zero traffic since he'd emerged from the shed until now. Though he was in a T-shirt, and wouldn't have turned down a jacket, he had thus far been ignoring the cold which nipped at his forearms.

As the lights increased, he made a point not to look back, but he was aware that it was more likely to be a police car than anything else. And that they were guaranteed to be on the lookout for the escaped convict, walking around with a gun in prison attire. So even before he heard tires turning over pavement and metal cutting through the wind, he began to wonder if he would get the keys back when he reentered Walla Walla. Or if he would even want them this time.

That also begged the question of how he could have been so wrong in thinking that God had moved him to leave Zack in control. But that wasn't such a mystery, now, was it? Gabe had failed at everything there was to fail at of late, so why wouldn't he fall short of hearing (or maybe just understanding) the voice of God as well?

Then it was next to him, driving at the pace which he was walking, and he still didn't look, focusing, rather, on the raindrops pixelating in the beams of the headlights directly in front of it. He considered thinking a silent prayer, appealing to The Lord for it not to be a cop, but then decided once again that he didn't care.

There was the electronic hum of a window sliding down, and though he knew it only looked more suspicious, Gabriel Brenton *still* refused to look until the occupant finally spoke.

"Gabe?"

Then he stopped in his tracks, his head snapped in the direction of the voice, and his eyes beheld a redheaded woman in a white dress that made his heart leap and attempt to fly right out of his mouth.

"Carrie?"

The car was a red nineties-model Ford that almost matched her hair. Its tires slid in the rain briefly, as it came to a halt and the driver's door opened. Carrie appeared over the top of the vehicle with her hair straightened and pale skin visible in streaks where the rain had washed over the makeup which had been applied for her funeral. Her high heels clicked as she stepped around the front, and didn't even squint when the headlights shone right into her face.

Even after what had happened today with Kim and the other children, Gabe felt his entire body begin to shake. She was as beautiful as ever, but she was horrible as well because she was dead. Dead and possessed, which meant that she wasn't Carrie.

But then she sucked in a breath, and said, "Gabe, baby. It's me. Please don't run." And another breath. "Just talk to me."

She stopped only feet from him, and that's when he found his voice. "You're not Carrie. Carrie's dead."

"I am Carrie, Gabe." Her voice was nothing like his daughter's had been today. It was exactly how he remembered it, though her face was expressionless. "And yeah, I'm dead. Thanks for noticing."

Every hair on his body erected and tried to uproot itself from his skin. Reaching behind his back, he removed the gun from his waistband.

"Oh Gabe. You don't know how to shoot a gun."

"Sure I do."

Finally, Carrie smiled, and it was so warm that he was tempted to believe that she was actually her. But her stomach heaved between every sentence that she uttered because she needed air to speak, and dead people's lungs didn't work on their own.

"Gabe, look at me." She held her arms out to her sides and spun around, causing her dress to flare, exposing milky-white calves that rivaled the preacher's at her funeral. "If I'm not me, then who am I?"

"You're the devil." He racked the slide and felt metal scrape on metal in his trembling hands.

"Do you remember how we met? At Josh's house? What was your goofy-ass friend's last name? Colbol, right? Josh Colbol? Remember I was there with Tina, and she was trying to get him to find somebody to buy us beer? You were wearing that dumb green sweater with the skeleton on the back, and then I saw you at school a couple days later and we had lunch together.

"I remember our wedding, too, Gabe. I remember the dress that your sister's kid was wearing. I remember making love to you on our front porch in the middle of the night and not caring if we were caught. And you know what else I remember? I remember you doing the dumbest thing you've ever done and leaving me to raise our little girl alone."

"You weren't alone," he said coldly.

"Oh, fuck off dude. Grow up. What did you expect? That I would just sit around on my hands and suffer because you fucked up? Ha! I always did wonder what it must be like in that fantasy world inside your head.

"But no. You're right. I wasn't alone. I wasn't sleeping around, either, though. Most girls would have jumped at the opportunity to justify having a good time. Me? I had one fucking boyfriend in two years, and you're gonna crucify me for it?

"Okay. I'll take it. Call me dead. Call me a whore. Who knows? They might both be true. It's a matter of perspective, I guess. But don't you dare fucking tell me that I'm not me." She took a step toward him, sucking in air. He took a step back, but didn't raise the gun, which was now hanging at his side.

"How are you here, Carrie?"

"How?" she snorted. "Are you really asking me how? Did you not see our little girl today? How about all those other kids? Maybe I don't know you nearly as good as I thought I did, because I would have sworn if you were gonna contemplate a question like that, it would have happened hours ago.

"We're all here, baby. Everyone who was at the funeral. They're all awake and wandering. Doesn't that tell you something, Gabriel? Doesn't it count for anything that I left Gus behind to come and find you? Don't you even care?"

"Convenience," he snickered. "That's all it is, Carrie. You didn't want me when it was inconvenient to want me. But now that you're dead and I'm free—" He shook his head because what the hell was he even entertaining?

Carrie sucked in another breath and snapped, "I always wanted you, you idiot! It was always you! You're the one who left me! You left me, and you left Kim, and we needed you, but you were gone! Look at us now! Look at yourself! Look at what our family has become because of your stupidity!

"But I forgive you, and that's what you don't seem to get." Her heels clicked as she advanced on him, and this time he didn't retreat. Reaching up, she took his face in both hands and said, "I forgive you, Gabe. I wanna be a family again. I want us to be together. Not just for now, either. I want us to be together forever and ever like we always planned. Just the three of us." She motioned subtly toward the car with her eyes, and though he refused to look, Gabe knew that she had his daughter inside. "Would you like that?"

His body stopped trembling and the fear seemed to drain right out of him like somebody had pulled a plug. But his lips didn't stop. They quivered, and there was a tingling in his chest like a spider was inside dancing on a hotplate as a warmth appeared below the surface of his eyes.

And there they were. The long-anticipated tears, which he hadn't yet been able to shed, not because he didn't care, but because sometime during his prison sentence, he had been broken. He had managed to fit in so well, and all the convicts looked up to him even though he was younger than them. But in the end, that only pointed to something very negative in nature because it meant that he had rapidly become one of them. So, he hadn't cried because convicts don't shed tears. Ever.

But it hadn't been prison that had broken him. It had always been Carrie. And his spiritual walk? It had been real. It was what he needed at the time to get him by, but it had never been complete, because he had never truly and completely forgiven his wife.

So, as she stood in front of him—and he was now convinced that it was, in fact, Carrie—he wasn't a convict anymore, and the tears were finally coming. He turned his face away from her, and pursed his lips. At first, he blinked, because it didn't feel natural to want to cry.

Then Carrie repositioned his head, so they were once again gazing into each other's eyes and when she took in air to speak, she got some of his breath as well. She repeated, "Gabe, do you forgive me?"

Her hand found his shoulder and ran lightly down his arm as the floodgates opened, and tears burst forth almost explosively. "I don't know," he moaned. "I don't—I don't know if I can, Carrie." He sniffed and hiccupped, attempting to choke the words out, but it felt good to finally feel something. "You took my daughter from me. If you didn't want to—if you couldn't wait—fine. But why, Carrie? Why did you have to take Kim? She was my baby too."

"Ssshhh." She stroked his face, causing his body to jerk against her cold hand. "Ssshhh. It's okay. I understand, and I don't need you to forgive me, baby. I just thought it might help you to be at peace."

Then before he even knew she was taking it, the weight of the gun disappeared from his hand, and she pressed the barrel to his chest and sent a bullet through his heart.

***

Benito Nunez slid out of the container on the wall and scanned the hospital's morgue. He knew exactly where he was because the monster knew. He also knew everything that had transpired around his two sons since they had murdered him and their mother last night. A few other parents were climbing out as well. Some were heavily mutilated. Others only had small gashes or bullet-holes in different parts of their bodies.

Once they were standing in the middle of the room in nothing but hospital gowns, they began to select sharp objects from trays that sat next to empty gurneys. Then, Benito took his wife's hand and they all left as a unit to find their children.

***

The monster visited the funeral home downtown next, waking the mommies and daddies and brothers and sisters so they could join the fun. Then the one on College Way. Then the others, and the homes where the babies had trick-or-treated. It brought back everybody whom the babies had killed. Even the cops. Then, when the streets were swarming with walking corpses, it floated, floated, floated and watched from above.

***

Kyle and Marie dragged Bartlet, unconscious, into the bathroom and handcuffed her to a pipe below the sink. Though Noel had begged to go with them, Margaret made her stay and make sure the detective was all right. Then they piled into the Dodge Caliber, because in light of everything they had already done, stealing a police-car seemed inconsequential.

Bridget's chair strapped easily into the middle-back seat, and she hardly reacted as they took off. Marie drove and Kyle sat in the passenger seat, hyper-aware that Margaret, who was seated directly behind him, still had Bartlet's gun.

As she pulled out of the parking lot, Marie leaned forward and gazed up at three choppers, which were circling the sky off to the left. "We'll have to take the long way," she said. "If we avoid where those news helicopters are, we shouldn't run into the children."

"Just get us there," Margaret spoke in a quiet monotone.

Gunshots and sirens could be heard in the distance, and every now and then, an explosion.

Kyle said, "They're trick-or-treating already."

"What the hell does that even mean?" Margaret asked.

"I don't ah—I don't actually know. I mean, on the video she—well the monster said it wanted to take my brother trick-or-treating. I wasn't positive, but when we linked up, I was able to think like—I mean—"

"Jesus kid. Just say her for Christ's sake."

"Right. I was able to think like her, and I'm almost positive that she didn't actually mean on Halloween, but on the night that it happened to her. And by trick-or-treating, I think they're going door to door looking for Marie's dad."

"Aaaaaaarguuuuuuuuuuuuuubuuuuuuuuuuh!" Bridget cried.

"It doesn't make sense," Margaret said.

Marie turned onto a residential street marked, "Pine."

Kyle thought about it, then asked why not.

"After your family was killed, didn't they leave town just so your brother could hunt you down?"

"I don't know if that was why, but yeah, they found me."

"Then why can't she find this guy just as easy?"

Marie's eyes narrowed and she turned her head ever-so-subtly, meeting Kyle's gaze in her peripheral. Kyle wanted to respond, but didn't know how. Before he could put any more thought into it, however, Marie's eyes expanded and zeroed in on Kyle's window. She shrieked, the car swerved, and something thumped right next to him.

Turning around, he looked out and saw a tall, dark-haired man with one orange eye in a hospital gown. His hands were both pressed against the window and the other eye was missing. He held a small metal object which Kyle recognized from rummaging through drawers at the doctor's office.

A scalpel.

"Oh, holy shit!"

Margaret shouted something that he didn't understand as the car scraped against him, turning his body and leaving him behind along with a small group of others who were all dressed identically to him. He didn't stop walking, and neither did they. Up ahead, three more did stop, however, right in the middle of the road. There were two men and an overweight woman, and they were pale under the streetlights. They stared with glowing eyes for a second, then walked right at the car as if engaged in a game of chicken.

"Hit it," Margaret said.

"What?" Marie asked.

"Step on the gas, girl! Come on!"

"Oh." Marie shook her head, laid her foot on the pedal.

The car zipped forward, picking up speed faster than Kyle would have expected. Then, the people who had to have been parents of the children, picked up their pace as well, sprinting fearlessly at the headlights. They all held objects that Kyle assumed belonged in the hospital, which was only blocks away, and one of them had fresh blood all over his gown.

Kyle tensed, and Marie cried out as she smashed into all three of them like bowling pins. He couldn't help but close his eyes. There was a hollow thump against the windshield, then crunching overhead, and he heard the bodies roll off the back window.

They're gone, he thought, opening his eyes and shouting at the sight of one of the males on all fours on the hood. His throat was wide open because half of his neck had been cut through with a precision that was almost surgical. His palms were pressed against the windshield and his light-brown hair tossed in the wind as he gazed inside, illuminating the car with his eyes. But he wasn't moving to attack, just staring past Kyle and Marie, directly at Bridget.

Marie slammed on the brakes and the tires screeched as the car slid for a while, then came to a stop, hurling the dead body onto the wet pavement where it rolled at least thirty feet and began to climb to its feet.

"GOOOOO!" Margaret screamed.

Marie set the vehicle back in motion, slamming once again into the thing. Only this time it went down and disappeared as the Dodge's tires trekked up and over, first in the front, then the back. Kyle watched in the rearview mirror, as they picked up speed, but it didn't move again.

***

Margaret listened to Bartlet's police radio and Kyle kept an eye on where the helicopters went. They had to take a longer route to avoid the trick-or-treaters, and it just so happened to lead them through Urban Ave. It was well past midnight, however, and Kyle never would have expected to see Claudia out this late.

Yet there she was, leaning up against the restaurant at the end of her street. He almost didn't notice her because a guy in a black hooded jacket stood in front of her, his arms around her waist, blocking the view.

"Stop the car!" he exclaimed.

"What?" Marie gasped.

"Just do it!"

"Okay. Okay." She pulled to the side of the road, causing Claudia and her companion both to look curiously at the vehicle.

"What are we doing?" Margaret barked.

But Kyle was already out the door where sirens and the *whomp-whomp-whomp* of helicopter blades filled his ears. He walked purposefully toward the couple, slipping his hand into his pocket as Silencer turned, reaching up and lowering his hood.

He held his own hands out to his sides and frowned. "What's up, puto? You got a—"

But before he had another word out, Kyle sent the brass-knuckles crashing into the bridge of his nose. He flew back into the wall of the restaurant, then hit the ground and curled into a ball.

"What the fuck, Kyle?" Claudia shouted.

"Shut up!" He raised his fist at her, causing her to stumble back a couple of steps and recoil. Then he pulled his fingers out of the weapon and threw it as hard as he could at Silencer's head. "You ever hit my girl again with these fucking things and I'll shove them right up your ass, mother fucker!" He spit on the cholo, who still lay in the fetal position, but didn't respond. Then he turned and jogged back to the car.

As he was climbing in, Claudia yelled, "*You're* a fucking cunt, Kyle!" But her voice was cut off as he slammed the door.

Marie smiled from ear-to-ear, her eyes beaming into his. "Your girl?"

Kyle nodded, attempting to catch his breath. "I mean, if you want."

"I want," she replied.

"All right. Very sweet," Margaret spoke up. "But maybe you two can consummate this thing later and focus on getting us where we need to be right now?" Kyle glanced back and saw her holding the crackling police radio in one hand, stroking Bridget's head with the other. Bartlet's pistol lay in her lap.

"Right." Marie put the Dodge in drive. As she pulled back onto Urban Ave, she smirked and said, "I told you that guy wasn't her cousin."

***

They passed Dobey's building, on College Way, where all the cop cars and news vans had disappeared. A few cars flew past, going the opposite direction, but otherwise it was deserted. When they made it to Waugh Road, Marie sailed around the corner, ignoring the red light. She grew noticeably tense in her seat, and Kyle wanted to reach over and touch her, but figured it wouldn't do well to help her relax right now.

He wondered what she must be thinking. Did she really think that her father was capable of such an atrocity? Or did she merely believe Kyle about his vision, and want to know the truth? *Or,* he wondered, *was she only complying because Margaret had a gun?*

As the car began to climb the steep hill, she picked up speed until they were going nearly fifty. Then she cut a left (so sharp that the smell of burnt rubber filled the inside) and pulled up behind a pearl-white Escalade, which was parked in front of the biggest house Kyle had ever seen.

The porch was covered by a high, steeple-like roof, and there were stained-glass windows above a huge wooden door. The place must have been four stories high.

Marie killed the engine, turned in her seat. First her eyes fell on Bridget. Then Margaret. "He'll be asleep at this hour. He may even call the police if he hears us outside. Not that it will do us much harm, as I'm guessing they're all occupied tonight. I left my house key in my purse, which is back in my car, so we'll have no choice but to knock. He keeps a baseball bat by his bed. He purchased it the day we arrived in the States." Her face remained solemn as she spoke. "Are we planning on bringing Bridget inside?"

"Kyle?" Margaret asked.

Swallowing a lump in his throat, Kyle said, "Yeah?"

"If it's him, you'll know?"

"Yeah."

"And if it's him, and we kill him in front of Bridget—"

"I don't know. Maybe, it'll work, but I don't think so. If her spirit isn't in her body—well, you know. I ah—I think we need to let the children do it. I think that's where she is. I mean with them or whatever."

"They're not all children anymore," Marie said. "Those were adults back by the hospital. They must have been the parents."

"You know what I mean. We should be close by, and we should let her watch—just in case. I ah, that's what I think at least."

"Then no," Margaret answered. "We're not bringing Bridget inside." She raised a set of chrome bracelets, which Kyle assumed was the second pair of handcuffs that Bartlet had mentioned. "If it's him, we'll bring his ass out to the car and follow those helicopter lights."

***

They knocked, and rang the doorbell for at least three minutes, before a light finally flicked on inside. Kyle's heart beat like machine-gun fire as the door swung open, and there stood the man—Bridget's Monster—in silky black pajamas, the shirt partially unbuttoned to reveal a hairy chest.

Kyle shouted. He cringed. A chill ran up his spine which made the hair on his head tingle as it went stiff.

The man ignored him. He held a shiny chrome bat in one hand and as soon as his eyes fell on his daughter, they narrowed and his olive-colored face flushed.

"Where are you been, huh? You must really want the trouble, because now you get it!" His hand shot out like a rattlesnake on the strike and latched onto Marie's hair, jerking her inside so fast that there was hardly time to react. Then the door was shutting, and Kyle didn't think, he slammed his shoulder into it, shoving with all his weight. It flew open and he advanced on the man, wrapping his arms around his waist and attempting to tackle him.

But the man was much bigger and stronger. The bat clanked noisily, dancing on the tiles as he let go of his daughter, picked Kyle up, and threw him at the floor. For a fraction of a second, he was Bridget again, being tossed at the hardened mud at Riverview Park, and he was terrified because of what came next.

Then he snapped out of it, and landed on his hands and his feet like a bear, stumbling into a staircase as he straightened up to see the man scooping his bat off the floor. Marie shrieked as he bared his teeth, gripping the weapon in both hands and advancing on Kyle.

POP!

Kyle's ears rang, and he grew painfully aware of how bright it was inside the Franco house. But it only took him a second to realize that he hadn't been struck. The man cried out, dropped his bat again, and clutched at his stomach before sinking slowly to the floor. Dark red blood oozed between his fingers.

"Oh! Oh you fuck me! Why you fucking? Why this to me? I don't want the trouble, please! I don't want—"

"SHUT THE FUCK UP!" Margaret strolled over with the gun in both hands, until she was standing over him and pointing it at his face. Looking at Kyle, she asked, "Is this him?"

Kyle nodded. Marie stood silently, her hands over her face, her eyes haunted as she stared down at her father.

"What is this?" A voice not unlike hers appeared at the top of the steps. "What in the world are you—"

Margaret pointed the gun at a woman whom Kyle presumed was Marie's mother, and told her that she had three seconds to get back to where she had come from. Without another word, she turned and disappeared around the corner.

The man groaned and complained as a puddle of blood accumulated around him, seeping between the tiles like tiny red streams. They rolled him over and put the cuffs on his wrists and it occurred to Kyle that Margaret probably hadn't brought the key, so he made a point to apply them as tightly as possible.

"Please." He stared up at his daughter desperately. "You want the money? It is yours. You and you friends. Everything is yours. Do not hurt your father, Marie. No more. Please you have kindness for me. I need the hospital, or I am dying. I do nothing for this."

That's when Marie finally reacted. Her jaw tightened and her eyes narrowed as she leaned down and picked up the bat. "You did nothing?" she cried. "You did nothing?" She lifted it overhead and brought it down in an arch like she was chopping wood, hitting him in the middle of the back. "WHAT IN THE FUCK DID YOU DO?" She hit him again. "WHAT WERE YOU THINKING?" And again. And yet again. "HOW MANY OTHERS WERE THERE, HUH? ANSWER ME, YOU SON-OF-A-BITCH!"

But he just screamed and cried, "PLEASE NO! PLEASE YOU STOP THIS, MARIE! I DON'T WANT THE TROUBLE!" until finally Kyle grabbed her from behind and pulled her away.

"Marie! No! Not like this! Come on, baby. Not here."

She fought and writhed in his embrace, but he held on until finally she stopped, but didn't drop the bat. When he let her go, she glared down at her father with tears in her eyes.

"I know," Kyle said. "Trust me, I know. But we need to get him to Bridget before he bleeds out."

***

Vanessa was dead because there was a nail in her ear, but she had a key to the Mount Vernon Juvenile Detention Center, where she worked as a guard. The doors were electronic, but they also opened with a universal key in case of a power outage. It was a big, heavy thing, which she used to let the Collins family into the building, then into Dobey's cell where Lucy Collins strangled her son with an electrical cord from the funeral home.

***

Kyle shoved the man out into the pouring rain, and watched blood pour from his pudgy belly, down his legs, and onto his front porch. They were halfway to the Dodge, when another Dodge pulled up next to it and Rivas stepped out pointing his gun with both hands.

"Margaret, what the hell are you doing?"

Margaret placed the barrel of Bartlet's pistol against the man's head. "Get back in your car, Chris, or I'll blow his head off!"

"I can't do that, Margaret, and you know it. Where's Christy?"

"She's back at my place. You might wanna go check on her."

"Please you help me!" The man frowned. "These people, they shoot me so hard!"

"Shut up!" Margaret barked.

"Margaret," Rivas didn't lower his weapon. "Think about what you're doing. You don't wanna go to prison. Let me do my job. Let me take this guy in."

Margaret's blond hair stuck to her face in thick strands as the rain fell on it. She said, "Chris, we're wasting time. Now I'm getting into that car, and I'm taking this mother fucker with me. So, either shoot me, or get in your own car and follow me, goddamn it!" Without another word, she locked eyes with Kyle. He nodded, pulled the man to the Dodge.

"Dammit Margaret! Kyle! Listen to me! I don't wanna have to—"

Another explosion rang out, echoed off the sky and the side of Rivas's head exploded, spraying blood all over the top of his vehicle like fireworks. His gun smacked the concrete before his limp body did. Kyle and Marie both glanced at Margaret at the same time, but she still had her pistol against the man's head. They all looked around for the source of the shot, Marie clutching the bat in both hands like a teddy-bear.

Kyle continued to scan the area, seeing nothing but huge houses with perfectly maintained lawns which were circled around the cul-de-sac. "It's one of them. I mean, it's her. She knows we're coming."

When nobody answered, Kyle looked back and saw every eye on the man, whose jaw hung as he stared down into the car, directly at Bridget. Bridget stared back, and for the first time tonight, her arms lay still at her side. Her head was tilted curiously. Her eyes were wide and alert.

Kyle stepped up behind the man and stood on his tiptoes. Placing his lips right by his ear, he said, "That's right. Now get in the car."

***

"Please. Please you don't do this to me. Marie, I am your father. I am your father, Marie!"

The man sat, bleeding, in the passenger seat. Marie was driving down Hilltop. The wipers were waving maniacally back and forth over the windshield. Kyle and Margaret sat on either side of Bridget, and though her limbs were once again flailing about, Kyle swore she was smiling.

"You stop this! You stop this fucking trouble right now, you little bitch! You stop! Stop! Stop! Stop! You want the trouble with me? Fine! I give you—"

"SHUT UP!" Margaret reached forward and hit him in the back of the head with the gun.

The helicopter lights were closer, and they were headed their way.

"Why?" Margaret peered over at Kyle. "I don't get it. Why didn't she just kill him back there, when she shot Chris?"

Kyle thought about it. "I don't know, maybe she wasn't there. I mean obviously *somebody* was there, and it had to have been one of hers. But I think she stays with the big group."

"But the radio's been reporting them all over fucking town. It sounds like there *is* no big group. They're everywhere."

"I really don't know, Margaret. All I know is that she didn't want Rivas to stop us, which means she knows what we're doing and it's what she wants, right?"

Margaret didn't answer, just turned her head and stared out the window.

Marie said, "How could you do this, Dad? How could you do such a terrible thing?"

"I do nothing," he whined. "What you think I do, Marie? You think I hurt the little girl? I never do this. I never do anything like this to little girl."

Marie's demeanor changed so subtly Kyle doubted anybody but him noticed. But her father had slipped, and she had caught it, because nobody had said anything about him hurting Bridget. Then he tensed and Kyle knew that he realized what he had done.

But before he could attempt to make a case for himself, Margaret gasped, "Oh sweet Jesus."

Up ahead, a humongous ball of orange light radiated around what must have been thousands of people. It was blurred by a thick layer of rain which was managing to accumulate in spite of being wiped away every second, but Kyle could see that they all had weapons and glowing eyes, and that they filled the three-lane road and the sidewalk as they marched directly toward the Dodge. The helicopters shone beams down on them, casting terrible shadows that looked exactly like Bridget's hair had in the river.

Marie slowed the car down, and at first nobody spoke except for the man, who continued to cry and beg for mercy. Then her eyes met Kyle's in the rearview mirror and her voice shook as she said, "What do I do, baby?"

"Keep driving."

"Are you sure?"

"No. But what choice do we have? This was the plan."

"Maybe we should reevaluate it."

Bridget ran the back of her hand over her nose. "Guh! Guh! Guh! Guuuuuuuuuuuuuuuuubuuuuuuuuuuuuuubuuuuuuuuuuuuaaaaa aaaaaag!"

"Please," the man coughed. "Please you don't have to do this to me. I give whatever you want. I am sorry. I am sorry. I am so sorry for this. Please."

Soon the orange light increased against the beams on the front of the car and the crowd of corpses was no more than a hundred feet away. Kyle told Marie to stop the car. She obliged, keeping her foot on the brake pedal, rather than putting it in park, and for a second all that could be heard were the wipers as they squealed over the glass.

Then Kyle opened the door and the rain appeared. He jumped out and was instantly soaked as he ran around the back of the Dodge and opened the passenger door.

"What?" the man asked. "What do you want?"

"Get out."

"No."

Then Margaret was beside him, shoving the gun inside and aiming it between the man's legs.

POP!

Kyle jumped as warm blood misted his face.

"Aaaaaaaaaaraaaaarrrrrrrg!" Bridget wailed, flapping her arms like they were wings and kicking her feet.

The man screamed. He bounced in his seat and then he rolled out of the car and onto the wet pavement where he curled up like a potato bug. Kyle dived over him, into the passenger seat and saw half of Marie's face covered in crimson splotches. Her features were hard, and he could tell she was attempting to stall what she was feeling.

But the crowd was close now. So close that Kyle could see Laura Cunningham marching in front. So close he could see the gaping holes in her neck. She held a shovel, which rested over her shoulder, and she was smiling from ear to ear, staring right at him. The children all wore Halloween costumes, but there were more adults, and most of them were in pajamas or underwear, and carried a weapon of some sort.

"Aaaaaaaaaaaaaaaarguh! Gubugubugubugubuh!"

Kyle tried to shut the door, but the man's body was in the way, so as soon as Margaret was back in the car, he shouted, "Go!"

"Where?" she shrieked.

"Backwards! Back up! They have guns, Marie!"

Marie put the car in reverse and stepped on the gas, turning in her seat wide-eyed. Kyle's door caught on the man, and dragged him a few feet, before breaking from its hinges and crashing into the road. Then the man appeared in front of the car and Marie slammed on the brakes.

"Gagagagagaaaaaaaaaaaaagabaaaaah!" Bridget's voice became a high pitched shrill.

"Why'd you stop?" Kyle turned around and received his answer when he saw another crowd, as big as the one in front of them pouring out of side streets and accumulating behind the car. "Oh fuck!"

Margaret stroked her daughter's face, and watched intently as the corpses finally reached the man. The ones in the front laid into him first, bringing garden tools down into his body and his head, but soon they were circled around him, and so many of them were swinging axes, shovels, hammers, and other objects, that Kyle doubted there would be any of him left when they were done. It only took half a minute, and then Bridget finally fell silent as they all turned their attention back to the Dodge.

"Baby," Marie sniffed. "What now?"

"I don't know."

"Wasn't that supposed to make it stop? Why aren't they stopping?"

But before she finished asking, the dead people were once again in motion, closing in on the car from every direction.

***

"Drive!" Kyle yelled. "Go! Go! Go! Go!"

So, Marie once again, stepped on the gas just as a sledgehammer crashed through her window, right in front of her head. The car lurched backward, tearing the weapon out of a small black girl's hands, then it fell to the road. The back window shattered next, and there was thumping overhead as bodies climbed up, causing the roof to indent.

The car jerked, then stopped because there were just too many back there to drive over.

"Forward!" Margaret cried.

But there were even more in front, and soon they were on the sides as well, trying to open the doors but unable because the ones on the outside were pushing the others against the car. But Kyle didn't have a door, so just as the windshield was being smashed by the black girl who had picked her hammer back up and now stood on the hood, cold hands reached in and wrapped around his neck.

He glanced over and saw his mother, completely nude with glowing eyes, her skin pale, her blond hair matted to her face. There was a deep cut on one side of her neck, but it hadn't penetrated her windpipe, so she took in a shrieking breath and hissed, "What in the hell did you do to your brother, brah?"

Then Marie's bat sailed directly in front of his face and the end slammed into hers, pushing her back a couple feet. Her nose lay flat against her cheekbone, but she smiled as she reached in again, wrapping her arms around Kyle and pulling him from the car.

Kyle was no Einstein, but it was clear what was happening. Death had come for him back at the cabin, and by some fluke he had cheated her. Now she was claiming what was hers, and Kyle had died just like everybody in the crowd.

The man had damaged Bridget, and in doing so, he had created Abel's Monster, but tonight had never been about finding the man. She had only wanted to find her doll, and she had been taken because nobody would help. They were all too busy to pay her any attention. But tonight, there would be no ignoring Bridget Newport.

As he hit the pavement his father appeared with a ball-pin-hammer. He tried to speak, but his windpipe *had* been punctured, so air whistled from the wound as he dropped to one knee and prepared to bring the weapon down on his son's head. Kyle heard Marie in the car, shrieking and grunting, then the horn blared for a long moment before finally stopping.

Metal clinked against metal. The car rocked noisily, and somebody stepped on one of Kyle's hands, grounding his skin into the blacktop. Flesh ripped from his knuckles as he pulled them out from under the shoe and rolled into a ball.

"Relax brah," his mother yelled over the commotion. "You're sixteen-years-old and you're acting like a big baby right now. You probably won't even feel it, for Christ's sake!"

Closing his eyes so tight that his head hurt, Kyle thought, *Why didn't they just shoot us? If Bridget didn't care that we were bringing her the man, they could have just shot us a long time ago. But why this?*

Then there was an explosion and Kyle saw red before he even felt the hammer crack his skull open like an Easter egg. The weight of the world fell on him and then there was nothing. Only darkness.

Until he realized that he wasn't dead. That he hadn't been hit. That he couldn't breathe. That something heavy was pressing his face and body against the cold pavement, but the commotion had stopped and all that could be heard were raindrops, helicopter blades, and the Dodge's engine.

He opened his eyes and still saw darkness. So, placing his hands flat on the road, he pushed himself up with every bit of strength that he had, and felt limp bodies roll off his back. Then he was on his knees, looking around, and they were everywhere. Motionless and strewn as far as he could see in every direction, stacked on top of one another with only streaming blood and their weapons between them. The handles of some stuck up like weeds in a terrible garden.

Every bit of orange light was gone, along with the shadows.

Marie panted from behind the wheel. A brown-haired girl in a bear suit, who couldn't have been older than two, lay face down in her lap.

Kyle saw Bridget in his peripheral before he even glanced in the backseat. Her eyes were wide, and she appeared alert, but her head lay on her shoulder, in a mess of brain and skull. The seat beside her was splattered with blood. Margaret clutched the smoking gun in one hand and stared at the back of the passenger seat expressionless.

"You shot Bridget?" Kyle panted.

"It didn't make sense." Her voice was cold and monotone. "I mean, why was she able to find you, but not him? And why were they attacking our car, but not shooting us? It would have been so easy to just shoot us, wouldn't it?"

Kyle climbed to his feet, making a point not to look at either of his parents. A dead man who could have been a body builder, wearing nothing but a pair of boxer-briefs was draped over the Dodge's back window. It was Principal Stack. Margaret still didn't look away from the seat as she went on.

"Then I started thinking, and I realized that she *could* have found him. She could have found him any time she wanted. Maybe she knew he lived in town," she shrugged, "maybe not. I don't think she cared though."

The helicopters grew louder, and their lights increased, glazing over the endless sea of bodies.

Marie said, "Baby, please get this thing off me."

Leaning in, Kyle took the baby by her hair and heaved her over the passenger seat and out into the road. Then he moved a hanging arm out of his way and sat inside to the sound of raindrops tapping on the roof.

Only then, did he take the time to consider how wrong both he and Bartlet had been. True, before tonight Bridget had only been killing the children, which she could stir up against their parents, but it wasn't because she hadn't had a choice. She could have taken anybody she wanted, and the evidence lay as far as the eye could see in every direction.

"And they weren't shooting us—" Margaret said.

"—because Bridget was in the car," Kyle finished her sentence. "They didn't want to hit her."

"They didn't want to fucking hit her," Margaret concurred. "It was so obvious. I don't know how we didn't figure it out sooner. Kids are abducted and killed every day, and this doesn't happen. You know why? Because they're dead. But my daughter wasn't. It was her this whole fucking time, because her spirit never really left her body. Not completely, at least. She was controlling everything from her goddamn chair, and you know what? There was no rhyme or reason to it either. She was just an eight-year-old throwing a temper tantrum."

"I don't know," Kyle said, finally catching his breath. "I think there might've been more to it than that."

Marie glanced over at him, tilted her head.

"She stirred the kids up against their parents before she killed them. She lied to my brother, Abel, at least. Told him I called him a retard, and that nobody would believe him about her. But I'm sure she did it to the others, too, just to put them through what she experienced the night she was taken.

"The abandonment. The thoughts that nobody cares that you're distressed. It's the same reason she connected with me when I was drowning in the lake. She just wanted people to feel what she felt."

Margaret took a deep breath, held it in, then opened her door, shoving it as far as it would go against the corpses, and wedging herself out. She dropped the gun on top of a dead woman in a medic's suit, then clumsily walked over bodies, in the direction they had been driving.

"Should we go after her?" Marie asked.

"I don't think so," Kyle said. "I think she needs to be alone right now."

"Then what do we do, baby? I mean we'll never be able to drive through this mess."

Taking her hand, he interlaced his fingers with hers and kissed her knuckles. "I don't think it matters what we do next, as long as we do it together."

Marie laid her head on her backrest and gazed into his eyes for a long moment. Then she smiled warmly and told him that she agreed.

Epilogue

Marie stood barefoot over the counter, slicing lemons in half and setting them in a neat line on the edge of the cutting board. She looked nice in boy-shorts. She had always thought that she did, at least. But in the UK, curvy girls had never seemed as widely appreciated as they were in the United States. Here, however, she couldn't even go to the grocery store without being hit on, and often it happened right in front of Kyle. Though he kept his composure, smiling and being polite, he sometimes told her when they were alone how much he hated it. She suspected that her accent was as much to blame as her body, and usually just encouraged him to take it as a compliment. She was his.

Summertime was nice because it gave her a handy excuse to wear shorts around the apartment, and she enjoyed the way that Kyle looked at her the most. Today, she wore a pair of white ones, which seemed to invoke more of said looks than any other she owned.

The apartment was cute. She liked it, mostly, because it was in New York, and her mother still lived on the other side of the country. They only had two bedrooms because it was all they needed, and one functioned as an office, which Kyle was currently in, clicking away at his keyboard.

It had been eight months since Marie fed her own father to the monster that he created when he raped and tried to kill an eight-year-old girl. At first, she had thought she would feel something because of it. Remorse? Sorrow? Perhaps relief? She had even sat alone from time to time, meditating on what had happened in an attempt to invoke anything but cold-hearted indifference. But there was nothing, and she wasn't sure if that revealed more about him or her, or if she cared one way or the other. Though she did often wonder how many victims he had left in his wake when he'd traveled alone around the world to appraise prospective properties.

Marie was a calculated girl. She was collected and level-headed, and hadn't needed to be told that her mother would dread the idea of what her husband had done being publicized. And since there was only a small handful of people who knew, Marie had made sure that Bartlet, Margaret, and Noel were paid generously to forget.

As there had been nothing of her father left with which to test his DNA and build a case against him, Bartlet had had little more than a shaky lead anyway. She never would have been able to make a claim based on Kyle's vision, so keeping it quiet hadn't breached any code of ethics. That's what she told them one afternoon before they left Washington, at least. It was during that same conversation that she revealed something, which she'd recently discovered.

"Your father did have a key to the Cinema Seven the night Bridget was abducted. He got it from the owner, so he could explore the inside while he was in town. The guy told me he thought Salvatore wanted to buy the place."

Marie hadn't needed her mother's generosity, so neither had Kyle. All they had requested was enough to get on their feet somewhere far away. Marie had contacted a few of her teachers back in London and managed to acquire an academic scholarship that would set her on the path to becoming a lawyer in just seven short years. Kyle never went back to school. Instead, he landed a book deal, with a very agreeable advance and first denial rights to the publisher on his next three.

He'd finished "Abel's Monster" shortly after they moved to New York, and the essay won a national award before it was even printed in literary journals around the country. But not before he started his debut novel which became the first in a series for young adults, was accepted by one of the top publishing houses in the world, and was set to be released sometime next year.

Marie hadn't spoken to her mother, or even her sister since moving away. It wasn't necessarily a decision that she'd made to shun them. She'd merely had no desire or reason to reach out yet, and apparently neither had they. Since his entire immediate family, and most of his friends were dead, Kyle hadn't looked back either. They had a few new acquaintances, and occasionally went out, but mostly they preferred to enjoy each other's company, which was looking like it wouldn't grow old anytime in the foreseeable future. For the first time that she could remember, Marie Franco was genuinely happy.

She squeezed the lemons into a pitcher, mixed the juice with water and sugar and split the contents into two tall glasses with ice-cubes in them. It was always silent in the mornings because that's when they both did most of their work. Marie, as it turned out, was an excellent manager, and she liked to think that her sharp business sense had contributed to her man's recent success more so than his award had.

Cleaning up her mess, she washed her hands, took the glasses, and made her way down the hall, cracking the office door and poking her head in. Kyle sat behind the desk, a thoughtful look on his face, which always made her heart leap inside of her. He didn't glance up until she said, "Are you at a point where you can rest?"

Finally, he took a deep breath and scratched his head. "Yeah. Come on in. I think it's about time to wrap it up for the day anyway." Then his eyes traveled over his screen and scanned her body, and he smiled so subtly that had anybody else been in the room, they wouldn't have noticed. "Lemonade?"

"Yes." She stepped in and shut the door behind her. "How's the book coming?"

Kyle stood and met her in front of a black leather couch, which sat along one wall. "Good," he said. "It's just that I think a sequel has to be better than the first. I mean they should get better as the books go on, right? And I'm sure it *will* be better, but there's always that pressure involved, and it can affect the free-flowing art, you know?" He took one of the glasses and set it behind him on the desk.

Marie smiled. "Well look who's the expert on writing serieses already."

"Series," he corrected.

"Pardon?"

"You don't say serieses. It's just series. Well—I think."

Marie giggled, raised the glass to her lips, but Kyle reached up and removed it from her hand before she could take a drink, setting it next to his.

Placing her wrist over his forehead, she said, "No coasters on your precious desk? Are you feeling all right?"

But his only response was to place both hands on her lower back. Then they found their way down and over the surface of her shorts until they touched her skin, and it sent a pleasant chill up her spine.

"Are you sure you don't want to get back to work?" she asked with a weak voice and a grin. "You wouldn't want to accidentally—" But before she could get another word out, his mouth covered hers. He kissed her long and deep, shoving her lightly onto the couch and peeling off his shirt. Then he climbed between her legs, and they didn't speak again for the next hour.

THE END

Other HellBound Books Titles
Available at: www.hellboundbookspublishing.com

Highway Twenty

An engineer from out of town disappears. Then Conor Mitchell's girlfriend. Then his parents. The townspeople of Sedrow Woolley, Washington are vanishing at a horrifying rate. But they come back. They all come back days later, and they're different: Hungry. Insectile. Creatures posing as humans. Because Conor knows the truth, and because the entire police force has already been changed, and because there's nowhere to run from an evil that only wants to spread, his sole option is to fight.

But they have no intention of letting him leave town.

Secret Harbor

Tony Carpenter loves Karina. It doesn't matter that they're only fourteen, because when they're together they forget about their abusive homes.

They run away, leaving a trail of murder in their wake, until Tony is caught and sent to Secret Harbor School - a boy's home on a remote island in Washington State's San Juan's.

Run by corrupt staff with no accountability to anybody who cares about the abuse administered daily to its residents, Secret Harbor School is among the state's best kept secrets.

Tony has no intention of staying. The first chance he gets, he plans to escape and do whatever it takes to get back to Karina.

Even if it means more people have to die.

Secret Harbor is a dark, fast-paced, psychological thriller that will make you laugh, cry, and scoot ever so slowly toward the edge of your seat...

The Toilet Zone
RESTROOM READING AT ITS MOST FRIGHTENING!

Compiled and edited by the grand master of 80's schlock horror, Bret McCormick, each one of this collection of 32 terrifying tales is just the perfect length for a visit to the smallest room....

At the very boundaries of human imagination dwells one single, solitary place of solitude, of peace and quiet, a place in which your regular human being spends, on average, 10 to 15 minutes - at least once every single day of their lives.

Now, consider a typical, everyday reading speed of 200 to 250 words per minute - that means your average visitor has the time to read between 2,500 to 4,000 words, which makes each and every one of these 32 tales of terror - from some of the best contemporary independent authors - within this anthology of horror the perfect, meticulously calculated length. Dare you take a walk to the small room from where inky shadows creep out to smother the light and solitude's siren call beckons you?

Dare you take a quiet, lonely walk into… The Toilet Zone

Invasive Species

A monster has come to Maldus, Arkansas, and the residents of the small mountain town are too busy to notice. With the monster comes something even more terrifying and threatening than gnashing teeth or razor-sharp claws.
The monster has brought change.
The residents of the small mountain town are too busy to notice at first. Busy with things such as addiction, racism, work, or land deals. Unnoticed, the change the monster brings in its insidious wake spreads like wildfire. Unnoticed, the town of Maldus falls prey to an Invasive Species.

Contents:

DATES FROM

HELL

6

Teenage Wasteland
By Victory Witherkeigh

He chose to die in the place where they had met. A part of his brain begged him to reconsider. After all, he was no longer the stupid boy who fled from this place. He knew he would not budge on his decision. He owed it to them to do it.

I've had a life, he thought, *But I was happiest here...*

They met on the sunny, sandy shores of Monterey Bay in California. Strolling along one of the small coves near a state park, two ten-year-old children, Neal and Maggie, were playing in the waves and trying to get Neal's dog, Keiki, to join them in fun. Keiki had been rescued a few years ago by Neal's family, a mutt who was mostly Greyhound and was terrified of the water. Maggie laughed when they met up at the beach. Keiki was wearing a doggie life jacket. Neal's plan for the day was to carry Keiki into the waves with him, holding her small body against his in the hope she would acclimate to the water. Maggie's role was to help lure Keiki into a false sense of security, cheering for her to come to follow into the smaller waves so Neal could sneak up on her.

Again and again, Maggie called Keiki, running into the water that just touched the edge of the sand, letting Keiki follow her to get used to the cold temperature. Maggie knew Keiki was unsure of the wet, mushy texture between her toes but would only giggle and kiss her nose to encourage her. Those big puppy dog eyes almost convinced Maggie to lead her away from the beach to their blanket fort for safety. She kept the ruse going just to smirk as Neal came behind Keiki, revving himself up to be able to pick her up. They were the oddest twosome on that beach. Maggie, vivacious and fox-like, would skip and tumble through the sand, practicing her gymnastics and ballet routines. Her long dark curly hair and chocolate brown almond eyes could have made her a shoo-in on some tropical island native in the South Pacific. Neal had white alabaster skin with dark hazel green eyes and vibrant red hair. His parents had come from England to work in California after living in Brazil. They became fast friends despite their different backgrounds due to their love of the ocean. Although he did not look like it, Neal was practically a shark in the sea, fearless and powerful. The idea that his own dog feared it was a horrible embarrassment to him.

"I got you girl!" he screamed, picking Keiki up and sauntering into the water.

Maggie just laughed and followed behind him. They slowly walked into the waves. The water washed against their bodies while they planted their feet in the sand. Neal was already slightly taller than Maggie, and so she was the first to feel her waist covered in water and felt the slick seaweed passing between her legs. Salt and sand brushed against her face, stirred by the gentle wind. Holding her hand above her eyebrows, she smiled to herself as Neal kept whispering to Keiki, walking her further and further into the water. It was only then that she heard him speak for the first time.

"S'up! I'm Bob…" said the voice.

Maggie looked over her shoulder to see him floating and bobbing on the wave next to her. He was so relaxed, going with the motion of the water effortlessly.

"Bob?" she asked inquisitively.

"Yeah, brah! Cuz I'm always just 'Bobbing' along," he smirked and laughed. He started rolling and spinning with the water, staying above water and near her but somehow in control. Maggie giggled back in response. It was a cheesy joke, but she thought it was cute. "Bob" had short brown hair with chocolate brown eyes accenting his smooth brown skin - just a shade darker than Maggie's. "Bob" splashed her with water when he saw her staring at him a little too long, starting a full-on splash fight. Her giggles made him blush. He liked her smile and that he was the one making her laugh. They were lost in each other's jokes before another set of splashing came up next to her.

"Did you see? Did you see?" asked Neal, who was no longer holding Keiki.

Maggie turned around to see him standing directly behind her and blushed. She wasn't sure why, but she suddenly felt itchy, darting her eyes away from him and bit her lip.

"No, sorry…" she mumbled quietly, blushing further, "I was talking to my new friend here - this is Bob. Bob, this is my best friend, Neal."

"Actually, pretty girl, my name is Hiri…" interjected the other boy, wading through the waves staring at the two of them.

Neal frowned, brows furrowed slightly, raising one of them inquisitively as he looked over at Hiri, still floating in the ocean along next to them.

"You missed Keiki actually swimming," Neal replied haughtily, not taking his eyes off him. "She's already back on our blankets refusing to come back…"

Maggie's shoulders dropped as tears came to her eyes. "Oh no! Poor Keiki!" she cried, "I'm so so sorry, Neal, I'll go make sure she's fine. You stay here and get to know each other!"

She took off, bouncing as quickly as she could to their blankets to cuddle with Keiki. As she moved farther away, the two boys squared off with each other, beginning a staring contest as if a duel to the death had been unspoken. Neal had squared his feet in the ocean, staring at the other boy's dark eyes, trying to tell his stomach to settle down from fluttering. He never saw the wave coming that knocked him over. Round and round, he tumbled until he felt Hiri pushing him up to the surface and dragging him to shore, laughing and giggling.

Neal flopped on his back after spewing up water from his lung, coughing and hacking away into the sand.

"It's not funny!" he coughed out at Hiri, "I totally was going to win!"

Hiri couldn't stop laughing, propping himself up on his elbow on the sand next to Neal, fully staring at him. They had to all be within a year of each other. He gave Neal a lopsided grin and a small pat on the belly.

"You okay, man?" asked Hiri, getting his giggles under control, "I know that wasn't the best way to meet, but you handled the wash beautifully…"

Neal looked back at Hiri and gave him a similar lopsided grin, acknowledging the other boy for the first time. Neal was definitely the bigger of the two as he was a swimmer, while Hiri was leaner like a surfer. They spoke about Neal adjusting to the California culture, how he missed Brazil and speaking Portuguese. Hiri told him how his parents were sailors, drifting from boat to boat, never on land for much of his life. He spent much of his time traveling up and down the coasts. Maggie soon came to join them, tagging Hiri, claiming he was "it" as the children spent the rest of the evening chasing each other as the bonfires lit and the stars rose. Neal and Maggie didn't remember when Hiri left; they just knew the next morning they had made a fantastic memory and hopefully, a lifelong friend.

The three friends met every year at the same beach. Each summer was always better than the last. Smores, stars, and waves were their mantra for so long it was a wonder there was ever any time they were apart. Often Keiki would get jealous and run in between them to try and get Hiri to pay attention to her as well. Neal and Maggie taught Hiri how to ride a bicycle. He, in turn, taught them both how to surf and stand-up paddleboard. If he closed his eyes, he could sometimes still see the way Maggie smiled at him over her shoulder as she stood up the first time. During the school year, they kept in touch through various letters and postcards, especially since Hiri was "boat schooled." It wasn't until the summer after before their freshman year of high school that things seemed different.

Maggie and Neal arrived at the beach, barely looking at one another. As Hiri strolled along the sand to wave to them, he couldn't miss the look of apprehension on their faces as he got closer. Maggie had her arms crossed under her perky, developed breasts. She was taller now and filling out athletically curvy. Her years of dance and gymnastics meant Hiri had found himself appreciating her curves more and more. He knew he'd never say so, but she was definitely one of the more beautiful girls he had come across. Neal was throwing rocks into the waves, standing at nearly six-foot-two. He had filled out the soonest between the three of them as he was put on the local swim team from an early age. Tall, lean legs connected to a nicely curved bubble butt on the boy. Last summer, he whispered to Hiri how some of the girls on the team had called him the "keel" - due to him coming out of the pool during one practice a little too "excited."

"Hey, guys!" exclaimed Hiri, "What's up?"

Both teens sheepishly waved to him and mumbled some kind of hello. Raising his eyebrow in confusion, Hiri tilted his head before asking again. "Is there something going on that I should know about?"

The two friends looked at one another in surprise before darting their glances away. Maggie shook her head, tapped her foot, stared at the ground, then threw her hands up.

"Ugh…. Yes, actually. Look, you should know I didn't want to come on this trip this year!" she sneered, giving a deathly glare to Neal, "Honestly, he stopped being my friend as soon as we started school this past year. I begged my mom to let me off this trip."

"That's not true!" yelled Neal, "You're the one who has been a shitty friend. I barely saw you with all your 'girls' around you... I can't even talk to you anymore."

"Oh, please!" Maggie yelled back, "As soon as you had Laurie's attention, you didn't even notice I was alive. As soon as the blonde, doe-eyed ditz told the whole school she was interested in you, you were all over her. And to hell with me, right?!"

Tears were welling up in her eyes, slowly pouring down her cheek now. Bringing her arms around her, she held herself as her lip quivered.

"I'm sorry Hiri, I can't do this...I can't pretend that it's still the same...that it doesn't hurt..."

She didn't even finish, she just turned and walked down the beach. Neal looked at the sand and then back at Hiri, who just watched her walk.

"What?" asked Neal, agitated, "What's that look about?"

Hiri shrugged, putting his hands on his waist and gave a pointed look to his friend. "Are you going to go after her, or will I?" He asked.

"I'm not going after her. She's the one who stomped off...acting like a baby," rebuked Neal.

"So.... who's Laurie?" asked Hiri.

"Just some girl at school. She's a tap dancer and one of the popular girls..." he answered, not making eye contact with his friend.

"Well...no matter who she is, I'll tell you what I know. I may not go to a 'normal' school like you guys, but I've traveled across the Atlantic by sailboat twice now. I've been up and down this coast of the Pacific more times than I can remember...And,"

He paused, taking his hand to bring Neal's chin up to meet his dark brown eyes, "I can tell you, unequivocally, that Maggie is one in a trillion. No matter who you meet or how cool they seem, they don't have a thing on our girl..."

Hiri let go of his face and started to walk past him when an arm reached out to stop him. Without turning to face his friend, Neal whispered, "Am I one in a trillion also?" and walked off. Hiri took off in a sprint, finding Maggie sitting on a bench near the beach parking lot, knees curled up to her chest with her arms holding them in place. Seeing Hiri coming close, she scowled and tried to look away from him, but he put both arms on her shoulders and gave her the biggest hug. Tears stained his arms as Maggie admitted to her jealousy of Laurie, that her hope was to have been Neal's girlfriend. He stayed with her until her mom came, telling her he'd always be there for her, as his stomach knotted, hearing how sad she was over the other boy in their lives.

Maggie did not return to the beach the following summer after that fight. Hiri tried asking about her once, which only caused Neal to storm off, so he did not bring her up again. He figured whatever they had to work out with one another was between them. Neal took some sailing lessons with Hiri, sharing his ideas of moving to another country after high school graduation and back-packing across them. His parents expected him to go to University, but in his gut, he knew he wasn't a college man. He figured he could take the money they saved for his college fund, set up a life in a college town, but travel instead - never letting his parents know the difference. It was that final summer, they were both eighteen, planning how they'd meet up for Neal's grand con. Laurie was going to be introduced to Hiri that evening as the final hurdle of acceptance. She had long bugged Neal about meeting him, and he had run out of excuses. The two boys were sitting in the sand, Keiki lazing behind him, staring off at the horizon as a group of pelicans swooped down towards the water. Following their flight path, they flew up just as a young woman was walking up the sand. Her long dark, curly hair flowing behind her, sundress hugging her gorgeous tan body against the breeze as she lazily followed the waterline.

"Damn, man," whistled Neal, "Look at that...just stunning..."

Hiri started to clap in approval when Keiki seemed to smell something and started to run. Both boys were stunned as the older dog took a full sprint towards the water at the woman they were ogling. Her laughter caught their ears as they both took off after the dog. It was only when they got close enough to her that they realized who they were looking at.

Maggie was standing before them in a light blue sundress, showing off her olive tan skin. Her eyes were bright and soft, confident even. She stood before them more beautiful than either could have imagined.

"Hi Keiki...I've missed you too..." she said before looking up at the boys. Neal looked the same as the last time they stood on this beach. Hiri was just a bit shorter than him, still lean and muscular, but tan and warm. She gave them both a shy smile.

"Hi...fancy seeing you guys here..." she said, a small smirk forming on the outside of her mouth.

Neither of the boys spoke for a full minute, utterly stunned.

"Wowie, wowzer..." breathed Hiri, "What happened to you?"

"Come here, stranger," she reached out, giving him a warm hug.

He held her, breathing in the scent of jasmine and honeysuckle in her hair. As she stepped back, she blushed before reaching out to Neal for a hug as well. Hiri could feel the heat rising in his face as he saw his friend's face looking down at Maggie's body as he hugged her. She did not hug Neal as long as Hiri, but Hiri saw him lightly brush his lips past her cheek. Maggie didn't seem fazed or at least hid it well before continuing.

"Sorry it's been so long...my dad got a job offer in Switzerland after we got back from that last trip," she said, Keiki chose to plant herself at Maggie's feet, "By the time my parents decided, I was all packed up and flying…"

Maybe that's what struck the boys. Maggie was calm and confident, radiant under the sunlight. Her eyes looked off in the distance as if older somehow before she looked back at them.

"How have you guys been?" she asked.

The two boys looked at each other before turning and grabbing her hand to drag her back to their blankets. Each animatedly told her of Neal's plan to con "the man and the system" by living in the University town but not attending University.

"Where will you be?" asked Maggie laughing.

It was almost like before.

"A small University in England...Hiri here will join me at points to help me sail as well…what about you?" asked Neal, edging closer to her.

Maggie smiled. "I'm still deciding actually...I got into UC Santa Cruz, which would bring me just a bit north of here. It would be interesting to do an American school again after so long…I did get accepted into the London School of Economics also...but a gap year does sound lovely though…"

As she spoke, both boys couldn't help but be entranced. Her lips and brightness of her eyes had a light that shone beyond what either of them thought possible.

Neal, at times, could barely answer. He was so distracted.

"What?" she asked, "you both have the funniest looks on your faces…"

Before he knew what he was doing, Hiri reached over and took her hand. "I'm so so happy you're here…" he said, "We should celebrate tonight. Let me take you out."

Maggie blushed a little before responding, "Like a date?" she asked. Hiri was the only one who could see Neal's face turning red.

Hiri nodded vigorously as Maggie smiled. She stood up, brushing the sand off of her lap. "I'm staying at the Sanctuary hotel…Pick me up at seven."

She walked off as Hiri started to dance and cheer silently before turning to high five Neal. His face was redder and sweaty.

"You okay, man?" asked Hiri, "You don't look so good…"

Neal gave him a look he didn't recognize and turned away.

"Dude...you aren't, like, jealous, are you?" accused Hiri, "You have Laurie for Christ sakes...you have a date with her tonight...and you know that I've always wanted Maggie…"

Before Hiri knew it, Neal whipped around and kissed him hard on the mouth. It wasn't romantic or sweet. The kiss tasted of ownership and anger with Hiri shoving Neal off and grabbed his stuff. He was shaking in disbelief even as he was getting ready for his date. The thing that made him snap out of it was seeing Maggie come down the stairs in a flowing white glittery dress. In various degrees of light, he could see the contours of her skin underneath, making breathing very difficult.

"You look like an angel…" said Hiri as he kissed her hand.

Maggie smiled and took in the sight of him in his blue chino pants with a black button-up shirt, still untucked. It was Hiri, after all.

"You look incredibly handsome yourself," answered Maggie, tucking her arm under his as they began to stroll along towards his moped. Handing her the passenger helmet, they set off for the main stretch of the boardwalk for dinner. Hiri got a table at a small restaurant overlooking the water and ordered sparkling water instead of still. He was going to pull out all the stops. His hands gravitated to her as if her whole body were magnetized. Any excuse he found to touch her hand, move her hair, gave him goosebumps, electrifying the little hairs on his arm.

"Sooo…" she said, snapping him out of his trance.

"Yes, mon Cherie?" answered Hiri.

Maggie giggled. "Something is on your mind, you've barely eaten. And if there is something, I remember distinctly, it's that something must be bothering you if you aren't eating…"

Hiri sighed, putting a hand through his hair, wanting to avoid the sentence coming out of his mouth.

"You haven't brought him up at all…" said Hiri sullenly, preparing himself for the worst.

"Brought up who?" asked Maggie, an eyebrow raised.

"You know who…" replied Hiri, staring directly at her now, "Neal. Your ex-best friend/love of your life?"

"Really? Hiri…" she reached out to touch his hand, holding his gaze, "I was fourteen years old. Going through puberty. You two were the only boys I ever talked to. EVER. Of course, I was confused. Things were changing, and I didn't like where I thought they were going. But I'm not fourteen anymore...I was able to see outside of our little musketeer hood, see a bit of the world you always talked about. See that maybe I wasn't the center of it like I hoped..."

Blushing sheepishly, she continued, "You are both a big part of my past...I don't know if I can really say I know what love actually is at this point...I just know it wasn't...It wasn't me being jealous or insecure in my friendship with him..."

Hiri thought his heart would leap out of his chest. Never in a million years did he think she would say something like that. He started to smile until she took a big gulp.

"Why did you feel the need to bring him up?" she asked, looking at him like she already knew.

"I..." started Hiri, "It was always the three of us for so long. When I met you, I knew there was something about you that was magnanimous and fabulous, and... then there was Neal. You two were a complete package...and I was the icing. A third wheel. But then you left...and it was just Neal and me..."

He did not know why he was getting choked up, why there was so much confusion in his heart when his dream girl was sitting here. He glanced over to see for the first time that Neal and Laurie were waiting for a table. His heart was pounding for a different reason, but he couldn't quite find the words. Without thinking, he got up and knelt next to Maggie's chair.

"What are you....?" Maggie never finished the question.

Hiri had taken her face in his hands and kissed her with everything he had. Feelings he carried the past few years - his hunger for her, the pain of her disappearing, the solace of time with Neal. His head exploded with fireworks of color, passion, light, but both his friends were in his mind as he kissed her. When the image of Neal kissing him crossed his mind, he bit down on her lip. She broke the kiss, pushing him back. He had bitten her hard enough to draw blood. Her hand covered her mouth, swollen from the kisses, eyes wide with horror as she saw Neal watching them for the first time.

"Is this some joke to you?" she asked angrily, "Am I just some joke to the two of you?"

Maggie stood up, backing away from Hiri, as he froze in shock over what was happening.

"No, how can you think that?" he asked.

"What am I supposed to think? You kiss me like that, and then I see him watching us...did you guys plan this?"

She didn't even let him start the next sentence. Maggie grabbed her purse and ran out of the restaurant, passing Laurie and Neal in a flurry. Hiri took some cash from his pocket and dropped it down on the table before grabbing his stuff to chase after her. When he got close to Neal, he shoved him out of the way as he ran out the door. Walking up and down the boardwalk, he could not find her. He stopped at her hotel, but she hadn't come back yet. Hours went by, and soon Hiri found himself wandering the beach again. Distraught and out of breath, he came upon their beach to see the silhouette of two shadows. A young woman, beautiful in the moonlight, leaning back from what looked like a hug, arms wrapped around her from a tall, strong man. Their eyes were locked onto each other as Hiri got closer. He knew in every fiber of his being these two people were in their own world, just about to kiss. It was only as he got within 10 feet that he realized who they were: Maggie and Neal.

Hiri could swear the vein in his forehead was going to explode. "What the HELL is going on, Maggie?" he screamed, knocking the two friends out of their bubble.

"Dude, you need to calm down," stated Neal.

"Don't you ever fucking tell me to calm down!! You're supposed to be my friend?! You knew that I've loved her forever - and you have screwed me over with her since the beginning!!" Hiri screeched, shoving Neal.

"Don't touch me like that again!" yelled Neal, pushing Hiri back.

"Guys, stop! This is ridiculous! Hiri! Neal!" yelled Maggie as the two began shoving and wrestling each other to the ground.

"You even kissed me, you son of a bitch!? Was that just so you could play games with me too?" taunted Hiri.

"SHUT UP!!" raged Neal. A nerve had clearly been touched as his fists went flying towards Hiri's torso.

"I said to stop this now!" yelled Maggie again, putting her hands on Hiri's shoulder to pry him off Neal. She pulled as hard as her petite frame could, digging her nails into his shoulders.

"Let go of me, you slut! You two - it's always you two. You played me and had me chasing you all night when you were with him!" Hiri saw red, hurt beyond reason, confused why he thought of Neal at all, swinging his arms back and forth to get Maggie to let go.

One hard swing was all it took, and she went flying back.

As soon as she was off of him, Neal wrestled himself around Hiri to attempt a sleeper hold. The two boys, grunting and swearing, did not notice Maggie's body lying in the sand, her skull cracked against a rock with blood dripping down the side of her beautiful face. Her wide eyes stared at them as they huffed, punched, and kicked - an unblinking soulless body witnessing a useless fight.

It was Hiri's eyes who first saw hers staring into the abyss. Mortified, he dove forward into the sand, ignoring Neal's confusion and screams. He couldn't hear anything except a small ringing. Kneeling next to her, sobbing and silently screaming, Hiri rocked back and forth on his heels.

"No..no..no...no...Maggie….Maggie...I'm sorry….Please ….no"

"What did you do?" whispered Neal, hand over mouth, "WHAT DID YOU DO?" dropping, reaching for her hand, cold in the shadows.

Both boys sat crying over her, stunned and unable to move.

"We weren't even doing anything, man," sobbed Neal, "I found her out here, and we were just talking... just apologizing to one another for all the stupid crap… I finally told her how much I love her..."

Hiri, eyes red, nose sniveling with snot, finally broke his gaze from Maggie's face to Neal. The girl of his dreams, the love of his life gone, and it was all HIS fault. If Neal hadn't shown up, the date would have been perfect. If he hadn't kissed him earlier and just gone on his way with his vanilla girlfriend, this never would have happened.

Hiri, bit into his lip, remembering the taste of Maggie's lips on his and clenched his fist around the rock that lay near her head. The last thing he remembered before the next morning was the sound of the rock smashing into Neal's face.

Hiri was on his sailboat out on the open waters before the sun rose. He sailed, port to port, living as a drifter and an urchin, never staying in one port for longer than

22

necessary. He avoided the U.S. coastline at all costs, and, at night, he dreamt of both their kisses. As the years passed, he came to realize that he was physically attracted to both of them and that he loved both of them. Time and alcohol only furthered his belief that Neal probably felt the same way. They were just too young, and neither of them knew how to express it.

When Hiri received the diagnosis that his liver was failing and that he didn't have much time left, the only thing he thought of was this moment - coming back to this beach. Standing on this sand again, the beach he met, fell in love with, then destroyed the two best friends he ever had. He walked into the same water he first met them all those years ago. His body naturally floated with the waves, just as it had done when she first saw him. As he closed his eyes and let the tide drag him further out to sea, he could swear he heard both of them laughing and giggling in the water with him.

"We've been waiting for you, Hiri," they said together, arms reaching for him under the tide, "Right where you left us…"

THE MEAN GIRL
By Michael J Moore

I'm here because my best friend Brittany has been missing for 5 months and I'm pretty sure she's dead. Well, that and because Kirk has abs in places I didn't even know abs could exist, and blue eyes that look so out of place below his jet-black hair that it makes him seem... I don't know, wrong I guess. But in all the right ways. So when I feel his hand on my leg below the cluttered wooden table, I grip the strap of my white purse which sits next to me and says "Chanel," on it, even though it's not a real Chanel. I gasp so subtly that I'm sure only he notices, but I don't move to stop him.

It doesn't matter that we're in a small, dirty motorhome, or that there's an old, fat woman with a raspy voice sitting across from us smoking a cigarette that's making my eyes water. It doesn't matter that there's a smelly mixed-breed dog with matted brown hair laying at our feet, or that I'm dressed like a catholic schoolgirl, and he's touching bare skin below my checkered skirt, because his hand is smooth, and it makes me wonder about his lips.

It's summertime—well, I'm not actually sure when the season starts, but today was the last day of senior-year, and though the sun's already gone down, it's still hot as hell outside. The window next to the table is shut, but I can hear a symphony of crickets chirping somewhere nearby. Or maybe they're frogs, considering Mobile Drive sits only a few-hundred feet from the Skagit River. Sometimes I get the sounds of their nocturnal songs mixed up. There are two separate fans blowing on either side of the R.V., and some cop reality-show playing on a small television set up near a bed that looms over the driver's seat.

Kirk's mother's name is Martha, and she's smoked two cigarettes already in the past half-hour. I don't smoke, never even tried, but I can't imagine this is normal. She tells me between long puffs that light up her brown eyes, about her other son.

"Sergio sleeps out in the car with the dog. I hate to have to keep him there, but there's just not room in the house. Not with Kirk and his sister in here. He's older anyway, needs to learn to figure things out for himself, ya know?"

I nod, say, "Yeah. Totally" as Kirk's hand glides slowly upward, sending an electric chill into my torso. It buzzes past my chest and stops at my eyes, which I'm sure glaze over as my toes curl atop a set of high heels that match my purse.

"You got any siblings, Stephanie?" Martha asks, and I can see in her face that she's noticed what's happening under the table, yet making a point to pretend otherwise.

"Just a sister," I tell her. "An older one. She moved out already, though."

"Tall blondie like you?"

"Taller." I smirk. "She's a model actually."

I met Kirk in the fifth, grade, and probably never would have interacted with him if we hadn't been stuck sitting together all year. It's weird when I think about it, because he looks pretty much the same tonight as he did then—taller, obviously—but he wasn't hot at 11. He didn't get hot until sometime during junior year if I'm being honest, and I usually always am.

This one time, during lunch, it was just Brittany and I, and she was staring over at his table while I was talking, so I was like, "Look at you, bitch," and she tried to play it off, but we made a joke out of it all year after that. In fact, I'm pretty sure that's what... okay, let's keep it real, that was definitely what planted the seed that caused her to eventually sneak around with the guy.

We have a motorhome too. I mean, my dad does. My mom jokes that it's his man-cave, because he goes out to it whenever he wants to be alone. He has to keep it in this parking-lot a couple blocks away because there's some rule in our neighborhood about having R.V.s or too many cars out front. I guess it makes the block look trashy and lowers the property value, or whatever.

Anyway, we went camping in ours once, when I was—I think I was 13? Maybe 14, and I found some nasty-ass oil in a red bottle from Lover's Package and it gave me a pretty fucked up idea of what he does when he's alone in that thing. I've made a point to stay away from it since then.

Kirk's motorhome is parked in a big gravel lot, though, among a cluster of others. It's actually similar to the lot outside our neighborhood, except that this *is* his neighborhood because the people of Mobile Lane live here, and the R.V.s are all old and beat up. I've learned in the past few minutes that Kirk, his mother, and his 7-year-old sister, who's visiting a friend in another R.V. somewhere nearby, cram into this cluttered aluminum box to sleep every night, and apparently his 30-something-year-old brother lives in the old station wagon that's parked out front next to my car.

He's quiet as his mother speaks, grinning and nodding, moving his hand slowly and softly until I feel my skirt brush the top of my thigh. I get the impression Martha doesn't have much company. She blows a long stream of gray smoke that fogs the window next to us, and scratches her breast over a darkened white T-shirt.

"They all got different dad's, you know? Obviously, Kirk's was the one to take the cake. He had the same damn eyes as my boy here, and I guess I don't gotta tell you what they did to me." She lets out a cackling laugh that ends in a fit of coughing. "Only thing he'd be good for these days is child-support if the son-of-a-fuck would get off his ass and get a job. Sergio's dad was—what's that thing again?" She takes a drag that causes ash to fall onto the table and eyes her son.

"Russian?" Kirk offers.

"Yeah. Whatever." She wipes the mess, leaving a streak on the wood. "The point is, these kids don't got no one to help 'em out, and get 'em on their feet. I gotta bear the brunt of parenting, and don't get me wrong, I don't mind raising my babies, but as you can see, I don't got much, and I don't like having to keep the older one in that damn car. He's fine for now, but it can get cold in the winter, ya know?"

Until today, I hadn't spoken to Kirk since the fifth grade. I don't mean to sound like a bitch... I mean, I'm really not one of those girls. It doesn't bother me that he's poor, or whatever. I hooked up with Zack Erickson after we hung out a couple times, and everybody at school knew about it. I wasn't embarrassed, either. Nobody cares how much money a guy has when he's popular.

I'm not making a strong case for myself, am I? I probably sound like the worst person to ever go to high school, but it's really not like that. I'm not Regina George from *Mean Girls* or anything. I'm actually not even that popular, and that's just it. I can't afford to be seen with someone like Kirk Tomlin.

Well, I couldn't until today. But high school is finally over, along with its social hierarchy, and the truth is, I wasn't surprised when he caught me outside the cafeteria and asked if I wanted to hang out.

I tell Martha I had a friend whose dad was a deadbeat, and instantly regret it because maybe it's not my place to say such things. My body tenses and Kirk's hand slides *up, up, up,* until his fingers are only inches from where they want to be, their tips pressing indentations into my skin that are soft, yet somehow firm at the same time. My legs seem to have a mind of their own as they drift apart.

Martha laughs, stubs out her butt in a black ashtray, where countless others sticks up like crooked tree-stumps. She exclaims, "They're all deadbeats, honey, just waiting to beat," and then slides her heavy body across the bench, stopping at the edge and glaring down at her dog. "Move it, Butch."

The animal raises its head from its paws and gazes tiredly up at her.

"Come on, stupid. Move." She nudges him with her meaty foot, and he climbs to his feet, yawns, stretches, and moseys toward the front of the R.V.

Kirk's hand crawls like a spider until one of his fingers—maybe his pinky—brushes my panties in a downward stroke that erects goosebumps all over my body. Using the counter to stabilize herself, his mother huffs to her feet, and his hand quickly retracts, leaving my skirt raised along with my heart rate. Maybe she notices, maybe not—I think she does—but again, she doesn't react, just meets her son's blue eyes and says, "I guess I'll go get your sister now. Probably stay over at Glenda's for a bit and catch up on my gossip. 'Bout ah—" she squints, purses her lips, "half-hour? Hour?"

Kirk nods.

She grins devilishly as she tells us to be good, then turns and makes her way toward the door, causing the R.V. to rock. The sound of the crickets—or frogs—increases when the door opens, and then she disappears into the night, taking their song with her. As soon as the door slams shut, Butch sniffs it, and then glances over at Kirk, who brings up one hand and sets it on an old newspaper on the table. The other brushes the tops of both my legs, before he slides off the seat, stands, and leans against the counter, staring down at me beneath eyelids that seem to have grown heavy.

We had kinda flirted for a while before he approached me today. I say kinda because, like I said, we hadn't actually spoken in years. We'd been making eyes in the cafeteria, though. In fifth period art. In the halls. We'd been doing it since the night Brittany hung out with him probably in this very motorhome—five months ago. Some of my friends had even noticed and flipped me shit about it.

His did the same. I know they did, because I heard the laughter after they were behind me. Normally, I would have assumed they were looking back over their shoulders, checking me out as I walked away, but it almost always came from the trashy whores in his circle. Some of them were pretty—or could have been—but they smoked cigarettes and stuck safety pins in their cheap-ass clothes, and got pregnant by older guys who went to prison for fucking them. Their loathing of the subliminal attention I paid Kirk didn't bother me. Actually, it made me smile most of the time, which only made them hate me more.

I can't help but wonder what they would think if they saw the swelling in his blue jeans right now, as he leans back and stares down at me all rosy-cheeked and glazed over like something from Krispy Kreme. I make a point to let him see me looking, and even smile a bit because it's bigger than I expected. He's tall, though, so that really shouldn't come as much of a surprise, should it?

A police radio cackles, and at first I think it's coming from outside. Then a robotic, female voice spouts numbers from only feet away, and I realize it's the show on his mother's TV. I thought that show was canceled after the de-fund protests across the country, but maybe I was wrong.

Kirk runs a hand over his bulge, and says, "You okay?"

I reach into my purse, feeling my gigantic iPhone, car-keys, assorted makeup, and two shot-sized bottles of Bacardi vodka. I tell him I'm fine as I bring out a lip-gloss and unscrew the cap.

"You sure?" he asks. "I mean, in your car you were all talky-mic-talkative, but since we got here you've been he-lla quiet. Maybe you're nervous?"

"Why would I be nervous?" I make a point not to break eye-contact as I run the tiny brush over my lips, then replace the cap and set it back into my purse. "Just because I'm hanging out with the only guy in the country still using the word 'hella'? I'm okay with it, I guess." When my hand re-emerges, both liquor-bottles hang between its fingers. I set my purse on the table, scoot toward the edge of the seat, and offer him one, making sure he has a good view of my hot-pink nails.

He laughs, accepts it, squints at the label. Pursing his lips, he says, "I didn't know you got down like that."

"I guess that's probably because you've never been invited to any of our parties."

I know I'm being a bitch now, but I also know he likes it because his eyes narrow and his lips curl into a subtle smile. This is what he was hoping for, because this is the preconceived impression, he had of me before today. It's the same thing everybody who doesn't know me thinks, and probably what he thought about Brittany too. I screw the top off my bottle, and wash down the liquid in one gulp, feeling it burn in my chest and willing my face not to express disgust.

He watches me with a smug expression, and I see a series of possible scenarios playing out just behind his eyes. Then he unscrews his own lid and sniffs the rim.

I couldn't give him my number today because he doesn't have a phone. This would have complicated things had he been a normal guy, because it would have made it hard to meet up later. I didn't want to be seen leaving school with him, so I told him to wait in the alley up the street after last period, and that's where I picked him up

We went out to the river and walked alone on the trails in the woods, and no, I wasn't a bitch to him then.

31

In fact, I think I was extra sweet with a cherry on top. And though he took his shirt off for a while on the beach, he was surprisingly shy. Then he brought me home to meet his mother, and that's when it got weird as fuck, but and I guess you could say I'm damaged goods because if you haven't figured it out yet, I'm kinda into it.

The dog wags its tail maniacally and makes its way across the R.V. It sniffs my feet, and then my legs. It tries to wedge its nose under my skirt, so I laugh and push it away.

Kirk says, "Butch! What have I taught you? You can't come off as too eager, or she won't like you. That's how girls like her are." The dog sits and gazes up at his owner all starry-eyed and pathetic as Kirk waves the bottle under his nostrils and smells it once more. This time his face scrunches and he coughs before dumping its contents into the sink. He meets my gaze and asks if I'm trying to drug him.

So this is it, and I'm kinda freaking right now, because no matter how many times I've played this scenario out in my mind, my imagination is no comparison to the thrill of what's about to happen.

His smile increases as he tells me he knows why I'm here. Then he says, "You know there are no cameras in Mobile Lane, right? I mean, like none. Somebody could drive in here and never drive back out and there'd be no proof she was ever here. So, whatever you think I did to your friend—to that fucking redhead—"

"Brittany," I cut him off.

"Yeah. Her. Whatever you think I did to her is only in your imagination unless you got some kinda proof. And I'm gonna go ahead and step out on a limb and say if you had that, you would've called the cops instead of flirting with me all year to try and play detective. I know you know she was with me that day, because that's what you told the police. And you know what? She was. Who gives a fuck?"

I swivel my legs so they're facing him, and I can stand should the need arise. He drops the empty bottle into the sink and takes a step toward me. He's still fully erect and so close now that it's only inches from my face. My heart is like a vibrator in my chest and my body is growing lighter with every passing second, but he's right, because this is exactly why I'm here.

The details are foggy in my mind. Not because it's been five months since Brittany disappeared, but because I wasn't there, and can only speculate about what actually happened. She didn't tell me she was gonna hang out with him, and no matter how much we had joked about it, I wouldn't have expected her even in my strangest dreams to do it. The only reason I knew she was with him that day was because she butt-dialed me and giggled his name. The connection lasted all of three minutes before she realized what had happened and killed it, and that's the last time I ever heard my best-friend's voice.

I don't know what motivates psychopaths, and I don't know why Kirk Tomlin killed Brittany. In my version of the story, he made a move on her and she resisted, so he raped her. After that, he freaked out and killed her so she couldn't report him to the police. I've tried not to get wet every time I've thought about it, every time I've inserted myself into her role in the scenario, but like I said: damaged goods.

So as he reaches into a drawer below the sink, and brings out an old, dirty revolver with a short barrel and shiny black tape on the handle, I only stand up because

I'm really hoping he'll push me back down. Grab me by the neck. Slap me or something.

And Kirk Tomlin doesn't disappoint. His lips harden and peel back into a sneer as he takes my white, button-down shirt in one hand and pulls so hard that some of the buttons burst and scatter onto the floor. Pressing the tip of the cold gun into my temple, he rips it all the way open and growls, "You thought you were so smart, didn't you, you little bitch? You thought you were gonna—what? Get me to confess? Are you that fucking full of yourself?"

I tell him, "No. I'm nothing," as his dog stands up on its back legs and presses its wet nose into my exposed breasts, which hang in a lacy, red bra that looks like it's from Victoria's Secret, but really came from Walmart. Kirk commands me to lie on the floor and take off my panties.

He says, "If you make a sound I'll put a hole in your pretty face and nobody will bat an eye because people fire guns around here all the time."

I don't want to because the floor is dirty (I was hoping this would happen in the bed, or even standing up). But Kirk is the boss now, so I make a show of sobbing as I oblige and hand him a size-six white cotton bundle from where I lie on my back, feeling the open air on my saturated labia, my stilettos digging into the dirty white linoleum.

He examines my underwear for a while, and then sets it on the table. That's when Butch comes sniffing again and I try not to break character as I shove his mangy head away, but Kirk tells me to leave him alone, because this is his house and I'm just a guest.

I cry, "Kirk! Please get this dog away from me! I'll do whatever you want! I swear! Anything!"

"What?" The word comes out as a shriek because it's mixed with surprised laughter. "Girl, I don't want nothing from you. What do you think this is?"

"Then what?" I sniff. "You're just gonna—kill me?"

He chuckles. Shakes his head. Scratches his balls with the gun, and then fetches a black cellphone from the drawer. "Don't get ahead of yourself, gorgeous. First, Butch is gonna have some fun with you while I record it with my mom's phone. See, we make these videos, and we get pretty good money for 'em online, so I'll need you to kinda get into it. No half-stepping and no crying. Don't mention this gun neither. You gotta be cool about it. You might get some scratches on you, but he doesn't bite much. I'll need to get some close-ups of him inside, so don't try and fuck me around, okay?" As he speaks, I feel my stomach turning inside-out. My tears have, at some point, run dry because they were fifty-two-fake anyway, I'm still trying to keep the smelly fucking dog away, but I'm staring up at the same time, searching Kirk's face for any indication that he's joking. "If you're cool," he continues, "and once Butch is done, if he looks like he had a good time, you can get into your car and drive away. I'll forget you tried to drug me, and as long as you don't run to the police, neither will I. How's that sound?"

I open my mouth to speak, but the words, whatever they are, are caught in my throat. The dog's tongue dangles from its mouth and it seems to be smiling as it resists my hands. It sidesteps, and for a second I catch sight of its genitalia, pink and protruding like an opened lipstick.

"It swells," Kirk asserts as he points the phone down at me, staring into its screen. "Dogs' dicks swell up to about the size of a softball when they're inside. You'll probably like it so much you'll come back for more. Now stop fighting him off or I'll have to give you something to help you relax. What was in that vodka you tried to give me anyway?"

This is wrong. This is not why I'm here. This isn't why Brittany was here either, and I'm sure now that she didn't resist. I knew my friend better than her own parents did, and she would have done what she had to do to save her life. She fucked this dog in this dirty, beat-up motorhome, and then Kirk Tomlin killed her.

The dog's head slips past my hands and before I can catch it again, its back legs wedge between mine. It places its front paws on either side of my waist, using them to hold me in place. Its face is so close to mine that I can smell its meaty breath as I tell Kirk between a fit of dry heaves that the bottle was full of scopolamine and acetone.

Then I feel it pressing against me, attempting to wedge itself inside. Some diaper commercial plays on the TV, and almost as an involuntary reaction, I take the dog's snout in both hands and twist, pull, squeeze. I try to rip it off its ugly face and wait for it to sink its pointed teeth into my neck.

But instead, it yelps. It sprays me with warm pee before it scurries back with its tail between its legs and its head down, looking at me like I just threw away its kibbles. Kirk doesn't react. He stands above, his hands now at his sides—the gun in one, the phone in the other—and stares down terrified.

Finally, my smile returns because *this* is why the fuck I'm here.

The dog continues to back up and watch me as I climb to my feet and fetch my purse. My chest heaves while I dig around and find a small zip-lock baggy with about a quarter gram of sparkling white powder.

"This," I say as I use my car-key to scoop out a tiny pile of the substance, "is scopolamine. I mixed it with acetone so when it evaporated from the bottle, you were breathing it in." My hand is still shaking as I place the key under his nose, so I press it against his face for stability. I tell him to sniff, and though his lips tremble, he does as he told.

"I learned about this stuff from a documentary," I explain. "They call it the devil's breath, and it's considered the most dangerous drug in the world. Criminals in Colombia slip it to tourists' drinks and it makes them do whatever they're told, I guess. Like puppets. They usually just take them to ATMs and get them to empty their accounts, but there was this drug-lord who loaded his own belongings into a thief's truck for him. In fact, now that I think about it, this stuff probably would have really come in handy for your little business here. I found it easy enough on the dark web."

The truth is: I wasn't actually sure it would work, and I'm still not convinced it's strong enough to aid what I have planned. I tell him to set the objects down on the counter, and he doesn't hesitate.

Flipping up my skirt, I say, "Your dog pissed on me. You're lucky I don't make you lick it off."

He doesn't respond, just stares into my eyes drooling on himself so I tell him I can see into his heart, and I know he was raised rough and just wants to be loved and taken care of. Then I cup his manhood and command him to fetch the biggest knife in the kitchen. Well, the kitchen area. Once he's done it, I slowly unbutton his pants and maneuver it out, which isn't easy because it really is huge and still fully erect.

"Now cut it off and feed it to that mutt. If you're cool, and he looks like he had a good time afterward, maybe I'll forget you tried to make me have sex with him. How does that sound."

Now I know I said I'm not a mean-girl, and I'm really not. I understand that this guy's poor and he did what he did to make money. I mean, I'm sure it was even his fat mother's idea. And believe me, I've never done anything like this before, and don't plan on ever doing it again. If I'm being honest, and like I said, I usually am, I really don't know what my future holds. I don't think I'll go to college, but maybe I'll do some volunteer work. Like food drives or whatever to help the less fortunate so they don't feel like they have to make videos of girls fucking dogs.

This guy killed my friend, though. Not just her, but he's probably done it to more girls than I can even imagine. He was gonna kill me, and if that's not enough, there is literally dog-urine on my vagina. Still, I tell him to be cool and try to get into it, but I don't watch as he saws into his penis with the serrated blade, because though the hunt excited me in ways I never knew possible, I'm not really into other people's pain.

Instead, I crawl around on my hands and knees picking up all the buttons from my shirt, and listening to him howl and cry unintelligibly. He hiccups and jerks, and I find myself more than a little surprised when the side of my face is misted with warm liquid and I look up to see him actually holding his now-limp member, bloody and plucked from his body like a weed in somebody's garden.

His crotch has become a freaky fountain, spraying lava-colored fluid in short spurts like a bottle of disinfectant. It paints the walls, the floor—even my face and body. I have to admit, it feels kinda nice against my skin, like a hot shower, so I kneel in front of him for a moment and stare up into his blue eyes as I let him do it on my breasts.

Kirk doesn't return my gaze, though, just examines the damage, tears and sweat streaming down his face. Wiping blood from my eyes, I stand and hold out my hand. When he doesn't respond, I say, "Come on, big guy. Give it to me," and finally he sets his penis in my hand with a reluctant groan. I toss it to the dog, who refuses to eat it, just cowers in the corner whimpering. So, I order Kirk to stab it to death, and then cut off its head.

As he does this, I rummage around the R.V. until I find a big, blue comforter and a towel, then I tell Kirk to pick up his gun. He walks bowlegged to the counter, while I use the towel to wipe bloody hand and footprints off everything I've touched or stepped on. He drops the knife and retrieved the gun, and I can tell by his sluggishness and loss of blood-pressure that there's not much life left in the guy.

So I run a hand through his hair and say, "I want you to go to the R.V. where your mom is and shoot her right in her fat face, okay stud?"

His own face slowly morphs into an expression of unhinged agony, and though he's still unable to form words, he begins to cry like an infant with a deep voice. It might be the most difficult thing I've ever watched, but his blood is still warm and it's spraying my legs, so I wait for him to make the first move, which he does. He turns and hobbles to the door, and once it's open, I hear the crickets again... or maybe they're frogs.

Then he's gone, the door shuts behind him, and I notice that the cop show has ended, replaced by some documentary about who knows what. I need to hurry now because though there are no cameras in Mobile Lane, Kirk Tomlin is about to make a scene. Just about every surface inside the R.V. is covered in dark crimson. It's splotched in some places, and streaked in others, and the dog's head sits about a foot from its body, its tongue still hanging from its open mouth.

I drop Martha's phone and the liquor bottles into my purse, and wipe away my tracks on the way out. Then, as an afterthought, go back inside and grab my panties, which sit next to the ashtray.

It's finally cooled down outside, and Mobile Lane is like a teeny-tiny ghost town. Light comes from inside countless R.V.s, but nobody is outside except for me and Kirk, whose feet drag in the gravel as he makes his way like a zombie to wherefore his mother is, leaving behind bloody pebbles. I use the comforter to cover my driver's seat. I mean, I've seen enough movies to know I'll end up leaving some kind of traces anyway, but I don't want to mess up my upholstery, and what are the chances I'm even questioned? Nobody even knows I spent the day with Kirk Tomlin.

I'll have to check and see if the phone was still recording before I destroy it, but I can do that at the river before I wash off. I start my engine and connect my own phone to the speakers so I can listen to music while I drive, and I can't stop thinking that maybe I *am* a mean girl.

The Tart

By Alexandria Baker

It began with a strawberry tart, of all things. Nellie had baked it a few days prior and brought the syrupy confection to my doorstep with that glow of condescension that can only come from an unexpected gift and the unspoken debt attached to it. Her ruby lips turned up into a simpering smile that matched the hue of the strawberries on the plate. I wanted to throw up.

"What's this for?" I managed to keep my tone light, but my eye twitched slightly as I spoke.

"Oh, well you know that strawberry bush in my garden? It has been growing like *crazy* this spring! I can't keep up with the darn thing, and Nick and I are both just about sick of strawberries. I can't give them away fast enough!" She laughed, and I swear I saw the tiniest flounce in her perfectly coiffed hair at the mention of Nick. The tart was a ruse. She had come over here to gloat.

"How thoughtful of you to come all this way for me," I said through gritted teeth.

"Don't be silly, it's a lovely day and the walk is good for my figure. I can't keep too many treats around the house!"

"Of course."

"But *you* enjoy that tart and bring the dish back whenever you're in the neighborhood!"

Before I could make a snide remark about how I was *always* in the neighborhood, she pressed the surprisingly heavy plate into my hands. With a trill of her fingers and an ostentatious "Ta-ta!" she turned in her red heels and clicked her way down the street to her house.

As I watched her swaying hips disappear around the corner, I sighed. In three minutes, she would be walking up the front steps of her tidy little love nest. It was a Saturday, so Nick would be at home, waiting for her. He would open the front door for her, wrapping his arms around her waist as she entered, and as the two of them slipped into the privacy of the house they would—I didn't let myself finish the thought. When I came to, I slammed my door shut for good measure.

I let the tart sit on my counter for three days before I threw the whole thing in the trash.

My sister, of course, was the one who reminded me I had to do my neighborly duties and return the dish.

She was bustling around my kitchen, pouring herself a second glass of wine as we settled in to enjoy a bit of after-dinner chocolate cake. It was a small indulgence we partook in every Friday, as neither of us had much going on in the way of romance or social lives to attend to.

"This is a lovely serving dish. When did you get it?" Laura had an eye for detail, and it was just like her to remark on the minutiae of my kitchen.

"Which dish?" I was sitting on the couch, more concerned with my dessert as I scraped my fork across the frosting.

"This one." She held the plate up for me to see, the intricate floral pattern on its center revealed since I had dumped Nellie's confection. I cut my eyes toward the plate in Laura's hand, letting out a sigh as I did so. She caught it, as she always did.

"It's Nellie's." I disliked even uttering her name in my home. This was supposed to be my safe place, my sanctuary.

"Ah, I see." As Laura returned to the couch, she set her refilled glass on the end table and held out her hand for mine. Ever the dutiful elder sister, she was a better host than I was—even when she was supposed to be the guest. She returned to the kitchen, and I could hear the wine pouring slowly into my glass as she asked, "And when did Nellie give you the plate?" Her tone was light, but she knew it was a sensitive subject. She lingered longer than necessary in the kitchen as she waited for my response.

"About a week ago," I muttered.

"…Do you think you might return it anytime soon?" she prodded.

"It's not like Nellie has a history of returning things," I fired back.

"Liz."

"I bet she's curled up right now with Nick. I bet she cooked a perfect dinner and ate three bites of it before telling him she was full. I bet she fixed him an after-dinner drink and some strawberry-flavored dessert even though she said they were sick of them." The wine was going to my head.

"It's none of your concern, Liz," Laura's tone was measured, but I knew where she was going with this.

"No, of course not. It's none of my concern what goes on behind closed doors, but I still have to slap on a happy face whenever I run into them in public like nothing's wrong."

"Exactly. Because as far as you're concerned, nothing is wrong."

"But it is!" The wine sloshed over my hand as I gesticulated. A few drops landed on the carpet, and Laura sighed as she reached over to blot them with a napkin.

"Leave it! Nick was supposed to be mine. I felt him watching me that day at the Sunday social. It was different than he'd ever looked at me before. Nellie saw I was about to make my move and she swooped in and seduced him with a damn pie. One bite was all it took. Why don't you figure out how to clean up that mess?"

Laura looked at me with cold eyes. Her disappointment hurt more than I thought it would, but it wasn't like I could unload like this at the book club. She put her glass down and stood up to leave.

"Wallow in your misery if you want," she said. "But don't take it out on me."

"Fine."

Laura shrugged on her coat and opened the front door. "And just remember that the longer you hold onto that plate, the more Nellie has to hold over your head. That's one mess I can't clean up for you."

And damn if she wasn't right.

It took another day before I worked up the nerve to walk the plate back over to Nellie's house. I had been content to let it fester on my kitchen counter, but Laura was right. I couldn't let Nellie have anything to hold over my head. She was insidious. She would find a time to use it and embarrass me in front of the whole neighborhood. Yes, the best course of action was to return the damn thing before she had a chance to bring it up.

Of course, that meant the possibility of coming face-to-face with Nick. If Nellie was a viper—coiled and ready to strike—then Nick was the forbidden fruit beckoning on her tree.

I spent several minutes carefully selecting my outfit before I left the house. It needed to be stylish but casual. Put together without trying too hard. It needed to show everyone that I was thriving, successful, and living my life—effortlessly.

I chose my best slacks with an airy button-up blouse, then threw a light spring jacket over the ensemble to make it look like I had been running errands all day. Nick needed to see that I was keeping busy.

Despite leaving the house ready for battle, I dragged my feet for the entirety of the short walk over to Nellie's. Her plate was like an anchor in my hands, dragging me down, down, and down until I finally turned the corner in front of her neat white house with its picket fence. She hadn't been lying about the garden. Though I found her to be poisonous, the plants were flourishing—threatening to overtake the fence in some places. As I opened the gate and walked up the steps, I noticed the cursed strawberry bush planted front and center in the yard. It was dripping with fruit, each strawberry more perfect than the last and all a uniform ruby-red.

I didn't have long to muse on the plant, because the front door opened before I had a chance to knock. It was Nick.

Though I had known there was a chance he would be the one to answer the door, I had desperately hoped he might be gone so I only had to deal with Nellie's insufferable niceties.

"Oh, hi, Liz," he said. He was gorgeous as always, blue eyes shining in contrast to his lustrous dark locks. I was tongue-tied.

He paused, waiting for me to piece my scrambled brain back together. "What brings you here?" His eyes glanced down to the plate still clenched in my hands, and at last I collected myself.

"I, uh, I just wanted to return this." I held out the plate, extending my arm farther than necessary to avoid stepping closer to him.

"Ah, thanks," he looked slightly puzzled. It was unlikely he'd even known Nellie had made a house call, let alone that she'd left the dish with me.

"Tell Nellie the tart was impeccable," I said. Though the words were right, my tone was wrong. My nerves had caused it to come out less like a request and more like a command.

He offered me a tight-lipped smile, nodding.

"I will—," he began.

"Tell Nellie what?" Her voice was a razor, cutting through the air. Like a kraken rising from the deep, she wrapped her cloying arms around Nick's waist, smothering the space between them with her curves.

"The tart. Was. Impeccable." I croaked. It was one thing to confront Nellie out in public, but here on her own turf, when she was literally twisted around the prize, I found it hard to speak through the anger that burned inside me.

"Well, I'm so glad you liked it! Looks like you cleaned the plate." Though naturally I couldn't have returned the pastry itself, I found myself thinking back to the chocolate cake and the fit of my slacks, wondering if she had a point. It was her most vicious power, the ability to turn a pleasantry into a weapon.

Nick clearly sensed the tension. He gracefully disentangled himself from Nellie's grasp. "I'll go put this away," he murmured.

Nellie took the opportunity to plant a swift peck on his lips. "Thanks, hon."

With a final glance in my direction, Nick raised a hand in farewell. "It was good to see you, Liz." He stepped back into the cool interior of the house.

Nellie lingered in the doorway, giving me a calculated once-over. "You'll have to let me know when you're around so I can bring you another treat," she said. "Looks like you were out and about today."

"I was." I seized the opportunity to look like I had been keeping busy.

She stepped closer to the edge of the porch, closing the distance between us. "I just wanted to let you know that you missed a button," she whispered. I glanced down in horror to realize that she was right. The second button from the top of my blouse was undone, creating an unsightly gap and revealing a tiny peek of my bra. My cheeks flushed, whether from rage or embarrassment, I couldn't tell.

"Anyway, I'll see you around. Have a good one, Liz!" She spun triumphantly on her heels and flounced back inside, closing the door in my face with a final click.

I wanted to scream. I wanted to fall to the ground and tear my hair out. I wanted to beat down Nellie's door and tear Nick from her arms.

Instead, sick with anger, I stomped down the short steps of Nellie's porch, preparing for the walk back to my house and the bottle of wine that would inevitably follow. As I reached the bottom step, a small breeze rustled the plants in Nellie's garden, and my eyes came to rest on her prized strawberry bush.

It truly was a marvel. The leaves were a thick forest green, and the berries were so ripe they nearly burst with juice, begging you to touch them. The plant had originally been placed with care, but its wild fertility had caused it to overtake its portion of the garden, easily growing over the small divider that had been placed in the ground around it.

In fact, it was nearly like a weed in the way it grew so wantonly over Nellie's picture-perfect garden. The thought gave me a terrible, incredible idea.

I glanced back at the house. I couldn't see any movement through the windows, nor could I hear their voices. They had likely retired to the living room near the back of the house.

Without giving it any more thought, I seized a portion of the plant by its thick, slightly fuzzy stem and yanked as hard as I could. Nearly half the plant burst out of the soft soil, shedding loose dirt all over my shoes. I had been intending to simply rip it away from the roots, leaving it to shrivel and die, but now I stood in Nellie's garden with a stolen plant and upturned soil.

I couldn't leave it—it would be obvious what I had done. I quickly scooped some of the loose dirt back into the hole, shaking out the soil from the roots as well. I tamped the dirt down with a firm pat and arranged some of the nearby leaves and stems to cover the area. It wasn't perfect, but Nellie's strawberry plant was so overgrown it was unlikely she'd notice the missing portion right away. I would be tucked away safely at home by the time she realized anything was amiss—with a new strawberry plant growing in my window box.

After all, Nellie's never been known to give back the things she takes.

I had mostly recovered from the incident, until the book club came around. It was my turn to host the group, and I thanked my lucky stars I had remembered they were coming ahead of time. Last month we met at Wendy's place, and the poor thing had completely forgotten we were coming until the five of us stood clucking on her doorstep like a flock of hens. She let us in, of course, but it was clear she wasn't really prepared to host.

She hastily cleared some clutter off the coffee table, attempting to artfully rearrange the piles around her home that everyone has but no one is supposed to see. The shriveled cherry on top of her embarrassing offering were the stale crackers and sweating cheese she set out. The rest of us graciously tried to pretend to enjoy the meagre snack, but as always Nellie had to open her big mouth.

"Oh, Wendy! You should have told me if you didn't have time to prepare anything. You know I'm always baking and I would have been happy to bring something along for the group." This scathing remark was accompanied by a firm little pat on Wendy's shoulder; Nellie's smile nearly engulfed her face as the color rose in Wendy's cheeks.

The rest of us attempted to make small talk about that month's book, but Nellie's comment hung in the air above us like a noose around Wendy's neck. It was weeks before she could look any of us in the eye when we crossed paths in the neighborhood. I asked her about it once. She said the whole incident really hadn't bothered her all that much—that Nellie was just being helpful. But then, she didn't know Nellie like I did.

After that, I made sure to triple-check the book club schedule.

Needless to say, I spent several hours that morning ensuring my house was spotless from top to bottom. I'd even tidied the bedroom, just in case someone wandered in. I couldn't take any chances with Nellie around. I had just finished laying out a rather impressive spread of h'ordeuvres—including fresh fruit, brie and crackers, deviled eggs, and the potato salad that the neighbors insisted they simply *must* get the recipe for—when the doorbell rang.

I ushered the book club inside to the usual niceties and small talk.

"This looks delicious, but I see there's no dessert." I could always count on Nellie to eschew the pleasantries. "I hope you don't mind that I took the liberty of bringing a little something over." She laid an icy hand on my arm as she slid a plate of cookies onto the end of the coffee table, jostling the careful arrangement of dishes. The chatter grew silent as the book club waited to see how I would respond to the invasion.

Luckily, I had prepared for this.

"Well, I certainly appreciate the gesture," I plastered a wide smile across my face. Laura would be proud. "But I've got a pie cooling on the windowsill. I figured we could share it after our discussion today. We can leave the cookies out to nibble on in the meantime, if you like."

Nellie's eyes flicked to the windowsill, where my pie waited in all its glory. Behind it, my stolen strawberry plant pushed up against the window. The leaves had turned a dark green since the transplant, and the berries, though still bright, had taken on bulbous shapes.

"I didn't know you grew strawberries," Nellie murmured.

"It's a recent addition." I let the implication hang in the air for a moment.

I watched as a beautiful, sour anger flashed on Nellie's face for a fraction of a second. Then her expression turned. "You know," she began loudly. "Gardening is quite a serious hobby of mine, and if you don't mind me saying, your plant looks a little sickly."

The other women in the room turned their attention to the plant. I could feel my heart starting to beat faster.

"Did you make the pie with fruit from that bush? It looks overripe to me," Nellie continued.

The silence of the book club members was beginning to build up like pressure inside a balloon. "No," I hastily interjected. "It's apple pie, with fruit from the store." But the damage was done. The misshapen, lumpy strawberries hanging on the plant were enough to turn everyone off the thought of fruit pie for dessert. As the color rose in my cheeks, I swore the hue of the strawberries darkened a little, matching the blotchy shame spreading across my face.

The afternoon wore inexorably on, and I was forced to watch as Nellie's cookies steadily disappeared, while my pie grew cold on the windowsill.

I nursed my wounds later that night with the darkest red wine I could find. I carried it around the house with me, not bothering with a glass and unable to settle. With each sip, I could feel the indignation growing in the pit of my stomach.

Why did Nellie get to win *everything*? Why did the world bend over backwards for her?

In my frustration, I opened the closet in my bedroom. From the top shelf, I pulled down a shoebox that no one else has ever laid eyes on. I sat on the floor, and took another swig from the bottle.

Inside the shoebox were photos of Nick. There was a group shot from the Sunday social, of course. And an old photo from when he was on the high school baseball team. But my favorites were the photos I had taken. The ones he didn't know about, when he was most himself, completely unawares. The back of his beautiful head as he walked down the street. His profile through the window as he sipped his morning coffee. And at the very bottom, my prized photo—a rare nighttime shot of him undressing in his room.

Nellie was always so paranoid with the drapes; it was hard to get useable shots after dark. I'd need to update my collection soon. Nick's hair had grown out a bit since some of these were taken. The thought made me angry. Nellie didn't have to settle for covert glances and flat images. She got to live the whole thing. She got *him*.

And even though she had Nick, she still had to come over with her false niceties and mock me in front of the whole neighborhood. How dare she?

As the anger rose inside me, I staggered to my feet. The room was spinning, but I stumbled my way downstairs to the intact pie that sat like an albatross on the windowsill. I leaned over it to open the window, and lost my balance as I did so. With a soft crunch, I crushed the pie underneath me as I slipped, staining my shirt with what had been an artfully crafted apple filling. As I stood up to take in the damage, the strawberry plant outside caught my eye.

It was an ugly thing, there was no doubt about it. This afternoon the berries had still been somewhat presentable, but now the fruit looked bruised and beaten. The strawberries hung low on their stems, bloated and misshapen. They had turned a sort of unseemly purple that I had never seen in a strawberry before. I wasn't sure there was anything else I could do to salvage the plant when I realized I needed to make a phone call.

The next day, I had Nellie over for tea. I arranged a simple affair, the pink floral teacups with the white tablecloth. Soft sunlight diffused through the sheer curtains, but instead of inviting me to bask, the light looked cold and sterile.

Nellie was punctual, as always.

She greeted me curtly, clearly on guard. It was the first time I had invited her over one-on-one. I directed her toward the table, which had a clear view of the yard through the window. I didn't bother with small talk as I put the kettle on the stove.

"It's a lovely day," Nellie began.

"Sure is."

"I suppose you'll be working in your garden later?"

I took a moment before I responded. I loved watching her squirm. Her curiosity was fraught with confusion as she nervously drummed her fingers on the table. Delicious.

"No. I've given up on gardening."

At this, Nellie glanced toward the empty window box where I had kept the strawberry plant.

"Hmm. Well, it's not for everyone." She carefully measured her words. "Perhaps your talents lie elsewhere." Oh, how she loved her cheap shots. I could hear the dull roar of the kettle in the kitchen as the water began to boil.

"In fact, I think they do. These days I'm much more interested in…domestic pursuits."

"Like what?" She perked up a bit at this. It was familiar territory for her, after all.

"Oh, you know. Baking. Blending tea. Hosting. Homemaking," I said. "All the skills a good wife needs."

"Is there someone in your life? Good for you!" She trilled. She reached into her purse and pulled out a gold compact mirror as she retouched her pristine lipstick. "Having someone to come home to really does make all the difference."

My eye twitched as the kettle unleashed its shrill scream. "I'm sure it does. There is someone, but there are a few things I need to take care of before we can be together."

"Oh." She gave me a long look. "I suppose it's good of you to make sure everything is in order first." Nellie replaced the lid on her lipstick, carefully returning it and her compact to her purse.

I fetched the kettle from the stove, and poured the loose-leaf tea through a strainer set in each cup. Nellie and I sat in silence as the tea steeped, slowly turning a deep purple color.

"What kind of tea did you say this was?"

"It's a special blend of my own creation. I want to make sure I've got it right before I introduce it to the book club."

As I reached for my teacup, Nellie did the same. She swirled the tea and inhaled, eyes closed.

"Strawberry?" She asked slowly.

"Well now, you can't expect me to go around giving up my proprietary blend," I said. "You've kept plenty of your own recipes secret over the years."

She cocked her head for a moment, eyes narrowed. Then she nodded. "That's fair." Her delicate fingers brought the tea to her lips. I lifted my own cup, but did not drink. Watching her ruby lips part as she sipped the tea was intoxicating. It seemed that that damned strawberry plant was good for something after all.

"It's a shame I never got the recipe for your strawberry tart," I said. "I know it was one of Nick's favorites."

Nellie's brow furrowed, and she choked on her tea. Her hand flew to her mouth as she politely tried to clear her throat, then cover a cough which quickly grew into full-body convulsions as her eyes widened. A smile crept across my face as I watched her lips gape open and shut like a fish dropped on the ground. She thrashed for another minute, but my recipe was perfect. She was dead in a minute, as intended.

Once she was still, I stepped around the table to double-check that the tea had done its job. The sunlight glinted off Nellie's compact in her open purse, and I reached in and grabbed it. I popped it open and gave my hair a quick flounce. I needed to look my best for when I gave Nick a visit later.

***

A Greenthorn Bride Comes Home
By Anna Haddad

His kitchen reeked. The smell was dense. She felt it like a fog as she stepped inside. It had a sweet layer, the familiar guy-kitchen haze of trash that was inside too long—and to be fair, plenty of girl-kitchens had that too—but there was a thicker stench underneath, like the wooden baseboards were seasoned with milk that had soured over decades.

The house must have problems with damp. Of course it did, it looked so old, and the foggy heat tonight didn't help either. Not pleasant, no, but absolutely not his fault, and anyway, she wouldn't be here very long.

"Sit here," he said, and pulled one of the four cane-backed chairs away from the round table. The tips of the chair legs clattered over the floor. As she came closer, the linoleum stuck to her sandal soles. Looking down, she saw the floor was grey.

At the chair she hesitated. A faded blue cushion with a faint brown smudge was fastened with ties to the seat. One of the four buttons in the middle had popped off, leaving a white-threaded impression. She had not expected to sit in this room.

"Ah." He sank into the chair across the table and sighed. He smiled, crinkling the skin around his huge brown eyes. He was older than her, by more than a few years. She'd figured that out already and was sure he knew it too. That was okay. It was all part of her trip. Part of the adventure. "Is something wrong?" he asked.

"No," she said. She sat, hooked her purse over the back of the chair, and rested her hands on the blue gingham placemat in front of her. It was gritty. She didn't draw her hand back. She'd wanted a bleach-hot shower at the next motel anyway. "This is nice."

The kitchen did look nice, in a way. The brass fixtures and wood cabinets seemed clean. A shining retro metal coffeepot sat on the back burner of the gas stove, and a painting of a pink-cheeked blonde girl with an old-fashioned bun on top of her head hung by the window over the sink. The white curtains were pulled back, showing blurred pine branches. Even now, after midnight, the room would be a homey place to sit and chat. If that was all they did, that would be okay. A connection between humans was always a good thing.

"Lexi," he said, dragging out the sounds like he had trouble getting his mouth around them. She frowned. Earlier, at the bar, he'd seemed sober enough to drive.

"Lexi," she repeated. "Short for Alexis." She was using the trip to try out new nicknames.

"Hmph." He shook his head, ran his fingers through the dark waves of hair that spilled over his ears. In this light, she saw how the stubble covered his pale, square

jaw in grimy uneven patches. She still itched to clasp her hands over it. "Alexis is some fancy city girl."

"Well, I am moving to Philadelphia." She tried to put a teasing lilt in her voice. Her own tongue felt clumsy.

"Nah, you're Lexi. Lexi's pretty."

"Thanks, Jarrett." She took her time emphasizing the *tt,* and shifted in her chair so her arm would be just a little closer to his. He'd rolled up the sleeves of his flannel shirt. She believed what he'd said, that he'd played football in high school and a little in college. "I like your name too. It's unusual."

"I know." He looked at her, frowning, but still didn't make a move to get closer. "Well."

"Well," she repeated. His look was heavy on her face.

"What will you do in the city?" he asked.

"Law school. I told you." She had told him half an hour ago. He was definitely drunker than she thought. It had been risky to ride with him, to give him her keys and let him get behind her wheel. But she was here now, and in the morning she could roll right out and move on. She looked at him again. His arms stretched forward a little farther. *Christ,* those heavy corded veins that snaked up to his elbows.

"Lots of college." He nodded slowly. "You have any family there?"

"No, I don't know anyone yet." They'd had almost exactly this conversation in the bar.

"All alone." He leaned back so his chair scraped the floor. His eyelids drooped a little. "It's dangerous."

"Some areas, yeah. Not where I'll be," she said quickly, and looked at the window again. He'd offered to take her in his car and leave hers back in town. No one would steal anything, he'd said. *Nice folks here. Good folks.* Sure, but she didn't know where his house was. It

58

was smarter to have her car with her. She insisted and he offered to drive it.

"Bad people in the city," he said. "They can hurt you."

She fought back a sigh. This conversation she'd had about fifty times already, with different people throughout the summer. She looked at the window again, then at the painting of the blonde woman.

It was surprisingly detailed. Fine gold and yellow curls spilled down past the woman's bright blue eyes and pink cheeks. Her deep rose lips curved in a little smile. The picture was textured with tiny bumps, too precise to be lumps of paint or a rough surface of the canvas, or whatever. She squinted. The bumps interlocked, making clear boarders between colors that blended back into each other when she didn't look closely.

"Did you hear me, Lexi?" He asked softly.

She turned back to him. He rested his hands flat on the table, staring her down the straightaway between his forearms. She froze, felt pulled forward.

"Yeah, I'll be fine. My neighborhood seems pretty nice." After a second she broke his gaze again and nodded toward the blonde woman. "Is that a cross stitch?"

"Oh, yeah." His voice got louder, more excited. She whipped her head back around. As he'd shifted his whole attention to the picture, his shoulders had relaxed, and his legs had stretched out to the side, so they almost reached the sink. "One of my grandma's fans made that and sent it to us."

"What? That's your grandma? She has fans?" This was it. This was the detail she'd tell people, people who weren't her best friends, when they asked about her trip. *You know, I wanted to explore, and really be a part of some local places. You never know what you'll find when you talk to strangers. This one guy was telling me about his grandma...* She'd say they talked about it in the bar, or set the whole conversation at a diner instead.

To listen to him, and make him remember she was still there—*Be available to him,* her friend Kristin had advised, *that's all it is*—she leaned forward.

"No, um." For the first time, he seemed thrown off. He looked at the floor and raised his fist to his mouth. His cheeks sucked in. She couldn't tell what expression he was hiding. When he spoke, he sounded calm. "My grandma. She raised me. She was an author. That was her first girl. Character, I mean."

"I'm—" She stopped herself before the *sorry.* She didn't know his whole family situation. He may have been better off with his grandma than his parents. If he was a little damaged, though, it would explain a few things. "That's cool. I minored in English. What was her name?"

"Her author name was Lorna MacDougall."

"No, sorry, I haven't heard of her. What did she write?"

"A whole series. Like, romance, but old fashioned. No sexy stuff."

Sexy stuff. She swallowed to stifle the cringe inside. Just one night. A good story for later. He was just a small town guy.

"It was kind of based on our house," he said. "There are 41 books. *The Angel Brides of Greenthorn Valley?*"

She shook her head, coughing to cover a laugh. "I haven't heard of it. I'll look it up, though."

"I don't know." He stared at the girl's glowing cross-stitched face. "It's not really published anymore. It used to be really popular."

"I bet," she said. Designing and stitching that picture must have taken months, if not years. Some fan.

"That's Angel, the first wife," he said. "She's an orphan, and she comes to the house and fixes it up. She learns the Bible. The second book is about the girl who works for her, and then it's about her daughter, and it keeps going."

"Oh." She imagined 41 books, recycling five plots and maybe eight or ten stock characters. All white, of course, maybe a few problematic ones who weren't. The heroines' hair colors might rotate. The writing would be laughable, but some people got comfort from that kind of thing. From the familiar. At least they were reading something.

"My grandma made Angel a woman every woman should try to be. She put that up there so she could see her face every day."

"I see." She guessed if she was living off a successful romance series, she'd want to be reminded of the people who loved her work and the character who started it all. "Why here, though? I'd put it by my desk."

"Grandma said her best work was right there. Whenever she filled up the coffeepot, she'd see Angel and remember to be a blessing like her for the rest of the day. Stories are make-believe, but she could make a real good place right here for anyone who stopped by. She made the best coffee. When she got sick, she taught me to make it for myself."

So Grandma was a woman of her time. So what? It wasn't like she, herself, planned to join this family. She continued to study his profile, his cut, stippled jaw. He looked sad, a little lost. Haunted? Grandma had raised him, after all, and she was gone.

"That's beautiful," she said. "Her characters must have inspired so many people."

"I guess." He lowered his hand from his mouth. He stared intently at the cross-stitch, at Angel. Angel reminded him of his grandmother. But it was still strange to see him look that way at a fictional character, a pretty cliché one at that, like she was someone real he'd lost.

That was alright. This guy was a little different, and maybe more than a little sexist. Maybe his grandma had raised him to think he needed an Angel to take care of the kitchen, and that's why it stank, and the placemats were gritty. But that wasn't her problem, and not her business to judge him anyway. All she had to do now was find a way to get through the night, until it was light out and she was sober. It couldn't be more than five or six hours now. *Stay in the moment,* Kristin had advised several times that year. *Have fun. Remember, he's more scared of you than you are of him. Think, what have you got to lose?* Kristin, who'd retire this fall to live near her worshipful fiancé, Dr. Duke Med School, and never enjoy an experience like this again. That's all this was. An experience. She had to relax, enjoy it. Have a meaningful human moment now and get his attention back. That heavy sculpted forearm resting on the table...

"So," she said. "You grew up in this house?"

"Yeah." He snapped out of it and turned back to her. "Just went for college. Not far from here."

"My college was in Virginia. A few states away from home. All girls," she said, and waited for him to ask more.

"That's best." He smiled slightly. At first, she smiled back, but something tightened in her lungs when he held the expression and didn't break his gaze. She wondered if this was her moment, if she should walk over and casually rest her hand on his shoulder. He didn't move. He didn't even blink.

Drunk, definitely, or maybe on something. Something scarier than pot. She should not have given him her keys. But he seemed cogent at the bar, and she'd felt safe as he drove through all those turns in the jagged woods so much more slowly and carefully than she would have done.

She looked behind him, to the chocolate brown fridge with its wooden handles. The upper door was dotted with a few photos, fruit-shaped magnets, a note or two. The biggest photo looked like a yearbook picture, in black and white. A girl with wavy box-cut hair leaned around the neck of a cello. She smiled crookedly, resting her bow on one denim knee, her open flannel shirt hanging long. Chain necklaces and cords spilled down her chest. Going by the girl's style, the picture was at least ten years old.

"Sorry, too many questions, but who's that with the cello?" She asked, to make him stop looking at her. A cousin or niece, maybe. Someone who shared their grandma.

He twisted his head back toward the fridge. "That's Heather." He sighed. "My wife."

Shit. Shit shit shit shit shit. She'd had no idea. She would never have done this if she had.

No one else seemed to be in the house right now. So, she could just crash on a couch tonight, not with him. That would have been the best plan even if he wasn't married. And then she'd bolt as soon as the sun rose. No cheating, no harm done, no drama with some weird couple out here in Nowhere, PA. A close escape. A story for Kristin and the girls next time they all saw each other.

"Oh. She's not here tonight?" She asked to confirm.

"No." He looked at the table, drumming his large fingers slowly on its surface. "It's over."

"Sorry to hear that."

She still shouldn't sleep with him. He still had Heather's picture up, and Angel's, and especially if he was so drunk or tweaked or whatever, she shouldn't mess around with his feelings.

But that hand, that arm, that jaw, those big staring brown haunted eyes…

"Don't worry. It was beautiful." He smiled at her again. Was it more normal, natural this time? "She was a marvelous musician."

Marvelous musician. It fit right in with *sexy stuff.* But she wouldn't have to listen to his weird alliteration much longer. She wasn't in this for the long run. And Heather, who looked sweet and ordinary, and probably was a talented person, must have seen something in him in the first place. Something she could enjoy for a little while too.

"I'm sure she was." Her smile felt soft and watery on her face. She tried to form a question that wouldn't cut too deep.

"Please don't worry about it," he said. She thought his hand inched a little closer. "That's all over now."

"Yeah. We don't have to talk about that." She focused her smile, tried to widen her eyes so they'd be sexy and appealing and draw him in. *Eye contact is key,* Kristin said late one night. That was a downside of an all-women's campus. All that theory and until now not much practice. Unlike Kristin, she couldn't visit other schools every single weekend and keep her grades where she wanted them to be.

She carefully fixed her eyes on his, willing him not to look away again. She waited a while, smiling at him smiling at her. The longer it went the easier it was to hold her gaze steady. As she looked at him, the pull inside her chest got stronger and stronger. She wasn't sure if he felt it like she did, but by the way he smiled, he must have felt at least *something* too. The pull grew warm as well as strong. Maybe it was her turn. Maybe she should reach for his hand, or even stand up, walk over, slide into his lap. What would he do, anyway, say no? Push her off? Even if he did, he was still a stranger, really. The rejection wouldn't count.

She set her hand on the table, inched it ahead with her fingers. She swallowed as her hand got closer to his, and she saw his knuckles flex. She'd never touched calluses that looked that rough.

"Lexi," he said, or almost sang. He laced his fingers together on his placemat. His face settled, became smooth and unlined.

"Jarrett." It was a little easier now to pronounce the *tt*.

"You're so beautiful," he said.

The warmth in her chest stirred. She shifted further forward in the chair, the remaining buttons on the cushion digging through her jeans as she moved. "You think so?"

"I know it." He cocked his head and smiled wider. "Where are you going?"

"I told you. I'm driving to Philadelphia. Philly," she said.

"Out to the big city." Like he was hearing it for the first time, again.

"Yeah." Seriously, was it booze, drugs? Something else?

"Bad people out there. They can hurt you."

"I'll be fine. I'll be careful," she said. She looked away, up at Angel, with the stitched-white sparkles in her eyes. What every woman should try to be. A blessing, Grandma said. A blessing every day.

"This is a good place here," he said. "You can be safe." He was talking louder. She heard his chair scrape the floor. This linoleum, it had stuck to her shoes as she'd walked in. "Lexi."

"Alexis," she corrected without thinking.

"That's not you." From the corner of her eye she saw him stand. He was finally making a move. He was so tall. So much broader than Dr. Duke Med.

She felt his warmth at her shoulder. She was about to scoot her chair away before he dropped to his knees beside her.

"You're an angel. Stay here."

"I— " A laugh snagged in her throat and died as his huge dead-serious eyes fixed on her face. Drunk. Strung out. Something. "What are you doing? Get off the floor."

"It's safe here," he said again, resting his hand on her placemat.

"I'll leave in the morning." She hovered her hand over his arm. Fuck, she still wanted to touch it. "I'll be okay to drive then. I can find the highway from here."

"It's wrong," he said. She sensed the table moving an inch or two as he clamped his arm down harder. "It's wrong for you to go. You're an angel." His face crumpled and he seemed genuinely in pain as he cringed toward the floor. "You're supposed to stay here."

She brushed her hand over his dark curls. His face was inches from her knew. *Poor guy.* It was sad. She glanced again at Angel's sweet stitched smile and then over at Heather, with her shy pose and grunge gear.

Something had truly messed this guy up, and it wasn't something she could fix.

"Hey, hey," she said soothingly. His hair felt softly wiry and tangled. "It'll be okay. I think you should talk to someone who can help you."

He looked up. His mouth was slack, a little open. His stare made her lean back.

"You," he said.

"I can't. You need someone who knows how." She dug her feet into the floor and scooted her chair back. Scuffling on his knees, he followed it. He dropped his head and planted the side of his face on her thigh. She froze. That didn't feel good.

"Will you marry me?" He asked, the words slurred and muffled.

"Okay. Maybe you should have some water." She tried to stand. He wouldn't move. He made a sound like a moan and pushed his face lower, against her shin. A guy had done something like this to Kristin once, during a party in someone's apartment. But Kristin had been almost blacked out, and she, Alexis, had been there to watch them both and keep him off, because Kristin hadn't liked that guy at all. "Can you let me get up, please?"

"Mmph," he said, looking up, his eyes startlingly wide and alert. "You're so beautiful. Angel."

"Thank you." She let her hand rest on the back of his head. Five minutes ago, in this position, she would have wrapped her fingers in his curls and, gently, pulled tight. Part of her wanted to even now. But she had to be the adult here. "I can sleep on a couch if you show me." It would not be as bad as driving through those jagged woods in the dark.

He jumped up and stood with his back to the sink. "No, you should have a bed. I can, you'll be…" His face went slack again. His head drifted from side to side, until he finally turned far enough that the cross-stich snatched his full, abrupt attention. "You see Angel? Isn't she beautiful?"

She took her purse from the back of her chair and held it in her lap. "Yeah."

"My grandma said she'd try to be a blessing. Like her."

"You told me." Outlined through the canvas base of her bag, the compact weight of her cellphone rested on one thigh. She could sleep with it in her hand if she had to. If this got really weird, if he wouldn't pass out and leave her alone, she could use it.

"She fixed the house." He spun around and fastened her with a very serious gaze. "You're so special. You'd fix the house. You can help me."

She almost laughed again, wanting to tell him he'd have to tear the whole house down to fix that sour milk smell. Instead, she stood and crossed to the chair he'd been sitting in, trying to casually drop her hand into her purse. "Um, sorry. Do you still have my keys?"

"I found you," he said. "I'm so blessed to have you with me."

"Okay." She stepped behind his chair. "I have to go now. I can drive. Give me my keys, please."

"You don't have to go. It's safe here." He started talking faster and faster. "The world is dangerous, but, I'm a gentleman. I'm safe. I'm safe. I won't hurt anyone. I'd never, angel, I'd never hurt—"

He wouldn't stop. She talked over him. "Give me my keys, please."

He kept going. "You can stay here. We'll talk about it in daylight. We'll rustle something up."

He sounded wrong, he didn't talk right, normal guys didn't talk that like that. "Jarrett, it's illegal for you to not give me my keys."

"Don't go. You're safe here. I promise you. You're safe."

"Okay." He wouldn't listen. Fine. So she'd speak his language, then get to a door with a lock. "I need your powder room, please. To – powder my nose. Freshen up." She slid her bag over her shoulder. She'd lock the door, dial 911. She'd tell them she did something stupid. They'd tell her what to do next, and give her a ride out. They might even call a tow truck for her car.

"Of course." He straightened and his smile got huge. His eyes didn't quite focus. "Through that door, keep going, then on your left. Is there anything you need? Food? Clothes to wear?"

"Uh," She forced herself to keep looking at him, to go along with whatever story was playing out in his head. "I would love some coffee if you have any now. You know, I'm shaken up after – tonight." If he made Grandma's coffee, used the old pot on the stove, he could be occupied a while.

"I believe you are," he said. "Go along now. It will be ready."

"Okay. Alright." She tried to turn away at a natural pace. She lifted one foot and set it down, then lifted the other. Foot by foot, the floor sucking her sandals down, she made it to the doorway at the back of the kitchen. She kept the same slowed rhythm through the short, shadowed blue hall, where the sticky linoleum switched to hardwood that squeaked under her step. The smell, which she thought would clear, briefly turned thicker and more soured.

The next room was light and larger, and seemed like it had been abandoned for decades. Reams of typing paper carpeted the floor and spread over the pink cushioned armchairs and sofa. Piles of clothes, all colors and shades, were scattered over the papers at random. She noticed acid-washed denim crumpled on the bay window seat and almost gagged. Panel blinds on the window shut out the night. They looked too clean. A long hippie-style white dress, yellowed ruffles spilling from its bodice and sleeves, swung slightly back and forth from a wooden hanger hooked on the upper sill. Small brown blotches dotted the ruffles on the chest.

She took a step. Papers crunched under her sandal, like leaves. She looked down. Pages and pages of typewriting, some fresher in black and white, some browning and fading into a yellowed background. Behind her, water gushed into metal. She glanced at the top of the paper stack closest to her foot.

VALLERIE

VALLLERIE was very pretty with brown hair and brown eyes. She was sad. Her family was very mean to her, so she wanted to run away. One day she was standing next to the river and she

There was a soft squeak and the water turned off. She jerked her head up and kept walking slowly, on tip toe, so she'd make less noise. She had to act like this was normal.

Up ahead, next to the pitch dark opposite doorway, was a small bookshelf stuffed with identical off-white paperbacks. Each had a single word on its cracking spine. As she got closer, she made out some names on the middle shelf. *Bethany. Clover. Judie. Harvest.*

Fucking Harvest? Grandma ran out of ideas. She looked to the upper corner of the shelf. Sure enough: *Angel, Martha, Joy.* She felt the ghost of an urge to pull a book down and open it to get a feel for the writing.

Some clattering and clinking from the kitchen. Her foot grazed a mound of cloth and a hard, cold chip of something slid under her toe and caught inside her sandal. She raised her foot to get it out. The cold thing was attached to a slim black woven cord with a silver clasp. She flexed her toe and caught the cord in her fist. Hanging from it was a black guitar pick, engraved with spiky silver letters whose edges had turned brown.

HEATHER

She dropped the necklace and kept shuffling through the papers. The room seemed longer now. She smelled coffee, good strong stuff. The best. Thoughts flipped through her head like slides.

A marvelous musician in the 90s. If she played cello, she'd play guitar. She must've saved for weeks to get that engraved. The girl who's still wearing that is way too young to get married. Okay, so she kept it when she got married, but she wasn't wearing it anymore. So why didn't she take it when she left? Why is it still in his house? Oh god oh god why the hell is it on the floor?

As she walked toward the doorway, she swung her purse forward and reached inside. Her fingers clutched at pens and softened receipts and her sunglasses before closing on the antenna tip of her phone. As she drew it out, the phone slipped from her hand. Her heart seized as her arm flew down and her hand caught the phone again before it could hit the floor. She slid her thumbnail under the screen to flip it open.

"Lexi, it's ready," he said.

She turned her head. He stood about a foot from the entrance to the kitchen, his shoulders filling the doorway behind him. He wasn't smiling.

"I—I have to call my mom and dad. My mother and father. They'll be worried. I have to check in with them each night." She dialed one number. She'd call and run. Couldn't get past him, had to make it to the front, through that black doorway, where she couldn't see anything ahead and *God knows what the fuck's in there.*

"You don't have to call them." He came forward. The coffee scent seemed to drift out ahead of him.

"Yes, I do," she said. She dialed a one. "It'll just take a minute." Another one, the beep as loud as an alarm, then she moved her thumb to the send button.

He lunged. She took a second too long to fall back. He wrapped his hand around her wrist and jerked it up toward him in one motion. At first, she felt nothing but pressure, but when she saw her fingers had opened, she realized her wrist was burning on the inside. She gasped. No one had hurt her like this before. There was a small *thud* as something compact hit a soft surface.

She tried to tug her wrist down, to twist it the way she'd learned to in self-defense class freshman year. It didn't work. She looked down. The phone had landed just six inches to the side of his sneakered foot. If she could distract him again—

He pivoted and kicked the phone with the side of his foot. A hard kick, at just the right spot, *and I believe you, I totally believe you, I believe you played football and you were good,* and the phone flew in a small arc across the living room, through the hall, where she heard it smack once on the hardwood and thud on the linoleum and then thud again and that was it.

He dropped her wrist. It tingled like it was filling with shards of glass. She massaged it in her other hand as she looked at him. He smiled now, focusing his eyes on her. Finally, he reached behind her neck and twined his fingers in her hair with gentle strength. She pulled back a little and he slid his other hand behind her shoulder. She noticed for the first time that he too had a smell, a scent. The woods. Pines and sweat. Dirt. Gas. A little alcohol or chlorine. A hint of coffee. In this light she saw warm flecks of copper in his eyes.

"Angel," he said. "I'm so blessed to have you here."

His scent overwhelmed her as he sealed her lips with his.

They Wrapped His Bones
By Marco Angelo

A week after Seth left me, I headed over to the South End. I had never indulged in clubbing, drinking, or picking up random men to fuck raw behind anonymous walls. Yet without Seth I felt liberated, and I would not let something so painful as my lover's departure restrict me from the freedom I hungered for. I cannot remember the exact details of how he left me, only that I was in a drunken stupor while we fought—and our daughter leaving with him.

The Menagerie: an obscure gay bar I frequently passed but never frequented myself. A speakeasy with no signs, no lights, wherein I sat during the night. The bartender's face drooped in suspicion when I ordered a triple shot of tequila and gulped it down with no help at all: no salt, lime, and no chasers, sir. Gasoline downed like water. The surrounding men patted my back and encouraged me to drink more. I ordered more shots. The world around me rendered itself a hazy blur while I indulged in higher spirits.

The red-headed bartender was a pale, freckled man who looked like a cheap porn magazine cut-out from the eighties. He did not cut me off after I reached my limit. Instead, he gave me drink after drink with enthusiasm, like he *wanted* me to pass out shitless, all the while devouring me with ravenous eyes. A strange sensation of danger overcame me; I looked around to see the other men eyeing me with similar hunger: a dangerous, predatory type of hunger as they watched me drink myself to oblivion. The further my world blurred, the further their hands crept up my thighs and snaked towards my groin.

I detached myself from the physical world for a moment. I looked at the rim of my shot glass, and there, Seth's face materialized as the only clear thing in this hazy fog: his pretty green eyes, peering at me not in his usual rage but in pity. Betrayal. *Do you understand that I did it for you?* his voice rang. Those were the last words I remembered from him, and I beat and beat myself in the head over what they could have meant.

The men's callused hands were now groping my crotch with unrestricted liberty, as if my body had belonged to them. As if it weren't mine.

A snicker. "He likes it," said some graceless voice behind.

With a scowl, I paid my tab and left that fucking place. When men aren't predatory pigs to women, we're predatory to each other and every-fucking-body else around.

Then down on Columbus Avenue, I glimpsed Seth walking as a spectacle of light amidst the backdrop of high-rise buildings cloaked in darkness. It was three in the morning; the streets had thinned out hours ago. I hiccupped and stumbled as I saw my ex-husband—what the hell was Seth doing out here? I swore I wanted to kill him, that fucking bastard! He was ruining my only free night by deciding to come back, returning to life in my deadened world. How dare he snatch the last strands of joy that I tried to grasp onto? How dare he sap the only integrity I felt for myself in this lonely hell?

I dashed after him. My impulsive hands stirred with life, thirsting to beat him to a pulp. He now stood in front of me, and I held a vendetta. I wouldn't let him leave without at least a cracked skull.

From behind, I pushed him towards the ground. His knees buckled and planted onto the cement, and I heard him grunt in a soft and high voice. A voice unlike Seth's.

"What the hell, bro?"

The man's eyes burned with hostility—and he looked *so* much like him: emerald eyes, a lanky figure that spoke of sophistication, a certain demeanor of self-assurance... sensitivity... but a high-pitched voice unlike his. No, this was not him.

"I'm sorry," I said as I turned to walk away. "Thought—*hic!*—thought, thought you were someone else."

His eyes batted over my body, then onto my crotch. The animosity and surprise in his eyes disappeared. The cracks of his fat lips upturned into a smile. A horny smile. *Hit me again, daddy,* his eyes begged, *you know I like it. Push my face into a puddle of your piss—*

Whisky dick found no place in my mental suppression that night. And that's why I took him home;

I wanted to pound this gorgeous man's asshole until it relapsed with the tenderness of a wilted rose. The kind of dying rose that the dead hold in their caskets after viewing hours.

I let the stranger sleep in my bed that night. He gave me his name—Francisco de León—after our escapades in the king-sized mahogany bed I had never replaced. My home had long been empty, so we had no prying eyes to invade our nightly acts, save for the empty wooden cross mounted on the wall.

I awoke the next morning before sunrise. Looking down at Francisco's body, I held back a surge of disgust. I was so drunk last night—his eyes, though green, held an icy hue unlike the dazzling malachite of Seth's. My subdued pain had caused me to see what was not really there. Why did I bring a stranger to sleep in my bed? I wanted to retch, but I needed to display some courtesy. I told him I would cook us some breakfast, and that he should follow me into the kitchen. He gladly obliged.

"I'll sit at the chair and watch you cook," he said as I left the bed, his voice wet with a hint of mildew. "See how that plump ass shakes in the kitchen."

I snickered. He leaned in to kiss me, but I veered my head away, pretending not to notice.

I sat up, ran my hands through my hair, donned a pair of blue low-rise trunks, then headed to the kitchen. Francisco followed my steps down the stairway, the ceiling low with a bar across the top: the perfect height to dangle a noose and hang a child-sized doll. Then he sat on the stool in the middle of the kitchen. And there... I had to blink, for my mind stirred upon glimpsing this spectacle who looked so much like Seth. Beneath this stranger, his doppelganger, blood seeped from the tiles—

"Antonio," he croaked, kneeling on the ground, eyes looking up at me in horror. "Antonio, I did it for you..." He stumbled, grabbing onto my shoulders as if to bring me down with him, to die with him. Then he lay limp, unconscious. Sprawled on the floor. Blood sprouted from the vertical mouth in his flesh.

I collapsed thereafter, and all that I recalled after returning to consciousness were the screams of our daughter Gabriela.

A flash of darkness. And I was standing over Seth as he lay sprawled, Gabriela nowhere to be seen.

"Hello? Are you there?" asked a shrill voice.

I turned my head and saw Seth sitting on the stool.

It was not Francisco anymore.

My insides churned with hate. Why was he alive? He betrayed me with his sudden departure and was returning to beg for forgiveness! He was not dead after all. He fucking lied to me. He only pretended to die.

Seth moved away from the stool, his foot stepping into the little rivulets of blood.

"Antonio," he said in a deeper, unnatural voice. "You alright?"

I snapped back.

The blood disappeared.

And there was Francisco, sitting on the stool above where Seth's corpse had dropped.

His eyes begot an icy hue once more, no longer warm. I blinked three times just to make sure my eyes weren't playing tricks on me. I remembered now, and all it took was an image of the dead upon its own deathbed to remind me of the events that transpired. Ever since Gabriela had gone, I attempted to get rid of all my memories of Seth by purchasing an island counter with two stools, right in the middle of the kitchen where he'd died.

But this morning was different. A random surge of sympathy found its home in the superficial shell of my heart. I did not yell at Francisco, or shatter plates and cups on the floor as I would have while married to Seth. I only let him sit at the island above the deathbed of my beloved, completely unaware that his bare foot touched the floor where blood once splattered the linoleum and a certain love had reached its perishing point: boiling then evaporating like a vampire's skin under high noon.

I took two small pans and started cooking our omelets. Spinach, tomatoes, mushrooms. And cheese just for him. Oh God, I could never stand the taste of cheese mixed with scrambled egg. Butter blocks greased the pans as they melted with the heat.

Francisco's eyes darted around, and he spotted a framed picture on the wall. "Is that your family?" he asked, pointing at the beautiful short man with emerald eyes who stood next to me in a business suit. In the portrait, Seth and I stood with Gabriela when she was six, a short while after I came into their lives.

How was that abandoned family picture still there? I swore that wall had been bare since Seth had died, save for the cracks—I swore I ripped the fucking portrait away and tore it to shreds, every bit and piece of it. I made a promise to myself long ago, to shred the paper into fragments, except for our faces because I could never tear our faces apart. My hand had trembled when I tried to slash Seth's face with my nails, knives, and even a hammer, but I couldn't do it. A torn-up family picture ravaged by the claws of a man engulfed in both grief and guilt, bodies and colors ripped apart save for the faces.

I lifted our omelets with my spatula and, one after the other, slapped them onto clanking plates. I didn't answer Francisco.

"Antonio?"

"What?"

"Is that your family?" he asked.

"Yes." *This persistent fucking weasel.*

"What's the story?" he asked.

"I don't know." And I didn't know.

"I have time to listen."

But I don't want you to listen. Don't you fucking get it? I don't want to talk about it.

"I'm gonna stay here all morning, and I really wanna know—"

I erupted in anger. I picked up his omelet plate and threw it across the room. The white porcelain shattered, little shards mixing with the spilling yellowy guts of the food. Francisco jumped from the stool with his eyes tensed, fixating upon me, and that pissed me off even more. How dare he look accusingly at a grieving man? How dare he question my authority? How dare he—

"What the hell?" he cried. "What the fuck was that about?"

I froze in place, my eyes widening in shame, and I started crying.

"I'm sorry! I didn't mean to do that," I sobbed.

"All I did was ask about your family. If you didn't want to talk about them, you could've just told me. But you didn't have to blow up on me like that. So goddamn insane, aren't you?"

"Gabriela," I sobbed. I didn't know the meaning of these words spilling out of my mouth, but they came anyway: *"I didn't mean for you to leave and for your*

Daddy to understand after everything that happened, I love you so much. . ."

I sat on the floor with my knees pulled into my chest, my arms wrapped around my legs as I rocked myself back and forth, mumbling as I stared at the broken porcelain pieces. My plates. Shattered. And in those shattered shards, the kitchen light had reflected millions of little faces: hallowed eyes which burned with fury—

"Seth." I caressed his face.

"Get the fuck off of me." He pried my fingers from his shoulders, but I pushed him even more forcefully into the wall.

It was not me who kissed him—he leaned in and devoured my drunken mouth, our wet lips engaging in each other's contrasting worlds. He kissed me with unspoken passion, a passion long extinguished, never to rekindle. Yet I had felt them, the embers, though the blue fire itself lay dead. Yes, those fiery strokes caressed me with the coarseness of bony fingers, an icy fire which ultimately bore no substance... no genuine love. But I was on high drunken spirits for I hadn't felt the embrace of another man for the longest time, and I could not recall the last time Seth had kissed me so hungrily.

He grabbed my ass and I cupped his stirring dick; I thrust my hands down his backside, my dick pushing against the tent of my crotch as if clawing out for escape. But amid all this hot sweaty shit, he pushed me off with an unrelenting force, scowling in disgust.

"I won't stoop so low as to have sex with an animal."

My ears pricked in rage, and my heart turned in disappointment.

"What just happened?" I asked, stunned.

"What?"

"Us kissing."

"Yeah. We kissed," said Seth.

"Care to explain? It was you who kissed first."

"I didn't kiss you because I love you. I kissed you because I'm sex-deprived. Don't flatter yourself."

"Seth, why do you have to be so harsh?" I gasped.

"Don't you get it, you thick piece of shit? I don't love you anymore."

My eyes brimmed with tears. When we'd once been tender with each other, his eyes never ceased to flash moments of brightness and color, but now all that reflected unto me was pure hatred, contempt, pity... no. This was not the Seth I had once known.

Why had Seth lost his love for me?

For my entire life nobody had treated me with compassion, but I will not wallow in pity or dare claim that I deserved compassion at all.

I didn't care, though. I was so fucked in the head.

"Francisco," I said, feeling empty, "I'll just let you know that my husband died."

Why am I telling this to a stranger?

"Oh, my—" his mouth gaped. "I'm so sorry, I didn't know. No wonder you reacted that way. Oh, my God. I'm so sorry." His jaw stayed hanging open as if he wanted to say something more, but stopped just in case he would offend me. He closed his mouth.

I glanced at him. "It's okay. I don't remember all the details myself," I said.

I knew he was thinking things like these: *Wow, he's such a damaged person.*

He's living with regret and thinks his husband's death was his fault.

But what about his daughter? What happened to her? Why isn't she here?

Antonio is a miserable man. He's torn up and has nothing left but his own empty shell. He proved that when we first met... I really wanna help him.

"Francisco, I'd prefer if you left me alone."

"Okay. I understand."

I could hear a mild offense in his response, but he slowly stood and offered me a kiss at the top of my scalp. My body reeled. He walked to the front door and left without saying goodbye.

***

I killed myself after Francisco left.

Or had I really killed myself? I had no fucking idea, but before I went to sleep, I looked in the bathroom mirror and saw a dead man.

The black and blue circles under my eyes became sallow in the days after Seth dropped dead, but they were now bloodshot. My face was pale with a grayish tinge; it had never looked this way before. On my cheeks there was the mold that turns into flimsy white stuff after growing on a corpse: edible mushrooms blooming in the rotten fauna of the dead. But despite these harrowing features, the most haunting part was that my eyes were that of a ghoul—so empty, *lonely*, as if I stayed in the dark for ten years.

As I leaned in to grab my toothbrush, the reflection in the mirror didn't move.

It stayed staring at me with those dead eyes.

I opened my mouth, but the reflection stayed still. Mouth closed.

I leaned to my left, but it didn't.

This dead man estranged from me in body, yet similar in soul, stood as frozen as a stillborn baby. I could not see my true self.

I turned around. And there, the dead man stood right in front of me, towering in the doorframe's space, looking down at me with no expression. Neck craned, black holes for eyes.

It did not speak. It spoke to my mind.

If you love Gabriela so much, why don't you find her? it asked. *Are you scared to find out what she did? What you did?*

Fire in my throat.

You would rather be me, wouldn't you? But you don't know why. Go ahead, retreat into your mental cobwebs like you always do, Antonio, Schrodinger's cat, a coward—

I took its head with both hands and snapped its neck.

It slumped onto the bathroom floor. No struggle.

Had I just killed myself?

I chopped my doppelganger's body into pieces. No blood.

I piled the body parts in my picketed backyard, leg on leg and arm on arm, set on the foundation of the torso with ribs. An acidic, dewy stench like an abandoned attic wafted from the cold-cut corpse. I doused the body parts in gasoline and set them on fire. I disposed of the head (*my head?*) in the trash. And it was at this exact moment that I cut my own heart in half, opening a blackened cave in the cavity where my heart had once been. Unfeeling. Cold.

I invited Francisco for a bonfire that night. There was no smell of burning flesh. We roasted marshmallows over the fire. They were delicious.

I gave him the raw-dogging of his life after we ate the marshmallows. As we kissed, he did not know that the flavor of my roasting flesh had stained his lips and his breath.

While I penetrated Francisco, a familiar, cold feeling wrapped itself around my cock. I imagined fucking Seth in a casket during viewing hours, and as I looked down, it was easy to imagine Francisco as his limp and lifeless self. My energy couldn't be contained, and I pounded him with the savagery seen only in predatory animals. My fantasies got me so excited, *too* excited. Sweat and mist, sex and embalming fluids.

A temptation swept me—to bash his head against the headboard, then pound away into the tight flesh that clenched so *tightly*, so *heavenly*, after all blood circulation, *all life*, was cut off. I imagined being inside him right as his body stiffened, entering the earliest stages of rigor mortis. But no—I let forth a wet moan as I finished inside him, resisting this primal temptation of mine. He said it'd be hot if I was that same sexual monster every night. I only chuckled, though. Francisco would tease me for days hereafter that I never pounded him like that. It was a perfect evening.

***

After a day of aimless strolling in downtown Boston, I came home to see Seth's family huddled around my doorstep.

All of my in-laws had gathered as a horde at the front door. But instead of angrily throwing fire at my house to burn me down and spite me like last time, they all sported radiant looks about their faces as if they felt relieved, but also apologetic.

They all held bright things in their hands.

I inspected the things they held, and I saw presents wrapped in various hues of paper and ribbon: neon pink, purple, green, sky blue, white. All these presents varied in size, from the size of my palm to hunky suitcases. I didn't know what prank they would play on me this time.

They all thought I had killed Seth, no matter how many times I tried to convince them otherwise. I knew I had to turn away these gifts; the last thing I needed was to face the vengeful wrath from the family of whom I supposedly killed. What I needed to do was run a cold bath and forget about everything and everyone— especially the justice system which condemned me through my unwanted liberation.

The verdict pronounced me innocent of Seth's murder, but that did not liberate me; it only released me into the wild. To the untamed depths of my sanity. To this day, I still do not know who killed him, and that has left me with an internal wound too deep for words.

I parked my Toyota Camry in the driveway. Past the passenger window, the horde of people stood still, as still as weeping angels in sleep. Yet as frozen in their state as they were, relief and pardon remained plastered on their faces like plastic, where moon craters adorned their faces and chests. Holes scattered among flesh that appeared brown from afar; tinged with gray as I narrowed my eyes.

I stepped out of the car.

"Hello everyone," I said as I approached, waving.

No response. They stood as the same statues. Unresponsive.

"Hello?" I asked again. I approached Jose, one of Seth's uncles. "Jose, I remember seeing you last month... at the wake," I added nervously. I eyed the small, bright gift he held. No response. I wanted to pry all those gifts away and see what the hell was inside them, what the hell these walking ghosts had to give me. "Are all these for me?"

Jose turned his head, saying nothing, and I jumped back in fright. His face held the same black holes for eyes as my dead self whom I'd murdered last night.

"Stop looking at me like that!" I stumbled to the door, tears suddenly in my eyes. "I know you all still think I killed him. But I'm innocent, I swear! Can't you just leave me alone?"

"Then where's his body?" asked an inhuman voice.

I turned around. It was Seth's mother, grinning.

Their mouths working in unison. A chorus of hallowed voices carved from rotten wood:

"Open them."

"Cut open his body."

"Carve him from the bones."

Icy stares. Looks of death. Flies buzzing, maggots squirming out of holes of standing cadavers. The overly *sweet* stench of decomposition in the air. Voices the texture of arid dirt. Skin pale and rotten like they were the walking dead. But my in-laws weren't zombies. They were spectacles. Projections. I didn't know what to conclude, except that I needed to get drunk quickly. I needed to forget all the surrounding madness.

I snatched each little wrapped box from their hands, hands that belonged to the morgue. There were twenty-four presents wrapped in bright colors: lavender and rosy surface art, cheesy quotes about God and love or some shit. I took two trips, taking twelve gifts per round, and I set the presents upon the welcome mat behind my front door.

"Will you all please leave?" I said to them, to nobody in particular. "Jose, Mario, answer me, goddamn it!"

Blank stares yet again.

I opened the presents.

Inside each gift were little assortments of bones: femurs and tailbones, rib-cages and brittle arm bones, all dusty and whittled. Shoulder blades so round they were small shields. Some bones still had leathery flesh hanging off of them—like skin and bone sex toys, the inventions of a perverted taxidermist testing the limits of his depravity. In one box was a skull that housed round, rolling eyeballs.

His corpse wrapped in bright colors. A voice.

The voice of the man in the mirror?

"What the hell is all of this?" I asked, my breath catching in my throat. I knew nothing about human anatomy, but I knew that together the bones were enough to create the frame of a human skeleton. "Whose fucking bones are these? Whose life is in this—"

Then a flashing remembrance. I knew without a doubt that Seth had died, but of the terrible aftermath save for Gabriela screaming her heart out... I could never recall a clear memory.

Until now.

Seth's body, still warm, lay in my embrace. I trudged over dirt and stone. His muscles still spasmed since the corpse was still in the earliest stages of transitioning into death. A forest surrounded me. A dark forest. I was all by myself, and I was sobbing. Black trash bags in the trunk. There was no forest for miles and miles away from our home. How did I even get here?

A car at the edge of the forest. A sedan, to be exact. I couldn't recall the make or model. A Ford, it looked like? A Chrysler? Even a Toyota Camry? It was all too blurry to tell.

Fuck, I knew nothing.

I turned to Helena, Seth's mother. "Are these Seth's bones?"

No response.

"What do you want me to do with them?" I asked the human statues.

Daggers in their stares. Mouths stitched with black thread, upturned in grins. Heads that looked like they would loll off their necks any time.

"Do you want me to bury them?"

Gradual nods of the head, cold neck muscles cringing like unoiled cogs, squeaking like accelerating tires. Soon everybody else started nodding in synchronization, their judgment as certain and capricious as the jury that failed to convict me.

Everything clicked.

I blinked, placing the bones back into the gift boxes and wrapping each of them carefully. "You want me to compensate for his death by turning my backyard into Seth's grave," I drawled, enunciating each word for clarity. "You want Seth's bones to rest with the burnt flesh of his slaughterer."

His bones to infuse with the flesh of his lover. A new birth.

They continued nodding, bones grinding like gears under their stiff flesh.

Carve his bones so they become flesh again—

"So be it."

They vanished in streams of mist and smoke, leaving me alone with his bones and the bright ribbons. No footprints left behind. I re-wrapped his bones.

I took a shovel and started digging under the wilted willow tree in my backyard. I dug and dug with the frenzy of a rabid raccoon, then threw all the gifts carelessly into the pit. I piled the dirt back up on these precious bones, remnants of death wrapped in light. My shovel was stained with the brown dirt that hugged his disassembled skeleton from above.

Right beside where I set my dead self ablaze in flames, Seth would forever lay inside the earth to crumble.

***

"I can see why you love this spot so much," said Francisco, chuckling. We sat sipping on glasses of Chardonnay atop a bench in my backyard, facing the wilted tree. His hand, painted with acrylic red nails, came up to support his chin. "It's so green here."

"Yeah," I said. *This is the most lively place on the property. Inside my home you can feel the distant memories of a family that is gone forever. The backyard reeks of neglect and overbearing weeds, but this one spot shines with the brightest green I've ever seen; too green for my soul to weep.*

Francisco laid down and rested his head on my knee.

I looked at him, startled. I swallowed the bile rising in my throat. Francisco and I had been seeing each other for around two months; we were not in a relationship, oh no we weren't. We were strictly on a no-strings-attached basis, but I loved to have these brief moments of tenderness every once in a while. Sexual escapades with whom I mistook to be the dead.

I thought he sensed my sudden tension, because he did a double-take before saying, "I don't have to if you don't want to."

Hell. What's the harm of having his skull rest on top of my leg?

"No. You're good," I said awkwardly. I shifted my leg a little to the left as he sat to my right, gapping the distance between us. He turned sideways, his dangling foot meeting grass, brushing Seth with his liveliness.

He kept silent, knowing fully well not to ask about my husband, after that episode of me erupting in anger over his probing questions.

He grabbed my hand and started caressing it. Oddly, I did not resist. I felt nothing while he probably felt something: a spark, an orb of love, perhaps a feeling that I did not share. He gave me little strokes on my hand, twirling his thumb and pressing it into my palm. Still, I felt cold. Just as cold as Seth's body had felt—as snowy as the frosty hue of Francisco's crystal eyes.

"I understand if you get mad at me for asking again, but we've been seeing each other for two months and you haven't told me anything about your family yet. If you're not comfortable with it, I won't push you, but I'm just curious—"

Oh, for fuck's sake.

"What do you wanna know?"

"Just... whatever you're comfortable telling me."

"Well..." I paused. "Gabriela was eleven the last time I saw her." Another pause. "Seth adopted Gabriela before he met me. Everything turned to shit only after I came into their lives. I loved Gabriela so much because I've always wanted to raise a kid, and I saw her as my own daughter. But she hated my fucking guts at first. She always saw me as the evil stepdad. We eventually grew closer, though, and she became comfortable calling me Papa. It was the happiest day of my life."

Yes, I can tell this part of my story to this stranger I've been seeing for two months. But I will dare not tell him anything else, especially not of my parents or his.

They had all disappeared now. Seth's parents and mine. I did not know why. Must I tell him that, too? It seemed that everywhere I went, the people I loved would always disappear.

I looked towards my arms—they were deathly pale. I was in shorts, and for the first time I really saw myself: a walking skeleton with a sorry excuse for saggy skin, expired meat struggling against plastic wrappings. My chest was concave; my stomach resembled that of a vulture who has come across no roadkill to feast upon for years.

I looked at the shovel underneath the tree, buried under a mound of dirt after months of neglect. It was the same one I used that night... and I remembered. I *finally* remembered. A knife and a shovel were in my hand that night he died—

"What happened to you?" asked Seth.

"Babe—"

"You were so bright and charming and intelligent... but when I look at you now, I don't even see my Antonio anymore. The Antonio I loved. And still love. But you're not that Antonio anymore, are you? Really, what happened to you? Who are you?"

"I—I'm gonna find a job."

He curled his fists, face fuming a bright red. "You say this every goddamn time, you stupid lazy fuck—"

"I'll go find a real job tonight. I promise, babe. Tonight."

"Don't you dare call me babe. Your head is so far up your ass that you think you're too good for minimum-wage jobs. I say get back on your ass and do SOMETHING."

Seth was screaming, his voice shaking the walls around as I trembled under his power. His words bounced incoherently as I waddled about, my head throbbing, slow to recover, as my mind sobered up. But because of the vodka, my world flew as a haze: obscure.

A flicker of time.

I looked at my hand, and I held a knife. Power coursed through my arm.

Where did I grab the knife? Why was it in my hand? Wait...

The words in me needed to spill out. I felt like keeping the secret of Seth's death meant betraying him. Betraying the only person in my life who I felt any love for besides our daughter.

"I have a... confession to make," I said to Francisco.

"What is it?"

"Come with me. Let's sit under the willow tree."

I took his hand and led him under the wilted branches, below which I heard the rumblings of—

(Seth's voice)

—caves and tunnels. Wordless words, soundless sounds.

We sat cross-legged facing each other, my face towards the tree trunk, peering past his head.

"I need to confess everything. I've been keeping some things from you," I said.

He looked at me and I felt only pity for the man. He caressed my hand with his thumb and said, "Antonio, what is it?"

"You know Seth was murdered," I started. "But I didn't tell you who murdered him."

Silence from his end. His fingers froze, as if he sensed what was to come.

"I killed Seth, Francisco. I killed my own husband."

I choked back tears. If I had killed Seth so mercilessly, then why did I feel even the slightest pang of remorse?

A long pause, his entire body still.

"Why did you kill him?" he asked in a restrained way.

"It was an accident. I swear to fucking God it was all an accident." I wanted to stand, take a shovel, and tunnel through the Earth, to where I buried Seth's bones wrapped in ribbons. I needed to rip him from the fucking ground. *Look at his bones, Francisco! Do you see how they speak? Do you see how the dust flutters to my voice? I killed him, but he's still alive, Francisco—his skull is right here! You see those pretty eyes in those sockets, those emerald eyes like yours? You see how those eyeballs spin and spin inside his skull?*

Francisco peered at me, his eyes gaping in newfound fear. He finally learned that I had only been using him to replace Seth, a live specimen to replace the corpse I so loved. I glimpsed that cute dimple on his left cheek, the one that flapped off the skull as I mounted it earlier—

This is proof Seth's still alive. His family gave me his bones, and I fucked the mouth of his crumbling skull with the rolling eyeballs. His dusty pelvis too. Then I buried those gifts which are bones: the gifts from—

(Seth's family)

—the dead man in the mirror.

"So, who's under this tree?" asked Francisco.

"Not him!" I barked. "*No no no no, not Seth! No!*" I jolted upwards and he jumped in fright, now standing. "Gabriela saw everything. But I remember now, Francisco. I remember now. I *remember*! She saw me kill her Daddy, so she ran away! Only thing is, I don't know where she went. The knife was in my hand—"

Parades of green leaves blindly tumbled to their deaths, led by the wind and not their own accord, to die above where Seth's dead eyes watched me from below.

"What do you remember?" asked Francisco. Voice far and detached. I looked at him no longer; I spoke only to the wilted tree, to Seth. I sensed Francisco's body recoiling away, as fearful and disgusted as if he just touched a dead rat without gloves: those types of dissectible rats in Biology class, drenched in putrid chemicals, their scent reminiscent of Aunt Matilda's room in the nearby nursing home.

"Everything. I remember the knife penetrating his guts. Telling Gabriela to go back. Driving Jose's sedan—it must've been Jose's, because it was a Ford Thunderbird!—that generous bastard. I stuffed Seth into the trunk and drove to a forest far, far away. But I didn't bury Seth's body, oh no, I didn't. I found a clump of deadfall where maggots burrowed homes inside the bark. I chewed at the bark, maggots and larvae and little eggs bursting onto my tongue, and I stuffed him into the tree stump by the deadfall.

"I cracked his limbs and bent his arms and legs into ungodly angles. Then I stuffed him into the dying tree trunk, fitting him in like a compression box. He was all done in. He looked like a mannequin that got manufactured all wrong, with the arms and legs coming out backwards.

"The maggots were fucking *pissed* at me, Francisco, don't think they weren't! I spoke to them. After I stuffed Seth inside the rotwood, though, the little shits became grateful. I had given them a new home: a shanty house upgraded to a mansion with endless food. I told the squirming shits that they were free to burrow and nest in Seth's body as long as they wanted. Slurp his flesh like soup. Carve hallways in his shrivelling veins. Most of them squirmed and died in a pool of my cum before I drove back home."

Francisco's disembodied voice from behind, floating further away, shrinking, until it would blend with the lithe rustle of green leaves far, far away. "Antonio, what do the reports say about Seth's death? What—"

"Ah, I was just getting to that part." I shifted my body. I was uncomfortable.

Francisco was now pacing away from me, heading for the street. I continued, "I went to court, and they pronounced me not guilty. At the time, I remembered nothing about the Ford I borrowed or the forest or stuffing Seth's body into the tree stump, so I didn't say that in court. Plus, I didn't want to self-incriminate—I gave them a lousy alibi. Said I drank myself shitless after I came home to see his body on the ground. I said somebody probably broke in and killed him before I came home.

"Gabriela was not in the courtroom. I never saw her again after she ran away. Oh, how naive she was. After the trial, there was still no concrete evidence that I killed him—they found no fingerprints on the knife. Our house had no cameras, so there was no visual proof. Some dipshit in the courtroom said this is why it's immoral for faggots to adopt kids, that we know nothing except killing ourselves and dying from AIDS, yadda yadda yadda.

"Like I said, Gabriela went away. She disappeared, I think. I don't know where she went—"

I knew what Francisco was thinking: *Antonio must've killed his child too. He killed his husband, and his daughter was his only witness; why wouldn't he have gotten rid of her either? Why is he confessing all of this*

96

to me, a random boy slut he picked up from the South End, why the fuck does he—

"—and then I killed myself."

"You know," stuttered Francisco, footsteps crunching over leafy ashes, "you're... you're not making a whole lotta sense right now."

"Oh, I know what I'm talking about." A pile of ashes: formerly green, mauve, and juicy orange leaves that only whiff through the autumn air at the brink of a violet sundown, piled under the wilted willow. "Before Seth's family came over to give me his bones in presents, I killed myself. In the bathroom I saw my dead self behind me in the mirror, so I snapped his neck. I cut his body parts up and set them on fire, and then you and I roasted marshmallows over it."

"Are you sure it wasn't yourself who you chopped up and set on fire?" Francisco asked, his poker eyes batting over the windblown grass, now understanding the depth of the evil that permeated here. "Antonio... think clearly. Have you ever stopped to consider that maybe it wasn't yourself who you killed... but someone else? Maybe, *Seth?* Your daughter?"

"No, Francisco. *I can't kill him a second time.*" The grin on my face widened. "Do you remember? They were good marshmallows, weren't they? But they had a particular... *human* taste. Think of pork—"

"Stop. *Stop!*" he gasped. "I can't listen to you anymore."

"Francisco, did you know that you look a lot like him?" I turned to look at him, his face pale and sinking. "That's why I brought you home to my bed, to my backyard, and above the grave I dug for him. Because you look like him, and that turns me on. I like to picture you so pretty, so *dead,* dead, dead, dead, dead, dead, inside that space, tucked so comfortably, so unresponsive. And did I tell you about the sloppy knife wound in Seth's stomach? Fuck, the guts make for amazing lube, especially when they're cold—"

"Antonio, I really have to go."

"That's fine." I cackled again. *"I can't wait for you to come back home."*

Francisco's footsteps trailed away, no answer from him as he ran.

His bones to infuse with the flesh of his lover.

What the hell did Seth's family want me to do with his bones? Did they go to the forest and take his body from the rotwood, ripping his bones through his flesh? Or did they go to that little old gravesite at the Mona Lisa Memorial over the hill and exhumed his coffin just to spite me?

Wait... if I disposed of his body in a dark forest, how did he even have viewing hours and a funeral—

Then it hit me. *Carve his bones so they become flesh again.* Oh, stupid me! Justice would only be rectified if I re-dug all his bones and made my lover whole again, to infuse with my roasted flesh. I had done Seth a disservice by burying him after I separated his bones; I needed to bury him *whole*, his skeleton reassembled.

They wrapped his bones, and I had to unwrap them. Perhaps he would come back to life; perhaps muscles would grow, skin and hair to vegetate as pasty batter, but it will be *his* eyes amid the renewed flesh.

His eyes to nestle in my burnt body, tacked on like a head on a pike.

I took my shovel and dug with renewed purpose. I kicked away at the pile of ash that was once the monsoon of leaves. The moon was bright; I looked upward and it was watching me, that nosy bitch, as

Seth's eyes watched me from below: soon to approach, whole, and devour me with foreboding fangs. Soon I would bestow upon the world a deed that would rectify all my evils and undo my insanity.

And so, I dug and dug again, battling against my muscles which strained and failed against my efforts.

The shovel hit paper. The cheap kind of wrapping paper found in Hobby Lobby. Finally, I had reached the gifts! Those gifts underground which were handed to me by —

(*the man in the mirror*)

— Seth's family.

But then, my daughter's voice rang through the air. Scintillating waves which throbbed my bones, my entire body shaking and vibrating with the low frequency of a broken bass. That voice: did it come from above or below? I couldn't tell; it seemed to call from a grave, nevertheless. An invitation to enter. To join him.

A church hymn that I vaguely remembered, with its verses sung out of order. Gabriela's earthy voice heavy yet squeaky, her self-assured echoes singing:

His dying breath brought me life
His death and resurrection
It was my sin that held Him there
My sin upon His shoulders.

The death song rang throughout the caves of my head, spitting incomprehensible nothings. I looked upward to the moon, poker-faced. I stood inside this deep pit that I dug. Seth's grave—my grave.

Ashamed, I hear my mocking voice
His wounds had paid my ransom
The Father turns his face away.

I can't wait to come down there to see you again, I thought. *Together, we can sing forever and ever, even with Daddy, who never died. Did I kill you, my baby girl? I can't remember.*

Sudden silence. A wave of bliss then came to replace this deep black grief in my heart; I knew it did not matter whether or not I killed Gabriela. I had already killed her in spirit a long time ago, when Seth brought me into their home. She had always been dead, or so she appeared. Gabriela spoke to me from the tunnels of my skull, from the soil. My precious daughter was *alive*, whether she spoke from caves or atop a mortuary table.

Daddy's mad, spoke the same singing voice. I listened to my mind while straining my neck. I turned my head to look at all the presents below, all still guarded by a thin film of dirt that I had yet to uncover.

Then I realized: her voice did not come from inside my head. She spoke from underground, from Seth's grave. My precious daughter singing from my lover's soil of bones: the pits of the earth, the depths of my insanity. That disembodied echo then screamed: *"Papa, you killed daddy! You killed Daddy, Papa, and you killed me too—"*

"Gabriela," I whispered. Her shrieks drowned out the volume of my thoughts. Tears were threatening to push through my eyes, but I resisted them. "Oh my God, Gabriela, I'm so sorry for everything..."

I knelt on the soft soil, my arms trembling as I grasped onto the shovel handle for support. Face wet. The dam holding my grief was now completely broken, collapsed, destroyed.

"The three of us can live inside Daddy's body, a happy family again—"

Then the world around me lit up in flashing streams of blue and red, ricocheting off the earthy walls like probing disco lights. I sobbed even heavier, tears spewing forth from the dusty cobwebs that were my eyes; surely, I had finally descended into hell, the last stage of my madness. I staggered and regained my breath. Those blue and red lights kept flashing, flashing... demons coming to grant me refuge, and then I heard radio dispatches. Blaring sirens. Cop talk. Police cars.

Luckily, I was tall enough that I could tiptoe and look above the edge of the hole, above the ground. I directed my eyes to the street in front of my house and saw a horde of police cars: a swarm of cops and figures with bulletproof shields running onto my front lawn.

"Come out with your hands up!" barked a woman who held a loudspeaker from the window of an FBI police Chevy. *"We have you surrounded, Antonio Rivera de la Cruz. Come out with your hands up and your face to the ground."*

And there behind the dashing SWAT agents I saw a beautiful man. His back faced me, and his body gestured frantically. A buzz cut dyed platinum-blonde. Francisco.

That motherfucker had reported me to the police. My lips curled in a snarl. I swore I'd murder him the next time I saw him! I should have cracked his fucking skull against the headboard or against the pavement on Columbus Avenue when I first saw him, when I had the chance!

I climbed up from the grave of presents, ready to pounce at Francisco and pummel his head into the concrete. The police, the FBI, and none of those law enforcement pigs could stop me. I taunted at the SWAT members and at Francisco, flipping the bird. He avoided my stare and continued talking to a police officer. That fucker, a snitch—

"He has two bodies in his backyard, like I said!" he screamed in the distance, the loudspeaker silent. *"He's killed more people than just his husband. That's his daughter under that fucking tree, I swear! That's why she's been missing for so long!"*

A *snitch* to whom I made the mistake of fully trusting, just because he looked so much like Seth. And that marked my biggest downfall: trusting another soul over my blind likeness for the flesh that housed it. I trusted his soul because I liked the appearance of his body, his pretty face and his eyes, a complete misjudgment that could only be made through failing to see beneath a facade of lies.

SWAT members bolted at me with their shields.

But in front of them all, a tall figure stood. A humanoid figure. And if my eyes weren't mistaken, it was headless. A dark, headless figure with the body of a man similar to mine. So similar to me in soul... yet, so *different.* He walked like the dead, *with* the dead.

Time slowed down. The SWAT agents now ran as snails amid a gray, invisible current.

The headless man walked toward the edge of the pit that I dug. He stood in front of me. The dead man in the mirror. My dead self. Except now, there was no mirror to grace our meeting—my real self-separated from my illusory image—I faced my own corpse head-on, that skeleton I tried to bury so long ago, when I died inside.

A stream of my daughter's garbled voice, warped noise marked by the grave:

"You can make Daddy whole again, Papa—"

"We can live inside Daddy's body and be a happy family again—"

I opened my mouth to speak, but the dark figure pushed me into the grave.

Time snapped back into focus. Those red and blue lights swirled and danced again amidst my blackened world. I fell into the burial pit—freefalling as the hellfire which sweeps and burns entire forests—and I spiralled, spiralled through the gifts. Bones now protruded from the sheets of bright colors, ripping holes through all the cheap surface art: skeletal arms, legs, and body parts all grasping at me, pulling me downward.

Seth's bones pulled me further and further into the earth as the soil under the wilted tree swallowed me whole, into those hollow caves which were his voice. Seth wanted me to lie with him again. Forever.

Soon the red and blue lights faded into dead hues, yellow-green shades of monotony and death, just as dogs saw the world. The headless man stayed standing at the edge of the pit as he watched me fall through the earth, his neck craned. Seth suffocated me as he pulled me downward, downward, bony chips and parts caressing my body. Then the visions of my world erupted into radio static.

***

Comforting darkness. The scent of vacuum-sealed rubber and embalming fluid embedded in my flesh... these were not unpleasant smells. I opened my eyes, my eyebrows fluttering, and life stirred in my dead limbs. I lay in the dark somewhere, my arms crossed over my chest. Was I under the earth? Skies? The wilted tree?

I bent my knees to stand, but they only met velvet. Soft, gliding fabric. I tried to push through the fabric panel above with my knees, but I met only a hard surface. I then tried to push through with my hands, but I failed. There was only solid, unbudging wood behind those velvet panels.

Panic grappled my heart as I felt around for an escape—a false wall, a click, anything!—all to no avail. Then I realized I lay entombed in a rectangle. A casket. Me, alive, in a casket underground. But I could not panic, even though my throat sunk into my heart and I was on the edge of a scream. I huffed and puffed, forcing the panic and fear inside me to subside and fuck off. I pried further for a loose screw or a wiggling panel, but this wooden prison remained unyielding, fighting against me the more I bloodied my knees and knuckles to break it.

My breath froze as the darkness above me incinerated with a dazzling light. A window in the coffin. A window into my life, surreal happenings.

And through that window to the world, I saw my dead self sitting in the kitchen.

My doppelganger sat atop a stool in the middle of the kitchen above where Seth had died. He restored his head, my head—had he picked through the trash to find it? Embedded in the figure's neck were horrible stitches, weaved in and out like zigzagging black ants, holding the head and the neck together. Just like those lolling heads of Seth's family.

Through the window, I saw myself gulp a shot of rum. Then, knocks came ringing from the door. The figure smiled. In its other hand was a chef's knife. The same one I held that night. Gleaming steel.

It downed another shot of rum before it approached the door.

Our family portrait still hung on the kitchen wall, unripped and whole. Except now, all our eyes were clawed out in red.

Another knock. My doppelganger's arm was bent behind its back as it walked, hiding the weapon.

That inhuman *thing* then opened the door. There stood Gabriela. Her hair was more kept than usual; she had dyed it a bright crimson red, like she had just returned from a surfing trip to Honolulu. She learned to cheat death. She looked healthier and seemed happier.

But as I watched the figure withdraw the knife from its back, fear materialized as a stone in my throat, scuttling to harden as cement against the walls of my veins.

"I'm so sorry, Papa," sobbed Gabriela to the towering figure, "for leaving you and Daddy. It's my fault, I ... I shouldn't have put the blame on you..."

"Don't you dare kill my fucking child!" I screamed at the window, somehow overcoming that burden of calcified fear. I tried to climb through the coffin window, but an invisible force had blocked me from entering. Enough damage had already been done with my impulsive hand many nights ago, and I could not let the only human being I loved more than life itself be taken away from me... not now. "She's the only thing I have left in this world! Oh God sweet Jesus our Father in heaven hallowed be thy name thy kingdom fall please rain destruction on anybody but my fucking kid—"

I continued my useless pleadings as I watched, powerless. Helpless.

The figure's knife-holding hand was raised high into the air.

It turned to look at me once more through the coffin window. It grinned widely. The stitches around its neck ripped as it turned to peer at me, those black threads ripping freely, blood flowing down the nape of its neck, over the collarbone then below in black-copper streams.

The most fucked up part? I felt like it was *my* own arm that raised the knife. I felt like it was not my dead self, but *I*, who controlled that knife-holding arm which drove into my daughter from above—

I looked away. I could not bear witness to the unspeakable.

Then beside me, I felt an invisible body take shape in the clumped air. Solid mass, long like a fallen tree.

And there he was: Seth, lying down next to me in the casket. Emerald eyes, a pretty face. I missed waking up next to him, under our velvety sheets as sun rays filtered through the blinds to caress our faces and naked bodies. Oh god, I missed us so much that it fucking hurt.

I looked towards my empty hand. No knife. *No knife. But a knife was in my hand...*

I was wrong. About everything.

Kitchen tiles. Blood that seeped through the floor. My eyes widened as I glimpsed the corpse of my beloved Seth beside me, cuddling me. A bloody knife in Gabriela's hand.

"I'm sorry. I didn't mean to do it," she said in a frantic whisper. "We were so happy till Papa came and everything turned to shit. I can't take it anymore. I can't take any of it, you two fighting and hurting each other every day. You don't know how many times you both made me want to kill myself and die."

She raised the knife to cut her own throat, but I ran towards her.

I snatched it from her; now, it was in my hand. My fingerprints wiped hers away from the knife handle. Seth's blood transferred from her fingertips to mine. Then, a brandishing glare of horror, of eternal betrayal from Gabriela's eyes. Yet within that unbroken scowl, there lay a mutual understanding.

"Go," I said.

A moment's hesitation. Then a dash. Small feet squinching upon carpet, thumps receding into the ceiling that was our only sky.

She ran away, to nowhere.

So did I.

Seth, her only refuge for love and peace, snatched away. She had meant to stab me, but Seth jumped in front and sacrificed himself in my place: the ultimate proof that he still held even the slightest hint of love for me. And now without him she had nothing to live for, no reason to ever find joy in this hell you call life. All that she had wanted was for the godforsaken suffering to end, and she saw no other choice but to take the knife.

It was so easy back then, taking the blame. But I could never bear to think—

"Sleep with me," the corpse beckoned with dirt and gravel in his throat. Yet just as lively and colorful as when he was alive. A sleepy voice, like it was another normal night as now I lay me down to sleep.

I pray the Lord my soul to keep.

"Seth," I said. My voice thin. "Is that really you?"

"Yes, baby," he said. Full of life.

Then his face morphed into a dead thing. His tan skin flushed by the second, and those jeweled eyes turned into black holes.

"Shh, sleep with me," he beckoned in a deeper, unnatural voice.

If I die before I wake,

Uncanny. His voice: the texture of maggots.

His rotting arms wrapped around the bulge of my bicep, in that same position as when I caressed him those many nights ago, as he lay dying. A fetal position. The smell of an abandoned attic.

I felt my cock growing hard.

I pray the Lord my soul to take.

Screams and shrieks of terror from the window, my arm feeling like it plunged into a soft cavity of meat. The sounds of dying swine in a slaughterhouse. But I could not turn my head to look. Seth was hugging me, suffocating me against his rotting chest. He did not want me to bear the pain of watching myself murder my daughter for my own sake. For all our sake.

But it wasn't my fault. I couldn't control myself after Gabriela ran. I just wanted us all to be happy again.

A few moments passed. I counted the ticks, the calling of time.

The screams stopped.

My arm felt as if it dropped, finally at rest. The sound of clinking steel against the kitchen floor. Then a colder, grating voice from that rotwood cage for flesh: *"She'll sing with us too, Antonio. Then we will sleep together, forever."*

OUT OF TOWN STRANGE
By Carlton Herzog

The Undertaker's Lament

To be a mortician—especially in New York City--you need a twisted sense of humor, a strong stomach, and a keen sense of fluid dynamics. Too much embalming pressure and you can blow out the eyeballs or blow off an arm.

Moreover, it helps to have a steady artistic hand. Some faces sink so much that applying Maybelline Blush Foundation is like trying to paint a portrait on a deflated basketball.

Remember that not everyone will share your cosmetic acumen or sense of beauty. I once worked on a crone who sported a grotesque facial wart festooned with long, grey hairs. The sorts of hairs you find on the testicles of withered old men. I felt aesthetically obligated to pluck them. At the viewing the family went ballistic claiming they didn't recognize her. I refunded their money.

Always remain open-minded on the ways people say good-bye to the departed. For example, I worked on a rodeo fanatic. His get-up made him look like Annie Oakley and Pippi Long-stocking had had a baby. At the wake, they wanted me to play tunes from Roy Rogers and Dale Evans *Songs of the Old West,* such as *Home on the Range, Wagon Wheels* and *Texas Plains.* The mourners came dressed as their favorite cowboy or cowgirl right down to the shootin' irons. The cherry on that Sunday was the square dance they held in the viewing room. They were swinging their partners round and round. I didn't know whether to laugh or cry.

Don't let their *rigor mortis* or the lack of a heartbeat fool you. Dead people do not always stay dead. Some can be obnoxiously chatty on the embalming table. Others like to get up and stretch their legs. I had one demand that I provide him with leotards and a skull so he could perform a scene from Hamlet one last time. Another grabbed a mirror, looked at her make-up, then ordered me to redo it, because "You made me look like shit."

One guy who went by the street name of Satellite Jack would babble incessantly about government conspiracies. So, I cut-off his head thinking that would shut him up. But he just kept on talking as if nothing had happened. That made me readjust my index of the weird to accommodate babbling disembodied heads.

What struck me as equally bizarre was the pettiness and triviality of the cadavers' discourse. One would think that they would reflect on the great existential questions of life and death. Not these turkeys.

Take Mrs. Cathy Garrity, for example. She would not shut up about the pests eating the fruits and vegetables in her garden. I got a shotgun blast by shotgun blast description of every rabbit, gopher, and raccoon she had obliterated with buckshot. Finally, I duct taped her mouth. That did not stop her in the least. She yanked off the tape and kept on babbling. Even after I slid her back into the freezer, I could hear here talking to me, all *Cask of Amontillado* like. A real chatty Cathy, if ever there were one.

The Dead Girl from Alabama

But she was mild compared to Jexx Adams. She didn't just talk. She wanted me to take her for one last ride, in more ways than one. Not in the hearse, but in my 65 Mustang, a cherry red convertible in mint condition. Said she wanted to feel the midnight air.

I said, "You know you're dead right?"

She said, "Fuck yeah, I know I'm dead. And when they put me in the ground that's the last time I'll ever be able to do anything but rot. So, grant me this one last indulgence. It will give you something to tell your grandkids. Think of me as your date from hell."

I said, "Fine. One ride. But you need to keep a low profile. I don't feel like explaining why I'm riding around with a reanimated corpse."

I waited until it was dark. I walked, and she stumbled out of the funeral home and into the parking lot. Even outdoors, I could smell the embalming fluid on her, not to mention a faint whiff of the grave.

She asked, pointing at the only car in the lot, "Is that your convertible? Can we ride with the top down? I want to feel the wind on my face and in my hair."

I should have said no. But she had power over me. Not mystical, but sexual. She had been an attractive woman, and still was despite her deathly pallor. She still had a vitality about her that not even death could completely erase, together with a wicked sense of humor and a manner like that of a prowling libidinous alley cat. If I had to guess, her family came from Trampsylvania."

She started reciting limericks as we drove through the city.

"Check this out dude:
There was an artist named Saint,
Who swallowed some samples of paint
All shades of the spectrum
Flowed out of his rectum
With a colorful lack of restraint.
I said, "You are quite the graveyard poet."
She said, "I know right. Listen to this:
There was a young lady from Worcester
Who dreamt a rooster seduced her.
She woke with a scream
But 'twas only a dream
A bump in the mattress had goosed her.
I said, "Admirable. You must have graduated with honors from Dixie's Trailer Park School of Rhetoric."

She said, "What's wrong Zippy, your blowup doll run off with a pool toy?"

I said, "Limericks are for simpletons who lack any refinement."

"Don't talk down to me Jiminy Cricket. Besides you ain't seen nuthin' yet."

Then she promptly stood up and rolled down her silk funeral dress giving cars and pedestrians a bird's eye view of my stitch work and her pendulous breasts.

"Hooters get your hooters here. Feast your eyes on these boys. They won't come this way again. I'll be here all night, so don't forget to tip your waitresses."

I said, "Jesus Christ, sit the fuck down before I get pulled over. Do you know how bad you're making me look?"

"That's not me. It's genetics and barber school haircuts. I need a drink. Maybe something or somebody to eat."

I said, "You're dead; you don't need to eat."

She said, "Just like a man to corpse shame a woman. You are what is known as an oppressive denier. By the way, you're the last person who should be commenting on another person's dietary habits. You have man boobs nearly as big as mine. Is that from too many lard-bombs at Paunch Burger?"

"You're hurting my feelings."

"Let me tell you about feelings. They're like your mother's breasts. You know where they are, but they're better left unfelt. Now how about that drink Tubby. I'm thirsty."

I drove around looking for a dark dive bar where Jexx would not attract too much attention. We slid through the seedier side of town where I found the Osiris Lounge. I parked the car. This time she did not have any trouble walking. She had a curious spring in her step for a bloodless undead person.

As we approached the bouncer, she said, "Look-it's lady's night. You get in for half price."

I replied, "Yeah, but not you cause you're no lady. I bet you've been on more hotel pillows than a chocolate mint."

Not to be outdone, she yelled, "Don't send to know for whom the booty calls, fir it calls for me."

"I can't take much more of this."

"You're like an Alzheimer's patient in a whorehouse. You're constantly surprised that you're being screwed."

When we got inside, she ordered a shot and a beer. The place was so dark neither the bartender nor the patrons gave her a second look. I had the same.

I don't know how she accomplished it, but Jexx gulped both her drinks down without batting a dead eye.

I asked her how it was possible for her to do that.

She said, "This is nothing I used to do heroin."

"Heroin?" I asked.

She said, "You have to be pretty high to rob a bank. And other left of center things. When one old flame dumped me, I dressed up as Robin Hood and shot his new girlfriend in the ass with an arrow."

I muttered, "What have I gotten myself into?"

"Well, if you must know, I'm a Wendigo, one of many in fact, who spiral around your funeral home waiting for an opportunity like this. Your funeral home is built on the old Leni Lenape graveyard. That's why all the previous tenants moved out. Too spooky for them. Guess they didn't mention the place was haunted when your mother bought it for you."

I asked, "So, why do you jump into the bodies of the dead? Seems like a being of pure spirit could find better things to do."

She smiled broadly and said, "Sugar, there ain't nothing happening in the spirit world. It is just a big incorporeal shitshow with nothing to do but watch the living. If you were in my place, you would jump at the chance to enjoy the sweetness of life's physical pleasures too. And for the record, a Wendigo can't hijack a body with a soul, so the dead are the only game in town."

All I could think to say was, "Okay universe, I give up: you win."

She said, "That's quitter talk. You need to fight for your right to party. Beastie Boys—remember them?"

Nothing seemed to affect her ebullience. All I could think of was that I had rubbed the cursed lamp, let the genie out in the process, and now had to get it back in before it could do any real harm.

I said, "We should be heading back now. Your viewing is tomorrow afternoon. It would be unseemly for you to miss it."

She said, "But sugar pie, I'm not ready to go back. I have things to do. Barkeep give us another round and keep them coming. Speaking of coming, when's the last time you got laid?"

I didn't know what to say. Both because I was, at the tender age of 40, still a virgin, and because I sensed where that question was leading.

"Come on spit it out goat boy. Oh, I get it. You've never seen a pussy let alone poked one. I know you're not gay because you keep gawking at my massive tits. So, what's the story my little fat prince of death?"

My face flushed beet red. I didn't have an answer. I just put my head down and hoped she would move on to another topic. But she didn't.

"Don't fret lover, my pussy is one size fits all. I'm not choosy. They used to call me Jexx Gets Around. If my vagina were a video game, it would be rated E for everyone. Maybe you'd like to take me for a spin. You could use the exercise, and I wouldn't mind a poke for old time's sake before they throw the dirt over me. Think of me as a wildfire that can only be doused by your seed."

"While the offer is tempting, there's laws against that sort of thing. Besides, your skin is brittle and dry. I don't want to damage your body before the viewing."

"Suit yourself, but at the rate you're going, you're going to die a virgin like Isaac Newton. Is that how you want to be remembered? I can see the epitaph on your tombstone now: **"Never Got Any**." Every now and then, somebody will write a puff piece about weird stuff in graveyards, and your tombstone will be front and center with a short bio that reads 'Pathetic funeral director never lost his virginity and decided to let everyone know it after he died'."

Just to shut her up, I said, "I'll consider sleeping with you if we can leave now. Otherwise, forget it. If you're not at the viewing, my reputation will go down the drain."

She said, "Okay Jughead. But remember—I'm like an Alabama bloodhound, once I get a whiff nothing can stop me."

We left the Osiris and drove back towards the funeral home. As we passed a dance club, Jexx screamed at me to stop.

"I want to go dancing one last time. Come on lover. Indulge me in this and I will be your willing love slave. After all, dance is the perpendicular expression of a horizontal desire."

I didn't feel like arguing. I pulled into the lot and we went inside.

It was a young crowd hopped up on Ecstasy, weed and booze. Oddly enough we almost fit in because Jexx's pale complexion was like that of the numerous Goth and punk chicks populating the bar and dance floor.

I wanted a drink. I needed a drink. But Jexx dragged me onto the dance floor where we were elbow-to-elbow with hot, sweaty writhing bodies dancing to Uber Jak'd's *Bounce and Bass*.

It didn't take long for Jexx's breasts to pop out of her dress. While she held the dress up, she made no effort to conceal her assets. She bounced and danced and hopped along until all that motion dislodged her right arm. It fell to the floor. She kept on dancing, tits a flopping as if nothing were wrong. I frantically snatched up the arm before it could be crushed by the dancing feet around us.

She grabbed the arm away from me. Next thing I knew she was using it to high five the other women on the dance floor.

I yelled, "We have got to go so I can reattach your arm."

She yelled back, "I'm fine."

I pleaded with her to leave with me.

She said, "I will go but only if you give me your solemn promise to fuck me."

I was desperate. I said, "Yes. Now for the love of God can we please go?"

"Sure lover. I can't wait to be the one who pops your cherry."

I groaned at that. But she followed me out laughing as she went carrying her arm.

When we got to the parking lot, a guy in a ski mask tried to rob us.

Not intimidated in the least, Jexx said, "Big man with a gun and probably a small dick. What's your street name, Small Dick, or is it dickless?"

The gunmen said, "Shut-up and hand over your wallet."

Undaunted by the robber, Jexx lowered the front of her dress to reveal the incision and stitches from her organ removal. Some of it had opened and was oozing embalming fluid salted with dried blood.

She pointed to the stitches and said, "I'm dead asshole. Here, listen to my non-heartbeat. This bozo is the mortician who's getting me ready to be buried. He's got to sew the arm I'm carrying back on my stump. Do you really think a bullet or two will bother somebody who is already dead? Besides, I already robbed a liquor store and killed a drifter, and the night is still young."

The robber said nothing. He turned and walked away. As he did, the streetlight illuminated him just enough for me to see he was wetting himself.

Jexx said, "See, having a dead girlfriend has perks, such as robbery protection."

We walked to the car. I needed to reattach her arm before we attracted any more attention.

I pulled a box of superglue cartridges from the glove box. I said, "Come over here, so I can glue that arm back on you."

She said, "Help me Obi Wan Kenobi—you're my only hope. By the way, do you always carry boxes of superglue with you?"

As I applied the superglue around her shoulder stump and on the end of the detached arm, I said, "Always. I learned the trick from a plastic surgeon friend of mine. Unfortunately, he got caught doing cosmetic surgery with superglue and lost his license as a result. I keep plenty in my car because I never know when I may need to stick somebody or something back together. Now hold still while I reattach your arm. Okay, we need to let it set for fifteen minutes."

"And after that?"

I answered with a curt, "I will bang you, and then stick you back in the freezer until tomorrow."

She pouted and said, "When you say it like that, it's very hurtful and very sexist. Don't you care about me at all?"

"You told me you were a spirit animating the corpse of a dead woman. I'm not sure what I'm supposed to feel. Besides, you blackmailed me into agreeing to have sex with you. So, you have the upper hand here not me."

"I feel like you are taking advantage of me."

"How am I taking advantage of you? I have done everything you asked. I took you for a ride, a drink, and a dance. I have promised to have sex with you and will if only to shut you up."

"See, that's the problem. You're treating this relationship like an algebra equation. I'm a woman. Granted, the wendigo thing makes me an outlier, but I'm still a woman with feelings that can be hurt. Didn't anybody tell that you're not gonna' get the virgin to the volcano by telling her you'll throw her in when you get there."

"How did you get so screwed up."

"My mother—the monster who bore me--never had a kind word for me. At my wedding, she said, 'I'm so glad you finally found someone who could love you."

"That's cold."

"She also said that God gave her me so death would seem more appealing."

"I'm beginning to understand."

"I went to a support group for people whose mothers had died, even though mine was still alive. Wishful thinking, I suppose. I know alcohol and drugs are poison, but there are things inside me I want to kill. Not the least of which are my memories of that soulless she-devil."

I sensed the only way this extended exercise in self-loathing could end would be for me to play along with her romantic nonsense. I moved towards her and took her in my embrace. Not too hard because I didn't want her to shatter like a potato chip. Then I kissed her, first on the neck then full on the mouth. She smelled and tasted of formaldehyde. I stuck to my guns and stifled my gag reflex.

She cooed, "That was so nice lover. I knew you had it in you. Now let's get back so you can poke me to death."

Corpse or no corpse, cunning manipulative bitch or not, I was turned on and couldn't wait to do it. I will not elaborate on the details other than to say, we did it in the back seat and I thoroughly enjoyed it. After that, we headed back to the funeral parlor.

We had not gone far when she pointed to a church.

"Look, there's a late-night service. Let's check it out."

At this juncture, I was far calmer, no doubt from our salacious interlude. So, I pulled into the church parking lot.

"This is it. We go in, and take a look and then back to your   coffin.
"Whatever you say Doctor Cyclops."

No sooner had we walked through the doors, than Jexx ran straight up to the pulpit, pushed the minister aside and began to preach.

"Brothers and sisters, I'm here to spread the gospel. Can I get an Amen? Come on brothers and sisters. This is the Lord's House. Can I get a Goddam Amen?"

Blasphemous though it was, she did inspire a thunderous Amen. But I knew it was just a matter of time before the lightning bolts started flying down from above and I was reduced to a pair of smoking shoes.

"Now the Lord wants us to be happy. Amen. He wants us to enjoy our earthly life. But most of all he wants us to laugh. Can I get an Amen?"

"Well then, here's a joke that will put joy in your heart, a smile on your face and a bounce in your step. Guy dies and goes to Hell. Devil meets him in the vestibule.

Devil says, 'You get to choose your punishment from behind one of three doors.'

The guy looks the doors up and down then opens the first one. He sees people standing on their heads on a concrete floor. He says 'Pass."

He goes to the second door. When he opens it, the scene is the same except in this case the floor is wooden. Again, he passes.

He opens the third door and sees people standing knee deep in shit. But otherwise, they seem happy as they drink coffee and smoke cigarettes. The guy says, "I'll take this one' and walks inside. He gets a cup of coffee and bums a cigarette.

He thinks that he made the best possible choice, since aside from the smell, the punishment was tolerable. But a moment later, the Devil sticks his head back in and says, 'Breaks over assholes! Everybody back on their heads.'

"Can I get an Amen?"

Half the congregation was laughing while the other half kept looking up waiting for the proverbial shoe to drop.

Before anyone could register their shock, Jexx opened her shirt to expose her braless breasts. If that weren't bad enough, she began gyrating and twisting her body to make them flop up and down. Then she turned around and twerked.

I was mortified. But before I could get her out of the church, the pastor approached Jexx. She was positively ancient. With her lunar face, so sunken and grey, she could have passed for the Crypt Keeper. I could see menace in her eyes, but before she could say anything, Jexx opened fire.

"Comes now Mother Time, so full of dust and undigested mastodon meat. Was your first Christmas the First Christmas? Your first car a chariot? Do you like to take long walks on the beach after crawling out of the ocean and growing legs?"

"Quite the acid tongue. But I'm not surprised since you seem crazier than a bag full of rats in a burning meth lab."

"Jesus cat dancing Christ. A cleric with an acid tongue and biting teeth. Bet they come in handy when you lure little kids to your gingerbread house. I take it that's your brown panel van parked out back, you know the one with all those buckets of chloroform-soaked rags."

"Leave or I will call the police."

Jexx looked at me and winked.

"You know if you get old Prudence here pregnant, then we can get a full page in Ripley's Believe It or Not."

"The police it is then. They will not be as patient as I am."

"Why don't you have God remove me. After all, it's his house, not yours. Speaking of God, I have a joke for you. This guy dies and is standing outside the pearly gates. Saint Peter strolls up and says, 'Sorry pal, you're too much of a sinner for heaven. You're going to the other place.'

The guy says, 'Hold on. I wasn't that bad. The worst I did was take the Lord's name in vain a few times.'

'More like a million six.'

'A million six! Jesus fucking Christ!'

No sooner had she finished than a bolt of lightning shot through the church roof and exploded the podium. I looked dumbfounded. Jexx looked delighted.

"Hey you up there. Yeah, I'm talking to you, asshole. You couldn't hit the broad side of a barn you cross-eyed fuck. Try again. I dare you."

I nearly wet myself. The thought of being split in two by heavenly lightning, and then summarily dispatched to a blazing inferno below held little appeal. I grabbed the front of her dress to pull her out, because grabbing an arm most likely meant pulling it off in the process.

As we made for the car, she was laughing hysterically.

"Now I can go into the afterlife with a skip in my step and a smile on my face".

After we finished, she got back on the gurney so I could wheel her into the freezer. We kissed one last time, after which she said, "I won't be in this body tomorrow morning. But I'm like herpes. One way or the other, I'll be back. I just don't know when and in whom. So, don't die, and don't lose your meat missile, and we can do this again lover."

"Just do me a favor."

"What's that lover?"

"Don't come back as a man."

"That's not very open-minded of you. Who knows, you might like it."

"Call me old fashion, but I like my reanimated corpse lovers female."

"Hey—if a man speaks, and there's no woman to hear him, is he still wrong?"

"I don't know. If a woman speaks, and there's no man to hear her, is she still lying?"

And on that snarky note, I wheeled her into the freezer and shut the door. I considered jumping her one last time but thought better of it. That dead woman had worn me out, a dead woman who was for all practical purposes my first girlfriend. My personal bar for weirdness had moved again, exponentially so, into the watery wild between the living and the dead. And so, ended my date from hell with out of town strange.

The End?

ALPHA MALE
By Adam Bell

Bound naked and spread eagle to the large flat stone deep in a wooded area, all Frankie can do is shiver as Marianne runs a fingernail down his chest. His wrists and ankles bleed under the hemp rope, and the pull of the restraints makes his joints ache. Five other smaller yet taller stones stand equidistant around the altar. Trees surround the outer ring, branches overshadowing Frankie, though the brilliant night sky remains visible. Abundant stars and a full moon glow through the leaves. He can't see the ground from his position, but the crisp scent of dry foliage and dirt tickles his nose.

"Please, Marianne, let me go." Frankie's voice is hoarse from whatever she'd roofied him with to knock him out long enough to get him here and tie him up.

"You should be happy. You're getting what you wanted." Marianne winks and pulls down the zipper of her ankle-length white robe. The fastener is long, going from the high neck to well below her naval. She cocks her hip in a stereotypical sexy pose as she takes a full minute to open the garment.

He can't help but stare in fascination at her brown, jewel-toned, flawless skin. So long has he waited. So long has he tried. So long has he schemed. To see her. To touch her. To fuck her.

It took him years to wear her down. Of course, she wasn't his only piece. Especially since she wouldn't put out. But she was and is so gorgeous that he couldn't stop trying.

She drew him to her like a man in a desert to an oasis. She exuded something powerful. Something mysterious. Something dark.

And if he's honest with himself, the main draw was the challenge.

More honesty demands that he acknowledge, only to himself, that he'd slept with many women, but did not have many long-term conquests. And no relationships. He's too much the player.

But for Marianne. For her, he would change his ways. Maybe.

Somehow, she had wormed her way into his jaded heart. It could have been as simple as lust turning to appreciation and then love, or perhaps it was more complex. Spending time with her, suppressing his player ways, he had opened himself to knowing her.

The zipper's movement ends with an inch of black curls showing. The expanse of skin revealed is lustrous and only blemished by a tiny scar at her lower ribs. A barely-there pooch to her stomach highlights her femininity. She's not one of those muscle-bound butches. A well-shaped belly button draws him to kiss. And the best of all is the inner side of two glorious breasts that he's wanted to ravage since the day they'd met.

"I don't know how you managed it, but you got what you wanted." Marianne teases by playing with the edges of the open cloth, giving small glimpses of skin. "I've fallen in love with you. Despite the horrible way we started. Despite the fact I'm not attracted to men."

He hadn't availed himself well in the beginning. He was too macho. Too arrogant. Too alpha male.

She was with another woman at a table in a popular pickup-bar he frequented for his one-night stands. The nightspot fit the stereotype. Dark but clean, loud music, and plenty of seating. It was too small to be a club but had a dance floor big enough for five couples, and a modest stage. That evening the platform hosted a live band. He later discovered her companion knew one of the musicians; it's the only reason she would visit a place like that.

As soon as he saw Marianne, he needed to fuck her. It had to be. The dress she wore showed a body that would make a model jealous. Her killer curves reminded him of Tyra Banks. Beauty and charisma, without being stick thin with huge fake breasts that so many seem to push as the ideal. Her presence drew him to her with such intensity he was standing before he realized he'd moved.

So, he approached her. He can't even recall the pickup line he'd used, nor the woman she was dating. Thinking back, he can come up with a blonde with a sporty androgynous look, but he couldn't remember significant details. All his focus was on Marianne.

"No, thank you." She placed her hand on the woman's thigh. "We're on a date."

"A lesbian? You're a lesbian?" Frankie's voice rose about the thump of the music.

She rolled her eyes. "Yes."

"You're too pretty. I bet you haven't had the right guy yet. I can show you what a real man can do. It's better than any plastic thing she can offer." He nodded his head at her companion.

Marianne growled. "No. Go away."

Frankie held no delusions. He was an asshole, and what he said was out of line, but forcing himself on someone isn't his kink. Rape was for sickos. Going further with the "men are better in bed than women" comments would only deepen the hole he'd dug, So, he'd left.

But he persisted. He could not resist that draw to her.

He looked for her, followed her. Probably stalked her. But he didn't send her creepy messages saying she was his, did nothing that would endanger her, didn't even approach her. He only watched and waited for an opportunity. Trailing her from a distance. Found out her name and researched everything about her.

He'd never chased a conquest before. It was not in the alpha male playbook. Sure, he was assertive and made the first move, but that was only "catching prey." But with Marianne, he discovered where she worked and where she lived but did not make the mistake of interacting with her at either location. She seemed to prefer straight bars and clubs to gay or lesbian bars, so he had more opportunities to watch her while she dated a woman who always wore sundresses.

And eventually it happened.

She was at a dive bar alone. There were only three other people there, including the bartender. Her back was arched, her shoulders drooped, and her head low. She looked moments from falling off the stool and crying. He took his opportunity, suppressed all his alpha male plays, and sat beside her.

The last time he'd felt the pain of loss was when he was a kid. Since then, he didn't allow anyone close enough to hurt him again. But he could play the part of a love-sick loser. "You look like someone broke your heart too."

Marianne glanced at him and grunted, then went back to rock her half-full beer bottle on its bottom edge of the table. The music from the jukebox was not too loud.

"I won't press. I'll listen, or I'll stay silent," he said. "There's no reason for you to be alone. I could use a little company myself."

And with that, he was quiet. He suppressed the urge to use his player tricks and just remained with her, peeling the label on his beer bottle.

An hour later, she stood, kissed him on the top of his head and left.

He waited a week and tracked her down again and again sat with her. This time not saying anything at all. As before, after sitting with him, she departed without a word spoken.

Third time was the charm. They spoke. It began with conversations about the pitfalls of dating women and moved on to the perilous topics of politics. They found they had much in common. Hated the same representatives, liked similar foods, and were both tired of the dating scene.

At least that's what Frankie let her know.

And this time, when the night was over, they arranged to meet again.

A friendship grew over a few years. They became closer, and Frankie began to like her as a person rather than as simply a chick he wanted to fuck. He might deny it, but he knew his feelings were true.

Her attitude towards him thawed, and they spent more time together. Eventually the innocent touches and friendly flirting went both ways. He even noticed that she would give him second glances when "he wasn't looking."

Both dated other people, though his "dates" continued to be one-night stands. If Marianne gave the slightest hint of becoming serious with a woman, he would sabotage the relationship. He couldn't risk losing her.

He was careful to do nothing overt. Never interfere in any way that could lead to him. Once he used a third party to help one of her dates to get a job out of state. He thought he was subtle enough that she never knew what he did, but maybe she found out? Maybe that's why he is now shivering in the cool air tied to a stone. Maybe this is his last night to be alive. No. It can't be. Must be some sort of kink, though the game would be better with cuffs instead of rope.

Marianne shrugs the robe off her shoulders. Her body is everything he dreamed. Not that her dresses in the clubs hid much but seeing her form without clothing is in no way disappointing. And her breasts are as magnificent as he expected. He wants nothing but to mash his face between her glorious breasts.

But his hands are tied.

She studies his body, looking him up and down and stopping with her gaze focused on his crotch. With no warning, she gives his dick a gentle flick.

"I thought you were going to show me what a real man can do. That little limp thing isn't up to the task." She caresses her breasts. "I thought you wanted my body."

"Um. I. I'm not into pain or fear." Frankie shivers. "And it's cold." He gazes in her eyes, attempting his best to convey sincerity. "I'm sorry. Trying to hook up with you when you were with someone else was an asshole move. What I said was out of line. I hoped you forgave me."

The glint in her expression doesn't comfort him. "So, the whole cold thing is true?" She caresses his balls. "Perhaps I can warm things up. Let's see what you can do before we start."

Her tone has an edge Frankie can't decipher. He wonders again if she's going to kill him. No matter what, after this night his life will never be the same.

Marianne runs her palm over her body in a manner that would inflame any straight man, and with her other hand, strokes him. Despite the fear. Despite the pain. And despite the cold, he rises to the occasion.

He is, after all, an alpha male.

"It's decent sized." She looks him in the eyes. "I've had bigger dildoes, though not much bigger, and, unlike them, it's warm. I played with a heated glass dildo once. While I enjoyed the heat as it filled me, the thing wasn't flexible at all. Your dick here is just right between hard and soft. A nice stiff core to hit the perfect spots with a cushiony covering of skin."

His male pride can't help but appreciate the compliment, even if conditional. But talk about dildoes doesn't chase away the fear. And that emotion pushes him to be brash and speak. "Heya, babe, why am I tied up? I can work my personal, warm, and well-sized cock into you better if my hands are free." Then maybe he can escape and get far, far distant from this person he thought he knew. What happened to her that made her do something so crazy?

"You're not going to like what's happening at first, but when it's all over you will."

Terror runs a trail of centipedes down Frankie's back. Will she break him? Torture him until he'll do anything to make her stop? Not knowing what she plans to do to him is driving up his heartbeat and causing him to sweat, even in the chill. His mind runs in circles, trying to figure how to escape.

"Come on, babe," he says. "You know I love you. You don't have to do this. And if you really want, I'll promise to never bother you again."

She releases his dick and moves to his side. He groans when she leans over him, her breasts pressing into his chest. She seems to freeze for a second then shimmies side to side, rubbing her glorious globes over him. Then, every muscle in his body stiffens when she straightens upright and has a knife in her hand.

The knife is only about six inches long. The blade has a serpent wave to it and shines silver in the scant moonlight. The tip comes to a sharp point and the cross guard and small pommel are gold. He's focusing on the blade so much he almost misses what she says next.

"Oh, that was interesting. I've never rubbed against a chest with hair." She shrugs. "I'm glad I experienced that once."

"What are you going to do with that knife?" Frankie hates the tremor in his tone.

"This will help you. Trust me. I mean, I've seen you try to hide it. Keep up your macho persona, but I'm more attuned to people than you think. Better than you believe any woman can be.

"I know that at first all you wanted was a good lay, but then you did the right thing. You came and comforted me when I needed it in a way that was not like the asshole I first met. It fit the situation perfectly. Simply one human keeping another company."

"Are you still mad at me?" Frankie racks his brain. He wondered if she discovered how he'd stalked her.

She presses a finger to his lips. "Shhh. You'll understand soon enough."

"Let me go! Please, Marianne, let me go!"

"This won't do. And I thought your pleading might be an issue." She leans down again; this time on her side of the stone, then stands with a small, maybe one ounce bottle, pulls out the little stopper, and brings it to his lips.

He clamps his mouth shut.

"I only need you to listen and stop interrupting." She keeps the bottle close so if he tries to speak, she can pour its contents into his mouth.

"Now, as I as saying," Marianne lays the knife against his chest. "You did a kind human thing, and you kept doing it. No matter your intent, you were what I needed."

She rests the tip of the knife on his skin where the neck joins his torso. No pressure on the blade. "Over the years, I've come to care for you more than as a friend. Of course, being a lesbian, I pretended to be a buddy. And, in the beginning, that was the truth. But, for whatever reason, you didn't pull any of that alpha male crap on me. Instead, you treated me as a friend.

"And, as can happen with long friendships, my feelings grew. I tried to make it brotherly love, and that worked for a while, but then I noticed that you no longer viewed me only as a hook up.

"Oh. You still want to fuck me. You're male, I'm attractive, and I'm not foolish enough to believe otherwise, but you care about me too. Of course, you hide it. You must keep up the macho male front, but I can sense it."

Frankie wants to deny it, but he is more self-aware than he gets credit for being. If he had a choice, he'd avoid discussing his feelings. Not think about them at all. But with a knife resting on his chest, he can't ignore the truth. Despite his love-them-and-leave-them nature. Despite the hurt of the past. Despite the insanity of the situation. He loves her.

Marianne looks away, as if deep in thought, "And the seed of honest caring finally broke through my resistance. Even I, someone whose doesn't find men attractive or arousing, have fallen for you. Love doesn't really care all that much about preferences." She gazes down at him. "But there's the rub."

Marianne sinks the blade into Frankie's chest. He gasps. Despite being tied up, with a knife touching him, he hadn't believed Marianne would stab him. They'd known each other for years. Forged a friendship. She had done nothing in all that time that would have made him think she would kill him.

She was kind to animals and strangers, and she helped friends in need. Her temper was average; angry when proper, but not beyond reasonable bounds. Her apartment was the typical bachelorette pad. No bondage gear. No knives or swords hanging on the wall. No magic circles. Nothing to show she would hurt someone out of anything but self-defense.

When his shock ends, he realizes the blade has stopped a quarter inch into his skin. He looks up at her. Then she draws the blade down his body, and Frankie screams. Pain rips through him like the knife she is using. She pushes the potion aside, apparently no longer worried about interruptions.

Frankie pulls at the ropes that bind him, but they are too strong, and he has no leverage, even with the help of a panic and a pain-inspired adrenaline surge, he can't get free. He's going to die here after she tortures him to death. Confusion joins the other fight-or-flight emotions. He doesn't understand why she'd hurt him like this.

Marianne doesn't stop cutting until she reaches the base of his penis. The long incision bleeds, but not in a gush. While significant, the cut is only skin deep. It harms nothing vital. No major vessels damaged.

She steps back and moves to the side of the rock where his feet are.

Horror jumps through his thoughts as the only thing he can think of her doing from that position is to emasculate him.

"Wait, please, please!" he yells. "Don't cut it off! Just kill me. Or tell me what you want. Please."

She grimaces. "No. I have something different in mind, don't worry. Slicing off your dick would probably kill you. And I don't want you dead. I love you. We only need a change."

Marianne turns the knife towards herself, says "Catlienne," then sinks the bloody tip the same distance in her own flesh over her heart. She hisses and drops the blade. Crimson wells from her chest.

Frankie's fright turns to shock as the blood doesn't drip out of the shallow wound on Marianne's chest, but pours out. She stiffens and her back bows, though she remains standing. Her body glistens, then turns red as blood seeps from her pores.

Blood all but erupts from her, more than any one person could hold. It floats in the air between them, then takes shape, beginning as an oblong blob that grows every second.

Frankie's primitive hind-brain jibbers at him that something horrible is happening. Something out of this reality. Something that should never be. His renewed frantic struggles do nothing but rip at the skin on his wrists and ankles and cause the long cut on his torso to bleed.

The shape continues to evolve, gaining a humanoid form. It's big, he guesses, nine feet tall. And it's female. Large, gravity-defying breasts protrude from the chest. Feminine hips flare below a narrow waist. No hair covers her sex.

Something is wrong with the knees, but his angle and the stone's height don't allow Frankie to see below them from where he is. Six-inch horns sprout from its head, as long black hair grows from the scalp. Gargantuan bat-like wings fold out from the back, and a tail with a spade tip wraps up around the red-skinned demon's waist and plays with its breasts.

"Does this fit the current ideal for a human female?" The succubus strokes a claw-tipped hand across its stomach. "I think I preferred the seventeen-hundreds. The women then were authentic. Had muscle from farm work. How am I supposed to stay stable with this ridiculous waist and these huge tits about to tip me over?"

The reality of a large, naked, red, bat-winged demon standing near him while he is on an alter freezes

Frankie's thought processes. It can't be possible. Is he drugged? Is he in hell?

"It will do for now, Catlienne." Marianne steps from behind the demon. There is no sign of the blood except a small scar on her chest where she cut herself. "So, are the conditions met for you to repay your debt?"

The demon steps to Frankie's side. "Yes. They were all delectable. I especially liked the, what do you call it, 'butch' one? The sense of betrayal she had as I consumed her was so… scrumptious."

Marianne flinches and looks away for a second. She takes a deep breath and turns back. "Good. Are you sure?"

The succubus dips a claw into Frankie's blood, then licks it clean. A small shiver of disgust passes through Frankie. The Demon seems to take a moment to savor, then faces Marianne. "Yes. And are you sure he loves you? That I cannot grant or force. The feelings must be genuine."

Marianne nods. "Yes. It's there. Tenuous for now but growing."

Frankie stops struggling. "Are you sacrificing me to some demon?" He looks between Marianne and the monster.

"In a way." Marianne turns to the succubus, "And he will like it? Will it feel natural and be functional?"

Frankie shouts. "What? What will I appreciate? Marianne, you're scaring me."

Marianne covers his mouth. "Hush, dear. You'll know soon enough."

"Yes. That I can do." The demon's tail strokes his thigh. "It's not stealing free will, not making him love, it's giving accceptance."

Frankie tries to bite the hand keeping him from speaking.

Marianne is deft enough to not allow it. "Make it so."

The demon nods. "Why did you change your wish?"

Marianne strokes his brow with her other hand. "I grew up. I realized eternal beauty is not that interesting and living forever might cause as many problems as it solves. One good life with a person you love is better."

The demon reaches toward Frankie's chest, then looks back at Marianne. "Aw, you removed some of the fun, some of the shock."

Marianne shrugs. "I do love him, so I didn't want his to be traumatized."

Sighing, the succubus worms its hand into the gash Marianne made earlier. Tearing pain distracts Frankie for a moment as the demon pushes aside his flesh. The fingers sinking into his breastbone doesn't hurt. The contrast of the sensation to the various hurts he is experiencing stops his scream before it can form. Pleasant heat radiates from the demon's hand, extending through his body. A less enjoyable ache throbs from his hips and chest, while an awful squirming sensation wiggles through his muscles.

A twisting, spinning strangeness takes over Frankie's mind, scattering conscious thought for an eternity that lasts moments. Then the demon pulls, and lifts Frankie from his old skin, which falls in a flaccid heap on the stone.

Frankie wavers and Marianne reaches for her and helps her stay upright. She strokes her face. "Sorry, love. I know that was frightening, traumatic, and jarring, but this will let us be together. You'll finally get to have me. All of me."

Frankie's lower lip trembles. "What did you do, Marianne?"

"Like I said, what we needed." She kisses Frankie.

Frankie leans into the kiss, savoring it. After years of waiting. Years of pecks on the cheek. Years of nights alone, rubbing one out in frustration, she's at last kissing Marianne. Her wildest imaginings don't even come close.

The warm, wet lip-lock sends electricity through her chest. Her breasts rub against Marianne's sending shivers down her spine. Her clitoris tingles in anticipation of more stimulation. She startles at the sensation.

Wait.

Clitoris!

Frankie leans away and looks down at her new, very female body. She's still muscular, though less bulky. Her breasts are small, and there is no longer hair on her chest. She has breasts? Her six pack is present, yet softer somehow. But the penis she used to be so proud of is gone. Kinky pubic hair hides her vagina from view.

"What the fuck?" The pitch of Frankie's voice is octaves higher than it had been that morning.

Marianne smiles and the succubus rubs its body against her from behind. "Well, it's your chance. Now you can show me what you can do. After all, I am a lesbian."

Frankie's much more feminine scream fails to drown out the succubus's laughter.

A Tiny Dribble of Blood
By Gerardo Serrano R.

The afternoon lied dying agonizingly, soaked in many filthy juices under a lead-colored sky. From the heights, the rain precipitated upon the city and saturated the hard biological mud that covered the pavement of the streets, like a second but brittle skin. The composition of that substance was finely pulverized dirt turned into the muck, trash, crushed and rotten food, and human and animal excrements. So, this rainwater, diaphanous and pure high above in the sky, with simply making physical contact with this mixture of filthiness, was transmuted; without any chemical reaction into a toxic and foul brew.

In those lethargic hours, the night irrupted with its battalions into this tragic kingdom of corruption, exterminating any shine and color which attempted to resist their invasion. They died slowly and vanished into a vast ocean of absolute darkness; each visible object made ill from the same sickness. First becoming blurred and then, its color dissolved into the intense shade of the sky, darkened until it became one with the rest of the universe. But the reign of darkness wouldn't be imposed without opposition. Their armies had to share its sovereignty along with the Pleiad of stars of the public lighting. Hundreds of vertical stairs of dazzling lights, all dispersed along the widespread landscape, conformed complex constellations that crossed the darkened ground. All of them with the same yellow hue of concentrated urine.

The sensation of death was patent everywhere; nevertheless, the sky was full of sparkles, reflected from distant places where life was more dynamic, energetic, and vibrant. The skyscrapers of Edyllica City were visible from that corroded zone. The helicopters hummed in the heights like monstrous dragonflies, and on the Highways, thousands of vehicles ran at every moment.

Edyllica City was something aside. It was protected by walls and guardhouses that stopped the access to whoever weren't members of that privileged kindred, leaving the rest of society like a nasty ghetto crammed with scum.

In the middle of such a landscape, a solitary figure sauntered upon the slippery sidewalks. His broken shoes were moistened as he waded into murky and smelly puddles. *Splish splash! Splish splash!*

More than a man, he seemed to be a spectrum. His hair was mostly gray, but black spots of resistance fought against his senility. His features seemed hewn out of a rock. He wore a brown raincoat that protected his wilted grey suit. The passage of time made his face look hard and folded, and his eyes were reddish due to the prevailing contamination of such a toxic environment.

The rain fell harder, dripping on his face and trickling down into his clothes, stealing heat from his gaunt body. From time to time, he coughed, expelling the phlegm that hampered his breathing. Still, he continued with his relentless ambling.

Irked people glowered at him. Their eyes were filled with blood and hatred. The man saw them but continued his endless walking. They coughed and kept on staring at him. Their anger gnawed their inflamed guts, but they knew him well and feared his revenge, at hands of his apprentice.

His suffering ceased at the moment he leaned on the rusty door of a derelict warehouse, taking shelter under its small frame. He grabbed a handkerchief and scrubbed his face, causing tiny scales of dead skin to float in the dank air.

He removed a key-holder from his pocket, selected a large key, and placed it in the keyhole. The creak of corroded metal produced a shrill and annoying noise. The mechanism resisted for some moments, but, in the end, was defeated, emitting a rattling sound. He opened the entrance and noticed that the doorframe had left behind an oxidized mark.

He closed the door and advanced slowly through a tunnel submerging himself into the darkness, which felt as oppressive as a crypt lost in the middle of a Mayan jungle. Dragging his feet, he expected to find the light switch, but didn't. He kept on advancing until he reached the bottom where a tenuous brightness showed him he was going the right way. His feet crushed all kinds of creeping vermin and debris, which gave to his footfalls a sound of incessant crackling and rustling. *Crackity-crack! Crackity-crack, splut-splat!*

Throughout his path, he heard shrieks of small furry animals begging him to spare their worthless lives, but he stomped them and silenced their exasperating pleads. As he approached his goal, the luminosity increased and illuminated his face. His hands became more self-assured. He advanced his steps confidently until he reached an enormous chamber.

In the middle of it was an enormous bed, illuminated by a gigantic reflector with the form of a bell tower that hung from the ceiling. The man looked all-around and sought a place to hang his raincoat, loaded with all kinds of instruments, firearms, a Taser, and doctor's tools. The floor was made of cement, immaculate and clean, sleek as a mirror.

The old man examined the bed. It was unmade, but the sheets and quilt were so immaculately white that they seemed to be illuminated from within.

The man looked up, but the light was so intense that it blinded him. He covered his eyes and returned to his perusal. He touched the bed at great length, even smelling it, seeing if he could discover a familiar fragrance. There wasn't semen, nor blood; no virgin was desecrated there; neither sweat, tears, liquor, or even the heat of the ones who had lain there. But there it was: a tuft of blonde hair. As he examined it, he noticed it had the scent of fresh flowers, perfume, and was intense… it belonged to *her*.

"Lizzie... Lizzie...

Where are you, little bitch? What did you do now?"

But there was no answer. His face seemed like a dried plot of land plowed by a farm tractor. The old man insisted, his voice thundered in the constrained chamber, "Lizzie…

Lizzie, where are you, little girl?"

He walked toward a door located at the other end of the chamber and opened it. Pale yellowish light illuminated his face. The man walked along a narrow but sumptuous hallway of what seemed to be a luxuriously furnished, secret apartment. The floor was covered with ceramic tiles, the walls decorated with white tapestries engraved with elaborate baroque designs, and at both sides were tables decorated with flowerpots and Chinese vases. Crystal chandeliers of what seemed to be the finest and precious Bohemian glass hung from the ceiling. As long as he advanced, he listened to the sound of a running shower. The sound spread like a low murmur along the dampened atmosphere. Steam traveled along with the air and made it thicker. The old man cut the air with his hand to see better what was in front of him. There was nothing more than an incessant humming, broken lights, a soft sense of heat floating, and a tiny dribble of blood draining from a bathroom door.

The man opened the door and listened to the sweet sound of a thousand violins. Inferring what occurred there, he followed the bloody trace. The marble floor was soaked with puddles of blood diluted with water. The lavatory was smeared with broken cosmetics jars and all types of flasks and vials, scattering their contents like lifeless bleeding things. He directed his steps toward the bottom of the room, toward the running shower. He opened the curtain, and there he found her, lying on the floor. The powerful spurt of water didn't stop sprinkling its fake rain upon her vulnerable naked figure, which rested downcast on the floor. She seemed to be unconscious but wasn't.

Here was the origin of the bleeding; the man could see the open lips of her wild orchid. Her face belonged to a lunatic, stained with red makeup as a mad depressed clown with absent-minded eyes. She was quite alive, masturbating with one of her fondling fingers. Although, it wasn't one of hers, since it belonged to another person's arm; one that had been clipped off. She was lying there, giving little bites to that arm from its most scrumptious part. She didn't stop sucking the flesh, tearing small pieces and swallowing them like a ravenous wolf. The mutilated arm was responsible for the scandalous bleeding.

"Lizzie, what did you do?" The man asked her with infinite patience.

"Nothing... I haven't done anything at all Dr. Sax." The woman rotated her head toward the man, twisting her body slightly until she lay downcast over his feet.

Her eyes remained set onto nothing, her face like a porcelain doll. At that moment, she began to piss, and the blood got mixed with the yellow fluid, mingling their dubious hues.

"I didn't do… anything. The scissors awoke inside of me and I had to make supper, but they got mad and sent me to take a bath... And, as you can see… I am bathing now… I just couldn't avoid it."

"Lizzie... Why can't you control yourself?"

"Nothing... Nothing... I haven't done anything. The scissors arose inside of me and cut my womb... yet again."

"Lizzie, when are you going to change? When will I be able to cure you?"

"I'm crazy."

"No, you're not."

"I am."

"You're not."

"Yes, I am..."

"For Christ's sake," the old man shouted, "How many times do I need to repeat this? You aren't crazy!"

"I want chewing gum," Lizzie cried fearlessly.

"What?"

"I want chewing gum," Lizzie insisted sluggishly.

"Why do you want chewing gum?"

"To put a plug into my ass."

"Why do you want to plug your ass?"

"Because I'm going away right there. My sphincters are... broken, then, I cannot avoid pissing myself out. What do you want me to do? The scissors cut my ass, and I'm going away down there."

"I only have strawberry. Does that matter?"

"No, I like strawberries, but... I like cherry even more... Or tutti-frutti, they're just yummy-yummy to my jolly tummy."

She took the pink cube delicately and placed it inside her mouth to chew it.

"The pleasure is all mine," The man responded, annoyed.

Lizzie's eyes were red. She was intoxicated and, apparently, there was a surplus of stimulants in her bloodstream, as usual. Yes, it was one of those crazy nights in the nightclub, filled with millennial's style of debauchery. Somebody had raped her, and she murdered him in response. Divine justice.

The man delicately placed a piece of toilet paper to stop her bleeding. The girl seemed bothered at the intrusive object but didn't do anything to avoid it. The doctor caressed her vagina and introducing into her mind a new stimulus, a soothing one.

The old man raised her and turned off the shower. He took her outside to the empty chamber, sat her down upon a stool next to her bed, and wrapped her in a plush white towel. He dried her hair and fragments of clipped tendrils fell off. She had cut her hair, almost shaving large portions of the scalp. He swathed her head carefully with towels since she had injured her scalp and bled.

He turned off the lights and switched on the headlamp. Quickly, the man injected the woman with a drug he had ready in his raincoat. The woman didn't fight when the needle pricked her. A begging moan emerged from her mouth. She was suffering a lot, but the drug flowed like a green ghost along her tormented neurons, filling her with heavenly peace. The girl's muscles were plagued with spasms; her vagina throbbed like an open wound.

Slowly, all her vital signs normalized as the drug made its desired effect. While the woman was sleeping, Dr. Sax checked her pupils to verify they dilated with regularity. Then, he verified that her blood pressure had also been reduced. After all of this, he certified that the beating of her heart was normalized. She was asleep; everything was okay again.

The doctor made his way toward a drawer at the other side of the bed where he kept his work instruments. He sought the small refrigerator for a water bottle, and he drank it to appease his thirst.

He could take advantage and rape her, satisfying his most basic instincts; but he chose not to, with the same temperance a Catholic priest should have. Maybe, he opted not to because he felt some kind of fatherly interest for the woman. Or perhaps; yes, maybe, that kind of body didn't awaken any desire in him.

The doctor pondered and examined a flask of pills placed upon the floor. They were her magical antidepressants. She hadn't consumed them regularly lately since the seal was intact. Opening and removing one of the pills, he sought a glass of water, dissolved the drug in the immaculate liquid, and gave it to the woman to drink. Magical drugs, they solve all sort of troubles, such as malaria, dysentery, and measles; also, exhaustion, nervous tension, anxiety, and schizophrenia.

She was sleeping, at peace, as if nothing had occurred there, as if she weren't responsible for anything at all.

***

...Liebe ist nicht echt,
in diesen Straßen Kohle gemacht.

Another night of *despapaye*, of cute and beautiful guys, all horny, all cutie, all preppy and pretty, dancing while the music rumbles in Lizzie's eardrums. She heard a song; she was so happy and followed the catchy rhythm. The name of the artist was Lady Peaches. She listened and sang along with the lyrics:

Love ain't real...
on these streets made of coal.
Everything is made of plastic, steel, and cardboard,
just like your heart is.
Your eyes look at me, what? Why?
Am I made of jelly?
Everything tastes like junk food,
Your knight in shining armor **eloped**
with a dominatrix witch,

Don't be naïve or everyone will use you.
I'm dead inside.
but I have to go to work anyway...
I'm dead inside.
but I must go to work anyway...
Nobody cares about your little tragedy.
The machinery of the world will continue to **work.**
Drinking fuel, sweat, and blood.
But you'll have to get up early anyway.
to go to work
*and bleed till you're **dead.***
if that's what they want from you...

She was taking a long hard look at everything. The stale air was imbued with that sweet stench of ugly, filthy worms. They were sprouting from the ground, twisting, and caracoling in her nostrils. Yes, they, the very unhappy ones. They were seafood soup, chowder, juicy and throbbing. She squeezed them between her fingers as a vengeful goddess, rejoicing in how she crushed them so easily, how she made them ground meat, dead and stiff. Meanwhile, she tore their skin and poured their fluids out, blood and excrement, lymph and phlegm, and snot, a lot of crazy snot. *Mucho moco loco.*

...Alles besteht aus Kunststoff, Stahl oder Karton,
genau wie dein Herz ist...

Lights dazzled her, lacerating her retinas with UV blades as these penetrated her pupils. Her eardrums beat with so much drumming, beat-beat and manifesto, and *traca-traca.* She scrutinized her kiln as they danced and laughed, free from the chains of normalcy. Do you want to dance? All those pretty boys were everywhere. There was a smell of sweet sweat, paired with floral essences. Shoddy perfumes they used instead of deodorant, believing they were *mucho* machos. Their faces had acne injuries, poor, poor pubescent boys! They were hidden in circles of pus under makeup plasters, under the skin of a lacerated, reddish, and infected skin.

...Deine Augen starren mich, was? Warum?
Bin ich ein gallertartige Blob?

She was thirty-five years old. She was pretty ahead of 'em, fifteen years, minimum. But she was luckily a MILF. Fortunately, she wasn't a victim of her hormones anymore, though, I'd be again quite soon, fucking menopause. Blasted men, they didn't suffer from this kind of shit. But I believe some do, ha! Andropause, of course, ha!

…Alles schmeckt wie Junkfood,
Dein Ritter in glänzender Rüstung hat setzten sich mit eine Domina Hexe,
Sei nicht naiv,
oder jeder wird dich nutzen.

They could be her cousins or her little children, products of unwanted teenage pregnancies. Luckily, she wasn't anymore, she thought. She was in a nightclub; the owner was a jerk who thought he was very gringo. Exuberance! Yeah, right! Exuberance her filthy but aerobicized ass! That song blasting through the speakers had a catchy chorus she didn't understand completely. Its words were in German. Of course! She didn't get anything, but these little boys sucked it all up as polyglot's daddy's boys.

...Ich bin innerlich tot.
Aber egal ich muss noch zur Arbeit gehen...
Ich bin innerlich tot.
Aber egal ich muss noch zur Arbeit gehen...
I'm so disappointed.
She was so disappointed.

There was no one there of her high caliber. They were all children who had never worked one single day of their stupid ninny lives. No one had made them feel like worthless pieces of shit, useless goods for nothing. They hadn't made them feel like Mr. Nobodies' pants. They were proud and believe they were important for studying college majors and that was why they had already made it big. They didn't know life was just the beginning. She had exceeded them, but she didn't have any friends to play with tonight. That was why she was so bored and... alone. All those pretty, pretty boys, so helpless and doomed. She was a lioness inspecting a herd of wildebeest and anticipating the taste of blood that soon would permeate her taste buds. So helpless and doomed. She hated them; they had no idea of how much she loathed them. They were stupid, cute, and spoiled. So spoiled and doomed. Ha! She had better go. She was fed up with so much filth. As she thought, she didn't have someone to play with.

The following day she must get up early, exercise, stay in shape; not letting her flesh succumb to the passage of time. She kept herself exercised, with no drugs or surgery, no Botox, and facelift. She removed calories from her diet, full of protein, minerals, and vitamins. She burned fats, kept her fibers firm, burned all traces of carbohydrates. Yes, she knew she was disciplined. She was a metrosexual and was still to the liking of the lofty yuppie. All those pretty yuppies who had come there to play with her. She was a dipsy-tipsy spider, and they'd all fall into her clutches. She wanted to tell them how much she needed them, she wanted to buy them a drink, whatever they like, and they could enjoy the good time that her company would bring them.

Oh, dear, God! She thought.

What a gorgeous stead has just arrived! Tall, refined, finely dressed, and with a hard hanger framing his shoulders. No belly. She would ride joyfully on his lap all night long. His knife-like eyes cross her uterus. What a lubricious fantasy!

His friends monopolized his attention, though.

She must find a way to get his attention.

He must be forty years old and still believed himself not so old as to go nightclubbing. Just like her. What a bodacious ass! Oh, dear Lordy! He was looking at her; yes, that's right, come here, she thought. Come here, I won't hurt you at all. Don't be afraid, darling, honey, sugar daddy-o, I won't hurt you at all, she kept thinking.

"Hello, do you know what time it is?"

"Twelve-thirty."

He raised his arm and showed her his platinum watch. A Rolex Pearlmaster. Then, he sat down and said:

"Doesn't it bother you?"

"What?"

"Don't you dislike that you have to make all kinds of excuses to introduce yourself with someone, all to get to the moment, to the time to say: hello."

The guy exhibited all his Latino Casanova skills. He told her about his work, he was a publicist and a marketer; about his metallic blue BMW M3 car, about his stocks on Nasdaq and Down Jones, about his membership in Edyllica City's most exclusive Country Club, about his expensive apartment in the Atenco Tower. Wow, they were neighbors! Sure, but she was strategically keeping this bit of info for her alone. They drank whiskey and tequila *caballitos*. Then, they swallowed proton accelerator pills, and everything became exciting. She looked at him, enraptured, you're exactly what the doctor prescribed me to keep my cholesterol low… or high, depending on if it's my expert in nutrition or my cardiologist, she thought. So as not to make him suspect, she played the dumb bimbo. He didn't know about all the joys she would feel when she put him right where she wanted him. Her heart anticipated as she segregated saliva, her blood hurried up, her heartbeats increased, lubricity took over her wet cunt. She wanted him. Just for her, absolutely hers, all hers!

…Niemand kümmert um dein klein Tragödie.

Der Motor von der Welt wird weiter arbeiten.

Kraftstoff, Schweiß und Blut zu trinken. They left and went to a motel room she had set ready for the occasion. They were in the apartment's bathroom. When they left the nightclub, the guys watched the left and smiled, knowing what they were going to do. That excited her. Her erogenous zones became hypersensitive. He took out a tiny box, opened it, and spread a white powder in a mirror smudged with greasy fingerprints. Okay, cocaine, all in line with the expected script, she thought. With a short knife, he made five lines. He inhaled two and left the others for her. She sniffed the alkaloid and her arousal accelerated. They kissed, she sucked the breath of the runaway stallion and tasted the flavor of its tongue. It got tangled up and twirled with hers. She felt his solid chest, rock, and flexible steel. She had flexed his muscles, deep down. Her breasts were crushed on the rigid surface of his chest, her nipples swelled and became tender. She felt underneath his groin and held his penis. The stallion exhaled. It was fast. She was just another lonely gringa, that was what he had to think of her, another bimbo he'd fornicate and then leave alone in a cheap-o hotel. Another spring breaker, another season of lonely gringas flying south.

Asshole.

So, she was just another cunt for him, well then, so she said to him: he was only another, another one for her, for her absolute joy and pleasure. And you'd see what awaited him, he, prick, he, absolute so-and-so, boring dunce.

Idiot, absolute imbecile.

She knelled before his shrine; she was a devoted follower of his purplish and bloody god. She kissed him and he beat at the contact of her lips. She opened the temple's curtains and penetrated the Sancta Sanctorum. Music infiltrated the walls, shaking them. She entered the altar where the god was, welcoming him with chaste kisses. He tasted like honey and manna. He looked at her and smiled. She removed the snake from the cocoon, freeing the reptile from the folds that had imprisoned it and she unleashed its mighty power. Its muscles turned serious, and the thang stuck out its tongue. She looked at the potato head and found out that its eyes had been ripped out. He looked at her, blind, willing to spit on her and leave me without dignity. The alien was preparing to throw up. From her back, she removed a sheath. Before the first bite, she placed the glowing blade next to it and decapitated the snake. He cried out, protested, but she stuck the dagger into his ribs and punctured a lung. He slapped her like a wuss, this was so unexpected for him, and she spat out the chewed meat. It fell to the floor, and she saw the marks of her molars on his severed glans. The dead alien bled out on the ground, full of towels and dirty water. As she climbed up his chest, she reached his face. She watched him watching her, terrified, and placed the blade on his throat and slashed it. He didn't expect it, none of this was in the script of his Hollywood movie, but she felt like improvising feminist dithyrambs.

She smiled and saw him bleeding to death. He didn't believe it, was simply incapable of believing it himself. He had always succeeded, had always been victorious, and mocked the defeated ones. Losers of the world, united. Not this time! I mean, I mean. The knife cut off his abdomen and it vomited guts. It stank of manure. She walked away.

...Obwohl du müssest werde früh aufstehen
und zur arbeite gehen,
und verbluten, bis du bist tot,
Wenn das ist was sie möchten von dich...

She opened ajar the door and glimpsed the outside world where she would be aborted in a few moments. There were still people loitering outside, selling drugs, whores offering themselves to the best bidders, all the night fauna that hung around the streets of the city at night. Yes, they were her dreaded enemy. She locked herself in and took off her bloody dress. With a rag, she cleaned her skin and left it all bloody. She put another on and pulled a jar out of her purse. She sprayed the corpse with it, luminol, a substance that made blood and other assorted bodily fluids shine as these were illuminated with ultraviolet light. She imbued her arms and legs with the substance. She put the guy in an obscene pose and took pictures of him with her iPhone. She photographed him and even took an HD video of him bleeding like a pig, like the animal he was. She uploaded them to the Internet and posted them on untraceable blogs on the Dark Web.

When she took her first step out, she almost suffered from a fainting. She closed the door and got out of the room. She advanced in the streets where the little ones strolled looking for having some fun in a nice place. They looked at her and clapped. She must be shining like a fucking Christmas Tree in a trans-trans rave. As she staggered, she grasped on the dresses of these little girls to avoid falling, leaving these painted and they protested. She just ignored them. She saw the entrance of a subway station, her way out, so she hastened her steps. She was getting closer and closer. The police officer looked at her, she gave him a bunch of bills of a thousand pesos, and he pretended to ignore her. She went in, the subway car welcomed her. She exhaled and started running.

After all, the naughty of her has planted the bomb, at any moment it would blow up in—

Ten, nine, eight seven, six…

But some of the guys had come along with her. Yes, it was a part of his anatomy, belonging intrinsically to his being. Yes, one arm, beefy and juicy, to be nibbled by the rodent girl in the sanctity of her private warren, her hidey-hole. She had packed it with his coat and was bringing it along with her.

That would be her supper for the night, yes, a beefy arm, juicy and swelled; before it could get spoiled. Yeah, dude. Spoilers, spoilers.

***

When Lizzie finally woke up, the first thing she saw was her face reflected in a mirror. She was covered with scratches and decorated with the few tufts of sheared blonde hair that had survived the deforestation by her own frantic hands. The only lighting came from the small table lamp, which gave off a golden hue. Lizzie slowly rotated her head and looked at the face of Dr. Sax, who was staring at her with accusing eyes. She closed her reddish eyes and swallowed before collapsing upon her pillow.

"What did you do now?" Dr. Sax asked her with a harsh voice, but he didn't get an answer, so he insisted harder: "What have you done now?" The voice echoed in the middle of the darkness like thunder, and something broke inside the heart of the woman.

"I don't remember... Leave me alone!"

"No, I won't! I won't leave you alone," Dr. Sax responded, forcefully, "The next time the police will discover what you did, and I won't be able to help you."

"It doesn't matter; anyway, nobody would have believed him. After all, ... I am a poor and handicapped lady."

The woman looked at the man who despised her; then, she rotated her head so the light wouldn't hit her in the eyes.

The doctor placed the mirror sideways, approaching it slowly and saying kindly: "I'm worried about your well-being; after all, I'm responsible for what you're doing, spoiled brat. I should make sure you take your medicine punctually, so you won't become mad again, as you did today."

"How did you know?

"What?"

"How did you know I would lose control of myself, Dr. Sax?"

"It was a hunch; I always foresaw that something terrible was going to happen. It's a trembling inside of me, a power that I have. By the way, where is the rest of the body?"

The woman kept silent for a brief moment and responded with a drowned voice: "It's under the bed. There, that thing won't smear my valuable sheets and duvet. I cannot afford to replace them every time I have a whim."

"How did you rip his arm off?"

"With the cleavers... as usual."

The doctor walked in circles as the moon glowed, penetrating through the windows. He walked around the bed with sonorous steps that tormented the woman. She sank her face into the sheets to try to appease the sound of its powerful clock's tic-tocking. His image vanished into the deep blackness and appeared again as a dead planet orbiting around a small dying sun.

Suddenly, he noticed that the woman was crying bitterly.

"What happened? Do you feel remorse?"

"I loved him," The woman said in a broken voice.

"Then why did you kill him?"

"I couldn't avoid it!"

The man approached and sat down at the edge of the bed. He caressed her head as her tears were shed.

Lizzie's face looked devastated by her pain, and she said with bitterness, "The medicine didn't work. I lost control again."

"So, the treatment didn't work. But you must first take it. If not, it won't work."

"This time all seemed to be going on well... I don't know what happened to me. I was a good girl... I don't understand."

"That's why you cut your hair because you didn't want to do what you did."

"I was going to spare his life; I was going to let him go free, to allow him to return to his home... He had suffered enough."

"How long did you have him prisoner?"

"Four months."

"But... If you had let him go free, wouldn't he have denounced you?"

"He wouldn't have... He loved me, too."

"How did you know?"

"Because he felt as lonely as I am... That's how I know."

"Do you know something? I think you're lying. One of your traits is that you're a mythomaniac. You meet that man yesterday and you're fabricating all this sad story, so you won't feel bad with yourself after what you did to him. Yes, after you sliced his throat so coldly. Yes, this man would never see again his family, his parents, or his wife and children."

"Yes! Yes! I know, but I was lonely. I felt so lonely."

"So what? What has that to do with any of this?"

"It has… it has to do with it that I wanted to keep him forever by my side."

"How? How could you keep him by your side if he was dead?"

"Because… If I keep him like a memento, like a souvenir, he would never be able to leave me forever, and ever."

"How could you keep him? How? Hum!"

"I can keep his skull clean and painted. Also, his penis, his heart, his liver, and kidneys. I can keep them in a jar with formol, that's how. Or I can tan his face and make a mask with it."

"Lizzie… you're a crazy bitch. If I wasn't being studying you, I would have let you rot in jail a long time ago."

"I know, Dr. Sax. I know. I know who you are."

Dr. Sax was surprised, looked at her mercilessly, and said finally: "Poor you."

The Lighthouse of Southerness Point
By Sergio "ente per ente" PALUMBO
edited by Michele DUTCHER

The swaying sound of the sea. The apparently unending twinkling of the waves in the near distance. Rising and falling as they reach the coast.

For many centuries men had fished the seas, facing storms and high winds to bring back food. Well, food wasn't what they needed, not anymore. Modern ships had become, with the passing of the years, much safer and comfortable than ever before, but vessels and boats kept being shipwrecked at times, and the crews and their passengers died. This was a fact that no technology seemed to be able to escape so far, or to prevent from always happening. Sadly, this was also what they had undergone, and this too couldn't be changed.

The visiting animals that approached the underwater portions of the vessel – where the sections of the ship became less and less recognizable year after year – while searching for shelters or the prey of the day, didn't mean much to them. And the varied weather on the surface that brought to the aft and the bow a pale sun, or rainy drops and the uninterrupted swash of the billows, didn't draw their attention either.

Standing next to what was left of the radio room, walking the full length of the half-destroyed upper deck, entering the hold full of stench below the surface of the waves, or also going to the upper level of the bow gantries where rust had weakened the metal could occupy part of the day, but it couldn't make you feel better. How could that be of any help, after all? Death had already come, to all of them, and this couldn't be modified, nor removed from the reality.

They were dead so they had no shore that called to them to visit. How could any of it be of any importance? And why should they care?

The group of the few presences slowly moved on, they came and went, again and again, looking like some cloudy vaporous shades with a swirling effect around their figures. Only for some brief moments their traits, and features, became visible, in full, but it didn't last long. Most of the time they looked gray in color, something which resembled a deep, hard breath let out of a man's mouth during a very cold weather. And nothing more.

Clinging to the sensation of discomfort and anxiety that permeated their very being, like elongating protuberances that came out of the darkness that arrived every day at sunset, here they stayed, and continued their otherworldly incorporeality.

And those endless days went on and on.

*****

The two men in their long overcoats were walking along the shore that went up to the old lighthouse. It was early morning, and the younger one with long blond curls, named David Baileguish, was well aware that the wind was becoming bracing as raindrops started hitting the ground around them. Looking ahead, he put his mind to the fact that Scotland was mostly known for its mountains and the beautiful wilderness so international tourists often forgot about the wondrous coasts and shorelines. Many visitors probably still thought of Scotsmen nowadays like people who only wore traditional kilts and marched onto battlegrounds trying to have their enemies scared by yelling and swearing. A nonsensical way of seeing the Scottish and their lands, clearly.

Southerness was a small coastal village in South West Scotland, located approximately two miles south of the A710 between Caulkerbush and Kirkbean. Though the town today was mainly a tourist village, it was only during the summer season that the local bus services to and from Dalbeattie and Dumfries became more frequent. So, this was a pretty lonely place.

The only local landmark was the Southerness lighthouse, built in 1749, making it the second oldest lighthouse in Scotland. It dated back to a time when roads in southwest Scotland were quite sparse so the bulk of trade even between local villages was mainly only possible by sea. It had been decommissioned in the 1930s, but in recent years, around two decades ago, Scotland had decided to make it active again for several reasons, one of those being tourism as it was open to visitors during certain seasons. After the 2020's crisis, certainly all the tourist attractions that came to mind had to be used, making them available to the visitors that started travelling again, hoping to spend their free days in the countryside.

Though wrapped in his overcoat, David felt the cold wind that blew across the expanse of water and, although his face was hit the hardest, the freezing blast cut through his clothes, chilling him to the bone.

Standing approximately 56-feet-tall the lighthouse was situated near a wide beach, with scattered rocks in the area where mud flats came to the surface at times, as well as a few interesting rockpools. At the time when it was completed, roads in South West Scotland were quite sparse, or so he had been told, and the bulk of trade even between local villages was carried out by sea. Dumfries was a major port and there were regular connections with Liverpool and Ireland. Construction on the lighthouse had finally ended in 1749.

This was going to be his new place of work from that day on, the young man considered.

"And up there, as you can see now, partly lying across the seabed and the sandbanks like a beached whale on the shore, stands the *Desna*. You'll get used to the rust of its upper hull that takes on a peculiar color at sunset…" the old lighthouse-keeper named Robert Fredericks told the younger David, while pushing aside part of his gray hair from his face. Despite being 67, he still had a long mophead that covered part of his wrinkled features as that strong and wild wind unceasingly ruffled it.

"*The Desna?*" the other eyed him and asked for more info about that.

"Aye, the *Desna*," the older one replied "A Container Ship flying a Russian flag, that got shipwrecked ten years ago. Didn't you hear about that? Okay, probably not, but its shape will keep you company while you are stationed here, and you'll learn how to appreciate it - the same as the rocks situated along the coastline or the spots of wild lush vegetation growing in patches across the sand, anyway…"

"Well, maybe I saw something about it on TV, but I was only twenty a decade ago, and didn't pay too much attention to it…" David lowered his head in a sneer.

"Aye, of course… you youngsters always bent over your smartphones or listening to music while playing electronic games. You think you're quick in the uptake, but I don't think so…Yer aff yer heid!" Robert conceded in a look of funny regret. "Anyway, you'll find that this seashore is a wonderful place to see wildlife, too: several seals, porpoise and dolphins are occasionally spotted if you like that sort of thing and you dare raise your head to have a look at the sea instead of your damn device…"

David openly smiled. He was thirty-years-old now, and he didn't consider himself to be a youngster anymore.

"About the *Desna*, there's another thing…" the old lighthouse-keeper added. "Well, I don't know, maybe for you it will be different."

"What is it?"

"At times, under the dim light of the sunset, it appears under different conditions…But I'm old, I'm too old for this…" Then, he said nothing more and flung the end of his cigarette into a corner between two rocks. "Anyway, we also had some divers, mostly tourists - there were just four, if I remember correctly - who went out there for

164

sport reasons and then died at sea a few years ago. Approaching a wreck like that from underwater is not always safe: there are metal parts and pointy surfaces, and the *Desna* has a bad reputation for people getting hurt out there. So, be wary!"

David couldn't figure out what his vague warning meant, but he thought it wasn't all that important, after all.

A brief bird's eye view of the history of lighthouses followed, as told by Robert in his own words, as the two entered the building and the younger man had his first look inside. He was certain he would get used to that place very quickly.

"Light at sea..." the old keeper said in his characteristic low and elongated tone. "It was a Frenchman, think of it! A French scientist named Fresnel who invented the special lenses necessary for the modern lighthouses. Made up of stepped concentric circles, those concentrated light into a powerful narrow beam. At that time, in the early 1800s, ships up to 20 miles away could see the light that came from a device that burned oil, preventing them from running aground or hitting the rocks. It was a long time ago. Now things are much better, and more modern, probably more to your liking. You young men of nowadays could never make one of those old contraptions work, so it's a good thing that technology has greatly improved since then."

David Baileguish noticed the clear meaning of his last phrase, that had the aim of poking fun at him.

"But there's one thing, however, that hasn't changed a lot from way back then: this is a lonely job, and despite all of your devices and smartphones, or whatever you are accustomed to reading as a distraction, days usually go by silently and repetitiously. Unless something bad happens…So, it's better when everything goes as expected, with no unwanted surprises, as you'll see, because the unwanted surprises, or accidents at sea, mean trouble. And in that case, *keep the heid*!"

Robert recognized this was the Scottish way of saying: "Keep your head or stay calm…"

The two spent most of the morning talking about what had to be done, and the must-know procedures the younger one had to learn by heart. Then, David asked the older man many things, and the other replied to him above-board and in great detail. After all that, the newly appointed keeper of the lighthouse made his way to the door, letting Robert out. They talked for a few minutes more, outside in the open, their features patted by the winds, and the older man once again flung the butt of another cigarette into a corner between two rocks.

"What are you going to do from tomorrow on?" the younger one asked the older man.

"You mean, after retiring? Oh, a lot of things! The things I was never able to do until this moment," the older man replied making a face, then he explained. "But truth is that mostly I'll be hoatching' doing nothing. Maybe I'll miss that wreck, the *Desna*, at times…but it's not something I want to talk about…you'll see by yourself probably, before long." Then the former lighthouse keeper wished the younger one the best days ahead and went away, eager to have a hot meal and a beer in the nearby village where everyone knew him.

Once back inside the lighthouse and sitting in the wooden chair in what had to become his new bedroom, David thought he'd better know something more about that half-destroyed ship, the *Desna*. He prepared and sipped a cup of coffee and started his search over the

166

internet. The man easily found the news he was looking for about that shipwreck a decade ago.

The wreck was the remains of a 1,700 TEU vessel, a large feeder with twin-engine propulsion and an unusual forward deckhouse. All holds followed an open-top design. Those were ships specifically designed for their trade: in order to sail year-round without problems, they were usually built to very high ice class standards. It reportedly came from St. Petersburg, Russia, bound for New York, U.S.A., and it was during the sea travel that it had gone shipwrecked not far from this portion of the shore where Southerness Point stood.

'*Wow!*' the man considered. '*From St. Petersburg…it might be really cold in Russia this time of year! Never been there, but after all, I've never even been out of Scotland yet.*"

It seemed that the ship had been driven onto the coastline facing the wind once the engines had unexpectedly stopped working during a strong sea storm. The disaster had occurred early in the morning and given its size and weight, the vessel had almost no way to escape from being wrecked. The seafarer's life was a dangerous one, David considered, and the high waves could destroy seacraft large and small. When help arrived, it was quickly obvious that the container ship was going to break up and that keeping its structure in one piece was impossible. The crew seemed to have been entirely saved in the end, at that time, or so the news said, but the wreck had later broken into five sections and was never retrieved – after all, it was still there on the rocks. Obviously, nobody had been interested enough to salvage it, both because of the high cost and the difficulties the operation would have required.

The young man knew that, especially in recent years, container feeder vessels like that, mainly employed in services to the Baltic Sea or to the U.S.A., had seen a considerable growth.

So, the remains of that shipwreck simply had to stay there, against those rocks, and would be in that place until its almost destroyed hull would be washed away from the billows one day.

Wasn't that also the same with the rocks and the shores that were uninterruptedly hit by the waves, and slowly, but assuredly, changed or were diminished until they simply disappeared because of the strength of the water? Almost as old as Earth itself, oceans dominated the planet's surface and all the continents, and modified them at will. The coastlines of every place also underwent constant change. But these were thoughts to be saved for some free moments later, before falling asleep, the young man told himself, and prepared another coffee before planning the next things to be done, of course.

*****

The next dawn came, after the first long and toilful first night of duty, and the new lighthouse keeper went down to the kitchen where he wanted to have a coffee before going to bed and getting some rest. He had done what he had to the night before, and now he was off-duty for a few hours.

When he woke up, it was already past 2 P.M. and he watched out of the window as a thick sea mist formed ahead when warm air blew across the cold ocean water. The man remembered that, before the invention of radar, thick mists like this had made navigation extremely insidious: he imagined himself as a wary helmsman from a century ago, trying to steer the boat while relying on the sound of ships' bells to escape grounding or collisions.

Undoubtedly, many things had changed since that time of old.

David Baileguish put-on his long-sleeved garment made of polar fabric, then went out of the lighthouse and took his time for a short walk around the site before he ate, and his next night's duty started. So, it was at that time that he spotted nearby the wreck of that ship again, the *Desna*. The young man wondered if he might go exploring the large remains of the damaged container feeder sooner or later. He was a good swimmer, he had always been, though the water was cold in that area, even in summer, and there were some strong and dangerous streams that should never be undervalued. But he was curious, undoubtedly. Besides, he was also a good diver, and his equipment had a camcorder to record his finds with a head-mounted camera. The young David had brought all that equipment with him, by chance, because you might never know, he had told himself. But if he ever did decide to dive into the wreck, he would need to pay careful attention, and be wary as there was no lifeguard here to save him if things went badly.

Who knows, maybe on his first free day he might try it, the man considered. He just needed to wait until he had his full 24 hours off duty.

He also wondered what he might find over there, and underwater, if he could reach that part of the ship which happened to be partly stuck in the rocks. The sea could prevent human exploration of a wreck for many long years, but it didn't really protect a vessel from marine life. Sea creatures, which could make a meal of woodwork that kept being eaten away with the passing of the time or chose to attach itself to the metal portions of the remains, might ruin what was left of the vessel as the whole structure slowly fell into visible decay. And he had seen a few wrecked ships covered in sea creatures during his previous diving explorations.

Walking back slowly along the path that led to the lighthouse, the man reached the entrance by 6:00 PM. He had to check to be sure that everything was ready for the night to come, so he made a quick inspection of the lower level.

Once again putting his feet up, the young man took another sip of his coffee and then placed the cup on the desk, his expression turning contented.

As his night of work was about to begin, the young man considered that he had a long time to go before crawling back into bed the next morning. And he never knew what night might bring along, as many things could happen at sea, or near the shoreline of course. He had to keep his eyes open and hope for the best. Many cups of coffee would be his best friends during those hours, anyway…Then, a pleasing sleep would finally be his when the sun rose again, maybe.

*****

David's free day had eventually come, and the weather was not so bad, although spring was still too far away to reach this part of the shoreline. Heavy undergarments were a must-have for a diving activity under such conditions, or it would be too cold for him below where the sun could be of no help in warming his skin. Therefore, David got to the point he had chosen to start his exploration at sea that late morning and began wrapping his body in his dry suit which gave protection from abrasion and possible bites from marine organisms. It was endowed with an air cylinder, the other usual tools he was used to bringing along with him, and a weight belt. That suit was very buoyant, helping swimmers to stay afloat, and for this reason divers needed extra weight based on the volume of their suit to achieve neutral buoyancy near the surface.

An unprotected person who didn't make use of such outfit could easily succumb to hypothermia in those waters, even on a warm day, and he knew very well that sea temperatures were substantially below comfortable, of course. Other than that, when he had first bought his dry suit, he had chosen the best one, though a bit more costly than the rest, as he had been warned that too loose a fit, particularly at the openings (wrists, ankles and neck), would allow cold water from the outside to enter whenever the wearer moved.

Seabirds were presently all around and the occasional great skua flew in the sky, looking for fish beneath the watery surface.

The young man checked the regulator another time, put his gloves on to keep his hands warm and immediately started his racing dive so he could be under the waves as quickly as possible. Soon many little bubbles of air, escaping to the upper levels of the sea surrounded him, quickly left at his back. They looked like small moons that became tinier and tinier, like a space probe on a TV show that was distancing itself from them at a great speed, and the eyes of the man were then able to see clearly underwater. The plastic that separated his cycs from the surrounding liquid was filled with a layer of air and objects around him appeared 33% bigger and 25% closer than they actually were.

The deepest human dive recorded with such a diving apparatus, so far, was 1,089 feet deep, and he surely didn't even want to think about having a try at that achievement. David knew that when sunlight shone into deep water, some colors were filtered out, leaving only blue. In the oceans, at sea and in deep lakes, the absorption of sunlight created varied light zones. Just below the surface lay the sunlit zone, where there was enough light for plants, and this was the underwater area that he usually contented himself with. Deeper than the sunlit zone there was just dim blue light, creating an environment which reached usually no more than 3,000 feet, but he had never dared diving there, because after that point there was only darkness. He mainly liked to explore the shallow seas, and at other times he enjoyed getting to the higher levels of the underwater seabed to collect samples of rocks. But no more than that, of course. For the present day, in a way, the young man hoped that he could also recover some valuable parts of cargo from the sunken ship, the *Desna*, that he had been staring at for a very long time during the previous months at the lighthouse. Of course, not that he imagined that he might really find anything which could be turned around for a profit, but maybe he could find some interesting objects.

As wrecked ships could themselves create problems thereby increasing the likelihood that another wreck would occur, there were a few floating markers that had been put around that damaged ship, displaying clearly where it stood and the danger it might be to other vessels in the area if they came too near the coastline.

Differently from the people who preferred to go inland off the beaten track, hiking difficult trails, he had always liked diving better, when he had some free time. Many lived to dive because they enjoyed the vastness of the underwater world, and it was commonly said that diving was more than just a sport or recreation, even for the few people who were normally qualified scientists and did their field research that way. It was a state of being - and a state of becoming. As David liked to say, becoming a diver made a person different, it made him special, too.

Minutes went by as he spent his free time underwater, heading for the wreck of the container feeder vessel and looking at the seabed while contemplating the streamlined bodies of the many fishes he spotted around. These were mainly twaite shads and European smelts, with their swirling groups changing in shape in an attempt to confuse predators.

He wondered how long humans would be able to see these endangered species before they might one day become extinct. The world's oceans and their climates were also inextricably linked through a very complicated web of interactions, and men and their civilization weren't doing all they could to help protect the marine life. On the contrary, most of the actions perpetrated day by day by humans made everything more complicated for sea organisms around the world.

At a certain moment, the changing color of the sea the young diver saw while staring at the higher level of the water, and the way it was darkening, made him figure out that the weather had already changed on the surface. This wasn't too strange, however, given the time of the year. In fact, once he came up, he found his head hit by a cold rain that had begun to fall from the now-gray sky, which became an apparently endless downpour that hurried David to immediately get back to the shore. Now, whether he was underwater or on the surface didn't make much difference, as he would be drenched all the same. But the young lighthouse keeper was undoubtedly afraid that the changed weather might also cause bigger waves and he certainly didn't want to be caught in the open, and the middle of high billows, if a real storm was moving in.

It seemed a pity though, as he had already reached the first part of the half-sunken ship. In fact, David was between two metal portions of that silent container feeder vessel, with his upper body and his gloves attached to what might have been in the past a portion of the railing, and it would take him some time to get back on land, which wasn't too far, truth be told.

As he opened part of his suit and his upper undergarments appeared – he immediately got hit by the rain. While giving his own chest a comfortable scratch, a detail made him be wary. There was something, or somebody, or whatever it was, not far from where he had resurfaced.

Almost immediately he was certain he had heard a soft breathing from a corner of the remains of the ship stuck next to the rocks, but he was also certain that this wasn't possible. David was definitely alone out there, at that time, and so it had to only be an impression and nothing more... After all, the man concluded that oxygen deprivation from the recent diving might have possibly caused it. Then, the young lighthouse-keeper thought he saw a figure of some sort, or maybe it was just a glimpse of soft light in the corner – but he didn't want to look back.

Anyway, the light gray presence appeared, regardless of what he thought, or wanted. And at that moment he couldn't believe what he saw! *How could he, actually?*

The image he saw before his eyes was real, though partly hidden because of the ongoing downpour, and he couldn't deny it.

With a straightforward shoulder-length cut, and some skinny features, an unknown female figure burst upon the view and she seemed to be staring at him, from the top of a half-open bulkhead covered in full rust. The female form didn't say anything, however. But there were many strange things about her body: the first one being that she was pale, and not well-defined, with faded clothing and two sad, almost lost eyes. Moreover, the young woman, maybe just a girl, seemed to be transparent, as if that was just a figment of his mind.

The man stood still, his feet in the water, as she kept staring in silence at him. Then, David heard different sounds around, and turned his head to check what it might be.

There were others…

Another blonde-haired young girl, half-naked and with a boyish cut, next to a tall one, with dark curls and a much more feminine and prettier haircut. Then, a fourth presence appeared, short and slim, fair-haired and very beautiful. All of them were very enticing…

David would have liked to remain longer in that place, ask one of them - maybe all of them! - questions about why they were here, who they were and so on, but the downpour got worse. He knew that soon the billows would become a real danger if he decided to stay beside the sea any longer. Anyway, it was as he turned his eyes again that he saw that everyone was gone, as if no one else had really been there, other than the diver himself, on the damaged portions of that ship. He became certain that he had only visualized those other-worldly beings in his mind.

Which was also very possible, and the most realistic of the answers that popped into his mind, indeed. Though, those images had looked so vivid, and attractive, and also sad, pale and silent, anyway…

He thought that he would like to know much more about the unusual and unexpected experience he had undergone. Because he wondered, or was perhaps afraid, that such a sight had to be much more than simply oxygen deprivation because of his previous dive, actually.

*****

Once back in his room inside the lighthouse, an out-of-sorts David took his time thinking again about what he had seen, or what he believed he spotted near the wreck of the vessel named *Desna*. He had never been one of those individuals who took ghost hunting seriously and had always thought that so-called paranormal investigators - who used specialized equipment such as EMF meters that detected localized changes in electrical fields and infrared cameras - were merely curiosities, good for TV shows or weird movies. But when he ascertained that his camcorder – the one he had brought with him during his dive that day – hadn't been able to record any footage of that first presence, nor of the others, he got worried. If those appearances had never been real, and he himself had imagined it all, did it mean that, possibly, he was going crazy? Were these the first symptoms of an illness of the mind? If this was the answer, well, that was something to be afraid about.

The young lighthouse-keeper researched the web and discovered that, contrary to his beliefs, there happened to be millions of people worldwide who thought the energy of the deceased was a fact and were passionate about such things, despite the fact that science hadn't been able to produce evidence that ghosts existed. The conclusion he had to draw, and that he found on many sites, was that, perhaps, it was modern science itself that hadn't evolved enough, or was too distant from common people, to entertain the idea of paranormal events. Who knows…?

Ghosts were as old as humanity itself, actually much older than religion itself. Or so legends from ancient times seemed to repeatedly say.

Contrary to what caution told him to do, and the fear he had felt that day, the man decided he had to go back there, at least one more time. He wanted to know! And he only let two days go by before he chose a sunny morning to try again. He put on his dry suit and started diving to get to that place where the lonely *Desna* was situated, not far from the shoreline. He had to see for himself what might happen…

And when he approached the remains of that ship, and got below the surface, he found that they were on the wreck, exactly as the previous time. The four young and beautiful women of unknown origins, those unearthly appearances were simply waiting for him. The first one, with her unmistakable shoulder-length cut, moved towards him while displaying her pale skinny body that happened to be perfectly visible as she was half-naked. She continuously stared at the diver as the distance that kept them apart became less and less. Finally, three more female figures came to the scene: the blonde-haired young girl with a boyish haircut; the tall woman with dark curls; and the fourth presence, short and slim, fair-haired and beautiful, as well.

All those women were wondrous, attractive and overwhelming. Despite the strange occurrence of them being there now, as they were unearthly creatures that couldn't be explained otherwise, the young man didn't feel worried, nor was he afraid of what they might be and of their otherworldly traits, or of what they could want from him. His eyes just couldn't be averted from their beautiful forms, and it was at that moment that he understood he was ready to do anything to be with them, to do whatever they wanted, and accept their will.

Of course, unbeknownst to David, he could imagine nothing about who those creatures really were. **Nelaikis** was the name of such ghosts, the souls of Lithuanian girls, people who had been victims of murder, or that had drowned or committed suicide. Such unearthly beings were well-known in their native country. Now that they were dead, this was what they had become, and this was the place where they now existed. Filled with sadness about what had occurred, wrapped in their strange conditions and with no purpose, and no end. They had been removed by force from their homes in far Lithuania, taken away from their parents and families, convinced through deception with the promise of a job abroad and then being hit, and hit again, eventually enslaved. They were finally brought at night in secrecy to the port of the second-largest city in Russia, where the few girls had discovered that their new residence would be New York, where they would be used there as sex workers forcibly and helplessly. And then the metallic walls of the container they had been sealed in, for the length of the sea journey to the U.S. They had experienced the terrible stench and dirt because no one had ever cleaned that place. Once imprisoned inside, and loaded onto the container feeder vessel named *Desna*, their desperate cries for help had been of no use as nobody ever came to free the poor females.

Their imprisonment continued for days, until the journey met an abrupt end. They didn't even know where they were, what part of the world they had arrived at, when the wreck occurred, and the water started entering everywhere once the ship rolled onto one side and then to the other before the sudden stop occurred. The watery deaths they had undergone in the end had been painful indeed. Only silence had ruled over the site for some time. But it hadn't really been the end to them, as their conditions indicated they were dead and yet, at the same time, also undead…

But nothing could make the bloody experiences they had faced, and the sad outcome they had met here, at sea, disappear from their mind, especially the night when the vessel had gone shipwrecked and the crew had left the decks. The other men aboard had been saved, but it was too late for them, as nobody else knew of their presence in the container, and no one would ever come on time to open it and let them out alive. Nobody would ever think of them again.

Now those girls were dead – and at the same time they weren't, at least not completely. They envied the existence of the living beings, whom they also disdained and hated because of all the suffering they had been forced to undergo, because it had been men who had taken them away from their land and had loaded their bodies like common merchandise ready to be sold elsewhere, at the other end of the ocean - the same as meat, or cheap products.

Certainly, they were unable to change their view, and their mind, nor could they forget their hatred, now that were not alive anymore, though not really blotted out.

Under the very strong incantation of those ghosts, and driven by that beautiful and surely overpowering sight, the young diver started removing his dry suit, and his protective undergarments, his gloves included, and despite the coldness of the sea that surrounded him, regardless of the sensation of pain and the growing torpidity of his arms, legs and the whole skin, he kept going, swimming through that water that enclosed his body, whose liquid reached his senses and clouded his mind, causing loss of consciousness, self-care, reason and the necessary attention he should have been paying. And so, he disappeared under the surface, never to be seen again. In the end, he was unable to protect and save his life.

*****

When Robert Fredericks got back to the lighthouse of Southerness Point after hearing the news about the disappearance of the newly appointed young man, David Baileguish, his mind was full of many thoughts, and he was a bit dejected. He thought that maybe he hadn't warned the new lighthouse-keeper strongly enough. The graying man also considered that, as far as he was concerned, he was too old to surrender to those beguilements, or too rational to follow those unearthly ghosts of the beautiful women.

Of course, he knew of those young girls, the fabled presences of the half-sunken vessel, who seemed to reside there, and he also knew of the previous strange deaths that had occurred near that area, when tourists had reached that site while diving underwater not far from there. Perhaps this was what had happened to that young man as well. The former lighthouse-keeper wasn't sure he would be believed by others, though he had been living and continuously working in that building for years and had seen many things and unexplainable sights. Maybe it was different for every individual, what people saw and the attraction they might have when it was put before them.

Or maybe it was just that his desire for sex, or his lasciviousness had long gone, given his present age, and he couldn't be tempted nor aroused anymore by the image of a half-naked beautiful young woman, and of her friends that might be spotted on those rust-filled bulkheads. Whether the beautiful ghosts he had seen himself years ago was merely the deceit of a feeble mind, the true souls of a dead person, or creatures of the sea that appeared under different shapes and characteristics at times, he could not say.

It was possible he had just been staring at the sea, lonely, for too long because of his job, and he knew the secrets of the water, the coldness and cruelty the sea held, and especially the particularity of that shoreline. Or probably he himself had just become too cold-hearted and irresponsive to that all after so many years spent in that place.

As Robert sadly looked at the expanse in the distance before moving away, in silence, he reminded himself of the words he had learned by memory long ago from the famous Early Naval Ballads of a time of old, that went, more or less, 'You gentlemen who live at home at ease, how little do you think on the dangers of the seas?'

She Has My Heart
By Sonny Zae

"Get up!" Ramon hissed, glancing around the mid-day alley. He poked through the layer of trash to prod Nash awake. "What the hell are you doing sleeping here?"

"Huh?" Nash sat up, bumping his head against the top of the dumpster. "Ow!" He scowled, brushing a layer of trash and rotten food from his partially-decayed body. "I was laying low, waiting for night, and ... well, fell asleep."

"Come on," Ramon gestured toward the open sewer grate in the middle of the alley. "You shouldn't be above-ground during daylight--even in Hollywood. If I wasn't looking out for you, the Living would have locked you away long ago. And you should *never* be so close to the edge of Cannibal territory."

"I'm coming, I'm coming," Nash grumbled, brushing off coffee grounds, a decomposing fish carcass, and globs of cooking grease. "Don't be so pushy. I covered myself in rot and filth. No one would've found me."

"I found you, didn't I?"

"Yeah, but only because you know me. No one else would have looked here."

"I don't think you were hiding." Ramon watched Nash sniff the fish carcass and nibble tentatively. "It looks like a hobo trap."

"What? No!" Nash climbed out and followed Ramon to the sewer. They crawled through the sewer until they arrived at a familiar spot. Metal rungs set into the concrete extended up a vertical shaft to a higher level. The lower rungs were buried in human skeletons.

"I thought you were going to clean up?" Ramon exhaled theatrically. "I took out the leftovers last time."

"I will." Nash grunted as his foot tangled in a ribcage. "Let go." He jiggled his foot free, then climbed the ladder, preceding the older zombie. "Got any food left? I'm feeling empty."

Ramon wasn't ready to let go of his proverbial bone yet. "What *were* you doing?"

"Uh, nothing," Nash replied, glad Ramon couldn't see the color rush to his face … assuming it could even happen. He'd lost his blood when he'd turned zombie. "Waiting for night, to hunt."

"What Living did you have your sights on? Were you lurking where trash addicts hang out? Near a concentration of Sewer Stevies?"

"No."

"Don't tell me you were trying to bring down a healthy member of the Living?" Ramon asked, an edge to his voice.

"No, no, of course not." Nash exited the vertical shaft and reached down for the hand of his friend and mentor, helping him up. He shouldn't feel wary about talking to Ramon. If it weren't for the older, more experienced zombie, he might not have survived. As Ramon repeatedly reminded him.

But the girl zombie he'd seen, well, she was special. And Ramon wouldn't understand.

Ramon brushed past him. "What the hell's the matter with you? You lose your mind in that dumpster?"

"Uh, thinking about food." Nash's guts clenched from the lie.

Ramon preceded him into the dead-end sewer section they called home. "We should go east on our next hunt. The Bonemarrow Gang is good at chasing food out of their territory. If we wait at the old, abandoned drugstore on Driftwood Lane, we'll be in ambush position when their prey escapes. I'd like some hot lunch delivery."

What the older, more experienced zombie really liked was the Bonemarrow Gang scrupulously observed the boundary. Bonemarrows wouldn't follow prey escaping into the unaffiliated territory of Putrefaction Palms, where Ramon and Nash lived and hunted--along with an odd assortment of other loner zombies. Ramon wouldn't admit such a thing, of course. Nash had argued the point with the older zombie many times, but Ramon always maintained his hunting preferences were based on years of experience and a well-earned sense of caution, that he'd survived more than a dozen years unnoticed by feeding on the homeless and dispossessed.

Ramon disliked and feared the zombie gangs, and would never declare fealty to a zombie lord, despite the protection and pack hunting such gangs offered. He was a bit stiff-necked about that. Ramon was a bit stiff about a great many things, being an old zombie.

Nash looked down at the semi-circular bite in his forearm. Ramon's precision was admirable. Another zombie would have tugged and pulled, tearing his arm off. Not Ramon, knowing proper bite placement and depth to excise a mouthful of muscle, without connective tissue getting caught in his teeth.

Despite the bite, Nash didn't remember Ramon chomping him. And he couldn't really remember much about his time as a Living. Probably due to head trauma suffered in the car crash.

"Well, it doesn't matter," Ramon said, sorting through the stack of bones and limbs against the end wall of the tube. "There's a spleen or liver here somewhere. We don't need to hunt tonight. I'd suggest we reconnoiter, instead. Since it's almost October, it's time for Los Angelenos to migrate, shifting from Hollywood spas and shrinks to those spas and psychotherapists farther east."

"Um, sure," Nash mumbled. "You go east. I think I'll prowl our neighborhood."

Ramon stared at him as if trying to read his thoughts. "Okay," he said at last. "Avoid the border. You know how territorial Corpsicana's soldiers are."

"I'm not worried about the Corpsicana Cannibals."

"Stay away from the border!" Ramon snapped. The older zombie's tone softened. "I don't want anything happening to you, kid. You know that." Ramon squinted at him. "You feeling alright?"

"Feeling a little weak from hunger. I'll take the liver, if you can find it."

Nash ate the liver slowly, waiting. Ramon finally left for the Sunrise Street manhole, but not until after one a.m., per his self-imposed safety rule.

Nash felt odd, despite acting normal. Something had happened while he'd been asleep. He didn't feel sick, more like his sense of well-being had been set a-kilter.

Nash pulled up the tatters of his dirty, bloody shirt, the one he'd been wearing during his fatal car crash. The shirt was patterned with wide red and white stripes, now torn and worn and stained until the original stripes were barely distinguishable--his lucky shirt. The diagonal tear in his abdomen was still there, unchanged. He reached in, feeling around. His stomach still resided in the correct spot, although the degree of rot on the lower portion had increased, despite his constant eating. One of Ramon's first lessons was that zombies had to eat constantly to replenish themselves. A zombie couldn't be killed, but a zombie who didn't eat could rot completely away.

He felt the bottom of his right lung. His liver was still there. Above that… Where was his heart? His fingers scrambled around inside his ribcage, searching for the blood-pumping organ, important even though it served no purpose in the undead. He found the torn-off end of an artery or vein.

The shock brought back a dream he'd had, a young woman's face framed in the opening of the dumpster's hatch, staring down at him. No, it hadn't been a dream, though it had seemed dreamlike because he'd fallen asleep afterwards. She'd been beautiful, her long hair exquisitely greasy and lumpy, tangled like she'd brushed with an eggbeater. A couple of teeth could be seen when her lips parted, protruding from grayish gums like scattered yellow gravestones in an abandoned cemetery.

Her hollow cheeks were untainted by any suggestion of blood, her skin more translucent than cheap toilet paper, real enough to be seen but too thin to hide anything. Something squirmed inside her cheek. It was her tongue, he realized, now a delectable blue-gray. Corpus delicti. The thought came to him, as if his subconscious were choosing a name. Though the term referred to crime investigation, it seemed perfect for this angelic zombie girl. He saw a distorted reflection of himself in the puckered skin of her eyeballs, a misshapen human form sprawled in the dumpster like another discarded item of rotten food, his mouth gaping like the fish carcass beside him.

She'd reached down and he'd felt a tug, followed by a sensation like a rubber band snapping. She'd held up his heart for a moment, staring at the purloined pump as if deciding whether it was worth keeping. He'd noticed the pendant on the necklace she'd worn, a small corpse figure dangling on a delicate silver chain. Then she'd disappeared and the hatch clanged down, leaving him alone in the dark with no heart.

He had to find her. Had to demand an explanation. Why had she stolen his heart? Was this some zombie ceremony Ramon hadn't told him about?

He had no idea where to look, so he headed toward the sewer outlet near the old shopping mall, where he'd seen her before. It was close to the border. Did her necklace symbolize membership in the Corpsicana Cannibals gang? Maybe he'd get lucky and stumble across her. He was a zombie after all, and stumbled over most everything.

Nash peered out from under a manhole cover. No Living were about in the Hollywood night.

He crawled up onto the street, then moved to the shadows behind a nearby store. An ambulance siren wailed in the distance, a hunter of another breed. He felt a kinship, as it also sought out freeway pileups where oil and radiator fluid mixed with the blood of the Living. Tasty blood! Nash licked his lips. Maybe he should have eaten more before prowling.

He moved down the dark alley. Ahead was an open space where homeless congregated. He'd found more than one good meal in the double lot between stores, a gap left by a long-ago fire, filled in with grass and trees. After ten at night, Shambledown Park was the exclusive domain of Outdoor Americans.

He slipped behind a dumpster to observe. A Gutter Guy and Park Princess walked arm-in-arm toward Nash. He pulled his head back. But they hadn't seen him, climbing into the dumpster, closing the lid and engaging in loud sex. Nash was tempted to make it a threesome (*menage a kill*?), but there was too much chance they'd scream before he could stab both. Instead, he endured the occasional squeeze against the brick wall as the dumpster bounced and jiggled.

Nash experienced a pang of memory, of making out in the backseat of his car, darkness and sweaty embraces, his tongue exploring the girl's mouth. He remembered the smell of her perfume as he pushed a hand under the waistband of her jeans, the fevered excitement as he'd unhooked the clasp of her bra.

His reverie was interrupted by the clang of the dumpster lid striking the brick wall above him. They'd finished already? The homeless woman cried out in alarm. The dumpster slammed him against the wall. The male derelict shouted, fear in his voice. Nash poked his head out. A figure raised an arm, a gleam of metal in its hand. The arm slashed down, followed by a bubbling groan and the frantic scratching of fingernails on the metal sides.

He peered around the corner again. The attackers were climbing in. They weren't from the Putrefaction Palms unaffiliated territory. Were they Corpsicana Cannibals? Nash suppressed a shudder.

The attackers feasted on the hobo lovers inside the closed dumpster. He smelled the fresh blood and licked up the trickle leaking out the corner. When they ripped open the peritoneum of a victim, the smell made Nash's mouth water. Since becoming a zombie, it was the sweetest smell, like flower nectar to a bee.

He thought of Ramon's rule: never kill more than you can eat--or stash. Ramon had lectured him about the dangers of the Living learning of zombies hiding among them and picking off occasional meals.

The invaders took their time. It had to be at least two hours before the dumpster lid squealed slowly open. They muttered softly to each other as they climbed out.

There were three. One had the flesh of his left cheek sheared away, as if in an industrial accident, and the left jaw joint hung free. Half-Face gestured for one of the zombies to scout ahead as he and the other zombie threw sacks of meat over their shoulders. "She'll be pleased with our hunt," Half-Face muttered. "No depleting our territory."

The "she" had to be the zombie girl. Nash followed as they went east, passing through a shipping district with high chain-link fences that offered no concealment. He could hear Ramon's admonishment. "Never be farther than two seconds from cover." But there was little in the way of lighting, the darkness punctuated only by an occasional security light.

When the trio neared the Corpsicana Cannibal border, they moved faster. They trotted when a city water treatment facility came into view. The invaders clawed their way under the perimeter chain-link fence and entered the main building. Nash followed shortly, slipping inside. He held still for several minutes. No sound. His eyes adjusted to the blacker darkness. The cavernous interior rumbled with the sounds of equipment. A light on the other side of the space dimly illuminated pipes and pumps. To his right was a control panel of flickering lights and illuminated dials. To his left were moving shapes. He crouched and moved forward.

He made out four shapes. The new shape was female, looking like the girl in his dream, the one who'd ripped his heart out. Nash's fists clenched. Time for payback. But first he'd get his heart back--assuming she hadn't already devoured it.

The three male zombies bowed and departed. The female looked to be about his age and carried herself with an air of authority. A jagged leg bone stuck out from the fabric of her jeans. He wondered what her marrow would taste like, then banished the thought.

Nash took several minutes to work up his courage. Were others nearby? He'd have to chance it.

He stepped out from behind the industrial cabinet he'd been lurking behind, hands raised. "Uh, hello."

She whirled, crouching in a defensive posture. "How did you get in here?"

"I followed your men. Are you part of the Corpsicana Cannibals?"

"Who're you?" she snapped, eyes ablaze. They were deep green, the color of an algae-choked pond.

"I'm Nash. I'm here because you … well, you stole my heart yesterday. I was sleeping in a dumpster near Sunset Boulevard. You opened the hatch--it was late afternoon, so I don't know what the hell you were doing out and about during daylight--and you looked down on me, laying there in the trash … and you ripped my heart out and left."

"Oh." She scowled. "What were *you* doing there?"

"I live in Putrefaction Palms. You, on the other hand, were out of your territory."

She crossed her arms. "What're you going to do about it?"

"I don't care about that, really. I want my heart."

The corners of her mouth pulled down. "And if I don't want to give it back?"

Nash hadn't considered that option. He could try to over-power her, but other zombies were probably within hailing distance. "Why did you take my heart?"

Her lip curled. "Don't get any ideas. You're no catch."

"Yeah, maybe not." Nash leaned against machinery. "If it's nothing great, why not give it back? Maybe you sense I'm a good person. Uh, zombie, I mean." He flashed a smile. "My friend tells me I'm too naïve, that a zombie who trusts others won't last long. But I don't think you wish me harm."

She stared at him for a long moment. "Maybe, maybe not. I don't know anything about you."

"I'm Nash."

"Carolanna."

"That's a pretty name for … for…"

"For an undead woman?" Her hesitant smile seemed genuine. "Your friend's right."

Nash held his arms out. "Well, if you were going to harm me, you could have done so by now. I'm unarmed … and alone."

She put an object on a nearby shelf, a knife she'd been holding behind her back, the blade crusted with blood. "I admire your honesty. You came here to reclaim an unnecessary organ?"

"Well, no." If he were one of the Living, his face would be turning red. "I also wanted to see you again. You … your face was so beautiful, looking down at me. I wanted to see you again, and…" Too bad he hadn't thought about what to say. "Um, have you eaten anything? I know this place where they serve the most wonderful carmelized cardboard camper, swimming in red gravy."

She licked her lips, her bluish-gray tongue traveling over the cracks in them as if searching for trapped blood. "Sounds wonderful."

Nash took advantage of the opening. "Last time, a guy had an array of skulls he tapped on, playing *Don't Fear the Reaper*."

"Sounds nice," Carolanna said, fluttering the eyelashes of her right eye. Her left eyelid lacked lashes, for some reason. It gave her an exotic, unbalanced look.

"How about tomorrow night?"

She frowned. "I gotta work." She blew a clump of hair from her face. "If I asked for a night off, the family would want to know. How could I tell them I met a zombie my age from neighboring territory and didn't eliminate him?"

Nash drew back. "Why would you do that?"

"We're the most powerful zombie clan because we eliminate the competition. How many zombies are in your territory?"

"I don't know," he hedged. "Look, I could have killed your men tonight. I could have killed you--if I were like your family."

"True." Her eyes narrowed. "You risked your unlife to find me?"

"Yes. Wouldn't you rather have an ally? I could have planted evidence of zombie presence in your territory for the Living to find. How would you feel if they came looking for you?"

She exhaled a blast of air. "You'd do that?"

"Putrefaction Palms may not outnumber you, but we can be ruthless, too!"

"Okay, you've made your point. Plus, you're kinda cute. But I still can't tell my family about you, Nash. It's better if they don't know I'm … going on a date."

"Why not?"

"Because then they'll want to know who you are!" she snapped. "And if you're not a Corpsicana Cannibal, there'll be trouble." She shook her head, causing an ear to swing alarmingly. "I'm the granddaughter of Carlito Corpsicana. I can't date some random zombie."

"Oh." His heart sank. Or it would have, if he still possessed it. "But is there any possibility…?"

She exhaled loudly. "Nash, I'll need to arrange some free time. How about we meet in a week?"

Nash straightened his shoulders. No sense in acting disappointed. "One week, then. But you still haven't answered my question. Why did you steal my heart?"

She tossed her greasy hair. "I'm a woman. It's what we do."

\#\#\#

A week later, he met her at the border at half-past midnight. Ramon would chide him for not waiting until after one in the morning, when he was unlikely to encounter the Living--there were worse things than zombies crawling around Hollywood's dirty streets in the middle of the night. But Ramon wasn't here, and he didn't feel like being careful.

She wore black yoga pants and a top with a stripe of black sequins. The sequins gave a rippling, distorting appearance in the dim light. Her hair had been swept to one side, clumped together in a shapeless mass. He wondered how much effort it must have taken her. The effect was elegant, stunning, like a Hollywood starlet in the process of decomposing. Good thing he'd worn his lucky shirt.

"Where to?" She slipped her hand into his. He delighted in the reassuring coldness.

"My favorite restaurant. They serve only the finest cuts of the Living. They have four Michelin stars … they serve roadkill run over by a car riding on four Michelins."

She laughed, like the tinkling of razor blades on a marble counter.

"Why did the zombie get a job as a waiter?"

"I dunno. Why?"

"He wanted to serve his fellow man."

She giggled. "You're funny."

He led her down alleys and through sections of sewer, stopping in another non-descript alley. "You can't see the sign, but we're behind the Hollywood Meat Cute butcher shop."

"Why here?"

Nash chuckled. "You know what they say in Hollywood, if you meet cute, then happily ever after is a foregone conclusion."

"You're a romantic?"

"Yeah." He pointed at a fenced compound behind the shop. "Kate-On-A-Plate's in there. They have a thigh meat skewer to die for, the *Bob Shish-Kabob*."

Nash leaned a shipping pallet against the fence and helped her climb up. "Mind the barbed wire."

"What do I do at the top?"

"Let yourself drop. There's a pallet on the other side."

Carolanna swung a leg over the fence. There was a thud and a curse from the other side. "You didn't have them lined up."

"Sorry!" Although zombies could absorb a vast amount of punishment, no zombie wanted to get hurt. It was a lesson drilled into him by Ramon, eat enough to prevent rot, even when you don't feel hungry, and don't take unnecessary risks. Although a broken leg wasn't painful like it was for the Living, it would slow one down.

Nash threw himself over, landing on Carolanna. One of her bones cracked. He leaped to his feet. "Oh, hell! I thought you'd moved. Can you walk?"

She took a tentative step, limping noticeably. "It's not too bad." She brought out a strip of cloth and tied it tightly around her calf. "Should hold for now."

"You want me to get you home?"

"No need," Carolanna replied. "Doctor Lee'll make a small incision and drip in super glue while holding my bones in place. I'll be as good as new."

"You've done this before?"

She drew up her sleeve to show a deep, open cut on her arm. "It's no big deal."

Nash rapped on the metal door of the waste disposal building, cinder blocks with a metal roof, built like a small fort. The butcher shop knew their food waste was a magnet for street eaters and dumpster diners, but remained unaware of the zombie bistro operating in the middle of the night.

"Table for two," Nash said, gesturing for Carolanna to precede him and slipping the maitre d' two homemade knives. The maitre d' led them to a table near the slurry tank where small bits of gristle and bone decomposed.

"Nice," Carolanna observed, sniffing appreciatively at the open door of the incinerator where a human leg turned on a spit. "I love the smell of burning hair and crisping skin."

"They serve meat with more than a touch of pink." He boasted, pulling out a chair. The interior was lit by candles at tables and the flickering, dancing flames of the incinerator. Through a door to another room, they heard the sounds of meal prep, sawing noises and occasionally the thunk of a meat cleaver. "I told Kate I was bringing a special lady."

"Oh?" Carolanna arched her eyebrows and fluttered her one set of eyelashes. "You must have some clout."

"Your hors d'oeuvres." The waiter slid a plate onto their table.

Carolanna picked up a skewer and took a bite. "I love finger food."

"Mind the nail."

The waiter brought sangria. It was sweet, despite the floating clots of blood and muscle fiber. Carolanna rolled her eyes at the delicate taste.

Nash tipped his goblet up as if drinking. Now wasn't the time to tell her he'd been a vegan while alive. As much as he craved the flesh of the Living, he still felt a secret shame. Normally he could press back his guilt, but tonight his stomach was kicking up a fuss.

"I'll have the *Hank steak*." Nash told the waiter. "The *Sven Ceviche* is also quite good."

"I'll have the ceviche," she said to the waiter. "You come here often?"

"Not as often as I'd like," Nash admitted. "Last time, my friend Ramon and I were celebrating my two-year zombie anniversary. How long have you been zombie?"

She shrugged. "Nine years. My family killed me at eighteen."

"They what?" Nash exclaimed, rising to his feet. He received reproving looks from the staff, who avoided calling any attention to the restaurant's presence. Kate's reputation was strictly word of mouth--but was also known for various other body parts served.

Nash shook his head in disbelief. "Your family *murdered* you?"

"You could say that." She twirled a wisp of greasy hair. "They wanted me to join them. How'd you become zombie?"

Nash took another sip of sangria slurry. "A car wreck, driving too fast, hurrying to pick up my girlfriend. I hit a tree and was pinned inside, time passing as I watched my blood drip. Then everything faded out."

"How many girlfriends have you had?"

"Only one. I'm not one of those *love 'em and eat 'em* types."

"I wish my change was accidental." She sipped her drink and nibbled another finger. "I was angry at my family for a long time." She chuckled. "No one can carry a grudge like a teenage girl. But I eventually forgave them. This Ramon, he's family?"

"No, he took me in after biting me and taught me to survive. I would have starved or been caught by the Living without his help."

She smiled across the table. "You must be grateful."

Nash shrugged. "Mostly. But he can be a bit bossy. He has all these rules, like no hunting alone, no hunting before one in the morning, and no going out during daylight ever."

"Very sensible." Carolanna laughed at his scowl. "Hey, he cares about your welfare. If he was a loner zombie, you gotta appreciate the effort."

"I suppose." Nash forced a smile.

Carolanna leaned forward. "I'm your first zombie girlfriend?"

"Yeah." He leaned forward too, pursing his lips.

She drew back. "Too soon. I come from a very traditional family."

Nash drew his shoulders back and pasted on a smile. "When can I meet them?"

She made a non-committal noise. "Let's focus on the present, okay? My grandfather is grooming me to take over, so my duties keep me busy."

"Fine. But when can we meet again?"

"In two weeks. I'll meet you here."

"Okay." Nash tried to sound nonchalant. Inside, something was gnawing at his heart. It would be the longest two weeks of his unlife.

###

"What do you mean, you met a girl!" Ramon roared. "You've been out flirting with some stranger, ignoring my rules of survival? You *want* to get caught?"

"I didn't intend to fall in love," Nash protested, surprised how well Ramon was taking it. Even though his initial impulse had been to keep Carolanna secret, sooner or later Ramon would suspect.

"You lied to me!" Ramon snarled. "Slipping out under my nose. Am I not good enough company?"

"I wouldn't do anything to hurt you. I owe you my Unlife." Nash spread his hands. "I met her by accident."

"And?"

Nash took a deep breath. "You're always telling me to follow my heart, right?" He waited, hoping Ramon would soften. But the other zombie stood there, a look of shock and anger on his face.

He put a hand on Ramon's shoulder. "You're still my best friend."

"Yeah, okay, I…" Ramon sat down. "It's just … I thought we'd be friends for years and years, sharing the hunt, roasting winos, scaring little children. Now…"

Nash squatted in front of Ramon. "We'll still be friends."

Ramon's eyes regained focus. "Who is she?"

"When you found me in the dumpster, remember me saying I felt odd? I encountered this zombie girl. But she did more than find me, she disappeared with my heart. I had to find her again."

"Now you're infatuated?"

"This is true love."

"You gonna marry this girl? This … this Polly Rot-Away?"

"Maybe. You still mad?"

Ramon stared at the floor. "No. I'm sure you care for her. Have you met her family?"

"Not yet. She's a Corpsicana, grand-daughter of Carl the Corpse."

"What?" Ramon screeched. "Are you insane?"

"No, why?"

"I've told you. They're the oldest and most powerful zombie mafia family in LA. They're vicious."

"I suppose you hate them because they murder the Living?" Nash snapped.

"I hate them because they killed friends." Ramon bared his teeth, his voice dropping to a growl. "I told you to stay in our territory, that leaving it would lead to trouble."

"I know. But I can't forget her. She has my heart, and I'm not talking figuratively. She took it. She has it. Has possessed it since finding me sleeping in the dumpster."

Ramon straightened. "You let her pry open your ribcage and take anything she wanted? You didn't put up a fight?"

Nash smiled dreamily. "It was over before I knew what happened."

Ramon sagged back. "That's the way love goes, kid."

"You've been there?"

"Of course," Ramon snapped. His voice softened. "I was married for twenty-one years. Bella was the love of my life. We were going to retire to Maui and enjoy a simple existence, ripping off tourists like the natives. But then I died … end of dream."

"What about her? You ever go visit her?"

"Not possible." Ramon scowled, annoyance crossing his face. "She was the first Living I encountered."

Nash's features registered shock. "You *ate* her? Why?"

"I was hungry. And she was there."

"You ever regret it?"

"Um, a little. But I got over it. And she *was* tasty." Ramon waggled a finger. "When you're a zombie, it doesn't pay to be sentimental. Remember that."

"You aren't going to help me?"

Ramon sighed heavily. "I don't know how I can help. We could never take on the Corpsicana family. You want my advice? Find another girl. I know there aren't many eligible zombie women around, but there has to be better than her."

"I want Carolanna."

"You willing to be part of the Corpsicana family?"

"There's gotta be a way to have Carolanna and not have to join their gang."

Ramon laughed derisively. "You think you can tell them to go to hell? If you marry into the family, you gotta *become* family. The only other option is to grab Carolanna and flee."

Nash put a hand on Ramon's shoulder--the good one. "Dude, I'm not fleeing. I'm staying here with you. With or without Carolanna."

Ramon's expression became hostile. "If you convince her to move in with us, you'll be putting me at risk--as well as yourself."

"What're you saying?"

Ramon's eyes took on a cold look, plus a glint of anger. His eyes always had a cold look, being undead. "I'm saying she's not welcome here!" Ramon roared, stalking away.

Ramon returned as Nash sorted through the bone pile. "I'm sorry about yelling at you, kid. And I didn't mean the part about her not being welcome. I'll help you win her. But you must either steal your heart back so you don't crumble away, or figure out a way to deal with the family." Ramon sighed. "Honestly, your best course is swallowing your pride and becoming a member of the Cannibals."

"You'd be okay with it?"

Ramon shrugged. "Seems to be the best compromise. You'd survive. I'd survive. We'd still be friends. And it wouldn't hurt to have an ally in the Cannibals. I know Carlito. He's honorable, though brutal as hell. Just promise you won't become a mindless eating machine, okay? It'd kill me if you turned into one of *those* zombies."

###

When they met two weeks later, Nash felt as if his heart was about to burst. But Carolanna brought it out of her handbag, still in its previous condition. He exhaled in relief. Why did it ache so much when miles away?

"How are you?" Nash asked before pressing his lips to hers. Hers were cold and rough and something wriggled inside, like a maggot annoyed by the contact. Nash's stomach rumbled in response to the putrefaction maggots indicated. No, if he took a bite of her lip, kisses wouldn't be the same.

She drew back, putting a finger across his lips, blocking another long, dreamy smooch. "We need to talk about our future."

"I thought you wanted to focus on the present?"

Carolanna tossed her greasy locks in a gesture of dismissal. "I've changed my mind."

"What brought this on?"

"My family wants me to marry." She frowned. "I must find someone before *they* decide who I marry."

"Cool. Let's marry, and you move in with Ramon and me."

She grimaced. "I won't live in your territory. I've eaten my share of Hollywood types. I can't look at tattoos, dye jobs, piercings, or implants without getting nauseous."

"Oh. I'm not good enough for your family?"

"Maybe not for my grandfather." She grabbed his forearm. "But you're good enough for me, my juicy T-bone. It's only my family we have to worry about."

"Oh." In her handbag hanging from the back of her restaurant chair he could feel his heart sink. "Why don't we run away together?"

She sighed. "I can't. I must take over the family business--and I take my responsibilities seriously."

"But I want to be with you," Nash moaned.

"Don't despair, my luscious meat bag." She tapped a fingernail on the table. "We're having a big dinner for the upcoming ThanksLiving holiday. Mother will make a stuffed Turk and mashed potatoes smothered in Open Gravy. You can join us."

Nash's mouth watered. "What does she stuff the Turk with?"

Carolanna grinned. "That's a secret. But you'll love the flavor. She bakes the Turk over a fire pit, but only enough to singe hair off and seal in the juices. He'll still be struggling when Grand-Pappa carves him."

"Oh." Nash felt light-headed with anticipation. "The screams of the dying make a good meal even better." He stared at Carolanna, taking in the curve of her cheek, the wild curls and twists of her hair. Her locks had the tangled, frazzled appearance of an electrocuted Living. The more he learned about her, the more he realized she was perfect in every way. "Then I ask your family if we can date?"

"No, you follow my lead. I have a plan." She put a hand on his chest. "Wear your lucky shirt."

###

Carlito Corpsicana was the first person Nash saw as he followed Carolanna into the family's dining hall. Carl the Corpse lived up to his name. The patriarch of the zombie crime family had a gaunt face pierced by black eyes that radiated cold menace. Streaks of grey in his hair showed his age. His narrow, hooked nose gave him the appearance of a hawk as his dark stare followed them. Nash gripped Carolanna's hand tighter, hoping he wasn't sweating too badly. No, only the Living could perspire.

Carolanna introduced him to one of her uncles, Carmelo … or Carmine? He also met uncles Marcello, Fiorenzo, Antello, and Enrico.

"You're the only one in line to take over the family?" he whispered as he scanned the room. "No cousins?"

"The only way to have children is when you're one of the Living." She scowled. "So, my birth was planned in advance. My parents were supposed to kill me *after* I was married and pregnant, then celebrate by feasting on my Living husband. But I'm a picky eater and rejected the suitors they found. Then the second cousin I agreed to marry ended up dead, killed in a turf war with the Necrotic Despots down south. So, my parents, zombie since after my birth, lost patience and bit me over."

Carolanna stopped to greet another zombie. "Nash, meet Uncle Luca, the family's financial expert."

Nash shook Luca's hand, adorned with heavy gold rings. An open gash extended across Luca's forehead. A few strands of Luca's hair were matted in the open wound, along with dead flies, as if the cut were ancient.

"Got that when a client wouldn't pay his monthly dues," Uncle Luca said proudly. "He thought he'd fight it out rather than pay."

"You got your money, though?"

"Oh, yes." Uncle Luca smiled proudly. "No one shorts the Family."

Carolanna tugged on his arm. "It's time for you to meet Grand-Pappa."

Nash clenched his teeth, trying to think up an excuse. "Is he going to get all protective and want to chop off my head?"

"Ha! He wouldn't dare." Carolanna propelled him along. "Not this time, he won't. I told you, I have a plan."

"Mind telling me what the plan is?"

"Can't."

By the set of her jaw--even accounting for missing teeth--there would be no changing her mind. He straightened up, determined to put on a good face when meeting the Family head. It had been a long time since he'd put on a good face. Last Halloween he and Ramon had worn the faces of their first victims to sneak into a frat party. The booze had flowed like blood, and blood had flowed like ... well, like the blood pumping out of a dozen dying frat boys. It had been a hell of a party.

"Grand-Pappa," Carolanna was saying. "I'd like you to meet Nash, the young zombie I've been seeing. He isn't one of us, but he's smart and brave."

Carl fixed him with a hard stare. "Brave enough to date you?" He uttered a short laugh. "Where you from, Nash?"

"Putrefaction Palms, sir."

"Ever eat a movie star?"

Nash wrinkled his brow at the odd question. "No, sir. My friend says it isn't smart to eat any of the Living who are famous and would be missed."

"True, very true. Have you applied for membership in the Family?"

"Uh…" He glanced at Carolanna, staring serenely at her grandfather. "No, sir, not yet."

"What are your intentions?"

He hadn't thought that far ahead. He was relying on Carolanna's plan.

"Well?" Carl the Corpse demanded, his eyes skewering Nash. "Can't think of an answer?" He turned to Carolanna. "My oldest meat cleaver is sharper."

Carolanna smiled, unperturbed. "He's a bit intimidated by your reputation, Grand-Pappa."

Carl turned to Nash. "Willing to become one of us?"

Despite his earlier uncertainty, his resolve gelled as he stared at Carolanna's features and halo of greasy, tangled hair. She'd brought him here and presented him, despite the problems it might cause for her. "Yes, Mr. Corpsicana, I'm ready to become a Cannibal."

"What was your toughest kill?"

"I … killed a clown once." No point in admitting Ramon had helped.

Carl's lip curled. "How is that tough?"

Nash shuddered. "You ever kill a clown? They're creepy as hell. They can also be surprisingly strong. After killing him, we found out he was an ex-con, wanted for extortion, aggravated assault, and copyright infringement. I stabbed him a dozen times before I got in a heart strike. The damn clown nearly tore my partner's arm off!"

Carl the Corpse grinned, a cruel expression on his hawk-like features. "I heard about it. You did the Living a service--although the police don't know and are still looking for Gore-O the Crimson Clown."

"He's captured my heart," Carolanna declared.

Carl turned back to Nash. "You did? Hold it out."

"He doesn't have it yet." She opened her purse and brought out Nash's battered but recognizable ticker. "I already have his. I intend to give him mine." She handed him a scalpel, pulling her blouse open. "Come and get it."

"Through the ribs?" Nash pointed the blade at her chest. "How do I get it out without damage?"

Carl the Corpse eyes' narrowed, waiting.

"Do it, do it now," Carolanna said under her breath.

"I've never removed a heart without smashing ribs up first," Nash murmured. Was this another test?

"Why are you hesitating?" she said out of the corner of her mouth. "Go on. Everybody's watching."

The scalpel sliced her skin. What if he slipped? No, no time to worry. He made a four-inch cut, following the gap between ribs.

"Good technique." Carl nodded his approval. "You know a Ramon?"

"My mentor," Nash puffed, not looking up.

"I recognize the technique," Carl replied. "Very precise."

Carolanna threw her head back and inhaled, expanding her rib gap. He pressed fingers into the cut. She grunted as he forced ribs apart. The ribs of the Living were difficult in comparison. He always ended up smashing and kicking until ribs shattered and he could chew his way in.

His fingers closed around the organ. He pulled. Her ribs spread, but not enough. He wriggled his fist, hoping if he got one knuckle out the rest would be easier. He pulled harder. Carolanna grimaced, bracing her feet. He gave another yank and the heart nearly pulled through his fingers. He became aware of the total silence in the dining hall.

"Hurry!" Carolanna said through clenched teeth.

He put a foot on her chest, under her right breast so it wouldn't slip. He nodded in warning, then yanked. His fist popped out. "Yeah!" he shouted, holding her heart high.

Murmurs rippled through the family.

Carolanna tugged her blouse into place with a satisfied smile. She lifted his heart. She hadn't dropped it, despite the struggle. "Nash, I give you my heart in exchange for yours."

"Time for the final step," she whispered. "Any doubts?"

"None." He risked a quick glance at Carl the Corpse, who had a strange expression of expectance mixed with protectiveness.

Carl nodded. "You might make a good Corpsicana."

Nash stared into Carolanna's lifeless eyes. "What now?"

She entwined her arm with his, like newlyweds toasting their vows. She took a bite from his heart, mouth wide and teeth extended as if biting an apple. "Go on," she ordered, chewing.

Her muscle fibers were tougher than expected. After a few seconds of working his jaw, he chewed off a hunk. Euphoria flooded him. He'd eaten a few hearts. None made him feel his Unlife had immediately and permanently changed.

THE END

Wears Her Heart on a Rope
By Eddie Generous and Theresa Braun

Vehicles and hydro poles and grassy shoulders disappeared at sixty miles an hour. Life whipped by in a blur of colors and shapes. There were no more truths and facts to existence in her current state. But then again, maybe nothing ever made any sense at all.

Air thumped against their eardrums. Paper and dust danced in the wind tunnel behind the cab. The man held his hat with his left hand. With his right hand, he stroked the fur of the beast's back.

The fur was fine.

The fur bore an unusual hue.

His way of flaunting its uniqueness.

The fur was hers, theirs.

But his 'dyeing' of it: another infliction of his power.

The bestial prison shackled her heart.

Her heart shackled her mind.

A rope leash lay coiled within quick reach, but she would never run.

~

The pickup had gathered us from an on-ramp just outside the city, reminding me of our first date.

I missed my humanity more than ever as I tried to get comfortable on the bed of the truck. In some ways, I felt the same as I always had. Fleetingly, I wondered if he remembered the old me, the one who wrote poetry, or that my name is Kira.

Of course he remembered my name.

Overcast grey with a hint of gold silhouetting the distant fluff fit my mood, a constant sense of instability since it had happened. The temperature remained warmish, given that it was mid-October. Leaves lined the gutter, glittering with a thin crust of frost. The browned foliage crunched as the wheels veered to the right shoulder. Knowledge that he was going to do it again fell to the wayside. The beauty of it all distracted me from this maddening imprisonment. I was by his side when he created the account and filled chat bubbles with flirtatious lines.

We all were there. We all witnessed the inevitable.

I always feel them, but they aren't quite like me. They are lost and I am found. They merely exist with me in this body, their awareness surrendering to the blood pumping through these veins. But he loves me, and it makes all the difference. He felt my soul aching for his attention. And he revelled in having at least one witness to the fulfillment of his plans. I have some control. He *needed* me with him in the truck.

The driver and his passenger craned their necks for a second look at the man with me. There was a time when I had an identity. There was a time when I had many things. Hands, for one. I hated him for doing this to me, yet being in his presence was like a drug. Until I learned that love is more than the highs. I loved him for keeping me close. I am forever his and he is forever mine.

That day he wore tinted eyeglasses, a sport jacket, straw clinging to his sleeves, and a battered fedora—grey, or maybe light blue, a very different hue than my exterior. My fur was something more along the lines of cobalt or new denim, bright and clean. At least he made sure I wasn't ordinary. He brushed me with long careful strokes before we left. That was something. It wasn't like the way he had caressed my once smooth skin when we were really together, and it made me long for it. No one had made me feel like he did.

"Never in all my days," said the passenger, eyeing me as if I was a sideshow. I didn't blame him. My body was not my body.

"I thought it was a dog," said the driver through the open cab window. "I thought it was black. Just a black dog."

My man hopped off the rear of the vehicle, waved with his free hand, and then tugged me down to the street. The men in the truck gestured in return. For a heartbeat, my motor memory almost had me waving before I recalled my cloven feet, feet that might as well have been the devil's.

I was at the end of the leash, my man walking without urgency. Pedestrians gawked and some pointed. Their other hands held various edibles. I am always hungry, have appetites for things that never interested me before—things like paper and garbage. The notion that everything is food no longer scared me.

Where we were going did scare me, though.

It angered me too. I wanted to scream and demand an answer. Why wasn't I enough? Why all the suffering?

It was beyond my power to stop it.

"Come, come, girlie," he said when I slowed, lost in apprehensive thoughts.

The scent of coffee filled the air as it did every morning, afternoon, and evening. A street stand steamed with heat from the urns and boiling water. I stared up at the proprietor, my wide, dark eyes reflecting like convex mirrors in the surface of his sunglasses. God, I missed coffee. I missed so many things. My carefree naiveté amid the rubble of my past.

"Large house blend, three creams. Thank you." My man smiled as he spoke.

The attendant was a smallish man--thin and of Middle Eastern genetics and accent. "That a goat?"

My master nodded as I shifted weight from hoof to hoof.

"It's blue. Why's it blue?"

My man merely grinned and raised his brow. That's the kind of attention he savored, yet he'd never answer the question, leaving them hanging. "How much?"

The attendant spilled coffee on his hand, unable to tear his attention from my unusual coat. "Ouch, geez! Ah, two and quarter," he said, sucking on the burnt patch of skin.

"Paper, too," said my man, lifting a copy of *The Times*.

"Three seventy-five," said the attendant, his focus back on me. His gaze shifted to the red rock on a gold band on the hand holding my rope. If you stared too hard, faces danced in the reflection of the stone. But apparently blue goats are infinitely more interesting than people or their jewelry, since the merchant looked at me again. If he only knew that this person with me wasn't really a man.

He was so much more. The skin on the surface does not dictate what dwells within. My man, my master, a creature of infinite torment and quiet provocation.

A thing I love and hate in equal parts.

My man paid and left behind a quarter gratuity.

I clopped along the cement sidewalk, imagining I still had my long legs and could wear heels, a surprisingly agonizing lament. No one would ever lust after my curves, run a hand over my calves, my thighs. The people in front of us parted, moving aside as if subject to a subconscious remote control. I expected my curled horns, long beard, jet-black eyes, and long ears jutting from the cobalt fur were something to see. It was like wearing an outstanding Halloween costume, but being unable to take it off.

My man paused at a bench to enjoy his coffee and the paper. While he slurped, the sun peeked around the edges of grey news. By now I was so used to waiting for him, standing idly, hanging on his every whim. The bittersweet torture of his company. It's not as if I had the tools to tell him what I wanted. Sometimes he revealed how much he cared. I knew he did. I saw it in his eyes, what appeared to be enlightenment, like he could read my thoughts while broadcasting his emotions into my skull.

He sipped until only a brown tint remained in the cup, then lowered his arm to let me feast on the flavored cardboard. Paper was one of those new cravings. When I finished gobbling the trash, I ate a page featuring a warzone action shot taken somewhere in the Middle East. I was still able to read, although war as a concern pales to existing as a goat. As my man recycled the rest, I realized how bottomless I truly was. I wondered if my man noticed, or if he ever would. Or maybe this is just how he wants it. Wants me.

We'd walked hours since the bench, passing throngs of people. They gawked at me. My man went mostly ignored, something he didn't seem to mind. The aroma in the air demanded he stop again.

"Two, please, one barren, the other with ketchup, mustard, onions, and relish," he said to a vendor, who peered over his wiener cart to see me at the end of the leash.

"Onions extra, that a goat?" the wiener man said.

"Yes, she is."

He always specified my gender. Clearly my man remembered womanliness covered in soft, tan skin. It was ecstasy and torment each time he called me *she*.

The vendor fixed the dogs without looking, staring at me the entire time. I stared back, working an empty mouth sampling an imaginary buffet. That emptiness again. Always an emptiness.

"Eight-fifty," the man said, accepting a ten. "Why's it blue?"

"She, the goat is a she. How much for a water?"

He hung on the word *she* again. It was moments like these I knew it was only a matter of time before he turned me back. He missed my feminine body as much as I did. In these sentiments he showed me that he loved me, still. It was in the flicker of his gaze, the purr of his tone.

"Buck and a quarter." The man looked down at the bills and coins in his hand, money breaking the spell.

"One, please."

The vendor handed over the dogs and turned to fetch a water from his cooler. My man fed the barren dog to me like I was a pet. I tilted my head and chomped, dropping not a speck of the feast. My tongue stroked his finger, and I tasted bliss, and yet I managed some manners. I ache for the sensations of my other mouth, the one with lips, the ones I'd smeared with wonderful Cherry Crave and Bombshell Pink. When I was a girl, I'd kissed the mirror in our bathroom. The greasy mess had made mother furious. But possessing soft lips is a thing to miss. One more on the list of many.

The vendor handed over the water and then tabulated the bill. He dug for the quarter in change, but we had already gone. My math skills and attention to detail were something worth grasping, not that anyone really gave a damn. But I do. I am scraps of humanity beneath this blue pelt, even if the others in here with me have given up. They've all chosen to forget any emotion—the love and the hate. Not me. It's what keeps me attentive, present. It's what searches my master's eyes when he gazes into mine.

It grew warmer once further into afternoon. The sun peaked, and my man stopped for another break. He patted my head. It was nice in the sun. I enjoyed the warmth. Still, I sensed we were almost at our destination, and that filled me with dread.

The others probably didn't notice the speeding of our heartbeat.

I watched the traffic and the world watched me some more. A florist with a basket of vibrant flowers hollered into the crowd, foliage held high. He stopped when he saw me.

"How much?" asked my master.

"Five spot each. Got a date?" said the florist. My man pulled his wallet, and the flower seller took in the image of his customer wearing loafer, an old hat, a dirty jacket, and had a massive ring on each hand. And me on a rope. "What's the goat for?"

My man ignored the question, pulling out a five. "There sir, and yes, a date."

In a brief breath, I let the words re-play in my mind, but ignored their meaning. He loved me. I was all the date he'd ever need.

But no.

"You pick." The florist held out his basket, and my man glanced at me for an answer. "How come the goat's blue?"

I latched onto a small bouquet of cobalt-tinted flowers and began to munch.

"She seems happy to me. See? She likes flowers."

I knew it was commonplace, but roses were always my favorite. Funny, I never ate them, though. The future pained me as much as the past as I devoured the bouquet. It was delicious. My human consciousness hated the barbarity of this moment. And that my skin would never feel like flower petals. No dainty nose would smell such a gift. They'd never die in a crystal vase.

The florist stood watching, frozen as if I were Medusa rather than dyed livestock. Then I understood what it was to turn men into stone.

People continued with their staring, eyes working on craning necks until the bodies passed and the chins could turn no more. My man pulled me along. It had been an exhausting day for both of us, but the end was near. That fact tightened my chest. The others here with me still oblivious to what was coming next.

There was an address on a slip of paper in my man's wallet. He pulled it out as he walked, and I read *4990 66E ST* as the sun made the paper translucent. I was so proud of myself for transposing it. Strange how the little things become big things when you've lost this much.

Face-to-face online dating, the wave of the present. If only I had stayed offline. If only I had taken my ex back. If only lots of things. If only love was fake. If only he didn't love me so much that he'd felt this need to test me. But I pass this test every time. Does he notice?

He read the next street sign with silent-though-moving lips. I let him navigate us toward the residential-industrial area where the poor don't have the funds to complain about the odor coming from the factories and mills. The crowds slimmed the closer we got.

A chicken-breading plant was next to a grade school; children heading home screamed and bounded around my man. He didn't talk to children. Me, a blue goat on a rope, wasn't so wild, not to their imaginative minds. They peered at me as if they'd seen one of me somewhere before, maybe in one of their picture books. They looked at him, drinking in his face, his clothes, and those rings.

The children thinned out as my man quickened his pace. I kept up, despite needing a nap, or at minimum, a rest. He yawned. See, we were so connected.

The signs foretold that dismal end approaching. As his heart pounded heavily, I swore I felt it through the rope. The palpitations seeped into my neck like magic fingers.

We neared the home of Lissie Porter. Lissie had said she liked farm animals, goats especially. I'd read her messages over his shoulder.

Me too! he'd typed in reply.

I'd liked to think he loved me especially. Even though I wasn't his first, nor his last, I'm dominant. That should count for something—for everything. When he took away my humanity and imprisoned me this frame, I refused to give into apathy and detachment. I am not a goat, but these others here with me, in this furry, hooved meat prison, they might as well be, since they've relinquished everything that had made them whole. They don't care about holding onto their human personalities.

Lissie's place was smack in the middle of a string of skinny, rundown duplexes. The entire neighborhood needed a bath and a coat of paint. Something to drive away the shadows.

My man glanced around. A woman outside a convenience store with a scratch ticket in her hands, mid-gamble, paused in wonderment before the yearning for quick money drew her attention away. We kept on. My hooves slowed, not wanting to arrive at our destination. I'd have dragged my feet, but it wouldn't have made a difference.

We approached the door early. My man tried Lissie's wooden door. The latch clicked and let go. He grinned at the simplicity of entry.

The Internet had all sorts, and to tell a man where you live and leave that bolt disconnected was a thoughtless peril. It was unwise to take risks with strangers, and more so, it was unwise to fall for their charms. I should know.

He'd pulled the same act with me. And with all the others that came before.

It was all a game with her, of course. He was real with me and only me. She didn't matter, never would. She'd disappear with all the rest. Just one soul in a sea of many.

The door creaked inward. My belly roiled. This was not the romantic encounter Lissie Porter expected. I wasn't sure it was in me to watch. That's what I'd told myself the last time. And the time before that.

That's how we got here.

That's how he'd collected us.

He had so much more than just my heart. I teared at the thought.

~

Thirty minutes early, the man dragged the beast into the home of the unassuming woman. She was in her bathrobe with an expression revealing her excitement, a silent plea of let this date work out, *please.* She did not hear the unexpected entry.

He closed the door behind him.

The room smelled of garlic and sausage. There was a greasy pan on the stovetop.

Saliva dripped down the goat's beard.

The man patted the head of his pet, holding it tight to his side. There was a rusty freezer chest and six pairs of shoes. Cheap and scuffed, four of which belonged to children. A mirror possessed a series of coat hooks. A single sweater dangled by its ratty hood, a small boy's.

She hadn't mentioned being a mother in her online profile.

The man wore an irritated expression. He took a step towards the hallway leading to the kitchen. The goat was a stride behind. Somewhere in the distance, upstairs and from a tinny source, an undiscernible rap track rattled. The man stepped into the kitchen, feeling in his pocket for a blade.

His safety blanket.

Step one.

On the yellowed refrigerator was a photo of the tired mama cradling two boys, both in their single digits, smiling and loving. It was the woman's fault she'd put them at risk.

Around the aged dining set, the man led the goat, with the leash choked tight to her neck. He withdrew the blade and shuffled over the pockmarked linoleum.

The goat had been quiet. Just like it had always been. It was as it was as when he'd put her in the hooved cell. This situation was different, but the woman's heart was the same. Hopeful, love-struck from the first traded messages, and utterly unsuspecting. Each victim ruled by the deep need for unconditional passion. All-encompassing acceptance.

Fury rose. It crept up her throat, and the goat wanted to scream like a woman, *he's mine!* Instead, a braying rat-a-tat-tat vibrated from between her thick, ivory teeth.

The man cast a glare upon his pet that made her retreat and shrink into all she'd become. She'd pray for forgiveness, the ache to impress him, to make him love her solely.

Had he read her thoughts?

This time he skipped the pleasantries, the seduction. The previous online chats apparently enough of a declaration of submission. Surely that meant this victim wasn't as worthy as Kira, who'd once shared a bed with her master. They'd exchanged breaths, mingled fluids. This mother was only worthy of collecting.

"What are you…?" the woman shouted, jumping to her feet and then stumbling over a coffee table, sending a can of Canada Dry to the rug of the living room floor. The man leapt forwards, swinging his blade.

The cut sank into the woman's neck. The strained tendons saved the jugular. She shrieked and staunched the gushing blood with her hand.

She kicked, aiming for the man's genitals. He skidded back and tripped over the goat that dashed and skipped out of the way. The corner wall separating the kitchen from the living room seemed to vault at him. The drywall cracked and a dusty asbestos puff wafted over them. The goat coughed and wheezed.

Up and on her heels, the woman hobbled to the stairs. The man regained his stance and slashed at an eye-level foot. The crusty, flaky sole took the blade. The flesh separated, spreading wide and bubbling a river.

"Boys!" the woman screeched. "Boys, lock your door!"

Tinny rap music was loud enough that her message missed its mark.

The man pounced on the stalled foot. The woman on the stairs flailed as the goat watched in terror. This was all wrong.

The blade sliced again, nicking and sticking, caught in the woman's tibia momentarily before she tumbled onto her ass. Her robe flopped open, and the man sneered at the lace panties and the uncooperative body that should've been an easy score. Her death and her assimilation into the goat should be as easy.

"Get out!" the woman shrieked, her voice approaching an octave audible only to dogs, and maybe even goats. She swung her unharmed right foot. The heel connected with the man's nose.

The goat brayed in pain upon witnessing the spillage of the man's black blood. Upstairs a door opened and the music quieted.

"Mom?" said a childish voice.

Auditory adrenaline. The woman leapt at the teetering man, driving him sideways into the ancient TV. The front-heavy box tipped and tumbled. It pounded the woman's shoulder. An *oooph* left her lips as she fell away. From there, the set dropped onto the man's arm and chest. The blade left his grasp, thumping onto the carpet.

"Mom, what's…?" started the voice.

The woman's agony evidently fled in the presence of potential harm to her children. Eyes fell on the bloodied blade. Her hand followed her gaze.

The goat opened her mouth to plea. No sound emitted.

Four inches of steel slashed into the man's neck. Then again. In his chest. Through his right eye.

His free hand swung, flapping, stupid. His lifeblood pooled around him like a midnight halo, seeping into the carpet. A curious indifference burned in his remaining eye.

She stabbed again. His mouth. His free shoulder. His scalp.

He'd ceased attempting to thwart her and still…

His mouth. His arm. The carpet next to his head. His ear. Black fluid splashed.

Finally the woman dropped the knife and slumped, her right arm dangling, the itty-bitty clavicle snapped.

"Mommy, what's going on?" asked one boy.

"Why he do that?" asked the other, the smaller.

The goat huffed and hopped at the sight. Never before had she experienced the purpose of her curved-and-pointed horns. Her only hope for freedom lay lifelessly on the ground, his last breaths gurgling from his throat. Her horns pierced the delicate flesh of the unsuspecting mama. It was like destroying herself, but the beast already missed him so much. No one would be left to love her. A new hell on the horizon.

Down the stairs the boys rushed and stopped on the landing. The woman turned to offer a hapless smile of better tomorrows.

Bending, the goat stabbed and stabbed at the soft woman in her softer bathrobe where she kneeled. The horns gored her intestines, stomach, lungs, and heart. Blood sprayed like from a sprinkler on a lawn, red rain everywhere. The beast's head and shoulders now purple, horns stained crimson. Droplets clung to her lashes, a fierce hatred shining in her eyes.

~

Die, you bitch! I screamed, but only the damned goat sound left my mouth again.

How could she?

He was all the light in the universe, and he'd wanted to share it with me, not her. How could she do it? He loved me…he will always be mine.

"Ma!" the bigger boy bawled.

I leaned down to withdraw my soiled horns.

The fur of my head was wet and heavy, my beard sopping. As I stared into the eyes of those boys, the younger one glared at me with recognition, cocking his head, lips widening into a toothy grin. He stepped forward, bending to retrieve the smoky, red rings from dead hands, and the slickened blade from the soggy carpet.

My goat heart thudded, and my little legs buckled as the youthful hand lifted my leash.

He studied my caked horns and fur with an air of admiration and pride. "Come on, girlie," he said with a tone of someone much older. "We'll have to try again."

"Cal?" said the older brother.

The boy replied with a "Shh." When his eyes locked with mine, I knew this was forever.

slriG, slriG, slriG
By W.P. Johnson

Ramsey was drinking beer on the couch in the midst of a *Halloween* marathon when Kristina called out to him from the kitchen.

"Hey, Ram… can you come in here?"

"What?"

"Um, you should see this."

"What is it?"

Silence.

Ramsey sighed and paused *Halloween III: Season of the Witch*. He used to think it was a severe drop off from the first two (Micheal Myers wasn't even in it for Christ's sake), but lately he found it was just as good as any horror flick to pass the time. Besides, Kristina hated scary movies, and after two weeks of dating he just wanted her out of his hair so he could get shit faced on the couch.

Cindy would've hung in there, he thought. *Maybe she would've been zonked out on pills, but at least she could hang.*

"Ram?"

He shook the thought and got up, trudging down the hall to the kitchen in his robe and slippers. There, he found Kristina in the midst of putting away a case of beer she picked up for him. She was doing that a lot lately; buying him beer, cooking him dinner, doing his laundry. It was that motherly thing girls sometimes did for him when they wanted to feel needed, not that he could complain. On the other hand, she was vegan and after they'd slept together, she started throwing out his instant dinners and offering to cook him vegan casseroles. Not a pain in the ass, unless you considered hiding Taco Bell bags like they were used condoms a pain.

But definitely annoying.

Which is all to say, it got Ramsey thinking that maybe Kristina's time in his orbit had finally reached its two week expiration date.

It's not you, it's me.

Too cliched.

I'm over this and you gotta go.

Too harsh.

I think I still might be processing my last relationship.

That one almost made him laugh. His last relationship? Some roller derby girl who broke her leg, so he made up something about hating hospitals and never visited. Before that there was a girl from Jersey whose car broke down, so all he had to do was stay in Philly. But the one before that was a real doozy. Goth

226

girl named Steph that lived in her dead parent's house out on the Main Line across from a cemetery. Did cocaine (a lot of it), unironically read books on witchcraft, owned a Ouija board that she frequently used, and fucked his brains out because her dead cat had communicated to her that he was 'powerful', whatever that meant.

It was fun at first, especially the coke, but when he found her dead cat in the freezer next to the ice cubes she'd put in her vodka, he decided to cut his losses. Thinking on it now, he wondered if he could go back for seconds now that he was breaking it off with Kristina.

No… you told her you were born again.

This time he did laugh.

"This isn't funny," Kristina said. She was on her knees, scrutinizing the inside of the case of beer.

"Sorry." He stood beside her. "What is it?"

"Look at this." She lifted the inner flap of the case of beer. Large black letters had been written inside.

im going to cut my wrists

Ramsey gave a nervous laugh. "Whoa… was it-

"It was glued shut."

"Really?"

"Yeah." She stood up beside him, hugged herself and shivered. "It's fucked up."

"It's definitely creepy…"

"I mean, it's fucked up that someone would do that. Cause someone with suicidal thoughts could have opened this and been triggered."

"Oh, right…"

Ding, ding, ding.

We have a winner.

Ramscy put on a sad face and walked back into the living room, sitting down on the couch. Footsteps were slow to follow, approaching with trepidation. He forced a sigh when she was close enough to hear him, letting his semi-long brown hair shift across his brow for that perfect emo sad boy look.

"Well?"

"I don't know…"

He closed his eyes and let out another practiced sigh.

She stood in the hallway, the kitchen light casting her sagging shoulders over the carpeted floor. "What are you thinking?"

What was his thinking? He was thinking about whether or not the leftover Chinese food he'd hidden in the fridge would still be any good. He was thinking about how long it would take for the beer Kristina just put away to get cold.

"It's hard to talk about."

He was thinking about whether or not *Halloween Six* had Busta Rhymes in it.

The couch sagged to her weight and she set a hand on his shoulder. Slowly, he lifted it off.

"Sorry," he said, looking away. "It's just… I was really close to this girl." He stopped, letting the silence do all the talking, Kristina filing in the blanks.

"Oh my god, did she-

She stopped, not wanting to even say it.

He uttered a simple, "Yeah," remembering that *Halloween: Resurrection* featured Busta Rhymes, following *H2O*, staring L. L. Cool Jay.

He closed his eyes, welled them up with tears while thinking he could always put a few beers in the freezer so they'd cool down quicker.

Maybe give Cindy a call too.

A tear drop slipped out and dribbled down his cheek, unplanned.

Focus Ramsey.

Don't overdo it.

"I never even got a chance to say goodbye."

"Oh my gosh Ramsey, I'm so sorry." She moved closer to hold his hand, but he flinched and she backed off. "I had no idea."

"How could you know?"

"What can I do for you?"

"Maybe…"

Almost there...

"Maybe it would be better if I had some time to myself. I don't know if I ever really processed it, you know?"

"Right."

The couch shifted as she got up, the sound of her grabbing her things; handbag, keys, jacket. She went to the apartment door, inches left of the flat screen, her back to him. She paused and half turned to face him.

"Listen," she said, "if you need to talk or whatever…"

"I think I just need some time."

She nodded and unlocked the door.

"Ram…"

He saw the flicker of her standing in his peripheral, waiting for him to say goodbye.

"I'm sorry… I-"

He turned the volume back up on the TV, blaring *Halloween III*.

Seconds later, the door clicked shut, locks slid in, and Ramsey was free. He waited, listening for footsteps to descend, for the front door of his apartment to open and close. After he was sure the coast was clear, he got up and went to the kitchen, putting four beers in the freezer so they'd be cold enough by the time the next movie came on. As he closed the freezer door, he saw a post-it on the fridge with Kristina's handwriting.

come back ramsey

He rolled his eyes and crumbled the note.

"No thank you."

He zapped his secret leftovers and went back to the couch to finish the movie.

He thought of Cindy.

She would've laughed about all of this... would've cut a line of adderall and spent all night drinking a case of haunted beer, talking shit.

He smiled, but then he found himself less happy for what he'd had and more miserable for what he'd lost. She had told him that she was leaving for California for a new job. Not tomorrow or next week or next month, but today, bus ticket purchased, apartment already procured. It struck him then as it did now that the reason she had waited so long to tell him is because how much she knew it would hurt, ripping the bandaid off instead of spending weeks peeling it off while sharing a one bedroom apartment.

Ram... I'm sorry... I-

It's cool.

He said goodbye to her from the couch, a *Hellraiser* marathon keeping his attention. The door opened, closed, his eyes always on the screen, always watching some other horror to distance himself from the Cindy shaped hole she'd left. The memory felt like some kind of incantation he couldn't rid himself of. Whether she'd meant to or not, she'd cast a spell on him, one he had tried to break with other women, but the spell never broke.

Eventually, the emptiness of that hole she'd left in him always opened up again.

Ram… I'm sorry… I-

He turned the volume up on his TV, drowning his thoughts.

When the beers were cold enough, he drank until everything went quiet and he passed out on the couch.

#

He went to work hungover (again), mainlining Excedrin and coffee until his fingers shook. He got the usual smart ass remarks from the other office drones that noticed his five o'clock shadow at nine AM, cracking wise about what (or who) he had been doing last night. Rushing past them for his corner office, he was able to hide in plain sight and phone it in, spending most of his day pretending to work, crunching numbers on the same page of data until someone actually stopped by to look at his computer screen.

Mostly, he scrutinized his dating app, wanting his dance card full for the weekend.

First message came from Miskittens, whose profile listed that she collected cassettes and loved vegan food, so zero for zero, not to mention that she wasn't much to look at as far as his taste in girls went. She had that 'let's move in together and get a dog' kind of look. Sometimes Ramsey thought about getting a dog to double his odds.

But not for you Miskittens.

Message deleted, user blocked.

Second message came from GooseGooseDuck. She was a cute redhead that worked part time as a barista in South Philadelphia while attempting Temple University, tree branches tattooed up and down her arms, vaguely suggesting some hippy dippy vibes that he wasn't so sure he was up for after dropping Kristina. Number three was KnittyKnittyBangBang, a self proclaimed fashion designer who sold hand woven scarves on etsy. She was also into baking but a former "bacon addict" that was "still trying to perfect a recipe for vegan bacon".

Holy shit, is every chick vegan now?

Cindy wasn't.

She swore and drank and never said no to staying up late and having fun, never turned down that extra drink, never failed to keep his bed warm no matter how cold he was to her. Never said no to one more pill, one more line, one more episode of some show they were binging until four in the morning, neither wanting to sleep. Because in dreams, they were alone, but in life, they had each other.

Had.

You had her.

Why didn't you tell her to come back?

"Ramsey?"

He jumped, looking up; his boss Sean stood right at the entry point of his cubicle, face pink and puffy, his baby blue dress shirt two sizes too big.

"Hey boss."

"You okay? Look like you've seen a ghost."

"Yeah." He shook his head, took a breath. "Sorry, just uh, focusing is all."

"Can you email me last week's recap? I need to send corporate a sales forecast for the next quarter. Bob wants it EOD," he said, rolling his eyes.

"EOD, heard that." He started clicking, clacking, opening and closing windows. He glanced up at Sean, finding him still there. "Yeah, I'll email it to you right away."

"Great." He walked off, visiting other cubicles on the way back to his office. After a few minutes passed, Ramsey opened his phone back up.

Where was I?

He reviewed his options thus far. He decided to save GooseGooseDuck and block KnittyKnittyBangBang. After that came a message from Misterious, a blonde who loved horror films and had enough pictures posted online to show him she wasn't pulling a fast one. Her message was short and to the point: *you seem fun, saw you liked horror films, top 5?*

Bingo.

He cracked his thumb muscles and got to work. A perfect top five was essential to preemptively "sealing the deal". It had always been his belief that one slip up could buy him a one way ticket to block island, while a perfectly curated list could have him in her pants before the weekend, which was crucial if he wanted to avoid spending those days alone.

Number one and two was a tie between *Texas Chainsaw Massacre* and *The Exorcist. "I know, I know,"* he wrote, having a duel choice was as much of a cop out as saying his favorite Beatles record was a split between *Revolver* and *Rubbersoul,* which was also his sneaky way of talking music without sounding like a pompous ass. Three went to *Halloween,* four to *The Thing.* After that he wasn't entirely sure, as he was always used to writing his "best of" lists in groupings of ten, but if he had to choose he thought he might give it to *Jaws* or *Alien,* but he also loved *Evil Dead, Psycho,* and *Suspiria.*

He left the fifth choice blank, asking Misterious to finish the list.

Or if you're up for it, he wrote, *we could finish the list over drinks.*

Number sent, seed planted.

He left his unread messages and clicked on his 'viewed by' link, curious to see who had cruised him.

Aside from the girls that had messaged him, one name was listed.

BaphometWoman.

"Speak of the devil…"

Aka, Steph.

#

Favorite food: Meat.

Favorite music: Mayhem.

Favorite movie: Haxan.

Religious views: Satanism.

He hadn't heard the sound of wedding bells, but after scrolling through a couple of her photographs, he started to brainstorm the various ways he could possibly get into demonic leather pants.

Turns out, it didn't take much. First date was over a cup of coffee at a nearby cafe wherein she spent most of the time staring intently at him while asking questions not of the first date variety. Have you ever astral projected? Do you believe in God? Have you ever really loved anyone? Who is your favorite serial killer? To the latter, he actually had an answer, Dennis Nielsan, which she found consequently *so obvious,* while the former he merely shrugged and made his usual witty banter to convince her that he was a good guy and not just out to hit it and quit it.

She'd read his palm as if taking notes, then they parted ways and he thought that was that. Flash forward to sometime after midnight when he'd had just enough to drink to make bad decisions. She interrupted his periodic viewing of *Reanimator* with a dozen text messages begging him to come over, photographs eroding any ambiguity as to what she had planned.

He made the drive, finding her coked up, her steely eyes shifting about the house as if spotting ghosts that hid in the shadowy corners. Mirrors laid throughout the living room, some covered in white powder, others in scribblings of red lipstick, which she dismissively explained were failed incantations. They had drinks, his suggestion, not hers, and when he found the dead cat in the freezer, he opted to enjoy his rum and coke without ice and possibly leave altogether before he got too drunk to drive.

Then he turned around and was face to face with Steph, who had decided that it was the perfect time to remove her clothes and get down to business.

She fucked him on a mattress on the floor in the middle of the living room, surrounded by candles flattened by fire. Her lips tasted like gasoline and she left bruises on him he spent a week trying to get rid of. When she finally came, she screamed so loud his ears rang.

After that, she rolled off him and fixated on a Ouija board to answer all those questions he had flippantly skated earlier that day. No to astral projection, yes to God, but more out of fear than devotion. When she asked him if he had ever loved anyone before, she began finding the letters on the board with her planchette.

"C… I..."

Ramsey got up then, slipping his clothes on and mumbling an excuse about having to get up early for work.

"...N…"

He stepped barefoot over a mirror, cracking it, his pace quickening as he rushed for the door.

"...D..."

Outside, he found his car at the bottom of the gravel drive, a trail of bloody footprints behind him. The cemetery surrounding her home held a swollen aura of darkness he felt was somehow closing in all around him. When he finally did get into his car, he pumped the gas barefoot and peeled out.

All the while, he heard her voice spelling the last letter of the name, screeching until it became a perpetual climax in his ears that left them ringing until morning.

#

He'd hadn't seen her since. Hadn't messaged her, hadn't heard from her. In fact, he hadn't even really thought of her until just a few days ago when he considered reaching out to fill in his weekend. Reliving the way he'd ran to his car made him think twice all of the sudden. Maybe his time was better spent barking up another tree, one that didn't look like it was the gnarled home of a warlock.

Still, he was curious. Had Steph changed at all or was she still looking for Mister Satanic Rites?

He amended his account to keep his views private and clicked on her profile. There, he found the same words written over and over again.

Favorite food: come back ramsey

Favorite music: come back ramsey

Favorite movie: come back ramsey

Religious views: come back ramsey

About me: come back ramsey, come back ramsey, come back ramsey, come back ramsey

Ramsey sat there, staring, feeling as if he were being watched.

A chat window popped open.

BathmoetWoman: come back ramsey.

He closed his phone, turned it upside down and slid it to the far end of his desk, ignoring it. Going to his computer, he opened up his email to send the recap Sean had asked for, trying to focus.

A loud rattle burst against the table.

It was his cell phone, vibrating. He stared, watching it ring. Slowly, he turned it over. It was a number he didn't recognize. It kept ringing and ringing.

He picked it up, answered it. "Hello?"

"Hi," a girl said. "Is this Ramsey?"

"Yes. Who is this?"

"Did you date Kristina?"

Ramsey furrowed his brow. "I mean… we went out a few times, but I don't know if I'd say we were ever really *dating*." A beat of silence passed and he leaned back in his chair. "I'm sorry, but who is this again?"

"I'm her roommate Shannon. I don't know if she ever mentioned me or not."

"I think so. What's up? Is something wrong?"

"Maybe you should sit down."

"Okay." He adjusted his seat, sitting up. "Did something happen?"

"Well… yes. I'm sorry to be the one to tell you this. And to be honest, I'm a little freaked out by the whole thing." She fumbled through her words, talking more than she should, speeding up and slowing down. After a time, she stopped short and took a breath. "There's no good way to tell you this, so I'll just say it. Kristina took her own life last night."

"*What?*" Ramsey stood, his chair sliding back.

Shannon continued. "She took a bath last night and she... cut herself."

He felt himself sink a little, falling back into his chair. Shannon's voice became small, distant, as if through a veil of sleep.

"I had to unscrew the hinges on the bathroom door to get in and by the time I found her, the water was cold. She didn't want anyone to stop her."

She talked for some time, walking him through calling the paramedics, having them take her away. She talked about how she had to clean the tub herself. Eventually, she trailed off, wanting to talk but not knowing what to say, searching blindly for some kind of closure.

"Anyway, I just thought you should know since you were the last person to see her. And I'm sorry to be the one to tell you. I know you two were really close."

"Oh..." Ramsey blushed, sighed. He nibbled on his chapped lips. "Listen, Shannon? I'm really sorry for what happened and that you had to go through all of this. But to be honest, we weren't that serious. I mean, we only went out a few times and then we broke it off yesterday and, well, I guess I'm just surprised to hear she was in such a bad place. I had no idea."

Silence, a hissing static through the phone.

"Hello?"

"Okay, so I'm confused," she said. "Because you're making it sound like she was just a fuck buddy or something when she obviously thought it was much more than that."

"Whoa, now hold on a second-

"Whatever," she said, anger and sadness fighting for control. "You know what? I wasn't going to tell you this because I didn't want to make you upset, but I think it's pretty obvious that you're the kind of person who doesn't think about how other people feel once you've decided you're done with them. So, maybe she didn't mean anything to you, but you obviously meant something to her."

"Shannon-

"And I think you should know that before she took her life, she wrote a suicide note. And you know what it said?" She was shouting now, her voice crackling in the tiny speaker. "It said, come back Ramsey. Over and over again. Come back Ramsey. Come back Ramsey." Her voice got louder and louder until she was screaming at him. "Come back Ramsey! COME BACK RAMSEY!"

He pulled his phone away from his ear, staring at it as she continued shouting at him, repeating the mantra over and over again.

"Ramsey?"

He screamed and jumped, falling back into his chair. Looking up, he found Sean staring at him, Shannon's voice crackling in the air through his phone. He cupped a hand over the speaker, feeling her voice tickle the palm of his hand like a finger searching his life line for meaning, reading him.

Sean furrowed his brow, nodding towards the phone. "Trouble in paradise?"

"Something like that."

He smirked, then gestured to Ramsey's computer.

"Can you send me that recap I asked for?"

"Uh, I did already..." He clicked open his email, searching the sent files. "Right?"

"You did email me, but it didn't have any files, just text. I thought maybe it was a joke or something, but I don't get it. Anyway, I really need that recap now, okay?" He knocked the cubicle wall and walked off, whistling some made up tune.

The voice on the phone continued, tapering off, losing strength. Through the crackling signal, she muttered '*fucking asshole*' and hung up, the dial tone whining.

Checking his sent email, he found what he'd sent to Sean. No subject, no files.

Just words.

Come back ramsey

#

He went home sick. It wasn't hard to convince Sean that he needed to; he had puked in his wastebasket just seconds before he came back to follow up on the recap. Minutes later, he was on the road, white knuckling the steering wheel while his mind raced.

He put himself on trial, acting as both defense and prosecution.

You killed her.

"No," he said aloud, shaking his head. "No fucking way is this my fault."

He kept replaying the past two weeks in his head, searching for some moment that justified his responsibility in all of this. Yes, he had misrepresented himself, pretending to like the same movies she did, being sure to play her favorite music whenever she was around. He even suggested that he'd be willing to go vegan if it made her happy. But he never said he loved her and he never gave her a reason to love him.

So, you lied.

You tricked her into having feelings for you.

"Absolutely not." He backed into a parking space, sitting there, talking to himself. "I didn't trick anyone into anything."

Okay, let me rephrase the question… you understand how it's possible to love someone when they don't love you back.

"That's not a question, that's a statement."

Did you love Cindy?

"I'm not answering that question."

And did she not love you back?

"I'm not answering-

Answer the court truthfully. On the night Cindy left, did you, or did you not make a pathetic attempt at committing suicide by drinking and taking sleeping pills only to wake up on the bathroom floor, covered in your own vomit?

Silence, save for the sound of his AC as it blew cold air on the sweat that broke out over his forehead.

"What about Steph?"

What about her?

Someone honked their horn at him, eyeing the space he was in with the assumption that he was just about to leave and not just now parking. He waved them away and turned the ignition off, sitting there another moment in the cool of his car.

"Okay, it's weird," he admitted.

In his head, he reviewed what he knew to be facts. Steph had changed her profile to the phrase 'come back Ramsey' and messaged him that same exact thing just moments before Shannon called to tell him that Kristina had killed herself and left a suicide note that said 'come back Ramsey' over and over again. But that didn't mean Steph had anything to do with what had happened to

Kristina. If anything, it made him wonder if Steph was next in line to slit her wrist over him.

So, you do admit that Kristina killed herself over you?

"No, absolutely not."

Your honor, the prosecution calls Steph… we don't remember her last name exactly. But we'd like to call her to the stand.

He suddenly saw Steph trudging up to the witness stand, her black hair covering her pale face in its dark tangles. Ramsey shook his head, feeling a dull ache behind his eyes, his throat burning from having puked earlier.

"She's got nothing to do with it," he told himself, wanting to clear his head of such insanity.

Silence then, Steph staring at him through the shroud of her dark hair.

If not me, then who?

His phone buzzed to an incoming message. He stared at it for a long time, fearful that it would be another message from Steph, or worse, news that yet another girl he'd slept with had decided to call it quits on life. Opening his phone up, he saw a text message from UNKNOWN, a preview flashing at the top of his cell screen.

Hey, this is misterious. My name is Jenny.

He opened up the full text, seeing the clipped end of the message.

Wanna get that drink?

"Court adjourned," he said, while texting her back.

One hundred percent.

As he restarted his car, "Mistrial."

#

They met at a rooftop bar in Rittenhouse Square that served Asian Fusion. He was early and sat at the bar, nursing Mai Thais while waiting for happy hour to start and for Jenny to arrive. It was the perfect fall day, the sun bright and warm, while a faint wind foretold the October weather that was waiting for them right around the corner. It was almost enough to make him forget that a girl he had dated had just committed suicide and that another girl was stalking him.

Almost.

He finished his Mai Thai, ordering another.

Jenny arrived an hour later, smiling and waving at Ramsey when she spotted him at the bar. He pulled back a stool, gesturing that she join him. Two drinks were already set out on the bartop and when she sat down, he slid one over to her.

"Tokyo tea," he said, taking a sip. "Vodka, midori, and pineapple."

"Very pretty," she said, noting the color. She took a sip and backed away from the straw as if it just tried to bite her. "And strong!"

"The best drinks are," he said. "And it's happy hour."

"Then I am very happy to be here." She raised her drink to his and they clinked glasses, cheering one another. "Also, I'm going to go with *The Shining* for my fifth choice."

"Oh yeah? Good."

"So, you approve?"

"I'm just relieved you didn't go with *Saw*."

She smirked, her pillow lips painted red. She eyed him, sly, nodding to herself, giving a satisfying "hmm-mm."

"What?" Ramsey smiled back.

"It's just that, you seem like the kind of guy that would have approved of any answer I gave, even if it was *Saw*."

"Think so?"

"I know so," she said. She sucked her drink down to the ice. "But that doesn't mean I'm not interested in another drink."

Ramsey sucked down his own drink. "Good thing it's happy hour then."

She eyed the menu. "We're gonna need some food if we're gonna keep doing this."

\#

Happy hour went by fast, the two enjoying pot stickers, bahn mi, and round after round of Tokyo Tea. Ramsey slowed down after the fifth drink, deciding he wanted to at least be able to drive home after their date, which he was almost sure this was. In fact, he couldn't remember the last time he'd had so much fun talking to someone. Their conversation came easily to both of them, the two discovering they'd had a lot more in common than they thought. She even made him laugh, which was rare, and when happy hour ended and Ramsey was about to ask for the check, Jenny cut him off and ordered dessert.

"Unless you don't want to spend any more time with me?"

"No, I…" Ramsey blushed. "Of course I do."

They picked at a plate of banana spring rolls with vanilla ice cream, a pair of fortune cookies sitting atop their check.

"I'm having a really good time," Jenny said randomly.

"Yeah?"

"Yeah." She sipped her cappuccino. "Listen… I live pretty close by if you wanted to come over."

"Oh… okay?"

She raised a stern finger. "Not a sleepover."

Ramsey laughed, mirroring her gesture. "Not sleeping over, got it."

"But maybe we could, you know have a glass of wine, watch a movie."

"As long as it isn't *Saw.*"

"I was thinking more like, *The Thing,* or *Halloween.*"

Ramsey smiled. "I'd like that a lot." He signaled for the bartender to come over, digging for his wallet. Before he could take his credit card out, Jenny grabbed the check, sliding her own card inside and handing it back.

"Hey now," he said. "You're not even gonna split it with me?"

"Guess you'll just have to take care of the next one." She leaned in, grinning slyly. "Unless… you never want to see me again?"

He looked into her eyes, lingering in that moment between them. She made him feel a certain way that he hadn't felt in a long time. More so, he hadn't even thought at all about the troubles he had that day. For some reason, she made him feel as if a spell had been broken and that he was finally waking up from a terrible dream.

"Don't bet on it."

She grabbed one of the fortune cookies and broke it apart, unfolding her fortune. When the bartender came back with the bill and thanked them, she quickly signed it and pushed her bar stool back to leave.

Ramsey stood with her. "So, ready to get out of here?"

She turned away from him and ran.

"Jenny?"

Dashing past the other tables, she gained traction towards the edge of the rooftop and jumped, clearing a row of planters and the guardrail behind it, diving headfirst and descending. The sound of her hitting the pavement was a faint thud followed by distant screams and several cars skidding to a halt.

Ramsey sagged in his seat, unbelieving his eyes. He looked towards the barstool she had just sat in only moments ago, trying to understand what it was that had just happened, debating the reality of it. A few couples rushed to the edge of the rooftop to see what had happened, a crowd forming where she had jumped. One woman screamed and soon the entire rooftop started to become aware that something terrible had just occurred.

Ramsey lingered on the bartop, looking at the lipstick on her cappuccino mug, at the bits of her unfinished fortune cookie. A small sliver of paper lay within the broken shell. Even from where he sat, he could see what it said.

He grabbed it and looked closer anyway.

Small scribbled words without punctuation covered the surface of the piece of paper.

im going to jump

"Sir?" The bartender stood there with the check in his hands. "Sorry to bother you about this, but is your friend still here?"

"What?" He felt dizzy, all those Tokyo Teas weighing him down all of the sudden.

"Your friend, the blonde girl?" He presented the check Jenny had signed. "I just need her signature instead of, you know, whatever this is." After setting it down, he looked towards the commotion in the distance. "Wonder what's going on over there…"

"Someone just jumped off the roof," Ramsey said, numb.

"Oh my gosh, you're kidding me. Who?"

Ramsey said nothing then. Instead, he looked down at the check, reading the space where Jenny had signed her name.

In place of her signature, just the same words, over and over again.

come back ramsey come back ramsey come back ramsey

#

He drove down 76 in the dead of night, his throat aching, his eyes sore. It had been over three hours of giving statements and explaining not who he was but who he wasn't. He wasn't family, or a boyfriend, or anyone important. No, she hadn't acted strangely prior to jumping. No, he didn't think she was on any drugs. No, he had no idea why she would do what she did.

Except, he did have an idea.

It was an insane idea, but insane times called for insane measures and he wasn't very much in the mood to sober up and make normal decisions. He very much wanted to make fucked up decisions in that moment. As soon as he left the police station, he barreled west towards Steph's house near the cemetery.

He sped, never slowing until he heard the gravel of her driveway under his tires, his car shifting sideways when he hit the brakes. From his vantage, he could see the yellow porch light before the front door and the candles that glowed throughout the house, a ghastly haze shining through the dirty windows.

Rushing up the drive, he couldn't see her through the windows into her house. He peered around the building, spotting a pale figure in the neighboring cemetery.

He marched over, shoving open the rusted gates, ignoring the dirt path set out to tour the gravesites. One marker nearly tipped over as he stumbled closer to the figure. When he was within talking distance, he stopped, looking. There, Steph knelt upon the ground before a gravestone as naked as the day she was born, a dark robe cast to the side. Whispers of smoke arose from her body, a cigarette nestled between her fingers.

He broke his silence.

"Well?"

Steph turned, seeing him. She grinned and returned her attention to the dirt at her feet.

"You really came."

He scowled, closing the space between them. "You asked me to."

"I did." She took a long drag and flicked the cigarette aside.

There came a rumbling knock by her feet and a whining Ramsey couldn't quite discern. He only knew that it grew louder the closer he got to her, as if she were wheezing through her grit teeth.

"I really wanted to see you again," she said.

"Why?" He stopped, the dull knocking going in and out, the whining faint but unyielding.

"Because," she said, looking back at him. "I told you before. You're powerful." She stood, her naked body aglow in the moonlight, slim and boney, her breasts swaying to her quickening breath. "Don't you believe me?"

The knocking sounded again. Steph smirked, biting her lip. She reached down and grabbed her robe, slipping it back on. As she did so, a high pitched wail sounded beneath her feet.

"What's that sound?"

"Come inside and I'll tell you all about it."

She walked past him through the graveyard towards her house. Ramsey lingered, looking back down at the dirt from where the sound emitted. It sounded almost like someone was buried alive, screaming, knocking their fists against the coffin lid. Only, the longer he stared, the less he thought that was possible.

The grass was fully grown, the dirt untouched.

Only her cigarette butts disrupted the space.

#

He followed her to her house where she opened the front door, shooing away her cat.

"Back, Lucifer, back." She glanced at him with grit teeth. "Sorry, he's just so happy that you finally came back."

"New cat?"

"No," she said. "He's just enjoying his tenth life is all."

She entered and he followed after her into the living room. Inside, the room took on a yellow-greenish hue, the candles flickering all throughout. It was the same as before; mirrors set upon the ground dusted with coke or incantations written in lipstick. She tiptoed past all the bits of broken glass and circular mirrors, settling onto the couch on her side, her black robe hanging loose over her pale body. Leaning out towards the nightstand, she snorted a line of cocaine, wrinkling her nose.

Ramsey remained by the entrance, staring at her. She gestured to the white lines.

"Help yourself, please."

"No thank you."

She shrugged and stretched, lighting a fresh cigarette. "I find I do my best thinking at night after I haven't slept for a few days." She crossed her legs, bouncing her knee. "That's when the world really starts to peel all its skin and show you the guts, if you know what I mean."

"Not really."

She pouted. "You know what you need? A drink." She hopped up off the couch and pranced into the kitchen, smoke wafting after her.

Ramsey said nothing. He looked at the various mirrors on the ground. Some were dusty with coke or pawprints, while others were marked with red lipstick. Several were shattered, as if she'd taken a hammer to its center. One oval mirror in particular had been cracked into a thousand tiny pieces. He took a step closer, looking down at the red lipstick that had been written over the glassy surface. Reading it, it appeared to be gibberish, red letters broken up by the hairline fractures of the shattered surface.

pmuj to gniog mi

Around that, circling it, the same series of letters over and over again.

yesmar kcab emoc

"Rum and coke, right?"

She sidled up beside him, holding out a tumbler of ice filled with his drink, a vodka on ice in her own glass.

"Yeah." He took it, stared at the drink, the bubbles climbing the inside of the glass. "This isn't the ice from the tray next to your dead cat, is it?"

"Not anymore."

Lucifer butt his head against Ramsey's leg, purring. The stench of him filled his nose. It was a mix of pus and wet fur, of something rotten in the dirt. When the cat looked up, he revealed his good eye, and to the left of that, an empty socket busy with tiny white maggots that fell out and crawled upon the ground.

"*Jesus fucking Christ!*" He backed away, stumbling over his own feet and falling, spilling his drink all over himself. Laying there, he looked up, seeing the room upside down. Turning over onto his knees, he spotted a tilted standing mirror, reflecting the floor. There, he saw the lipstick writing in reverse.

im going to jump

And around it, written over and over again:

come back ramsey

He looked up at Steph, backing away, shifting to avoid any of the mirrors.

"You killed them," he said, pushing himself onto his feet. "I don't know how you did it, but you killed them."

She rolled her eyes, drinking a sip of vodka. "I never killed anyone."

"She jumped," he said, pointing at the incantation. He searched the ground. "Here," he said, pointing at Kristina's name. The command was there, written backwards in red lipstick. "I'm going to cut my wrists."

"All I did was plant the seed. Just like you plant your little seeds, right Ramsey?"

"What are you talking about?"

"Like you really gave a shit about any of these girls," she said, waving a hand at all the mirrors. "Tell me this… did you ever really listen to Mayhem? Have you even seen *Haxam*? Did you really think it was interesting that I was into the dark arts? Or were you just trying to get into my pants?"

Ramsey shook his head, seeing all the broken mirrors that surrounded him.

"I never killed anyone."

"And neither did I." She strolled over to the couch, sitting back down. Her robe parted and she set her cold glass of vodka between her legs, shuddering. "I just… gave them some dating advice, that's all."

"They're dead!" Ramsey shouted. He threw his tumbler against the wall, shattering it. "I barely knew any of these girls and now they're all dead!"

She rolled her eyes again. "Big deal… it's not like you were in love with them." She parted her legs, shifting the icy glass deeper, biting her lip. "If it weren't for me, they probably would've died without you even knowing. Besides… now I can have you all to myself."

"I didn't come here to fuck you."

"Well, then what are you good for?"

"I came here to tell you that it's over. I want you to stop interfering with my life. Cause if you do…"

She stood, her robe slipping off her shoulder, drink sloshing out. She cocked a stink eye at him.

"If I do *what*?"

Silence.

Ramsey waved a dismissive hand at her and turned to leave, careful to not step on another mirror.

"You're not going anywhere."

"Watch me."

"I do," she said. "I watch you drink alone on the couch. I watch you watch the same movie over and over again. I watch you play all these pathetic little games with these other girls, playing their favorite music whenever they're around, laughing at their jokes, making sure the books they like are dog eared on your nightstand. I watch you stop talking to them when you want them to leave while texting some other girl that you want them to come over. And for what? So you can fuck them a few times until you get bored?" She snorted and sniffed, chuckling. "So banal, I'm surprised you haven't offed yourself yet."

He stopped, pausing before the door.

"Everything I've done was the price I needed to pay in order to do something incredible, which is definitely more important than what you do to avoid feeling alone on the weekends."

"Like what?" He turned, carefully shifting his feet to avoid the glass on the ground.

She shrugged. "I see things. Things that haven't happened yet. Things that could happen. I've gone places without moving. Ever leave your body and travel to the edge of the universe? It's worth the trip." She knelt down and lifted up Lucifer, stroking his sore ridden head. "And after one night with you, I've managed to raise the dead."

He looked out through one of her windows towards the cemetery, thinking of the undisturbed grass and the cigarettes strewn about on the ground.

She took a step closer, crossing one pale leg before the other, the distance between them closing. When she was nearly within arm's length, she set Lucifer down and looked Ramsey in the eyes.

"Isn't that worth the lives of a couple of dead girls?"

He pointed a stiff finger at her.

"You're crazy."

"Am I?" She looked down at the mirror between them. There, written in red lipstick:

ydnic

"Or do I just know how to get exactly what I want?"

Ramsey felt his vision go white, his hands clenching. He inched closer, avoiding the glass, unsure what it would do to Cindy if he accidentally broke it. Steph backed away in kind, the two shifting further into the living room towards the back wall. All the while, Ramsey felt his knuckles crack as he flexed them.

"Now hold on," Steph said, smiling. One last step backwards, and her head bounced against the wall. She looked left, right, searching for an escape.

"I'm going to bury you," he said, inching closer. "I'm going to bury you with whatever the fuck it is that's out there screaming under the dirt."

"I wouldn't," she said, eyes darting left and right.

"You haven't given me much of a choice."

"Then you'd be killing her too."

He stopped, hands still poised to strangle her.

"How?"

"It starts with a name. Then once they respond, there's a command." She looked past him towards the various broken mirrors. "Cindy lives far away, right? In another time zone? That's probably why I haven't had a response to the spell yet." She tilted her chin towards another mirror, the one used for Kristina. It was broken and spotted with dottings of blood he hadn't noticed before, but the one marked for Cindy was without stains or cracks. Just her name written backwards, and around the edges, a scribbling of letters he struggled to read backwards.

Take all the pills.

"I can stop the incantation before it reaches her." She reached out and touched his chest. "If you like…"

He stepped closer, nose to nose. "Don't you hurt her."

"I won't." She took his hand, set it over her breast. "Just give me what I want."

"Why?"

"Because…" She set both her hands upon him, staring down at his chest. "There's something about you that's awakened something within me. It's powerful. More powerful than anything I've ever felt in my entire life. Without you… I'm just another girl. But with you… I can raise the dead."

Ramsey looked back at the mirror with Cindy's name on it.

"Promise me she won't die."

"I promise."

"Okay then." He turned back around and started unbuttoning his shirt. "After tonight, I never want to hear from you again. And if I do, I swear to god, I'll put you in that fucking graveyard myself, dead or alive."

"Of course." She unbuckled his pants, greedily pulling them down. Kneeling, she looked up at him, tugging his boxers off.

"But make it last," she commanded before putting him in her mouth.

Ramsey did.

He thought of Kristina slitting her wrist in a bathtub.

He thought of Jenny's collapsed face.

He thought of Cindy emptying every pill bottle in the house and flopping around on the floor like a dead fish, alone as her heart stopped beating.

He imagined every girl he ever kissed dead and rotten, clawing their way out of a coffin for one last dance with Ramsey.

All the while Steph rode him, her black shroud of hair obscuring her white face as she screamed to all the power he gave her.

#

At home, he tossed his car keys onto the ground and stumbled into his bedroom, sleep hitting him like a baseball bat. He slept without dreaming, cold and dark.

Come morning, the alarm cried out, waking him. He groaned, smelling Steph on his skin, the gasoline burn lingering on his lips. Shifting, every inch of his body ached as he sat up.

There were voices in his apartment.

He got up, went to the door, listening. It sounded like the TV, but he didn't remember leaving the TV on.

"Hello?"

More voices, louder this time.

He opened his bedroom door and walked down the hall. The living room was dark, lit solely by the glow of his television as *The Shining* played. A lone figure sat on the couch, watching.

"Who the hell are you?" he shouted. He flicked the lights on and the darkness was swept away.

The stranger turned to face him. It was Jenny. Only, it wasn't the Jenny he had gone on a date with days ago. It was Jenny who jumped headfirst into the pavement, her face broken apart, her head split open. A flap of skin hung from the side of her skull and blood flowed around her neck like a scarf. Her right arm was bent, bone jutting out of the skin, while her right leg was backwards, sinewy muscle showing through torn jeans.

She spoke, her jaw swinging about.

"Uh oo on da ining," she said, attempting a grin. She gestured towards the TV.

"Hey Ram, want a beer?"

Kristina looked to him from the kitchen, putting away a case of beer. "I can put a few in the freezer to cool them down for you if you like."

Ramsey stared, eyes adjusting. There, he could see that Kristina's face was pale and blue. When he focused, he could spot the open wounds on her wrists.

"Breakfast will be ready in just a minute," a third girl said.

Ramsey walked down the hall, approaching. He found her stirring eggs and turning bacon over in a frying pan. Two slices of rye jumped out of the toaster.

She turned around. She was gray, with foam lingering on the corner of her lips, her eyes red with burst vessels and blood caked around her nose.

"You're gonna need your strength," Cindy said, turning back to the stovetop.

"No," Ramsey said, shaking his head. "No, no, no, no." His legs wobbled and he stumbled back down the hall.

"Oh, it happened a while ago," Cindy said offhand. "Long before what's her face tried to get me." She half turned to him, gesturing with her spatula. "I mean, you *could've* called to see how I was doing."

"Wa ee u auss ed?" Jenny asked.

"Oh yeah," Cindy said. "That's a good idea. You should pause the movie before she gets here, otherwise she'll just want to start it from the beginning"

Ramsey clenched his eyes and fell to the ground, praying he'd wake up in bed and that it will have all been a bad dream. Instead, he heard the hiss of a fresh beer, opening his eyes to see Kristina's slit wrist as she held out the bottle for him to take.

"Here you go babe."

Cindy came around, helping him up, the smell of vomit on her breath, half digested pills dotting her cheek.

Ramsey started to cry.

"Oh, come on now, get ahold of yourself," Cindy said. "She won't like it if you're like this."

"Yeah," Kristina said, "have a beer Ramsey." She shoved it into his hand. "It'll calm your nerves.

"Eeeass," Jenny said, half her face falling off.

"Okay," Ramsey said, catching his breath. He took a sip of the beer. It was still warm, but it was beer, and it made him feel light. They took him down the hall into his bedroom. As they did, Ramsey kept drinking, feeling as if someone were making him transparent, disappearing. In bed, they pulled his socks and pants off. Cindy caressed him and kissed his head while Jenny nuzzled his legs and kissed his inner thigh with a mouth that was split in two. Kristina left the room and came back seconds later with a rum and coke, setting it in his hand. After, she pulled his boxers off and took him in her cold dead mouth.

"There you go," Cindy said. "Just relax, okay?"

"Okay…"

He drank, wanting Cindy's voice to become just another dream. For the first time ever, he wanted to wake up alone.

"You'll make her real strong Ramsey," Cindy said, setting her hand over Kristina's head as she bobbed up and down. "Strong enough to raise up as many girls as you like."

"Irls, irls, irls," Jenny said, giggling.

Down the hall, the door creaked open. Following that, footsteps.

"Oh," Cindy whispered, watching the shadows as they crept closer. "Here she comes… and I think she brought a friend with her too!"

At the door, he heard the high pitched whine and closed his eyes, picturing the unturned grass and the pile of dead cigarettes, wishing somehow he could leave his body without moving, wishing somehow he could go to the edge of the universe where nothing at all could touch him.

Cindy cupped a hand under his chin.

"So," she said. "What are you thinking?"

Bloody Good Times
By Serena Daniels

'*L*eft, left, left...oh come on!*'
Ryan almost threw his phone down in disgust at his lack of options, he just wanted a date and there were slim pickings to be had. He had been through every dating app on his phone and either one that he had chosen had yet to message him back or they just didn't seem his type and the craving had set in, he needed to do something about it now.

'*What the hell am I going to do?*' He snorted out as he flopped back first onto the bed with an arm on his head. He felt like dying and he didn't seem to have many options that would help him…until his phone chimed a message from one of his buddies and he opened it.

"*Hey man! Check out this new brand new app! It's going to make our lives so much easier now, I guarantee it!*" John was always such a drama queen, but he wouldn't have sent this message if he wasn't serious about it. Ryan opened up the app page and a wide smirk appeared on his face as he read its features.

'This is just too perfect!' He wouldn't need Dave's hacking skills with this baby installed! Self-deleting messages…someone must really like people like him! This was perfect, a little too perfect…

'What if this is some kind of hoax?' He wondered as his finger hovered over the download button. *'What if they just look deleted and they're actually being stored for blackmail or something? That would really spell trouble…on the other hand, what if it's all real? Besides, if there is trouble than we have people that would take care of it if blackmail does come through to me…'* Decision made, he tapped the button and waited.

#

Bighani was alone and so she did not repress the urge to raise her eyebrow at the message that appeared in her app inbox.

'That was quick, I just put up my profile a minute ago!' She clicked on the little envelope and read the message, her other eyebrow joined its twin.

The Filipino beauty read through the message of the man who called himself Ryan and snorted; it was just the kind of message that she was waiting for, the kind that was saturated with flattery at how gorgeous she was, and she gave a smirk as that was exactly how she had planned it. The photo that she had put up was meant to maximize her sexiness, to show off her long legs and emphasize her modest bust; she wanted to lure the flies with her honey and even she was amazed at how quickly one had flew in.

'No matter,' she thought as she opened his profile. She scanned over him carefully, and made her decision. *'He'll do for this evening...'* She began to type out a reply.

#

'Yes!' Ryan had thought when his eyes had landed on one of the few female profiles that were available on the app; he could only guess that it was because this was so new that only a small pool of people knew about it. Damn she looked smoking hot!

'Never had an Asian before...' he mused as he stared at the picture on the screen. She was petite everywhere, breasts, hips, stomach and she seemed to be well aware of how beautiful she was and wasn't shy about showing off her goods. He'd had petite women before and he'd had big women and every kind of woman in between, but this woman had such an allure about her that he just had to have a night with her.

'Bighani,' he read the name silently and groaned quietly. Damn, he hoped that he wouldn't screw up the pronunciation when he talked to her; but he didn't really have any other option at this point, he would go insane if he didn't do something about this craving and it was early enough in the evening that he could spend a few hours seducing her first so he could have a little before he had to end things…

'Here goes nothing,' he thought as he quickly typed out a message to her; desperately hoping that she didn't already have plans tonight.

"Hi there, you're gorgeous!" He waited with bated breath as he saw the message go through and refrained from squealing in joy as he saw the indication that she

had read it; cautious optimism bubbled up in him when he saw the three dots that showed that she was typing out a response and crossed the fingers on the hand that wasn't holding the phone.

"Hello handsome," the message didn't have a voice to go with it, but Ryan could easily picture a very seductive voice that no doubt went with the messages' sender, maybe even some kind of accent to go with it? Ryan couldn't be sure but all he could do to find out was to plow through the conversation and hopefully that would later become a plowing of a different kind…

"How's it going tonight?" He knew that he had to be patient, he didn't want to scare her off so soon.

"Not a lot," was her reply. *"Just sitting around bored at home, waiting for something fun to come along, how about you?"* Oh, she sounded desperate alright.

"Looking for someone to take to that late night aquarium show," he typed out. He always did this kind of research when he was planning a date, he didn't really care about what was going on, he just looked at what he thought would be interesting to his date; or in this case, it was the only event going on this evening and he had hoped that this would be enough for whoever he would be taking out this night.

"Oooh, sounds interesting!" She answered. *"I love looking at fish, there is something so soothing about seeing them moving back and forth through the water!"*

'I could probably have shown her a small version of a shiny disco ball on a keychain and she would more than likely have the same reaction.' He thought smugly. *'This is actually going to be easier than I thought it would be!'*

\#

"I hope I'm not overdoing my act," she muttered as she saw that her last reply had been read. "The last thing I need right now is for him to be onto me and run off, having to chase him down wouldn't be fun at all, or in my nature." Her Filipino accent was slight, but just as musical sounding as the rest of her voice. "Then again, this is the easy part, I could pretend to be however I want to be when I'm just messaging, I can see why some unsavory people like doing it, and this is fun in a way! No, the hard part will be playing out this role."

His reply came up.

"Sounds good gorgeous! I hate to have to ask this, but how exactly do you pronounce your name?"

'At least he asked beforehand,' she thought before she started typing.

"Just call me 'Hani', it'll be easier for the both of us!" She smiled as she pressed send. His reply came swiftly.

"Alright Hani, how about we meet here?" He attached a picture from Google Maps that showed a small restaurant that she was familiar with, she'd passed by it numerous times while she went out on her nightly walks. She'd never gone inside, she hadn't needed to, but she was more than willing to go along with this if it meant getting what she needed.

"Sounds good, handsome."

#

'Okay, how do I want to look tonight?' Ryan asked himself as he examined his closet. He had to be a chameleon, so he'd filled his closet and drawers with a variety of outfits to fit his chosen woman, depending on what kind of vibe that he got from them. Businessman,

Slacker, Rocker, Goth, rich or poor he felt that he had an outfit for any woman that he came across. However, he couldn't quite get any kind of vibe from Hani, true he was sure that she might be a bit of a simpleton, but what kind of outfit should he go for that would maximize the effect he would have to have on her?

'Would going casual work wonders?' He looked over his casual wear with a frown. *'Or would I need something a little more high class? Businessman? Banker? Or would going too high up the social ladder be too much? Then again, when has any of my dates complained about the way I've dressed before? Surely anything I'll pick out will be worth it, maybe I should go with the safest route and wear something in between?'*

Ultimately, he went with his fail safe and chose one of his business casual outfits; while he was giving himself one last once over in the mirror, he wondered what she would be wearing.

'Hopefully, something that can be easily torn off!'

\#

'I need to find an outfit that can keep up with my ruse,' Hani thought as she looked through her sparse wardrobe. She had packed light when she had left the Philippines to come to the States and hadn't really had any inclination to do any clothes shopping despite having money to do so. That was fine with her, she didn't want to have to try hard enough to attract a date, she preferred to save her money for moving around to wherever she pleased, just like she'd saved up to come here from such a far off country.

After careful consideration, she chose a pink and white sundress and white kitten heels that she felt made her look as innocent as she tried to portray herself as.

'Let's see how long he keeps this girl waiting.' She thought after one last look in the mirror before she left her place, making sure to lock it up tight, she didn't need anyone snooping into her secrets. She did somewhat feel uncomfortable in her outfit, it wasn't her usual style, she usually dressed to blend into the crowd wherever she went, and didn't want to draw attention to herself. Unfortunately, she felt like she was doing just that as she felt eyes on her, she knew that she might as well have been screaming that she was on a date.

'This isn't good,' she thought with trepidation as she turned onto the street where the restaurant was. *'I am drawing too much attention to myself dressed like this!'* Hani knew that she was a very attractive woman, it was what made doing what she did all that much easier, but she couldn't afford to have that kind of attention on her now! She would just have to be extra vigilant this night, be more aware and extra sure that no one would be following her movements.

In front of the restaurant was a beautiful, small, iron fence that was all twisted in filigree patterns, it was clean looking enough that she leaned against it and took out her phone to text Ryan.

"I'm waiting outside, I'll be the only woman leaning against the fence."

'I wonder if that sounds silly enough for him.' She wondered as she pressed SEND.

#

Ryan was on the message right away, he'd had his phone in his hand since he'd left his haven and there was only one page open; he'd even ignored the text messages that his buddies had been sending him in favor of keeping the app open, waiting with trepidation as to whether or not she was going to change her mind or go through with this.

'Yes! Someone likes me!' He cheered inside as he read the message twice over to make sure that he wasn't hallucinating, as that was a symptom of his condition that cropped up when one like him didn't take care of their urges. But he was sure that the message was real, and he licked his lips with some subtlety in order to avoid receiving any strange glances from the people around him, especially the women, who he could sense were stopping and staring at him; his outfit was really making him stick out and it could be a good or bad thing this night.

'It's almost a shame that I can't hunt this way,' he thought as he looked over the message one last time. *'But that would be how I would draw attention to myself, this isn't like the olden days when few people went out at night, this is the era of late night dates without judgement and technology to make that much easier to do; it's why I had to take to these dating apps to begin with! At least I get to attract all kinds of women, I do like a little variety, like Hani here, I mean look at this message! Holy shit is this kind of lame, this might be easier than I thought!'*

He carefully typed out a message:

"Good, that'll make it easier to see you! I'm on my way!" He looked up as he hit SEND. He technically didn't have to as his superior senses could warn him of any potential obstacles in his path, human or otherwise,

and he knew all the statistics of people being hurt or injured from not looking up from their phones, but at least he thought to at least look almost normal if he were to occasionally look up and around.

Also, it gave him a chance to look around at the women, his next potential target? Or perhaps not, true he did recognize a few of them from the various dating apps that he had on his phone, but he wasn't going to risk trying again, he'd been in this town too long and now he'd definitely been seen walking along the street heading somewhere and there would more than likely be a few witnesses who could say that he'd been with Hani if questions just happened to pop up.

True, he always made sure to thoroughly get rid of the bodies, whether it was by burning, acid or just leaving it miles away near another jurisdiction, there was always that chance that technology could make law enforcement catch up with him; this was still a low chance of happening as he had no DNA to speak of anymore. But, there was always witness statements that could get him caught, however, more than likely he himself would be done away with by his people's own law enforcement if they even caught a whiff that he was a wanted man.

Self-preservation always came first for their kind, more than the loyalty towards the individual, hell, he knew that he would not even count on his own friends to shelter him if that time even came. Not only was that dumb, it was also hypocritical as he himself had once turned in an acquaintance that had made too many mistakes with their victims and had been on the run from the humans. At least the clean-up was easy after one of their own would be dispatched…

In any case, it was best that he get out of town as soon as he was finished with Hani, too many witnesses could identify him if she were to be uncovered and he need to lay low for a good long while before he could start hunting again, at least he could stave off his urges for a while after tonight…

He breathed a small sigh as he turned up the street, he felt himself weakening by the minute and was glad that he finally had some prey to catch now that he'd spent his nights hunting fruitlessly until now; he could finally breathe a little now, but he could only hope that he still had enough strength to be able to subdue her when the time came. This was a rock and a hard place for his kind as they needed their strength to take down their prey, but their strength weakened just the last final hours before their hunger related madness set in.

He still couldn't emphasize enough to himself that this was his last chance to curb his urges for a little while longer and that he had really lucked out on this new app; and to have found Hani's profile.

He didn't look at his phone again the rest of the way, he knew that he didn't have to as surely, she wasn't going to send another message when he was on his way, right? She didn't seem that intelligent to him, but she didn't look to be the clingy type either, at least, that was what he had hoped, not because it made things harder, rather clingy women made things a little easier to take them home, but because taking too many of them home after a certain amount of time just got plain annoying.

His excitement rose as the restaurant came into view, the crowd of people were still thick as people were either heading home or coming towards some event that was going on that night and it definitely put him on more intense alert as he had a strong inkling that more than a few of these people were also heading to the same aquarium event that he and Hani would be attending and that made the situation even more dangerous, but there was no other option and he had strongly felt that any kind of change to their already made plans would make her suspicious and maybe make her run, then he would really be fucked!

'Just calm down,' he scolded himself. *'You are a hunter, just get into hunting mode and think about satisfying your hunger only, do not doubt yourself!'* His eyes carefully scanned the area until he was able to see the restaurant fully, and much to his delight, they landed on the hot lady in pink and white, leaning against the railing like she said she was going to.

As much as he wanted to, he didn't go to her right away, he wanted to look her over first, to try and get a better feel of how he should approach her. She was looking at her phone sure, like an ordinary person, but what was she looking at? She looked…quite bored, was it from waiting for him? Was she regretting this date? It was driving him nuts that he still couldn't figure her out, her aura was as mysterious in real life as it was with her picture.

'Fuck it, I'm just going to have to wing it…' He was forced to decide before he puffed himself up in as unseen a way as he possibly could and moved forward.

#

She had felt him coming as soon as he had turned up the street, she pulled out her phone just to look as bored as she possibly could; she couldn't describe the feeling, she just felt something coming, something that was…off. No, Ryan was no ordinary man, and she would have to remain on complete alert until this night was over. She couldn't just pretend to look at her phone screen, so she brought up the dating app to check out the stats.

'Wow, 500 people from around the country have already joined and a dozen couples have already hooked up with another 100 already messaging, not bad for something this brand new!' She saw Ryan begin to head in her direction out of the corner of her eye; she kept her side gaze on him until he was close enough for her to decide to put her phone away, look up and "happen" to see him. *'Here we go…'*

"Hi Ryan!" She shouted when he was in earshot to allow herself to be heard above the crowd; giving a friendly wave to really sell it, also practically bouncing against the fence.

#

'At least she appears to be excited,' he mused as he gave a smooth hand wave in return and giving her his most charming smile, the one that he knew would blind people if it was possible. "Hey Hani," he said when he was right next to her. "You hungry?"

"Starving!" She said with a giggle and placed her hand in the one that he offered. "I'm just glad you came! You're the first one in a while that hasn't stood me up!" She wasn't dragging him to the restaurant, letting him take the lead but it felt like she desperately wanted to.

'I honestly can't imagine why,' there wasn't any sarcasm in his inner statement, he was genuinely puzzled as to why anyone would turn down a chance with this hot piece.

"Some guys are just dicks," he told her coolly with a small shrug. "Personally, I never keep a lady waiting." She let out another giggle.

"Dick, I love that word!" She made a happy noise. "But, I'm just glad that I have a real gentleman tonight; it's been way too long!"

'Wow, this is going to be easy...' "That's a real shame!" He said soothingly. "You seem quite a lady! I'm amazed that you were even alone tonight!"

"I don't mind being alone!" She said with a shrug. "But I have urges too you know, and it just frustrates me when my time is wasted and I'm alone when I don't want to be." She shakes her head, as if to banish the morose thoughts that were creeping up; she then plasters a huge smile back on her face. "Anyway, let's not ruin this by talking about such depressing things! How long have you lived here?"

"I just got in town myself," he replied carefully. "I'm just here to visit some family, but they had forgotten that I was even coming to I'm just staying in the house alone while they are out of town for the weekend." That was only a partial lie, the house that he was staying in did technically belong to family, but it was more of a haven that was a more of a pay the landowner to use than a free for all, however, it did belong to another one of his people so he knew that it was relatively safe to use when cravings set in; that was the whole point of having homes like these to begin with.

"Wow, that's harsh!" She gasped as they reached the door. "I can never imagine my family doing that, we're all so close!" They had reached the front podium at this point and neither spoke until the hostess requested the number of guests and led them to an open table, what seemed to be one of the few left in the place.

"Is your family all here?" He asked after they had been left alone with the menus.

"No," she said with a shake of her head as she opened her menu. "They are all back in Manila, I'm just touring around the world until I get back home."

"Then why are you here?" He asked with genuine curiosity. "In this town, I mean. Why wouldn't you be visiting one of the bigger cities that this country has to offer?"

"That's just the way I prefer it," she replied as her eyes continued to scan. "I like visiting smaller places, I like to think of them as 'hidden gems' compared to bigger cities, plus, there's less tourists in the smaller towns. I've run into enough jerk tourists back home, I don't want to have to deal with them while I'm travelling myself." Her previously happy tone had become slightly bitter, and the switch caused him to raise an eyebrow that luckily went unseen.

He was saved from answering by the waitress appearing and taking their drink orders; he was grateful as it gave him time to think of an appropriate thing to say to this.

'Maybe there's more to this girl than meets the eye...?' "Has tourism really soured your opinion of travelling that much?" He asked with genuine sounding curiosity.

"It hasn't completely driven my love of it away," she corrected still without putting down the menu. "Otherwise, I wouldn't be doing it at all, I know that not all tourists are terrible, one day I might be able to handle bigger cities without grinding my teeth, but for now I would rather not run into the same type of morons who mistook me for a sex worker on a regular basis." Her eyes appeared over the top of the menu now, as if waiting to see his reaction.

He'd met women like this before, the kind who complain about being harassed over their looks in one way or another, and they usually came in two categories. The first was that they secretly enjoyed the attention and just wanted some kind of reaction from him; the second was the type who were genuinely aggravated and just needed to vent. The question was, which category did she actually fit into?

'Time to guess,' he thought as he inwardly took a deep, unnecessary breath and simply stared her straight in the eye over his own menu and raised a brow; this seemed to have been the right call as her eyes almost seemed to sparkle before she lowered her gaze again and said nothing else and neither did he for the time being.

#

'Oh, he's good,' she inwardly complimented him. It was now even more obvious to her that Ryan was no ordinary man; but whoever he was, it was clear from his mild reaction to her sadly all too true rambling that he was careful, yes, there was something sinister about him…and the things that she wanted to do to him…

'Down girl,' she scolded herself as she felt herself become really excited at the prospect, but it wasn't time yet, they were in public so she had to settle down; yet it was so difficult because the flashbacks of what she used to do to those stupid, disgusting tourists were beginning to bubble up from the depths of her mind and she was having trouble keeping her breaths even and her excitement from showing.

Instead, she pretended to concentrate on her menu and opened her senses to try and take stock as to who Ryan could possibly be and she was puzzled, but did have an inkling as to what the truth was, but she would have to get him alone to be absolutely sure. Her hands really felt like twitching at the remembrance of how…chilly his hand felt when she'd held it earlier, she took a small sniff with her now open senses and he didn't smell…alive for a lack of a better term, and there was she did (or rather didn't) pick up with her ears…

'I always wondered if his kind even existed, then again, only locals of my country are even capable of believing in mine,' she carefully closed the menu and put it down. In truth, she had chosen a light salad to eat and had just been buying up time to keep from talking to him, analyzing him instead; plus, the salad was the only thing that she knew that would be able to choke down, that was from firsthand experience.

An experience that had almost revealed her true nature…

She watched as he also lowered his menu before he looked at her again, and she wondered just what he was going to order that wouldn't give himself away, she saw that it was fortuitous that their waitress had returned with their drink orders and swiftly took out her notepad once she had set their drinks down.

"Ladies first," he said smoothly, and she gave the most perky smile she could muster before she ordered her salad and she looked at him, trying not to look expectant, nor to look puzzled when he ordered a rare steak as she tried to connect the dots.

'Maybe because it is only a step above raw?'

#

'Maybe she's more ordinary than I thought?' Ryan wondered after the waitress swiftly left to deliver their

order to the kitchen. It was in his experience that few women actually ordered real food that wasn't vegetable dominant, then again, maybe she was a vegetarian? Her figure was very thin, but not eating disorder thin, so he wondered if her being a vegetarian, or a vegan was the truth.

He, on the other hand, was capable of consuming meat, but only of the rare variety at most as it was only a step above raw and bloody, and technically he could eat other things, but they would have to be drenched in blood to do that. Luckily, he always carried around small bottles for occasions like this, he never used them when he was hungry because they could never sustain him on the long term like an actual body would. However, some sleight of hand was going to be required to pull off getting away with putting blood on his food.

"You must like the taste of blood or something," she interrupted his thoughts with a giggle and he froze as his thoughts raced, he could have even sworn that his heart was racing, if only that was even possible…

"It's okay," he managed to shrug. "I just personally find anything that's cooked more than that to be a little tough on the teeth and I don't particularly feel like having to work to chew my food." *'Or to actually get it.'*

"I don't mind anyone else's dietary habits," she shrugged still smiling. "As long as no one tries to tell me how to eat, I don't try to pick fights over it." He decided that it was better not to ask about her salad choice than, he didn't want to accidently offend her and lose this last chance for satiation, so he decided that he needed to change the subject and quickly.

Somehow, he managed to finagle a bit more out of her as he gave the usual lies when she asked about him before their food came. They talked about their families

276

(his were actually long dead) and she still seemed sympathetic when he expanded on his lies about the absent-minded family that left him behind; she, on the other hand, seemed to be very close with her family.

They ate in silence and that was fine with him, and her too it seemed, things only took a turn after they had left the restaurant.

#

"How about we skip the aquarium and go back to my place?" Hani asked into his ear in a seductive voice before she could stop herself. If she could sweat, she would, but it was too late to take the words or the tone back. Shame, she genuinely wanted to see the aquarium, but she needed to take care of him as soon as she was able to and she was tired of dragging this out; she had to be careful though, as her theory seemingly had been confirmed when she noticed that he had taken out a small bottle of red liquid that he hid behind the ketchup bottle when he poured it on his food.

She had to give him credit, he knew how to be sneaky, she admittedly wouldn't have even noticed his actions if she hadn't been secretly looking at him directly.

If he was shocked by her proposition than he gave no indication as he turned to look at her in the eyes before he said smoothly, "If the lady wishes, then lead the way." She almost shivered as she grabbed his hand to lead him, but not to her home, no she couldn't do that with the risk of being seen, not she would anyway, she always led her prey astray…

She felt anticipation build up in her as she led him to a series of back alleys in the opposite direction of her temporary haven, where there were no streetlights and would give him the perfect chance to make the first move, after all he was a creature of the night like she was. He took full advantage of the darkness quickly and removed his hand from hers and tried to grasp at her neck and pull her to him.

But she was quicker and grabbed both his wrists and pushed them back until she heard the snap and his cry of pain that he was trying to muffle to avoid being heard; she didn't know how long it would take for the bones to heal, but she didn't want to take the risk of it being quickly enough to overpower her, yet she couldn't resist wanting to walk circles around him as she gloated like the villains in the movies. So, that's exactly what she did.

"I have to admit, I never thought that I would ever run into one of your kind, even while in your part of the world…"

#

If Ryan had been human than the pain would have been overwhelming, but he managed to keep his wits about him as he listened to her speak and her feet walk around him.

"I can tell that you are the arrogant type, that's probably why you didn't open your senses and figure out what I was," she continued. "Such a shame, but I can never turn down an opportunity for blood, and it would be interesting to try something new."

'What the fuck is she talking about?!' He mentally cried out as his wrists only became more painful, there was no way that he could heal them when he was so low on blood; he was well, and truly, fucked.

"When you've lived as long as I have, you might get tired of the same old routines," she was still speaking. "After so many centuries, you get tired of just sticking your tongue into a pregnant belly just for that little bit of blood that a fetus holds…" something tickled in his mind at this statement.

"Then those asshole tourists finally came and oh they were so much fun to induce fear in," he pictured her eyes gleaming as he heard the happiness in her voice.

"But…" she trailed off for a moment before resuming. "I grew tired of that routine too and that was when I started travelling, going to those quaint places and drinking whoever I was able to grasp; it was fun and yet I still wanted more…and then I got an idea. I figured that since dating apps were getting so popular nowadays, I would learn enough programming to launch my own…"

"The app," he managed to rasp out despite the pain.

"Exactly!" Her tone was kind of excited. "I never expected it to be so popular on launch night, nor to find a victim; never mind one like you." She made a small noise before continuing, "Sorry, I need to be more comfortable before I continue." He heard rustling and out of the corner of his eye he saw her dress fall; he was so shocked that he took his gaze away from his injured wrists to look up, and his eyes almost popped from their sockets.

Oh, she was naked alright, but that wasn't the most shocking part, it was the artificial legs that she was still walking around with the heels still on; if that wasn't enough, that gorgeous flesh that made up the top half was beginning to change, it was becoming more shriveled and bat-like wings were beginning to emerge from her back. Also, she was unstrapping the legs from herself, and the top half hovered above the discarded legs.

Shit, he'd heard of these kinds of creatures, the ones who feasted on blood as he did and could separate themselves from their lower half and were from the Philippines, fuck what were they called again?…Right…

"Manananggal," he hissed out as she stopped in front of him.

"Exactly, little vampire." Her red eyes gleamed before her fangs descended upon him.

\#

She never dreamed that she would feel this good from feeding.

Hani finished dressing and putting her prosthetics back into place as she stared at the pile of ash that was left of her date. She was feeling very euphoric, she wondered if she was feeling the equivalent of a human being "higher than a kite".

'I should be finding other blood drinkers more often,' she told herself as she carefully stepped out of the alley, but didn't head home just yet.

She still wanted to see that aquarium show and she hoped that it was still going on.

The Girl Who Loved Senpai
By Scott McGregor

There he is, seated at the front of the classroom as a proper senior should be. All the boys in school wear the same seifuku uniform—the standard buttoned black-jacket with a stand-up collar and dress pants—but none of them spot it with such dapper and sophistication like he does. Everything about him reeks of elegance, from the way his gelled, ink-black hair glimmered, the way his chiseled jaw compliments his tastefully red dimples, the way his tan brings out his gorgeous brown eyes, and the way his pearly-white teeth help showcase his majestic smile. I especially adore how he leaves the top two buttons of his shirt undone, granting me a peek at what's beneath.

He's so succulent.

So mouth watering…

His name is Senpai, and soon, we will be together. One day, we will get married and spend the rest of our lives together. We will abandon the crowded city of Tokyo and find a perfect minka on Tsunoshima Island, with tatami matted floors and wooden engawa verandas, like I've always dreamed. All the girls at school will be jealous of Senpai and I. They will refer to us as the true staple of romance, the perfect evocation of intimacy, and above all, the greatest couple in Japan. No love story shall compare to ours.

But for now, Senpai is too busy gawking at Hana-chan. Too busy to realize the love of his life sits a mere three desks behind him—so close, yet so far. Unlike the distance that separates me from Senpai, Hana-chan gets to sit at the front beside him, all thanks to a coincidental, unfair alphabetical seating arrangement by Tanaka-sensei. I hear Hana-chan's obnoxious, insufferable giggle at every one of Senpai's flirtatious comments. What I wouldn't give for Senpai to make me laugh instead of that superficial, worthless Hana.

It's too unbearable to watch them any longer, so to relieve my pain, I drift my gaze away. I look out the classroom window into the chilly October day—at the moribund decay of leaves entering a calm autumn in Tokyo. I can't let this beautiful scene slip past me, so I pull out my camera and capture as many fleeting moments as I can. This will be perfect for the yearbook.

The clock strikes 8:45 AM, and the bell follows. Myself and the rest of my classmates arise from our seats and sing the Kimigayo national anthem. If I focus closely, I can drown out the rest of the class and hear only Senpai, listening to his perfect soprano tone. Even his voice is heavenly. Once the anthem finishes, there comes another voice I must hear, one not nearly as pleasant as Senpai's.

"Students of Hokkaido High," principal Sato begins on the overhead, "I have dire and disheartening news that has been brought forth this morning. Another one of our own has gone missing. Mira Hashimata."

Whispers amongst my classmates start to flutter.

"This now makes a total of three students at Hokkaido gone missing," principal Sato continues. "As a result, we are now administering new protective measures and curfews to prevent more disappearances from arising while the authorities look into this pressing matter. After school hours, students are to head straight home and travel in groups of four or more. Lunch shall now remain indoors. The teachers and staff here at Hokkaido care deeply about the wellbeing of—"

As Sato continues with his blabber, I notice Senpai passes Hana-chan a note, and she responds with a blush. That blush makes me dig my nails into my wooden desk.

Eventually, the principal finishes with his little announcement, and the day commences as normal. For the first twenty minutes of class, I pay no mind to Tanaka-sensei's lesson. Instead, I examine Hana-chan closely, trying to figure out what makes her tick. Senpai is known as the class flirt, so it was only a matter of time when Hana-chan reached his radar. As revolting as it is to admit, I understand the appeal Hana-chan offers, that sort of charm the boys crave: popular, intelligent, shy but not distant, and of course, drop-dead gorgeous, with her light complexion, silky hair, and curly eyelashes. To top it off, she kept her skirt an inch shorter than the dress code requires, making her the sort of girl who abides by the rules while simultaneously breaking them. Perhaps that's what Senpai likes about her. Perhaps he likes a girl with a dark side.

But, what is it about me that he doesn't like?

It's been over a year since I first laid my eyes upon Senpai. It happened on my first day at Hokkaido, the moment I stepped through the front door as a freshman student. There he was, so handsome, so majestic. First, I assumed love at first sight was merely a superstition, but the pleasant burn of endearment in my eyes from Senpai's presence proved me wrong.

But not once has he shown me the same appreciation. Not once have we spoken, and I haven't stopped wondering why he hasn't noticed me. I never cease to ask why he didn't grant me the attention and affection he gives the other girls. Is it because my hair is dyed orchid purple? Is it the fact I'm only 5'2? Is it the fact I'm a junior and he's a senior? To this day, I don't know why I've gone unnoticed, but nonetheless, he will be mine.

And I know exactly how to make him fall in love with me.

***

During the lunch period in the homeroom, I sit at my desk and nibble on soybeans and fried almond fish. Everyone—besides me—is talking to someone, and as I chew my lunch, cleansing my palate with veggies and fish, I watch Senpai converse with our social studies instructor, Ichiku-sensei. They are talking about upcoming 2002 entrance exams for seniors, and Senpai is confident he will land a perfect score. This is the only time of day I catch Ichiku-sensei smile. Even the women instructors in their 40s can't resist Senpai's charm. That is just the kind of effect Senpai has on people, capable of wooing women in all their wonderful forms and ages. Hell, even the boys seem lured to Senpai, some by appreciation, others from jealousy.

"Akari-chan!" The girl who calls my name and sits down on top of the desk adjacent to me is Niko-chan, senior class president of Hokkaido High, and one of the most persistent, pestering, and downright insufferable girls I have the displeasure of being acquainted with. "I was hoping to catch you alone. I think it's about time we discuss the yearbook. I know you've been working extra hard. I'd love to run some ideas by you."

"Mhmm," I usher, not taking my eyes off Senpai.

"There's the fall catalog that'll be out in a month, and then of course we've got the upcoming volleyball season—"

"Mhmm."

"—obviously the cherry blossoms don't bloom till April, but it'd be smart if we plan ahead in preparation for that."

"Mhmm."

It's at this point I zone out, knowing words continue to spew out of Niko's mouth, but I can't register what she says. I don't want to. More often than not, I deal with this inconvenience on a weekly basis, whether from classmates or teachers. My role as the school photographer holds certain obligations, one of which includes constant communication and updates on the progress of the yearbook. Such a pain.

Even though I have to put up with the vermin that is the Hokkaido community, I love taking pictures. I have ever since I was a child. I love it almost as much as I love Senpai. Sometimes I'm able to have the best of both worlds when I take pictures of Senpai, even if he doesn't know it's happening.

As much as I want Senpai to lay his eyes on me, there were plenty of times I prayed he never noticed I was around to take pictures: Those times I followed him between classes; those times I followed him after school; those times I lurked outside his home, praying he'd leave his blindfolds open so I'd have a new picture to add to my collage of him; he is the reason why photography is equal parts exhilarating and terrifying, and it makes me love him even more.

For a second, Niko-chan finally stops blabbing, and from the corner of my eye, I can tell she takes notice of what I'm staring at.

"Oh, you like him, huh?" she says, referring to my Senpai. "If I'm being honest, I have a crush on him too. The school dance is coming up, and I would love it if Sora-kun asked me, but he seems more interested in Hana-chan by the looks of it."

His name is Senpai.

"Anyways," she continues, "let's talk soon about the yearbook. I look forward to it."

I don't respond back, and Niko strolls away to go bother someone else. I lean my head back in relief, then start to devour my lunch and keep watching Senpai.

For a second, I believe I can spend the rest of the lunch period in a peaceful trance, but not a minute later, someone else hovers over my shoulder. They whisper, "Uhm, Akari-chan?"

I glance over, and to my surprise, it's none other than Hana-chan. What does this stuck-up, tease of a pretty girl be doing speaking with me?

"Can I help you with something?" I ask, mouth full of soybeans.

"Well, see, I know you're the school photographer, and I've seen your work. You're really talented. So, I

286

was wondering… well… would you mind maybe taking some photos of me?"

I stop chewing, take a big gulp, and say, "You want me to cover a photoshoot for you?"

"If you wouldn't mind? There's a certain somebody I want to impress." I see her glance over to Senpai and blush again, and I'm tempted to risk getting suspended on the account of breaking her nose, but I keep my composure. She faces me again and says. "If you're too busy, I totally under—"

"Meet me after school and we'll do it then. I know a great place where we can take photos. Don't keep me waiting."

***

After school, Hana-chan does as I instruct, and we ignore Hokkaido's four-person group rule and depart alone. At first, she assumes I am taking her back to my house, but I have other plans. I know of a better location for the session—somewhere private, secluded, isolated. A place where nobody will interrupt us.

By the time we cross into Kamezawa street, she starts to shiver and rub her arms from the cold breeze. That's what she deserves for wearing a skirt so short, all to impress a boy that belongs to someone else.

"Thanks again for doing this," Hana-chan says. "I really appreciate it."

"Mhmm," I mumble.

"How much further is this place?"

"Not far."

"Are you sure about doing this for free? I really don't mind giving you some sort of compensation?"

"That won't be necessary."

It takes us fifteen minutes to arrive outside the abandoned Yigglo building: former laundromat, now abandoned warehouse. We step through the door, walk past the old washing machines, and go to the very back where the elevator is.

"Here we are," I say. "Below is where we'll conduct our photoshoot."

"Are you sure about this?" Hana-chan asks. "We could get in trouble."

"Don't worry." From my pocket, I pull out a rusty key. "As far as I know, I'm the only one who has access to this place."

"Where does it lead?"

"You'll see." I unlock the gate and enter the elevator shaft. I can see Hana-chan is reluctant, so I extend my hand and say, "Do you want your photos done or not?"

She takes my hand and enters the elevator. Then, I press the downward button that starts our descent. There is nothing but the sound of the elevator's creak and Hana-chan's nervous breath to hear.

After a minute, we reach the bottom. When I open the gate, Hana hastily takes the first step out into the dark basement, seemingly wanting to leave the elevator as quickly as possible. I understand the feeling, since I felt the same months ago when I first entered this place. But now, there is nothing for me to fear, so I follow behind Hana.

Then, Hana-chan covers her nose in disgust, likely from the pungent odor. "What is that awful smell?"

"Don't worry about it," I say. With a match, I light the nearby lantern, granting the basement with some mild luminescence. The floor is damp from a dripping pipe. Not much can still be seen, but it's enough to conduct the job I came here for.

"This is where you do your photoshoots?" Hana-chan asks. "Down here?"

"Correct." I lock the elevator gate behind me.

"It's a bit dim, don't you think? I can hardly see anything."

"I wouldn't worry about that." I take a step forward and examine Hana-chan. "I've seen the way Senpai looks at you."

"Senpai?"

"It's that same look he gave Ichika, and Yui… and Mira. But never to me."

"Akari-chan?"

"Shall we get started?"

"No," she says as she uncomfortably rubs her arms up and down, clinching to the light. "I'm sorry, Akari-chan, but I'm a bit confused. How are we supposed to start taking photos in a place like this?"

"I wasn't talking to you." I glance past Hana-chan, raise my voice, and say to my friend, "You can come out now."

First, Hana-chan is confused, then she turns around. "Who're you talking to?"

"Him," I say as I point to the corner of the room.

From the shadows, my friend emerges. He is twice the height of Hana-chan and myself, nearly reaching the ceiling. He wears a long, black yukata that hides his feet and drags against the ground, moistened by the wet concrete. As he comes closer into the light, he reveals his face; his eyeless, noseless, earless, lipless, mouthless face that glimmers against the lantern's shine, blank as a piece of white paper, smooth as a baby's bottom. He lifts his dry, shriveled index finger and points to Hana-chan.

Hana-chan is quiet, paralyzed by the sheer sight of my friend, just as the other three who came before had been.

"Hello, Noppera-bō," I say. "Sorry to have kept you waiting."

"A-Akar-ri-ch-chan," Hana-chan sputters. Noppera-bō looms over Hana-chan, leaning his head toward her. As they meet *face-to-no-face*, I see a trail of urine run down Hana-chan's leg.

"Be still, Hana-chan," I say, as Noppera-bō wraps his arms around Hana-chan and embraces her. "It'll be easier for him if you're still."

Noppera-bō brings his index and middle finger below Hana-chan's jaw, then presses his thumb against her chin. His nails extend, digging beneath her skin. Then, in one quick tug, he pulls upward and removes Hana-chan's face like snakeskin. There is no blood when he does so, nor does Hana-chan scream when it happens. How could she, since she no longer has a mouth to do so. Her faceless corpse hits the floor, and in Noppera-bō's hand is another mask for his collection.

Once Noppera-bō finishes with Hana-chan, he cranks his head toward my direction. In one of Noppera-bō's hands is Hana-chan's face, and with his other, he raises four fingers.

Four down, six to go.

I grab Hana-chan's legs and drag her corpse to the corner of the room, away from where the lantern's light shines and with the other three faceless bodies. By now, Ichika's corpse has mostly been reduced to a skeleton, but Yui and Mira still have a ways left to decay. No getting rid of that odor anytime soon either; not with a fresh batch to rot away down here.

I walk back up to Noppera-bō. "The deal we made… the promise, does that still hold?"

Noppera-bō's neck twists and twirls counterclockwise, and then he wear's Hana-chan's face. "Of course," Noppera-bō says in Hana-chan's voice. "Ten faces for one wish of your choosing."

Ten faces, and Senpai shall be mine.

***

Ten minutes past the new curfew for students, I walk into my minka on Nakano Ward. My parents ask what kept me out later than expected, to which I respond by saying I stayed after school for a photoshoot. I avoid mentioning the name Hana at all costs, as her name will soon join the list of missing people on the news. By the time I finish with my elaborate lie, my parents allow me to be excused to my bedroom. Wasting no time on small talk, I run upstairs, lock my bedroom door, and remove my collage of Senpai photos I keep hidden in my closet.

I'm not normally one to brag, but my collage is what people would call a true work of beauty, far more captivating than anything in the Mori Art Museum. Senpai's life story was practically captured onto this amalgamation of photos, from Senpai eating lunch at Hokkaido to Senpai running laps on track team to Senpai walking home from school.

For the past year, I've been assembling this majestic work of beauty, and it grows better with each new entry. I dare not show this piece to anybody, for I can already imagine the sort of responses I'd receive. *Akari-chan, you can't take someone's picture without their consent. Akari-chan, this is incredibly creepy and inappropriate, so you need to stop. Akari-chan, you're a total stalker.*

Akari-chan, have you considered mental therapy? These fools can think whatever they want. They've likely never been in love the way I have.

Still, I often wonder what Senpai would think of my collage—hell, of my love of him in general. Certainly him of all people would be flattered by everything I've done. Or, would he think I'm a freak. What if he files a restraining order on me? What if he finds out I'm the one who killed Ichika, and Yui, and Mira, and now, Hana? What will he think of me then? What if he'll think I'm a monster?

Maybe I am a monster, and maybe I don't deserve Senpai's love after all...

No, I mustn't think of such things. Now is not the time to abandon everything I've worked toward. I must believe love comes with some kind of happy ending, and I will stop at nothing to achieve it. I will show Senpai my collage at some point, but only after we're together. Only then will he understand why I did what I did.

So long as my special friend keeps up his end of the bargain, I shouldn't have to wait too much longer.

***

I still remember the first day I met Noppera-bō. It was five months into my first year at Hokkaido; four months into my infatuation with Senpai. At this point, I'd developed a habit of following him after school, taking whatever pictures I could from secret vantage points to craft my collage.

One day, Senpai walked down a different route than usual, so I kept my distance and followed. Eventually, we wound up outside the abandoned laundromat. I didn't know why Senpai came to this place, but he strolled inside with no hesitation.

I waited outside for twenty minutes, and still, he hadn't emerged. This is where I began to feel a bit anxious. Then, my unease shifted to nausea, and my nausea quickly shifted into unrelenting fear. Fear that maybe something terrible happened to Senpai without anyone knowing.

So, I decided to ditch the whole *stay out of sight at all costs* routine and enter the laundromat to ensure Senpai was safe and sound, but when I stepped inside, he wasn't there. The building was vacant, all to myself. At this point, I suspected maybe Senpai realized someone followed him, and his entry into the laundromat was his way of shaking off his tail. If that was his intention, it certainly fooled me. Or, perhaps his visit to the laundromat was simply out of curiosity and boredom, with no knowledge somebody followed him. To this day, I pray for the latter.

That's when I found the key to the elevator, lying on the floor right in front of the gate. I figured maybe Senpai took the elevator down, which, of course, led to me unlocking the gate and travelling down myself.

It wasn't long after that I reached the basement and met the faceless demon for the first time.

As expected, I was paralyzed with fear upon meeting a creature without a face. How could someone not react to such a bizarre abomination? I half-expected to be attacked, maybe even eaten alive by whatever this thing was.

Instead, it waved at me, and when I gained the sense the creature didn't intend to harm me, I relaxed a little. Then, it cranked and twisted its neck, spotting the face of an elderly man I didn't recognize. "Hello, I am Noppera-bō," he—or should I say IT said in a hoary tone. "What is your name?"

A part of me wanted to stay silent, but I gulped in fear and sputtered, "Akari."

"Tell me, Akari, if you could have one thing in this world, what would it be?"

Without needing to think about it, my mind drifted to Senpai—to his luscious face and angelic aura. Even in a deep, dark, secluded place below the laundromat in front of a monster, his existence plagued my thoughts. But, instead of telling Noppera-bō of my desires, I asked, "Why is that your business?"

"Because I can grant you whatever it is you desire, so long as a price has been met."

"And what price is that?"

"Ten faces for one wish of your choosing," the creature whispered to me. "Bring ten people here before my presence, and I shall do the rest."

For a moment, I stared into the elderly face, perplexed with what Noppera-bō asked of me. I read about mythical spirits capable of granting wishes in some of my children's books, though I never believed they existed, nor did I believe those wishes came at the cost of a life. I chose not to entertain the creature with a response, merely turning around and heading back up the elevator in haste.

Four months passed after the encounter, and I stayed as far away from the laundromat as I could. I kept the key with me, for I couldn't let any other poor soul stumble across Noppera-bō. Quite often, I thought about the deal he offered me: *Ten faces for one wish.* That meant I needed to lure people inside the laundromat and sacrifice them to Noppera-bō. At first, the idea appalled me. How could anybody offer up people to a creature like that, all for a silly wish?

Of course, Junior year began, and I saw Senpai chatting with this senior called Ichika.

Ichika Yayoi, leader of the mathematics team, member of the debate club, and support on the volleyball team, otherwise the first girl to be a royal pain in my ass. For reasons unbeknownst to me, she garnered Senpai's attention. He relentlessly flirted with her, made her laugh, and focused his attention onto her instead of me, the love of his life. I couldn't stand it, and I walked home from school every day engulfed in rage. I knew there was zero chance of Senpai falling in love with me if he was crushing on Ichika.

So, one day after class, I mustered the will to speak with Ichika, and before I knew it, I found myself taking her back to the laundromat basement, and Noppera-bō received his first face.

Now, as I gaze into my collage of Senpai, I repeat the words, "*Four down, six to go.*"

***

The week following Hana-chan's sudden disappearance proved rather irritating. Frequent announcements from principal Sato, new protective measures, student locker checks, and shorter curfews after school. This all made my job for Noppera-bō more difficult. If I am to continue delivering him faces as he requests—and I shall, for nothing will stop me from acquiring my wish—then I am to operate with more caution, finding candidates on the weekend rather than the weekdays and careful not to be seen.

To make matters worse, I see Senpai has gotten over Hana-chan without a second's thought. I catch him flirting with Sakura-chan between classes, some sophomore girl from the swim team. They don't share any classes together, and yet, somehow, she lands on Senpai's radar while I stay unnoticed as usual.

It's unfair.

It's sickening.

It's enough for me to snap my pencil in the middle of mathematics class.

Every student in the room turns their attention onto me. Botani-sensei's face shows concern, along with some mild annoyance at me interrupting his lecture, and he asks, "Akari-chan, is everything alright?"

If I speak, I know I'll scream out of frustration, so I merely nod in silence. I'm thankful Senpai is not in this class, for the last thing I want him to see is me throwing a temper tantrum. That's not how I want him to notice me.

The bell rings, and as everyone scrambles to get to their next class, I search for Sakura-chan. Whenever Senpai flirts with someone new, I take special precautions to learn everything about that person, including their schedule and locker number, so finding her is easy.

"Hello, Sakura," I say, sneaking up behind.

"Hi?" she says, a tad startled.

"Sorry, we haven't been properly introduced. I'm Akari, the school photographer. Say, how would you like to do a photoshoot this weekend?"

***

In the course of a month, the progress towards my wish comes together quite nicely. I delivered three more faces to Noppera-bō's grand collection, granting him a total of eight to wear as he pleases. They were all girls I went to school with for years, girls who caught the eye of Senpai: Tanji, Senpai's chemistry lab partner; Chiyo, Senpai's personal tutor; Ishida, Senpai's fellow teammate on the badminton team. Some were easier to lure to the laundromat than others, but I managed to offer them to my friend nonetheless. I even tried to offer Tanaka-sensei a photoshoot, though she turned it down, no surprise.

There's been times I'm afraid someone will catch me, but I've been careful and taken the extra precautions. Besides, people in Tokyo disappear all the time. Hell. Even before my freshman year, a bunch of students at Hokkaido went missing and were never found, and to this day, nobody knows why, how, or who was responsible—certainly not by my doing. Nobody suspects what I'm up to, and as far as the authorities are concerned, this is the work of some perverted old man who crushes on underage girls. People are so easy to fool these days.

Just two students left until Noppera-bō grants me my wish.

Just two students left until Senpai is mine.

And as I walk through the front door of Hokkaido on a Monday morning, I see Senpai flirting with another girl, and I acquire my next target. She has her back turned, and I can't quite make out who it is. It didn't matter who, for her face would soon belong to Noppera-bō regardless.

I can't help but picture it's me he's flirting with. Him finding me by my locker, leaning in close enough for a kiss, and then walking me to class. His enchantment is too powerful to handle sometimes, but soon enough, it will be I who enchants him.

Senpai departs to class, leaving my target alone. Once she turns around, I realize that it's none other than Niko-chan.

She catches sight of me and strolls over. "Good morning, Akari-chan!" she says.

"Morning, Niko-chan," I say.

"You won't believe it, but Sora-kun just asked me to the school dance!"

My eye twitches. "You don't say?"

"Yeah, I'm so happy. It sucks to hear about Ishida-chan, but between you and I, I thought Sora-kun was going to ask her to the dance, so I'm a little glad my competition has dwindled a bit. Anyway, you and I never got a chance to talk about the yearbook. We should do that soon."

"You're right, we should discuss it. How about this weekend? I know a great place where we can chat."

***

On a chilly Saturday morning, Niko-chan meets me outside the Yigglo building. She's too enchanted by her own voice to question where we're going, so leading her into the elevator shaft is easier than I assumed. As we descend, my ears nearly bleed as the sound of Niko-chan's toxic, infuriating voice continues.

"So the yearbook is clearly our number one priority to discuss today. There's still several sections that need to be developed."

"Uh-huh," I say.

"Then we also need to go over the swim team. Not to be a bother, but I hear you haven't taken any pictures of them yet."

"Mhmm."

"There's also the matter of the school dance. Now that I have a date, I'll be too busy keeping track of everything, so the photographs will need to be taken under your supervision."

Does this girl ever shut up?

Finally, we reach the basement. I lead her out and lock the gate behind, not sure how much longer I can tolerate listening to her.

"Wow, I know you said peace and quiet, but this place is a bit much, don't you think? And what is that terrible smell?"

I clap my hands and say, "Alright, let's get this over with, quickly, please."

"Sheesh, Akari-chan, I'm just being thorough. You know, with a more can-do attitude, I think you'd be—"

"Niko, do me a favor and keep your mouth shut." I point to the corner of the room. "You can come out now."

Noppera-bō emerges, then moves up to Niko-chan, and this is the first time I see her stay quiet for more than a few seconds.

"Akari-chan, what is—"

He slips his two fingers beneath Niko-chan's chin and removes her face, and I'm thankful I'll never have to listen to her insufferable nagging again.

"She might have a nice face, but her voice is worse than nails on a chalkboard," I say. "Use it sparingly."

Noppera-bō tucks away his new face beneath his cloak, then raises nine fingers.

One left.

I smile as I stare up at the ceiling. Only one face left until Senpai and I are together at long last. I normally wait at least one week before I pick another target, but now that I'm so close to my wish, I might have to find someone tomorrow. I should be able to find one more person to lure down here, and then I can finally have what I've craved since I started high school. A boyfriend who loves me. Somebody I can talk with. Somebody who understands who I am. Someone who notices me.

As I daydream of the life I'll receive after my wish, I hear someone say, "Hello, Akari-chan."

The tender, eloquent voice I've admired for so long comes from the corner of the room, and the figure steps out of the shadows for me to see.

It's him.

It's the man I love.

"Senpai?" I usher.

"It's nice to finally speak with you after all this time, Akari-chan," he says.

My heart nearly stops. Hearing him say my name is heaven to my ears, something I've dreamt of since I first laid my eyes on him. I'm left without words, simply hanging my mouth open in awe, nearly drooling.

"I thought you'd be happy to see me," he says.

"I-I am," I stutter. "I just didn't expect we'd meet here of all places." For so long, I've wanted this moment to come to fruition. Yet, I can tell something is off. I glance away from Senpai and turn to Noppera-bō. "Is this your doing?"

He nods his head.

"But I haven't delivered you the tenth face yet."

Senpai chuckles. "Don't you understand, Akari-chan? You're the tenth face."

My body grows cold, and my stomach turns. "What do you mean?"

"Did you think you were the only person who knew about Noppera-bō? Him and I have known each other since I was a freshman at Hokkaido. Back then, I was nothing but a lonely, miserable, and undesirable kid who nobody wanted to be around. No friends, no popularity, no girls or boys asking for my attention. I hated it.

"That's when I found Noppera-bō, for he has an act for turning up to those who will stop at nothing to get what they want. He told me that if I delivered him ten faces, he would grant me any wish of my choosing. So that's what I did. I gathered anybody I could lure and offered them to him until I reached ten. Do you want to know what I wished for, Akari-chan?"

I gulp, then ask, "What?"

"I wished that everyone who lays their eyes upon me will fall in love with me, so now, I'm irresistible to everyone, including you. Of course, once I saw what Noppera-bō was capable of, I knew I couldn't stop there. I wanted more. I wanted another wish. The problem is, I knew if I kept scouring for people, the police or whoever would eventually catch onto me and I'd get into trouble. So, I figured I should get someone else to do it for me. That's when you came into the picture."

I think back to that day I followed Senpai to the laundromat and say, "It was you that left me the key?"

"I did, and you've done exactly what I hoped you'd do."

"But why me? Why not have another girl do your dirty work?"

"Because, Akari-chan, unlike the other girls at school, you're the only one that reminds me of myself. You really think you went unnoticed? I've seen that look in your eyes—that one of lust, passion, and persistence. Those eyes that scream ambition to acquire what you desire, and it seems I was right. You've delivered nine beautiful faces to Noppera-bō, just as I knew you would, and once he has yours, he'll grant me another wish."

Senpai takes a step forward, close enough for us to kiss. Even after all that's been said, I still love him, and I want nothing more than for us to be together like I always have. But from behind, I can sense Noppera-bō looming over me.

"Senpai-kun?" I whimper.

"Be still, Akari-chan," he says, voice warm and endearing. "It's easier if you stay still."

The Flood

By Mason Gallaway

When Celeste awoke among the purple hearts, monkey grass, and Japanese Maples, she knew she'd broken her promise to herself not to drink too much on the job. Her head ached, her stomach twirled, and she was surrounded by vegetation and darkness. Which part of the sprawling yard she now lay in was a bleary mystery.

There had been a party. Celeste had escorted client number God-only-knew. A well-respected, well-connected plastic surgeon named Nate. She hadn't bothered to ask for his last name, nor had she asked why someone as pleasant and rich and handsome as he was even needed an escort. Celeste knew the real reasons went far beyond sex and were probably too complicated for even an educated doctor to explain.

The party had been grand and impressive, as she'd expected. Most of the festivities had poured from the house into the backyard. There were lush, colorful gardens and a circular pool sporting a massive stone grotto, whose waterfall curtain gave just enough privacy for the horny and daring. Dr. Nate had introduced Celeste to everyone he knew, without even trying to mask their arrangement. Her ear had been filled with drunken whispers of various guests he'd worked on. Her glass had been filled with drink that never ran dry. Celeste had smiled and drank and spat off wry comments. After some fumbling, half-blind sex in a remote part of the yard, Nate had disappeared to take a call, and Celeste had kept drinking and schmoozing…

Now, darkness and silence blanketed her. Thin, broken light slipped through the dark foliage near her face, teasing her eye. The purple leaves, like black tongues in the dark, tasted her nose and lips. The pungent, moist aromas of earth and mulch began flooding her senses as her head cleared. She hoisted herself up on an elbow.

She was in a shadowy corner of the backyard garden, far from the pool. Next to her was a small, dark clearing with a dry fountain at its center. A large shed of some kind blocked her view of the pool and patio. As she rose to her knees, her brain slammed into her skull. Celeste winced and paused to let the pain pass. Then she got up and stumbled to a stone bench by the fountain.

The fence was nearby. She could probably climb over it and call an Uber and call this night a job well done. But her purse. She looked around the garden. No purse in sight, which meant no phone. She might have dropped it during the sex on the other side of the yard, but one of her last memories was grabbing her purse and going for another drink.

"Shit," she said, taking a deep breath. She listened to the backyard. It was quiet. The party was over. All the guests were gone, and the homeowners were surely sleeping off the night. Though she didn't want to risk being seen like this, she could probably search the yard unnoticed.

She dusted herself off as best she could and peered around the corner of the building. The patio lights were still on, and plates and abandoned glasses sprinkled the pool deck. The water seemed remarkably clear of debris, its surface smooth and still. The porch was empty, and the house's back windows were engorged with shadow, save for traces of dim light from somewhere deep in the house.

Seeing that the yard was clear, Celeste stepped out from the shadows and began her search.

The purse was nowhere on the grassy lawn. She moved toward the pool deck. No purse there either. A glass of champagne, whose sides were still moist with condensation, sat abandoned on the stone bench that wrapped around the back of the grotto. A single bubble rocketed to the drink's surface. Celeste felt like spewing and had to turn away from it.

Suddenly, the water of the pool stirred, as if someone had broken the surface after a long breath-holding contest. Celeste gasped and dropped down behind the rocky grotto. She crept around and looked in the pool, expecting to see a sopping head, arms resting on the pool's side, someone gazing into the night, contemplating successes and mistakes.

But the pool was empty. Celeste's eyes swept back and forth over what she could see of the pool's surface.

The waves and ripples spoke that the pool was not empty. After doing a quick scan of the house's back windows, Celeste moved closer to the water.

The pool was free of life, but not of strangeness. There was something at the bottom, below the grotto. It appeared to be a large, vertical crack in the concrete where the side swooped into the bottom. A fissure surrounded by a greenish-black, mold-like stain.

Celeste cocked her head, studying the black marring as it gently swayed from the movement of the water. It occurred to her that she had probably heard bubbles breaking the surface. It didn't make sense, though. People this rich with a monstrous blemish in their pool. It was so obvious and disgusting that Celeste wouldn't have considered hopping in even on the hottest day or the sexiest night.

There was a flicker of movement in the corner of Celeste's eye. As if the dim light from within the house had winked off and on. Celeste looked up and saw shadows floating within the house, blinking the dim light. People were entering the living room, approaching the double back doors. Celeste dropped down again and crawled behind the grotto.

The back door flew open violently, and fierce voices and frantic footfalls followed.

"No, no! This can't be happening!" said a shrill, nasally voice.

"We looked everywhere," a softer voice said flatly.

"Just shut the fuck up, okay!" A booming voice. "Let's think about this."

"But we did everything right. There has to be someone here. *There has to be!*" The first voice again.

Celeste crouched with her heart pounding, listening but not really listening. She just wanted those voices to float away so she could find her purse and get the hell out of there without humiliating herself.

"Okay, okay," said the booming voice. "Didn't you say your prayers, pay respects, didn't you all do what the fuck you were supposed to?!"

"Yes!"

"Of course."

"Okay then. The sacrifice should be here. It's not always so easy, remember? This is a big house. Maybe there's a lesson here, you know? Maybe it's some kind of test."

Now Celeste was listening, her purse forgotten… Sacrifice? What the hell were these people talking about? She should have been able to say they were twisted drunk or blasted stoned, but they sounded ice-cold sober. Like they were discussing poor sales performances or an indictment or something worse. LSD, maybe? It was quiet for a moment. Celeste crept around the grotto to catch a glimpse of the people, and to get a better idea of what was going on.

The voices began again as she rounded the stone structure. As she moved, she realized how clear their voices were. The waterfall in the grotto had been flowing during the party, but now it was dead.

"The Flood is just making it harder this year. Testing us. Maybe you're right. Maybe our faith hasn't matched our indulgences, our rewards. But we'll find the sacrifice, and everything will be fine."

Celeste rounded the grotto and the people came into view. There were three: all about her age but maybe a few years older; one man, petite with a neat beard and glasses and smart-casual clothes, built like a jockey; a woman, blondish and pretty in a summery cocktail dress, slimmer than Celeste; another man, tall and tan and clean-shaven, with muscles showing through a partly buttoned Oxford. His swim shorts were long dry.

The tall, muscular man turned to the small bearded man. "Now, before you all start panicking, have you checked the *entire* backyard? Not just the usual places. Maybe the gardens over here?"

The big man held out his arms in a half shrug, his would-be tutelary gaze jumping from the woman to the bearded man. The bearded one sighed and ran a hand through his hair and nodded.

"Yeah, you're right. There's still land to cover." He scanned the yard, his eyes fixating on the area where Celeste had been.

"I prayed, I did everything right. I swear," the woman said as she began to pace.

"Did you, Colleen?" The larger man asked, his gaze sharpening. He then turned in the direction of the shorter man, who was now frantically walking to the shadowy garden where Celeste had been. After a moment of his rummaging, he shouted, "Fuck!"

"It was Brian," the large man said quietly. "I know it was him. He's been so obsessed with his stupid book. His nut-job fans. Since he was the first to hear it, he thinks he's got some kind of special rights or something."

"Shh!" The ~~woman~~ Colleen hissed as Brian approached.

"Nothing! Fucking nothing. Oh God, I don't want any of us to die. Not after all this!" Brian's hands clawed at his hair and pulled, as if he were trying to pull off a tight mask. Colleen went to him.

"Hey, calm down," she said, putting a hand on him but not looking at all calm herself. She turned to the larger man.

"Corey, you want to check your workshop?" Her voice trembled with feigned calm and sweetness. Corey, whose head was low, gave her an ominous upward gaze.

"It's been locked. There's no one here. No one to sacrifice. And it's too fucking late now." His eyes dropped from Colleen to the pool as if he'd seen something down there. "And it's because of Brian and his stupid fucking pride!"

Brian threw his head up and stiffened.

"No! I was reverent. I prayed every day! The Flood knows that. The Flood knows the truth, and it's that *you're* the arrogant, greedy one here. All of this part was your fucking idea! Thirty years of this shit? The money. The drugs. The whatever-the-fuck-we-want. And for what? Death? Murder? Sacrifice? Don't you guys fucking see! There was never any deal. Never any sacrifice. *We* are the sacrifices, because we're gluttonous, egomaniacal fools. And you, Corey, are the biggest fool of all!"

Brian, a good foot shorter than Corey, suddenly took a breath and seemed to go inward, as if he hadn't intended to exhaust so violently. He said nothing, but his eyes took on an apologetic, placating look.

"You little piece of shit!" Corey stormed toward Brian with boiling blood in his eyes. Colleen cried out, made to step in between them but flinched, knowing she'd do nothing but get herself injured. Celeste watched on from behind the grotto, transfixed, confused, and horrified. Her hand shot up and gripped the bench before her. Instinct told her to run, to scream, to get up and stop Corey all at once.

She maintained the presence of mind not to do any of that, but the movement of her hand was enough. Her index and middle fingers bumped into the bottom of the champagne flute and it toppled off of the bench and crashed onto the deck with a wet crunch.

The commotion before her halted. Corey stopped just before Brian, his hands poised to shake or choke; they all turned to the grotto. Celeste tried to duck down and hide, but it was too late.

"Who—Who's there?" Corey asked.

"Oh, thank God! I knew it. I knew it!" Brian sounded on the verge of tears.

They all stood there a moment, hesitating, waiting. Then Corey called out again, coming closer. Celeste didn't answer, but she knew she'd been caught. Slowly, she stood. Before she'd been afraid of humiliation. But now she was afraid of something else, something she couldn't name. As she appeared, she offered a humble, diffident smile and raised her hands in conciliation, bundling a surrender with an awkward greeting.

All three of them stared at her in disbelief, their expressions unreadable. Then Corey's face broke into a flagrant grin, and his mouth exploded with gleeful laughter.

"Hey! See?! See?!" He pointed to her, looking at his bemused friends. Brian's lips quivered into an almost smile while Colleen stared with wide, unbelieving eyes.

Corey laughed again, pointing, stabbing the air in Celeste's direction. When he locked eyes with Celeste again, he grew serious. But not in a threatening way. He looked shameful and fearful.

"I'm—I'm sorry. I passed out," Celeste said with a nervous laugh.

Corey's eyes shot back and forth from her to his confused friends. He held out his hands as though to keep Celeste and the others from attacking him or each other.

"Okay," he said turning back to Celeste, eyes raised. "It's actually good that you're here. Don't be scared. Um, can you come here, please? We just want to ask you something."

Corey motioned vigorously for her to come closer. Instinct kept Celeste in place, but she couldn't pinpoint all the unease she felt, beyond that she'd crudely overstayed her welcome. These people seemed scared, more intimidated than she felt. Though the air held currents of danger, she couldn't deny their wealth and attractiveness served as a salve on her fears. And she felt as though she owed them by intruding. So, she stepped out from behind the stone structure and walked toward them, skirting the pool's edge. As she did so, Corey's eyes dropped to the water once again.

Celeste followed his gaze, again seeing nothing moving in the pool. But the strange blemish, the crack, was there. And it seemed bigger. The water seemed cloudier than it had been too. When she rounded the pool, she stopped a few feet from Corey.

"I really just need to find my purse, and I can go. I must have had too much. I'm so sorry—"

"No, it's okay. We have your purse inside. We just need you to help us with something." Corey's eyes were pleading, a cross between *put down the gun* and *please give me a chance*. Drugs certainly had to have been involved. Corey turned back to his friends for approval. They continued to stare, blankly. Brian and Colleen looked at each other. Brian shrugged, his face blank.

"Um, sure," Celeste said. "What is it?"

"Well, it's kind of a game," he said smiling. And just as he did, a gurgling sound filled the air, followed by popping and splashing. The pool's surface broke with more bubbles, larger than before. Celeste turned to the water, startled. The gases seemed to have risen from the dark fissure below the grotto. The air suddenly filled with an odd odor, an ammonia and ozone cocktail, with a hint of something that made Celeste think of night's she couldn't sleep as a child.

When she turned back, she saw that Corey's face was stricken with terror. His eyes skipped from the water to Celeste and back.

"Oh God," Brian said with a whisper.

"No, Corey," said Colleen. "It's not supposed to be like this. She's awake. Something isn't right here. Let's just take a moment to—"

"There's no fucking time!" Corey roared. He looked sidelong over his shoulder without turning his head. Then his eyes slid back to Celeste. They burned with a cold, unemotional aggression. More animal fear than human hate.

Then he spoke in a taut, fierce voice. A chant. An incantation.

"Blessed be the waters. Blessed be the nourishment. The water gives. The water destroys. To you, we dissolve our flesh!"

Celeste stood transfixed, watching Corey, looking to the others who looked as scared as she. As she began to back away, scaling the fence in her mind and running far, far from here, Corey charged at her.

His hands seized her before she could move and began dragging her toward the others.

"Hey, what the hell! Let go of me!"

"It's okay. It'll be okay," said Corey through heaves of breath. When they were closer to the others, Corey turned Celeste to face the pool. She tried to flail her arms, but his grip around her waist and chest was too much. She began to kick his shins, step on his feet, slam herself into his iron chest.

"Stop that!" he screamed, and his fingers dug into her skin. Celeste winced and eased her thrashing. She looked to the others, pleading.

"What is this? Make him stop!" They looked horrified but did not move. Corey turned to them.

"Come help me, godammit!"

Brian just shook his head, his mouth open, words balled in his throat. Colleen began to cry. Thoughts stampeded through Celeste's head as fast as her heartbeat. *Where was Nate? Who the fuck cares? Why did I come? Because the money. Maybe this is all—*

"No, Corey. I think it's too late," Brian said, voice trembling, eyes welling with tears.

"What?!" Corey screamed, his grip tightening as he did so.

Celeste managed to turn her head to see Brian. His face appeared bloodless, and his eyes were bloodshot. She expected blood to flood from his eyes instead of tears. His mouth quivered, like a child trying to be tough after a good whipping. He lifted a tremulous finger, pointing at the pool.

Celeste turned, and she felt Corey turn too. The strange crack in the pool's bottom was now open like a gaping mouth, bearded by the strange, moldy, mossy substance. A silent moan. For a moment, there was only the yawning black, as more bubbles containing their antsy gases raced upward from the opening and popped through the pool's surface.

"Oh God. No!" Corey said.

Sounds like retching, gagging, vomiting filled the air. More bubbles rose from the gaping hole, escaping, fleeing something. And suddenly, behind the globular bubbles, that something appeared.

The dark of the hole came alive, reaching upward, outward, into the pool. What appeared to be appendages, long, restless fingers maybe, reached into the pool, feeling the light, feeling the pool's bottom as if it were a fine satin. Then the rest of the apparition emerged. It was a vaguely human form, but it moved how no human could, undulating along with the anxious waters. Arms and legs and what might have been long garland-like tatters, or diaphanous fins, waving and swaying.

As the apparition emerged from the hole, a thick cloudy mass rose up from behind it. It seemed almost solid one moment, then going transparent. Celeste thought it might be hair—long, abundant, smoky tresses that bloomed outward and came together in ghostly motion. The strands curled and stretched and reached. And as they moved the water began to roil more intensely, as though imbued with a charge.

"Oh, shit!" Corey suddenly released Celeste and ran to the others. His voice rose in pitch. "Guys, come on! Let's throw her in. We have to all agree!"

Brian shook his head.

"Why not?"

"It'll make it worse. Maybe it'll go easy on us if we…" Brian broke off and began to sob.

Celeste's eyes were on the water, and the thing that had just appeared below. It moved with the grace and rhythm of the ocean. But its form became more and more unclear as the water began to boil. The being seemed to emanate a faint flash of light. But other than that, it was a deep mass of darkness.

"Coll! Please, you have to agree!"

Colleen shook her head, her eyes blank. "I can't do this. I can't do any of this anymore. I think we had our fun. It's over, Corey."

"Fuck you guys! You have no faith. You're weak. I'll do it myself." Corey went to Celeste and seized her once more. She felt his fingers dig into her flesh again and she knew that this time those hands meant to throw her into that foul, boiling water—with that angelic devil.

"No! No!" Celeste screamed.

Corey dragged her to the edge with a power and determination that couldn't be bargained with. But before he could throw her in, the churning water began to rise.

It flowed over the sides of the pool, rolling over their feet in a cool rush. Corey stopped speaking, and his fingers slackened and fell away from Celeste. He stepped back, in both defeat and awe, moving closer to the others as the water flooded the area.

Celeste looked down and realized that the water around her feet was rising along with the surface of the pool. The water was not just overflowing and pervading the yard and patio; it was rising as a single mass, and it stopped at a certain radius—as though there were an invisible wall enclosing the four of them, the pool, and the patio.

"What the fuck is this?" Celeste looked at them, seeing vague understanding in their faces but also paralyzing terror. No one answered her.

"What do we do?!" Colleen screamed at the men.

"It can't seriously want us. Not all of us." Corey's voice had lost its steel and bravado.

"We knew this would happen," Brian said. "We got careless!"

"What will it do to us, Brian?" Corey asked desperately. "What did it say it would do!"

Brian didn't answer, so Corey turned to the rising water and screamed. "Fuck off! Do you know what we've become!? You freak!"

Brian rushed Corey and got in his face. "Shut the fuck up! See, it was you! It was you!"

Colleen broke from her emotional stupor and pulled Brian out of Corey's face.

"Chill out, godammit. We have to run!"

"Someone tell me what the fuck is going on, now!" Celeste screamed. They all looked at her, as if they'd forgotten she were there. But still no one answered. She looked down and realized the water was almost at her waist.

"What the—"

The rest of the yard, beyond whatever invisible field had been created, was totally dry. The walls of the pool had risen, turned invisible, and expanded to encapsulate all of them. It was more than Celeste's brain could handle, and she tried to convince herself she was still drunk-asleep on her bed of mulch, beneath her blanket of purple hearts.

They all turned to the house, then to the rest of the yard where it was still dry.

"Come on!" Colleen screamed. She waved them onward as she trudged through the water that gripped her waist, toward the backyard. Celeste followed. The guys hesitated, not believing they could move. Then they too pushed through the water. But before they all could pass the pool proper, the hideous devil-angel appeared over the pool's brink.

The snaking, thick, billowy strands rose upward, dancing, caressing, reaching. Then the faceless head, the wispy arms, the teasing fingers. The thing floated from the pool into the rising waters beyond it, now nearly deep enough for it to negotiate freely.

The sight of the shadowy thing, its terrible beauty and grace, made Celeste's bowels loosen and her bladder quiver. This was what her worst childhood nightmares had been like. What dawned before her echoed ghosts, sharks, octopuses, angels, devils, and other nameless, confounding threats she once believed were always waiting to seize her.

And now for the part of the nightmare where Celeste tries to run but can't for the life of her.

"Fuck!" Colleen screamed. She whirled around and began charging toward the house. "Go, go!"

They all turned, stricken with fear, and began to wade-run to the back doors. Celeste found she could move despite the nightmare of the situation. They all looked ridiculous as they ran, and the insanity welling up within Celeste caused her to chuckle as she pushed through the water. She kneed and kicked, throwing her body through the liquid. It resisted like cool sludge.

At any moment, that swarm of hair, the flourish of ethereal tendrils, would enwrap her. Gentle at first. A tickle, a caress. Then that caress would tighten to an excruciating squeeze, as the strands burned their way into her. Into her skin and into her soul.

They all broke through the rising wall of water and ran to the glass doors. Corey threw one open and they all filed in. Celeste was the last through the door, half expecting Corey to slam it in her face. But he did not. Terror had somehow initiated Celeste into their strange group.

She almost slipped on the tile floor as she entered and caught herself on a leather couch. Brian slammed the door shut and locked it. Everyone stood back from the window and watched as the wall of water rose and moved closer to the house as a slow and deliberate tidal wave. It lapped against the back windows of the house, as if the backyard had been turned into a giant aquarium. It rose and rose, until yard, deck and sky were completely obscured by water. The porch and yard beyond became a watery haze.

"Come on!" Corey shouted as he turned and ran to the front of the house. He went straight to the front door, ready to pull it open and run.

"Wait!" Brian grabbed him by the shoulder. There was a faint rumble and the sound of brushing outside the front door. Brian pointed downward. Water was trickling in over the door's threshold, down the sides and through the door jam, puddling outward over the tile. Corey went over to the shades of the parlor and drew them upward.

The view was flooded with water.

"Fuck!" Corey screamed. Colleen and Celeste joined them, saw that the entire house was surrounded by a flood. Celeste's eyes jumped over the parlor windows, the dining room windows, trying to see some sign of trickery, some element of design, some sign she was still asleep in the garden. But no matter how she looked at it, she was in a house that seemed to have been shrunken and dropped into a pool.

She turned to the back bay windows. Most of the porch was visible, with its floating debris, trash, and potted plants. The pool's edge and the grotto were vague shadows. But beyond those was a haze of blue, a strange, unearthly blue. It was not unclear if the entire yard had been flooded, but something told Celeste that the blue she was seeing went far, far beyond the yard.

The dark apparition was nowhere to be seen.

Then a shape appeared, just beyond the grotto. The thing moved in a slithery, wavy motion that reminded Celeste of a giant, slow-moving Beta fish. Its whispery, ethereal appendages flowing and pluming like slow flames. At any moment, she knew the thing would turn and do its slow, graceful dance to the glass and shatter it and pour itself into the house.

Celeste looked away, turned to the others. Colleen was staring out the back window with her, watching the dark phantom pace. Corey was still looking out the front windows as if they might magically clear of water, like a kid glumly waiting for the rain to stop on the first day of summer. Brian had disappeared, perhaps to check other windows. There was no cry of excitement or triumph, which meant all the other windows showed the same watery view.

He reappeared a moment later, his face drawn.

Celeste couldn't take anymore.

"What the fuck is this?! Tell me?! You all know what this is. Fucking tell me!"

The voice that exploded from her mouth sounded alien to her. Flooded with a ferocity and desperation she'd never felt or heard before, from her or anyone. Thankfully, they seemed to sense it too, and broke from their trances and looked at her. Then they all shared a resigned glance.

Corey and Colleen nodded at Brian. He closed his eyes, in quiet defeat, and took a deep breath.

"Looks like its's all over. Might as well run through it all again. Let's have a seat, shall we?"

***

"We were all kids, teenagers," Brian began.

They were all sitting in the living room, awash in a spectral blue glow. The house's interior writhed and slithered with shadows and ghostly glimmers. Every so often, a deeper, more insistent shadow would stir up the glimmer, sweeping over the furniture, the floor, and their terrified faces. Celeste resisted the urge to look at the apparition head on. She did not want to see its finer details.

"We'd meet at this secret spring as often as we could," he continued. "No other kids knew about it, not our friends, our parents. And we tried to keep it that way. But one day, this kid, this snotty rich kid we hated, who hated us, was there when we got there. He's looking at the water as if he'd gone to heaven. He starts mumbling to us how he's going to tell his parents, have them buy the land, all the stupid parties they'd have. Now, we wanted to kill him, but instead, we just messed with him. Just trying to scare him, you know? Things get a little out of hand…he goes in. And doesn't come up."

Brian sucked a breath through his teeth. As though his memory were dragging him back into the spring, to chilly depths. The sound made Celeste wince.

"For a long time. All we can do is just stand there. Maybe he was trying to scare us. But he wasn't coming back up, and we were too shocked to swim after him. Maybe a part of us didn't want to save him, I don't know. So, I started praying. And I told them to pray too. To let the kid live, to let him forget about us and the spring. But the funny thing was, I didn't pray to God. I figured God would have no mercy on us stupid, bitter, selfish kids. Instead, I prayed to the water, to the *spring*. I got us all to pray to it. Not for the kid's life. But for *our* lives. For the life of the water."

Before he could continue, another phantasmal shadow swept over them. Everyone seemed to flinch, but no one looked up. Celeste was seated so as to see the windows in her periphery. It was there, dark and beautiful and horrible. Close now, close enough to see. To really see. And it hovered there, *wanting* her to see. Instead, she looked at Brian, his terrified gaze. After a few moments, the shadow passed and the thing, *The Flood*, moved out of Celeste's partial sight.

"So, what? What happened?" Celeste asked, hurrying him along.

Brian blinked and nodded, as if he were wedged between not wanting to continue and not wanting to acknowledge what was circling the house.

"It told me, all of us, to jump in. I don't remember doing it, but we must have."

He stopped and looked at Colleen and Corey.

"And we sank. The water became so cold, so dark. Something like black hair surrounded me. I just knew I was dying, and this was some demon coming to take my soul. But then I heard it speak, or felt it. The understanding just arose within me. It would help us, give the kid back, for a price. But only so long as I, we, never forget about it. And it says we could have so much more than Ezra's life, than the spring's waters. We all could. If we show it reverence, remember it, we would have riches and success and ease until thirty years had passed. Then, all the success will only continue if we feed it every year. The Flood. That's what it calls itself. The Flood wanted our attention, and then it wanted an offering, a sacrifice…"

Brian cringed and shook his head.

"Or clse.." Celeste said.

"It would come for us."

Celeste had so many questions, but her belief in every detail was as sure as the water outside the windows, trickling inward, threatening to make wet whatever was dry.

"How old?" she asked.

Brian looked at her, eyes welling shame. "Fifteen. We're forty-nine now." His eyes flickered, as though he wanted to turn away. But he made himself look Celeste in the eyes.

"I know. We look a lot younger."

"So these parties—I was supposed to be—" Celeste felt faint and took a moment to breathe. "But, I just drank too much. It happens a lot."

"When—" Colleen began, clearing her throat. "When we remember it, The Flood—when we pay reverence to it. Every time we pass a body of water, or take a drink, then the sacrifices are fairly easy. Someone just passes out. Stays behind. Turns up. " Colleen's eyes go distant, and they begin to fill with tears and a mix of longing and guilt.

"Makes it easier for us," Corey spat out in frustration.

Brian and Colleen nodded.

"So, what now?" Celeste asked, going to her feet. "Just wait until that thing floods this place and drowns us all?"

Brian was looking at the floor wistfully. He began to laugh quietly, his shoulders bouncing.

"What?" Celeste asked.

His laughter suddenly ceased. "It's not going to drown us," he said coldly.

"I think we're supposed to figure out which one of us broke the…covenant. Right?"

Brian lifted his head, his humor and pensiveness evaporated, and narrowed his eyes at Colleen. Corey stopped his pacing and turned to her also.

"And let me guess," Corey said with a sneer. "It wasn't you, was it? You were little miss pious the whole time."

Colleen threw up her hands. "I think I was respectful enough not to incur some shit like this, Corey."

Corey turned to Brian. "What about you, Bri? You willing to admit it was you who fucked this for us? Huh? Isn't all of this kind of your fault anyway. I'm pretty sure you said the first prayer. That stupid kid would have come up. Why'd you have to drag us into your stupid, sick game, huh?"

Brian's mouth quivered and his jaw muscles twitched, and his eyes, locked on the floor, darkened. He suddenly threw his gaze at Corey.

"Are you fucking serious, Corey?! Did you hear yourself out there? Right now, even!? We all know it was your arrogant, foolish, self-sucking ass who fucked this all up!"

"Stop it!" Colleen shouted, but her voice carried little charge, like a parent who'd resigned to letting her kids fight themselves bloody and hoarse. Of course, it didn't stop them.

"Oh," Corey huffed and smiled a cold, humorless smile. He began to sway side to side as if the anger and fear were surging through him, looking for an outlet. "That's just fucking rich, man. What about your writing gigs? All the offers? You never mentioned The Flood once!"

Corey paused, as if choked. He stepped back, took a breath, and then turned his eyes to the watery gloom outside. Then he began to cry. It was the sob of someone experiencing every dark, heavy emotion possible. His eyes gushed, his nostrils flared, and his jaws flexed. "Why man? Why did you bring us into this?"

"I was a kid! I was scared! We all were!"

"Ok! Get a fucking grip!" Celeste screamed. Part of her wanted to crumble and blubber along with them, at the nightmarish madness of it all. But a greater part of her felt almost insulated, as though she were a mediator at the fringes, observing the dynamic, the conflict but impervious to its flares and its blows. This was not her problem, and if she could keep herself convinced of that, she might be able to get out of this alive.

Celeste rose to her feet and grabbed the first breakable thing she could find. It was a glass figurine on the mantle: a tastelessly rendered Buddha with a manic smile. She hurled it to the marble floor. It shattered into pieces all around them. Then she went for something bigger and heavier—some kind of shield. A family coat of arms, made of bronze. Probably a dubious claim to Corey's ancestry. When her hands seized it, she saw Corey flinch, his fear and turmoil vanishing for a moment to make room for his usual materialism and territorial impulses.

"Whoa, what are you doing?" he asked, showing only half concern. "Take it easy, we can—"

Celeste walked over to the back window and lifted the escutcheon over her head, making to send it crashing through the glass.

"No!" Colleen cried.

"Don't do that!"

"Hey, easy now!" Corey said, taking a step toward her.

"Shut the fuck up! I'm the only real victim here. I've made mistakes, but I don't deserve this. Find a way to

324

make this right. Pray, meditate, toss chum out there, something. Make this fucking thing go away!"

It was quiet for a moment. Colleen crossed her arms. Corey rubbed his chin.

"She's right," Brian said. "It's worth a try."

"Maybe that's what it wants. I'm pretty sure it's not even trying to get in here," Corey said.

"You don't think so?" Brian waved at the windows. Water puddled below them, fed by small but steady trickles from the minute spaces between the glass and the frames.

"It's pushing its way in, trust me," he said. Then he turned from the window and stretched and swung his arms, as if preparing for an obstacle course. "Alright, fine. Let's get on this."

"Where should we do it? Right here?" Colleen asked, eyeing the broad and bleeding windows. There was still no clear sign of the creature, though Celeste caught sight of pacing shadows every few seconds.

"Upstairs?" Celeste said. "In case those windows bust."

"Yes," Corey said. He stood by the windows, very close, gazing into the cerulean nothing. He'd gone quiet, almost submissive. Celeste didn't like that, but no one else seemed to be worried.

"Corey? How does that sound?" Brian asked. Corey didn't respond. "Corey?" Brian went to him and shook his shoulder; Corey jumped as if Brian's hands held a charge. He turned to Brian, his eyes distant and bleary, as blue and hazy as the flood outside.

"Yeah, sure. Fine."

They all filed upstairs. When they reached the upstairs landing, Celeste noticed no difference in the lighting. It was still a dim, elven blue. A window at the end of the hall confirmed that the water had risen to the second story.

"Okay, how about we each go to different rooms?" Colleen said. "We can just pray, meditate, whatever the fuck we have to do."

Corey and Brian nodded. Colleen turned to Celeste, who was trying her best to merge with the situation, to be one of them, though she knew that was impossible. She was supposed to have been, at least in their minds, the sacrifice that would have spared them all this, helped them preserve their affluent, plush lives. Whatever happened, Celeste was easily a chip to be played. She eagerly nodded at Colleen.

"Whatever you guys have to do," she said.

"Don't worry. We're done with the sacrifices, right guys?" She turned to the others, her gaze unyielding and authoritative. Brian closed his eyes in resolve and nodded frantically. Corey gave a single nod, less pronounced and less reassuring, but it was enough for Celeste, at least in the moment.

"I just need to sit and process all this. You guys do what you have to to get us out." Celeste paused and looked around at several windows, the blue realm beyond. Then she turned back to the others. "Do you guys think it still—" She caught herself, not wanting to put the thought in their minds, even though she knew that they were already thinking it.

"What?"

Celeste cleared her throat. "—think it's still out there."

They all sighed and chuckled and then turned away, going to their separate rooms, offering half-hearted farewells.

Celeste was left in the dim blue dream light of the hall. She let herself fall against the wall and she slid to her butt. She just wanted to look around, to find a way out. But first, she would close her eyes and let her mind clear so that she could figure out how to get out of this. She did not intend to go to sleep.

But that's what she did.

Her sleep was a dreamless, cold, flooded void. She floated in place, as though in water, seeing nothing, feeling nothing but cool wetness. She wasn't in any pain, but she felt a distant discomfort that reminded her of nights when she needed to wake up to relieve herself but couldn't bring herself to do it. Maybe there were whispers, soft creaks and faint gusts of movement around her. But otherwise, Celeste's sleep was cold and empty and unsatisfying.

When she awoke a while later, her head and back felt melded to the floor and wall. She was still in the mansion; the windows were still portals to a hungry flood. The water from her dream had evaporated, but the strange whispers had not. As the sleep receded from her brain, Celeste heard soft voices coming from downstairs. Hushed, conspiratorial.

Celeste got to her feet without making a sound and crept down the hall toward the stairs. When she reached the head of the stairs, the whispers rose to greet her: *I can't do this...Can still work...have to try...open the door, run for the stairs. It will be enough.*

Celeste slowly descended the stairs, trying not to get distracted by what was being discussed. She already knew. Because the house was solidly built, she worried little about the steps betraying her presence.

She saw them, kneeling before the large windows of the back doors. It appeared as if they'd sat down to pray together and had instead fallen into tense chatter. Celeste might have laughed if it wouldn't have given her away. These poor people were right where they belonged. They deserved each other, all of this. But Celeste did not. She'd made mistakes and put herself in harm's way, but her selfishness and greed had never amounted to a willingness to commit cruel acts and murder. Celeste did not belong, and she was getting the hell out of this. The shield Celeste had wielded earlier lay on the couch. The others were maintaining posture, facing the alien, ominous water, possibly with their eyes closed, while they prattled away. Celeste knew what she had to do, though it terrified her. It would be one of the hardest things she'd ever done, aside from seeing her mother off to death—and her first, fumbling, trembling night with a client. But it would be far less horrible than killing these wretches herself—or being fed to that thing.

While her eyes remained on the three, her hands found the shield. She gripped it and lifted it like a frisbee. Then the watery blue outside wafted and broke. A shadow began to take shape, first the bulk of it, then the trailing mass of blooming flame-like, tendril-like tresses. The thing—a fusion of fish, of woman, of ghost--approached the glass.

The Flood had finally come to face them.

Celeste didn't want to stare too long, but she marveled at the way it moved. It didn't so much as swim or float but rather became the spaces ahead of it. Celeste stood frozen as the thing grew clearer, more than watery shadow. The arms and legs, seemed to dissolve at the tips, washing away without ever fading. The body now emitting strobes of candescence, creating a dizzying pattern of light and shadow. The light revealed what could have been a human chest—breasts male or female—but any details seemed to wash away in Celeste's mind when she tried to focus on them.

And the face. Maybe there were eyes to see her, a mouth to sing mournful, entrancing songs. But when Celeste tried to focus on the facial features, the shadows followed the flashing, and all she could see were fathoms. Down and down. Abyssal trenches. Ready to swallow her.

The only thing Celeste could have compared the sight and feeling to was the time she'd gone swimming in a rock quarry with a crush she was trying to impress. She'd known how deep it was, could feel its chilly nothing nipping her toes. But when she went under and peaked at the depths, she hadn't seen two hundred feet of dark water. What she'd seen was a rich cobalt infinity that sent her loins and bowels into a spin.

She'd known that looking upon that nothing for more than a couple seconds might send her tumbling to that desolate, unforgiving void forever. That's how she felt now, looking at the face of The Flood. Celeste ripped her eyes away.

"Oh, oh!" Corey called out, seeing The Flood at the window. Its movements were as soothing as they were threatening. "Here, here!" Corey said, suddenly throwing his gaze downward, away from the water, as if he too could not look for long. Colleen and Brian looked up and gasped simultaneously. Both of them gazed at the entity, their bodies rising and falling in quick, vigorous respiration. They seemed to struggle to keep their gaze.

"No, Corey. Look! You have to, goddammit! Just try to focus on the light." Colleen first grabbed Corey's shoulder and shook him. When he didn't budge, she clawed his hair and ripped his head upward. Corey whimpered and complied. When his eyes fell on the thing, he moaned.

"I—I think she's listening. It's listening," Brian said in a breathy, ecstatic voice.

Celeste knew she had to act fast, but now, with the thing just beyond the glass, she felt her resolve withering. Then Brian's head suddenly cocked to the side. Maybe he'd seen Celeste's reflection in the door, or maybe The Flood had given some kind of signal. But Brian turned and saw Celeste, his eyes going wide.

Now, she thought. She raised the shield and sent it spinning toward the glass. The glass seemed to dissolve just as the metal made contact, and it crumbled and rushed inward along with a deluge of water. For a moment, The Flood was obscured, as were the three acolytes who were completely enveloped in the rushing wave.

Celeste broke for the stairs, but the wave crashed into her and sent her spinning. She struggled for a moment, kicking and grasping, but the power of The Flood was overwhelming. She gave in and let herself be taken by the current. For a few seconds, she tumbled and spun, her eyes closed tight. The water was cool as in her dream, though it was anything but empty and still. Thousands of bubbles and bits of glass and dirt swarmed her, tickling and pricking her skin.

And then things began to settle. Celeste found her bearings and righted herself underwater. For a moment, all was a cloud of bubbles. But then the bubbles cleared, revealing a slightly muzzy, newly flooded living room and foyer. Celeste found that she'd been swept to the head of the foyer, and she could see the living room and part of the kitchen.

Colleen was floating behind the couch, looking dazed, frantically spinning and looking around for the others or The Flood. Corey and Brian had been pushed to the kitchen, but The Flood was out of sight. Corey frantically grabbed Brian and motioned for the stairs. Brian nodded and they began to swim toward Colleen. As they swam out of the kitchen, the ghostly Flood emerged from behind the kitchen island.

Brian didn't turn, but he moved with a desperation that indicated he knew it was there. Corey turned and released an abject cry of terror that was muffled to a pitiful squeal by the water. He swam to Brian, who then turned and saw The Flood, its strange, fin-like, tattered appendages waving and flapping. Its body with its flashes of humanity and life, its shadows of fathomless fathoms, and its strange, smokey coiffure pluming outward toward them.

Brian brought his hands together, in prayer, in supplication and desperation. Corey did the same, though more clumsily, fervently, pitifully. The Flood stopped and hovered before them. Celeste and Colleen watched, mesmerized with terror and wonder. Celeste realized she could tolerate The Flood's strangeness, because the flashes of light gave her just enough reprieve from the shadows of infinity that followed.

She knew she should be trying to get to the stairs, but she couldn't move. Her lungs began to ache, but still, she couldn't move. Though she expected The Flood to go for Corey—the obvious fool, the heretic, the blaspheme—The Flood swept its strange arms and turned its faceless face toward Brian. The thing didn't move, but its strange hair gathered together in a single thick lock, and then the bundle swung itself toward Brian's neck, coiling around it.

Brian's head was obscured, and when The Flood pulled away, Brian's head was gone. Replacing it was a smoky geyser of blood, but it too disappeared into The Flood's reach. It wasn't as if The Flood had ripped Brian's head off, more that it had pulled his head into its depths. And after the head, it had sucked in his blood too. Then the thing's appendages and the rest of its coif cloaked Brian's entire body, and then Brian was gone.

The Flood then turned to Corey, who was kicking and paddling toward the door to the backyard. But the water demon was faster and was on him in a second.

Celeste felt a hand clawing her shoulder. She turned to see Colleen, her eyes electrified and her hair a suspended mass of shimmering blonde seaweed. Despite Colleen's ravaged gaze, her floating skin made her look like a teen. She motioned for Celeste to follow her to the stairs. Celeste did so, feeling that she'd drown before the demon even got to her.

As they approached the stairs, Celeste peered up at the surface. It was unclear how high the water went. From where she was, it could have risen all the way to the ceiling. But Colleen reached the stairs and she scrambled upward out of the water. Celeste followed.

The water had risen to about the second to last step. Colleen and Celeste stood on the landing, coughing and gasping. For a good twenty seconds, neither of them focused on anything other than breathing and readjusting to dryness. Then Celeste looked at Colleen warily.

"The water's going to rise," Colleen said.

"Just stay away from me," Celeste ~~staid~~ said, holding out her hands. Colleen smiled sadly.

"I'm not going to try to sacrifice you. I'm done with this. I've been done for a while now." She glanced at the rising water, and then winked at Celeste without humor.

"You ruined it? You set all this up?" Celeste asked, still feeling silly. She spoke as if she'd been in this all along. Colleen nodded.

"But, they were your friends."

"I didn't kill them, if that's what you're saying. They wanted this. They may not have known it. But they did. They weren't happy. None of us was happy." Colleen looked around the landing and then up to the ceiling. Searching for dryness. "Nothing was ever enough."

"But you're here," Celeste said.

"No, I'm done. I just need a moment. To help you. To prepare myself. To do a decent thing maybe."

Colleen looked back down at the water. Her eyes suddenly broadened and twitched with fear as her teeth clinched and her face tightened. Celeste looked down and saw the amorphous, angelic shape of The Flood rising up the stairs. It moved upward a few steps and then stopped. Waiting for the water to rise further and give it passage. It no longer flashed; it showed only its dark depths.

"Maybe there's a way. Maybe it'll let you go—"

"No!" Colleen looked at her fiercely. "We were kids, but we knew better. We were selfish and jealous and cruel. I have to do this." Her face softened and she took a calming breath. The tension seemed to leave her. The water was now rising up to the final step of the stairs.

"But what about me? Am I still…?" Celeste couldn't finish.

"I don't know," Colleen said. "But your decisions did bring you here, not us, not that thing." She turned to Celeste and smiled. "Just be wise."

Then she turned back to the water and dove in.

"Wait!" Celeste called. But it was too late.

Colleen flew toward the water and crashed into The Flood. Instantly, she went down into the hungry depths. It must not have swallowed all of her at once, because the water beneath the stairs bloomed red with blood. But as soon as the red cloud plumed outward, it imploded, swallowed up in seconds. Sucked into the depths of The Flood.

Celeste said no more. She moved no more. She lowered herself to the ground and sat on the newly soaked floor. She did not move as the water rose up the stairs and through the balusters behind her. And when the water was high enough, The Flood, in all its terrible, nightmarish grace and beauty rose up to meet Celeste. And she tried not to look away.

***

Celeste looked herself over in her vanity once more and was satisfied. Even while escorting, she'd always been careful to keep the gleam and flash to a tasteful minimum, opting for an easy, natural glow. That's what she had now, only it was perfect, and she was ready to meet her date.

A real date. A comely, gentle, smart man she'd met in her last semester of film school. An older student like her, who loved noir and mystery almost as much as she did. She grabbed her designer purse and coat and walked through the condo she might have never been able to afford. Passing a note reminding her to call her agent about the screenplay she'd optioned. There would be more, she knew. And the fees would rise.

But before she stepped out of her door, she stopped next to the small fountain she'd had installed. Surprisingly, it hadn't been as expensive or problematic as she'd expected. The contractor had installed it with precision and an odd look of pride. She stared into the gently rippling waters. Not to admire it like everyone else did, but to humble herself.

To remember.

Thirty years. She would be sixty. Two years older than her mother was when she died, after a life of sterility and rigid purity. Death comes either way, so what would it matter? Celeste would be right here to meet it, proudly. Right here, or near her pond or her pool or her private lake, outside the mansion she'd undoubtedly have soon. Celeste had spent years believing she'd never even see fifty, so this was not such a bad deal. Not a bad deal at all. No wondering, no waiting, no mystery of how or when. It would come and it would come fast and painless.

When the waters did finally rise, she'd sink into them, bathe in them. Let them flow over her, into her. And when The Flood rose up to face her, to hoist upon her its infinite depths, she would not look away.

She would give herself to the deep.

Quality Meat
By Fulvio Gatti

Marcello had a feeling that he would remember that night forever. He was sitting in a luxury restaurant in Alba, the Italian truffle capital city, at the same table with a gorgeous blond woman, Giulia. A delicious smell of freshly braised beef, cooked with Barolo wine, reached him as the waiter passed by to bring the dish to a nearby table. Marcello poured the red wine into Giulia's glass, then into his. They toasted, exchanging an intense glance.

The date was going even better than he could expect. He had picked up Giulia in front of her house, in Torino Mirafiori. The very moment she had stepped out of the door, his heart had missed a beat. She looked stunning.

As she had slipped into his car he'd glimpsed at her perfect, long legs, very little covered by a cyan silk dress. She had kissed him on his cheeks. She had looked at him with her bright blue eyes and Marcello had felt his blood boil.

But then, just with the appetizer–a thistle flan–in front of him, his phone rang. Marcello looked at the screen. It said "Mom". Marcello sighed, apologized and walked out of the dining room to answer the call.

He went down the stairs until he was in the street. The official reason was that he needed to be outside to properly hear the voice of the caller. In reality, he was ashamed to talk to his mother in front of Giulia.

"Your Snake Plissken costume is here, hon, you forgot to take it back," was Antonia aka Mom's first sentence as Marcello answered the phone. "Or maybe you had a better idea for your costume?" She used to be very straight to the point, and things had only gotten worse as she became older.

"Well, yeah... sort of..." Marcello replied.

"I know that tone and I don't like it," she said. "Put on something scary enough, take your car and go to Mr. Coletti's Halloween party, now," she ordered.

"I just can't," he said in a single breath. He complimented himself for being able to state it with such clarity.

"What does it mean you can't? It's Mr. Coletti, your boss. You know how much of a goth he is. You know he expects you, like any other employee of his, to celebrate Halloween with him. Those who arrive late will play the zombies in the zombie hunt, but you must be one of the survivors!"

The words came out of the phone as powerful as bullets from a machine gun. They hit Marcello's brain one after another, and he didn't scream in pain just because he was out in the street and people would see him. He took a deep breath as he looked at the tidy stoned street.

"But, Mom..." Marcello muttered in despair.

"What exactly wasn't clear in my words?" Antonia asked, the severe voice just hinting a shade of anger. "Do you want me tomorrow to get an upset phone call from my good old friend, Mr. Coletti, the man to whom I strongly suggested to hire you five years ago?"

Usually, Marcello would have followed his mother's orders. He was about to give up when he found himself staring, and smiling, at Giulia's blue eyes. She had sneaked out the dining room and stood gracefully on the first step of the entrance stairs.

"Everything all right?" she mouthed with her perfect lips.

Having a beautiful woman looking at him in concern caused a sudden wake up. He was a man, not just mama's boy.

After five years of careful and thorough work at the Banca di Asti, attending every single darn game night at Mr. Coletti's mansion–from Star Wars Day Rebel Assault to Die Hard Christmas–this time he had something better to do. Nothing on Earth could have him change his mind.

"Sorry, Mom, I'm busy," he said on the phone, then hung up.

Marcello took a step closer to Giulia. "Here I am, it was just some sucker from work," he said.

"Shall we go back?" the blond woman asked.

"Just one minute."

Drunk on hormones for winning the fight against his tyrannic parent, Marcello grabbed Giulia by her chin and kissed her passionately. After a few seconds of surprise, the woman's warm lips sunk into his, showing appreciation.

Their tongues touched each other and he caressed her hips, drawing her slender body closer to his while feeling the excitement rising.

Marcello stepped back, his eyes locked into hers.

"That was... unexpected," Giulia whispered in awe.

"I hope in a good way," he commented.

"Oh, yes," she replied, lowering her eyes in embarrassment.

He took her hand. "Let's go back to dinner, shall we?" His voice sounded very manly.

They went back to their table. They ordered tagliatelle with truffle and waited for the dish while they chatted charmingly. To prevent any further call, Marcello turned his phone off. The night was his and he didn't want anybody to bother him.

There was a short, unexpected visit at the table by Fulvio, one of his frequent customers at the bank. He noticed Marcello while walking toward the exit to pay the bill and stopped by for a quick chat.

Fulvio introduced them to his girlfriend Filomena, a short, curly-haired brunette, and complimented Marcello for being such a great bank accountant. He smiled in modesty as Giulia looked at him in awe.

"You're a celebrity," Giulia said as the couple left.

"Not at all," Marcello replied. "I just helped Fulvio once, solving a tax issue of his."

"You are my hero," Giulia whispered, touching his foot with hers below the table.

Marcello's mind imagined the many, delightful ways in which that night could continue after the dinner. The bold move of kissing her had been made with perfect timing. Still, he forced himself to stay focused and enjoy the dinner first.

He didn't expect to get the tagliatelle into a closed platter. Also, it had been a middle aged woman who had taken their orders. Seeing that tall, pale and skinny man, appearing out of nowhere at their table, handing a platter with a lid over it, seemed out of place. Marcello and Giulia exchanged a frown.

When the waiter lifted the lid, they both screamed in horror.

On the platter, the decapitated head of Fulvio stared at Marcello with empty eyes. His mouth was wide and unnaturally open, like he had been yelling the very moment he had been killed. Fresh blood was dripping into the platter from the ripped off neck.

Giulia was the quickest in standing up. Her seat was the closest to the exit door. Marcello stumbled behind her only to reach the nearby door a few seconds after.

The door was locked. Giulia punched hard on it, screaming for help. But there was a long stair between the dining room and the street and no chances that anyone could hear.

With his back on the wall, Marcello scanned the dining room. All the walls were decorated with medieval fight pictures, with some life-size swords and knives replicas hung on a wood rack.

The main entrance was on the shorter side, about twelve foot wide. But the room was four times deeper. All the windows were not a good way out, but they could try to reach the door at the other end.

Everything, from tables to furniture, was tidy and empty. Chairs and tablecloths had been put back in place so carefully one could swear nobody had been there recently. Marcello had clear memories of a crowded room. Except he and Giulia had been so focused on each other that they didn't notice that every other patron had left.

"What's up, pals. You don't like your meal?" the tall waiter asked, upset. He took a deeper look into the decapitated head. He grabbed it by the hair and turned it to them. "It's fresh human meat, with the brain of a very smart guy. How can you not appreciate it?"

Marcello and Giulia were side by side, their backs glued to the door. He slipped his hand into hers and he felt her trembling hold.

"Don't worry, we'll get out of here," he whispered. "Somehow."

Giulia sighed and nodded. There were three tables between the waiter and them. The tall pale man, still holding the head, stepped towards them going over the first table. He kept getting closer in his casual stroll.

"I think it's all a misunderstanding. I think you haven't seen this good meat close enough," the waiter said. "Please, help yourself!" He tossed the head at them. It was what Marcello had been waiting for.

"Go!" Marcello yelled to Giulia, while rushing to the closest table and pushing it over. A loud crash broke the silence as the cutlery fell to the floor and the glasses were reduced to smithereens.

Giulia slipped past the waiter to a safe hideout in the other side of the room. The waiter didn't move. He stood fists on his hips with an astonished face.

"Is it like that you plan to survive? By wreaking havoc in my tidy dining room?" the waiter asked.

Marcello ignored him and tried to outrun him as well. But the other performed an impressive rugby catch and stopped him. Marcello couldn't help falling down on the floor. The guy was strong. He tried to kick himself out of the awkward embrace with very little result.

"Come on, you jerk! Can't you fight for your woman?" the waiter scoffed while holding tighter.

"Let me go!" Marcello cried.

"Why, exactly? You just offended me and my family by refusing the delicious meal we prepared just for the two of you, love birds".

"Should I… say I'm sorry?" Marcello exclaimed in despair.

The grasp softened. Marcello was still lying on the floor as the waiter stood up, brushed off some dust and stared at him.

"Well, it would a good start," the waiter said.

Marcello pushed himself back in a sitting position. He could stand up at any moment and run away, but he wanted to try and play the crazy man's game first.

"I'm sorry if I offended you," he said.

A faint smile appeared on the pale face of the waiter. Before Marcello could react, the strong hands of the waiter were on his neck. The pressure felt like steel.

"I was kidding. I'm not offended. I just want to kill you," the waiter said.

Marcello tried to fight back, he moved his hands around and grabbed the waiter by the shirt and the wrist. He tried to hit him in the eye with his index but the other turned his head quick enough to avoid it.

Marcello coughed and gasped.

"Please! My mother is rich, she can pay you whatever you want," Marcello managed to say in a harsh voice.

The waiter flinched and grunted. He freed one hand, focusing on something on his back while frowning. After some fumbling, he got back with a bloodstained knife.

When he turned, Giulia slammed a dish on his face.

The waiter lost control and fell on the floor. Giulia stretched her hand and helped Marcello up. Scruffy and restless, she still glowed like an angel.

They rushed to the door, slammed it open to see a narrow brick stair heading down in the dark. Holding hands, they followed the staircase as it bent to the right. They found themselves in a hall. A door to the right seemed to lead to the kitchen. Another to the left to more stairs.

"The street should be over there," Marcello said, pointing at the left door.

They descended more steps, still frantically and with their hearts racing.

The final destination turned out to be a large cellar, split into four sections by an archway. The light was dim and the air cold and wet. All over the walls were huge wine barrels, marked with numbers and signs over the stained and consumed wood.

Marcello and Giulia took a few careful steps in the cellar. They both jumped at a sudden bang. A bullet hit the wall behind Marcello while the echo of the explosion slowly faded out. A short armed figure emerged from the darkness.

"In fact, my aim is better than that," the newcomer said in an amused acute voice. "But if I had killed you with the first shot, I wouldn't see your hilarious scared face!"

It was a short woman, as pale as the waiter and wearing similar white clothes. Her long black hair was tied in a ponytail, her eye bags and a scar going from her left cheek to the forehead gave her a disturbing look. The gun she held was a Luger of old design.

"We mean you no harm, Miss, we just need a way out," Marcello said, holding up his arms, partly shielding

Giulia with his body. As a reply, the waitress shot again. The bullet hissed close to Marcello's ear.

"You're not going out. You'll die!" the waitress screeched.

Marcello and Giulia turned to the stairs just to see the waiter stepping in.

"Hey brother! I'm finishing your job, here!" the waitress said to the waiter.

"Sister, please, don't bother me and let me work..." the waiter replied.

"No way! The cellar is my hunting ground. If you wanted them, you shouldn't have let them leave the dining room."

Marcello and Giulia took advantage of the family reunion to slip away. There were a lot of places to hide but no way out. They squatted behind a barrel, the last of its row.

Both of the main hallways were visible. Sister and brother were out of sight. The quarrel between them, that they could barely hear, was apparently going longer than expected.

"Let's hope they kill each other," Giulia said. "Did they mention the psycho personnel on TripAdvisor?"

Marcello swallowed. "I swear, I have no idea about what is going on here. I've been at this restaurant many times."

Giulia smirked. "I bet you bring all the girls here."

Marcello blushed. Not that he had dated so many women recently. Certainly, none of those he had been hanging out with in the last ten years had ever been as charming and smart as Giulia. The sad truth was he had been eating there many times with Mom.

To break the awkward moment, Giulia kissed him lightly on his lips.

"Next time, I choose the place," she said.

Marcello brightened at the idea of a second date with Giulia. Then a gunshot brought both of them back to the crazy reality. The bullet had crossed the barrel from side to side and now a gush of red wine was spilling out. Still crouching, Marcello and Giulia withdrew along the row of barrels.

"I wasn't aiming at you, love birds," the voice of the waitress announced. "I was just testing my gun."

All they could do was keep moving while trying to reach the stairs. They carefully crossed the hallway with quick steps and took cover behind the next row of barrels.

Two more gunshots rumbled in the cellar. Marcello and Giulia walked past another pierced barrel. It was wasting precious Barolo. They sprinted and avoided the next two bullets, which caused more spilt wine.

Marcello and Giulia were just a few steps from the stairs. He quickly glanced beyond the corner just to see the waiter standing in his usual pose. Fists on his hips, piercing gaze over an otherwise bored face.

"We have to go another way," Marcello whispered.

Another gunshot missed Marcello by a few inches. He looked up to see the waitress sitting on the other row of wine containers, madness flashing in her eyes.

"Exactly. Stay there", she said.

Giulia stepped back and another bullet streaked in front of her nose.

"I said you stay there," the waitress ordered.

Marcello felt his feet wet. He looked down to see that wine had begun flooding the floor. Some liquid had entered his shoes.

The crazy woman had broken so many barrels that now the whole cellar was wet. He imagined some kind of desperate plan to set the wine on fire and he realized he didn't even know if it could catch fire.

He looked at the waitress. She was staring at them, grinning and swinging her legs down like a little kid having the time of her life.

Marcello raised his hands. "What now?" he asked.

"Now you die," the waitress announced. She took aim, then lowered it as if she were uncertain. "Is it most fair if I shoot you first and your girlfriend last? Kind of a girl power statement?"

Marcello and Giulia exchanged a look.

"I'm not sure," the waitress muttered. "If she dies first, you'll suffer more. What I want is to make you suffer." As she pondered, the waitress scratched inside her left nostril with her middle finger.

"Kill me first, I'm OK with that," Marcello said. Giulia touched his arm, mouthing a "No". Marcello smiled to her and shrugged.

"Well, good for you, good for me," the waitress said. She took aim and held her breath.

"Sister, please, you cannot always spoil the fun," the waiter said. He had walked around the barrels to appear to their left. Marcello realized the way to the stairs was to their right.

As the siblings quarreled, Marcello took Giulia's hand and pointed her towards their way out.

"Get ready to run," he whispered.

"I hope you have just told her goodbye," the waiter said to Marcello. "Your neck and I have some unfinished business."

The tall man took a step towards them. Marcello pushed Giulia. She bolted. The waiter slipped on the wet floor and lost balance. An opportunity to survive. Marcello ran, deafened by the gunshots all around.

Giulia first, Marcello second stepped on the stairs. He gently slapped her ass and she smirked back. They reached the hall. Mad yells came from downstairs.

"The kitchen!" Marcello said.

"What if we go to the dining door and we try to get out of the main door?" Giulia suggested.

"It's still locked," Marcello retorted.

"Can't you throw it down?"

Marcello shrugged. "I don't know how. I'm no movie hero."

Giulia gave him a sad look. Steps echoed.

Marcello put his hand on the knob of the kitchen door. "It's on street level," he said, hopeful. Giulia sobbed. They broke into the kitchen to find it very dark. Marcello searched for the switch and pulled it.

He wished he had kept the lights off.

A huge bald man in a dirty white vest, large tattooed shoulders ending in two muscular arms, sneered at them while clashing two long knives that screeched loud. His figure stood in the way towards what definitely looked like the exit door.

"Hey, glad to meet you! I'm the cook!" he said.

The room was small and filled with shelves, ovens and kitchen tools. Marcello glanced at another, narrow door and wondered if it could be a way out or at least buy them some time.

At that very moment the waiter reached them and froze in the doorway.

"Oh, hey Dad! They're with you..." he said with blatant indifference.

Giulia yelled. "I'm so sick of all this!" She launched herself towards the cook and kicked him in the crotch. The big man bent while screaming in pain.

Marcello took advantage of that to run to the door to the right. He pulled it while trying to grab Giulia's hand– and missing it. They entered and closed the door. Only after a few seconds they realized it was an ice house filled with human corpses.

Also, no knob from the inside.

Giulia started punching the door and screaming. "Get me out!"

Marcello tried to stop her. "Are you crazy? They'll kill us."

"You'd like to die here, instead?"

"Yes, maybe. Later."

Giulia gave Marcello a death stare.

"We're certainly not opening the door, for how kindly you may ask," the cook said from the other side. "In fact, the ice house was exactly where I wanted to put you."

Marcello swallowed.

"Too bad the game is already over. I was having fun," the waiter said.

"I still wanna shoot the man! I wanna see him dying!" the waitress said.

"Shut up!" the cook said. "What did I do wrong to have such morons as children?"

Marcello gently knocked on the door. He kept hopping to fight the cold.

"I have a question," Marcello said.

"What?" the cook asked.

"I'd like to know why..."

"What?"

"Why you do this!"

The cook pondered.

"Long story short. Human meat is delicious, as long as people don't know it's human meat. I'm just an entrepreneur meeting a very specific niche of the market. That's all." His tone was a reasonable tone.

"Why us?" Marcello asked.

"Well, sometimes we run out of meat and you looked tasty."

"Oh, yeah, this explains everything," Marcello moaned, feeling energies fade away. He leaned to the door and let himself slip to the ground.

Giulia sat a few steps away, arms around her knees, facing away. As she noticed him, she stretched her arm and pulled him to her. She wrapped his arms around her body.

"Warm me up, you jerk," she said.

"With my naked body?"

"Oh, come on!"

Outside, fading steps hinted how the happy family had lost interest in them.

"I don't want to die here," Giulia complained. "I'm too young and beautiful to die."

"You definitely are," Marcello agreed.

Giulia turned to him expectantly. "You really think so?"

"I've lost count of how many times I've been looking at you tonight, thinking you are the most awesome woman I have ever seen in my life," he said. Confessing it made him feel better, even in the cold of the ice house.

"You've seen many?" Giulia asked.

"Let's say I look around a lot," Marcello replied.

Giulia pondered for a while.

"That's very nice of you," she said in a tender voice.

She guided his arms around her shoulders, then her arms, then her hips trying to produce some extra warmth. Eventually she put his hands on her breasts making Marcello blush heavily.

They stood in the same position for long, empty minutes. They tried to move at first, then they gave up and simply breathed softly, slower and slower as their conscience started fading away.

Marcello, half frozen, thought that if he had to die, it was a nice way to do it. Still better than the crappy Halloween party.

Suddenly some booms from the outside woke Marcello up. He shook Giulia, getting no reaction. He clumsily stood up and put his ear on the door.

"Something is happening!"

Giulia muttered a curse. But in the restaurant some new event was really going on.

There were gunshots from an assault rifle, along with other thumps and crashes. Marcello heard human screams and thought he recognized the waiter's voice, even if into some extreme distress. Later everything reverted back to full silence.

Eventually Marcello heard steps in the kitchen, a hand turning the knob and saw the door opening in front of his very eyes.

He found himself looking at Antonia, his mother, dressed as Mary Poppins. Her costume was perfect aside from with some drips of blood. At her side his boss, Mr. Riccardo Coletti. He wore a leather jacket and a brown wig covering his bald head. Behind the Ray-Ban sunglasses, what appeared to be an injury was instead a Terminator make up.

Coletti held a smoking hunt rifle. Marcello blinked to be sure it wasn't some hallucination.

He grabbed Giulia by her shoulder, shook her hard until she groaned.

"Giulia! Giulia! We're free!" he said excited.

Mr. Coletti helped them both out of the ice house while Antonia headed out and got back holding blankets and table cloths. She wrapped them around Marcello then, after a careful check, did the same to Giulia.

"Poor Marcello, don't worry, everything is OK now," Antonia said. She looked at Mr. Coletti. "It was clear, since you would never miss our friend Riccardo's Halloween party, that something bad had happened to you on the way back."

That was how they had set up the rescue party.

Antonia continued. "I knew this restaurant, you even posted on Facebook you'd be here". She stopped and looked into the ice house and sighed. "Who knew that good old Sergio had such dirty secrets?"

Mr. Coletti grimaced. "People who don't celebrate Halloween are not trustworthy," he stated.

Antonia smiled at him and caressed the gun barrel. "You know, Riccardo, this weapon fetish of yours always comes in hand..."

Giulia gave Marcello an astonished look. He couldn't help shrugging.

THE END

Zara-Lena's Surprise Dinner
By Eowen Valk

It was just past midnight when Cedric Shard struggled through a pile of letters to pick a winner for his contest. There were two hundred fifty-seven pieces in which their senders explained why they wanted to win a meet & greet with him at a location of their choice. He thought it was a great way to self-promote in the run-up to the publication of his next horror novel. He yawned, wanted to call it a day until his eye spotted a black envelope. He opened it. It contained a piece of paper with scorched edges. The poem was decorated with red dried spatters.

#

To my favorite author Cedric Shard.
Each of your stories is a real piece of art.
I've read every single one, until the last letter.

Themes that you describe truly matter.
I invite you to a place that suits your desire
and will cook for you, maybe make out by the fire.
Choose me if you have nerves of steel
to experience something truly surreal.
Not scared of dust, ghosts, spiders, or blood?
Bring your old shoes; there's also mud.
Do you trust me? Are you in for a game?
Zara-Lena Witsier is my name.

#

Zara-Lena's phone number and address were written under the poem. He put it aside and drank the last half of his beer. No matter how hard he tried to read the other letters, Zara-Lena's words kept buzzing through his head. He would give her a call come morning.

#

Two weeks later, Cedric arrived at the train station close to Zara-Lena's home. As he walked to the exit, he spotted a woman, dressed in a black jacket and tight jeans, holding up a sign with his name. Black hair with snow-white highlights fell in wavy strands across her shoulders. He guessed she was in her early thirties, a few years younger than he. She caught him with her intense gaze.

A few minutes later, they sat in her car, an old model Fiat. She stared at him with dark-gray make-up eyes. "I'm so happy to meet you. I've read all your stories. This day means a lot to me. We will have a great time together. I have big plans for today."

He smiled. "Where are we going?"

She giggled and started the car. "You will see soon enough."

He didn't ask further because he let her decide the location of their date. She had a friendly face, no ring, skull-shaped earrings. Her perfume smelled like lemons. As if she felt that he stared, she turned her head and stared back. He smiled again.

"Your entry was creative. How did you put those red splatters on the paper?"

"I wanted to give the poem a personal touch." She showed her palm with a scar from a knife wound. "I cut my hand and collected some blood in a bowl. I splashed it on the paper with a toothbrush. I'm glad you like it."

Cedric swallowed. *Great, a chick who mutilated herself.* He watched the plants and trees passing by at the side of the road.

After a long drive over country roads, along fields and streams, Zara-Lena parked the car at the edge of a deciduous forest. She took a cooler and an overnight bag out of the trunk. Cedric took the cooler from her. They followed a hiking trail into the woods.

She led him away from the main route over narrow paths covered with leaves and grasses. After a while, they came to a fence. Zara-Lena opened it as if it were hers. Cedric grabbed her arm.

"Wait. That sign says *Private Property*."

Zara-Lena smiled and came closer. She stroked his cheek with her warm fingers. "Don't worry. No one will notice," she whispered.

He gently pushed her hand away, looked around to be sure no one saw them. The path led to a sandy beach with a jetty. A rowboat was moored there. In the middle of the lake was an island with a lonely wooden house, partially hidden behind leafless trees and bushes. A pile of rubble, probably the remains of a collapsed shed, stood nearby. The lake was surrounded by forest. Zara-Lena walked onto the jetty. "That's our destiny, my grandparents' house. My family still owns that island."

"So," he said, "no trespassing."

She smiled and shrugged, then stepped into the rowboat and put her stuff in the front. The paint of the boat peeled on every side. Cedric glanced nervously at the island, then at the boat. The idea of traveling in that rotten coffin made his guts itch as if insects crawled through them.

"Is there another way to reach the house? That bridge, maybe?"

Zara-Lena shook her head. "The bridge collapsed long ago. My family is responsible for maintenance, but no one wants to pay for the repairs. The house has been uninhabited for years."

"Why did you choose that place for our date? Why not a cafe? Or your house?"

She grinned. "Too boring for you. I read in an interview that you like old houses. This house breathes history. It might inspire you."

Cedric stepped into the rowboat. The vessel wobbled. He almost fell, but Zara-Lena grabbed him. He would not let his fear of water ruin his day, especially in the presence of a fan. She slapped his shoulder. "You're not afraid of a little water, are you?"

He put on his poker face, loosened the rope, and pushed the boat away from the jetty. Zara-Lena rowed. Cedric tried to ignore the nerves. He listened to the sounds of oars sloshing through the water and focused on the island. His feet suddenly felt cold. Water flooded his new sneakers. Two loose floorboards floated from their spot, revealing dry rot at the bottom of the boat. Five branch pieces served to plug the holes.

"The boat is sinking! Do we make it to the other side?" He rolled up his pants.

"No sweat. We are halfway," Zara-Lena said calmly.

Cedric went to the side of the bench, trying to determine if there was a current. The boat wobbled.

"Calm down and keep still!" Zara-Lena said. "There's a bucket behind you in that pile of rope. Use it to get the water out if you're scared." She bared her teeth in a mocking grin. Cedric suppressed the urge and sat quietly.

While Zara-Lena attached the rowboat to the remains of the wooden bridge, Cedric climbed out of the boat. As soon as he was on solid ground, his nerves subsided. He took the overnight bag from her.

"Wow, that's heavy. What did you put into it?" He pulled the zipper.

"Don't open it!" She grabbed the bag and closed it. "It will ruin the surprise." She gave him the cooler. "Carry this and keep it closed." She stared at him as if angry. He looked away. Like it mattered that he saw a piece of rubber or cloth tarp. He wasn't sure.

They walked along the narrow sandy beach and came to a large garden. Long blades of grass rustled rhythmically on gusts of wind. Eight grey headstones stood next to a collapsed shed. Cedric laid his hand on the weathered stone of Jacoba Witsier, who apparently lived for one hundred and fifteen years, and closed his eyes. He hoped to sense more than the green and yellow lichens under his palm, like an image or an emotion. Zara-Lena put her arms around his waist and pressed her chest against his back.

"All of them lived in that house. Jacoba was my grandmother," she whispered.

Cedric opened his eyes. "I always get story ideas when I touch a headstone."

"She was a great witch. I've inherited one of her notebooks. It contains dark spells. She used them to harvest the souls of dead animals."

He smiled. "You're kidding me."

She pointed at another part of the garden, where many old wooden sticks were stuck into the ground. "Over there is an animal graveyard. Grandma and her mother harvested the souls of animals and captured them in crystal. Soul energy is powerful. They lived a very long time."

Cedric walked towards the area with dozens of rotting sticks. "Could they harvest human souls?"

Zara-Lena took his hand. "Let's go inside the house. We have a lot to do."

They passed a wooden outhouse and a well with a water pump. The faded paint layer of the house showed that the original color was red. Weather and dry rot had scourged the boards so severely that the wood was full of cracks and splits. The jerkin head roof lacked a few tiles. Cedric looked at the broken window on the first floor. He hoped to see an appearance between the half-open curtain; a pale face, a hand hitting the glass, or a sudden movement. Zara-Lena opened the front door. The hinges creaked in protest.

"After you," she said.

A trail of footprints was visible in the dust layer on the floor. The wooden floorboards creaked under his feet as he walked further into the dark hallway. The house was cold and musty. He came past a staircase leading upstairs and stopped in front of a closed door. The footprints disappeared underneath it. He attempted to open the door, but it was locked. He walked into the living room. Zara-Lena opened the curtains. A sea of light expelled the darkness. Giant cobwebs hung in the corners and along chains of petroleum lamps. Cedric put the cooler on a low table in front of a three-person couch. He sat down and made himself comfortable by putting his feet on the table, right before a silver-colored candlestick. He breathed deeply. The air smelled of old wood, decayed rug, and dust. God, he loved these deserted places, hotbeds of inspiration.

Zara-Lena giggled. "I want to show you something." She took his hand and pulled him off the couch.

In the kitchen was a coal stove with four shutters and a thick black pipe through the wall. Cedric slid his hand across the enamel top. A dark-gray smudge remained on his fingers. He wiped his hand on his pants. Zara-Lena lit the petroleum lamp above the table. A brown chair with a high backrest and two armrests stood behind the table. There was a tangle of scratches in the leather upholstery as if someone carved a childish-looking spider web in it. Two dark brown wooden chairs stood at the other sides of the table.

"Have a seat," Zara-Lena said, pointing at the biggest chair.

Cedric sat down and put his arms on the armrests. The upholstery groaned under his weight. Zara-Lena disappeared behind him. A scraping sound came from the backrest of the chair. Metal arm straps shot out of the armrests and snapped shut around his arms.

"What the..." Cedric tried to move his arms. The metal bracings around his wrists didn't move.

"Do you like it? Found it on eBay," Zara-Lena said close to his ear. She pulled her cell phone out of her pocket and took a selfie with him.

"Untie me," Cedric said.

Zara-Lena took a clock from the overnight bag. She set the timer to four hours, pressed a button on the back, and placed it on the kitchen counter. It started to count down.

"What happens when the time is up?"

Zara-Lena took logs out of a basket near the kitchen door and put them into the stove. "This beauty burns coal and wood," she said while lighting a fire.

Cedric tried to pull his hands through the braces. The openings were too small. "What are you up to?" He tried to keep his voice light but could not avoid a tremble.

"We're going to have dinner together. Just sit back while I cook." She left the kitchen with the cooler. The sound of her boots faded away. He heard a key turning in a lock, followed by the sound of a door cracking open.

"Hey! Don't leave me!" He pulled and turned his wrists until his skin became sore. The brackets didn't move.

Zara-Lena put a pan full of water on the table. "Fresh from the pump." She opened a bag of baby potatoes, dropped the contents into the water, then placed the pan on the stove. She put a small saucepan next to it and emptied a bottle of sunflower oil into it.

"Untie me so that I can eat," Cedric said.

She kissed him on his forehead. "No need for that. I will feed you," she said with an almost sensual smile. She put a plate and silverware in front of him. She added the contents of a small plastic box into the saucepan. The hot oil sizzled.

After a few minutes, Zara-Lena put a bowl of fried worms in front of him. She sat down next to him, scooped some up with a spoon, and brought the fat-smelling pile to his mouth.

"Eat. These little fellas are very healthy."

"I don't eat insects. Let me go!"

"Don't tell me you're afraid of a few maggots. You use them so often in your stories that I didn't think you would have an aversion. They are protein-rich." She pushed the spoon against his lips. He kept his mouth tightly shut. Zara-Lena held his nose.

"I'm more patient than your lungs." She almost sang the words.

He moved his head while holding his breath, but Zara-Lena moved her hand along. The urge to breathe became unbearable. He kicked her shins. She spread her legs and waited patiently with the spoon in front of his face. His lungs couldn't take it any longer. As soon as he opened his mouth for a new load of air, she forced the spoon with crispy little bodies inside. He spat everything in her face. She let out a slow sigh and wiped her face with her sleeve. She got up, disappeared behind him, and put her hands firmly around his neck.

"I put a lot of time and energy in this day. Unfortunately, you don't care, so I must encourage you a little. I want this to be a memorable day." She tightened her grip on his throat. Cedric struggled, kicked. The chair opposite him fell to the ground.

"Eat everything I cook for you. If you refuse, I will correct your behavior by doing something to you that happened to one of your story characters. Do you understand?" She released his neck. Cedric coughed and gasped for breath.

"Damn, bitch! Why are you doing this?" Adrenaline rushed through his veins. Zara-Lena rubbed with her hands through his hair, scratched with her nails over his scalp.

"Stop whining, dear. You chose me to take care of you today. I'm grateful because I admire you, but you need to obey me." She held a new scoop in front of his mouth. "Eat."

Cedric obediently ate what Zara-Lena fed him. Drops of sweat slid down his armpits. He wanted to puke the fried pulp and push Zara-Lena's face in it. A rat walked along the wall. Zara-Lena giggled.

"I can use that little fella." She took a knife and crept like a lion to its prey. The blade whizzed through the air. The rodent stopped moving. Blood flowed from the decapitated body and covered the brown fur. Zara-Lena grinned. "I can bring his soul back. Grandma taught me. I'll show you later." She cleaned the blade with a napkin.

Zara-Lena took a dark brown butcher's apron from the overnight bag. She put on rain boots and yellow plastic gloves.

"Oh God, what are you going to do now?" Cedric groaned. His heartbeat rose.

Zara-Lena took a large carving knife from the cupboard and pointed the weapon at him. "Get our meat, of course."

"Geez, not a piece of me, I hope?" Cedric wrestled with the metal arm straps.

"No, silly bun, it's for you." She took a plate from the closet and put it, together with the carving knife, into the overnight bag. Next, she grabbed an ax from the top of the cabinet.

"You're not going to kill someone, right?" He imagined a person hanging on a hook in the enclosed room. "Tell me what you're going to do."

Zara-Lena left the kitchen with the ax and the overnight bag. Her boots pounded through the living room. Elsewhere in the house, a door slammed shut. Cedric wrestled with the chair and tried to stand up. The chair fell to the right. He hit his head against the floor. A dull pain radiated through his brain. Dust itched in his nose. He sneezed. He listened if Zara-Lena reacted to the sound. In another room, chains rattled against one another. A woman screamed. Cedric froze. She didn't sound like Zara-Lena. Sounds of someone chopping flesh and breaking bones dominated the frightened voice. He shuddered. *Oh Hell, that lunatic was cutting someone into pieces for his meal.* The woman's whining became softer until it ended in silence.

Cedric pulled, pushed, and turned his wrists. The metal arm strap on the left armrest moved a little. The sounds of Zara-Lena's boots came closer and closer. When she came into the kitchen, her smile disappeared immediately. She put the plate on the table.

"Why are you on the ground? Tried to escape, eh?" She struggled to get the chair up.

He glanced at the meat. Zara-Lena stroked his cheek with a bloody glove. The sickly smell of iron took his breath away.

"Do you smell that?" She kept her glove under his nose. "Fresh blood. You can't get meat that fresh from the supermarket." Blood spatters formed red freckles on her face. She took the potatoes off the stove. She hummed while she put the flesh in a frying pan with a large chunk of butter. Within minutes the kitchen smelled of fried steak. It became dark outside.

"What kind of meat is that?" Cedric asked.

Zara-Lena lit an extra petroleum lamp. "You will taste it in a minute. How do you like your main course; rare, medium, or well done?"

He took a deep breath. "Please, untie me. I've had enough of this!" The situation reminded him too much of his story *Behind Closed Curtains*, in which the neighbor fed the main character human meat. He looked at the countdown clock. "Don't keep me chained to this chair for two more hours, bitch! Let me go!"

"No." She put her hand on his cheek and rubbed it affectionately. "You look so tense. I love it. So intense. I suppose you want the meat medium-rare. A guy like you likes his meat bloody."

"You are imitating a scene of *Behind Closed Curtains*. Why are you doing this? We could have done nice things together."

Her eyes twinkled. "This is fun. I read that your greatest fear is to fall prey to a murderer who executes his sick fantasies on you before he turns you into worm food. I would love to see how you react once you realize that you are in such a situation."

His lower lip trembled. His strength flowed from his limbs and disappeared into the floor. "What do you mean? Are you going to kill me?"

Zara-Lena turned the meat, grabbed a bowl with pre-cut mushrooms, and threw the slices into the frying pan. Cedric began to hyperventilate. All kinds of nasty things he had done to story characters buzzed through his head. That crazy bitch was inspired by it. He forced himself to breathe more calmly to prevent fainting. He bit his tongue, sharp pain. His eyes searched the kitchen for an escape, something he could use as a weapon; a fork, a knife, a broom, anything.

Zara-Lena put two plates with meat, fried mushrooms, and baby potatoes on the table. She cut off a little piece and held it in front of his mouth. He kept his jaws firmly together. He refused to eat anything human. She hit with the serving spoon on the table.

"Eat it! I wrote forty letters for your competition to get you here. So don't turn our date into a disappointment."

"Untie me so I can eat by myself," he said.

Zara-Lena took the bloodstained carving knife. "No. You eat everything I feed you. Don't be such a wimp. You're a horror author, so you shouldn't fear a little meat."

"You will not use that knife because you're a fan. You gain nothing killing me."

Zara-Lena's eyes turned dark. "Watch me." She stretched her left arm. She let the blade slide slowly over her wrist but didn't flinch. The fabric of her pastel-blue sleeve turned dark red. She moved her hand slowly in front of his face. "Look what you made me do." Thick drops slid down her fingers and splashed on his pants. "Eat your dinner, or else I'll make the next cut in you on the same spot as Alan from your story *No Place for Seers*." Her wet finger slid from his temple to his right eye. Warm drops fell on his cheek. Cedric shivered.

"Do you promise to let me go if I eat everything?" He pressed his fingers tightly into the leather of the armrests. She smiled. Cedric swallowed the meat piece with difficulty. He would puke everything as soon as he set foot outside again. The meat tasted like steak, but he knew better. Even Zara-Lena ate it.

"I need extra iron now, don't you think?" She grinned.

Cedric looked at the pool of blood near his shoes. If that bitch bled to death, he would be stuck here forever. "Zara-Lena, you're losing too much blood. Let me help you bandage that wrist."

"I'm glad you care about me." She rolled up her sleeve and licked some blood from her wrist. Two little hoses with red liquid inside were fixed with tape to her forearm. She opened her blouse and pulled an emptied blood bag from her armpit. "Fake blood. The expression on your face was priceless. I'll never forget that." She grabbed his head and kissed his lips.

Cedric boiled with rage. He fantasized how he would hit her head against the table repeatedly. One hour left on the clock. "Tell me what happens when the time is up." He tried to let his voice sound as confident as possible.

She grinned. "I'll show you some cool magic, but I want something in return."

With a proud smile, Zara-Lena put the dessert on the table. A shiny red skull, of which the skull cap was missing, lay on the plate. A light pink mass with grooves and ridges on the top side was inside. Cedric gagged but not strong enough to vomit. He would report her to the police if he got out of here. Zara-Lena took a picture of him with her cellular phone.

"I forgot the whipped cream." She took the knife and left the kitchen.

Half an hour left on the counter. Now or never. Cedric used all his strength to push the left arm strap further up. The metal arm strap slowly opened a little. He got his arm out of the opening. Next, he pulled the right arm strap open with his free hand.

He pressed himself against the wall next to the passage to the living room. Zara-Lena's boots sounded closer and closer. Three. Two. One. He jumped her. She fell to the floor. He rushed past her into the living room. Zara-Lena grabbed his leg. He fell on his belly.

"Don't go! It's dark outside. You won't find the way," she said.

He kicked his leg free from her hands. "Leave me alone!"

"No, stay with me. I have put so much effort into this day that I deserve a night with you."

Cedric grabbed the silver candlestick off the table and held it like a sword. "Stay away from me, crazy hag!"

"Kiss me. Then you're free to go. I promise!"

"Go to Hell." He walked away from her.

The sound of her boots approached quickly. Cedric turned around. Zara-Lena rushed up to him with the knife pointing at his chest. He hit the weapon out of her hand with the candlestick. She screamed. He grabbed the knife from the floor. Zara-Lena hit his face. He pushed her away. She fell back and banged her head against the small table. She came slowly upright and leaned with her back against the table. A dark red stain grew under her left shoulder. She breathed heavily, touched the wound, and looked at her fingers. Cedric looked at the blade in his trembling hand. Bloodstained. He became lightheaded.

Zara-Lena groaned. "How could you do this? I would never kill you. I admire you." Her eyes filled with tears. Cedric dropped the knife on the floor and rushed to the front door.

Thousands of stars twinkled in the sky. He ran through the garden. As soon as he spotted the moon's reflection in the water, he ran to the waterfront.

He rowed as fast as he could over the ink-black water. The moonlight showed him the way to the other side. A sudden scream broke the silence. Cedric froze. Zara-Lena staggered onto the bridge remains, one hand pressed against her chest, her other arm stretched out to him.

"Come back! You misunderstood me. I love you! I only wanted to impress you by scaring you, like you scare readers with your stories!" she yelled.

Cedric hesitated. Was it for real or another trick with blood, just like that blood bag under her armpit? She probably wore more bags on her body to fool him if he didn't react the way she desired. She could choke on it. He rowed away from the island.

"Come back! Don't leave me here!" Zara-Lena yelled.

#

The days after his escape, his conscience gnawed at him. At night he woke up drenched because Zara-Lena haunted him in his nightmares. Memories of their date kept resurfacing in his head. He tried to analyze them to get a sense of her real meaning. *What if she had told the truth and didn't plan to kill him?* Maybe she was injured for real. When he couldn't take it any longer, he sent a message to her cell phone.

#

Cedric waited for a response for three days. Zara-Lena didn't answer his calls or messages. Maybe she was in the hospital or worse. He opened a can of beer and drank as fast as he could. That hag had ruined everything with her idiotic behavior. Memories of her taking pictures of him flashed through his head. If the police found her cell phone, they would come after him. That would end his career, his life. He needed that phone today.

#

Zara-Lena's car was on the same parking spot. A gray blanket of heavy clouds blocked the sun. Cedric ran into the woods. He wanted to reach the house before the rain would soak him.

He came to the sandy beach, where he had left the rowboat that fearful night. That heap of rotting wood was half ashore but so full of water that the rear had submerged. The oars were on the jetty, where he had left them. The bucket was gone. Cedric pulled the boat on the beach and pushed it on its side to get rid of the smelly water. He inspected the leaks.

He found a few thick branches that looked suitable enough to plug the holes. He cut the wooden sticks to the correct size with his jackknife and pushed them into the gaps. He took the oars and stepped into the boat. The vessel wobbled. Cedric sat down carefully in the middle. He stared motionless at the small island to keep control of his nerves. "I can row, I can row," he whispered repeatedly. Once his heart rate was back to normal, Cedric pushed the boat away from the beach using the oars.

The front door was open. Cedric went inside. "Zara-Lena?" He looked along the stairs. No reaction. He went to the kitchen. The used pans still stood on the stove. Cedric opened the curtains to dispel the darkness. The countdown clock showed 0:00. Zara-Lena's grotesque dessert grinned at him from the table. The skull was a tourist attraction for an impressive column of ants.

Several ants clung to the dried pink layer that covered the entire head. The color was too light for blood. Cedric carefully took the dessert from the table without putting his fingers on the ants. The material felt lighter than he expected from something made of bone. It felt more like plastic but very sticky. The stuff on his fingers smelled of strawberries. The contents of the brainpan had been transformed into a pink mush with a green fungus island. He found a small, transparent, empty box on the kitchen counter. The label on the cover stated: *edible buffalo worms*. Cedric threw the package on the floor. It was her fault that he had nightmares about getting eaten by maggots.

Zara-Lena's overnight bag stood next to the couch. Cedric emptied the bag and inspected the contents. No cell phone. He found a piece of paper with notes about her plan for the date, the blood trick with her arm, the menu. There was no human flesh on the list but beef. He shook his head and tore up the notes. Lies. Those sounds of slaughter didn't come from a cow. He was sure of it. It sounded so real. A door opened with a cracking sound. Cedric turned around. "Zara-Lena?"

The door of the room, which he previously could not enter, was open. It was a bedroom. An empty meat package lay on the ground. There was a sticker on it: Beef rump steak 520 gram. He found a receipt with the price of the skull in a plastic bag. Inside the cooler, he found a box with melted strawberry ice cream. A bottle of strawberry sauce stood next to it. A red tape recorder stood on a table in the corner. Cedric pushed the *play* button. No sound. He rewound the tape and pressed the *play* button again. A heart-rending scream emanated from the speaker. Nauseating sounds of an ax cutting through meat and crushing of bones were unleashed into the room. A woman's crying turned into groaning and rasping. Cedric pushed the *stop* button. A horrible realization struck him like a lightning blast. Zara-Lena spoke the truth when she said that she only wanted to scare him. She succeeded all too well. He grabbed the flask of strawberry sauce and smashed it to the wall. The red mush splashed in all directions. He sat down with his back against the wall and rested his hands against his face. He banged his head against the wall a few times. "I'm so sorry, Zara-Lena." His eyes became watery. Warm tears slid down his palms.

Dripping sounds came from another part of the room. The air turned heavy and ice-cold. Cedric shivered. Nails scratched on the floor. He peeked carefully between his fingers. Zara-Lena crawled towards him from the other side of the room. Two black eyes in an ash white face stared back at him. She left a trail of water and blood on the floor. Cedric gasped. He sat as if frozen. She grabbed his leg with ice-cold fingers and bent over him.

"Kiss me," her blue lips whispered.

He swallowed. "No," came out as a whisper.

Zara-Lena screamed. Cedric panicked. He pushed her away, then fled to the living room. He stepped on the knife, slipped, and fell on his back. He hit his head against the floor. Zara-Lena groaned and gasped while she crawled toward him. Cedric rolled on his belly, got up and fled the house.

Zara-Lena moved inhumanly fast through the garden, fading and reappearing in the process. Cedric made it to the bridge remains. He went into the boat and rowed quickly away from the island. Zara-Lena appeared on the bridge and pointed accusingly at him.

"I'm sorry! I misunderstood you!" Cedric yelled. "I didn't mean to stab you. It was an accident!"

Zara-Lena disappeared in a blink of an eye. Cedric looked around, hoping she would give up. The rowboat stopped abruptly. Cedric fell backward. "Damn!" He rubbed his back. It almost looked like the back of the boat was held back by an invisible rope. Water flowed underneath the floorboards and pushed two of them from their spot. Cedric picked up one of the planks. A branch piece floated near a hole. Cedric grabbed it. While he pushed the wood piece into the gap, another stick rose from its rotten spot. He hesitated. His heart pounded like it tried to break out of his chest. A white finger withdrew into the hole. A third stick rose from another spot until it floated freely in the puddle of water. The pale finger slid back into the gap. Cedric quickly pushed the sticks back into the holes. He took off his shoes and used them to get the water out of the boat. He heard water dripping on the bench, right beside him. Somebody breathed heavy and bubbling near his ear. A dark silhouette appeared in the corner of his eye. His heart hammered so fast it felt like it was trying to crush his ribs to escape. He wanted to look aside, but the muscles in his neck refused to move. Slowly he turned his head and looked at Zara-Lena's gray-white face. She jumped at him, grabbed him into an iron-like embrace in the process. The boat capsized.

Zara-Lena pulled him into the depth. He hit her face, pulled her hair, kicked her legs. Zara-Lena clung to him like a block of concrete.

"Give me what I want, then I'll let you go," her voice said in his head. She repeated her demand louder and louder. His lungs hurt. The urge to breathe became untenable. He stared into her pitch-black eyes. Everything was better than drowning. He hugged her firmly and kissed her stone-cold lips like she was the girl of his dreams. She released him. He hurried to the surface.

He climbed on the jetty and lay down on his back to rest. When his heart rate was back to normal, he came upright and looked at the private island of Zara-Lena's grandparents. He burst out into euphoric laughter. "My dear Zara-Lena, I will make it up to you by writing a story about you!" He wiped some tears from his cheeks. "You know how I treat my characters, so it will not have a happy ending."

A shadow approached him under the water surface. Cedric swallowed his grin away. Two hands shot out of the water, firmly grabbed his ankles, and pulled him off the jetty. The cold water swallowed him again. He desperately waved his arms as he got further and further away from the surface light.

"What Are the Odds?"
By Wayne Faust

You're probably not going to buy this. I know I wouldn't. I mean, what are the odds? But hear me out.

I was pissed. What about? I'm still not sure. My teenage hormones had kicked in full time, and I didn't yet have a love life. I was stuck with Kerkoran for third period, the rottenest Geography teacher ever. To top it off, that morning I'd gotten cut from the summer baseball team so my chances of playing in college had just taken a dump. In fact, my baseball stuff was still in the back seat, reminding me of my failures. So, there were lots of things to be pissed about. But soon there was gonna be more than teenage angst to worry about.

It was a warm Saturday night in late May, and I was out on a date with Gretchen Miller. She had finally said yes and gone out with me. That should have made me happy. But all night she'd been acting as if she'd wished she'd just said no like all the other times. We'd gone to see 'The Exorcist,' the most popular movie the Christmas before. Now it was finally at the bargain theater. Gretchen had spent the whole two hours with her hands over her eyes. When the closing credits came on, she looked at me with eyes like laser beams. She was definitely not happy with my choice of movie or my choice of theaters. After that, she wasn't happy with my choice of a late night snack either, Village Inn on free pie night. Who wouldn't be happy with free pie? Gretchen wasn't. And now she just wanted me to take her home.

We were cruising down Nagle Avenue with the windows down in my first car, a blue Chevelle. No bucket seats. Gretchen could have slid over and snuggled up close to me like most high-schoolers out on a date. But no. She sat as far away from me as she could, practically hanging out the window and watching the streetlights and the elm trees go by. Whoopee. What a scintillating date it had turned out to be.

I sighed and popped in a cassette. Remember those? I do because I'm an official geezer these days. 'In-A-Gadda-Da-Vida' started blasting from the Radio Shack speakers embedded in my door panels, which were covered with baby blue, fake fur like in a pimpmobile. Remember when everybody did that? I remember it like it was yesterday. I also remember 'In-A-Gadda-Da-Vida.' In fact, I'll never forget it because of what was about to happen. The song was seventeen minutes long and I had recorded it onto the cassette three times in a row. That's fifty-one minutes, almost the whole first side of a two-hour cassette if the machine didn't eat it first. I loved that song, with its bizarre lyrics, screaming guitar, and, best of all, the drum solo that sounded like somebody pounding on a coffin from the inside. It was my soundtrack in those days.

We stopped at a red light on Northwest Highway behind a rusty, black Buick. The driver was tapping the fingers of his left hand on the steering wheel waiting for the light to change. He had his right arm around a woman. *She* was snuggled up next to her date as close as could be, her head pressed tightly against his shoulder, long blonde hair flowing over the back of the seat. Boy did that piss me off. They were probably heading out to find a nice place to park while I was getting ready to bail on the worst date of my life.

I tapped my own fingers on my steering wheel in time to the drum solo, which had just started up:

Thump-thump-thump-thump-thump-thump-thump.

Thump-thump-thump-thump-thump-thump-thump.

It really did sound like a guy pounding on the inside of a coffin.

The light finally changed. The Buick turned left. Gretchen's house was straight ahead. I hesitated for a long moment.

I turned left.

"...ere...w...ing?" shouted Gretchen.

"What?" I hollered.

"Where are we going?"

I reached over and turned down the music. "Let's follow this car."

I don't know why I said it. To this day I still don't know. I mean, what are the odds? The night had been a disaster. So why did I want to prolong it?

"What for?" asked Gretchen.

"Just for kicks. It'll creep them out."

Gretchen didn't answer. I glanced over. She was looking right at me. Instead of the usual hostility she had been showing me all night, there was something else. A little bit of confusion. And a spark of interest.

"Okay?" I asked hesitantly.

"Okay," she said. "And you can turn the music back up."

So, I did.

What are the odds?

I stayed close behind the Buick. He continued down Northwest Highway going 45 in a 30. I knew the cops would be hanging out down on Milwaukee Avenue where the bars were getting ready to close so I wasn't worried about getting a speeding ticket. Besides, my Dad was a cop so he could fix it if I did. When the Buick sped up to 50, I kept pace. By now the song was heading into the screaming guitar solo, where it sounds like rusty nails shrieking open the coffin lid. I stole a glance at Gretchen. She had her hands on the dash like we were riding a roller coaster, her eyes wide in the quick flash of green neon from the All-Night Laundromat as we raced by. But she looked happy, or at least excited for a change.

We crossed into Park Ridge. The Buick slowed down and turned right onto a side street. I knew exactly what the guy was doing. Park Ridge was aptly named because it didn't have nearly as many streetlights as Chicago and the houses were all set back from the road. It was as good a place as any to find a spot to park unless you wanted to drive all the way out into the country.

The Buick crept along, the driver craning his neck left and right, looking for a dark place along the curb. I stayed about ten car lengths back and turned my music way down, leaving the creepy, church-like organ solo to mix with the sound of my tires rolling slowly along the pavement. I couldn't hear any music from the Buick up ahead. I wondered why that was. Did he have his windows rolled up? It was a hot night, and most cars didn't have air conditioning in those days. Surely a rusty piece of crap like the Buick wouldn't have it. But the girl up there didn't seem to mind. Her head never moved from the guy's shoulder. I wondered what her hands were doing down below. Was she teasing him, getting him ready for when they would pull over? The thought of that was pissing me off big time.

I was mad enough to forget about keeping my distance. My headlights caught the Buick's rear view mirror and the driver looked up and noticed me. I saw his dark eyes at the same time, reflected in the glass, narrowing as he shook his head. Then he sped away with a roar, muffler dragging on the pavement amidst a shower of sparks. I stepped on the gas and followed. I heard Gretchen giggle beside me. She even scooted a little closer.

Now it was a chase.

He turned right at the next street.

I turned right to follow.

He turned left.

I turned left.

And on and on.

We continued through the dark, leafy neighborhoods of early summer, our tires squealing as we raced around turns. I caught a whiff of burning rubber. He seemed to be avoiding Northwest Highway, sticking to side streets. Park Ridge has a lot of side streets so we could have kept this up all night. My heart beat faster and my hands began sweating all over my steering wheel. I'd never driven like this before.

By now Gretchen had moved right up next to me and turned the music back up. The song was nearing the end, all the instruments playing together, building and building toward the climax. Gretchen was actually squeezing my thigh as we squealed around turns. It should have been exciting, sexy, just what I wanted. I mean, what are the odds? But I was seeing red, focused on that bastard up in front of me. And I was *pissed off...*

To this day I don't know why.

And then everything happened fast.

The driver in front of me slammed on his brakes. The Buick fishtailed as it screeched to a stop, leaving zigzagging black marks in the pavement. I hit my brakes too, almost too late. Good thing my tires were in a lot better shape than his because I was able to stop a few feet short of his back end.

His door flew open, and he climbed out, slamming the door hard behind him. He stomped toward my car. He was wearing a gray t-shirt with no sleeves, and he had short, slicked down, black hair. His face was pockmarked, looking like the moon in the harsh glare of my headlights.

And then he was on me.

"You got a problem, Pal?" he shouted over my music, leaning down like a cop at a traffic stop. His face was nearly touching mine, sweat dripping off his forehead and onto my shoulder.

He shouldn't have stuck his head up close like that. Mr. Vitale used to do that to me when I messed up in gym class in 8th grade. I didn't like it then and I *really* didn't like it now.

I thrust my left fist up and caught him under the chin. His head snapped back. He reared back to throw a punch of his own through the open window, but I had already unlatched the door. I kicked it open with my foot and hit him in the midsection, knocking him back before he could strike. I scrambled out of the car and stared him down.

I hadn't been in a fight since I was seven years old. And here I was facing off against a guy I'd never even met before. And I wasn't even scared. I was just pissed. To this day, it's amazing to me how pissed off I was.

So, I punched him in the stomach.

Evidently, he hadn't been expecting that. Maybe he thought I was gonna say something first. I even surprised myself with how quick I threw that punch. There was a *whoosh* of air as his cheeks puffed out. He bent over, wheezing. I brought my knee up as hard as I could and heard a crunching noise as I connected with his nose. His head wobbled and blood dripped onto the pavement. He coughed and made a gurgling sound, bending over at the waist. I clasped both my hands together and slammed them into the right side of his head. He spun around like a top and fell onto his side, curling up into a fetal position. The side of his unshaved face was covered with blood and stubble, looking like strawberry jam in the harsh glare of my headlights. But I didn't care. I brought my left foot back and lashed out, kicking him once, twice, three times in the stomach, with him hugging himself to try and block my kicks.

For the fact was, I had decided to kill him.

I'd been pissed before. But *murder?* For no reason? I've thought about this a lot since then. What drove me? It was like a brush fire in my brain that had flared up into an full-fledged inferno. And nothing was going to put it out.

But then he pulled out the knife.

It had been sticking out of the top of his boot. Amazingly, after the beating he had just taken, he was able to roll over and get to his feet. He weaved in front of me, wielding a gleaming switchblade. "You've had it now, Pal," he said in a gurgling rasp.

From inside my car, I heard the song end on my cassette player. Then it started up again for Round Two, intro on the organ, pounding beat and blaring guitar. Then the lyrics:

"In-A-Gadda-Da Vida baby, don't you know that I love you..."

I couldn't help feeling a rush of fear. No one had ever pulled a knife on me before. I backed away.

His face formed into a bloody smile, and he jabbed the knife at me a few times, toying with me, beginning to laugh. "Shouldn't have followed me, you prick," he said, spitting out blood. "You didn't know what you were getting into." He was certainly right about that.

Not taking my eyes off his face, I felt behind me for the open car door, trying to put it between me and the knife. But he was too quick and kicked it shut, forcing me farther back, away from the glow of my headlights. The knife was no longer gleaming but I could still see it along with the outline of his skinny body, closing in fast, jabbing. My belly puckered as I imagined what the knife would feel like going in.

I could have turned and ran. But something kept me there, backing away and keeping my eyes on him. For the fact was, I still wanted to kill him. I wanted him *dead.* I held my arms out to the sides and dodged back and forth, letting him advance but staying out of his range, heading around the back of my car and then up the other side, looking for an opening so I could knock the knife out of his hand. Through my open windows the music played, loud and insistent.

"Oh won't you come with me and take my hand..."

Round and round my car we went like in some sort of twisted dance.

Three times around.

Four.

"Come on, you pussy," he said.

I didn't care if he called me names. It only stoked my anger.

But then, as I was backing once more around the rear of my car, I tripped.

My arms pin-wheeled and I hit the pavement. All the air was knocked out of me, and I found myself lying on my back, trying to breathe. He hovered over me, blood streaming from his nose and over his smiling mouth. He raised the knife high with both hands and brought it down. I put my hands up and just managed to catch his wrists. I held on for dear life, trying to fend him off and catch my breath at the same time. My eyes began to dim. Sweat poured out of my armpits. I smelled sour wine on his breath as his face got closer, sour wine and blood.

Something loomed behind him, a white shape seeming to come out of the dark canopy of elm trees overhead. There was a loud, liquid crack and his head snapped to the side in a blur, his hands letting go of the blade. He fell away from me and the knife dropped to the ground.

I looked up open-mouthed to see Gretchen standing over us with my baseball bat held high. Her thin, white blouse was covered with splatters of blood, black in the red glow of my taillights.

"W...w...what?" I managed to wheeze.

"Get up," she said. "I think he's dead."

I turned onto my side and coughed. Then I staggered to my feet, my breath coming back to me in gasps. I looked down at the driver of the Buick. He was splayed out on his back, one side of his head crushed like a melon. Chunks of what could have been brain matter were leaking onto the pavement. I turned my face away and threw up the last of my free pie from Village Inn.

"Are you finished now?" she said.

My knees turned to water as the adrenaline left me. I tried to say something, but my throat felt like it was closed off.

"Help me drag him into his car," she said. "And then we need to get out of here."

"Huh?" I sputtered.

"Come on! Somebody in one of these houses is bound to see something if we hang around much longer."

Her sense of urgency rubbed off on me and I bent down to grab his hands. She took his feet, and we began to drag him around the driver's side of my car.

"Wait," I said, and reached through the open window to turn off my headlights. Now we were lit only by the glow from the Buick's taillights. I craned my neck, trying to see into the car. "He had a woman in there with him," I said. "She probably saw the whole thing."

"Then we'll have to kill her too," said Gretchen.

I shook my head. Who *was* this woman, this seventeen year old girl who I had been out on a date with?

I let go of the driver's hands and crept cautiously up to the Buick, peeking in through the side window.

What I saw there changed everything.

A woman was lying on her side in the front seat. She had long, blonde hair, just like I had already seen. But what I hadn't seen was the rest of her. Her wrists were bound with duct tape. Ankles too. There was another piece of duct tape over her mouth. Her eyes were closed, and the lids were fluttering as if she were asleep and having a bad dream.

"Is she in there?" asked Gretchen.

"I think you need to see this."

Gretchen came up and stood beside me. She let out an audible gasp. "That sick pervert," she muttered under her breath.

"We should take off the duct tape," I said.

"No!" said Gretchen.

"She's asleep or something. I don't think she saw a thing. We should at least take the duct tape off her mouth. Then she'll be able to breathe better."

Gretchen didn't say anything, so I opened the door. A wave of hot air wafted out, smelling like stale tobacco and piss. I thought I might be sick again but willed it back down. I reached out and touched the woman. She didn't respond but I saw her breathing gently, up and down, up and down.

"I think she's drugged," I said. "There's no way she could have seen anything. And she seems to be breathing okay."

"Then let's put the guy in the back seat and get out of here," said Gretchen.

We dragged the driver the rest of the way to his car. He was a scrawny guy, so it didn't take long. His head left a trail of gore but this time it didn't make me feel sick at all. It's funny how that works, how we can get used to almost anything.

"What now?" I asked after we had gotten him into the back seat.

"You go back to your car and wait for me. I'm gonna run up and ring the bell in that house over there a couple of times, the one with no lights on. They're probably in bed. Then I'll run back to the car, and we'll get the hell out of here before anyone has time to see your license plate. They'll look out from their porch and see this guy's car sitting here. Eventually they'll come out and have a look. Then they'll call the cops."

By now my legs had stopped shaking and I walked calmly back to my car. The drum solo was kicking in for the second time. It suddenly sounded much too loud, and I switched it off. I sat there tapping on my steering wheel, making my own little drum solo until Gretchen came back, opening the door, sliding in and saying, "Go!" I backed into an open parking spot and did a three point turn just as a light came on in the house. I kept my headlights off as I raced away. I wasn't exactly sure where we were, but we managed to find Northwest Highway after a couple of wrong turns. Then I switched on my headlights, and we headed back down to Chicago.

Neither of us said a word all the way to Nagle Avenue. My stomach felt sour and there was a bad taste in my mouth. As I turned left onto Nagle and headed down the last few blocks to Gretchen's house, she finally spoke.

"I think we did something good tonight."

"Huh?"

"That guy was going to kill that girl. It's obvious."

I simply nodded my head and swallowed hard. We pulled up in front of Gretchen's house, a brick bungalow with a postage stamp lawn in front. The streetlights were bright here and I could see every bloodstain on her clothes.

"What are you going to do about that?" I asked, nodding toward her formerly white blouse.

She looked down. "I'll toss it in the dumpster behind the drug store tomorrow morning. My parents are out of town. Wanna come in?"

She looked at me sweetly. This was a dream come true. Gretchen Miller asking me into a house with no parents. What are the odds? But all the air had been let out of me and I just wanted to get home.

"Uh, no thanks," I said. "I gotta sort through this. And I gotta get rid of my clothes too."

"See ya' Monday?" she asked, as if it had been just a normal evening.

"Yeah," I answered. "See ya' Monday."

No goodnight kiss. No walking her to the door. Nothing.

***

What happened next was in all the papers. It turned out that the guy we bumped off that night was Frank Joseph Janus. Not the most prolific serial killer of all time, but a budding wannabe. The girl we saved, Saundra Stubblefield, would have been victim number six. He'd committed five murders in just over a year, all over the Chicago area. Who knows how many more there would have been if we hadn't stopped him?

The best the cops could figure, his M.O. was to simply cruise around the city looking for women walking alone. He'd drag them into his car and stick them with a hypodermic full of Narcozep. That would knock them out almost immediately. Then he would tie them up with duct tape and drive to the suburbs to find a dark place to park. I don't have to spell out what he would do to them then. When he was finished, he would take a plastic sheet out of his trunk and lay it down on the back seat. Then he would carve them up like pumpkins with his switchblade, the one he had tried to use on me. Afterward he would throw their bodies into dumpsters.

No one knows why he didn't take them out into the country, away from houses. Maybe he got a sick thrill from doing it all in front of sleeping suburbanites. Or maybe he couldn't afford the gas money. No one will ever know for sure because he was dead. Thanks to me. And Gretchen.

The papers were full of speculation about the mysterious hero who had come to Saundra's rescue and then fled the scene. Saundra didn't remember any of it of course, only how this skinny guy had stopped her and asked for directions, dragged her into his car, and then stuck her with a needle. Rewards were posted for anyone with information about that night. That made me a little nervous because I thought it might make Gretchen go public. But she never did. I didn't either. I knew enough from my Dad to know that we'd committed murder, even if the guy turned out to be a serial killer.

As for Gretchen and I, we never talked about that night. I saw her in school once in a while, but never asked her out on another date. Best to try and forget the whole thing.

She went on to have a happy life. Last I heard, she has seven grandchildren. And of course, Gretchen Miller is not her real name. I'm never gonna spill that information. I owe her that much at least. And I'm not gonna tell you my name either.

I've had a good life too. Eight grandkids. I didn't go into law enforcement like my Dad. I've done something else for a living all these years, traveling the world. And no, I won't tell you what my job is. I suppose you could try to find me through my Dad, since you know he was a Chicago cop. But there have been a *lot* of Chicago cops in the last forty years. Go ahead and try to find him if you want.

As to Saundra Stubblefield, well, you might have heard of her. She's dead now (from cancer a couple years ago) but she was Cook County D.A. for a bunch of years. In that time, she put away a *lot* of bad guys. So maybe we saved more lives than one.

So why did I write this? It was time to get it off my chest. To try and understand that night. Because the fact is, I have *never* come remotely close to feeling like that again, that blinding, red rage. Sure, I get mad about things once in a while. But not like that. I had no way of knowing that the guy in the Buick was a serial killer. How could I? But still, I decided to follow his car. And to kill him.

The more I think about it, the more I think that someone, or some *thing,* was moving me around like a chess piece that night. Moving *us* around. Because as far as I could tell, it got to Gretchen too. What else could have made her do what she did, cool as a cucumber?

So, what was it? God? He probably doesn't work that way. Well, maybe in the Old Testament. The Devil? He would have wanted the guy to keep on killing women. So, what could it have been? That's the million dollar question. Maybe we were possessed or something, like in the 'Exorcist,' only instead of being possessed by Satan, it was by the spirits of the women Frank Janus had already killed. It's as good an explanation as any.

All I can say is, something truly remarkable happened one late spring night in May, a whole bunch of years ago. I was a normal, All-American kid. Gretchen too. And we killed a guy. A guy that needed to be killed. And I have to admit, I'm not really sorry. I suppose I should be wracked with guilt and remorse. But I have daughters. And granddaughters.

Sometimes I still listen to "In-A-Gadda-Da-Vida" on my IPod. I can set it to repeat all day if I want. I never dreamed they'd have technology like that.

I mean, what are the odds?

END

Club Ludillo
By Robb T. White

I was standing in a corner nursing a glass of white wine, a beverage I've never had much use for. I'd been to parties like this one before—too many, truth be told, and for similar reasons: I was lonely or I was bored. I wasn't even sure how I found out about this one or why I was there when every guest looked unfamiliar.

I remember sitting in a bistro in Chelsea close enough to smell the Hudson, not a boon to my appetite, believe me. I was overhearing several conversations at once: a middle-aged couple were exchanging monosyllables like exhausted tennis players barely able to get the ball past the net. A student wearing an NYU sweatshirt was earnestly trying to impress a girl with quotes from Schopenhauer, and two young baristas were kibitzing to my left, and I think one of them mentioned the Ludillo. I've lived in Manhattan most of my life and made it past some of the hardest doors in the city like Provocateur, but I'd never heard of that place.

Of course, I was an old-timer by their standards. Besides, clubs open and close all the time on the west side and word of mouth can make or break an entrepreneur as fast as those columns by gourmands can propel a fancy restaurant into hot-spot status overnight— or kill it with a snobby *bon mot* like the one I'd read earlier from "Franco," whoever he was, when he skewered a place I often frequented: 'Because thou art lukewarm, I shall spew thee out of my mouth'—so says the bible of tepid Christians and so say I about the brasato-vitello and Romano beans I experienced Wednesday at Christie's on 34th St."

I'm not handsome, never pretended to be, but I clean up good, as they say. She eyeballed me a few times in passing among the crowd with drink in hand, stopping here or there to say a word to someone or a couple. She was olive-complected, maybe Portuguese, maybe Creole. Very striking eyes and her hair was cut expensively and stylishly to enhance an oval face.

It was an artsy crowd, not exactly rough bohemian, like some of the parties I'd attended in Soho. The apartment was spacious by Manhattan standards, tastefully decorated, but there were too many people to hear more than a few words uttered in excitement or distinguished by an unusual voice. I was getting bored by the general din of conversation. It reminded me of my last trip to Beijing. People everywhere you looked from dawn to dusk and all speaking into their cell phones or to each other and me unable to parse a single word out of that non-stop ribbon of language. At the end of my trip, I tried out a phrase in Chinese and the young female clerk laughed behind her hand at my ignorance of her tongue.

Besides, I had just about had it with the saccharine dollops of Adele, Fiona Apple, and Annie Lennox that piped from the speaker system I never did locate in the room.

"Not having much fun, are you?"

Her English was flawless except for the slightest whisper of another language, one with spongy vowels, lying just beneath it. I couldn't tell until she introduced herself to me as Neci from Brazil. It turned out she was from Fortaleza, where I'd been just a few years ago. I was a kite-surfing fiend until I destroyed the meniscus ligament in my right knee in a gorgeous kite lagoon in Jericoacoara. I hadn't been back on a board since and now damp weather made it ache.

It also turned out she was a fanatic of the sport. Suddenly, my boredom and loneliness slipped from me in an instant. We talked about records people had set, whether the "sport" would be recognized in the next Olympics, and kiteboarders who had set records for speed and distance.

"Last year I caught some good wind in Paracuru," she said; "it took me up to fifty knots in seconds. It was exhilarating, a fantastic rush."

She made it sound orgasmic. I was suddenly aware of her lush mouth and the sensual lips enclosing a perfect set of white teeth. The tiny little pulse of a vein in her neck, the delicate way she moved her hands when she spoke and the teasing scent of her perfume that wafted straight through my nose into my neocortex with her movements. We had to stand close to be heard.

She mentioned getting out of there and going to a club.

"I heard of a new one today," I said. "New to me, anyway. Ludillo. It sounds Italian."

"No," she said, "definitely not Italian. It's really different, like no place else I've ever been."

It was said with an odd kind of inflection, somewhere between nostalgia and regret. Before I could ask her what either the name or her response meant, she said: "Let's go there. Right now."

I finished the drink I'd been warming for the last hour in my hand and made a face.

"I'm not fond of our hosts' wine selection. This stuff is awful." I looked about for a place to set down my plastic flute, something you'd get from Amazon.

"I'm not much of a wine drinker myself," she said, reaching for my hand. We threaded our way through the bodies to the door.

"Where are we going?"

"Hunt's Point."

You don't have to be from New York to know that is one of the most blighted sections of the Bronx, whose denizens rival Bed-Stuy for crime, drugs, and violence. Crack whores, teen prostitutes and their pimps lurking nearby, and a whole motley crew of unsavory types wander those bleak streets every night.

I have a clear memory of lying back in the cab we'd flagged down outside the apartment. What bothered me was my lackluster behavior. I had a beautiful woman, an exotic Brazilian flower, who had picked me out of a crowd to go clubbing, and I was acting listless and dull once we hit the brisk air of the street. I wondered if I had unintentionally gotten drunk despite myself. I didn't eat much before leaving, I was sure of it, but for the life of me, I couldn't recall what I ate for supper or when I ate it.

Neci did most of the talking in the cab and seemed not to notice the change in me. I tried to snap myself out of it with a silent pep talk, and being a single man with some dating experience, I knew I wanted to sleep with her when our little club adventure was over. Everything's a game, almost a predetermined pattern we follow all our lives. I've sometimes convinced myself there's no such thing as free will. I'm no philosopher, however, and if we were going to make the beast with two backs, as Shakespeare says, I didn't much care about how the universe's electrons and molecules are supposed to work.

We passed under streetlights that gave Neci's lovely face a chiaroscuro effect as she passed into and out of the light in the rear of the cab. I was about to tell her how attractive she looked in this slow-motion strobe light, but as I opened my mouth to speak, I glimpsed her face in profile under a passing light and she looked aged, a crone with glittering eyes.

"What's wrong?"

"N-nothing," I stammered. "I was just wondering where we were. I'm not familiar with this part of the borough—"

"We're almost there," she snapped.

The clipped, dismissive tone jarred me. I didn't know what to make of it.

He pulled to the curb. I didn't remember Neci giving him a destination. I saw her pass something through the plexiglass slot, but it didn't appear to be money. As we stepped out of the cab, I leaned over to the driver's side and tapped. I had my wallet out because I was sure she hadn't given him money, whatever the object she passed him might have been.

"I already paid him," she said. "Let's go. This way."

I stood there rooted to the sidewalk in a part of town I didn't recognize. That abrasive tone was too much. All the eroticism I had felt for her back at the party had evaporated like smoke. I watched her walk ahead, and I had an urge to let her keep going and find my way back home. But, like most single men who don't get nearly enough sex without a lot of work and phony acting, I still felt I had a sure thing before the night was over.

I followed her into that alley between a pair of brick warehouse structures that might have dated from the last century. Club Chic, this was not. She was waiting for me, half-turned, and as I approached, she skipped up to me, all schoolgirl-flirty now, and grabbed my upper arm and squeezed it while she bumped her hip into me in a way that was sexually promising.

The alleyway stank of piss. Styrofoam packing, papers windblown against the walls on opposite sides. A pair of eyes glittered up at me from the interior of a cardboard house--some derelict's home. The smell of rotting fruit reminded me of the filthy conditions during one of our garbage strikes.

"I know, I know," she said. "It doesn't look like much but once you're in there, you'll see what a crazy place it is."

She pushed open a rusted-out metal door. A bare bulb hanging from a wire gave a cone of illumination inside a bleak warehouse. No one manned the door. No security staff or anything that looked like a normal club entrance, even the ones that wanted to remain discreet to keep a certain clientele, the sort that existed at the opposite pole from those wannabe Kardashian cliques.

Crazy. That was her word. Once inside, I had other words for it: surreal, bizarre, disturbing. Strobe lights and black lighting made vision difficult. I assumed the owner didn't get the memo that the sixties weren't coming back. I wondered if this was a theme night and

I'd see plenty of tie-dye shirts and elephant pants among the crowd.

"You said this was a Halloween party," I shouted to her. "Nobody's in costume."

I couldn't have been further off with one exception: wide-open drug use was rampant everywhere I looked: snorting, smoking, and acid tablets passed around and placed on tongues like communion wafers at high mass in St. Patrick's. One man was shotgunning reefer smoke into a couple girls' open mouths like a mother robin feeding her babies.

The snap of cigarette lighters and swirls of tiny flame erupting here and there in the darkness lit the way deeper inside like a fairy tale I had read as a child where fireflies lit a path through the woods—except that in that case they were assisting a boy's escape from a witch who intended for his organs to be the primary ingredients in her ragout. I lost count of the number of people who would have to be paid off to turn a blind eye to the violations I took in at a glance.

For another thing, the place was darker than any club I'd ever been in. It started out like a normal bar with a cavernous space for dancing. The DJ started with some basic house music, lots of synths, then shifted to a progressive house with a mix of nu disco—you know, that same 4/4 beat you find in every club between New York and Chicago. Then it changed.

"What is that music?" It was a grimy-sounding, funky, squeaking series of short- and high-pitched notes.

Neci had just returned from the bar with a couple drinks and a lit blunt. She handed me the grass and I toked it just to be sociable

"Here," she said and handed me one of the drinks. "Cheers."

We drank. It was sweet going down, yet it left me feeling as light-headed as I was in the cab. She maneuvered us to a table against the back wall. Over our heads track lighting on a computer timer crisscrossed over the tables like searchlights trying to find a man overboard in black waters.

"I think it's fidget house," she said. "Or maybe some new Euro thing."

Before I could argue, her voice was drowned out by the music, only this time it was unrecognizable to me. By now, every Manhattanite is familiar with the EDM in clubs but this was musical chaos, a caterwauling, erratic, skitchy beat with jarring percussions fused to a repetitive bass line; it all added up to a hypnotic beat that set the crowd on the floor wild in an animated frenzy I had not seen since I let a goth girl talk me into catching Pinkish Black at the St. Vitus Bar in Greenpoint, a metal bar with ear-bleed decibel music.

"Who the hell are these people, Neci? What is this place?"

The people were not your typical west siders or club goers. Every now and then, a burst of flame in front of a face would outline someone at a table, but this crowd looked to be the kind who slept rough like that homeless citizen outside in the alley. The men had a Neanderthal look to them, something tribal about their preference for black clothing, and displays of tattoos, piercings, and studs. Tattoos that go past the neck always make me think of one semester's lecture at NYU on aberrant psychology. The women were similar; most sported an edgy look like the men they kissed and groped. The lesbians in clubs I'd noticed always seemed to prefer a feminine partner. Here, it was impossible to choose which of these hatchet-faced kissing fish was the butch and which the molly dyke. On top of the numerous code violations, the rampant sexuality in the place was a leavening influence. I was about to formulate a bit of cheap wit along this line to impress Neci when I took in the fact that the woman's warm body next to mine, in close contact with my arm, wasn't Neci but a total stranger.

The first words of the *bon mot* I had cleverly arranged in my head were barely out of my mouth when I found myself looking into the face of a blue-eyed blonde, a classic California girl from a bygone era, in fact. An image snapped in my neocortex. She was the spitting image of Donna De Varona, Olympic swimming champion from a 1964 *Life* magazine cover I had seen as an undergraduate. The college library did a retrospective exhibition of magazine covers from the sixties to the present. Even in this din, how had Neci slipped away without my seeing her? I blamed the grass and whatever it was laced with—maybe formaldehyde if I was having this kind of hallucination in this kind of place.

"I'm sorry," I said to the blonde beside me. "I thought you were—I thought you were someone I came here with."

My befuddled brain was trying to gin up that old *Life* photo of Donna in the pool, her short hair tousled in a practical swimmer's style. This girl could have been an identical twin. I flashed to that moment in the library when I gazed at that image of the girl in the water, now a middle-aged woman and sportscaster. I had not thought of her before or since. Yet here she was, sitting beside me and smiling at my confusion.

"Did she abandon you? That's so sad," the blonde said.

"It—it doesn't matter," I stammered. "I can't make any sense out of anything right now."

"Let me help you," she said. "I can read palms. I can tell you what your future holds."

"Sure," I said. "Why not?"

I offered her my hand, palm up. The *non-sequiturs* of the evening were already piling up around my feet like the unread books under my bed. *What did one more matter now*, I thought.

Her fingers were cool to the touch as she pressed them into my palm but extraordinarily strong; she gripped my hand to turn it over and trace the network veins with a long fingernail. Then, without a word, she turned my hand over and pinned it to the table in an iron grip. Her eyes bored into mine; she looked intense and her voice dropped an octave and the words came out in a throaty ripple.

"You're an only child. You were spoiled by your parents. Your mother died of breast cancer at forty-one. Your father remarried a much younger woman and she fleeced him of all his wealth and assets in the divorce except for a stipend that allows you to live in an expensive city without working. You dropped out of law school because you were bored—"

I jerked my hand away as if a tarantula had crawled over my skin and stood up. I backed away from her. She sat there, no longer the demure California girl with the wholesome looks but an apparition, someone who had made herself up to look the part. But how did she know me to say what she did? I had held that magazine in my hands for no more than ten seconds and I was alone, at night, in the library with a few students studying in carrels or looking at the cell phones. The only reason I remembered it at all was because I was mentally contrasting the cynical and sexually experienced youth of my own time with the Donna De Varona generation.

She was reading my mind. They were all in it together. Suddenly, I was panicking. It was Oliver Stone and *JFK* time—one massive conspiracy to—

—*to what?* I asked myself, trying to calm down and stem the flow of adrenalin shooting all over the nerves and muscles of my solar plexus. That was crazy! Neci's word.

I had to find her and get out, go somewhere, anywhere, and make sense of this place. It had to be my imagination overreacting with the alcohol. Then I thought: *Neci must be in on it,* whatever "it" was. She brought me here. She could have spiked my drink and set up that little fortune-teller act between her and whoever the blonde imposter was. Maybe a friend, someone who knew me or who had access to the circle of people who did know all about my past. Granted, an extremely limited number and no one who would have run in Neci's circle came to mind.

But every word of my so-called fortune was true— even the last part about me dropping out of Cardoza Law School. Living off a trust fund like some effete dilettante or a *fin de siècle* poet. The truth was I didn't have enough to live as freely as the scions of rich New York families, but I had too much to force me to go to work. The money in some ways was a curse. I usually lied at parties or to strangers about having a real profession to avoid seeing contempt creep over their eyes no matter what they said to my face.

I had to find Neci. She must have some answers. None of this was an accident.

I pushed and jostled my way through the crowd looking for her everywhere. The dancing was even more frenetic now,. Being right up against people, I absorbed some hostile stares and noticed a common tattoo among both genders: spiderwebs. The males looked grimmer, older than at first, more like a rogue species I had never noticed in the streets before. Daylight and night time bring out different types in the city, but these were altogether unlike any groups I had seen before in my travels across the city's eclectic neighborhoods. They belonged to no class I recognized and made all those self-selecting mavericks of the recent past—the mosh-pit fighters, the goths, the gays, bikers, Mohawk, or spikey-haired punks, metalheads—all seemed archaic by contrast with this crowd.

I finally worked my way to the bar. A girl came over to take my order. She was typical of the women in the place in that nothing seemed to fit: her nose stud, the lip ring and eyebrow piercings clashed with her milky white skin. She wore a black lace bra beneath a leather vest, exposed generous cleavage when she leaned over to hear my order, and asked me what I wanted.

"Bourbon, any kind," I said and placed a twenty on the bar. She brought my drink and made the money disappear. I made the drink disappear in a swallow. She made no effort to make change. Unlike every female bartender who had served me from the clubs in the meat-packing district to Irish bars on Gansevoort Street and Houston, she moved in time to the music, dancing solo behind the bar, when she wasn't busy serving. I was scanning the crowd for Neci when she leaned into me and said, "I like your tattoo."

"I don't have tattoos," I said, but she had already drifted away, rolling her hips, heading for a customer waving a twenty over his head and flagging her.

That's when I noticed my face in the cracked mirror behind the bar. A blemish just under my right ear. It looked like a tattoo. A tiny spider web tattoo—thin silvery strands dangling from my ear lobe. I slapped at the side of my neck as if I could brush it away. My heart thumped a counterpoint rhythm to the bass line in the music. This was impossible. *"That's not me! That's not me!"*

Fearful, no longer curious, I just wanted out of there.

Jumping off the bar stool and bolting through the crush of gyrating bodies, I shoved my way through the crowd which pushed back; hands shoved me this way and that. I avoided flailing limbs. I knew I had to get out of there.

I came to the center of the dance floor amid the gyrating bodies when suddenly the music stopped. People stopped dancing and formed themselves into two lines with an open space between them running down the center of the floor.

The music started up again. It wasn't dance music this time. It was the theme song to "Gilligan's Island," that moronic TV show from the 1960's. The quiet in that place was unbelievable; it had gone from an eardrum-shattering crescendo to a cathedral-like silence in seconds. The people who surrounded me would not let me pass. Instead, they forced me closer to that corridor of open space. The people on both sides began to scream curses at one another across the opening. They were furious, spitting ferocious and vile curses where they had been dancing just moments earlier.

The DJ started to play disco music. I don't mean nu disco but the old-fashioned Club 54 kind, the funky soul music of that glam generation long before I started going out. There was no reaction from the crowd. This was war. People from each side tried to pull someone from the other side over the corridor and stomp that person, man or woman, into a bloody pulp on the floor.

I couldn't go back because of the press of bodies pushing me from behind and the realization that, once I crossed over that "corridor of death," I would be swarmed and beaten with fists and feet, too. I cursed Neci, whoever she was, for dragging me into this ghastly tableau, like that time I witnessed a "rat king" exiting the 42nd Street subway station—a nest of rats with their tales snarled together, snapping at one another in a frenzy, something out of folklore or a Grimms' fairy tale.

Then I saw her. She was in the line opposite me. She didn't see me, but I saw her face contorted with rage like everyone else. The girl with purple hair beside Neci jumped out and grabbed a smaller girl by the hair from the opposite side and pulled her across, her legs kicking wildly. I watched her disappear in a melee of flying kicks and punches. Gripped by her hair, the small girl twisted toward me and revealed a bloody face, one eye pulped closed, and teeth missing from the blows. A girl in a black Lycra skirt with spiked heels was about to launch a devastating kick to the victim when that girl disappeared in a squirming vortex of attackers.

I was sick to my stomach. I had never seen such incredible violence. I knew intellectually human beings anywhere were capable of this horrific and vicious malevolence, but I'd never seen it up close and personal like this. Being robbed at gunpoint on my way home from Cielo's was nothing; that's a rite of passage for every New Yorker who rides subways at night. I was dizzy, terrified that the swaying line of screaming combatants would nudge me into the open and some arm

HellBound Books Publishing LLC

**A HellBound Books LLC
Publication**

http://www.hellboundbookspublishing.com

Printed in the United States of America